WILLIE MAE

WILLIE MAE

Joseph D. Manzer

ᚼᚱᛒᚢ
McMann Publishing LLC

ISBN-13: 9780692578285
ISBN-10: 0692578285
Library of Congress Control Number: 2015918756
McMann Publishing LLC, Camdenton, MO

IN MEMORY

OF

CAROLYN CATHERINE

MANZER

Acknowledgements

———✦———

To EVERYONE WHO READ THIS story before it was finished, (and you know who you are) and encouraged me to keep writing, thank you. As a first time author who jumped into the literary world without a clue as to what I was doing or how to do it, your comments and suggestions were well heeded and greatly appreciated.

To Captain Jeffrey J. Manzer of the Southern Belle, my brother, who provided all of the maps from the early 1930's of Mobile and the river in which I drew upon in an effort to depict Willie's early life upriver, thanks dude. And last but not least to my loving wife, who, and with a snicker I might add, was always there to critique my spelling.

Author's Note

THERE IS NO DOUBT THAT Washington is corrupt beyond any sense of the word and has become nothing more than a cesspool of thieves, liars and whores. Greed and power, however it is disguised or subtle it may be, drives everything and everyone there. It is our nation's greatest disease, a cancer that has grown and spread into almost every branch of government we have. It is sad but true, and although the players seem to change from year to year, the game they play and how they play it is still the same.

'We the people' no longer applies. Empowered by rules of their own making they care not for the unthinking masses of this country, which lends credence as to how some of the political shenanigans and dealings portrayed in this book, although fiction, could very well have went on. That is my opinion, and also my hope that some-day the people of this great nation will avail themselves of the truth and wake before it's to late.

MOBILE ALABAMA

———◆———

IT WAS LATE MORNING AND already hot by the time the big rig diesel had pulled into the compound. Noisily rolling to a slow and jerky stop with its empty lowboy trailer, it sat for a moment then released the pressurization from its brakes and shut down its motor. A second later, a small cloud of dust billowed into the air and covered the truck's rear axles then slowly disappeared across the grass on the warm gentle breeze.

They had been given specific instructions on where to go and who to see, yet still the two men perched high inside the cab seemed lost and confused. As if they had stopped at the wrong place. Gazing across the grounds in search of their cargo, they grabbed their work orders and carefully re-read their directions. This was it, wasn't it, they wondered as they eyed each other then turned and surveyed the grounds once again?

"There it is!" Earl finally exclaimed, pointing to a single story cottage sitting amongst a cluster of shady oaks. Unassuming in its appearance, the red bricked home with its low-pitched roof and small front porch was almost completely covered in ivy. Surrounded by lavish beds of flowers, all still in bloom, it was neatly manicured and sat quietly at the far end of acres of well-kept grass. Knocking firmly on the door, the two men waited until it finally opened and a distinguished looking gentleman, slim and with graying hair, appeared on the other side.

"Ah, Father Finnegan?" Kennard, the bigger of the two drivers drawled hesitantly.

"Yes...?" the man in black answered as he cautiously eyed the pair.

Standing humbly before the priest, the two disheveled and overweight truck drivers froze in a state of uncertainty. They were rough and tough, yet still they were intimidated and quickly looked to each other as if there were something you were suppose to do when you first stood before a priest. Suddenly, and as if he'd just been enlightened from above and knew what to do first, Kennard pulled his cigar from his mouth and snatched his ball cap from his head, then bent at his waist and bowed. Exactly why he wasn't sure, but he did.

It was an action that quickly caught his buddy's attention and after a quick but hesitant glance back to the man in black, Earl clumsily followed Kennard's lead. He wanted no chance of being sent to hell for offending God and with the whisk of his hand he removed his cap and bowed like his friend. A few moments later, the mismatched pair sheepishly raised their heads and looked to each other with confident smiles, certain in their thoughts that they'd done the right thing.

But Father Finnegan held a different view and could only shake his head and roll his eyes to the sky, for it was painfully evident that the two before him had very little, if any religious upbringing. And as far as he could surmise, they had probably never even seen the inside of a church let alone attended Mass. Yet still, here they were, and even though they had come for a good cause, as he gazed upon them he wondered how they had ever made it this far in life.

"Ah, we're here ta get..." Kennard began as he held up his clipboard.

"Yes, yes I know," the priest interrupted. "Just a second and I'll be right there." Closing the door in their faces, the man in black disappeared only to return a few moments later and step out on the porch. "This way gentlemen," he gestured as he descended the steps.

Following the priest across the grounds, the two overweight drivers labored to keep pace as they made their way towards an old storage building sitting at the other end of the compound. Walking briskly, Father Finnegan smiled at their attempt to keep up, but even the best of priest had their faults and as he gave into the temptation of just a little orneriness, he quickened his stride even more.

"Come, come," he quipped with a mischievous grin. "Let's keep up! We haven't all day now!"

Huffing and puffing, the two men lumbered behind him until they reached the front of the building and stopped.

"Damn," Kennard huffed as he threw his cigar to the ground. "Ya tryin ta kill us?" Looking upon the man gasping for air, Father Finnegan just smiled and turned to the doors then lifted the large iron latches from their slots and pulled.

Sixteen feet high and twelve feet wide each, they were constructed from a thick tongue and grove lumber that ran in a vertical direction. Chalky white and peeling from years of neglect, the doors had small rectangular windows running horizontally across them just at head height.

"Well," he finally exclaimed as he stepped inside and pushed the second one open. "There it is. I just can't understand why we've had it this long."

Focusing his eyes into the darkened building, Kennard stared in awe at the timeless classic. "I'll be damned," he uttered beneath his breath as he jutted past the priest. "Look at that Earl."

"No shiiiit," Earl exclaimed, but then instantly cringed. "Oh, sorry Father," he apologized with a sheepish expression as he slowly turned back to Kennard. "How old ya think she is?"

"Don't know exactly, but she shor is a classic ain't she."

"Yeah, she shor is," Earl continued as he gently rubbed the palm of his hand along its side then pounded his fist against the wood. "Man oh man, whaaat a beauty. An it's solid too! We shor better be careful with this one don't ya think?"

"Yeah… yeah I do," Kennard grinned with his hands on his hips. "But I think we're gonna need a little help gettin it loaded, ya know." A second later the big man dropped to his hands and knees and began to study the supports underneath.

"Excuse me," Father Finnegan said of the man on his knees. "But did I hear you say you could use some help?"

"Yeah, we could actually," Kennard turned his head and answered.

"Well I don't know how much help he would be, but we have a caretaker here on the grounds that could help, if you'd like."

"Yeah that'd be great," the man replied with a heavy groan as he struggled back to his feet. "Just another pair of hands an eyes is all we need really," he added as he brushed the dirt from his hands.

"Well good, then let me see if I can find him while you get your truck, okay?"

"Shor Father," Kennard replied with his gaze still fixed to the boat only to jerk it back to the priest. "Oh Father," he called out before the man could even take his second step.

"Yes," the priest stopped and turned.

"I was jus wonderin," he cocked his head with a growing curiosity. "At, well, I mean. Jus where'd you guys get this? I mean, how long's it been sittin here?"

Smiling with an almost childlike amusement at his question, Father Finnegan slowly approached the big man. "Well," he began. "From what all I've been told, I believe it was given to the church some time around the late forties by a woman of very considerable wealth. I think a close personal friend of the Bishop's actually. They said that the two of them used to take rides together after church and that when she moved out of state, she just up and gave it to the church.

"Now the Bishop I'm told, really liked boating, and for the next ten years or so he used it almost every Sunday after services. They say all the way up until the day he died. Anyway, after that I guess it didn't get used a whole lot except for a church function here and there and it just kind of sat in the water. And then after about a year or so, and when no one else seemed to want to use it, the new Bishop had it put here in this old barn.

"Now that was all fine and good, but after a couple of years it seemed that everyone just kind of forgot about it, and to tell you the truth, it's been sitting here ever since. And now that the church property is being sold for the new water front development, it's really time to do something with this as well. So the church has decided to auction it off and donate the proceeds to charity."

"Well," Kennard shook his head then turned toward his truck. "It's gettin moved now." It was Friday and neither he nor Earl wanted to be there all day. "Jus let me get the truck backed on over here," he said as he began walking away. "An we'll have it out in no time."

"Good," Father Finnegan replied as he turned and took off in search of his caretaker. "I'll meet you back here in a few minutes."

Once again crossing the grounds, Father Finnegan finally found Otis behind the church cutting grass. He had his back to him, but when he turned to make his next pass he looked up to see his boss waving his arms.

"Yes sir Father," Otis yelled as he shut down his mower.

"We need your help Otis," Father yelled back with an arm gesture to follow. Nodding his head, Otis instantly dropped the handle to his mower and started toward the priest.

Getting the 1926 40 foot cruiser onto the trailer and pulling it from the barn turned out to be much harder than what had anyone thought. It was a precarious task, but after hours of tedious work they finally succeeded and had it firmly secured. Hot and sweaty, the two burly drivers bid them farewell and then climbed into their truck. A moment later, and with a huge puff of smoke coming from their big diesel motor, they left Otis, Father Finnegan and a young newspaper reporter standing in the grass as they slowly made their way back through the grounds.

Watching as they carefully weaved through the compound to the road, the reporter, who'd been sent to do an article on the church's history and its impending sale, lifted his camera to his eye. He needed a picture for his story, and with a shot from the rear and slightly to the side, he captured the truck, the boat, and the church behind it. It was a great shot, and with a contented smile he lowered his camera then watched with Otis and the priest as the boat left on its journey to New Orleans and next Saturday's auction.

The following Sunday a woman in her late fifties casually stepped through the patio door of her beachfront home. Beautiful and elegant, the years had been kind to her and she looked much younger than she actually was. Her day was just beginning, and as she re-tied her bathrobe, she set her gaze out across the white sandy beaches of Destin Florida and greeted the morning. Smiling brightly, she took another sip of her coffee, swallowed with a sigh then inhaled the fresh clean scent of early morning air. "Aaah yes," she uttered with a quiet contentment. "Another beautiful day."

Stretching with a yawn, she glanced once again back out to the ocean, stared for just a second, then turned and walked to the table. It was time to read, and without another thought she took a seat in one of the oversized wicker chairs and sank into its plush cushioned comfort. Picking up her Sunday edition of the Mobile paper, a paper she had read for years, she laid it on her lap then closed her eyes and tilted her face toward the morning sun. It was peaceful, and in the tranquility of the moment, she couldn't help but listen to and then smile at the eclectic mix of sounds emanating from the beach. The light wind and constant yet subtle roll of the surf lapping at the sand, the children already at play and milling about. A large fishing boat leaving from the pier on its morning run, and of course, the always present and noisy gulls looking for a free meal. They were the sounds of the beach. Sounds, that'd been transformed into small but vivid pictures inside her head. Sounds she knew all too well, for it was this stretch of sand that she'd called home for years.

She'd come a long way since her days in the cotton fields of Alabama and she knew it, and with that in mind she slipped on her glasses and opened her paper then began browsing the pages just like she'd done for years. The classifieds and the business section, until she had turned to the real estate section with a picture that just so happened to catch her eye. A picture of a church and its impending sale for a new real estate development.

It was a place she knew well, and with an ever-growing sense of curiosity, she narrowed her eyes and began to read. Turning to the next page to finish the article, she froze at the sight of yet another picture. One of an old wooden cruiser, cradled on a trailer behind a big rig diesel as it was leaving the church. Taken from the side and the rear, the boat had a name on the back that she knew all too well. A name that had actually been conceived because of her.

She'd often wondered what had become of it and now she knew. It had survived, even after all of these years. Staring for just a moment longer, she finally resumed reading and finished the article. The boat was to be sold next Saturday at auction in New Orleans, but as she lowered her paper and looked out to the ocean, she couldn't help but think of her friend and wonder what had become of him as well. A few moments later, she turned her gaze back to the picture, smiled a knowing smile then picked up her cup and downed her coffee.

Standing on the pier at Bellingrath Gardens the next day, Captain Jeffrey Manzer watched as the last of the young school children boarded the Southern Belle for their afternoon field trip. It was a beautiful day and the gentle breeze blowing across the river gave a shimmering sparkle to the water as it reflected Mobile's late September sun. Looking down from the pilothouse, Jim Williams waited until he had received a thumbs up and an all clear nod from Jeff then engaged the boat's powerful diesels. A second later, he smiled and reached up to pull on the knotted rope.

It was what all kids really liked, and with three long pulls to the Southern Belle's massive horns, he signaled their departure from the dock. Resonating sharply across the placid waters and grassy marshes, he turned to see their smiles and chuckled. Churning the mud from the shallow silty bottom with its giant propellers, the one hundred six foot riverboat slowly pulled away from the pier.

Watching as his helmsman skillfully navigated the tight turns of the Fowl River, Captain Jeff picked up his microphone and began his narration of the river and the surrounding bay to the crowd of children. Talking between themselves during breaks, he couldn't help but smile at Jim's repeated request to attend the old boat auction in New Orleans that coming Saturday.

"Ya know Jeff," Jim began with a hopeful drawl. "I really would like to go if it's okay with you?"

"Well, I don't see why ya can't," Jeff replied with a shrug. "Hell, you've already worked enough Saturdays lately. I'll just get Melissa and Clair to help me next week. Besides, they need to get out of the office anyway."

"Are ya sure?"

"Absolutely, you just go on down to New Orleans and buy you a boat, but make it a good one, okay. An old classic or something. You know, something with lots of history."

Laughing at his request, the old riverboat pilot just turned back to the wheel. "Aye Aye Captain Jeff," he uttered with the confidence of an old salt. "That I will..."

It had been advertised as one of the largest selections of old wooden boats from the thirties and forties to go up for bid and Jim certainly knew the importance of arriving early. There would be a lot of people vying for that rare and perfect find and he would need time to check out the inventory and make his inspection if he found one. Thinking of the many boats that he'd lovingly restored over the years, he smiled to himself and then turned back to Jeff.

"So what-a-ya think ol Meredith will say when she sees me pullin another boat home to set in the yard?" he asked with what was more of a sheepish concern than a question.

"Oh my God," Jeff coughed into laughter at the thought. "I don't know, but I sure hope you're done reproducin."

"Well, not exactly," Jim drawled with a hearty laugh and a twinkle to his eyes.

It seemed that Jim just couldn't stay away from the old wooden boats, and every time he brought one home it was another battle with his wife. She hated his 'stupid boats' as she'd come to call them, and he knew that this one would be no different than the others. A few moments later, and after their laughter had settled, Captain Jeff stepped from the pilothouse and continued with his narration.

Jim had waited all week for this day, and after a nice hearty breakfast, he loaded his new Chevy truck and prepared to leave. Setting a thermos of coffee on the seat with his lunch and a cooler full of Bud on the floor, he squeezed his oversized frame behind the wheel and started his truck. His wife still wasn't happy, but as she blew a loving kiss from the door, he pulled from the drive and began on his journey to New Orleans.

Arriving at the shipyard with the mid-morning sun, Jim couldn't help but grin as he drove through the chain-linked gates, for sitting before him on acres of aging blacktop were more than a hundred vessels to choose from. It was the auction of all auctions, and with all due haste he parked his truck and quickly made his way to the large metal building at the far end of the lot with his cooler in tow. Rusted and worn with openings at both ends, the building had people already milling about and was obviously the sight of the registration desk. Registering took only a few minutes, and as soon as he was done he took his listing sheet and headed outside in search of the perfect boat. Smiling with anticipation as he entered the yard, he slowly surveyed the range of boats. From twenty four to sixty feet in length, the once idyllic symbols of wealth sat cradled on stands like giant antiques in an out-door museum. Gazing upon them, he could easily see that there were ones nearly perfect and ones that were almost beyond repair. It was just what he'd hoped for and with that he began walking the yard in search of his next purchase.

Scouring the lot, he searched without success. Nothing seemed of interest, and with each row of boats his hopes diminished a little more until he turned the corner on the very last row. Immediately catching his eyes at the far end of the row was an old forty-foot cruiser from the late twenties or early thirties. Sitting nicely on stands, it called to him in a way he couldn't ignore. Could that be the one, he wondered as he took off toward it?

Beautiful in its design, it sat reminiscent of an era that was long gone, a history book into the past. Assessing its condition as he climbed in and around the boat, he quickly surmised that its chalky white hull and varnished wooden top, both peeling from years of neglect, looked much worse than it actually was. Walking around it one last time, Jim thoroughly checked the hull just to be sure of its integrity and then stopped at the stern. It was still amazingly solid and with a glance to the transom, more out of curiosity than anything else, he stared at the name on the back and wondered. Old and faded, and covered with dust, he grabbed a rag from inside the boat and began to wipe the wood.

Working enthusiastically, he quickly finished his task then stood back and read the name, *WILLIE MAE*. Yes, this is it, for not only did he like the boat, he liked the name as well. It was perfect, and with a confident sigh he set his cooler in the stern and then excitedly returned to the building to await the bidding.

There were plenty of bidders, but with the condition of the boat looking far worse than it actually was, it was Jim's knowledge of old wooden boats that finally proved to be his most valuable asset. Hanging tight, he stayed in the game until one by one people dropped out and he was awarded the highest bid. It was a good price, and after a few congratulatory handshakes from some of the other bidders, he made his way to the auctioneer's desk.

One of the last people in line, Jim waited patiently to pay for his purchase and get the title. But as he waited, he grew increasingly uncomfortable for out of the corner of his eye he'd noticed a man watching from across the room. An old black man who stood not more than sixty feet away, and who seemed to shadow his every move. Progressing slowly to the front of the line, Jim turned once more to view the man still standing to the side. A little older than himself, the man waited patiently, but looked nervous with his head slightly lowered and his hat in his hands, as if he had something to say.

It felt strange to be watched and as soon as his paper work was completed, the crusty old riverboat pilot headed straight toward the old black man and sternly confronted him. "You need something there my friend?" he asked with a scowl. At 6' 4" and 275 lbs., his towering presence was clearly an intimidating factor causing the man to shrink ever so slightly.

"Ah, a no sir," the man replied in a hesitant tone. "I, I mean, yes sir," he instantly corrected himself. "See, I use to be the captain of the boat you jus bought an I--"

"Whoa whoa whoa, just hold it riiight there," Jim interrupted. "I don't need a pilot okay. So if you're looking for a job, you're out of luck. Now just go on an ask somebody else," he gestured with his hand to go away. "There's plenty of other people buyin boats."

"Yes sir, but you see," he continued on in a humbled but insistent voice. "I made a promise to someone a long long time ago to look after it, an I--"

"Look my friend," Jim interrupted again. "I'm a licensed riverboat pilot and I don't need a captain or anything else. Now, if you'll excuse me," he turned and started walking.

"But I was," Jim heard before he could even take a few short steps. "I really was the captain, an I promised to..." his voice trailed off as Jim's distance increased. "Heck, I even helped name it."

It was the man's insistence and sincerity that caused Jim to finally stop and turn. Staring with an inquisitive gaze, he looked at the man with his hat still in his hands then slowly approached with a gnawing curiosity. Stopping just short of him, Jim cocked his head and narrowed his eyes. "You really the captain of that boat?" he asked curtly.

"Yes sir," the man answered matter of factly. "In fact, I even helped name it," he boasted proudly.

Standing straight and tall with his hands on his hips, Jim stared for a moment longer then suddenly began to smile. The man was telling the truth, he knew that now, and he also knew that he probably held a wealth of information with regards to the boat. He had to, for he had once been its captain. So with an extended hand and another smile, Jim introduced himself and invited him outside.

Casually walking through the crowds of people and boats as the auctioneer continued to call out numbers, the two men talked and became acquainted. It was a huge event with hundreds of people, but before they knew it the noise had faded into the distance and they'd reached their destination.

Standing just behind the stern, Otis looked first to Jim and then up to the transom. Smiling at the sight before him, he quietly stared at the faded black and red lettering outlined and bordered in gold. Reflecting back to days long gone, he whispered the name then reached up and lightly brushed his hand across the letters still clinging to the thick mahogany transom. A moment later, and after a nod from Jim to go first, Otis Brown grabbed the ladder and climbed into the back of the boat.

Climbing in right behind him, Jim looked to Otis with a grin then instantly began with an endless round of questions. Beginning with the engine and drive, he asked about everything, including the steering and water storage. Taking his time, Otis proved to be just what Jim had thought, but after an hour he finally called it quits, thanked the old man and then exited the cabin. It was time for a beer, and after finding a spot to sit and relax in the stern he reached for his cooler and pulled two cans of Bud from their icy confines.

It was a gesture of gratitude, and after popping their tops, the unlikely pair quickly guzzled the first half of their beers, belched loudly, then wiped their mouths with the backs of their hands and smiled at one another. Yet as Jim took another swig from his beer, Otis could see that the expression on his face had changed. As if his mind were consumed with some sort of unanswered question. "Are you okay there Mister Jim?" he asked with a curious concern.

"Yeah," Jim nodded and smiled. "I'm just fine," he added as he turned his can upside down and drained what was left of his beer.

Belching once again, he then cocked his head as if he were going to say something, paused for just a moment then crushed his can and threw it into the corner of the boat. Clanging its empty hollow sound as it bounced off of the side of the hull, it twirled for just a second then came to a rest on the floor. Reaching into the cooler, he grabbed two more beers and handed one to Otis. Blowing the water and ice from its top, he pulled the tab and took another long swill then wiped his mouth with the back of his hand and looked to Otis.

"Otis," he began, as he reflected back to what the man had said in the auction house. "You said earlier that you'd even helped name the boat. Well I got a tell ya," he scoffed and shook his head. "Quite frankly, I find that just a little hard to believe if ya know what I mean."

"But it's the truth," Otis postured forward in defense. "Really!"

"Well then," Jim persisted with a growing hint of cynicism. "Tell me there, Mister Brown. Just how in the hell did a young black man in the South, all the way back in the thirties do such a thing? I mean, come on..."

It wasn't so much as what Jim had said but how he'd said it that caused Otis to relax and lean back against the boat. He knew exactly what the man was insinuating. It was an unheard of thing, and with a long final swig from his beer Otis crushed his can and threw it into the corner by Jim's. He really had helped name the boat, and with a long deep breath as he drifted back in time, he popped the top to his beer and took a sip. He'd never told the story to anyone, but today, sitting in the back of the boat, Otis Brown began to tell of how he'd come to be the captain of the boat and of the first time he'd met the beautiful little girl it had been named after... Miss Willie Mae Dawson.

1 9 3 0

THE GREAT DEPRESSION

———⬥———

GROWING UP IN THE MIDDLE of the Alabama black belt on a small desolate cotton farm, life for Willie Mae was harsh. The child of a poor uneducated sharecropper, she grew up in the worst of times, and as cotton prices plummeted and the boll weevils came to feed, life for the young girl became even harder.

Raised by her mother and an abusive unemployed stepfather, they struggled to make a living against all odds. Uneducated and really nothing more than dirt poor, she had been pitted against life's adversities from the start, yet still, and even though she lived a life of hardship and squalor, she would often dream of a better life as she worked in the fields with her mother. Strikingly beautiful and already developed years beyond her age, the young girl carried with her a sultry innocence that as of yet, was still untouched by the rest of the world.

Born on September 11, 1915, Willie Mae Dawson was just about a month away from her fifteenth birthday when she tragically left home. No one was really sure of just where she came from except that she showed up in the city of Mobile sometime around the late August of 1930 and the beginning of the Great Depression. Most of the people from the upper crust of Mobile's society, speculated that she came out of the bayous and the deltas; some from the cotton fields up north... and others. Well, they just didn't care.

CHAPTER 1

AUGUST 1930

———◆———

"COME ON WILLIE, YOU CAN do it." Sara encouraged as she stood and wiped her forehead.

"But Momma I'm hot," Willie drawled with a frustrated whine.

"I know sweetie, I know," her mother agreed as she bent back over and resumed her work. "But jus a few more pounds an we're done okay," she said. "I promise."

Groaning in disappointment, the tired young girl stood to stretch and bend her aching back. A few seconds later she reluctantly bent back over, picked another handful of cotton balls and stuffed them into her bag.

Soaked in sweat, Willie Mae and her mother struggled to pick their day's quota of cotton from their small sharecroppers plot. And with the sweltering summer sun now at its hottest, the two women labored against its unrelenting intensity. Knowing full well the consequences of coming in short of their quota, Sara and her daughter, now with bloody fingertips, continued to pick the little white balls of cotton from their bolls. Smiling as they stuffed the last bag full, the two finally returned from the dusty fields long before sunset with their two hundred pounds of cotton.

Quietly walking back to their small home, the exhausted women strolled with their arms around each other like best friends. Tucked mid way up on the hill overlooking the fields, the house with its two small bedrooms, kitchen and large front porch, really wasn't much more than a twenty by twenty box that had been covered with a rusted corrugated roof. Poorly constructed, un-painted, and weathered from the elements and sun, it suffered from years of neglect. It was a shack and nothing more, yet it was where Willie lived and the only home she'd ever known.

They were hot and sweaty and as they continued to walk, Sara casually leaned down to her daughter's neck and inhaled through her nose. It had been days since Willie had bathed and she smelled.

"Oh dear Lord girrrl," she began with a laugh as she released her breath and fanned her nose. "You stink."

"Momma!" Willie instantly turned with a playful push and an indignant cry. "I do not."

Smirking at her daughter, the two stood for a moment facing each other until they both finally broke into laughter and began to giggle. It had been a long hot day and they were tired, but still they seemed to find a bit of humor in their lives that they could laugh about. It wasn't much, but it was all they had and with that they put their arms around each other like sisters and resumed walking.

A short while later they climbed the steps to the porch, but Sara still had the giggles and as they stepped inside and the screen door slapped behind them, Willie turned and grabbed her mother by the shoulders. "Okay Momma, I'm really serious now, you hear?" she scowled in an effort to look and sound stern.

"I'm sorry honey," Sara apologized as she tried to appease her daughter and end her laughing. "But it's jus that you ain't had a bath in days."

"Mommaaa!" Willie called and stomped her foot.

Coughing and clearing her throat in another attempt to finally suppress her laughter, Sara inhaled a heavy breath and then looked to her daughter.

"Do I really?" Willie asked in a drawn out drawl.

It was more than she could bear, and with an ever so subtle nod, Sara covered her mouth and then broke into laughter once again. Frowning with her hands on her hips, Willie tried hard to maintain a serious demeanor, but her mother's laughter was contagious and it wasn't long before she joined in with her. She was right, and as they stood together and laughed, Willie slowly raised one arm and dropped her head to her shoulders.

"You're right Momma," she exclaimed as she sniffed one arm and then the other. "I do... I stink real bad."

Swelling with pride, Sara grabbed her dirty, sweaty daughter and then hugged her tight. "Willie," she said. "We've worked hard today so why don't you jus go on down to the creek an make yourself beautiful while I make supper."

It was music to her ears and without a second's hesitation Willie turned and took a step to get her clothes but then suddenly stopped and turned back in a moment of uncertainty.

"It's okay Willie," Sara quickly assured in an effort to appease her look of concern. "I can make supper jus fine."

But Sara was exhausted from their day in the fields and it showed. The heat had taken its toll, and with an ever-growing concern at the thought of leaving her to prepare dinner all alone, Willie slowly stepped back in front of her mother. "Are ya shor Momma?" she drawled in a sweet but somewhat guilty tone. "I can stink another day if'n ya want me ta help."

It was the unselfish gesture and sincerity in her daughter's voice that caused Sara to smile and her eyes to water. "Yes, I'm shor," she said with a reassuring nod as she wiped her eyes and cleared her throat. "Really, I'm okay," she insisted. "You jus go an enjoy what's left of the day. I jus need to rest a bit an then I'll be fine."

She'd said it with all of the conviction in the world, yet Willie could see that she was tired and didn't move. "Now go on," Sara insisted with a push to her daughter's chest. "I mean it, get out-a-here. I'll be jus fine."

Slowly stepping backwards, Willie finally turned to her room and retrieved a brush, a clean dress and panties. Returning to the kitchen a short moment later, she bent and grabbed the bar of soap next to the washtub then stood and turned just as her mother cleared her throat.

"Yes ma'am?" Willie asked as if she were now in trouble.

"Willie," Sara began. "Have you ever seen your daddy shave?"

"Yes ma'am," the young girl answered. "A whole bunch a times."

"Well good," she quipped as she held up her husband's straight edge razor. "Then you know how to use this right?"

Gaining an immediate smile, Willie instantly reached for her mother's hand. "Now don't cut yourself," Sara warned as her daughter pulled the razor from her grip.

She'd suspected for some time that Willie had wanted to shave just like she did and her expression confirmed it. "Oh Momma," she said and hugged her tight. "Oh thank you, an I promise I won't." Beaming with joy and without another word, Willie turned and stepped through the screen door. "I love you," she yelled as it slapped behind her and she bound down the steps.

Quickly picking up the path to the swimming hole, Willie skipped and hopped through the dry dusty fields until she'd reached the far side of the hill. It was where she always stopped and waved before disappearing behind the trees, and today was no different. Smiling at the sight of her mother's arm waving back through the opened door, she instantly spun back to the forest and disappeared.

To Sara it was a moment of pride to think that her daughter was maturing into a young lady, but as she turned and stepped back into the sweltering kitchen, her thoughts quickly changed to her task at hand. John would want dinner when he got home, and with that she threw a few more sticks of wood into the stove then wiped her brow and stared down at the food she was about to prepare with a mix of emotions. Blessed to have received it yet saddened at how she'd earned it, she gazed upon the chicken, the green beans and the potatoes all sitting on the table.

It was hard to believe she'd prostituted herself for a better life, but she had, and she hung her head at the thought of what she'd become. Life was supposed to have been different, but it wasn't. It was harsh and cruel, yet because of her once a month liaisons with Mr. Johnson, one of the largest and wealthiest plantation owners in the county, they lived in a much nicer shack and at times ate a little better than many others. In short, they were one of the lucky few in a changing world that was rapidly becoming harder and harsher.

Intelligent, wealthy, and still handsome, his position in life combined with his gentleness and soft-spoken demeanor attracted her immensely. Even in spite of their twenty year age difference and after all these years, Sara still looked forward to her visits. She liked the way he made her feel when they made love. Unlike her cruel and sadistic husband, Mr. Johnson was caring and refined and always seemed to make her feel like a lady when they were together.

Leaving early in the morning under the pretext of cleaning his house in return for their living in a larger than normal shack, they would abscond to one of his far off properties where she would spend most of the day with him. Often receiving food as a sort of bonus for her services, she would many times receive money to buy goods when food wasn't available. Hiding it from her husband in a jar inside the pantry wall, Sara was frugal and saved for years. Glancing toward the wall, she stared for a moment and then slowly shifted her gaze back down to the food. She had dinner to prepare, but as the tired and over worked women bent and reached for a potato, she suddenly found herself overcome by a dizziness she'd never felt before. It scared her, and as the overpowering wave of weakness consumed her, she frantically grabbed for the table's edge.

Staggering as the blood from her head began to drain, she leaned against its edge for support but the heat from the day had taken its toll and she faltered. Losing her balance as the table abruptly slid, she dropped to her knees and grabbed wildly for the chair sitting neatly in its place. Clutching its top as her eyes rolled into the back of her head, she exhaled with a heavy moan and then fell to the floor.

She felt as if she were dying, and as everything began to darken and fade, she desperately cried out for her daughter. But Willie never answered, and as the last of the tiny blinking white stars swirling and flashing around in her eyes faded and her vision went dark, the world around her became ghostly quiet. Weak and frightened, Sara laid on the floor of the sweltering shack, drooling from her mouth and trembling in a state of unknown. Unable to speak and now unable to move, she quietly dropped into a state of unconsciousness.

———◆———

Descending into the clearing at the bottom of the hill, Willie smiled at the clear pool of water sparkling in the sunlight below. Sixty feet wide by eighty feet long, the oblong pool had a six-foot waterfall that gently flowed from its upper end onto a pile of smooth round boulders below. Fed by an underground spring, along with the fact that it drained the surrounding countryside for miles, it always had water in it even in the driest of times.

Running slowly, even though it hadn't rained in weeks, it was still full and still the perfect swimming hole. Surrounded by ancient oaks with giant canopies that reached for the sky and gnarly roots that drank from the water's edge, it was filled with minnows, crawdads and frogs. To say the least, it was a hidden oasis set in the middle of hundreds of acres of cotton fields. And with its smooth round pebbles and boulders that had been polished by mother nature for hundreds of years covering the banks and the bottom, it was just plain beautiful.

Setting her clothes and soap onto the rocky bank, Willie turned with an anticipating grin and stepped into the water. Stopping knee deep, she looked down as the water settled and cleared then wiggled her toes. It felt good, especially after her long hot day in the fields, yet even so the thought of someone watching worried her and with a cautious eye she looked around and checked her surroundings. Satisfied that she was alone, she crossed her arms and grabbed the waist of her dress. Shaking her head as she pulled it high above her, Willie looked to the sky and then quickly lowered it back to her chest. Looking around a final time, she smiled and dropped her dirty garment into the water then bent and slowly removed her panties.

Standing beneath the rustling canopies of the giant oaks, bathed by the filtered rays from the late afternoon sun as it shimmered and reflected off of the water, Willie by all outward appearances looked as if she'd been sculpted by the Gods themselves. Young and lean and hard, with small yet curvaceous hips that flowed sensuously into long and slender legs, she was exotic and alluring and stood as a living testament to their divine and unrepentant skills. A sultry green-eyed Goddess of uncompromising beauty poised just at the cusp of womanhood.

Gracefully stepping out of her worn and tattered undergarment, she stood for just a moment with it in front of her then finally dropped it into the water with her dress. Yes, it was time to swim, and even though the water was cool and caused her to shiver as she stepped in deeper, she took a big brave breath and lunged headfirst beneath the surface.

Playfully jumping and splashing, she swam for just a few minutes then returned to the bank and grabbed her bar of soap. Washing her thick mane of auburn hair under the little waterfall, she then washed her dress and panties on one of the smooth round boulders then hung them from a branch of one of the oaks. Standing tall in the sun and right at the water's edge, its low hanging limb jutted just over the water and made for the prefect clothesline. Satisfied that her clothes were clean and they would stay, she finally turned toward her clothes on the bank with an anticipating grin.

Walking back, she reached between the folds of her dress and carefully grabbed the razor then turned and sat down in the shallow water. Soaping her legs, she carefully began the tedious task of shaving for the very first time. Finishing with only a dozen nicks and cuts, seven on one leg and five on the other, she deemed that she'd done pretty good. But Willie was far from finished, and without a moment's hesitation, she lay down on her back with her head on a boulder and soaped up her left armpit. Carefully removing the hair with only one nick, she smiled at the rapid conquest of her new-found skill then looked to her right armpit. Okay girl, she thought as she stared with the razor still in her right hand. Now what-a-you do? Maybe this shaving stuff wasn't so easy after all?

It was a dilemma she'd never imagined, but with a determined effort she soaped up her armpit. Staring with an uncertain look at just how to start, she took a heavy breath then carefully began the awkward task of shaving left-handed. Cutting herself on the very first swipe, she shook her head in frustration but continued on. Seven more cuts and a few minutes later, the young novice finally succeeded with her task but knew that more practice was needed. Splashing water onto some of the still bleeding wounds, she wiped her cuts then shook her head at the thought of her mother's words. '*Now don't cut yourself,*' she remembered her saying. Grinning at the thought of what her mother would say when she returned, she lay back down in the water beneath the afternoon sun.

Savoring in its radiating warmth, she closed her eyes and let the burning orb's rejuvenating qualities penetrate into her body. Immersed in a world of silence with her head resting comfortably on the shallow bottom, Willie smiled to herself as she drifted off and envisioned her future. The wife of a doctor or a lawyer, with a big white house; just like Mr. Johnson's, with pillars and a yard. Yes, that is what she wanted. With a car and kids too.

———◆———

She was really unsure of the time that'd passed, but it was the sound of a woodpecker hammering on the side of the house that'd finally awakened her. Gradually stirring, Sara moved her arms and legs then raised her head from the floor. Yes, she was still alive, but what'd happened? She tried to think but couldn't, she could only think of the over-powering thirst now consuming her. Struggling from the floor to her knees, she grabbed at the table's edge and a nearby chair then pulled herself up and took a seat. She was dehydrated and needed water in the worst of ways. Her day in the fields had overheated her and her body had shut down, yet with a determined effort she rose and then slowly made her way outside to the well.

Pulling a bucket from its darkened depths, she gulped the cool refreshing water straight from the pail. Spilling out and around her mouth, the water fell to her shoulders and down the front of her dress. Setting the bucket down with her thirst partially quenched, she wiped her chin with the back of her hand and exhaled a satisfied sigh. Looking out across the fields, she stared for a moment then dipped her hands together into the bucket. Splashing more of the water onto her face and neck, she cooled herself a little more then returned to the house and picked up where she'd left off.

———◆———

Returning from her dream of a better life, Willie slowly raised her head from the silent world and cautiously surveyed her surroundings. She couldn't hear a thing with her ears below the water, but after a few moments, convinced and relieved that she was still all alone, she rolled over onto her stomach and faced the bank.

Spying a small bullfrog right at the water's edge, she instantly went after it. Frogs were neat and it would make a great pet, but before she could even close half of the distance between them, it sensed her intentions and dove beneath the water. Quickly chasing after it, Willie scanned the underwater terrain but the frog had disappeared.

A little disappointed that he had vanished, she abandoned her search then changed her thoughts to something else and reached for a small flat rock just below her. There has to be a crawdad under here, she thought as she turned it over and stared. Scanning the underwater cracks, she looked but saw none then continued on in search of the little crustaceans.

Dragging herself into even shallower waters, she shuddered at the touch of her breast now gently rubbing across the smooth round rocks of the bottom. The feelings were new and exhilarating, and she relished in the tingling sensations that were beginning to race throughout her. What were these she wondered, as she pushed her chest across the slippery bottom again?

Now consumed by an overwhelming curiosity, she closed her eyes and rolled onto her back.

Lured instantly into a desire to further explore these new and wonderful feelings, she began to rub and caress her breast. Flush with excitement, she writhed in response to the new sensations that were now flowing through her. She liked the feelings, especially the growing heat that came from the depths of her loins. But all too quickly, she abruptly and grudgingly stopped. Why, she really didn't know, yet with a heavy sigh she finally rolled back onto her belly and continued on with her search.

Reaching out in front, she turned another rock over. Nothing. Another, and still nothing. Where were they all? Looking around as the water cleared, she scanned the bottom until she saw another nice rock. Yes, she thought as she lifted it up, certain that this one would make a great place to live if you were a crawdad.

Smiling at the thought that she was right and the sight below her, she gently slid the rock to the side. He was the grand daddy of all crawdads and with his large red tipped pinchers raised high and his antennas waving back and forth in defiance of the invasion, he boldly stood his ground. Wisely reaching for a stick, Willie turned back in hopes of doing a playful underwater battle. They would battle like warriors, but before she could even bring her stick to bear, he disappeared with the flick of his tail into the scattered cluster of large round boulders.

Scampering after the tiny underwater giant, she pulled herself along the bottom until she rose up and onto one of the hot sun-baked rocks protruding partially out of the water. Quickly retreating in response to its surprising heat that had been stored from the afternoon's sun, she gently splashed water on top in an attempt to cool it down.

A few moments later she slithered up and over the smooth large rock like a snake. And although it was still hot, Willie slowed her forward motion as its incredible warmth began to radiate deep into her. It felt wonderful and relaxing, but there was also another feeling. A feeling she'd felt just a few moments ago, that seemed to invade her body as before but now with a greater intensity. A churning warmth and desire that propelled her to continue on, inch-by-inch over the hot wet boulder until the boulder itself had parted her legs.

Falling to either side as she slid into the water, she closed her eyes with a softened moan as the rock's pent up warmth instantly invaded and bathed the inside of her loins. The feelings were intense, and as she supported herself on her elbows, she slowly raised her hips from the water. She wanted more, and as she sought out that same feeling, that radiant glow she'd just felt, she gently pushed herself back onto the wet smoldering stone.

Shuddering as the intense heat permeating from the ball of granite penetrated deep into her sex, Willie closed her eyes then tilted her head and sucked her breath. It was hot and it stung, but there was pleasure in the heat that beckoned to her. It was something she couldn't ignore, and as a trail of drool escaped from the corner of her mouth, she arched her back and pushed against it even harder.

Gasping sharply as powerful waves of pleasure began to surge into her body, she slowly but brazenly began to undulate her hips. Coating a small area of the smooth sparkling stone with her own natural wetness, she gradually quickened her pace. She had only one thing on her mind, and as the burning desires between her legs continued to rise, she knew she wouldn't stop.

Raising and lowering her hips against the hot heavy boulder, she relished in the feeling of its intense heat and then the coolness of the water. Gasping and groaning, the soon to be fifteen year old, still so innocent, but now without shame, roughly began to massage herself against the hot heavy stone. Desperately seeking the secret release to this new and hidden pleasure, to extinguish the burning desires that were simmering between her legs, she steadily quickened her pace.

Shuddering as the gates of her adolescence finally began to open, releasing and giving way to the forbidden pleasures of womanhood, she could feel the muscles in her stomach as they slowly began to tighten and constrict. Knowing that she wouldn't stop, that she couldn't stop, she shamelessly continued as she sought out an end to her unknown pleasure. A few seconds later, Willie cried out in an unmuffled moan of pleasure.

Convulsing as powerful surges of ecstasy clawed at her body, the sultry young girl, that afternoon in the cool clear waters of the pool, took one of her first small steps toward womanhood. Satiated in a way that she never could've imagined, she slowly rolled onto her back and collapsed in the afterglow of her new experience.

Exhausted, but now with a contented smile stretched across her face, Willie closed her eyes and savored in the last twinges of pleasure as they slowly ebbed from her body. Resting with her head on a stone and with her body floating limply in the shallow waters, she listened to the sounds around her. The leaves rustling in the canopies of the giant oaks as they swayed in the hot summer breeze. The waterfall at the far end, lazily splashing onto the rocks below it.

They were the sounds of the water hole, soothing sounds, and with a contented sigh she slowly drifted off into a state of tranquility. A dream world that took her away from the life she lived and into the one that she wanted. A dream world that was suddenly broken after only a few short minutes by the loud sharp snap of a stick that came from behind her.

Horror stricken that someone had seen her, that someone had actually watched her, the young girl bolted up in fright and quickly tried to cover herself. Sitting in the water with her arms across her chest, she frantically looked around in search of her intruder. She felt sick with embarrassment, and for a few short moments she sat frozen until she exhaled with relief and even smiled at the sight of a lone but very startled white tail deer bounding over a fallen tree. Unaware that she was even there, the big buck, which had only come to drink, quickly disappeared over the hill with its tail held high.

It was nerve wracking to think that someone could've seen her, and with that thought weighing heavily on her mind, Willie decided that she'd stayed long enough. Rising to leave, she dried and quietly dressed in a clean new dress and fresh panties that she and her mother had made from their left over flour sacks. The fit was perfect, and after she'd brushed her hair, she gathered her clothes and belongings, and then began on the long slow climb back up the hill.

It was always easier going down, but Willie was young and after only a few minutes she reached the summit and the edge of the trees just as the sun had dropped to the horizon. The day was finally over, and as it painted the landscape with the last of its burning rays, she marveled at the fields glowing in a strange and eerie silence. Thinking of how they possessed such beauty, yet at the same time such harshness, she stared with a mix of emotions. There was more to life than just picking cotton and she knew it, but what? They worked so hard yet had so little, but as she looked to the house and resumed her walking, her thoughts quickly changed to that of showing her momma her newfound shaving skills and eating their special dinner. Bounding up the steps and in through the door, Willie held her arms high for her mother to see.

"Momma, I'm back," she yelled as the screen door slapped behind her.

Turning to see her daughter as she spun and proudly showed off her legs and underarms, Sara smiled at the obvious nicks and cuts. "Let's see here," she laughed as she looked closer and began to count. "Six, eight, nine, twelve," she continued.

Unamused by her mother's obvious enjoyment, Willie stomped her foot in protest. "Momma," she cried out halfheartedly.

Humorously unfazed, Sara continued counting. "Sixteen... seventeen," she laughed some more.

"Stop it Momma," Willie pleaded as if she were insulted. "I'm serious," she added with an embarrassed look as she lowered her head.

Now holding her at arms length, Sara stared for just a second then tenderly reached under Willie's chin and gently raised her head. Gazing into her daughter's light green eyes, she pulled her tight into a warm embrace. "Oooh baby," she whispered and squeezed then pulled back away to arms length again. "Jus look at ya now would ya. Ya've gone an grown up ta be such a pretty girl... I'm so proud of you," she added with another hug just as her light-headedness returned.

Hitting harder than before, Sara hastily grabbed for a chair by the table then dropped onto the seat and laid her head into her hands. It was an action that instantly gained Willie's attention, and without a second's hesitation she dropped to her knees and reached for her mother's face. Lifting her head from her hands as she struggled to breathe, Willie gasped at her complexion that had turned pale and void of all color.

"Momma are ya'al right?" she asked as she brushed the hair from her mother's face. But Sara didn't answer; she just stared in a daze. "Momma, are ya'al right?" Willie asked again.

"Wha..aaat?" she finally replied as if she'd just been awakened.

"Are ya'al right?" Willie repeated with an ever-growing concern.

"Yes honey," she said. "I'm fine, I jus needed ta sit a bit," she added as she reached for her daughter's hands and squeezed them. "Really."

It was a reassuring effort, but as soon as she spoke she closed her eyes and slumped back in her chair. She was sick and Willie knew it, and without another thought she reached under her mother's arms and helped her up. "Come on momma," she groaned and pulled her from her chair. "Let's go lie down okay, I can finish dinner jus fine, hear," she assured as they shuffled into the bedroom.

Laying her mother on the bed, Willie left but quickly returned with a washcloth and laid it on her forehead. Removing her shoes she told her to rest then went back to the kitchen and picked up where her mother had left off. Finishing the green beans, potatoes and gravy like a pro, she set the bowls of food onto the still warm stove just as a truck came to a stop at the end of their long dirt drive. Looking out of the window into the fading light, Willie watched as the all too familiar figure that she'd come to both fear and despise emerged from the back. Hoping that tonight would somehow be different, and that he would appreciate how hard they'd worked, she stared for a moment and then dropped her head in dismay.

CHAPTER 2

———◆———

LAID OFF FROM THE SHIPYARDS in 29, John Dawson hadn't worked since, and after a final wave to the other men in the truck, he turned and began on his long walk up to the house. Watching as he staggered and weaved, Willie could tell that he'd been drinking and was returning home drunk once again. It had become a regular thing and with a heavy sigh she prepared for the worst.

Angry and wallowing in self-pity over his inability to get a job in the toughest of times, John had taken to the making and running of white liquor. There was money to be made, but in his quest for riches the former steel worker had gotten caught up in his own disgusting world and had become nothing more than a mean belligerent drunk. Thinking of how she wished he could find work, she listened to his footsteps as he slowly ascended the steps and then to the screen door as it slammed behind him and he entered the house.

Fearful that anything she might say could set him off, Willie greeted him in the kitchen with a cautious apprehension. "Daddy," she said as she clutched the back of the kitchen chair. "We made you a special dinner tonight."

But John never replied, he just stared at his stepdaughter in her new clean dress and then stepped toward her. "Well well well," he finally growled in a low lewd voice as he reached up and brushed her cheek with the back of his fingers. "Ain't you jus somethin preeetty."

Stepping back with a guarded caution, Willie tried to gauge his mood. "Daddy please, not tonight."

Looking around for his wife as he contemplated her plea, John finally turned back to Willie with a disgruntled sigh. "Where's your momma?" he demanded in a tongue that was thick and heavy with liquor.

She knew her mother was supposed to greet him every night with dinner and ask how his day had been, but Sara was sick and Willie was determined to defend her.

"Momma got sick today," Willie replied in hopes he would understand. "She got real sick, an she's layin in bed asleep. But we still made you a real nice dinner," she added in hopes that he wouldn't become angry. "See, it's on the stove."

Turning and raising his head ever so slightly John sniffed the air with a heavy breath. The aroma was incredible and the thought of a really good meal instantly changed his mood. He no longer cared about his wife, and with a step toward the stove, he gazed down at the golden pieces of chicken, potatoes and green beans. He was famished and without another word he turned and took a seat at the table. "Bring me some food goddammit," he barked in an ugly tone. "I'm hungry!"

Hastily fixing his plate like a servant, Willie then made one for herself and joined him at the table. Watching meekly, she quietly ate her dinner as he disgustingly inhaled his food like a pig. Clanging his fork onto his empty plate as he finished, he licked and sucked the tips of his dirty fingers then wiped them on the front of his overalls and demanded another.

Consuming the second just as fast as the first, he finished his meal then pushed his chair back and relaxed. Belching loudly, he wiped his mouth with the back of his hand and grinned. His belly was full and as he sat with a contented smirk, he lewdly eyed Willie as she too finished her supper. He'd all but forgotten about his wife, but just as he was about to rise and retire outside for a smoke, Sara slowly shuffled into the kitchen with a blanket draped across her shoulders.

Rising to help her ailing mother, Willie quickly pulled out a chair and helped her settle. "Momma how do you feel? Are ya hungry?" she asked as her mother took her seat. "There's plenty left."

"Oh, thank you sweetie," Sara nodded. "But jus a little okay, I'm not real hungry."

Making her plate, Willie returned and set it down then took a seat beside her. "Come on momma," she encouraged. "Eat some supper, okay. It's good."

Picking up her fork, Sara took a bite of her food, glanced to John now staring as if she'd done something wrong, then quickly looked away.

"What's wrong with you woman?" he demanded in a cold uncaring voice.

Raising her head back up, Sara slowly finished chewing then swallowed her food to speak. She was clearly exhausted, but John was impatient and furious that she did not immediately answer, and in an over-reaction to her presumed insolence, he slammed his fist onto the table.

"Goddammit," he yelled as the plates and glasses bounced and rattled. "Answer me woman."

Jumping in fright, the two women cowered in fear then waited, afraid now more than ever to speak. It was just what he'd wanted and with a sort of demented joy, he began to laugh. A moment later and after he'd settled, he leaned across the table and glared at his wife.

"Now, I saiiid, what's wrong with you?" he growled.

Gently setting her fork back down on her plate, Sara emitted a heavy sigh and cleared her throat. "The heat must of gotten to me," she coughed in a raspy voice. "But we made our quota," she added as if he'd be pleased and pay them a compliment.

"Well you better of goddammit," he snapped. "Cause you know good an well what'l happen if ya don't. You know ol man Johnson don't allow no slackers durin the harvest," he glared and pointed his finger. "An I shor as hell ain't gonna have the two of you goddamn lazy asses a ruin'n my good name, ya hear."

Nodding her head as if she understood, Sara took a labored breath then exhaled with a long drawn out sigh. "Yes John," she finally replied. "We know," she lowered her head in an attempt to avoid his burning glare and any further confrontation. "An we'll make our quota tamorrow too. I promise."

Satisfied that they both understood and would continue to pick the cotton on schedule and in the quantity required, John finally rose from his chair and walked outside for his smoke. Listening as the screen door slapped behind him, Willie reached up to comfort her mother.

Stepping out onto the porch, John quickly found one of the half broken chairs and took a seat then began to roll a cigarette. To him his tobacco was a must, especially after a meal. They went hand in hand and with a long hard pull he inhaled the nicotine laden smoke deep into his lungs. A second later he tilted his head and blew his smoke into the air then yelled for Willie to bring him a bottle.

His words were ugly and demanding, and with the look of dismay painted across her face, Willie took in a long deep breath then turned toward the door and exhaled with a heavy sigh. "Jus a second Daddy," she finally answered in disgust. "I'm helpin Momma ta bed," she added as she turned back to her mother and reached beneath her arm. "Come on Momma," she groaned as she pulled to help her up. "You need ta lay back down an rest okay."

"No Willie," Sara shook her head in an effort to warn her daughter of something she feared. "He's drunk an he don't need no more liquor an you--."

"I know Momma," Willie cut her short as they shuffled toward the bedroom.

But Sara wouldn't let it go, for it was her very own husband, a man who'd taken her in at the age of sixteen and married her even though she was pregnant with another man's baby that frightened her. Ever grateful but ever regretful, and now hopelessly and helplessly trapped in a life of cruelty, she was doing her best to protect her daughter from what she perceived as John's ever growing intentions. Intentions that if he were to actually act upon would be far more devastating than any of the beatings she'd ever suffered. Willie had grown into an alluring young girl and she'd caught him more than once looking at her in ways in which he shouldn't.

"No baby, you don't understan," Sara tried again to explain as they shuffled into the bedroom. "You don't need to be alone with him, he, he's..." her voice seemed to fade until she quit speaking.

"I know Momma, I know," Willie assured as she laid her mother down. "But you don't need to worry, daddy's on the porch. An all I'm gonna do is go clean up the kitchen an then go to bed," she added as she tucked her in. "So you jus rest now ya hear," she finished then rose and returned to the kitchen.

Filling a pan with hot soapy water, she began washing her dishes but then stopped to the sound of John's voice once again. "Willieee," he snarled in a drunken slur. "Where's my goddamn bottle?"

Dropping her head with a heavy sigh, Willie hesitated for a moment then slowly pulled her hands from the pan of water. Shaking her head in disgust, she flipped the water from them then reached for a towel. She knew that he wouldn't stop, and even though she remembered her mother's warning, she bent and retrieved a bottle of rotgut from beneath the cabinet.

Stepping onto the porch, Willie called to her stepfather in a concerned voice. "Daddy," she said as the door slapped behind her. "I'm worried bout Momma, she's sick... real sick. An I think she needs to see a doctor," she added as she crossed the porch with his bottle.

"Oh you dooo, do you?" he scoffed and rolled his head then watched as she approached.

"Yes, I do," Willie stressed as she stopped next to his chair. "She don't feel good at all."

"Well, that's just a shame ain't it," he drawled in a cold uncaring voice. "But why are you tellin me? It's harvest time an I really don't give a shit how she feels." He smirked and then pulled on his cigarette. "Jus as long as she picks that cotton like she's sapose to."

For as long as she could remember John had always been mean and cruel, but it was his utter lack of concern and compassion toward the only person she'd ever loved that cut into her like a knife. Filling her with despair, Willie for the first time in her life shot back in defense of her mother.

"No Daddy, nooo. You don't mean that," she argued. "I know you don't. I jus put Momma to bed, an I don't think she can do nothin she's so sick," she added in hopes he would show some concern.

"Oh really?" He smirked and then stared. "Nothin, huh?"

"Yes," Willie asserted as if to admonish his lack of concern. "Nothin. She's sick I tell ya, really sick, an she needs help. She needs a doctor."

John knew that Sara was sick but he could've cared less, and as he eyed Willie's long lean legs and curvaceous lines, he licked his lips and began to smile. "Well well well then," he growled beneath his breath. "I guess you'll jus have ta do now then won't ya?"

Cocking her head, unsure now of what to say, Willie just held out her arm with his bottle. "Well, here's your whiskey," she said in disgust.

But John never moved; he just stared in a way she'd never seen before until she spoke again in a much firmer tone. "Daddy, I said here's your whiskey!"

"Well then step your ass closer girl," he finally demanded. "An hand it to me."

Frustrated that he hadn't taken his whiskey, Willie reluctantly did as she was told then held her arm out once again. "Now here," she said as he raised his arm from the chair.

She had expected him to grab the bottle, but before she knew what was happening, he'd reached up under her dress and grabbed the inside of her thigh.

"Daddy?" she cried out as she tried to pull away. "What are you do'n? Dooon't!"

Holding her tight in an attempt to keep her from escaping, John quickly reached around to her buttocks with his other hand and jerked her closer. "Therrre," he growled again. "That's better."

Now completely helpless under his overpowering grasp, Willie dropped the bottle to the porch and pushed against his hand. "Stop Daddy," she begged as he boldly continued his assault. "Stoppp... pleeease."

He heard her pleas, but John wasn't listening, and in an action that was driven by lust and fueled by alcohol, he continued to inch his rough and callused hand ever so slowly up Willie's thigh. She was his and he wasn't letting go, and as he inched ever so closer to her sex, Willie frantically wiggled to break free.

"Mommaaa," she cried out in a quivering plea as she turned toward the house.

"Your momma ain't gonna help you none tonight girl," John's drunken slur instantly shattered her hopes. "Now you jus keep still, ya hear."

Consumed with a sick and sinking feeling growing in the pit of her stomach, Willie cringed at the thought of how truly alone and utterly helpless she was. Her mother was sick and there was no one else to help. It was a horrible feeling, and as she trembled and prayed and looked up into the night, she listened as he began to question her.

"Willie?" he whispered with a vile hiss as he continued to inch his hand up her thigh. "I wanna ask you somethin. I wanna know if you know how babies are made?"

Closing her eyes in hopes that his assault and the nightmare she was enduring would end, Willie stood in a state of helplessness. She was completely frozen but John wanted an answer, and after what

nightmare she was enduring would end, she dropped her head and began to cry. She could take no more, and as the tears of her innocence gently overflowed and fell down her cheeks, John knew that he'd pushed her far enough. He had broken her, and as he released his grip and lowered his hand down and out from under her dress he looked up at her with a cold uncaring gaze and reminded her of her impending lesson. "Ramember Willie," he drawled in a raspy growl as he reached down and grabbed the bottle. "Sooon... reeeal soooon."

As soon as his hands were off of her, Willie bolted like an animal that'd been held against its will and rushed into her bedroom. Slamming the door behind her, she threw her back against it and then completely broke down. She was traumatized beyond belief and it was some time before she regained control of her emotions and quietly slipped into bed. Lying with her eyes wide open unable to sleep, Willie stared at the door. Fearful that he would come and take her, she listened as the night wore on until she suddenly jerked and bolted up in bed to the sound of the screen door slapping hard against the house.

Breaking the eerie silence of the night, the frightened young girl quickly huddled into a ball and shook with a pounding heart for it meant only one thing. He was coming to show her how babies were made just like he'd said, and as the sound of his footsteps drew closer and closer across a creaking floor; Willie swallowed hard and began to pray. He was almost there, and as she stared at the thin wooden barrier that separated them, she could see the flickering light from his lamp cast its soft eerie glow beneath the crack of the door and into her room.

Moving slowly from side to side, she watched in horror as it increased in size and spread out across her floor like a growing pool of water. Shivering in the quiet dark, she concentrated on the sound of her rusty doorknob as it slowly began to turn. She was trapped like an animal and there wasn't a thing she could do about it. It was a horrible feeling, and as she waited for the confrontation she knew was coming, she listened in a state of frozen fear to the sound of the steel mechanism as it slowly continued to turn.

Staring intently at the black round knob, Willie held her breath and watched. It seemed like forever but it was only a short moment, until, and for some unknown reason, it suddenly stopped and turned back to its original position. A second later, and just as ominously as it had arrived, the soft yellow glow beneath her door slowly receded along with his footsteps.

He was leaving, and with a sigh of relief the tormented girl dropped her head to her knees. But why, she wondered? Why had he stopped after what he'd done and told her he was going to do? She tried to think until she heard the sound of him in their adjoining bedroom. Affording little if any privacy through the thin wall that separated them, Willie suddenly realized the answer to her own question as her mother's soft yet desperate pleas rose from the other side.

"Nooo John," Sara begged in a raspy whisper. "Please, not tanight... pleeease. I don't feel..."

But John didn't care and with a slap across her face, Sara fell silent. Weeping at the cruelty she was enduring, Willie tried her best to block the sounds from her head as he hit and forced himself upon her mother. Knowing that they could very well have come from her own room, she reflected back to the last words he'd spoken to her and how they'd struck such a nauseating feeling.

"Soon Willie," was all she could hear again and again. "Reeeal sooon."

Agonizing and tormented with a desire to help yet frozen with fear and unable to move, Willie sat in her bed and listened. She hated him for what he was doing, but finally, and after what seemed like an eternity, it was over. Shortly after that the house grew quiet except for the sound of her mother's crying. Resonating through the thin wall, Willie listened and wept along with her. She should've helped or at least have tried, she knew that, and now with a sense of guilt consuming her, the distraught young girl began to well with anger and hatred.

———•———

CHAPTER 3

THE NIGHT WAS LONG AND even though neither one had gotten much sleep, the next day Willie and her mother rose long before sunrise for breakfast. It was still dark, but under the dim glow of the lamp Willie could clearly see the results of her mother's ordeal. John had brutalized her until she'd quit fighting and he'd gotten what he wanted. Her lip was swollen and one eye was blackened, and in a heartfelt voice that was filled with sorrow Willie began to cry. "Oh Momma," she sobbed between heavy breaths. "I, I want'd ta help but Iii--."

"Hush Willie," Sara cut her short as she stepped toward her daughter. "Don't ya worry none baby, ya hear," she said through a swollen lip and a battered jaw as she pulled her into a warm embrace. "I'll be jus fine," she whispered. "Really... jus fine."

She was trying her best to reassure her daughter, but her words of comfort fell on deaf ears and as soon as she had finished Willie looked away and began to cry all over again.

"What's wrong baby?" Sara asked in an attempt to comfort her again. "Come on, I told ya I'd be okay. John was jus a little drunk las night, that's all."

But Willie knew differently, and with a labored breath she turned back and stared into her mother's eyes. "No Momma," she cried and shook her head. "It's not that. It's somethin else, I need ta tell you somethin. Somethin that..." she stopped and turned away again as if she were ashamed.

"Willie?" Sara called. "What's wrong baby?" she pried as she slipped her fingers beneath her chin and turned her back.

"I hate him Momma," she seethed with a burning glare. "I hate him!" she repeated with an anger that rang into her mother's ears.

A little surprised and confused, Sara quickly tried to pacify her daughter. "Oooh honey, I know, I knooow," she began with a fabricated smile. "But look, I'm okay... seeee."

Shaking her head again as if to deny her mother's claim, Willie finally choked out the truth between her sobs. "Nooo Momma!" she cried. "You don't understand, last night while you was in bed... he touched me! Daddy touched me!"

It was an unconscionable act that hit her harder than anything else in her life and for a few fleeting seconds Sara could only look upon her daughter and stare in a state of despair and disbelief. "Whaaat?" she asked in an attempt to digest what she'd just heard.

"He touched me Momma," Willie repeated. "Daddy Touched Me!"

It took only a second for the true meaning of what Willie had said to sink in and almost instantly Sara began to swell with the tears of both guilt and pain. She felt as if her heart had just been ripped from her chest and in a hopeless denial of what she knew was true she began to shake her head.

"Oooh baby," she cried as she turned and stared at the bedroom door. "I'm so sorry Iiii," she quit speaking and grabbed her daughter. She knew there were no words of comfort to be had and that they now had to get away just as far as they could. John had finally crossed the line and she had to protect her daughter, and as they held onto each other and prayed, she whispered her promise.

"We'll leave baby, ya hear me. We'll leave him right after the harvest. I promise," she said with thoughts of how Mr. Johnson might help. "I mean it baby. "Right after the harvest."

Her words were comforting, yet even so it took a few moments before Sara finally gained a smile and a nod from her daughter. "Good, now come on an let's get somethin to eat," she said as she reached down and grabbed her hand. "I think it's gonna be another hot one."

Shuffling to the table, the two women took their seats and under the dim light from the lamp, ate their cold meager breakfast. Finishing without another word, they left the shack and returned to the fields just as the new day began. Tired and weak from yesterday's heat and her night's ordeal, Sara labored into the beginning of what they both knew would be a long hot day.

Later that morning as they stuffed their bags, the two women stood and turned to the sudden sound of the screen door slapping against the house and then to the voice of the man they'd both come to hate. "Hey," he bellowed across the field as he descended the steps. "You two ramember what I told you last night don't ya? Ol man Johnson don't allow no slackers an neither do I, so you better have that goddamn quota done when I get back, ya hear!"

Looking on with disdain, the two women said nothing and only watched as he began on his walk down the long dirt road with a bottle in his hand. He was leaving, but they knew he'd be back, and with that thought in mind Willie turned back to her mother with the look of dismay etched deep into her face. "Momma," she pleaded hopelessly. "What're we gonna do?"

"I don't know baby," her mother replied as she shook her head. "I jus don't know..."

Saddened at the thought that for the first time in her life she was truly unable to provide an answer, Sara watched as her husband slowly walked down the long dirt road and climbed into a waiting truck. Taking off in a plume of dust, she turned to her daughter as it sped away and stared with the look of despair. There were still no words of comfort to be had and they both knew it, and after a long and silent gaze, she slowly dropped her head. A few moments later, and as if they were one, they bent in unison and return to their work.

Struggling in haste to beat the morning sun, the two women worked hard but even so they slowly lost their battle. There wasn't a cloud in the sky and as it continued to rise and broke over the trees on the hill, the burning orange ball quickly replaced their precious shade with its unrelenting heat. Signaling the onslaught of another scorching day, the sun's blistering rays burned onto the landscape and across the fields.

Doing her best to ensure they made their quota, Sara worked hard but began to slow as the day drew on. She was weak and tired, but even so she struggled. She was determined to meet her quota and avoid another beating, but her efforts were to prove in vain. Standing for a breath and to ease her aching back, Sara's vision suddenly faded and her world went dark. A second later she stumbled and cried out for her daughter then collapsed into the dirt.

Turning just as she did, Willie screamed for her mother and rushed to her aid. "Momma!" she called again as she dropped to her knees. "Wake up!" she demanded as she rolled her over then brushed the hair and dirt from her face. "Momma, what's wrong?" she asked as cradled her mother's head in her lap.

It was a heartfelt plea, but Sara didn't answer, she couldn't. She was unconscious, and in a moment of panic Willie shook the lifeless woman. "Momma... pleeease!" she sobbed as her tears began to fall. Waiting for an answer that still didn't come as they baked under the late morning sun, Willie's patience quickly ended. She had to get her mother out of the heat and with all due haste she stood up and pulled her from the ground. It was a task that proved much harder than she thought, but with all of her strength she managed to get her up. Struggling with one of her mother's arms draped over her shoulder, and one of her own around her mother's waist; Willie began the long and arduous task of dragging her back to the house. Back through the fields until they had reached the steps where Sara seemed to regain a semblance of consciousness and then turn to her daughter with a ghostly gaze.

"Willie wha...?" she tried to speak as they slowly ascended the steps to the house. "What happen?"

"You fell over Momma."

"I diiiid?"

"Yes you did, but you're gonna be okay now cause I've got you. Now jus hush okay, we've got ta get you up these steps."

"But I don't ramember."

"I know Momma, I know, but come on now I need you to help me," Willie encouraged. "Come on, you can do it."

"But I feel real bad Willie," Sara replied.

"I know Momma, but you're gonna be jus fine ya hear. Jus as soon as ya lie down an rest," she assured as they made their way through the screen door and into the house. "Now come on," she said as they reached the bedroom and collapsed onto the edge of the bed. "Let's lie down."

Exhausted from her struggles, Willie gently coaxed her mother to the center of the bed then picked up her feet and laid them out.

Removing her shoes as she groaned and labored to breath, she left and quickly retrieved a bucket of water from the well and a rag from the kitchen. Returning to the room, she sat on the edge of the bed then tenderly wiped the dirt and sweat from her mother's face and neck. "There ya go Momma," she said as she dipped the rag back into the bucket and placed it across her forehead. "Does that feel better?"

Rolling her head to the side, Sara reached for her daughter's hand then squeezed it and grimaced in pain. "I hurts baby," she said with another groan. "I hurts all over."

"I know Momma, I know," Willie's voice quivered as she tried to reassure her. "But you're gonna be okay, ya hear." She squeezed her hand back with watery eyes and a smile pulled tight. "Ya jus need ta rest a bit an you'll be fine in the mornin," she added as if she were trying to convince herself.

Gazing intently at her daughter, Sara smiled and exhaled a heavy sigh. "I'm really tired baby," she said in an almost inaudible whisper as she rolled her head back and closed her eyes.

"No Momma," Willie instantly pleaded. "Wake up. Momma, please," she called again and gently shook her. Waiting for a reaction that never came, Willie, in a moment of hopelessness, gently laid down next to her mother and began to weep. She was afraid and uncertain of what to do, and in the deathly quiet of the house, with only the sound of the clock on the dresser and mother's steady breathing, the frightened young girl finally fell asleep.

Hours later, she awoke in a panic and rose from the bed. It was late and getting dark and John would be furious if there was nothing to eat when he got home. She'd seen it before, and without another thought she quickly built a fire in the stove and began making dinner. But between her mother's needs as she drifted in and out of consciousness and her efforts at the stove, she burnt what little food they had.

Unattended for just a moment, or so she thought, on a fire that was way to hot, her pot of beans quickly lost their water. Agonizing over her misfortune, Willie frantically fanned the air with a towel in an effort to rid the house of its thick white smoke. Succeeding in part with the help of a soft breeze, the house cleared but remained heavy and pungent with the smell of burnt food.

It was a mistake that carried consequences, and with that in mind the exhausted and emotionally strained girl took a seat at the table. Consumed with grief, she laid her head in her hands and quietly began to cry. A few moments later, she raised it back up and listened to the soft coo of a morning dove as it called for its mate again and again. Thinking of how pleasing it was, she smiled but then anxiously stirred as another sound broke the quietness of the house. Turning to the sputtering sound of a vehicle stopping and then starting again in the far off distance, Willie stood and peered out of the window. Gazing through the dirty pane of glass, she watched for a moment then hung her head at the darkened silhouette that was now walking up the path.

Returning home in his usual state, John finally reached and then slowly staggered up the short set of steps. Working to maintain his balance as he stumbled through the door, he entered the house and immediately raised his head. Breathing deep through his nose, he sniffed the air and the odor of burnt food then instantly turned toward the stove. "What in the hell is this shit?" he bellowed as he looked at the pot and then back to Willie.

"I, I tried ta make supper cause momma got sick agin. Real sick, an I was tryin to help her an..." Willie tried to explain but quit talking as he reached for a spoon and then boldly took a taste.

Cringing with disgust, he instantly spit the beans back into the pot then turned to Willie with another burning glare. "Did ya make this slop?" he snarled. Waiting for an answer that didn't come quite quick enough to suit him, John raised his voice and yelled again. "Well Goddammit, did ya?"

Jumping in reaction to his outburst, Willie cowered in fear but managed to stutter a frightened reply. "Ye, yes sur," she admitted. "I tried ta make diner, but Momma got sick agin an," she tried to explain but stopped and began to plead as John grabbed the handle to the pot. "Oh no, Daddy. Dooon't, pleeease." she begged and retreated against the wall. "I can make some..."

She wanted desperately to appease him but before she could finish John had picked up the pot and slung it across the room. Crashing against the wall with a heavy thud, he then vented his angry rage. "Now clean it up!" he screamed.

Confused and petrified at just what to do, Willie could only stare at the splattered mess as it dripped and ran down the wall onto the floor. "Ye, yes sur," she said in an effort to calm his anger. "I'm sorry

I ruined your supper, but Momma needed my help," she tried to explain as she began to cry. "She got sick agin today, real sick. But I can make you somethin else if'n you want?"

Glaring at Willie, John contemplated her offer for just a second then turned and looked around for his wife. "She's sick?" he finally asked as if what she'd said was some sort of new revelation. "What-a-ya mean she's sick?" he sneered in disgust. "Aginnn?"

"Ye, yes sur, real sick. An she needs ta see a doctor," Willie replied, still fearful as to what he might do next. "She's been lyin down in bed sleepin almost all day."

"All day," he repeated in a disgusted voice as he turned and stomped to her room. "An so you didn't make your quota?"

"No sur," Willie replied as she followed. "I'm sorry, but Momma can't work, see," she added as they entered then stopped and looked down at the unconscious woman.

"So what's wrong with her?" he demanded with an uncaring gaze back to Willie.

"You hit her too hard last night," Willie asserted along with a disgusted look. "An you hurt her, an I'm not gonna let you do it agin," she boldly added as she stepped between him and the bed.

"What?" John said with a surprised step backwards. "What'd you jus say?" He narrowed his eyes and glared, clearly incensed by her tone.

"I said, I'm not gonna let you hit Momma no more," Willie raised her voice in a defiant stand.

"Oh is that sooo?" he drew in a heavy breath at the thought of her insolence. "Well let me tell you somethin little girl," he snarled in a drunken slur. "This is my goddamn house, an if I think your momma needs ta be smacked around, I'll do it. I'll slap the shit right outa her an you too if you don't watch yourself," he warned and pointed his finger. "An ain't nobody gonna stop me."

Drawing upon all of her courage, Willie for the first time in her life boldly and angrily confronted her step dad. "Nooo!" she yelled with an assertiveness he'd never seen before. "You already hurt her bad enough last night an I ain't gonna let ya do it agin! Now leave Momma alone you hear!"

Caught off guard by both her defiance as well as her posture, John took a shallow breath and began to speak. He was going to assert his dominance, but for some unknown reason his mind went blank and with an awkward step backwards he stopped. He was drunk to the point where he just couldn't think anymore, and even though he wanted to say something, he didn't.

It was a standoff, and as the two stared at each other in a tense but fleeting moment of silence, John could clearly see that the young girl meant every word she'd said. She'd asserted herself in the most defiant of ways and now unsure of just what to do or who to yell at, and too drunk to really care, he slowly turned back to the door with a disgruntled huff and headed for the porch.

Watching as he disappeared, Willie stared and waited until the sound of the screen door slapped against its jam. A moment later it was followed by that of a chair being drug across the porch until it too stopped with the sound of his body flopping into it. Looking toward the ceiling with her eyes closed, she finally exhaled a sigh of relief then slowly lowered her head and turned back to her mother. Her confrontation was over, yet she knew at any moment he could return. He was like that, and as she sat on the edge of the bed contemplating that thought, she dropped her head and began to cry. She felt lost and afraid... afraid that her mother was going to die.

"Oooh Mommaaa," Willie pleaded as she took the damp cloth from her mother's forehead and then tenderly applied a new one. "What am I go'n to do?"

Stirring to the sound of her daughter's voice as she laid the rag across her brow, Sara finally opened her eyes. "Willie," she called in a raspy whisper.

"I'm here Momma," Willie smiled and took her hand. "I'm herrrre. How do you feel? Can I get you somethin?"

Shaking her head ever so slightly, Sara grimaced and then turned her gaze toward the window. "It's daaark," she said with a worried look.

"Yesss," Willie nodded. "You've been sleepin all day."

"I have?"

"Ah-huh," she nodded again. "Ever since I brought you in this mornin."

Staring at Willie as if she were trying to recall the day, Sara gazed at her daughter then suddenly began to panic. "Oh baby," she inhaled and pulled on her hand. "Your daddy, is he home yet?"

"Yes Momma, he got home a bit ago."

"But his supper?" she asked with a growing sense of anxiety. "What about his supper? I have to make his--."

"It's okay Momma," Willie interrupted. "It's okay. Daddy's already eatin. I took care of it an made supper while you was sleepin." She fibbed in hopes that her mother wouldn't worry. "An everything's fine. He's sittin out on the porch havin a smoke, so don't you worry none okay. Now tell me, how do you feel?"

"I hurts baby," Sara tightened her face and swallowed. "I hurts all over."

"I know Momma, but we're gonna fix that," she whispered along with a gentle squeeze to her hand. "Cause tamorrow I'm gonna go into town an get the doctor an he's gonna make you all better," she added with a smile. "Very first thing in the mornin... so you jus hang in there okay."

Comforted by the thought that her daughter was there and that she was cared for, Sara exhaled a contented sigh and then closed her eyes. She was weaker now than ever before, and the few words that she'd spoken had exhausted her, but before she could slip back into her dream world, their quiet was broken by the sound of John's voice bellowing for more whiskey.

It was a harsh and ugly tone that left little doubt as to his state of mind and before Willie could move, Sara reached out and grabbed her arm. "Don't you get it Willie," she grimaced as she squeezed and pulled. "You hear meee? He don't need no more."

But John was insistent, and after only a few moments he yelled again then cursed them both as he rose and walked inside. He was mad and his patience was gone, and as he staggered and banged into the walls, he entered a mean belligerent drunk looking for more whiskey.

Rummaging through the cabinets, he finally found a bottle after a short but noisy search then took a seat at the table and pulled its cork. Taking a long hard pull of the home made mash, he swallowed the burning liquor with a satisfied sigh then set it down hard and wiped his chin.

His world was spinning, but even so as he sat at the table he couldn't help but stare at the door to Willie's room. Smiling at the thought of the tasty young innocence lying just on the other side, he contemplated his desires for just a moment then noisily rose and grabbed his bottle of corn mash. He could barely stand let alone walk, yet he was determined to have her in a way that he shouldn't. It was all he could think of, but just as he reached the other side of the room he crashed into the doorframe. A second later and in an effort to keep from falling, he quickly fumbled and found the doorknob then rolled his back to the door to steady himself.

He needed a moment to collect himself, and with a big deep breath in an attempt to replenish his oxygen deprived brain and slow his spinning world, John gradually regained some semblance of control. He was drunk beyond any sense of the word and he knew it, yet still he turned his head against the door and called for his stepdaughter.

"Willieee," he whispered with a sickening hiss as he slowly turned the rusty knob and pushed it open. It was time she learned how babies were made, and with the most depraved of smiles, John Dawson quietly slipped into Willie's room.

They'd been listening since he'd entered the house but as the sound of Willie's door slowly creaked open and the man they both feared and hated entered her room, their looks of fear quickly turned to disbelief.

"Goddammit girl," he called as he shuffled and stumbled in the dark. "Where are you, you little bitch?" he laughed with a heavy slur in search of his desires. "It's time you learnt how babies are made... ramember?"

Waiting for an answer that never came, John quickly took another breath and continued on with his search. "Goddammit girl," he growled with a salivating anger as he spun in the dark. "You hear meee?"

Listening as his words cut through the wall and into her soul, Sara writhed in heart wrenching pain. It was a sick and nauseating feeling to know why he was there, and as she lay in bed unable to rise and defend her own daughter, she shook her head and began to cry.

Bending ever so slightly, John looked under the bed for his precious treasure but lost his balance when he stood back up. Smashing into the dresser with an agonizing groan, he dropped his bottle of corn mash to the floor and grabbed his ribs. He needed to sit, but as he turned back to the bed, he lost his balance and fell. Hitting his head on the nightstand, he emitted a painful cry and then hit the floor with a heavy thud. Sprawled face down beside the bed, he lay unconscious as the blood from the gash in his head slowly puddled onto the dry cracked planks of the floor.

There wasn't a sound now, and for a few agonizing minutes Willie and her mother lay in bed wondering and waiting, listening to the eerie quiet, until Willie finally rose to investigate. Stepping softly onto the floor, she quietly made her way to her room then cautiously opened the door and looked inside. Gazing into the dark, she looked down at the silhouette of John's body lying on the floor next to her bed. Staring for just a moment, she wondered if he were dead then stepped through the door for a closer view. Looking down at the unconscious drunkard, his head lying in a small but growing pool of blood, she stared with a burning hatred then dropped her head in disappointment at the sound of his breathing. He was still alive, yet even so she exhaled a sigh of relief and then quietly returned to her mother.

"What happened Willie?" Sara asked.

"It's okay Momma, Daddy jus fell an he's sleepin now," she answered as she crawled back into bed and closed her eyes with a heavy exhale.

She was completely exhausted from the day's events, but before she could slip into the dream world, she stirred to the sound of her mother's voice calling her name. "Willie," Sara whispered along with a gentle nudge.

"Yes Momma?" Willie rose to her elbows and stared. "What's wrong? Are you okay?"

"Yes, but I want you to get somethin for me."

"You whaaat?" she asked as if she'd misheard.

"I said, I want you ta get somethin for me. I want ya ta get my bible," she said and pointed to her dresser. "Pleeease."

Gazing at her mother, Willie stared for a moment then began to shake her head as if she could actually sense what she was thinking. "Nooo Momma," she argued. "You don't need it."

"Yes baby, yes I do," she said with a pleading gaze. "I need ta make my peace... pleease."

For a moment it was a battle of wills until Willie reluctantly rose from the bed and retrieved it from the dresser. "Here ya go Momma," she choked as she returned and handed it to her.

Taking it from her hands, Sara pulled it to her chest and closed her eyes. Clutched tightly in her left hand, she reached out with her right and cleared her throat. Grabbing her outstretched hand, Willie squeezed it tight then dropped to her knees by the bed. She knew her mother was slipping, but the words that came next broke her heart and filled her eyes with tears.

"I think the Lord has come ta take me Willie," Sara hushed with a frightened look in what was clearly a fear of the unknown.

"No Momma, don't talk like that, you hear me," Willie pleaded. "I told ya, I'm go'n to town tamorrow ta get the doctor an you're gonna be jus fine... ramember."

Nodding ever so slightly as if to appease her daughter, Sara's thoughts slowly drifted back to what she knew was the truth. She was dying and she knew it. The life within her was fading and with that thought consuming her, she pulled Willie's hand to her chest and laid it on top of her bible.

"Willie," she said as she intertwined her fingers with her daughter's. "I want you ta promise me somethin okay."

"Yes ma'am," she answered as her tears began to fall.

"I've been thinkin, an if..." she paused and took a breath. "If somethin happens ta me, I... I want you ta promise me that ya'll leave this place okay. Leave jus as fast as you can baby, an don't never come back. Go to the city an get an edjacation, an make a better life far yourself, you deserves it."

"What-a-you mean Momma?" she asked with a quiet uncertainty. "Where would I go? I, I don't know nobody."

"I know baby, I know, but still I want ya ta leave, you hear," she insisted.

"But how would I live Momma? I ain't got no money."

"Yes baby," she refuted emphatically. "Yes you do, you have lots of money."

"I do?"

"Yes, you do."

"But I don't understand?" Willie shook her head. "Where'd you get money? We're sharecroppers Momma... we ain't got no money!"

Hearing the hopeless desperation in her daughters voice along with the confused expression on her face, one that was now laced with a deep and growing curiosity, Sara finally confessed as to her long and intimate relationship with Mr. Johnson. Listening at first in shock and then with an endearing smile, Willie fondly reflected upon the man she'd known most of her life. He was a good man, and as she thought back to the many times that her mother would either leave and or return with him, she now realized why she always seemed so happy whenever he was around. Finishing with what was clearly a contented sigh, Sara lifted her arm and pointed to the kitchen.

"Now, there's a jar hidden in the pantry that I want ya ta get."

"A what?" Willie turned her head toward the kitchen.

"A jar," Sara repeated. "Where I've been savin, an it's full. I've been savin far a long time baby, an I want you ta take it an go to the city. Go to New Orleens an get an edjacation. I've heard it's a wonderful place, an if God'll let me when I get ta Heaven, I'll try an help you an show ya the way."

"But why, Momma?"

"Cause ya deserves it baby," she said as she looked on with pride. "You're smart, I know you are, an you deserves a better life. A better one than what I've given ya."

"But I don't wanna leave you Momma."

"But you have to," Sara raised her head from the pillow. "Dammit Willie," she grimaced as she labored to speak. "Ya have to listen ta me. It's not me... it's him. You've got ta leave him, ya hear. Your daddy's a bad man an I want ya to promise me, okay. I want you to promise me that ya'll leave him if I die."

Slowly shaking her head, the sad young girl finally broke down and sobbed at the thought of what her mother was truly asking. "I promise Momma," she cried as she crawled into bed and lay beside her. "I promise."

CHAPTER 4

HOURS LATER, WILLIE WOKE ONCE again to the sound of her mother's voice and a gentle nudge to her side. "Yes Momma?" she quickly asked.

"I love you sweetie," Sara said with a groan as she raised her head from the pillow. "An don't you never forget it, ya hear."

Somewhat surprised at her mother's warm and loving words, Willie smiled. "I know Momma, I knooow. An I love you too," she yawned as she snuggled back into her side. "Now let's go to sleep okay," she said as she closed her eyes.

Slipping as the night wore on, Sara's condition continued to weaken until Willie woke to the twitching of her body. Convulsing as the life within her slowly but steadily drained, Sara Mae Dawson took her final breaths of life and then quietly died in her sleep.

Welling with tears as she exhaled for the very last time, Willie cried out in agony then shook and begged her mother to wake. But she couldn't, she was gone. She'd left this world and had gone to another, to a better world. To one that would give her the ever-lasting peace she'd always desired as she took her place in the kingdom of heaven.

A short time later, Willie finally rose from her mother's side, lit the lamp on the dresser and walked outside for some much needed air. Gently closing the screen door, she crossed the porch to its edge then stopped and looked up at the stars. They were bright and twinkling, and after a long deep breath to quell her emotions, she lowered her gaze and stared out across the fields. To the ones that'd taken her mother's life and that all too quickly filled her mind with the haunting vision of them walking back in from their hard days work.

She remembered the sound of her voice, and how she'd laughed and told her she smelled. She remembered it all until the memories themselves seemed to pull the strength from her legs. Dropping to her knees, Willie stared out to the spot where her mother had fallen. She missed her already, and as the overpowering emotions of grief took hold, Willie slowly lowered her head and began to cry.

She was heartbroken, but there was no changing what'd happened and as the reality of her situation became clearer and clearer, she finally rose and turned to the house determined to fulfill her promise. She would leave, but for some reason as she walked back to the door, she felt drawn to the side of the house. Why she wasn't sure, but with a strange and somewhat overpowering urge now compelling her, she descended the steps as if in a trance and continued until she'd made her way around the corner. Stopping just short of the neatly placed border of rocks, Willie looked down and smiled at the sight of her mother's small flower garden and its late summer blooms.

Gazing at the garden, she thought of how her mother had always loved fresh flowers on the table, and of how she would fuss and pick over the various types until she had the prefect ones. Taking a step forward, she bent for a closer look, and under the dim light of the moon, began to pick a variety of the prettiest ones. Finishing with a half dozen of her nicest daisies, her favorites, she returned to the kitchen, made a lovely bouquet in a vase, and then placed it in the center of the table.

It was something her mother had done for years, and after she was finished, she took the daises she had laid on the table, pulled a ribbon from her hair and tied them together with a delicate bow. Then with a heavy breath as if to summon her will, she turned and slowly walked back into the bedroom. Taking a seat on the edge of the bed, she tenderly folded her mother's hands over her bible still on her stomach and slipped the flowers beneath them. She was at peace and resting with God, and after she'd smoothed her dress, Willie slid from the bed to her knees and said a prayer.

Finishing with a promise to fulfill her mother's wish, she rose without another thought and quickly made a shoulder sack out of blanket. Gathering her clothes, some odds and ends, and an old picture of them together, she then went to the pantry and took what little food they had. Easily finding the money her mother had spoken of in the wall, she dumped it all into a leather pouch then went to her bedroom where John was lying. Looking down upon the man, the drunkard, Willie couldn't help but seethe in anger. She hated him now more than ever, and before she even realized what she was doing, she'd returned to the pantry and retrieved the jug of lamp oil.

She knew as soon as she had grabbed it that what she was about to do was wrong, yet even so she unscrewed the lid and began to douse the house. Concentrating heavily in her bedroom, she saturated the floor around the man she hated then finished with a heavy trail to the front door. Returning to her mother's bedroom to say her final goodbye, she sat and spoke as if she were still alive.

"I'm leavin now Momma, jus like ya told me to," she whispered as she fought the growing lump in her throat. "An jus as soon as I get ta New Orleens, I promise ta get an edjacation."

It was a promise she intended to keep, and with that she rose from the bed, grabbed the lamp from the dresser and walked to the door. Stopping for one last look, she turned back with a trail of tears running down her cheeks. She knew that this was the last time she would ever see her mother again, and after one last lingering gaze, she rushed from the room.

Grabbing her shoulder sack from the table, she slipped it on then stepped to the screen door and pushed it open. Stopping in the threshold, she turned back with her lamp held high and stared with a glaring hatred at her bedroom door. Her mother was right, he was a bad man, and he would never stop in his ways. She knew that now, and with the thought of how his cruel and uncaring ways had killed the only person she had ever loved, Willie dropped the burning lamp to the floor.

Shattering as it hit the thick wooden planks, she watched in a surreal daze as the blue and yellow flames quickly began to spread and engulf the home. Quietly yet ravenously feeding on the dry cracked wood, the flames crawled across the floor like a growing serpent now possessed with a life of its own. Quickly filling the house with a thick white smoke, Willie finally turned and let the door slap behind her then slowly descended the steps and took the path to their drive.

Illuminated now by the burning blaze behind her, she easily found it and began walking with determined strides straight to the main road. She was leaving, yet for some reason she suddenly slowed and then stopped as the fire began to roar and crackle behind her. Breaking the quiet of the night, the house, now completely ablaze, cast an eerie orange glow along with a flickering shadow that danced hauntingly across the snow-white fields. Staring for just a moment, she finally turned back to the house and watched as the flames, fueled by the oil and overly dry timber, began to lick higher and higher into the night. Lashing at the stars with giant yellow and blue serpentine tongues, the fire soon began hurling bright sparks and burning embers high into the sky. Glowing brightly for just a few moments, they would then slowly fade and disappear into the dark.

Reflecting upon her mother peacefully lying on the bed but now consumed by the growing inferno, Willie looked up to the sky and past the stars into the never ending black abyss of the heavens. "Take care of my momma, God," she choked as she dropped her head and began to cry.

She was sad beyond words, but with a tenacious resolve to carry out her mother's wishes, she wiped the tears from her eyes and turned. A second later and before she could actually take a step, she jerked back to the blazing structure as the screams of the man she hated suddenly rose from inside. The flames had finally reached him, and as his bone chilling cries for help penetrated into the night and echoed across the valley floor, Willie knew that his time had come.

Begging and pleading as the fire engulfed and consumed his oil soaked body, John E. Dawson laid on the bedroom floor. Trapped by the burning blaze, she listened to his screams in the coldest of ways until one long last horrifying scream of death finally ended in silence. He would never hurt her again, she was certain of it. Then slowly turning away as if in a daze and without remorse, Willie Mae Dawson, overwrought with emotions and now all alone, quietly walked into the night and into the beginning of a new life.

Reaching the main road, she finally stopped then looked up and down the road. Which way she thought, as she looked first one way and then the other? Contemplating her choices for just a short moment, Willie finally turned to the south. This way, she decided. Yes, south, the big cities are south. New Orleans is south.

Satisfied with her decision, she slid her hands under the straps of her shoulder sack and took her first steps. Determined now more than ever to fulfill her promise to her mother, she began a slow but steady pace down the road. Cresting a high rolling hill a half hour later, she stopped and turned to view the house one last time. Now nothing more than a pile of glowing embers shimmering in the far off dark, she dropped her sack to the ground and then quietly stared.

It was a surreal moment, and as she drifted back with her thoughts, she remembered her mother's last words as they lay together on the bed. *'I love you sweetie.'* The haunting sound of her voice echoed in her head. *'An don't you never forget it, ya hear.'*

"I won't Momma," she promised as her mother's voice faded and she began to weep.

Her heart was broken, yet just as quickly as she'd begun to cry, she wiped away her tears with the back of her hand and cleared her throat. She had to remain strong, and with a long last look at the only place she'd ever called home, she picked up her shoulder sack and then turned to continue.

She was ready, but before she could even take a step, Willie suddenly jumped in fright at the unexpected sound that came from the other side of the road. Hooting loudly at the intruder below him, a large grey owl suddenly broke the still of the night. She knew what it was as soon as she'd heard it, and even though it had frightened her, she turned in search of the feathery winged raptor.

Finding it high above her in a large dead tree that stood just off the road, it hooted once more then spread its wings and dropped from its jagged perch. Silently taking flight across the field below her, Willie watched as the nocturnal bird of prey glided effortlessly with the descent of the land until it had disappeared into the forested border below. It was gone, and with one last quick glance to the house, she turned and quietly walked over the hill.

Hours later a completely exhausted Willie finally stopped at the crest of another rolling hill. She needed sleep in the worst of ways, and with the sight of a large lone oak standing majestically at the edge of a field she crossed the ditch and climbed over the fence. It was perfect, and as she took her refuge beneath its giant canopy, she laid a blanket on the grass and made a bed between the gnarly roots of the ancient wonder. Fluffing her shoulder sack into a pillow, the girl who could go no further, curled into a ball and cried herself to sleep.

———•————

The night seemed to pass all too quickly and before Willie knew it, the coming dawn was at hand. Waking to the new day, she slowly stirred and raised her head then marveled at the pink and crimson sky as it began to brighten. She felt rested yet still she was tired, and as she continued to stare at the growing light, she began to reflect on the fact that for the first time in her life she was truly alone. It was a daunting thought and before she knew it she began to weep at the thought of her unknown destiny. A moment later, she called to her mother in a broken voice. "Momma," she pleaded in search of an answer she knew would never come. "What-a I dooo?"

It was a heart wrenching moment, yet even so she waited and hoped for a sign. But it was not to be, and as she stared blankly toward the horizon and replayed the night's events, she pulled her legs to her chest and wrapped her arms around them then gently dropped her head to her knees.

It wasn't until the sun had peaked above the horizon and through the distant wispy clouds that Willie at last raised her head. Shedding its light across the rolling landscape with an almost instant and unremitting intensity, she rubbed her eyes then watched as the burning ball slowly ascended ever higher into the sky. It was beautiful, but along with it came her morning hunger. Reaching behind for her sack she dug into the middle and grabbed a small piece of salt pork wrapped in paper. Gnawing on the tough dried meat, she quickly swallowed her bite and took another but then suddenly stopped to a strange sound emanating from the far off distance. What is that, wondered as she curiously stood and walked from under the tree?

Surveying the vastness of the valley before her, Willie stared in awe as she looked first to the distant hill and then to the grassy field in front of her. Dotted with large trees and small groups of cattle, the field sloped all the way down to the edge of a dried up creek. Now nothing more than small random pools of water left from the long summer's drought, it snaked lazily through the valley and gave precious water to the grazing animals. Past it the field continued on until it reached a barbwire fence and a set of railroad tracks. Running along the valley floor, the iron rails continued on towards a small sleepy town that seemed less than a mile away. A short distance past the tracks, the opposite hill rose steeply and was thickly forested all the way to the top.

It was beautiful, but with an ever-growing curiosity she turned her gaze away from the rising sun and focused on a sound that was emanating from the far end of the valley. Increasing at a slow but steady pace, Willie concentrated and then smiled at what was clearly the faint yet unmistakable rumbling of a train. A few moments later, she watched as a big locomotive belching its thick black smoke finally appeared at the far end of the valley.

Serving as its lifeline to the rest of the world, the long slow moving freight train meandered like a slithering snake along the valley floor toward the little town. Appearing and disappearing behind clusters of trees as it drew ever closer, Willie began to reflect upon all of the stories she'd heard of people riding the rails. It was her way out of Hale County and she knew it, and with all due haste she rolled up her blanket and set off for the iron rails.

She had to get on the train, and with a new sense of urgency she ran down the hill and across the field. Scattering the cattle, she crossed the creek then rushed up the other side toward the tracks. Reaching the barbwire fence just as the train rumbled past, she hurriedly but carefully climbed over the thorny strands then scrambled up the gravel embankment to the tracks. Reaching them just as the last car passed, she stood behind the train and watched as it slowly lumbered on. Catching her breath after arduous run, she rested for a few moments then took off in a trot toward the town.

Slowing as it pulled into town and approached the station, the big locomotive continued on until it came to a stop beneath the water tower. Screeching and clanging with the sound of metal against metal, it finally ceased all forward motion when the big engine dumped its pressurization along with a huge cloud of steam. Breathing and panting like a giant steel dragon that'd just come to rest after a long long journey, it waited as it was fitted to take on its precious liquid.

It was just the break that Willie needed, and as she hurriedly ran down the tracks and approached the rear of the train she began to smile. She'd closed the distance and it was still there, and with the thought that this would take her to New Orleans, she stepped to the side in search of the open boxcar she'd seen when it had passed. It would be perfect, but just as soon as she spotted it the train blew its whistle and jerked forward.

To Willie it was the thought that she wouldn't make it that scared her most, and as the train began to slowly roll she panicked and began to run. Passing coal car after coal car, she struggled on the loose gravel to catch the accelerating boxcar. Running as hard as she could, she finally succeeded and threw her shoulder sack into the open doorway.

Certain she could climb onboard, she jumped and grabbed at the floor of the boxcar only to realize that she'd made a mistake and was now in serious trouble. Unable to pull herself up, and now unable to let go, she hung with her body swinging perilously from the car. Stuck with her arms stretched out across the floor, she desperately clutched for something to hold as she slowly began to slip and drop in front of the rolling wheels.

Scratching and clawing at the rough wooden planks, she frantically searched for a crack between the boards in which to embed her fingertips. Wide eyed with fear that she'd be cut in half by the giant wheels, she scraped at the floor, driving splinters deep into her hands and arms. It was the fight for her life but it was useless and she continued to fall, and as her feet began to drag across the ground, Willie closed her eyes and cried out.

It was a cry that instantly bolted him into action, and with an unbelievable quickness Duncan Haywood bounded like a cat and lunged across the floor of the boxcar. Reaching Willie just as she slipped from its edge, he grabbed her upper arm and clenched it in a powerful grip.

Feeling his vise like hold on her bicep, Willie opened her eyes as her fall beneath the wheels abruptly stopped. Looking first at the huge hand that was wrapped tightly around her arm, she then looked up and into the eyes of the largest black man she had ever seen. Met with a smile as broad as his shoulders, she frantically reached for his forearm with her other hand.

"I's got ya missy," his deep baritone voice drawled over the rumbling of the wheels as he lifted her from certain death.

He was huge, and with an arm that was larger than her leg, he slowly turned back into the train like an enormous crane then effortlessly set her down away from the edge. Towering in the doorway, in dirty overalls and a t-shirt stretched over his huge muscular frame, Willie stared at the man for just a moment then turned her gaze back to the spot from which she'd hung. Shaken beyond belief at the thought of her near death experience, she stood in a daze unable to move until Duncan reached up to steady her.

"Are you okay there missy?" he asked as he bent and grabbed her arm.

Brought back into reality by the sound of his voice and the touch of his hand, Willie slowly turned and looked up at the man. "Yesss, yes I am," she replied with a nod. "Thank you mister. You jus saved my life," she continued gratefully.

"Yes um, an you's quite welcome," Duncan replied and shrugged his shoulders. "But it weren't nothin really."

"Well still, I'm much beholden to ya. Thank you... an I want ya to know that I won't never forget it either."

Standing in the doorway the two silently stared at each other until Duncan gently tugged on her arm and pulled her from the edge. "Well, we bes sits down," he said as he turned.

Crossing the boxcar as the train continued to accelerate, the two took their seats at the far end and away from the other riders. Settling onto the floor with her back against the wall, Willie crossed her legs and then guardedly placed her sack on top of them. Yes, she'd made it. She'd made her train and she owed it all to the man standing next to her. Her savior who'd pulled her from certain death, and who was now slowly sliding down with his back against the wall. Watching as his big limbs bent under his incredible weight, she wondered for a second as to how such a large man could have gotten to her so fast.

Hitting the floor with a groan and a sigh, Duncan made sure he sat several feet away then quietly smiled at the newest member to the boxcar. Smiling back yet still unaware of the other riders setting in the shadows, Willie boldly extended a hand to the big man. "I'm Willie," she said with a confident voice and a grateful smile. "Willie Mae Dawson."

Hesitating for just a moment, Duncan cautiously eyed the other men sitting at the far end of the car. It was a dangerous act for a grown black man to be sitting with a young white girl and he knew it, but even so he slowly reached out and took her hand.

"I's Duncan, Miss Willie," he drawled as her hand disappeared inside of his giant palm. "Duncan Haywood. An I's pleased ta meet ya," he added as they shook.

He was the first black man she'd ever met, and after they shook Willie leaned back against the wall and turned to survey her surroundings. Adjusting her eyes, she focused on the half dozen men sitting in the shadows at the far end of the boxcar, all white, all silently staring at her. Riding the rails was crime enough, but a young single white girl sitting and traveling with a black man in these times was not the wisest of things to do. It was how things were yet even so she didn't care for he'd just saved her life. A moment later, she turned her gaze back outside.

She'd never been more than a few miles from home her entire life, yet here she was on a train leaving the only town she'd ever known. Watching as it slowly fell behind, Willie stared out at the passing landscape with an ever-growing sense of trepidation. She had absolutely no idea as to where she was going or what she was going to do, and as she silently said goodbye to her mother and the only life she'd ever known, she quietly began to weep.

Wiping the single tear rolling down her cheek with the palm of her hand, she bit her lower lip in an attempt to repress the others that were trying to follow. But the gates to her salty reservoirs were open and there was no stopping the tears that they held. They were coming, and as the overwhelming feelings of emptiness and grief began to build inside of her, Willie pulled her knees to her chest and wrapped her arms tightly around them. It was her attempt at preventing the inevitable but it failed, and with that she looked to the ceiling and took in a breath then dropped her head into her knees.

It was something that quickly caught Duncan's attention, and for a few quiet moments he watched as she wept. Something was wrong and it worried him. "Miss Willie?" he finally drawled with the concern of a father. "Is you okay?"

Slowly lifting her head, Willie turned toward the man then nodded and smiled. But it was a feigned smile and Duncan knew it, and with an ever-growing concern he questioned her again. "Whut's wrong Miss Willie? Did someone hurts you?"

"No," she shook her head. "I'm fine," she added as she wiped the tears from her cheeks then turned and stared back outside.

She'd said she was fine but Duncan could sense that something was terribly wrong. The father of two young girls himself, he knew that something had happened to her and that it was hurting her. Her tears she'd just wiped away had already returned and after a moment of silence, the gentle giant now more concerned than ever, questioned her once more. "Where's your momma Miss Willie?" he asked. "Does she know dhat you's on dhis train?"

His question was a simple one yet it seared into her head, causing her to choke and gasp for air. Her heart was broken, yet even so she turned back and then summoned the words that hurt so bad. "My momma's gone," she finally managed between heavy sobs. "She died last night an left me."

As a father Duncan wanted nothing more than to hug and comfort her, but he was black and she was white, and although his desires were strong he could only sit and stare in a moment of silence then politely offer his sympathies. "Well, I's truly sorry bout yer momma Miss Willie," he said in hopes that she would find some comfort. But Willie never responded, and as he sat and watched her cry, he began to wonder about her father. If her mother was dead and she wasn't a runaway, then where was her father and where was she going? Tilting his head, he thought for a moment longer and then cleared his throat.

"Miss Willie," he called then waited with no answer. "Miss Willie," he called again after only a short moment. "Where's yer daddy? Don't you's have a--"

"I don't have no daddy," she snapped with an icy glare before Duncan could even finish. "An I never did!"

Caught off guard not only by her tone but also her ice-cold gaze, Duncan instantly dropped the subject and ceased with his questions. And even though he knew there was more to her not having a father than she'd said, he let it be and just watched as she stared out of the boxcar. Brushing her tears away every so often with the palm of her hand as she stared at the landscape and the train rolled on. Marveling at the vastness of the countryside as the miles disappeared and they slowly rolled across the state, Willie finally wiped the last of her tears from her dirty cheeks then rose and walked to the edge of the door. To the spot where she'd hung just less than an hour before.

Holding onto the side of the car, she looked down and thought of just how close she'd come to dying, and then of just how lucky she was. She should be dead but she wasn't, she'd been saved by a stranger. By a man whom she'd never met before, by a black man. But why, she wondered? Hadn't she just committed God's ultimate sin? Shouldn't she have been taken for what she'd done? The life of another person? Contemplating the reasons with no answers, Willie finally shifted her gaze back to the rolling hills and fields then shook her head into the wind and stared at the passing scenery.

It was a whole new world opening up to her. A world that up until now she'd never seen nor ever imagined. It was so big and intimidating, yet she knew as she stood in the doorway and took it all in that she'd find her way. She had to, for she'd made a promise to her mother she was determined to keep and with that, she slowly turned back to the man who'd saved her. He was watching her like a guardian angel, and with a comforting smile as she gained his eyes she slowly walked back to her spot beside him.

Settling onto the floor just as he reached into the sack by his side, Willie curiously watched as he rummaged around and then finally turned back with a large canteen in his hand. "Dhis is if'n you don't minds drinkin after a black man," he grinned as he loosened the cap and handed it to her.

Thinking of his words and what they really meant, Willie smiled again and shook her head. "No sur, I don't mind at all," she said in a raspy but grateful tone as she grabbed the canteen. "Thank you, I ain't had nothin ta drink since last night," she added as she unscrewed the cap and then tilted it upwards. Guzzling from the little hole, she took four big gulps then set the silver container back down between her legs with a satisfied sigh. A second later, she screwed the top back on and then handed it back to Duncan. Politely thanking him again as he took it in his giant hands, she quickly turned to her shoulder sack and pulled it to her lap. She wanted to return his gesture of kindness, and with that she reached inside and pulled out her package of salt pork. Unwrapping the paper covered meat, she grabbed one of the largest pieces she had and held it up to a very surprised Duncan.

"Here," she quipped with a mischievous grin and a gleam to her eyes. "This is if'n ya don't mind eatin after a white girl,

Gaining a smile along with a hearty laugh at her quick witted remark, Duncan, for a fleeting moment, could only sit and stare as he reflected upon the times that they lived in. She was white, yet here she was without any of the bigotry that was so common of their day, sharing her food with a black man. He liked that, for it was a refreshing change from how he'd always been treated and without another thought he reached for the meat. "I don't minds at all Miss Willie," he shook his head and took a bite. "Nots at allll."

A short while later Willie slowly turned back to Duncan and cocked her head. "Mister Duncan," she asked with a hint of trepidation to her voice. "Do you know where this train's a go'n?"

"Oooh yes um," he drawled as he swallowed his last bite. "I shorly does. It's a go'n ta Moobile. To where there's work. An you can jus calls me Duncan if'n ya wants."

"Oh nooo!" she cried in a panic. "It can't, it jus can't. I'm sappose ta go to New Orleens... to a big city so I can get an edjacation."

"Not on dhis here train you ain't," Duncan assured. "Dhis here train's a go'n ta Mobile."

"But it can't, I promised my momma..." her voice waned as she turned and stared out the door.

He knew it was hard on her, yet still Duncan did his best to ease her mind and assure her that Mobile was big enough to get an education. They talked for the longest of time, and even though Willie seemed pacified when he'd finished, she leaned back against the wall with a disappointed sigh. Her journey had not started off very well and it seemed as though it'd just gotten worse, and as she sat and contemplated her situation, the train, to the discomfort of its riders, slowly turned south. It was already hot, but now with the late afternoon sun shining directly into the open boxcar, it became even hotter. They were trapped in a rolling oven, and with only the open door and the continuous breeze providing any comfort, the group rode on and slowly baked in the afternoon heat.

CHAPTER 5

IT WAS JUST BEFORE SUNSET when the train gradually slowed and then stopped for another of its much-needed drinks. The town was small and quiet with only the far off panting of the locomotive and the sounds of a lone rail worker checking the train to be heard. He was banging a heavy hammer on the under carriages of each car, and as he slowly approached and then stopped at theirs, they listened as he banged on the pins and springs beneath their car. Fearful that he would also look inside, the group hid in the shadows and corners against the walls until he'd passed. It was a huge relief, and as the man in dirty overalls continued on, the group slowly settled back into their respective spots. Minutes later, the sound of his hammer fading in the distance finally stopped and the yard became quiet.

But the quiet didn't last long before Willie and some the others suddenly jumped back up to the sound of voices and running footsteps then watched as three young men ran across the tracks toward the boxcar like a pack of wild dogs. Reaching the car just as the train jerked and began to roll, they threw their sacks inside and easily jumped onboard. Dirty and lean, they appeared as if they were looking for trouble. Searching for a spot to sit as the train began to accelerate, the trio looked to the one end and spied Duncan sitting in the shadows.

"I ain't sittin by no nigger," the smallest one said with a mouthy disdain.

"I ain't either," his older bother immediately chimed in as they both turned to their leader.

Staring for just a second at the huge figure sitting on the floor, Lester jerked his head with a disgruntled huff. "Over here," he ordered and turned. Walking over to the windward side of the car, he looked down at the older men and then smiled through a set of dirty teeth. "This is our spot now," he growled. "So you all need ta move, ya hear."

His demand was clear yet the men didn't move and without a second's hesitation, the belligerent leader flew into a rage. "I said now Goddammit," he screamed as he began to kick the closest one in the legs.

Laughing as the rest of the men quickly scrambled in hopes of avoiding any farther confrontation, the three thugs slowly took their places and settled down. They were an unruly bunch that'd quickly brought an air of discontent amongst the men, and even though they all rode on edge, they all seemed to welcome the setting sun and the unrelenting heat that it took with it.

Now resting on the hazy horizon, Willie watched as the burning ball cast the last of its rays across the quiet scorched landscape. Illuminating the darkened boxcar, but now with a greatly diminished intensity, she watched as the light eerily crawled along the walls of the train as they began on their long slow turn back out of town.

Now radiating a deep burnt orange, she wondered as to how something so beautiful could be so harsh. She thought of her mother and how the heat had taken her life, then wiped her eyes and stared as the sun's iridescent glow ever so slowly swept across her face. She missed her terribly, but as the train rolled on and she slipped back into the shadows, Willie suddenly changed her thoughts and turned her head then focused her eyes toward the far end of the boxcar. A second later, she locked eyes with one of the three thugs.

Shivering at the sight of his dark and beady eyes that were staring back at her, she quickly dropped her head and looked to Duncan. And although he was now lying down just a few feet away, she knew he would protect her. She could feel it, yet even so, and even though the three thugs were at the far end of the car, she scooted a few inches closer to the big man.

Shocked at what he thought he had just seen, the smallest of the three slapped his brother. "Jack!" he exclaimed in a whisper. "Look! That's a white girl sittin wit dhat nigger."

"Wha-uut?" Jack opened his eyes and turned with an annoyed expression.

"That's a white girl sittin wit dhat nigger, look!" Carl pointed, his voice now an octave higher.

Leaning forward, Jack strained to see into the shadows then instantly began to smile. "I'll be goddamn Carl, you're right," he drawled as he eyed the pretty young girl.

"Yeah, but what-a-ya think she's a do'n sittin wit him?" Carl cocked his head and turned back to his brother.

"Don't know," Jack chuckled as he wiped the tobacco drooling from the corner of his mouth. "But she shor is awfully fine lookin ain't she."

"Goddamn right about that," Carl snickered. "But check out that buck she's wit," he raised his head with an upward nod. "Ya think they're tagether? He shor is a big som bitch."

Eying the mass of flesh lying on the floor, the two men stared with a kind of uncertain awe. Duncan was huge, yet even so they smiled at the thought of their impending fortune and then turned to their leader.

"Lester... look!" Jack said with a nudge.

Rolling his head toward the two, the cruelest of the three opened his eyes and grinned. He'd already seen her, and with a growing smile that seemed to emanate from the thoughts already brewing in his mind, Lester slowly turned his gaze back to Willie and snickered. "In due time boys," he drawled with a quiet self-confidence the other two lacked. "In duuue time. Now gimme that bottle of shine Carl."

Quickly doing as he was told, Carl reached into his sack and pulled out a brown quart bottle stuck in a paper bag. Handing it to Lester, he and Jack watched as their leader uncorked the top then tilted it to his lips. Pulling on it long and hard, he gulped the white-hot liquor in giant swallows then slammed the bottle down into his lap with a whoop and a smile.

"Goddamn that's potent," he winced and coughed then pounded his chest. "Did your uncle make that?" He exhaled and shook his head in an attempt to extinguish the fire from his throat.

"He shor did," Carl replied with a proud but stupid grin. "He made it special... jus for our trip. Ya like it?"

Nodding with a smile, Lester greedily took another short nip then wiped his mouth with a satisfied sigh and jutted his arm to Jack. Drinking as the miles slowly disappeared beneath them, the three men quietly talked of taking the young girl for their pleasure. Looking around as they made their plans, they carefully assessed the other six men onboard then wisely turned their attention to Duncan. Unsure as to whether or not he was really with her, they stared and continued to drink.

"I don't know Lester," Carl finally said with an uneasy voice. "He's pretty goddamn big an I think he's with her."

"What-a-you mean?" Lester snapped as he grabbed the bottle from his hand.

"Well it's jus that. I mean, I was jus thinkin."

"You was what?" He glared in disbelief. "You was thinkin? Shut up you sniveling piece of shit, you know I do the fuckin thinkin far us. Jack!" He barked and then turned to Carl's brother. "Kick your stupid ass brother for me."

"Yeah Carl, you know that," Jack said with a boot to his younger brother. "You know Les knows what he's do'n."

Glaring at Carl with a disgusted look, Lester finally rose from the floor, downed what was left of the bottle and then slung it out of the door. Shattering faintly on the rocks as the train rolled on, he winced and shook his head then stared down at the two with a determined glare.

"Well I don't know bout you boys, but nigger or no nigger, I'm jus about sick an tired of this shit," he said with a huff. "Come on, it's time we got us some pussy!" he added as he stepped only to instantly turned back with a smirk. "An ramember, ain't no nigger gonna fuck with three white men over no rail ho. Besides if he does, we'll jus whip his ass an throw em off the train."

To Carl and Jack, Lester's words were an instant confidence builder, and without another thought the two enthusiastically rose to their feet. Approaching like a pack of hungry wolves closing in on their prey, Willie watched as the three quietly crossed the boxcar. She knew what they wanted just by the looks on their faces, and as they stopped and closed in around her, she turned to Duncan in desperation.

It was a look that instantly caught Lester's attention, and with an ever so cautious glance over his shoulder, he eyed the big man still sleeping then turned back to the girl and bent at the waist. "Well hello there little lady," he drawled in a quiet tone. "Me an my two friends here were jus wonderin what you were do'n sittin with this here nigger?"

Turning away in an act that infuriated him, Lester stood and inhaled a long deep breath then bent back over and questioned her again. "I saiiiid, what are you do'n sittin with this here nigger? You're white, an you should be sittin with us."

The stench on his breath was nauseating, and even though she'd turned her head away in disgust, she finally answered. "No, I'm fine right here," she said as she tightened her arms around her legs. "Jus go away."

Standing once again as if he were suddenly enlightened, Lester turned back to the others. "Well boys, did you hear that?" he laughed and slapped his leg. "We're sapose ta jus go away."

Gaining a chuckle from the two brothers, Carl instantly repeated Lester's words. "Yeaaah, jus go away, jus go away!" he mocked again and again.

But Lester had no intentions of going away for he wanted her now more than ever. Willie was beautiful, and with a renewed and determined effort, he turned back to the girl then bent once again with his hands on his knees. He was drunk, it was hot, and his patience was at an end. "Now you listen ta me little girl," he began with a snarling growl. "I really don't like it when you turn your head away while I'm talkin, so I want ya to turn it back an look at me," he demanded.

Reluctantly complying, Willie slowly turned and stared at the man with dirty teeth.

"There, now that's much better," he said with a smile. "Now, like I was jus sayin, you know an I know that ya need ta be sittin with white folks. It's the way things are, so why don't you jus grab your little sack there an come sit with us?" He finished and then held out his hand.

Although that is what he said, Willie knew what he really wanted. She could tell by the look in his eyes, a look she'd seen before in her stepfather's and she wanted nothing to do with him. "Thank ya kindly," she said with a stern resolve and another glance to Duncan. "But I'm fine right here."

It was her final rejection that caused Lester to instantly stand and turn to his friends. "Okay boys," he declared. "I'm tired of be'n nice, it's time we jus had our fun. Grab her ass."

Hollering with a whoop and a whistle, Jack and Carl quickly stepped forward and grabbed an arm then yanked Willie from the floor. Screaming for Duncan as they drug her to the center of the car, she fought with all of her strength but the men were strong and drunk, and easily overpowered her.

Instantly waking to Willie's cry, Duncan quickly rose from the floor and took three giant strides straight toward the liquored up trio. Enraged at their actions, he thought of his own two daughters and immediately confronted the three thugs, now against the wall and directly across from the door. "HEY!" he yelled ferociously as he stopped behind them.

Startled at the intrusion, the three men instantly stopped then turned and stared at the black giant now towering before them.

"Leave's the little Misses alone," Duncan demanded with a commanding growl, his body poised as if ready to strike.

But Lester wasn't about to stop, and in an act emboldened by the homemade mash he immediately and very unwisely took a stand. "What'd you jus say?" he growled as he defiantly stepped toward the man. "Did I jus hear you right?" He raised his eyebrows and glared. "Did you jus tell me what to do? A nigger tellin a white man what to do?" He sneered with an incensed expression. "Well, did ya?"

"No sur," Duncan replied as he cautiously eyed the three men. "I jus wants ya ta leave the little Misses alone. You don't needs to be a do'n whut yer do'n."

"Oh really, an jus who the fuck's gonna stop me... you?" Lester crowed.

"No sur, I don't wants no trouble. I jus wants you to let her go."

"Oh really, jus let her go?"

"Yes sur," Duncan nodded as he continued to eye all three.

"Well that jus ain't gonna happen," Lester assured with a glance to the two behind him. "Cause ya see... we ain't had our fun yet, have we boys?"

Gaining an instant and enthusiastic reply from the both of them, Lester continued on undaunted. "Now you listen to me," he poked the man in the chest. "I've had jus about all the shit from you that I'm gonna take, so if you know what's good for you, you'll set yer black ass back down before I lay an ass whoopin on ya." Satisfied that he'd made his point, Lester quickly turned back to Willie and grabbed her arm. "Now come on goddammit," he said with another jerk. "I told you that you need ta be a sittin with us white folks."

"Noooo," Willie cried as she began to struggle. "Mister Duncan!"

Instantly answering Willie's call for help, Duncan took another step closer then reached out and grabbed the man's forearm. Encircling it in a crushing grip, he stopped the liquored-up bully dead in his tracks. "Now I said ta leaves the little Misses alone," his deep voice boomed.

Grimacing as the giant hand began to pull, Lester instantly released his grip on Willie then turned back to Duncan with a seething glare. He was furious, yet even so he could see that the big man meant business. He could see it in his eyes that were filled with a glassy fire and in his veins that were pulsing and bulging from his neck. He was intimidated, yet even so, no self-respecting white man was going to let a nigger tell him what to do. Especially Lester.

Over confident with too much liquor, he smiled with sort of a crazy look then brazenly spit his chew onto Duncan's foot and clenched his fists. "Niiigger," he yelled back ferociously. "I tried ta warn you but you wouldn't listen, so now you's in far one hell of an ass whoopin."

It was a warning that Duncan quickly heeded, and as the man rolled his neck and shoulders and prepared to swing, he reacted instantly and with unbelievable speed. Dropping Lester's arm, he quickly lowered his stance and then reached straight for the man's chest. "I don't thinks so," he objected matter of factly.

Slowed by the alcohol and surprised by the man's quickness, Lester tried to react but faltered. Now the victim instead of the predator, the drunken bully suddenly realized all too late that he'd unleashed an unstoppable and powerful rage within the black giant.

Grabbing Lester's overalls square in the chest, Duncan yanked with an almost superhuman force. Pulling the man almost out of his shoes, he hurled the two hundred pound bully through the air and across the boxcar. Watching in horror as their buddy screamed and flailed helplessly out of the door, Jack and Carl listened over the rumbling of the train to the sickening thump of his body as it hit the ground with an agonizing groan, and then the faint but unmistakable twang of barbwire strands snapping as he tumbled into the fence.

To Duncan it was a befitting end to the bully, but there were still two more and without a second's hesitation he spun back and confronted them. "Now I said, ta leave's the girl alone!" he roared as the veins in his neck continued to bulge and pulsate.

Shocked by what they'd just seen, the two instantly dropped Willie's arms and then cautiously stepped backwards. They'd never seen such a display of strength, and with their eyes locked with Duncan's, they guardedly yet hurriedly made their way to the door. Looking back into the fading light, they caught just a glimpse of Lester screaming at the edge of a field, horribly entangled in an old rusted fence. Snapping the four strands of wires as he tumbled into them, they had coiled around his body like deadly constrictors. Helplessly trapped with a dislocated shoulder and a broken leg, Lester lay in the middle of nowhere all alone, unable to free himself.

Bleeding profusely from the hundreds of tiny barbs piercing his body, he teetered on the verge of unconscious. And as the train rolled on and the true reality of his situation sank in, a quivering fear knowing that the night and its creatures would soon close upon him took hold. He was doomed, and with the thought of his own impending death now consuming him, Lester Crawley for the first time in his life looked to the sky and began to pray.

Turning back to Duncan and Willie after their friend had disappeared, the two men quietly stared until Duncan took a giant step toward them.

"Now ju… jus hold on there mister," Jack stuttered as he held up his hand. "We… we ditn't mean the little gal no harm. Heck, we was jus havin us a little fun, ya know," he said with kind of a smart-ass grin as if Duncan was going to agree.

"Yeah, that's right," Carl quickly added with a stupid laugh.

Gazing back and forth between the two, Duncan searched for the sincerity in their voices but found none. They were lying and he knew it. "Well dhat don't matter none cause yer baaad men," he said as he took a step toward them and narrowed his eyes. "An you don't needs ta be a ridin on dhis here train."

Slapping his leg with a laugh, Jack turned to Carl. A lot like Lester, he'd never really learned just when to keep his mouth shut.

"Oh really?" he smirked as he began to taunt the raging giant. "Did ya hear that Carl? This here nigger says that we ain't sapposed ta be a ridin on this train," he crowed. "An jus what the fuck are you gonna do about it," he dared as he turned back to Duncan.

"Juump!" Duncan's deep voice boomed again as he took another step toward the man.

"Wha-uut?" the two half drunks uttered in unison, only to realize just as quickly as they'd said it what he'd meant. They could see it in his eyes, and in his body that was poised and ready to strike. They were in trouble and they knew it, but with six other white men on board they anxiously looked to the far end of the car. They were looking for support, but the men staring back never moved and with disheartened expressions the two slowly turned back to Duncan's burning glare.

"I said Juuump!" he roared once again.

Infuriated, but also emboldened by the effects of his uncle's homemade mash, and maybe just a little to stupid too know better, Jack puffed up his chest and daringly leaned forward. "Fuck you," he yelled, determined that no nigger was going to tell him what to do either. Smiling as if the words themself had stopped the giant, he turned to his brother. It was a defiant stand but one that was poorly considered for just as he turned back to Duncan the man's huge fist came rocketing at him.

Punching him square in the nose with the force of a hydraulic ram, Jack's face violently snapped backwards and exploded into a bloody mess. Catapulted into the air from the powerful impact, the man flew helplessly out of the door and into the tops of several small saplings growing along the tracks. Watching as he fell through the trees and then hit the ground with a groan, Duncan instantly turned his attention to the last of the three now cowering in fear.

"Now you," he yelled with a step toward the man.

"Aaah no man," Carl began to whine in a sniveling voice. "Co, come onnn now…. ya knows we was jus funnin," he pleaded as he shrank a little more and grasped at the opened edge of the door. "Really… that's all."

But Duncan wasn't listening, and nor did he care, they'd tried to hurt Willie and with another step toward him he narrowed his eyes into a merciless glare. "I said Jump!"

To Carl he was demanding the unthinkable, and as he held onto the door and debated his choices of hitting the ground or being punched by this monster, he began to plead even more. Seconds passed like minutes, and with a deep and sinking feeling growing rapidly in the pit of his stomach, he frantically looked outside. They'd just begun to cross a small river, and with the jerk of his head back to the sound of Duncan, Carl Mosley made his decision.

"I said Juuump!" Duncan bellowed and stomped his foot then cocked his giant arm.

Choosing the river some thirty feet below over the blow from the man's mighty fist, the last of the three thugs jumped from the train. Landing in the water with a splash and a scream, Duncan and Willie watched under the light of the rising moon as he thrashed in the water far below. He seemed to be hurt but the train rolled on and before they knew it, they'd crossed the bridge and he was gone.

To Willie it was a moment of relief, and with a step to her protective giant, to the man who'd just saved her twice in one day; she opened her arms and wrapped them around him. "Thank you Mister Duncan," she said as she laid her head against his chest and squeezed him.

Surprised and touched by her actions, Duncan nervously looked to the other six men still sitting at the end of the car. What Willie was doing was unthinkable, but to his surprise the men remained seated. "You's quite welcome Miss Willie," he said with the tenderness of a father as he awkwardly patted her on the back. "Ain't nobody gonna hurts you no more."

———◆———

He'd jumped in hopes that the river would break his fall, but when he landed in the stagnant waters still down from the long drought, Carl fractured his femur on a submerged log. Screaming in agony as the bone penetrated through his skin and overalls, he flailed and thrashed about then grabbed at the bloody and splintered object sticking out of his leg.

The pain was excruciating, and he knew that before he lost consciousness he had to make it to the shore some thirty feet away. He was hurt, and bad, but Carl was completely unaware of the four gators that he'd just awakened on the opposite shore. And as he continued to struggle and thrash about like the wounded animal he was, he quickly gained their unwanted attention. A few seconds later, he turned and froze with a sickening fear at the sound of splashing that'd come from down and across the river. Focusing his eyes onto the smooth dark surface now painted in a yellow light from the rising moon, he instantly vomited at the sight of the four large reptiles that had entered the water.

They were coming for him and he knew it, and he knew what it meant. They were predators and he was their prey, and as the rumbling of the train quickly faded into the distance, the reality of being truly alone instantly burned into his brain. Shivering in absolute horror, he turned back in a desperate attempt to reach the shore. Glancing behind him with every other stroke, he watched as the scaly skinned creatures continued to close in.

They seemed to be coming faster, and with that Carl frantically renewed his efforts and pushed hard on the bottom. He had to reach shore and get out of the water, but it was a mistake that would cost him for without his other leg to free himself his foot became stuck in the thick gooey mixture of Alabama mud. Twisting in desperation, he finally freed himself but then froze just as all four gators silently submerged beneath the blackish waters. Whimpering and shaking in both fear and pain, now deathly afraid to move, he listened to the river which had become eerily quiet. A quiet so quiet that it screamed into his ears and burned into his brain. That is until it was finally broken by the screams of his own death as the four large reptiles set upon him and began to feed.

Returning to where they'd been sitting, Willie looked at Duncan just as he dropped to the floor. Watching as he settled in with a heavy sigh, she wondered if there was anyone who could ever really stop him. He was without a doubt the biggest and strongest man she'd ever seen, and although she was still a little shaken, she found a soothing comfort in his protective nature. "Thank you agin for helpin me," she said gratefully.

"Dhat's quite al right Miss Willie," he replied as if it were nothing. "Those were baaad men."

Nodding as if she agreed, Willie smiled and then reached for her shoulder sack. Punching it like a pillow, she took a spot next to her protector, laid her head on her sack and then gazed outside at far off horizon. Dusk had arrived, and as the train rolled on she watched as the flashes of lightning shot through the boiling clouds and illuminated them with an ominous glow. It was a storm and a big one, and they were headed straight for it. But Willie was unconcerned for the day had finally taken its toll, and with darkness quickly closing in, she yawned great big and closed her eyes. A few minutes later, lulled by the gentle rocking of the train and the rumbling of the wheels beneath the floor, the tired young girl quickly fell asleep.

It seemed like only minutes, but in reality it had been hours when Willie suddenly awoke to the bright flash and cracking boom of a lightning bolt that'd hit close by. Bolting straight up as if she'd just awakened from a terrible dream, she cried out then quickly turned and searched the boxcar. Wide-eyed with fear that the men had come back to get her, she stared into the darkened corners until another far off flash of lightening dimly illuminated car. Sighing with relief at the sight of just the six men at the other end, she patted her chest then turned back to the sound of Duncan's deep comforting voice.

"Is you okay there Miss Willie?" he asked as he raised his head off his sack.

"Yeah," Willie replied and nodded. "I jus think I had a bad dream that's all. I thought that those men were comin ta get me agin."

"Well, dhat weren't no dream," Duncan said, affirming her inner thoughts and fears. "Those were bad men, but they's gone now," he continued. "An ya don'ts haf ta worry none see."

"I know," she sighed as she watched the storm and its flickering lightening dance outside. It seemed to be growing in its intensity, but after a few moments she turned back to Duncan.

"Mister Duncan?" she called as if she were contemplating some great question.

"Yes um Miss Willie."

"I want ya ta know somethin."

"Whut's dhat?" he asked with a curious gaze.

"That I...," she began but then stopped in an effort to choose her words. "That I won't never forget what ya done for me today, ya hear. Not ever."

"Well, dhas quite al right," Duncan replied. "Like I said afor, those were baaad men an they really ditn't needs ta be on dhis train."

"Well still, I jus wanted you ta know that," she reiterated. Then rising from the floor, Willie looked down at the man with her hands on her hips. "An I mean it too!" she added as if she'd just gotten in the last words of an argument then turned with a satisfied smile and walked to the door.

Grabbing the edge of the doorway, Willie steadied herself and stared out into the night. They'd finally reached the edge of the storm, and for a few moments she watched as the brilliant flickering forks of lightning silently danced from cloud to cloud. Illuminating the landscape without a sound, she marveled at its beauty then turned and stared in the direction of the train. Shaking her head into the wind, she put her hand to her hair and pulled a few wispy strands from her face. Gazing toward the darkened horizon and the far off lights of yet another city, she stared for a moment and then turned back to Duncan. "Mister Duncan," she whispered excitedly. "Come look!"

Rising from the floor with a groan, Duncan slowly made his way toward the door.

"Look," she said again as he approached.

"Ooh yeaaah," Duncan drawled as if he instantly recognized the far off glow.

"Is that Mobile?" she asked with a glance up to the towering giant.

Pausing for just a moment, Duncan grabbed the straps of his overalls and took a big deep breath. "Yes ma'am," he finally answered. "It shorly is. Dhats Mobile al right... Moobile Alabama. Where there's work."

Standing in the door as as the train rolled on, the two quietly stared and wondered with their thoughts as to what fates their city of hope would bring. A half-hour later and long after midnight, the train slowly rolled into the dark and barren Mobile yard. It had been a long long journey, but they were finally here, and with the screeching sound of steel against steel, the long, slow rolling freight train finally came to a stop and fell silent.

"We're here Mister Duncan," Willie said as she looked out the door.

"Yes ma'am Miss Willie," Duncan grinned in hopes that the city would somehow bring him work. "We shorly is."

Turning back, Willie began to speak but before she could utter a word she was pushed aside by one of the six men as they began to jump from the boxcar. They were anxious to get away before they were seen by the railroad bulls and for good reason, for once one had been caught, one rarely escaped unharmed and they all knew it.

Ready to follow, Willie hurriedly grabbed her sack and slung it to her shoulder. "Come on Mister Duncan," she said as she pulled her hair from under the strap. Shaking it free, she turned back to Duncan and stared at the man standing flat against the wall. "Let's go," she insisted with an anxious but somewhat agitated voice. "What are you do'n?"

"Waits Miss Willie," he replied and jerked his head as if to motion her against the wall.

"What is it?" she asked with a curious step closer.

"Dha bulls Miss Willie... dha bulls."

"The what?" She scrunched her face. "The bulls?" she inquired innocently. "What kind-a bulls?"

"Dha railroad bulls!" Duncan repeated with a frustrated hush as he grabbed the strap on top of her overalls and pulled her to the wall. "Now gets in dha dark so they don't see's ya."

Completely confused as to why anyone would let a bunch of bulls run loose in a train yard, and that they would actually look for people, Willie slipped into the shadows then looked to Duncan. Just what kind of bulls were these that had him so concerned? Was he losing his mind, or was he just afraid of cows? He was a big man and she couldn't imagine him being afraid of anything. And another thing, why weren't those other men afraid? Consumed by curiosity, she finally leaned from the wall and stared out of the boxcar in search of the cows.

"Well I don't see no cows," she said in an aggravated tone as she turned back to Duncan. "An besides, why in the heck are they a runnin loose anyways? They ought a be fenced up." It was an innocent question but before she could continue, she heard a man yelling for the six to stop. His voice was harsh and demanding, and after a glance outside to see who it was, she turned back to Duncan with a curious gaze.

"Dhat be da bulls Miss Willie," he answered before she could speak. "Dhaaat be da bullllls."

Startling the men that'd just jumped from the train, they all stopped and turned then stared at the bulls five cars back. Eerily vanishing and then reappearing like ghosts with the flashes of lightning, the two groups stood as if they were frozen until another long pulsating flash broke their moment and the men took off.

"See," Duncan whispered along with another tug to her shoulder. "Whut they do is watch dha train, an dens chase after you when you gets off. Dhat's why we needs ta wait right here, till dha coas is clear," he finished in hopes that she understood.

Shaking her head, Willie slid against the wall and into the darkened corner with Duncan then listened as the men were chased. Yes they were safe, but before she could even thank him, she shuddered at yet another order being barked by the yard boss. "Check all the cars goddammit," he yelled at the remaining workers as he slammed his axe handle against the side of the train. "I'm tired of these freeloaders use'n us."

Listening as the men instantly carried out their orders and began opening doors two cars back, the two stood motionless against the wall. They were trapped with no way out, and the bulls would soon be upon them. Frantic with a desire to run yet fearful of being caught, Willie looked to the ceiling and began to pray. They needed a miracle, and no sooner had she begun, than she smiled at the sound of heavy droplets that'd begun to pelt the roof. A second later, another bolt of lightning split the sky and struck the ground with a heat so intense that it sizzled the air.

Hitting the steel tracks on the other side of the train, the giant electrical charge traveled the iron rails until it dissipated itself beneath a waiting coal car. Showering the undercarriage in a brilliant explosion of blue and white sparks, an ear-shattering crack of thunder instantly followed, violently shaking the train. An instant later, the overpowering sound of rain took its place and a torrent of liquid began to fall onto the hot parched earth. The clouds had finally opened into a downpour, and with that the yard boss called off their search. "Let's get out a here," he yelled as he began to run, his voice barely audible over the pouring rain.

Immediately followed by the other men, Willie sighed with relief then cautiously slid to the door and peered out into the rain. Watching as they passed and their feet pounded the ground, she stared until the last one had disappeared like a ghost in the rain. "They're gone Mister Duncan," she said excitedly as she turned back.

"Yes ma'am," he said as he dropped to the floor to lie down. "But they'l be back in dha mornin, you can count on it, so until then we bes makes our self comfortibal. Mornin al be here afor ya knows it," he added as he laid his head on his sack and closed his eyes.

It was clear that Duncan had every intention of going to sleep and with that, Willie took a spot between him and the wall and settled in for the night. It had been a long hot day and they were both exhausted, and now with the noise from the rain lulling them into the dream world, the mismatched pair finally found what they needed most.

CHAPTER 6

——◆——

WAKING EARLY THE NEXT MORNING in a panic, Willie bolted up to the sudden jerking of the train. The bulls had returned to get her and she knew it, but when she turned to the door and stared she saw nothing. The train was dark and quiet except for the sound of voices that seemed to be coming from far away. Was it the bulls she wondered as she rose and stepped to the door?

Peering out into the gloomy yard and down the tracks, Willie focused her sights on the men with lanterns, just behind the engine. They were talking and banging their hammers against the train when it suddenly jerked again. What were they doing? Were they leaving? A second later, she heard one of the men yell and the train jerk once more. Yes that was it, they were leaving and they had to get off. She had to hurry, and without a moment's hesitation she returned to Duncan. "Mister Duncan," she whispered as she knelt and pushed his shoulder. "Wake up." Waiting for a response that never came, an anxious Willie pushed again and called a little louder. "Mister Duncan, wake up!"

Slowly stirring to life, the big man yawned and stretched then finally opened his eyes. "Whut is it Miss Willie?" he asked in a groggy voice as he looked around.

Grinning with a contented smile, Willie leaned a little closer. "Come on Mister Duncan," she said impatiently. "Get uuup. They're do'n somethin to the train."

Rolling to his side, the big man rose to one elbow then slowly lifted his massive frame from the floor. Walking to the door, he looked out into the dark just as the train jerked again. Grabbing the edge to steady himself, he stared at the men working under the dim light of their lanterns then turned back to Willie. "We bes be on our way Miss Willie while they's busy an dha coas is clear," he said as he stepped past her to get their sacks. "Da bulls al be back soon," he added as he returned and then held out her sack. "So we needs ta go now."

Slinging her sack across her shoulder, Willie smiled and then nodded as if to indicate her readiness. A second later, Duncan sat on the edge of the train then slid off and dropped to the ground. Quickly turning back with his arms up high, he grabbed Willie under her armpits and then gently set her down. Scurrying under the train to the other side, the two quietly made their way past the workers and through the yard. A few minutes later they finally reached the edge of town, looked around as if they were lost, then turned back to each other and stared in a moment of silence.

They'd come to the crossroads in their journey together and they both knew it. And even though it would carry on for both of them in ways they could never imagine, they each knew that it was time to say goodbye. Their time together was over, and with that Willie took a shallow breath then turned and looked toward the city. Dark and desolate looking, with only a stray dog trotting beneath a street light a block away, she stared with a growing sense of trepidation.

She would be alone again and that worried her, and even though she had only known him for just one day, she didn't want him to leave. She was afraid and heartbroken, and in an attempt to remove the lump now growing in her throat, Willie swallowed hard. She liked the big man, and not just because he'd saved her. He was kind and gentle, but the attitudes of the day would not allow nor tolerate such a thing, especially in the south. Sitting and riding in the same boxcar was one thing, but traveling the streets of Mobile with a young white girl was another, and Duncan knew it better than anyone.

"You can't go with me, can you?" Willie finally asked in a solemn voice and face to match.

"No Miss Willie, I can'ts," Duncan replied as he slowly dropped to his knees.

Staring at each other now eye to eye, the big man reached for both of her hands and took them in his, then gave them a gentle squeeze. "But ya'l be jus fine," he finally said with the tenderness of a parent trying to reassure her. "Somebody al helps ya, I'm shor of it."

His words were comforting, but even so she turned back toward the city once more and wondered at the unknown. What would happen now? Were three more men waiting in the darkened streets to take her? It worried her immensely, but after a moment she turned back to Duncan and nodded as if she understood. "Well," she finally said with a heavy sigh. "I guess I bes be go'n."

"Yes um," he replied as he dropped her hands. "I thinks we both needs ta be a go'n."

It was their final goodbye but before Duncan could move, Willie lunged at him and threw her arms around his neck. "I want ya ta know that I won't never forget what ya done for me," she choked in a whisper as she squeezed him and his powerful arms wrapped around her. "Ya hear me? Not ever."

It was a heartfelt hug and as painful as it was for Willie to say goodbye to her protector, it was just as hard for Duncan to see her continue on. Knowing that she would be all alone, he worried about her like a father. A moment later she released her squeeze and stepped back then turned to her shoulder sack as if she'd forgotten something.

Reaching into the dirty bag, Willie dug for the leather pouch hidden deep in the middle of her clothes. Finding it after a short search, she grabbed a handful of coins then turned back with a smile. "Hold out your hand, Mister Duncan," she said with a gleam to her eyes as she held out her hand and then nodded for him to take her gift.

Gazing at her with an ever-growing curiosity, Duncan finally reached up under her outstretched hand. Gasping as she opened her fist and dropped a handful of silver into his hand, he stared in disbelief then quickly looked back at Willie. "Miss Willieee," he smiled.

"That's so you can buy somethin ta eat," she drawled before he could utter another word.

Quietly smiling with an air of satisfaction, Willie stared for just a moment then turned without another word and picked up her sack. Slinging it onto her shoulder, she glanced back to Duncan one last time, smiled with watery eyes and then bravely began walking into the dark colorless streets.

It was hard to leave the big man, yet step by step she slowly walked away toward the unknown. She was sad and felt lonelier now than she ever had. Her mother was gone, and now she was leaving the only other person in her life who'd ever helped her. Yet even so, and even though her heart seemed to ache a little more with each and every step she took, she slowly continued on with an unyielding will.

Hopelessly lost at what to do or where to go, she aimlessly wandered into the quiet sleepy town but then stopped at the first corner and turned back to Duncan. She'd hoped to wave goodbye one last time, but when she looked to where she'd left him, Duncan was already gone. Scanning the edge of the train yard in search of her friend, she stared for a moment hoping and looking then sadly turned back toward town. A moment later the light mist that'd been falling turned back into a drizzle, and with a glance to the sky in disgust, she quickly took off in search of shelter.

Finding a corner building at the end of the second block, Willie took cover beneath its storefront awning but then instantly stopped. She'd seen them before in catalogs that her mother had brought home from Mr. Johnson's house, but never in real life. They were beautiful, and as she quietly stared through the panes of glass, she marveled at the window's display of dresses. Thinking of how pretty they were, she smiled and then thought of her mother and of how nice she would've looked in one twirling and dancing. It was a haunting thought, and an attempt to free her mind Willie dropped her head and turned away then slowly slid to the sidewalk. Looking out at the dark empty street as the light but steady drizzle continued to fall she pulled her knees to her chest and then wrapped her arms around them. She missed her mother now more than ever, and as she huddled beneath the awning, she lowered her head and began to cry.

It was almost an hour before Willie finally raised her head to the breaking dawn and stared at the colorless streets still shrouded in mist. The tears that'd fallen earlier, had all but dried and gone, and now that the rain had almost stopped, she slowly stood and walked out from under the awning. Gazing up at the gloomy overcast sky, she looked to the distant horizon and watched as the morning sun struggled to pierce an opening in the low-lying clouds.

Succeeding in part, the gleaming ray of sunshine instantly bathed the city in its morning light, and although it was for just a few short moments, it brought a welcomed brightness and color to an otherwise dreary morning. Briefly lifting her sprits along with it, she looked up once again and then stared transfixed. How beautiful she thought as she gazed at the glowing array of colors.

Created by the sun reflecting off of the misty rain, a beautiful rainbow hung in a sweeping arc just above the city and ended somewhere in the center of town. Was it a sign from her mother? Her heart leapt at the thought, but all too quickly the fast moving clouds on the horizon obscured the sun's rays and the shimmering ribbon of colors began to waver in its intensity. Regaining some of its radiance with one last unfiltered ray of light, it brightened once more for just a few seconds then slowly faded and disappeared.

Watching and waiting in hopes that it would return, Willie thought of what her mother had told her just before she died. *'An if God'll let me when I get ta Heaven, I'll try an help you an show ya the way.'* Certain that it was a sign from above and that it had come from her mother, she returned to the awning and grabbed her sack. Slinging it onto her shoulder one more time, she stepped back into the street with a resurgence of energy and took off in search of her rainbow.

Hungry, wet and tired, she quietly walked through the empty streets meandering in the direction she thought it had been. A half hour later, she abruptly stopped at the corner of an intersection and lifted her head. Sniffing the air, she smiled at the smell of breakfast carried on the soft morning breeze then turned to find its source. Gazing down the street, she watched as a nicely dressed man and a dark haired woman casually walked up the steps and through the door of a small corner diner. An eatin place, she thought as another waft of the incredible aroma invaded her senses. Then, and as if she suddenly recognized the area, Willie's mind began to race. Yes, this is it, she thought as she looked to the sky and then down to the restaurant. This is where it had ended, she was certain.

Staring down the long empty street, the hungry young girl wanted nothing more than to walk straight through the door and get something to eat. Her belly said go, but she was hesitant, for in all of her fourteen years of life, she'd never eaten at a restaurant. It was a daunting thought, but before she knew it the intense gnawing in her belly and her desire to get out of the weather prevailed. Setting her fears aside, she nervously stepped forward and began walking. A few minutes later, she climbed the three short steps to the entrance and then slowly reached for the doorknob. She was still nervous, but with the squeak of steel against steel, she turned the worn and tarnished knob and then pushed the door open. Looking up to the ding of the bell, she smiled and entered then lowered her head and surveyed the room.

To her it was an amazing sight, even though it was nothing more than a simple diner. A row of booths sitting against a wall of glass faced the sidewalk, and adjacent from that, a row of swiveling bar-stools anchored to the floor on heavy silver stands lined the long counter in front of a kitchen. Beyond that, there was another small room with tables and chairs and behind the counter, a lady with plat-inum blond hair piled high, worked at rearranging donuts beneath a glass case. A little heavier than what she probably wanted to be and dressed in a uniform that seemed just a bit too small, she had a grainy hardness etched across her face from years of hard work. Obviously a little past her prime, she looked much older than she probably was.

Watching as she gently closed the case and raised her head, Willie closed the door and took two short steps but then suddenly stopped to the sound of her voice. "The soup kitchen's down the street at the church," the woman hollered as she reached for her cigarette on the counter. "We don't serve free loaders here," she continued in a cold but nonchalant way as she took a heavy pull and then blew her smoke into the air. "So just turn on around an get."

Somewhat confused, Willie took another small step forward then stopped. "Whaaat?" she asked as if she'd misheard.

"I said the soup kitchen's down the street honey," she exclaimed again and pointed toward the door. "We don't serve free loaders, now beat it!"

"But I'm hungry," Willie argued with the look of despair. "An this is an eaten place."

"Look sugar, I don't care how hungry you are," the waitress raised her voice and glared as she extinguished her burning stub into the ashtray. "We don't give our food away. That's what the soup kitchen's for, now beat it ya hear!"

"But I got money!" Willie replied emphatically. "An besides, I'm hungry!"

Their confrontation was short, but it had instantly gained the attention of everyone eating, including that of Foster K. Siler, who now and along with all of the others, couldn't help but stare at the young girl. God she was beautiful, he thought as she stood with her hands on her hips and waited for a reply. Dressed in torn and dirty overalls, and worn out working shoes, she had a long thick mane of untamed hair that'd been pulled straight back and tucked behind her ears. Hanging just a few inches below her shoulders, she stood defiantly in what seemed like a stalemate as the waitress carefully studied her.

"Well then," she finally said in a gentler voice along with a gesture to enter. "If'n you gots money, then ya might as well come on in an have a seat."

Sighing with relief, Willie instantly began walking straight toward the counter to the eyes of everyone there. Watching along with everyone else as she confidently crossed the room, Foster stared with an ever-growing interest for there was something about her that captivated him. Maybe it was her defiant stance combined with her sultry and alluring innocence, or maybe it was the ghostly aura of a mature woman masked delicately just beneath her child-like features. Whatever it was, dirty and wet, Willie Mae Dawson carried with her a sophisticated and hypnotic beauty that was far beyond her years. She was amazingly beautiful and the thirty-five-year old lawyer, try as he may, could not break his gaze until she'd reached the counter and he'd turned back to his clients.

Taking her seat without a word, Willie watched as the woman wiped the counter and then quietly prepared a place setting. Grabbing her silverware and a cup from the lower tub, she set it down with a muffled clunk then reached for a menu in the napkin holder. Laying it on the counter just as Willie had settled, she stepped back and folded her arms then stared as if she were waiting for something.

"Whaaat?" Willie looked on as if she were in trouble.

"Money," the waitress snipped. "Let's see it," she added as she held out one of her hands and flicked her fingers.

Staring back with a frown, Willie slowly turned and reached into her sack. Digging for her leather pouch, she pulled out a handful of change and then smacked the coins on the counter. "There," she yelled with glaring gaze. "Now can I get somethin ta eat?"

A little surprised by her tone and the fact that she actually had the money, the waitress's voice and demeanor instantly softened. "Ya sure can honey," she replied. "You can get whatever you want. I'm Connie, an you just call me whenever you're ready."

Smiling triumphantly that she could now get something to eat, Willie picked up the menu and opened it. Staring for just a few moments, she slowly raised her head in the most inconspicuous of ways and turned to the other diners. Unable to read, she curiously looked from plate to plate until the gentle tapping on her menu caused her to jerk back.

"Ahem," the waitress cleared her throat.

Sheepishly looking over its top as she held it in front of her, Willie, fully expecting to be yelled at, was instead greeted with a smile of kindness.

"Honey," Connie said softly as she leaned toward her. "You can't read can you?"

Somewhat embarrassed, Willie looked around and then shook her head. "No ma'am," she admitted and sighed. "I ain't never learnt how."

Smiling compassionately, Connie reached up between the folds of the menu and then gently pulled it from her hands. "Well then, how about if you just tell ol Connie here what ya want okay," she asked in a voice that sounded more like a mother than a waitress. "Are ya real hungry?"

"Yes ma'am," Willie nodded and grinned. "I ain't ate hardly nothin in two days."

"Two days, oh my my. Well then, how's about if we just get you the number one special ta fill that little belly of yours."

Quickly nodding her head again, Willie watched as the lady jotted on her order pad then put the pencil behind her ear and turned to the kitchen. Ripping the ticket from the pad, she stepped to the pass through and laid it with the rest of the orders. "Billll," she yelled. "Another number one." Then turning back to Willie, she smiled and grabbed the coffee pot. "It'll be just a few minutes honey," she said as she hurried off to her other two patrons at the end of the counter.

Emptying her pot into their cups, she quickly took their orders then turned to the sound of a man calling her name. "Miss Connie," he drawled in a polite but commanding way. "I believe you forgot our coffee?" He smiled and then shrugged his shoulders with an open set of hands. "If you don't mind," he added with an insinuating look.

"Oh, yes sir," Connie replied. "I'm sorry, I forgot, give me just a minute and I'll be right there." She nodded toward his table. "I have a fresh pot that's almost done."

"Thank you Connie," he replied with a smirk as he stuffed his hands into his pockets. "That'll be just fine," he added as he turned and stepped toward the young girl setting on the barstool.

To Connie it was an act that infuriated her, for now she knew why he'd come to the counter. The girl was beautiful and he was nothing more than a womanizing bastard who wanted to add her to his list of conquests. But with a confidence level that bordered on the threshold of arrogance, Foster K. Siler was actually Mobile County's most sought after attorney. A razor sharp litigator with a smooth southern style, he had a cunning and ruthless reputation that both clients and adversaries knew all too well. The biggest cases were his, and it was said that he would do anything to win.

Born and raised on a farm in the hills of western Tennessee, his family was poor and Foster labored hard his entire youth. Yet even so, his parents kept him in school. Incredibly gifted, he struggled and worked his way through college and then law school. After law school and then his parent's untimely death, they say he took a short vacation to the white sand beaches of the gulf coast and just never went back.

Settling in Mobile, he set up practice in a one-room office and for years on Sunday held his own brand of court at Connie's Diner with potential clients. Always on Sunday morning, and always at the same table. Stories of him taking his pleasures with wives, ex-wives and girlfriends of clients and foes alike were rampant. Rich, smart and ruggedly handsome, he had a slick and polished underside to his well-armored exterior and Connie knew it.

"And good morning to you young lady," he greeted in a voice that exuded a confidence and charm she'd never heard before.

"Mornin," Willie replied as she looked up and stared, only to be cut short by an overly loud voice that radiated out from the kitchen.

"Order Up!" The cook yelled as he set a plate of food onto the pass through.

"Oh, it's your food honey," Connie quickly chimed in.

Turning to get the plate, she hastily returned and set it down. "Here ya go sugar," she said, unfazed by the glaring gaze from Foster. "Would you like a glass of milk to go with that?"

"Oh, yes ma'am," Willie replied with an enthusiastic nod.

Returning just a quickly as she could, Connie set the milk down and then turned to Foster. "An I'll have your coffee right over," she said with another nod toward his table. "Just as soon as it's done."

Staring at the woman for just a moment, Foster dipped his head as if to concede defeat then turned to Willie. "Enjoy your breakfast Miss," he said with a disappointed sigh. And although he wanted nothing more than to find out who she was, he had clients that were waiting and with that he turned away and slowly crossed the room to his table.

Taking advantage of the poor and the unfortunate in their times of need had become Fosters stock and trade. He was a predator and a good one, and since the depression had hit, business was good. All that was needed was money, and as he took his seat back at his table, he calmly looked at his clients and smiled. "Well now," he began as he pulled a pen from his pocket and then laid his hand on his tablet. "Tell me about your son."

CHAPTER 7

———•———

ONCE ONE OF THE WEALTHIEST families in Mobile with a life of privilege and social prestige, Howard and Katherine Davenport had, like a lot of people, lost everything in the crash. For years, Howard, through his immense wealth and influence, had been able to buy their youngest sons way out of trouble, but this time the spoiled little rich kid had gone too far. Now sitting in jail for the beating and rape of a seventeen-year-old girl, their son waited in a ten by ten cell unable to even make bail. Distraught that he was languishing in such dreadful conditions and with nowhere else to turn, they'd come to plead for Foster's help.

A woman of unparalleled beauty in her early forties, Katherine Davenport personified the very essence of the word like no other woman in Mobile, and Foster instantly took note. In short, she was everything that any man could ever want. Sophisticated and elegant with a sprinkle of fine jewelry and a tailor-made dress, it was clear that she was a woman who was accustomed to wealth. Yet there was something more to her that led him to believe she had another side. Maybe it was the way she looked or acted, or that she was married to a man fifteen years her senior and he'd heard rumors of her infidelities. Or maybe it was the fact that her foot was now discretely and lightly brushing against his. Either way, he felt an immediate and strong magnetic pull towards the beautiful woman sitting across from him.

Looking up with a questionable gaze, Foster instantly knew by the look in her eyes that her touch was no accident. "Mr. Siler, please," she drawled in a honey smooth voice. "We do so desperately need your help," she paused and glanced to her husband then redirected her eyes back to his. "Why everyone in town has said that you're the one to see."

"Well, that's very flattering Mrs. Davenport," Foster replied curtly, a slight smile tugging at the corner of his mouth. "But the simple truth to the matter is, is that you and your husband are broke. And quite frankly, I don't work for free. Besides, from what I've heard of your son's troubles, I don't think you could get a jury to acquit him anyway, even with my help."

"But you must help us," she begged and then boldly pressed her foot to his leg again. "Tell him Howard," she demanded as she reached for her husband's hand.

Squeezing it as if it would compel him to speak, she stared into his eyes for just a second then turned her gaze back to Foster. She was reckless and brazen, and he thrilled at her methods.

"We'll do anything," she implored as she slowly and sensuously slid her foot up his calf.

Instantly responding to her caress, Foster discretely slid his leg a little closer as her foot encircled and then hooked on his calf. Her touch was electric and intoxicating, and the more she continued the more he wanted. He was enthralled, for now it was abundantly clear as to what the lady across from him really meant. Yet even so, he shook his head with a heavy sigh. "I just don't knooow," he finally said as if he were still unsure.

"Now just hold on a second there, Mr. Siler," Howard instantly protested and dropped his wife's hand. "We still have a couple of assets left that I've managed to hide, don't we honey. Maybe we could trade some of these for your fees? That is of course, if you'd be interested in them."

"And just what would those be?" Foster asked with a discrete glance to the man's wife.

"A small house and two hundred acres up river that we used to use as a weekend getaway, you know, for hunting and relaxing. It ain't much, but it's all ours."

"Whoa whoa whoooa," Foster shook his head and then held up his hands. "Let's just hold on a second here." He chuckled beneath his breath. "First, I really don't need or want two hundred acres of swamp land. And second, how in the hell would I get to it if I did?"

"With our boat," Katherine interjected. "We have a boat too."

"A what?"

"A boat... a nice boat," she said proudly. "A forty-foot cruiser. It's just three years old and we could include it too, so that you would have a way of getting there. We even have a captain to go with it. Well, that is, if you don't mind having a negro work for you."

"A forty foot boat, and a captain?" he repeated as if he couldn't believe it.

"Yes, a boat," she reiterated. "And a captain. At least take a look at it before you say no," she asked. "That's all we ask."

Taking a sip from his coffee, Foster couldn't help but smile as her foot, now without her shoe, once again began to caress his leg. Glancing up, he caught her smile and lustful gaze as she stared from across the table. God she was determined, but was she doing this for her son or for herself because she was married to such a selfish slob? Or, was she just really hungry? He had heard rumors about her but had always dismissed them as just that. But this was different, this was real, and it was he who was the object of her desires. He liked that. In fact, he liked it a lot.

"Please, Mr. Siler," she finally said as she slipped her foot up under the cuff of his pants. "We're begging you. I'm begging you. Our son needs your help. Now what we would like to do is to show you what we have tomorrow, but unfortunately Howard has to leave for New Orleans in the morning and won't be back until Friday. But maybe we could show it to you then."

"No no, that won't do at all," Foster shook his head. "I have a really big case that I'm working on and I have to be in court later this week. I'm sorry but we'll have to do it tomorrow or wait and do it in a couple of weeks."

"Oh nooo," Katherine protested. "We can't leave Bobby in jail any longer. I just won't have it; it's such a dreadful place. Howard, do something, pleeease. Change your plans and go on Tuesday."

"I can't Darling, you know I've got to be in New Orleans tomorrow for that interview. Hell, I set it up over a month ago... you know that," he said and shook his head. "Nooo, I think that this time little Bobby is just going to have to wait; besides it just might do him some good."

Dissatisfied with his reply, yet still determined to free her son, the woman brooded for a moment then widened her eyes and turned with a smile. "But wait a minute, I have an idea," she exclaimed as she looked back and forth between the two men. "Maybe I could show Mr. Siler the property?" she volunteered as if asking. "I know where the boundary lines are and Otis could take us up by boat."

Taking a deep breath, Howard looked to Foster and then to his wife as he slowly digested her idea. "Well," he finally exhaled as if he'd clearly thought it over. "I really don't see why that wouldn't work? Actually, I think it's a pretty good idea... good thinking dear. I'll have Otis get the boat ready first thing in the morning before I leave. That is, if it's okay with you Mr. Siler," he added.

Still determined to get her way, Katherine once again applied the use of her magic and daringly slid her foot up even higher. Staring with an unflinching gaze through her hazy blues, she sensuously curled her toes and then caressed his calf. She was as persuasive as she was beautiful, and as he stared back into her eyes, he could see that she was offering to show a little more property than what her husband was expecting.

"Well, I guess it wouldn't hurt to just take a look," he drawled wryly. "Tomorrow afternoon would be just fine," he continued on. "I'll clear my schedule, and let's saaaay... around two."

Now content that she'd gotten her way, Katherine slowly and seductively slid her foot back down his calf and then gently pulled on his sock in a discrete yet tantalizing gesture of gratitude. A second later, she carefully withdrew it from under his pants and picked up her coffee then smiled at her husband and took a sip.

Sitting back in his chair with an anticipating grin, Foster casually reached for his cup then shook his head and set it back down. It was cold and half empty, and with an aggravated look, he turned to find Connie just as she stepped to the table.

"Coffee everyone?" she asked with a pot held high. Pouring their cups, she took their orders and left.

Greedily preying upon their misfortune and enticed by an offer he couldn't refuse, Foster agreed to look at their house and acreage in lieu of his fee. It was a good deal, but what he really wanted now was the dark haired beauty sitting across from him. He liked the idea of taking another man's wife, and he smiled at the thought. She had invited him to dine and he had accepted. The menu was clear, and now he wasn't going to stop until he'd eaten his fill, regardless of ethics or morals. She was beautiful and mysterious, and in his arrogance he knew that the only way he would turn Katherine Davenport down... was face down. The forty-foot cruiser along with its captain were just icing on the cake as far as he was concerned, and he could've cared less about either one.

But their son was in serious serious trouble, and as they ate their breakfast and conversed, Foster listened carefully and took notes. He was their lawyer now, and devoted all of his attention to them until the beautiful young girl sitting at the bar rose from her seat and downed her glass of milk. Regaining his eye, he turned his head ever so slightly and then watched as she conversed with Connie. Wondering with a growing curiosity as to just who was she and where she was from?

"So where ya headed honey?" Connie asked, as Willie slung her sack onto her shoulder.

"I really don't know," she replied with an uncertain glance toward the door. "I don't know no one, an I don't know where I'm go'n."

"What-a-you mean?" she asked. "Are ya new here?"

Receiving a nod, Connie smiled. "Well ya just can't go wanderin the streets in the rain now ya know."

"I knooow," Willie sighed and then sat back down. "But since I ate all that food, I'm tired now an I'd jus like ta find a place ta sleep," she added. "Ya don't know where I might go do ya?" she asked in a voice growing with apprehension.

Smiling, but with her heart now aching, the gruff old waitress reached across the counter and gently laid her hands on top of Willie's. There was something about the girl that touched her and made her want to help for she'd seen a lot of young girls just like her when she'd lived in New Orleans. In fact, a long long time ago she'd been one herself. Destitute and all alone, she knew better than anyone what the pitfalls were for a pretty young girl on the streets, especially with a man like Foster who was now watching. A man she resented in the most vehement of ways for who and what he was. And if she could, would keep from Willie.

"Actually I do," she said with a gentle squeeze to her hands. "But why don't you tell me what your name is first.

"It's Willie," she said as she looked down at her hands. "Willie Mae Dawson."

"Well Miss Willie, I want you to listen to me, okay. I have a friend that has a boardin house about half way across town. It's cheap an it's a little run down, but it's clean an there ain't no riff-raff. I want ya to go there an ask for Miss Shelda, an make sure you tell her that Connie from the diner sent you, okay. That's me."

"Yes ma'am," Willie replied and nodded.

A few moments later, certain that she knew how to get there, Willie finally rose from her seat and walked to the door. Turning the tarnished knob, she pulled it opened with a ding and swung it wide. Glancing up at the bell, she stared for a second then lowered her head and looked back to Connie. Gazing at the woman behind the counter, she smiled and waved then turned back to the door and quietly stepped into the wet gloomy streets.

She was leaving and it bothered him, and he wanted nothing more than to run after her. Especially after she'd passed his window and he'd caught her gaze. Yet even so and as hard as it was, Foster remained seated until he'd concluded his business with the Davenports. Assuring them both that he would be at the pier at two, he shook their hands and bid them farewell. Waving a final wave as they walked through the door, he downed his coffee then walked to the counter to pay his bill.

"Well Connie," he said with a contentious smile as he placed both of his hands on the counter. "And just what do I owe you today?"

Finding his ticket, she quickly punched the numbers into the cash register and rang up his total. "That'll be $4.25," she said as she pulled the lever and opened the drawer with a ding.

Pulling his wallet from his coat pocket, Foster smiled again then curiously glanced to the street. "Sooo," he asked as he handed her a five-dollar bill. "Just where'd the little gal run off to?"

Rolling her eyes in disgust as she counted his change, Connie thought of how much she despised him. "Wellll," she finally replied as she handed him his money. "I'm sorry, but I really don't recall jus where she was headed."

It was a lie and he knew it. He could see it in her eyes and with another glance to the street; Foster quickly counted his money then slapped his hand on the counter with a disgruntled humph. "There," he said as he gained her eyes. "That's for your troubles," he smirked then raised his hand and turned to the door.

Looking down more out of curiosity than anything, Connie stared at the single dime that he'd left behind with a mix of emotions. Was it an insult, or just his cheap ass ways? She wanted to throw it back at him, but she didn't for it was the depression and a dime was a dime. Watching as he opened the door, the poor woman swallowed her pride and slipped the thin silver coin into her pocket.

Stepping into the street, Foster turned and hastily headed in the same direction as the girl. Stopping at the corner, he looked up and down the empty streets in hopes of seeing her. Dammit, he thought as he crossed from one corner to the other. Where in the hell did she go, and most importantly, who was she and where was she from? A little disappointed and somewhat frustrated, he finally accepted the fact that just too much time had passed and walked back to his car. Gazing once more at the streets as he opened his door, he finally abandoned his search completely and dropped into his car. Backing out from his parking spot, his thoughts soon waned from the young girl to that of Mrs. Davenport and their meeting tomorrow afternoon. Yes, life was good for Foster K. Siler, and as he casually drove back home, he smiled at the possibilities that awaited him.

———————

Finding the place that Connie had told her of just as a light mist began to fall again, Willie stepped up onto the front porch and knocked on the door. A beautiful building in its day, the white two-story structure sat framed inside of a wrought iron fence with giant oaks dotting the yard. Bearded heavily with Spanish moss, they surrounded and shaded the grounds and kept the summer's heat at bay. Yet as she waited and looked around, she could see that Connie had been right. The place was run down, but even so, it was far nicer than what she'd grown up in.

Waiting for a few moments with no answer, Willie impatiently knocked again.

"Go away," a harsh raspy voice suddenly came from the other side.

"Bu... but I'm looking for Miss Shelda," Willie replied as she looked at the door. "I have to see her. Is she here?"

"She ain't here," the voice cut sharply. "Now go away."

"But I have to see her."

"I said she ain't here, now go away an leave me alone."

"Bu... but Miss Connie from the diner sent me. She said that she could help me. I jus need a place ta stay for a while," Willie pleaded. "So I can res..." her voice trailed off as if she'd run out of hope.

Waiting, with only an on going quiet coming from the door, Willie's hopes quickly diminished. It was a horrible feeling, and even though she waited and prayed that it would open, it didn't. She felt a sense of hopelessness and wished she'd never gotten on the train and come here, and that she were still at home with her mother. But she wasn't, and with the sound of the rain returning as it steadily began to fall, Willie turned and looked back out into the street. This time it was more than she could bear, and as the gut wrenching pain of being so utterly alone returned, the devastated fourteen-year-old, now hopelessly lost at what to do or where to go, slowly dropped to her knees and began to cry.

She was all alone, and even though it seemed like an eternity, it was only a few fleeting moments before the heavy latch on the door broke the sound of the falling rain. Turning with a jerk, Willie immediately rose as the door slowly opened. Brushing the tears from her eyes, she anxiously waited until a crusty looking woman in a dirty pink bathrobe appeared on the other side. A little older and a little taller than Connie, with a face still painted in yesterday's makeup, it was funny as to just how much they looked like each other.

Staring at Willie for just a second, she took a long hard drag on her cigarette then pulled it from her lips and blew her smoke into the air. "An just who might you be," the woman asked with a cough as she tossed her burning stub into the yard.

"I'm Willie," she said, clearing her throat and extending her hand just like her mother had taught her. "Willie Mae Dawson."

"Well, Miss Willie," the woman replied and took her hand. "I'm Shelda, an did I hear you say that Connie sent ya?" she asked with a curious gaze.

"Yes ma'am," Willie nodded. "I jus had breakfast at the diner, an she said ta come here an you could help me. That you could give me a place to stay."

"Oh she diiid, did she," Shelda crowed with a cynical chuckle and a glance to the sky. "Well, I reckon so since I got all these rooms just a sittin here do'n nothin."

"But I got money," Willie instantly retorted. "An I can pay for my keep… please Miss Shelda. I really need a place to stay."

"Well you shor look awfully young. You ain't in trouble with the law or nothin like that are ya?" She raised her eyebrows. "I don't put up with no riff-raff."

"Oh no ma'am," Willie assured and shook her head.

Crossing her arms in front of her, the woman studied the girl's face with a critical eye. A few moments later, she finally exhaled with a heavy sigh. "Well, I guess if ya passed Connie's muster ya must be halfway okay, but ya better not give me no trouble, hear? Now why don't ya come on in an let's see if we can't get you settled."

Stepping into the foyer as the woman gently closed the door behind her, Willie couldn't help but smile for she now had a place to stay. And although it smelled old and musty, it was clean, just like Connie had said.

"Now come on an I'll show you your room," Shelda said as she started toward the stairs. "Oh, an just so ya know, it's thirty-five cents a day, an that gets ya a small breakfast between seven an eight, an not before an not after, ya got it," she emphasized.

"Yes ma'am," Willie answered as she hurriedly followed.

"Or, if you take it for a week, I'll do thirty a day; an that's as good as it gets, got it," she added, then abruptly stopped and turned with one hand on the railing and one foot on the bottom step.

"Yes ma'am," Willie replied and nodded.

"Good! Oooh, an ya did say ya had money didn't ya?"

"Yes ma'am," Willie replied with yet another nod.

"Good," the woman said as she turn backed and resume climbing. "We'll just settle up later after ya figure out what ya wanna do, okay."

"Yes ma'am," Willie said as she followed her up the steps.

Creaking under their combined weight, the two finally reached the top, turned down the hallway and took the second door on the left. It wasn't much, but still it was clean, with a bed, a dresser and a nice sized window for air and light.

Stepping inside, Willie smiled at the sight of the bed, then yawned and shook her head. "Excuse me," she mumbled with a hand over her mouth.

"Are ya tired sugar?" Shelda asked as she turned and stared into the girl's heavy eyes.

"Yes ma'am," she replied with another yawn. "I ain't had much sleep the last two nights, an I'd jus like ta lie down for a bit if I could?"

"Well this is your room, an you can sleep all you want now."

"Yes ma'am, thank you."

"Now you just rest that pretty little head of yours an I'll come back an check on ya later, okay."

"Yes ma'am," Willie replied as the woman gently closed the door behind her.

Listening as she walked down the hallway and descended the stairs, Willie threw her sack on top of the bed then opened the window and stared outside. Sighing with relief, that at least for now she had a safe dry place to sleep, she stared for a moment longer then turned and walked back to the bed. Sitting on its edge, she slowly took off her shoes and then her damp dirty socks. She was tired beyond any sense of the word, and without another thought and a big final yawn, she laid her head on her pillow and closed her eyes. It had been an exhausting two days and now with her belly full and the rain pattering outside, the heartbroken young girl quickly drifted into a deep, deep sleep.

CHAPTER 8

———•———

MONDAY MORNING BROUGHT WITH IT a bright blue sky scattered with small but fast moving clouds. The cool northern front that had collided with the hot moist air over the weekend and brought the heavy rains had finally passed and a pleasant coolness now blanketed the city. The unrelenting stale and stagnant heat of the gulf was gone and a clean refreshing breeze from the north carried with it a substantial drop in temperature. All of Mobile had suffered from months of record temperatures and it was to go without saying that it was a welcomed relief that resonated throughout the city.

Turning under his sheets, Foster finally opened his eyes and greeted the morning. Stretching with a giant yawn, he smiled at the fact that he wasn't stuck to his sheets and then threw back his covers. Lying with his eyes close for just a moment longer, he slowly rolled to the edge of the bed and sat up. Gazing at the opened window and the curtains blowing lazily in the breeze, he inhaled a deep breath of morning air then rose and walked to the bathroom. His day was going to be a long one and he wanted to start it early, for if things went as he hoped, it would end with Mrs. Davenport right here in his bedroom.

Yes, the beautiful Mrs. Davenport he envisioned as he studied his face in the mirror and waited on the hot water. 'We'll do anything,' he remembered her saying as he splashed water onto his face and then grabbed his shaving cup. Swirling his brush in the bottom, he quickly made a lather then looked back into the mirror. "I'm sure you will Mrs. Davenport," he mumbled with an anticipating grin. "I'm sure you willll," he repeated as he lathered his face and continued with his thoughts, reflecting back to the look in her eyes.

Oh, yes. God, the look in her eyes, he thought as he started to shave. How could he forget? The clear unspoken message that'd come from those beautiful hazy blues. She was a bold sophisticated woman with an obvious agenda, and now all he could think of was her and the promise of her unbridled passion. He took another swipe with the razor and smiled.

Climbing the two flights of steps to his third floor office, Foster finally stopped at the top then turned and gazed at the view. A vicious gladiator in the sanctity of the courtroom, he had a winning record with a reputation of going straight for the kill. And although his methods were sometimes questionable, they'd provided for him very very well. He occupied the top floor of the most coveted building on the square and it sat directly across from the courthouse and county seat. It was a great location, and was one that served him well, but most of all it was the best and he owned it. Walking through the frosted glass door with his name on it, he found his receptionist already working.

"Oh, good mornin Foster," Dawn greeted cheerfully.

"Morning Dawn," he replied as he shot past her counter and entered his office. "Is Vicki in yet?" he asked as he quickly reversed his steps and peered back out of his doorway.

"No, she called in just a few minutes ago and said she'd be late. Something about the kids or something, you know."

Nodding his head as if he understood, Foster scrunched his eyebrows and stared for a moment then turned back into his office. He had ton of paper work and a pile of calls to make, and one of the first on his list was to the prosecuting attorney of Mobile County, Cyrus Buchanan.

A puppet of sorts for some of the local big shots, Cyrus was really nothing more than an self-serving pompous ass who always seem to preach with an overzealous voice of moral indignation and self-righteousness. Often times quoting from the Bible in his trademarked wrinkled white suits that he wore to trial, a lot of people within the legal community, including most of the judges, had gone to calling him the preacher. It was a name that stuck, but Cyrus wasn't a preacher, he was the prosecutor, and a greedy one at that. And as often was the scenario in his dealings, money could make or break a case in his office. But Foster had dirt on him and it was good dirt, and if there was ever a time to use it, it was now, for the prosecuting attorney of Mobile County had blood stained hands and he could prove it.

It was just over three years ago at the trial of a man who'd been wrongly accused, convicted and sentenced to death for the murder of a local prostitute. Ignoring the overwhelming evidence that had been provided prior to the man's trial, clearly proving his innocence, Cyrus knowingly accepted and introduced during the trial, tainted evidence and perjured testimony to sway the jury. Bowing to a group of local wealthy businessmen in an attempt to protect one of their own, an innocent man was put to death. A vagrant and a nobody, but still an innocent man; his life ended at the end of a rope.

Kept incredibly quiet and behind closed doors, it was Foster's unique intuition for behind the scenes, closed-door double-dealings that'd alerted his senses. After all, he had basically written the book on dirty ethics. And as one who was always the consummate opportunist, he acted with all due haste. There was potential in possessing such incriminating information, and even though the trial was over and the man was dead, he quietly and doggedly investigated. Unraveling and piecing together the complicated web of evidence that they'd buried, he finally found his smoking gun. Eyewitnesses who were questioned, but never mentioned or called during the trial that could prove the man's innocence and implicate the prosecutor in his deceit of the court. Remaining cautiously quiet as to just what he knew, Foster carefully secured his evidence and waited.

"Dawn," he yelled from behind his desk.

"Yes sir," she answered from the other room.

"I need you to get Cyrus Buchanan on the phone for me and bring me a cup of coffee would you. Oh, and when did you say Vicki was coming in?"

A little flustered by all of his questions at once, Dawn quickly grabbed a note pad and rushed to his office door. "I'm sorry Foster," she said holding her pad in front, ready to write. "What'd you say?"

"I saiiiid... oooh never mind," he shook his head with an agitated voice. "Just get me a cup of coffee first, okay."

"Yes sir, black?"

"Dawn!" he glared.

"Oh yeah, I forgot, cream and sugar."

Watching as she left, Foster sighed and then shook his head once again. She was a ding-a-ling all right, but he had guessed that when he'd hired her, and even though she worked hard and never complained, days like this really tested his patience.

Returning a few moments Dawn set his cup on his desk. "Will that be all?" she asked as she stepped back.

"No," Foster replied as he reclined back into his chair. "I still want you to call over to the prosecutor's office and see if you can get Cyrus Buchanan on the phone for me, I need to talk to him. Oh, and tell him it's important too."

"Yes sir," she nodded and turned. "I'll get him right away."

Turning back to the windows after she'd left, Foster stared at the courthouse and began to smile. He was about to blackmail the prosecuting attorney of Mobile County, but he didn't care. All he cared about was getting his client out of jail. He wanted to know the particulars of the Davenport boy and what it would take to bond him out. His goal was simple, to secure the boy's release before he met with Mrs. Davenport that afternoon. In short, he wanted to impress the hell out of her.

"Foster," Dawn called from her desk, breaking his gaze at the courthouse. "I have Mr. Buchanan on the line for you."

"Thanks Dawn," he said as he spun back to his desk.

Grabbing the heavy receiver, Foster put it to his ear and then leaned back in his chair. "Cyrus," he drawled as if he were talking to a long lost friend, "Foster Siler herrre."

"Well well welll… Fossster Siler," Cyrus sneered with a nasally twang. "For whatever reason do I owe the pleasure on such a fine mornin?"

To say that the two men really didn't like each other would have been an understatement, and everyone in town knew it. And their run ins with each other over the years, in the courtroom and out, were legendary to say the least. Cyrus despised everything that there was about Foster, yet still, the man was an attorney and he'd called.

"Well Cyrus," Foster said in a tone that'd suddenly turned serious. "I need to see you this morning. It's kind of important, actually, it's real important."

"Well I don't knooow Foster," Cyrus drawled. "Ya know I am kind of busy an all this mornin, but maybe I could break away later this afternoon just for you... you know, in the spirit of co-operation an all."

"No nooo, that won't do at all," Foster argued. "I really need to see you this morning," he insisted. "Like I said, it's important."

"Oh come on," Cyrus replied. "What-evvver could be so damn important that it can't wait until this afternoon?"

"Well, I'd rather tell you in person."

"Good God counselor," he snapped. "Just tell me what in the hell ya want. You called me, remember?"

"Yes, I did," Foster replied and took a breath. "Well, it's about the Davenport boy."

"Whaaat?" Cyrus blurted. "The who boyyy?" He continued an octave higher as he began to snicker into the phone. "Did you just say the Daaavenport boy?"

"Yes Cyrus, the Davenport boy, I need to know the particulars on him and what his bond is?"

"The Davenport boy," he repeated again, but now in a voice dripping with curiosity. "What in the hell are you doing with this one Siler? Shit, they ain't got no money. Hell, they lost it all in the crash last year, everyone knows that. And besides, what they didn't lose ol Mrs. Davenport's probably already spent. You know that, don't ya?" He snickered.

"Yes Cyrus, I'm perfectly aware of their financial situation, but I'll still be representing the boy at the request of his parents."

"Well let me tell you something mister fancy pants," he began with an adamant huff. "Before you even waltz on over here an get yours or their hopes up, the boy is going down this time! I ain't takin no more shit off this kid or his parents, ya hear! No sir! I've had enough of little Bobby Davenport and ain't nobody buying his ass out of this one, I'll see to that personally. Besides, they ain't got the kind of clout they use to have to get him out anyway," he finished almost joyously.

"No they don't," Foster replied solemnly. "The Davenports have come across some very difficult times and that's why I've agreed to take on their case and help them."

"What... pro bono?" Cyrus laughed. "Foster Siler doing a pro bono? Goddamn, what in the hell's next?" He crowed, but then quickly settled and cleared his throat. "Ya know counselor, you're just wastin your time. The boy's as guilty as sin and I'm gonna put him away. But I guess if you're that insistent, then come on over at ten and I'll give you fifteen minutes and just fifteen."

"Thank you Cyrus," Foster replied with an icy coldness. "Believe me, fifteen is all I'll need."

Setting the phone back onto its cradle, Foster slowly pulled his fingers out from under the heavy handle with a nagging uneasiness and reclined back into his chair. There was something about their conversation that just didn't sit well. Maybe it was something that Cyrus had said while they were talking or the way he'd said it that made him uneasy. Concentrating, he locked his hands behind his head and then closed his eyes. What was it that made him hate the Davenports so much? What had they done? He wondered and tapped his foot; he had to know before their meeting for no self-respecting lawyer would meet unprepared. Slowly spinning his chair, he shifted his gaze once again out through the glass and stared at the court-house with its flags on the lawn. Dammit, what in the hell was it? He concentrated harder; he needed to know, he had to know.

Deep in thought, he tapped his fingers on his desk like a gallop-ing horse then tilted his head to the ceiling and stared at the rotat-ing fan. Hypnotized for just a few moments, it was the nine dings from the clock on the wall that finally brought him back to reality. Looking over, he glanced at the time and shook his head. God, he still had another five hours until he met with Mrs. Davenport. Yes he smiled, the beautiful Mrs. Davenport. Her husband was gone and they were going up river all alone. It didn't get any better, but just as quickly as he envisioned her and their impending afternoon, his mind suddenly flashed back to the past. Yes, that was it, he gasped excitedly. It had to be, it all added up, and now it made sense.

It was just under two years ago at the mayor's second inaugura-tion party when she had embarrassed and humiliated him. All of Mobile society was there, and at the time, the Davenports were still both very wealthy and politically powerful. It was a grand affair, but as the party continued on into evening, Cyrus, who by then was half drunk, made a serious error in judgment. Emboldened by rumors he'd heard of Mrs. Davenport, he approached her as to her son's impending litigation. Insinuating in the most salacious of ways as to how she could get the charges against him dismissed, the incensed woman threw her drink into his face.

Humiliated as she then loudly berated him in front of a crowd of onlookers, he now knew why Cyrus held such contempt for the woman, and why he was now using her son as a means of payback and punishment. Smiling at the thought of Cyrus's face covered and dripping in some sort of fruity concoction of homemade punch, he now knew where he stood. And now that he knew where he stood, he knew exactly what he was going to do.

Digging into the bottom drawer of his desk, Foster pulled a thick heavy folder from its confines then closed the drawer with his foot. Dropping it onto his desk with a thump, he stared at it for a second and then smiled. Damn, this is going to be fun, he thought as he untied the string and opened it up. It'd been almost three years since he'd looked at it, and now he was going to do what he always did before a trial: study and prepare for battle. He had just forty-five minutes until his meeting, and with that he quickly began skimming the pages of the folder.

He was going to play a game with the prosecutor, a game of poker to see just how far the arrogant ass would go before he threw down his royal flush. He wanted him on his knees, willing to do whatever he asked. He wanted his questions about the Davenport boy answered. He wanted the house and the two hundred acres, and the boat. But now, and more than anything else, he wanted the beautiful Katherine Davenport.

Looking up at the clock, he finally folded the contents of the folder back into place and then rose from his chair. It was nine forty-five and it was time to leave.

"Dawn," he yelled as he reached for his suit coat.

"Yes sir," she answered then appeared in the doorway.

"Is Vicki in yet?"

"Yes, she just got in about ten minutes ago. Do you need her?"

"Yes I do," he said as he brushed his sleeves and straightened his coat. "Tell her to come in would you."

A few moments later, Vicki appeared in the doorway and greeted her employer.

"Mornin boss" she grinned with a cigarette in one hand and a cup of coffee in the other. "Who we gonna behead this week?" she asked as she approached his desk.

Laughing at her remark, Foster just shook his head then watched as she stopped in front of him and waited for his reply. At just over five foot two and a hundred and ten pounds soaking wet, she was a walking fireball with a quick wit and a dry sense of humor that he never tired of.

"The Prosecutor," he finally said with a grin.

"The Prossssecutor," she repeated and rolled her eyes. "Wellll, isn't this going to be an interesting week."

"Yes it is," Foster replied with another smile. "But here," he added as he handed her a list of things he needed done. "I want you to check this out for me first, okay."

"What's this?" she asked as she pushed her glasses back onto her nose and scanned the list.

"There's a two hundred acre parcel of ground about twelve miles or so up river that I want you to do a quick title search on. I believe it's held under the Katherine Davenport Trust. I want you to make sure that it isn't tied up in some way and that there aren't any liens or mortgages on it. Oh and Vicki, do it first thing will you, I need to know right away."

"You got it boss," she replied and turned to leave, but then quickly stopped and turned back. "But what about the prosecutor?" she asked with a disappointed look.

"Well," he said as he grabbed his briefcase and headed for the door. "We're about to find out.

Bounding down the steps and out the door, he quickly crossed the busy street and stepped onto the courthouse lawn. Cutting through the grass like everyone else, he wondered as to why no one ever put sidewalks where people used them? Shaking his head as he continued on, he followed the well-worn path that led right past the two flagpoles and a small flower garden that ringed it. Stopping as if he'd suddenly forgotten something, he stared down at the late summer blooms then bent and picked a single flower. Yes, this is perfect, he thought as he held it up for a closer inspection. Delores would surely be surprised. She was Foster's favorite secretary at the prosecutor's office and whenever he had a chance to tease or give her a hard time, he did just that.

Climbing the steps to the second floor, he finally strolled through the office door. "Good morning Dolores," he said as he handed her the flower.

"Why Foster Siler," the woman exclaimed as a light blush crept across her face. "If I didn't know better, I'd swear you were tryin to entice me into do'n something that I shouldn't," she laughed as she took the beautiful bloom and inhaled its scent. "Why whatever would people say if they knew?"

"Entice?" Foster leaned across the counter and teased in a whisper. "Ah hell Delores, you know me, I don't want to entice you. I just want to drag you right over there into the back room and then pull that pin out of your hair."

Completely flustered, Delores could only grin with an embarrassed but knowing smile and then clear her throat. "Well under any other circumstances I jus might be tempted, but since Mister Buchanan is already waitin," she fanned her face with a note pad and nodded toward his door. "Please... won't you."

Turning with a wink, Foster cross the room and stepped through Cyrus's door. "Morning Cyrus," he greeted as he closed it behind him.

Looking up as Foster strolled across the room, Cyrus smirked then slowly pulled his feet from the desk. "Well well welllll... Foster Siiiler," he drawled as he pulled off his glasses and then rocked back in his chair. "It's been awhile."

"Yes, it has," Foster replied and took a seat.

"So tell me, what-a-ya doing fuckin with the Davenports?" Cyrus wheezed with a snicker. "Or have you already done that, I mean, you know, with the Mrs. and all that is? I heard she's been given it up lately and I know how you are. So tell me, just how is it?"

"Well, that's something you'll just never know because who I do or do not fuck in this town isn't any of your goddamn business so let's just get back to the real reason I'm here."

"Ooh, and what's that, I forgot?" Cyrus smirked again.

"Well, it's actually pretty simple. I want you to release the Davenport boy."

"Release the Davenport boy," he exclaimed with another laugh. "Are you serious? I mean, are you really serious?" He sat forward in his chair. "Goddamn Foster, I already told you on the phone that the boy wasn't going nowhere or did you forget?"

"No Cyrus," Foster smiled and rose from his chair. "Actually I didn't," he added as he placed his hands on top of the desk and leaned toward him. "Because you see, you've just changed your mind and now you're going to release him."

"Oh really?" Cyrus cocked his head as he sat back. "I've just changed my mind and I'm gonna release him? Are you crazy?"

"No, I'm not. In fact, you're even going to see that all of the charges against him are, shall we say, conveniently dropped and that he's released," he paused and placed his hands on his hips then looked to the ceiling as if in thought. "Oooh, let's say by Friday morning. I think that should give you plenty of time to fabricate some sort of story to tell the girl's parents and the judge. You know, kind of like you did with the Atwell case a couple of years ago."

It was at that very moment that the true audacity of Foster's demand sank in and an angry blush crept up the back of Cyrus's neck and then spread across his face like a giant red wave. A second later, the man sprang from his chair and exploded into a rage.

"What'd you say, you son-of-a-bitch!" he snarled. "Just who in the fuck do you think you are comin in here demanding this shit?" He continued loudly as he shot a burning glare directly into Foster's eyes. "I'm the Goddamn prosecutor around here! I'm the one that says who and who ain't gonna get charged or released. Why in the hell should I drop the charges on that spoiled piece of shit when I've got him by the balls?"

"Well, since I knew you'd ask," he chuckled as he reached into his briefcase and grabbed the folder. "I brought you a little present with the answer," he added as he threw it onto the desk.

"What's this?" Cyrus asked as he stared down at the folder and then slowly opened its cover.

"You'll remember," Foster quipped with a smile as he stuffed his hands in his pockets then watched as the man slowly turned from page to page. He knew that it wouldn't take long, but before the thought could even register, Cyrus looked up and exploded into another uncontrolled tirade.

"You son-of-a-bitch," he screamed in a blazing rage, his eyes glazed and boiling with anger. "Do you actually think that you can just waltz in here and threaten me?"

"Yes!" Foster snapped back. "Actually, I do!"

"Whaaat? What'd you say? You son-of-a-bitch! Do you have any idea as to just how much shit I can rain down on top of your ass? Don't fuckin mess with me counselor, I'm warning you or I'll have your goddamn sorry ass arrested for obstruction of justice and have you sittin in jail in less than ten minutes!"

"I don't think so, you self-serving piece of shit!" Foster bit back just as loud and viciously. "You're not going to do anything except shut your goddamn mouth and listen to me. And then you're going to do exactly as I tell you, or I swear to God I'll take every bit of this evidence to the Attorney General. And believe me, when it's all said and done," he lowered his voice and then glared with an icy gaze. "I'll make sure that your pathetic fat ass hangs from the same rope that you put around James Atwell."

Foster's evidence was overwhelming, and for a few fleeting moments, Cyrus could only look down at the folder and stare in disbelief. Foster had him and he knew it, for in his haste to accelerate the man's trial years ago, he'd made too many mistakes with too many loose ends. Yet even so, he pushed once more.

"You wouldn't," he looked back up and narrowed his eyes.

"Just try me Cyrus," Foster growled as if itching to strike. "And I swear, I'll see you hang!"

Swallowing hard, Cyrus slowly dropped back into his chair and exhaled with a defeated sigh. Foster wasn't bluffing and he knew it, he could see it in his eyes. And even though what he was asking was almost certain political suicide, Cyrus cleared his throat and then exhaled another sigh. "And just what is it that you want?" he asked and shook his head.

Taking a seat, Foster smiled triumphantly for this was the part he liked best, not only victorious in battle, but also dictator of his conquered adversary. It just didn't get any better than this, especially with Cyrus, and for the next fifteen minutes he went over his plan on just how he wanted everything to unfold throughout the week.

"It'll probably take all week because of the way I want to use the press," he began. "But the bottom line is sometime before noon on Friday, I want to walk out of the county jail with Bobby Davenport a free man. So I want you to take today and tomorrow to start putting everything in order. And then on Wednesday, I want you to issue a statement to the media. I'd like you to say that in light of a new witness that has just come forward that your case has weakened dramatically. Then on Thursday, I want you to issue another statement that says that only after the careful review and consideration of all of the new evidence, you are now considering dropping all charges. And then on Friday morning, you will issue your last statement that says you are dropping all charges of wrongdoing and release Bobby Davenport to me sometime before noon. Are there any questions?"

"Yes, just one," Cyrus answered and then stared with a perplexed expression pulling at his face. "Why wait until Friday?"

Rising from his chair, Foster gazed down at the prosecutor and smiled. "Well hell Cyrus," he began as if he were gloating. "That's when Howard returns from New Orleans, and I can't very well have Bobby running around loose all week now while he's gone, can I? Why that would just ruin all my plans with Mrs. Davenport," he finished with a smirk then grabbed his briefcase and turned for the door. Strolling across the room, he grabbed the knob and pulled it open, then with a final glance to Cyrus he stepped through the door and left him to his own.

Returning to his office, Foster sat in his chair for a few quiet moments and stared at the court-house. He'd been right, that was fun, but his day was far from over and with glance to the clock, he quickly calculated the time that was left before his meeting with Mrs. Davenport. Yes there was plenty, but even so he would have to hurry if he were to make his two o'clock at the docks. He still had to review Vicki's title search of the property and prepare a transfer of deed.

"Dawnnn," he yelled.

"Yes sir," she answered and sprang from her chair.

"Come in here."

"Is Vicki back yet?" he asked as soon as she appeared in the doorway.

"Yes sir, she just got back before you did. Do you want me to get her?"

"Yes, please."

The boat would be just a simple signature on a title they should already have, and with a quick trip to his house for a change of clothes, he would be off to the newly completed state docks.

CHAPTER 9

———◆———

THE BREEZE COMING IN FROM across the bay that afternoon was refreshing, but still it was the bay and it smelled as such. Walking to the end of the first pier as the wind blew and tussled his dirty blonde hair, Foster finally stopped, slipped a small leather binder beneath one arm and then stuffed both of his hands in his pockets. So this is what ten million in government spending will get you, he thought as he turned and surveyed his surroundings.

Large concrete fingers with huge cranes jutted a thousand feet out into the water. Three hundred feet across, they created new berths for giant ships that waited for their arrival. Gargantuan warehouses stood like massive monuments ready to store the precious cargos that would come from afar. And opposite of them, the railroad tracks lay waiting to deliver everything to the rest of the country. It was a good set up, and it was abundantly clear that it'd been well thought out. The people involved had certainly done their homework and they'd done a good job. Mobile was now one of the largest ports in the country and certain to bring a much-needed economic boost to the city, but even so, where all of the ships were. Turning back to the bay, he scanned the waters, and although there were no ships to be seen, he did catch sight of a beautiful wooden cruiser that was slowly approaching.

A new looking vessel with a clean white hull and three small portholes that were evenly spaced towards its bow, they were ringed in brass and were complimented by two mahogany strips that trimmed its sides. Sitting topside, a tall-elongated box like cabin with large panes of glass sat back from and overlooked the large open area of the bow. Behind it, a lower cabin sided with long narrow panes of glass, stretched almost to the stern. And on its roof, a small white row-boat sat in its own custom cradle, ready and waiting to be dropped into the water by its own launching mechanism.

Is this the boat, he wondered as he raised a hand to shield his eyes from the afternoon sun? If it was, it was nice. A hundred yards from shore, it approached at a steady speed, slicing through the water with a few noisy gulls following just behind in search of a free meal.

Catching sight of a figure standing in the stern, Foster waved with his arm high above his head. Waving back in response, the sputtering boat blew its horn and slowed then veered towards him. Reducing its speed to an idle as it approached and prepared to dock, Foster couldn't help but smile at the radiant beauty standing in the stern.

Truly a vision of elegance, Katherine stood in the back coiling a length of rope. Dressed in a trim fitting white blouse with her sleeves rolled up, she had it neatly tucked into a beige cotton skirt that stopped at her ankles. Bordered and hemmed in blue embroidery, the skirt hung delicately from her hips, accentuating her still youthful and voluptuous figure. Her long dark hair that had been twisted and pulled back into a messy bun had a loose tussle of hair that hung just beside one eye. She was casual and ready for boating yet still she was incredibly stunning.

"Now I wasn't a day over twenty-five when I pulled along side that pier with Mrs. Davenport," Otis began as he fondly thought back to his days as a young man. Handing him another beer, Jim sat back and continued to listen while the auction, still a steady buss of activity, droned monotonously in the distance.

"I remember it real well too, cause that was the first time I ever saw him."

"Saw him, saw who?" Jim asked.

"Foster Siler," Otis replied. "I remember he was standing there, a tall fellow; lean an strong an nicely dressed, waitin patiently for us to pull along side. A confident sort, you know, with a look an presence that gave ya the impression that... well, that he wasn't gonna bow to nobody.

"Now up until then I had no idea as to who he was or why we was gettin him. All I knew was that ol Mrs. Davenport sure was excited. In fact," he popped his top and took a sip. "It seemed like the closer we got to that pier, the worse she got. Heck, I don't know how many times she looked in the mirror

an fussed with her hair," he laughed. "Yes sir, she sure was excited all right, an jus as soon as we'd picked him up an I saw the two of em together, I knew why, specially with ol Mr. Davenport not around."

"Good afternoon," she yelled as they pulled along side and threw a line. "Caaaatch!"

Awkwardly grabbing the flailing rope as Otis brought the boat to a stop, Foster did his best to pull the boat to the pier.

"Juuump," she called out with an extended hand.

Hesitating for just a second as the boat settled, Foster summoned his courage and then jumped in the back. Catching his hand as he landed, Katherine stepped back slightly but held her grip. "We're good to go Otis," she yelled as she bent and looked through the walkway.

"Yes ma'am, Mrs. D," he yelled back and then pushed the throttle forward.

Sputtering back to life in response to its command, the powerful motor quickly pushed them away from the pier. "Well, welcome aboard Mister Siler," she greeted as she released his hand and then pulled a long wisp of hair from her eyes. "I'm so glad you could make it."

"Why thank you Mrs. Davenport," he replied as he steadied himself. "And so am I."

"Oh pleeease," she pleaded. "You must call me Katherine... why I insist. We're boatin, and boatin is an informal pleasure, so enough of this formality."

"Well Mrs. Daven... I mean Katherine," he replied with a grin. "It's your boat and your rules."

"Good, now that that's settled come with me, I want you to meet your captain."

Ducking beneath the doorway, Foster followed as Katherine made her way to the front of the boat and began to point out the accommodations. A nice salon with long built in sofas on both sides sat just off the stern. After that, a bathroom, and then a small galley with a sink sat to one side. Tucked nicely against the side of the boat and the bulkhead that separated the pilothouse from the salon, a table for dinning sat anchored to the floor. Neatly configured into an L shaped booth, the entire interior was hand crafted from the finest Honduran mahogany and varnished to a bright shine. Climbing the two steps up into the pilothouse, Katherine finally stopped and turned to Foster.

"Well?" she asked with a smile. "What-a you think?"

"I like it," he replied as he continued to look around.

"Good, then you'll really like this."

Quickly turning, she stepped to the left of Otis and then descended into another stairwell. Looking as he followed, Foster, to say the least, was again impressed. A separate sleeping quarter, along with yet another bathroom consumed the entire bow of the boat. Furnished with a nice sized bed and built-in closets, it had three small portholes on each side that provided the room with a cozy light. Turning back into the main room after viewing the bathroom, he smiled at the sight of Katherine lying on the bed. Stretched across it on her side, she stared with a beckoning gaze, her head and shoulders raised with an elbow pushed deep into the mattress.

"Come try it," she invited as she patted and smoothed the covers with her free hand.

It was an invitation he couldn't refuse, and as they stared into each other's eyes, communicating yet still not talking, Foster slowly and silently crossed the tiny room. He liked her game of foreplay and the way she was playing it, and in his desire to have her, he was more than willing to play along. Stopping beside the bed, he looked down at the elegant beauty, her eyes unflinching as she turned her head upwards and met his stare. She was more than beautiful, and as he lowered himself onto the bed and stretched out beside her, Katherine, her heart pounding with a nervous anticipation, smiled and cleared her throat.

"So tell me," she finally asked in a seductive whisper as she sensuously drew the back of her hand down the buttons of his shirt. "Do you like everything you seeee?"

Quietly studying her face, Foster delicately traced a finger across her rose-colored lips then slowly rolled his hand and drew a line from the crook of her mouth to the side of her face. Trembling at his touch, Katherine closed her eyes and tilted her head. She liked what he was doing and it showed, he could tell by the way her nostrils flared with each and every breath. Caressing her cheek with the backs of his fingers, he then slipped them beneath a long strand of hair that hung from her temple. Twirling it around one finger, he tenderly tucked it behind her ear then lowered his face to the side of her neck and inhaled the scent of her perfume. There was no doubt she smelled as good as she looked, and as her intoxicating scent invaded his senses, he raised his head and then hungrily cast his eyes across her voluptuous curves.

As far as Foster was concerned, there was a little sluttiness in every woman, and beneath the facade of Katherine Davenport's prim and proper exterior, he knew she concealed another side. A side he was certain, was wicked and decadent. She was a married woman and yet she was offering herself to him, and that was the part he liked best. The taking of another man's wife; the addition of another trophy. It didn't get any better than that, but as he brought his eyes back to hers, he couldn't help but think of how beautiful they were. Dazzling and captivating hazy blues that pulled heavy and hard at the hearts of men. He wondered how any man could look away? A moment later, he reached for her hand and intertwined his fingers with hers then ever so slowly leaned towards her.

Yes, he was going to kiss her, and with an almost inaudible gasp, she closed her eyes and readied for his lips. She wanted nothing more than to embrace and savor in the moment, and as she inhaled his cologne and waited, she could feel a moistened heat stir from the depths of her loins. A second later, she felt his breath on her lips and quivered like a schoolgirl then suddenly opened her eyes wide to the sound of Otis's voice.

"Mrs. Davenporrrrt," he yelled from above. "Where's we headed taday ma'am?"

Rolling her eyes with an exasperated groan, Katherine fell to her back and then pounded the bed in a miniature mock tantrum. A second later she sat upright, shook her head with a laugh then turned and looked to Foster. "Well Mister Siler," she said wryly. "I do hope we can continue later on, don't you?"

"Oh please Katherine," he fenced back with a bit of humor. "It's Foster remember... we're boatin."

"Oh yesss," she apologized with a laugh. "How silly of me to have forgotten so quickly."

"Well good," he stood and held out his hand. "Now that that's settled, shall we see what your captain wants?"

Sliding from the bed, Katherine straightened her clothes and yelled toward the stairway. "Up river Otis, I wanna show Mr. Siler the house and acreage," she said as she turned back to Foster. "Now come on and I'll introduce you to our negro."

Following Katherine back up the two steps and into the pilot-house, Foster was more than happy to meet the young captain. Peering out into the harbor with a calm but serious gaze, Otis navigated the busy waterways with the skill of a seasoned harbor pilot. Medium in stature, he'd been hired about five years ago to care for the Davenport's house and two hundred acres. Quickly proving to be a talented and loyal employee, he was then given the task of refinishing their old boat as well. Finishing three months later to the elation of Howard, he soon began driving them whenever they went boating. It was a great job and one that he excelled at, and so right after the purchase of their new boat, he was given the keys and became their full-time captain.

"Otis," Katherine called as she stepped up and touched his arm. "I'd like you to meet someone."

"Yes ma'am," he turned and politely pulled his hat from his head.

"Otis, this is Mr. Siler."

"Yes ma'am," he nervously replied as he twisted his hat in his hands. "I... I's pleased ta meet ya Mister Siler."

Gauging the man as he stepped closer, Foster reached out and extended his hand. To him it was nothing, for his views were just a little different than those of the deep South, but to Katherine it was a shock, and she could only stare in a moment of disbelief. A man of Foster's stature shaking hands with a black man; why it was unheard of. In fact, Otis thought the very same thing, but even so he released the hold on his hat and took Foster's hand.

"I'm Foster Siler," Foster said as they shook.

"Ye... yes sur," the young black man stammered. "They calls me Otis, Mister Siler," he added with a jittery nervousness. "Oo... Otis Brown."

"Well Otis," Foster said as he released his grip. "It's my pleasure, and I'm sure that we'll get along just fine."

"Yes sur," Otis agreed along with a nod. "If'n you says so," he added, only to instantly cock his head and scrunch his eyebrows. "Huh," he uttered with a perplexed expression.

"Oh yes," Katherine quickly interceded. "Otis, I forgot to tell you that Howard and I have been thinking about selling the boat and Mr. Siler is here today for a ride. See, he's thinking about buying it, and I'm sure if he does, he will most certainly be in need of a captain. Isn't that right, Mr. Siler?"

"Oh absolutely," Foster laughed. "Heck, I don't know anything about boatin."

"Well I shor would do a good job for ya Mister Siler if'n ya'd give me a chance," Otis said in hopes of keeping his job.

"I'm sure you would Otis," Foster replied. "I'm sure you would."

A second later and with what was clearly a sigh of relief, the young man turned back to his wheel and applied more throttle.

Looking at Jim, Otis took another short sip from his beer then continued on with his story. "Now in all of my years of livin an up until that time, no white man had ever shaken my hand. So to say that I was jus a little confused an a whole lot intimidated, well, that would've been an understatement. An then when I realized that the Davenports were a sellin their boat, well, that's when I started to think that my whole world had jus come to an end. Hell, at that point, I really didn't know what I was gonna do. But that young lawyer feller was smooth, an he had a way of makin you feel real comfortable. An after the two of them went to the back an we started up river, I got to thinkin that somehow, maybe everything was gonna be okay."

"Well now," Katherine began. "Now that that's all over, how about if we retire to the stern and make ourselves comfortable?"

"Yes, by all means," Foster replied as the boat increased in speed. "That sounds wonderful," he added as he followed her down the steps and into the lower cabin.

"Excuse me, but do you drink wine Mr. Siler... I mean Foster," she laughed as she turned and then stopped at the icebox.

"Yes ma'am," he nodded and smiled at the thought of how there was nothing like a little liquor to loosen things up. "I love wine."

"Oh good," she said as she looked down and opened the lid. "Well, if I remember right, I believe we have several to choose from. Do you like white?" she rambled on as she reached inside and grabbed a bottle then turned and handed it to him before he could answer. "Here hold this," she said as she spun back to the counter and began searching the drawers and cabinets.

"Aah yesss, there it is," she said as she held up the corkscrew and then pushed the drawer closed with her hip. "Now let's go and enjoy this beautiful day, shall we?" she said as she grabbed their glasses from the counter.

"By all means," he nodded. "After you," he insisted as he stepped aside and gracefully extended an arm toward the stern.

Stepping through the doorway onto the stern, Katherine set the glasses and corkscrew down on the small wooden table sitting between two Adirondack chairs. A little closer together than what she liked, she stepped behind one, grabbed the back and turned it ever so slightly toward the other.

"There we go," she said with the clap of her hands. "That's better."

Taking their seats, Foster reached for the corkscrew then sat back in his chair and stuck the bottle between his legs. Unwrapping the seal from around the bottle as they began on their journey up river, he picked up the corkscrew and twisted it into the cork.

"Oooh Foster," Katherine sighed as she settled into her chair. "This is so nice, don't you think?" she went on as she closed her eyes and then tilted her head toward the sun. "You know, I really do love it out here."

Relaxing with thoughts of times long gone, Katherine quickly drifted off into a dream-like state. For months she'd been plagued by worries; her failing marriage of some twenty years, their financial ruin and fall from social prominence, and most of all her spoiled son who was completely out of control. But for now, they were all gone. Out here, it was just her and the boat and a few noisy gulls following close behind. A soothing blend of noises that lulled the senses, until the sound of the cork being pulled from the bottle brought her back to reality.

"Well," she said as she opened her eyes. "I do believe that that was just about the most pleasant sound I've heard all day, don't you?" her refined drawl raised slightly in an effort to overpower the sputtering of the motor.

"Yes ma'am," Foster laughed and poured their glasses then set the bottle down. "Shall we toast?" he asked as he handed her one and then raised his glass.

"Yes, by all means, we shall," she said as she sat forward and raised her glass. "Here's to the rest of the day," she smiled with an inviting coyness. "And may it bring us both what we desire most."

"I couldn't agree more," he added with a knowing smile as he touched his glass with hers.

Savoring its taste, Katherine closed her eyes and tilted her head toward the sky, held the wine in her mouth for just a moment, then swallowed and slowly reclined back into her chair. "Aah yesss," she sighed. "Now that is truly a wonderful expression of a perfectly balanced bouquet," she mocked as if she were a connoisseur then laughed.

Laughing along with her, Foster just shook his head then tilted his glass and gulped his wine. "Yep," he agreed with a satisfied sigh as he held up his empty glass. "Not bad at all."

Gaining a smile, Katherine casually draped one leg over the other and set her glass on the arm of the chair, then turned and looked out across the river. There was no doubt that she was a vision of elegance, and he couldn't help but stare, yet even so, he could sense that something was on her mind. Her mood had changed, but after just a few moments, she turned back and narrowed her eyes.

"Tell me about my son," she asked with a deep concern and another sip from her glass.

"Well Katherine," Foster began in a solemn voice. "I think you already know that Bobby's in some very serious trouble."

Cringing with an anguished expression, Katherine lowered her head and stared at the floor. "But you can help him," she finally asked as she raised it back up. "Can't you?"

"Well quite frankly," he sighed as he began to play his cards from the bottom of the deck. "I really don't know. It's serious, and the prosecutor really has him. But there's something else," he went on as if he were deeply troubled. "There's something more, and it's been bothering me. And actually, it wasn't so much as what he said, but what he didn't say that really caught my attention. I'm not sure, but for some reason I get the feeling that Cyrus Buchanan has some sort of grudge against you. And even as wrong as it is, it could very well affect the outcome of your son's case. So I'm concerned," he paused with another sigh. "Does he?"

It was as if the question itself had brought back the past, and for a moment Katherine could only look on as if all hope of freeing her son had just disappeared. "Yes," she sighed and lowered her head. "He does. It... it was about two years ago, when Howard and I--."

"It's okay," Foster interrupted as he reached over and squeezed her hand. "You don't have to explain it to me, I just needed to know if he did," he added as she raised her head and returned his gaze. "See, I know exactly who and what kind of man Cyrus is, and now that I know he has a grudge against you, it helps me."

Biting her lip in an effort to quell the emotions rising inside of her, Katherine stared for just a moment then slowly began to shake her head. "No, you don't understand, the man hates me," she said in a voice filled with despair. "He literally hates me, and I just know that he's going to take it all out on Bobby. You see, when he was arrested and we went to see him, Cyrus just laughed and told me that by the time he was done with my son, I'd be dead before he was out of jail. You've got to help me," she pleaded and gasped for air as she rolled her hand over and clutched his fingers.

"Now just calm down a little," Foster said as he squeezed her hand back. "Everything is going to be just fine, you hear. Just take a deep breath and relax, because I will get your son out, I promise. Trust me, somehow, just somehow... I will get Bobby out."

Staring deep into his eyes, Katherine searched for the reassurance and comfort that she needed, that would convince her that everything was going to be okay. "But how?"

"Well, let's just say that I have a few tricks up my sleeve, how's that."

"Are you sure," she asked in a voice still filled with uncertainty. "You do know that the man absolutely despises me."

"Yes ma'am," he drawled confidently. "I'm sure. I have some favors that are owed to me. Some pretty big ones that are long over-due and it's time I collected them. Remember, you hired me to get your son out of jail and that's exactly what I intend to do. Now it may take me all week to do it considering your case, but trust me, by Friday, I really think that I can have Bobby out."

Squeezing his hand with a tight-lipped smile as if to express her profound sense of gratitude, Katherine cleared her throat and then stared deep into his eyes. "Well if you do Mister Siler," she began in a sultry voice, her eyes unflinching with some hidden promise. Her grip on his hand now a sensuous caress. "If you can get my son out by Friday, and before my husband returns from New Orleans. Well," she paused and cleared her throat again. "Let's just say, shall we, that you have no idea as to just how truly grateful I would be."

It wasn't so much as what she said but how she said that gave Foster pause. "Well then," he finally replied with a knowing smile. "I had better get to work, hadn't I," he added as he rose from his chair and returned to the cabin.

Retrieving his leather binder with the deeds and papers for the two hundred acres, he returned a few moments later to find Katherine standing at the side of the boat, waving with her arm high above her head. He'd heard the rumbling from inside, and as he focused on the shoreline, he could see the freight train running along the river's edge. Belching its thick black smoke as it labored to pull the heavy cars, the giant locomotive barreled on towards the city.

On its afternoon run into Mobile, it carried just some of the precious resources that kept the city alive. Consisting mostly of heavily loaded coal cars and flat cars that were stacked with steel and lumber, there were also a few open empty boxcars. Occupied with destitute men riding the rails in search of a better life, the train finally blew its whistle in a long and loud response to her wave.

Overjoyed that the conductor had seen her, and had actually blown the whistle, Katherine finally turned to find Foster refilling their glasses.

"It's the Louisville and Nashville" she exclaimed over the distant rumbling of the wheels.

"Yes, it is," he agreed as he handed her a glass.

Taking it from his hand, Katherine took a sip then turned and watched the train until it had crossed the trestle at Chickasaw Creek. Disappearing a few moments later, it left only the rumbling of its wheels until that too had disappeared and was replaced by the sound of their own motor. Now nothing more than a distant memory, she sighed and turned back to Foster. "You know, I really do love watching them."

"Yes, I can tell," he grinned then extended an arm towards the chairs. "Shall we?"

Returning to her chair, Katherine gracefully took her seat, draped one leg over the other then smoothed her dress and looked to Foster. "And what have we here?" she asked with a curious glance to the folder.

"Well," he began as he pulled the documents from the binder and then held them out. "These are the deeds to your house and the two hundred acres that you need to sign. You know, that will transfer the ownership of your property to me in lieu of my fees. You see your husband actually had everything set up quite nicely in a trust in your name; and I believe that is why the creditors failed to seize it and you still have it. And since you are the trustee of that trust," he continued as he handed her the papers. "All I need is your signature to complete the transfer."

A little surprised at the revelation, Katherine took the papers from his hand, stared at them for just a moment then shifted her eyes back to Foster. "Just me?" she asked. "I don't understand. Why would Howard do that?"

"Well, I think that he may have been doing some estate planning," Foster answered casually. "But I really can't say for sure. But what I can say for sure, is that the house and the acreage is all yours and no one else's. And all it requires is one signature, and that is yours," he flipped his pen and then held it out.

Looking back down at the papers, Katherine blindly reached for the thin silver cylinder and took it from his hand.

"Right here," he said, turning the papers slightly and then pointing to the bottom of the first page. "And there are others on the following pages as well."

"But I've never had to sign anything before," she hesitated with a nervous glance back to Foster.

"Yes, that very well may be. But now you have to. You're the only one who can."

Nodding her head as if she understood, Katherine looked back down at the papers and set the pen where she was shown. She was about to transfer one of the last possessions they had, yet even so she drew in a breath and began her signature with the beautiful swirling of a capital K. Suddenly, and with the thought of how another piece of her life was being stripped away, the woman who'd already lost so much, stopped and raised her head. "I cannn't," she cried. "It's all we have left." A second later she turned away, and as the onslaught of tears came rushing from inside, she dropped her head into her hands and quietly began to cry.

A little uncomfortable at first, Foster stared for just a moment then sat forward in his chair and pulled the papers from her lap. "Katherine," he said as he set them on the table and then gently placed his hand on her shoulder. "Come on, it's going to be okay. You're going to be okay, you hear."

But Katherine never responded; she just curled her body and shunned his touch. She was upset and embarrassed, for she'd never cried in front of anyone over her losses or troubles. Not anyone, yet now here she was, crying in front of a man she barely knew, and try as she may she couldn't stop. It was more than she could bear, and in an effort to clear her mind, she rose from her chair and walked to the side of the boat. Grabbing the edge of the cabin for support, she steadied herself then lowered her head into her other hand.

Watching from his chair, Foster stared for just a few moments then slowly rose and stepped behind her. "Katherine," he finally said as he touched her shoulder. "Come on, it's going to be okay. Everything is," he stopped as she turned and fell into his arms.

Comforted by his embrace as his arms wrapped around her and tightened, Katherine slowly found relief from the incredible grief she was feeling. He was tender and kind, and for the first time in her life she began to feel a kind of compassion and comfort she'd never known. Even from her husband of twenty some years who treated her as nothing more than an ornament. Cold and uncaring, he hadn't touched her in over ten years, yet in Foster's arms she felt safe and secure, as if everything was going to be okay. Regaining a bit of her composure, she raised her head from his chest and stared long-ingly into his eyes. It was the look he'd been waiting for and without a moments hesitation, he lowered his head and touched his lips to hers. Softly at first, he explored the outer smallness of her mouth; tasting and savoring then slowly and tenderly moved to her neck and nipped at the softness of her flesh.

His breath was hot and moist and with a tingling shiver running through her, Katherine closed her eyes and sucked her breath. She hadn't felt these feelings in years and wanted nothing more than to be kissed hard and passionately. It was what she wanted more than anything else in the world, and without another thought, she tip-toed to the balls of her feet and pulled on his shoulders. Frantically seeking his lips with hers, she grasped at the back of his neck, and in a moment of passion as he pulled her tight, the two melted into a hot and greedy embrace.

It was a long and heated kiss and after it was over, Katherine smiled and inhaled a much-needed breath then turned away and looked out across the river. Watching as a gust of wind rippled the tranquil waters into a million tiny waves, she gazed at the glittering reflection of the sun as it danced across its surface. A little ashamed and worried that she'd been too brazen, she wondered if he would now think less of her. Maybe it was that their kiss had affected her more than she realized, or that the mindset of her prim and proper upbringing was overreacting. After all, she was a married woman, and she was still cradled in the arms of another man. It worried her, and it showed.

Sensing her discomfort, Foster slipped a finger beneath her chin and then gently turned her face back to his. "It's okay," he said with the gentle kiss to her forehead.

"Please don't think ill of me," she mumbled into his shirt as she tightened her arms around him. "It's just that my husband..."

"Shhhh," he hushed in a comforting voice. "You don't have to explain anything to me,"

"Yes, yes I do. I know that I'm married," she began as if she were ashamed. "But you see Howard, well..." she lowered her head and voice, then continued on. "You see he hasn't touched me in over ten years. That is, I mean... you know, really touched me. And it's just that I've been so alone for so long and just so lonely, that I...," her voice trailed off into a muffled mix of saddened gibberish.

Looking down into a face that was filled with despair and loneliness, he wondered how any man could leave a woman like this alone. He certainly couldn't, hell, no man in his right mind could or would. After all, she was without a doubt still one of the most attractive women in all of Mobile. So was her husband sick or just crazy, or... did he like other men?

He'd heard of those types before, but had never actually seen one. But now, and in light of the circumstances, he was growing with his suspicions. After all, Howard sure didn't seem sick the other day. In fact he was fine, so if he wasn't sleeping with a woman as beautiful as his wife, it stood to reason that he just might be one of those fellows. Yes, that was it, and damn lucky for him too, for if not, she just might not be here.

"Well, I think your husband's a fool," he said in an attempt to lighten her mood and reassure her. "And I'll tell you, if you were mine, I wouldn't leave you alone for ten minutes," he added in hopes that she wouldn't change her mind; that emotional female kind of thing where they regret what it is they're about to do before they even do it. That, *'Oh I'm sorry, but I just can't do this kind of thing right now. That this is wrong.'* No sir, it would kill him if she did, especially after he'd just tasted and felt her hunger.

"Thank you," she said graciously. "You know, sometimes a woman just needs to be reminded that she is still desired."

"Well Katherine," he drawled and smiled. "I can assure you... you arrrre most certainly desired. Now," he said as he pulled on her hand and turned toward the chairs. "Let's sit back down."

Grabbing her glass of wine as she sat back down, Katherine took a sip then reclined into the comfort of her chair. Gathering her senses, she looked to Foster as he pulled the papers from the binder and extended his hand toward her. "Are you okay?" he asked."

"Yes," she nodded and cleared her throat. "Just show me where again."

Pointing with the pen at the beautiful swirling K that she'd left just moments ago, he flipped it in his fingers once again and then held it out for her to take.

Staring at the paper for just a second, Katherine finally picked up where she'd stopped and finished her signature with the beauty and flare of old-world calligraphy. "And the others," he said with a shuffle of the pages. "Aaah... right here."

"And what are these?"

"Those're the resolutions to your trust, basically verifying that you're the trustee. You know, all that legal mumbo jumbo stuff."

"Oh okay," she nodded again as if she understood.

Signing wherever Foster pointed, she quickly finished her task then handed the papers back. Carefully placing them back into the binder, Foster took them into the cabin then returned. "We can do the title and the bill of sale to the boat tomorrow," he said as he dropped into his chair. "I would imagine Howard probably has that somewhere around the house,."

"Well then, you'll just have to come by tomorrow evening when you get off work and get it won't you," she grinned invitingly. "Maybe for supper?" she added and stared.

Grinning at the thought, Foster picked up his glass and held it toward the woman. "To supper it is then," he said in a casual toast.

"Yes, to supper," she repeated as she clinked her glass with his.

Basking in the afternoon sun as they continued up river, the two quietly shared the bottle of wine and idly talked of nothing. Occasionally pointing out landmarks as they went, of who owned what and where, Katherine gave Foster his first history lesson on the upper delta of the Mobile River. He liked it, and he was enjoying the day, and as they motored up river he'd all but forgotten where he was until the boat suddenly slowed and blew its horn.

"What's wrong," he asked as he sat up and looked around. "Are we here?"

"Oh nooo, it's just the trestle for the Louisville and Nashville," Katherine replied. "You know. We have to signal it so they can turn the tracks and let us through."

Standing up with an amazed expression, Foster grinned and then watched as the giant mechanical bridge slowly began to spin.

"See, they do this every time."

"Amazing," he said with a child-like awe, turning slowly in a circle as they passed. "How much farther now?"

"Well the property starts just around the next bend, but the house is about another ten minutes or so. Why, are you getting anxious?"

"Yes actually," he replied as he walked to the edge of the boat and looked across the river. "Yes I am," he went on as he surveyed the vast expanse of wilderness and then downed his glass. "And I like this boatin stuff too," he said as he turned back with an empty glass.

"Me too," she added as she pulled herself from her chair. "You know, ya just get up here and it seems as if all your worries just go away," she stepped beside him and emptied what was left of the bottle into his glass.

"Yeah, I can tell," he chuckled with a glance into his glass. "Sure ain't gonna have any worries today are we?"

"Well, that was the first part of my plan," she said with a gleam to her eyes as she turned and then stepped into the cabin with the empty bottle.

"Oooh? The first part?" He raised his voice. "And just what pray tell, was the other half?"

"Just a second and I'll show you," her muffled reply came from inside.

A few moments later Katherine reappeared in the doorway and presented the other half of her plan. "Well, what-a-ya think?" she beamed with another bottle held proudly between the palms of her hands.

"That's the other half of your plan?" Foster laughed and shook his head.

"Yes sir," she smiled and then sauntered toward him. "Would you care to do the honors again?"

"Well, I don't see why not," he laughed again and took the bottle then stepped to the table to retrieve the corkscrew.

Turning back to the river as he opened the wine, Katherine stared at the passing shoreline for just a moment then suddenly turned back to Foster. "Oh look," she said excitedly. "We're here! This is our property; this is where it starts. Right here at that little offshoot, see!" she turned back and pointed to the shore.

Walking up behind her, Foster pulled the cork with a pop. "Right here," he asked, gazing at the grassy peninsula separating the two bodies of water.

"Yes, right there," she pointed again.

"But where's the house?"

"Well, it and the pier are way up that tributary. We wanted to keep it off the river, you know, out of the way of all the barge traffic," she added but then stopped as the boat began to slow and turn. "Otis," she turned and yelled through the doorway. "Keep going will you, I want to show Mr. Siler the river front first, okay!"

"Yes ma'am Mrs. D," he replied as he turned the wheel back and applied more throttle.

Continuing up river, Katherine scanned the shoreline in an effort to locate the property lines. She'd thought she knew where they were, but it had been years since she'd seen them and with what was clearly an uncertain guess, she did her best and then turned the boat around. Making their way back to the tributary, they finally turned and headed toward the pier. Half the width and depth of the river, it was bordered on both sides by a thick forest of old growth Cypress. Dotted with idle eddies and tree-covered pools along its banks, it meandered for almost a mile toward the house.

Gazing at the land as they continued on Foster began to sense that something wasn't right, for based on what she'd already showed him, he was certain he'd seen way more than two hundred acres. He wondered if he'd misunderstood or just not heard correctly? Surely not, in fact, he remembered Howard saying clear as a bell, two hundred acres. Maybe it was just Katherine not knowing where the boundaries really were, or maybe it was the wine.

"How many acres did you say there was?" he asked nonchalantly.

"Two hundred... isn't it big?"

"Yes... yes it is," he replied as if he were trying to sound impressed, yet still harbor his thoughts. For if there was a mistake in the acreage and it was in his favor, he certainly wasn't going to let on. "I guess I just never realized how big two hundred acres was," he lied.

"Well, it's all yours now," she said with a carefree laugh. "House, furniture, pots, pans... everything." Then downing what was left of her wine, she set her glass on the table, stepped to the corner and picked up a coil of rope from the floor.

CHAPTER 10

———◆———

APPROACHING FROM DOWNSTREAM, OTIS SLOWED the boat, veered hard toward shore and began his big question-mark turn into the pier. He liked to dock with the bow pointing out and the stern toward shore, and he liked to dock on the down-stream side. Hitting reverse as they pulled along the edge, he kicked the stern sideways and then went to neutral. Bumping slightly as they settled and stopped, Katherine quickly stepped onto the pier and began tying the boat.

Wrapping a line around one of the massive pylons embedded deep into the bottom, she secured the stern and then the bow. Newly constructed and solid in its making, the pier held firm against the constant flow of water. About twelve feet wide and seventy-five feet long, it ended on an expanse of grass that sloped up and toward the house. Beyond the open grassy area, a small two-bedroom home with a nice screened in porch sat neatly behind a clump of several large cypress trees.

Jumping back into the boat, she threw a glance to Foster and grabbed the half empty bottle of wine, then ducked her head into the doorway. She knew Otis loved to fish, but more importantly she knew it would keep him occupied while they were gone. "Otis," she yelled. "I'm going to show Mr. Siler the house and the grounds and we may be a little while. So while we're gone, why don't you just relax and do some fishing. See if you can catch us some catfish to take back with us? And if you get enough, I'll have Miss Bessie fry them up for supper tomorrow. How's that sound?"

"Oh, yes ma'am Mrs. D," he replied and shut down the motor. "That sounds great."

"Now I knew that ol Mrs. D liked to drink," Otis began with a chuckle. "But boy I sure didn't know she could drink like that cause by the time we'd finally pulled up to that pier those two were already on the bottom half of their second bottle. Yes sir, they was havin a hell of a time an jus as soon as we were all tied an she'd told me what she was go'n to do, I knew right then an there that she was gonna show that young lawyer a whole lot more property than what ol Mr. Davenport had bargained on."

"You know, I was just thinking," she began as she turned back to Foster and then scooped up their glasses from the table. "Otis is such a good negro, you should really consider keeping him on with you, you know." She finished and handed them to him, then made her way to the edge of the boat.

"Yeaaah, you're probably right," Foster replied as he followed. "I mean, I don't see why I couldn't, he seems nice enough. Besides, who in the hell else am I gonna get to drive this crazy thing," he chuckled and shook his head.

"Well, I'm glad to hear that," she laughed as she stepped onto the pier. "Cause I'll tell ya, out of all our help, he sure has been about the best. And I'll tell ya another thing," she added as Foster stepped onto the pier and she pulled the cork from the bottle. "Good help is hard to find. Now hold up those glasses," she grinned with a twinkle to her eyes.

Doing as he was told, Foster just shook his head and held up the glasses.

"So he's my negro now?" he asked as she filled his and then hers.

"Yep," she nodded as she pushed the cork back into the bottle and then reached for her glass. "I'm giving him to you, along with the boat. Now," she said and turned toward the house. "Shall we?"

She was doing her best to appear in control, yet beneath the facade of her carefree demeanor, Katherine was a ball of nerves. She was about to do the unthinkable, and even though she knew it was wrong, she took in a breath for courage and began walking down the pier. She felt like a schoolgirl, and as they reached the end and stepped onto the grass, her heart began to pound with a nervous anticipation.

Finding the key in its place under a stone, she turned and inserted it into the lock then opened the door to the dark and musty staleness of a closed-up house. "Ooh myyy," she exclaimed and fanned her face. "We better do something about this."

Scurrying into the kitchen, she set her glass of wine on the counter and then hurriedly opened several windows throughout the house.

"Well," she said as she returned and picked up her glass. "What-a-you think? I know it's no mansion, but it's nice and clean, and well-built," she added, but then stopped as if she'd just run out of words. This was supposed to be her moment, but now that it was here she suddenly found herself lost at what to do. Fidgeting in a moment of uncertainty, she cleared her throat and set her glass back down onto the counter then turned and looked out to the river.

It was clear she was uncomfortable, and without a moment's hesitation, Foster quickly stepped toward her and reached up under her chin. Gently turning her back, he gazed into her eyes for just a moment then slowly lowered his head and kissed her.

Tasting and testing with a tender passion, he once again explored the outer folds of her mouth until the heated hunger within her had removed any and all doubts as to what it was she was about to do. The burning heat in her loins screamed with a searing need, and almost instantly they were pulling and tearing at each other's clothes in a spinning and twisting duel.

Yanking his shirt from his pants, they stumbled and crashed against the counter and then the table. And as her desires took hold, fueling and driving her aggressions, she gripped at the cotton fabric and ripped it open. Exposing his chest to the sounds of buttons hitting the floor, she sighed with desire then felt his arms wrap tightly around her. A second later he lifted her from the ground, and with her arms draped around his neck, carried her into the bedroom.

Kissing her again as her feet touched the floor; they renewed their efforts and continued to tear at each other's clothes. Ripping and peeling the layers from their bodies, she finally stood before him in all of her naked glory, an erotic vision of loveliness. Bathed in the afternoon light, her soft olive skin glowed with the look and luster of a Greek Goddess.

God she was beautiful, he thought as he feasted his eyes upon her and then lowered his mouth to her breast. Full and womanly, they were pointed and firm and heaved with desire. Cupping his head as he sensuously worshiped one and then the other, she pulled him tight then closed her eyes with a moan. His touch was electric, yet even as she relished in the feeling of his mouth on her breast, she felt yet another sensation as one of his hands slowly slid down from the curve of her hips. Shivering as it settled between her legs, her heart fluttered then surged as he gently began to stroke the softness of her curls. It felt good to be touched, yet still as she concentrated on his hand between her legs, she could feel his other as it slowly slid up her spine. Rising ever higher, until he had reached the base of her neck and grabbed a handful of hair then jerked her head back.

Startled by his direct and sudden forcefulness, Katherine whimpered with an uncertain yet elated pleasure as the dominance of his desires instantly consumed and excited her. And although she tried to hide her feelings, she failed, for he could see it in her eyes and feel it in her body as she began to shiver. Smiling at the thought, he ravaged her neck with his mouth then embedded his middle finger deep into her. She was his now, and he was going to use her as he saw fit.

Flinching and then gasping as he slipped into her, Katherine, propelled by feelings she'd never felt before and in a completely unconscious act, instantly began to move her hips. She should've felt ashamed and been incensed by the vulgarity of what he'd done and was doing. Or at least, have protested. But she wasn't and she didn't. She liked the sleaziness and the decadence of his boldness for most of the men throughout her life, including her husband, had treated her like a porcelain doll. Fragile and afraid, that somehow they might break her. But Foster was different, he was carnal and raw and forceful, and her body thrilled to his touch. Closing her eyes as he continued to work her sex, she blindly found his mouth with hers then slowly and sensuously raised one of her legs along the outside of his.

Grabbing the outside of her thigh with his other hand, Foster pulled it high and held it against his waist. Now allowing his complete and unencumbered access, she welcomed his second finger then lewdly began to move and undulated herself. Thrusting her pelvis upward and on him in an act that simulated sex, she smiled at the excesses now invading her until Foster abruptly pulled his hand from between her legs and pushed her onto the bed. God she was amazing, he thought as he looked upon her; a lustful and stunning example of femininity sprawled on her back with her hair in a sensuous disarray. She'd mothered two children and yet here she was, still one of the most beautiful and desirable women he'd ever seen.

Lifting herself ever so slightly, she rested on her elbows and stared as he slowly began to unbuckle his belt and removed his pants. A few seconds later, she inhaled a sharpened breath and then smiled as they hit the floor. It had been a long long time since she'd seen a sight such as him, and as he hovered beside her she stared with a lustful gaze at a body that'd been sculptured and honed from years of hard labor. Muscular and tight he stood hard and ready with eyes that were fiery and wild.

It was a look she'd never seen before, a ravenous look, and she felt helpless under his gaze. Yet even so she needed and liked what he had, that edgy boldness, that sexual power and confidence that her husband didn't. And now like that of a new bride on her wedding night, she waited to be taken as he knelt on the bed and then crawled between her legs.

Slithering over the top of her body, he slowly lowered his face to hers then gently brushed and nipped at her lips. He was teasing her, but Katherine wanted more than just kisses. She wanted to feel him again and he knew it, he could tell by the look in her eyes and the way she'd lifted and spread her legs then pulled on his shoulders. Answering her unspoken request, he kissed her neck and then moved to her breast. Moaning as he took one and then the other, he slowly continued on working his way down her body. She was in heaven and as he moved from the flat of her belly to the crease between her leg and her sex, she grabbed his head and writhed in pleasure.

Trembling with desire as he stretched out and wedged himself between her thighs, he smiled and shoved his arms up under her legs. Laying his hands on her belly, he pulled her skin taught and then lowered his mouth to her sex. Nuzzling her mound, he inhaled her scent then slowly and sensuously traced his tongue along her opening. Delicately perfumed, she smelled flowery and delicious but still carried the intoxicating muskiness of a mature woman that he liked.

Gasping sharply, Katherine suddenly stiffened, for no man had ever kissed her there before, not ever. Not even her husband. It was a sin and a violation of the very morals she'd been raised and had lived by all of her life. She couldn't allow it, and as she shook her head and battled her thoughts she pushed at his head. "Nooo," she cried as her fingers slid through his hair.

She was saying no yet Foster persisted and continued on. Feeling his breath hot on her sex, and then his kisses and his tongue on the insides of her thighs, her resistance quickly faded. Welling with a desire she'd never felt before, overpowering any and all misgivings she had, she slowly relaxed her legs then grasped at his head and pulled, urging him on.

Now desperately seeking the forbidden and unknown, she gave herself over to the pleasures of his oral desires and slowly pulled her knees into the air. Lewdly exposing herself like never before, she shuddered as the fleshy organ of his mouth began to lick and separate the folds of her womanhood. His touch was erotic and unlike anything she'd ever felt, and in a moment of unfettered passion, she obscenely rolled her hips to meet his mouth. Gasping sharply as his tongue plunged deep inside, Katherine froze and clutched a handful of his hair, then exhaled with a heavy moan.

Quickly finding her most sensitive spot, Foster began to manipulate her in a way in which she'd never dreamed. Circling, flicking and sucking, he tenaciously worked his magic as she squirmed beneath him and dug her heals into the small of his back. She wanted to scream and cry out with pleasure, but she didn't... she couldn't. Unrelenting in his assault, he lashed with his tongue again and again, and as her moans of mewling whimpers slowly changed into incoherent pleas, he felt her body begin to tighten. Clutching his head with both of her hands, she drove herself onto his mouth and began to rock her hips. A few moments later he felt her constrict, and as the first golden ripples of her release flowed into her, Katherine stiffened and rode a long rolling wave of pleasure.

It was certainly a newfound pleasure and after she'd settled, she smiled with a deep contented sigh and began to shake her head. "Oh my God," she drawled as she propped herself up onto her elbows and looked down at the man still between her legs. "Wherever did you learn to do such a thing?" she laughed then dropped her head back to the bed and stared at the ceiling. "Why I do believe that that was the most wickedly delicious thing that anyone has ever done to me."

Smiling at the thought of her undying gratitude, Foster just stared then silently rose and crawled over the top of her. Supporting his weight on his elbows, he lowered himself and kissed her then pressed his manhood against her sex. Thick and veiny and hard, it pulsed with a virility and life of its own, and as he slowly slid it across her opening, she spread and lifted her legs in an effort to receive him. Hooking her feet around his legs she pulled at his back, but to her chagrin, he pulled away in a move that was sudden and teasing. Opening her eyes in a moment of disbelief, she stared for a second then closed them and pulled at his back once again. "Don't," she pleaded as she lifted and undulated her hips in search of the object she so desperately craved. "Pleeease."

It was exactly what he wanted to hear; yet even so Foster had no intentions of giving her what she wanted... or at least not yet he didn't. He wanted to take her to the edge, to see if he could lower the puritan values in which she lived by and push her to the point where she would beg to be taken. It was a game he liked to play, especially with the prim and proper socialites of the city. He loved to corrupt and violate their morals, and to conquer their will. But most of all, he loved to expose and exploit their deepest and darkest desires, and to prevail upon them until they had toppled from their pedestals of purity. Willing to do whatever he wanted, whenever he wanted. And as demoralizing as it may have been or seemed, he didn't care for he derived almost as much pleasure out of it as he did the sex itself.

Squirming beneath him as he continued to tease and drive against her, Katherine suddenly felt one of his hands slide beneath her head and clutch a handful of hair. Gently pulling it back, he quickly covered her mouth with his other then rolled her head flat against the bed and bit her neck.

"Now Katherine," he hissed into her ear as she began to whimper. "Tell me what you want. Tell me what you want me to do... I want you to say it. Do you want this?" he asked as he brazenly rubbed against her again.

Nodding her head in a silent response, he groaned as she raked her nails across his shoulder and pulled at him once again. She knew what he meant and now what he wanted; yet somehow she couldn't say it. And although her body was saying yes, her mind, still imbedded with the morals of decency was saying no.

"Then say it. You know you want to," he whispered as he rose to his knees then reached around low and grabbed the front of her thighs. "Tell me what it is you want."

"I… I caaan't," she cried and shook her head.

"Yes you can," he growled. "Just say what you want me to do."

Roughly pulling her hips into the air, he slid his hands up her thighs and then placed them behind her knees. Driving them forward toward her chest, he exposed her then slowly began to grind and rub himself against once again.

"You want this don't you," he hissed as he simulated the act of sex. "You need it and you know it… now say it!"

Whimpering once again, she blindly reached between her legs and grabbed at the thickness of his manhood. Encircling it in her hand, she rocked her hips upward then pulled with her legs and impaled herself onto him. "Oh God!" she gasped as he entered and she clawed into his shoulders. "Yes!"

Cringing as her nails went deep, Foster couldn't help but smile. He was right; she did need it. And what's more, she wanted it and she wanted it bad. Her actions said it all but still she hadn't asked, and as hard as it was to do, he pulled from within her determined to prevail. "Is that what you wanted?" he taunted as she lay beneath him in a state of disbelief.

Numbed by the shear intensity of the erotic euphoria, she tossed her head back and forth then let out a tortured moan. "Yesss," she cried out in a breathless whisper.

"Then say it," he hissed again. "Say the words and tell me… tell me what you want."

He knew she was close, he could see it in her eyes and feel it in her body as she writhed and whimpered beneath him. Clawing and pulling at him with her legs and hands, delirious with desire and intoxicated by the decadence of what he was really asking, she finally surrendered her pride. He had diminished her to the point where she just didn't care, and as she slipped ever deeper into the folds of his moral decay, completely inflamed with a desire she could no longer endure, she exhaled with a heavy sigh and closed her eyes. Digging her nails into his back, she pulled on his shoulders and brought her mouth to his ear then lifted and spread her legs ever so slightly. A second later, and in a low sultry voice, she finally whispered the words he wanted to hear.

"Fuck meee," she pleaded. "Pleeease."

To Foster her words were a Godsend, and without a moment's hesitation, he kissed her fervently then drove into her with a groan of pleasure. Forcefully raising her hips to meet his thrust, he shuddered and rolled his eyes as the inner walls of her silky depths instantly and greedily gripped him like the coils of a python tightening inexorably around its prey. Squeezing and pulling, she manipulated herself in a manner and unlike any woman he had ever been with before. Pushing into her with long powerful strokes, he knew in an instant he would never get enough of her. She was incredible, and he moaned in blissful agony at her vise-like qualities.

Grinding and rolling together in a heated coupling, it wasn't long before Katherine abruptly stopped their movements with him beneath her. Lifting her body from his with a wanton smile, she sat straight up and straddled him. Pulling her hair from her face, she placed her hands on his chest as he instinctively grabbed at her waist and she slowly lowered herself back onto him.

Coupled now in her new and dominant position, she began to undulate and grind against him. Slowly raising and lowering herself, she relished in the feelings of his engorged sex as it filled and penetrated deep into her. Touching her in places that no man had ever touched before, she moaned with pleasure then moved her hands from his chest to the sides of his head. Gripping the bedspread for support, she shivered as he took one of her breast into his mouth. Cupping his head with one hand, she pulled him tight then steadily drove herself onto him as she sought a release to her own carnal pleasures. Impaling herself against him again and again with an ever-increasing aggression, she continued until the first glorious waves of pleasure shot through her and she cried out. Arching her back as they began to rock her body, Foster pulled down on her hard and thrust up into her. Throwing her head back as he went deep, she shuddered then emitted a long low primeval moan as the tremors of her release surged throughout her.

Smiling as the feelings of pleasure slowly ebbed from her body, Katherine suddenly found herself weak. Deliciously and deliriously drugged, she slumped her head forward then collapsed onto his chest unable to move. Gasping and panting for air as the last remnants of strength gradually seeped from her sweaty body, he could feel her heart and the contractions of her womanhood pound and pulsate around him as she slowly settled.

Pulling the hair from her face as she continued to calm, he gently took her head in his hands and then lifted her face. Kissing her tenderly, he stared into her eyes for a moment then rolled her over. Pulling himself from within her as she lay beneath him, he gazed down at her then smiled with a devilish gleam. "Now," he said with a demanding gruffness. "Turn over... it's my turn."

Flipping her over like a rag doll, Katherine gasped at the sudden and violent abruptness of the movement. She'd never been exposed like this before but quickly smiled in obvious approval. His demanding forcefulness was something new, and it instantly lured her back into the sordid depths of ecstasy. Dizzy with excitement, she felt completely taken as torrents of submissive pleasure instantly ripped through her body. Kneeling behind her, Foster easily parted her legs with his then grabbed at the curves of her hips and jerked them into the air. Turning her head, she caught his gaze and smiled, then and in an almost inaudible guttural demand, unfettered by the moral restraints of earlier, she arched her back and cried out for him to take her.

Obscenely exposed and insanely aroused, Foster instantly responded and pushed himself deep into the smoldering depths of her loins. Driving her hips into the air, he held himself for just a moment then slowly and steadily began to rock. Moaning with an ever-increasing pleasure, Katherine blindly reached between her legs and encircled his thighs with her hands. She liked being taken this way and it showed as she pulled herself tight and then ground against him.

Seeking an end to the pleasures building inside her, she demanded it harder and faster until she felt the grip on her hips tighten as he drove into her like never before. She was his toy now, and she gloried in how he was using her. They were animals mating, noisy, raw and wild, and now nothing else mattered but their own steamy gratification. And as her moans of pleasure gradually turned into a frenzied gibber, he slowly brought her to a level she never knew existed.

Unable to maintain her grip on his thighs, she quickly brought a hand to the headboard and braced herself then reached up between her legs with her other and grabbed at his manhood. Caressing and dragging her nails across the tenderness of his flesh, he knew that he wouldn't last long, no man could. Panting, heaving and sweating, he continued on until he felt her muscles began to tighten and a long raspy moan escape from her throat. A second later, she curled her back as massive jolts of pleasure began to surge from within. Mumbling incoherently to God and to Jesus, he increased his efforts even more, determined to ensure her pleasure and satisfy her like no man before. Pummeling into her without mercy, he ravaged her inner sanctum until a second wave of spasms hit her with an intensity and duration she never could've imagined.

Screaming as her body exploded, and in a reaction to her own contractions, she clawed deep into his manhood. Her nails were sharp, and as they dug into the tenderness of his flesh, Foster's struggle to last ended instantly. Bellowing like that of a raging beast mating in the wild, he threw his head back and then emptied into her with a pulsating force that rocked her once again. Quivering together in an uncontrolled union, their passions finally boiled over in a moment that seemed to last forever.

Collapsing on top of her in a sweating heaving heap, Foster finally rolled to her side and slumped to the bed. Gasping for air as he caught his breath, he could feel her body and the snug inner reaches of her arousal squeezing and nipping at him as she slowly descended from her pinnacle of pleasure. Twitching and pulsating like tremors after an earthquake deep below ground, he could feel the last of her contractions gradually fade until she'd returned to a state of normality. Still curled and coupled together, they laid for a moment in the afterglow of their experience until he slowly pulled himself from within. Shuddering as he did, she slowly stretched out and rolled on her back.

Fulfilled and satiated in a way she'd never imagined, Katherine lay limp with a euphoric grin, sprawled on her back like a sailor that'd been washed ashore. Her skin was wet and flush, and her hair clung to her cheeks and neck in dampened strands. Her chest heaved with each and every breath, and her breast, still taut and red, glistened with droplets of sweat. She was a wreck, and as the final sensations of bliss slowly ebbed from her body she rolled toward Foster.

Smiling as she propped herself up on one elbow, she stared into his eyes then reached up and softly brushed his cheek with the back of her fingers. Drawing them tenderly down the side of his face, she rolled her hand and brushed his lips but then suddenly stopped and stared at the brilliant sparkle of afternoon sunlight reflecting off of her wedding ring. A glittering symbol of the vows that she had promised to keep so long, long ago.

Instantly jolting her senses back to what she'd just done, she suddenly found herself at a loss and without words. She'd done the unthinkable, and now in a moment of guilt and regret, she began to think of herself as a whore. How could she not after what she'd just done? She'd just given herself to a man unlike any before, and only as a married woman should or would give to her husband. And as the incredible blanket of shame slowly engulfed her, she turned away and reached for the bedspread then pulled at its edge. Dragging it over her shoulders in the hopes of preserving what remnants of dignity she still had, she lowered her head and covered her body.

"Don't," Foster said as he rose to one elbow and slipped a finger beneath her chin. "Don't do this," he said again as he lifted her face. "Look at me. It's okay."

"I can't, I'm so ashamed. I... I just don't know what got into me," she stopped then pulled from his grip and lowered her head again.

"Hey, listen to me. You've done nothing wrong you hear," he said with a tender concern. "And besides," he added in an attempt to ease her mind. "You're way too sexy to be covering up."

Blushing, but with a smile, Katherine watched as his eyes slowly roamed across her body and then back hers. Somewhat relieved, she laid her head back down with a heavy sigh and stared into his eyes. "You know Foster Siler," she said as she reached up and brushed his cheek again. "For all of the bad things that people say about you, you're actually a very kind man."

A little surprised by her compliment, Foster stared for a second then lowered his lips to hers. It was a tender and reassuring kiss that gave her a kind of solace, and when they broke she gazed into his eyes and smiled. "And I'm a very hungry lady."

"Yes ma'ammm," he replied coyly. "That you most certainly are, aren't you."

"No silly, not like that! I'm talking about food, you know… all this drinking and fooling around has made me hungry. How about you?"

"Yeah, I am too," he laughed and nodded his head. Actually I'm famished, but where in the hell are we going to get anything to eat out here? We going to go shoot something?"

"No smarty britches, all we have to do is go to the boat and get the basket that's in the ice box."

"Really?" he questioned like a child. "What's in it?"

"It's a surprise, but I'm sure that you'll like it."

"Well then," he said as he rose from the bed and began to dress. "Give me just a few minutes, and I'll be right back."

Food was now at the forefront of his mind and as he turned to leave, Katherine rose from the bed completely unconcerned as to dressing and followed him into the kitchen. And even though she was a mess and smelled of sex, she didn't care. She felt decadent and free, and with a carefree motion she grabbed the bottle of wine from the counter, emptied it into their glasses and then held it up.

"There's one more with the basket," she said as she handed him his glass. "Oh, and don't forget the corkscrew. And hurry too, okay… you do know how hungry I am."

Quickly gaining a knowing smile, Foster gulped his wine and kissed her, then turned and headed for the door.

CHAPTER 11

———◆———

STEPPING OUT INTO THE LATE afternoon sun, Foster took a huge breath of air and then smiled with a grin that stretched from ear to ear. God, life was good he thought as he looked out toward the pier and started walking. What a great day it had turned out to be. And as best he could recall, since this morning he'd managed to decapitate an archrival; secure ownership of a huge piece of ground, a house and a boat; get about half drunk and have some of the greatest sex he'd ever had with one of the most stunning woman in the state. It just didn't get any better than that, and he was certain that it would go down into the annals of glory as one of his all time greats.

Leisurely making his way through the group of cypress trees separating the house from the river, he finally emerged on the other side then stopped and surveyed his surroundings. Looking across the river and over thousands of acres of untouched wilderness, now painted in a dark burnt orange, he could see that is wasn't a swamp all. It was nice, and he was surprised at just how much he liked it. And now adding to the final scene like icing on a cake, were the soft sweet sounds of a harmonica rolling down the pier and up the grass. No doubt coming from the boat, Foster raised a hand to block the setting sun and glared toward the pier. Spying the darkened silhouette of Otis sitting in the back, he smiled again and resumed walking.

Reclined in one of the Adirondack chairs with his feet propped up on the side of the boat, he had a couple of poles in the water and was slinging out a low rolling blues. A catchy melody that reminded him of his days as a child on their farm in Tennessee, and the music that some of the old black men use to play. How after supper when they would sometimes gather on their porches with their guitars and harmonicas, and of how he would sit and listen as they played into the evenings. He loved that music, and as he walked down the pier toward the boat, shaking his head and sashaying to the tune, he could tell that Otis wasn't just good, he was damn good.

Stopping just behind him as he continued to play, Foster quietly stood and listened until Otis, still unaware he was even there, stopped to eye a pole. It was the break he'd been looking for and without a thought as to what he was doing, he jumped into the boat right behind Otis. "Unbelievable," he shouted as he landed.

Screaming as if he had just been struck by a bolt of lightning, the poor unsuspecting Otis rocketed out of his chair and almost went overboard then instantly turned to view the horrors that awaited him. "Oh my God! Sweet Ja-e-sus," he gasped as he clutched his chest and tried to stuff his heart back in. "Mister Siler, you scared the heck right out-a me."

Now to Foster, the sight of Otis damn near jumping overboard was funny as hell, and as he stood and watched the young black man slowly regain his color, he began to laugh. Maybe it was the alcohol or the look on his face, he really didn't know, all he could think of as he gazed at the man still gasping for air was... that it was damn funny.

"Aaah, I'm sorry Otis," Foster apologized even as he continued to laugh. "I... I really didn't mean to scare you like that. It's just that when I got down here you were really kicking it up, so I just kind of stood on the dock listening. And then after you quit to check that pole, well, it just seemed like the right time to jump on board. Didn't mean to frighten you. Oh, and I gotta tell you something, that's some pretty fine stuff you're belting out there. Reminds me of back home."

"Ooh yes sur," Otis grinned. "Thank you. I's been a playin now for bout ten years."

"Well, it sure shows, you've got a good sound there. You should keep it up."

"Oh yes sur, I shorly will."

"Good, now the real reason that I came back down here was to get some food that Mrs. Davenport said she'd brought along. So if I was to accomplish that task, where would I find it?"

"Ah, that'd be in the icebox down below," Otis replied and turned toward the doorway. "Jus a second an I'll get it for ya."

"Oh no," Foster held up a hand. "That's okay, I can do it," he said as he stepped to the doorway. "You just go on back to your fishing."

"Yes sur, if'n ya say so."

"Oh, an by the way," he suddenly stopped and turned. "How is the fishing?"

Grinning broadly, Otis stepped to the stern, grabbed the stringer hanging in the water and pulled up three large catfish. Wiggling and slapping their tails as they hung in the air, Foster smiled and nodded then turned and disappeared into the cabin. Opening the lid to the icebox, he quickly found the containers of food and began pulling them out. Three medium sized bowls, the last bottle of wine and a wicker basket covered with a red and white-checkered towel. Setting them all on the counter one by one, he emptied the icebox except for the six brown bottles lying in the bottom. Curiously opening the containers, he smiled and licked his lips. Cole slaw, potato salad, and beets in the bowls; and in the basket, a pile of golden fried chicken and a half dozen rolls. Yes, everything he liked. She had certainly planned her day, but how in the hell did she expect him to get it all to the cabin.

Contemplating his dilemma, he stared for a just second then began looking for plates. Pulling three from the cabinet in front of him, he set them on the counter then grabbed a spoon. Dipping from the bowls, he filled their plates then reached for the chicken and rolls. Placing three large pieces on each plate, he wrapped the remaining chicken back in the towel, removed it from the basket and returned everything to the icebox. Taking two of the plates, he carefully put them in the basket and covered them with a towel. Then grabbing the third, he turned to the doorway.

"Otis," he called from inside. "When was the last time you ate?"

"It was this mornin afor I got the boat," he replied as he set his pole back down. "Why?"

"Well," Foster said as he appeared in the doorway. "I just thought that you might be hungry."

"Ii... is that for meee?" Otis stared in disbelief as Foster set the plate full of food on the table like a waiter.

"Sure is," Foster drawled. "Ain't no man needs to go hungry, and I don't care what color he is. Now go on and help yourself."

Otis was hungry, and without a second's hesitation he quickly took his chair and grabbed his plate then set it on his lap. Overflowing with three big pieces of chicken, a generous scoop of potato salad, coleslaw, and beets, it was finished off with a couple of rolls plopped on top.

"Oooh Mister Siler," he gushed. "Thank you."

"Well, you're quite welcome Otis," Foster replied nonchalantly. "Like I just said, no man needs to go hungry, and besides, it looks like Mrs. Davenport really went to a lot of work here. I guess she must be some kind a cook, huh?"

"Cook?" Otis quickly looked up with an amused expression. "Ooh no sur," he shook his head as he set his chicken back down. "Mrs. D didn't make this here food, Miss Bessie their cook did. She's the best cook in all of Mobile, an she made it special, jus for you."

"Oh she did, did she?" He grinned and raised his eyebrows.

"Yes sur, she shorly did. In fact, I helped her packed it all up in the kitchen this mornin. Why Mrs. D can't even boil water. An heck if she did actually try an cook somethin, I can tell ya right now that we jus might as well be eatin this here table."

"Is that so," Foster laughed.

"Yes sur," Otis replied and nodded. "It shorly is."

There was a lighthearted humor in not only what Otis had said, but also in how he'd said it, and Foster took note. He was genuine, and with that in mind Foster turned one of the chairs toward him and took a seat. He'd already surmised that the man before him would work out fine, but even so, he wanted to talk to him about his intentions for the property and boat.

"Otis," he began as he crossed his legs. "I want to talk to you for a minute okay?"

Nodding his head, Otis looked up from his plate then quickly swallowed and cleared his throat. "Yes sur, Mister Siler. What can I do for ya?"

"Well," he quickly went on. "I was wondering if you really knew why I was here?"

Cocking his head, Otis sat for a moment in thought then slowly began to shake it. "No sur," he replied. "I mean... not really."

"Well, I'm here because I was thinking about purchasing, aaah, I mean buying the Davenports property and this here boat. Actually, I've decided that I am just going to go ahead and take them both which means that from now on you'll be working for me... that is if you want to."

"Oooh, yes sur," he widened his eyes. "I'd be pleased ta works for ya."

"Well good Otis, I'm glad to hear that, cause I'll tell ya," he chuckled with a quick glance around. "I'm definitely going to need someone to drive this crazy thing, that's for sure."

"Yes sur, I can shorly do that. An I can work on everything too, an fix stuff. Lots of stuff!"

"Good Otis, that's good," Foster replied. "Then why don't you come by my office around ten next Monday and we'll get things started."

"Yes sur, that sounds great."

"Good, now there's just one more thing that I need to talk to you about."

"Yes sur, what's that?"

"Well, I was thinking that since it's getting kind of late, and since we've been having problems with the motor all day, I'd really rather not boat at night. You know for safety reasons and all."

"Yes sur, but--."

"No no, just listen to me now," he interrupted and continued on as if he were leading a witness. "So I think that we should just stay here tonight, and since we are so, how shall I say, unfortunately stranded, Mrs. Davenport and I will stay in the house and you can just fish as long as you want and sleep here on the boat."

"But Mister Siler," Otis insisted. "This ol motor here ain't missed a lick all day, an I know the river like the back of my hand if you's worried about the dark. An heck if we took off right now, why go'n down stream we'd be home in no time."

"Otisss," Foster cut him short. "You're not listening," he raised his eyebrows and then rolled his eyes toward the house.

Turning his gaze toward the house, Otis stared for a moment as if there was actually something to see then slowly turned back to Foster and began to smile. "Ooh yeaaah," he beamed as if he'd just been enlightened. "We was broke down right!"

Satisfied that Otis finally understood, Foster rose from his chair and then dropped back into the cabin. Grabbing the basket and bottle of wine, he returned to the stern and grabbed the corkscrew from the table. Stepping back onto the pier, he began walking but then suddenly stopped and turned back to Otis.

"Oh an Otis, I almost forgot," he added with a casual nod toward the cabin. "There's about a half dozen cold beers in the bottom of the icebox. I'm not going to drink em, and I know Mrs. Davenport sure as hell isn't. So if you want em, just go ahead and help yourself." Then without another word, he turned and left the young black man to his own.

Walking back down the pier, Foster slowly made his way up through the grass and to the house but then stopped at the door and turned back to the boat. Gazing into the sun now on the horizon, he caught a glimpse of Otis just as he stood to check one of his poles. Straining against the glaring light, he watched as the darkened silhouette pulled his harp from his pocket and put it to his lips. A second later, the sweet sounds of his harmonica rolled up the grass on soft gentle breeze and filled the air. Smiling with a nod, he listened for just a few seconds then opened the door and stepped inside.

Greeted in nothing but an unbuttoned shirt, Foster couldn't help but smile as he stepped through the door. "Where've you been," Katherine asked as she grabbed the basket and peeked inside. "I'm starving. Oh, and what about Otis?" But before he could answer she looked back up and froze. "Oh my God," she gasped and rolled her eyes. "What's he going to think of me now? What's he doing? Is he okay?"

"Oh hell Katherine," Foster drawled as he sat the bottle of wine on the counter and began to open it. "Otis is just fine, he's down there catching the hell out of fish just like you told him to. So he's happy. Besides I made him a big ol plate of food and told him he could have all those beers in the bottom of the icebox. Sooo," he added. "You don't need to worry about him."

"Whaaat? You fed my negro?" She mocked as if she'd just been offended. "And now you're going to let him get drunk. Why Foster Siler, I'm appalled!"

"Well look at it this way Mrs. Davenport," he turned and raised his eyebrows as he pulled the cork from the bottle. "Which would you prefer, a happy negro down there fishing and drinking until he goes to sleep? Orrr, one who's kind of discontented and wondering when in the hell the lady he work's for is going to come back down and want to go home? Now I can't even imagine what all he'd be thinking by morning, could you? And besides, he's my negro now, you gave him to me remember. Now shut up and kiss me."

Pulling her tight, Foster embraced her with a renewed and heightened passion, and in the blink of an eye they were back in the bed. A short while later, they sat at the table in the fading light and devoured their plates of food then started on their third bottle of wine. It'd been a glorious day, but now with their appetites satiated, the two returned to bed completely exhausted and succumbed to the excesses of the day.

"So he came down an made you a plate of food an then jus went back up?" Jim asked.

"Well that an to tell me that we was stayin the night," Otis nodded. "Anyway, an jus as soon as he had gone inside, I finished that plate of food then grabbed me one of those cold ones an went back to fishin. I'll tell ya I really had it good, you know, a twenty-five year old black man fishin an drinkin beer on the back of a forty foot boat at the beginnin of the Great Depression. Yes sir, it jus didn't get any better than that for someone like me an I knew it. Anyway, the fishin that night started out kind-a slow, but as the moon climbed higher an higher into the sky I really started catchin em, an big ones too. So I kept on fishin an before I knew it, it was way late, the moon was high in the sky, an I'd just opened the last one of those beers.

"I remember it was jus about as peaceful an quiet out as you can ever imagine. Yes sir, there wasn't nothin stirin really, that was all except for a couple of hoot owls way out across the river callin to each other. I'll tell ya, I guess those two birds must of really had somethin to talk about cause they were a chatterin back an forth like a couple of ol hens when I all of a sudden I thought I heard somethin else."

"Something else?" Jim cocked his head. "What-a-ya-mean?"

"Well, at first I wasn't real sure," Otis began with a chuckle. "Cause I'd been listenin to those damn owls for so long, but then I stood up an concentrated. An that's when I began to hear screams comin from the house, an they was comin from Mrs. Davenport."

"Oh my God. What happened?"

"Well, at first I wasn't sure an was ready to run right on up there. But then, the more I listened the less likely I was inclined to interfere. Cause I'll tell ya, it sure didn't sound like she was needin… or for that matter, wantin any help. In fact, to tell ya the truth, it almost sounded as if she was prayin."

"Prayin?" Jim quipped curiously.

"Yes sir... prayin. You know, Oh Goddd take me, an Dear Lord Pleease, an Ooh Jesus. Why hell, she had a whole list of requests. I'll tell ya, it seemed like right then an there that woman was tryin awfully hard to get into heaven. An quite frankly, I'm not so sure that she didn't jus make it." He chuckled. "Anyway, when I heard all that an then realized what was go'n on, I jus shook my head an laughed, then downed what was left of my beer an went to bed."

———◆———

Their mid-night tumble proved to be the final straw for the both of them, and after that neither one stirred until late morning. Until, and with their heads pounding from the three bottles of wine, they finally emerged from the house and then ever so slowly made their way to the boat.

"Okay Foster Siler," Katherine whispered and shook her head. "Now what-a I do?"

"About what?"

"About Howard," she sighed. "You know he's going to hear about this the instant he gets back don't you. Employee's love to talk, so tell me, just how in the hell am I going to explain this one?"

"Well," Foster replied. "As I recall, we were broke down."

"What?" She turned and narrowed her eyes.

"We were broke down," he repeated with a grin. "But hopefully Otis has got us fixed since I asked him to work on it last night and this morning. So really... we should be good to go again."

Stopping with a heavy exhale, Katherine slowly raised a hand to her forehead and squeezed her temples to ease her pounding head then turned to Foster. "Foster," she exclaimed with a confused expression pulling at her face. "Just what in the hell are you talking about? If I recall, there wasn't a thing wrong with the boat... and we weren't broke down."

"Well," he replied with another grin. "Last night we were."

Staring with her mouth slightly agape, Katherine stood for a moment as she digested what he'd said then finally began to smile. "Wellll... aren't you just the clever one," she replied then resumed her walking. "But it still isn't going to stop the gossip, you know that, don't you?"

Approaching the pier, Foster couldn't help but smile at the sight of Otis filleting the last of his fish. He'd really slaughtered them from the looks of it, and as he and Katherine neared, the young black man stood and tipped his hat.

"Mornin Mrs. D, mornin Mister Siler," he greeted with a grin. "Look Mrs. D, I did jus like you asked. I tell ya, they was a really bitin last night."

"It sure looks that way Otis," Foster replied with a wink. "That's one hell of a mess of fish you got there. Ought-a make a fine dinner for a whole lot of people too, don't you think? Oh, and did you get that little problem with the motor taken care of?"

"Oh yes sur Mister Siler, I shorly did. I started workin on it right at first light, jus as soon as I could see an got it fixed jus like ya wanted."

"Good Otis, good job, thanks."

"Yes sur, you's most welcomed," he replied and then turned to Katherine. "So is we ready ta leave ma'am?"

"Yes Otis," she whispered as the pounding in her head continued. "Mister Siler has to get back to town, so I think we should really get going."

"Yes ma'am, jus let me get all this here fish mess cleaned up an I'll get right on it."

"Thank you Otis," she said as she turned her gaze back to Foster and rolled her eyes. "And so just when did you come up with this little idea?" she asked with a kind of lofty but appreciative curiosity.

"Oooh," Foster chuckled. "When I was getting our food. You know, I had a little talk with Otis."

"A talk?" she cringed. "Oh my God... so he knows?"

"Yes, he knows, and to tell ya the truth," he leaned toward her and whispered. "The way you were screaming and carrying on last night, I'd say that all of Mobile does too."

Gaining an immediate jab to his ribs from her elbow, along with an embarrassed glance, Katherine shook her head and then jutted ahead to the boat. Rinsing the pier as they walked away, Otis quickly threw the thick slabs of meat into a bucket and then followed. A few minutes later, Foster stood in the stern, and as they idled away he watched as the house and pier faded into the distance. It had been a great trip and he wanted to thank her, but when he turned to do so, he found himself alone.

Stepping to the cabin, he poked his head just inside to find her already stretched out on one of the sofas. Lying face up with an arm draped over her forehead, she was completely out. Shaking his head with a smile, he finally turned back around and grabbed one of the Adirondack chairs. Their night together had been an absolute marathon of carnal pleasures and now with sleep at the forefront of his mind, he spun it until it faced the other, then took his seat and plopped his feet into the other chair. Wiggling until he'd found a margin of comfort, he took a deep breath then exhaled with a contented sigh and closed his eyes. Minutes later, lulled by the steady noise of the motor, Foster quickly drifted off to sleep under the mid-morning sun.

There was just something about the steady drone of a motor when you were tired that seemed to keep one in the depths of sleep, and for a little over an hour that sound didn't change until Otis had pulled the throttle as they approached the docks. "Mrs. Davenport," his voice resonated from up front. "We're herrrre."

Instantly waking, Foster opened his eyes and looked around. It was just before noon and they were back, and without another thought he rose from his chair and walked to the front. Passing a still sleeping Katherine, he made his way through the salon and up into the pilothouse. "Wow, that was fast," he said as he stepped up behind Otis and placed a hand on his shoulder.

"Oh yes sur," Otis turned and grinned. "That's cause we was go'n with the current."

"Yes I see," he said as they slowed a little more and approached the pier where they'd picked him up. "So I guess the ol motor ran just fine after you worked on it, huh?" he asked with a telltale grin.

"Yes sur," Otis replied with another grin. "It didn't miss a lick all the way back."

"Well that's great," Foster replied. "But still, I'm curious. What exactly was wrong with it?"

"Aaah, it was the carburetor," he replied.

"Yes, that's what it was," Foster feigned and rolled his eyes. "The carburetor. How could I have forgotten? Good work Otis... that's real good," he added with a pat to Otis's shoulder. "You know, I can see right now that you and I are going to get along just fine, isn't that right."

"Oh, yes sur," Otis beamed and puffed up his chest. "Aspecially if'n you say so," he added as he pulled the throttle to reverse and brought the boat to a stop.

"Are we here already?" Katherine's groggy voice suddenly resonated from behind.

"Yes ma'am," Otis replied as he jetted out the door to tie the boat.

Immediately taking advantage of her opportunity, she pulled Foster to the lower salon, pushed him against the counter then cupped his neck and pulled her mouth to his. Kissing him as if it were the last time she would see him, she finally broke when Otis stepped back on the boat. Smiling as if she had just gotten away with something, she quickly composed herself then escorted Foster out to the stern and onto the pier.

"Well Mister Siler," Katherine finally said as she graciously extended her hand. "I really do thank you for coming... annnd, I do hope that you enjoyed your ride."

"Oh, yes ma'am," he drawled with a laugh as he took her hand. "That, I most certainly did."

Her innuendo couldn't have been any clearer, and although he wanted to say more he didn't, he just smiled and dropped her hand then turned and began walking away.

"Oh, and Mister Siler," she called after just a few steps. "Don't forget supper tonight, say six thirty?"

"And just what are we having Mrs. Davenport?" he asked as he spun back and stared.

"Why catfish silly," she retorted with a grin. "I had Otis catch some right after he fixed the boat."

Shaking his head with a laugh, Foster turned without another word and resumed walking then looked to the sky. "Six-thirty it is," he yelled after just a few steps. "See you then."

Watching as he slowly walked across the vast open expanse of the pier, Katherine quietly stared until he began to fade amongst the workers milling about. A few moments later, unable to distinguish him from any of the others, she finally turned and rejoined Otis on the boat.

CHAPTER 12

IT WAS JUST A LITTLE after noon by the time a worn out Foster puffed up the steps and opened the door to his office. His head was still pounding and he was running on fumes, but as he stepped through door he suddenly stopped to the sound of Vicki's voice.

"Eeeew Fossster," she began to laugh. "What in God's name happened to you, you look like hell!"

Looking at the two behind the counter, Foster just shook his head then instantly dropped into a lengthy charade of his horrible breakdown. "Oh my God," he began. "You two aren't gonna believe what I've just been through. Why we got up there... and then we got... and after we looked at the property and were ready to leave... and then the damn boat wouldn't start and..."

Listening as he rambled on, both Vicki and Dawn couldn't help but laugh. To them, his night stuck on the river was funny as hell, but after a few minutes, Foster finally finished then turned and walked into his office.

"Wow, did you see that," Dawn squealed beneath her breath. "He looked like hell!"

"I sure did," Vicki snickered as she lit a cigarette and took a pull. "I just hope he got the property like he wanted."

"Oh yeah, me too," Dawn agreed. "I can just imagine what he'd be like if that didn't go through."

"No kiddin," Vicki shook her head.

"Oh Vicki," Foster called as he reappeared in his doorway. "I have the papers to the Davenport property and I'd like you to get them recorded for me."

"Yes sir boss," she said as she turned. "I can do that… no problem."

"Good, now if you don't mind, I need to see you for a minute. There's something else that I want to discuss with you before I leave."

An hour later, Foster left his office and headed home. He needed sleep in such a way that he didn't even know his own name, and as soon as he entered his house he headed straight to his bedroom. Striping down to his underwear, he crawled into bed, collapsed face down and fell sound asleep.

Four hours later he woke to a brilliant beam of sunlight crawling across his bed. Radiating directly into his tired slits, he blinked his eyes open then did a quick internal check of his body and smiled. Yes, he was human again, and with a great big yawn and a long giant stretch, he rose and began to get ready. Katherine was waiting, and if everything went as he hoped, he would be back in her arms in a couple of hours. Well, maybe a little longer with dinner and all, but not long. And tonight was special, for not only was he taking another man's wife again, he was going to do it in the bed that they shared. And that was something that Foster loved most, no matter what the risks.

───────

To say that the Davenport home was impressive would have been an understatement, but Foster knocked without a care and in short order was greeted by a pleasant heavyset black woman.

"Miss Bessie," he presumed. "I'm Foster Siler," he added and extended a hand before she could answer. "I'm Mr. and Mrs. Davenport's attorney."

"Oh, yeas sur Mista Siler," she replied in a raspy drawl as she took his hand. "Mrs. D's been aspectin you. Pleease pleease, come on in an I'll gets her far ya."

Following her into the foyer, Foster stopped in the center then watched as she continued to the bottom of a beautiful stairway that curved up to the second floor. Stopping at the first step, Bessie put her hand on the banister and then turned to Foster. "Ya know Mista Siler, I may be a talkin out a turn here, but I shorrr do hope you can help poor ol Bobby. Ya know, he really ain't that bad, even if he is a spoiled little shit."

"Well, I'm sure gonna try," he laughed.

"Well I shor hope so, cause ol Mrs. D. shorrrr does have her hopes up. I'll tell ya, she really thinks highly of you."

"Oh she does, does she?"

"Oh yeasss surrr," she emphasized. "Specially after yestaday. I guess you mus really be good at that lawyer'n stuff."

"Really?"

"Oh yeas sur," she nodded.

It was an unexpected compliment, and for just a moment Foster seemed to stand a little taller. It felt good to be appreciated, and while he savored in the moment he watched Miss Bessie turn back to the stairs, take a big deep breath and yell up the stairway. "Mrs. Deeee," her raspy voice boomed from within. "Misssta Siiilers herrre."

"Oh thank you Bessie," Katherine's refined drawl emanated from a far off bedroom and drifted down the steps. "I'm almost finished, but would you be so kind as to offer him something to drink an make him comfortable? And tell him that I'll be down in just a few minutes okay."

"Yeas ma'am Mrs. D," she replied and turned back to Foster. "Well," she remarked as she plopped her hands on her hips. "I guess jus comes with me Mista Siler. Would ya likes somethin ta drink?"

"Yes ma'am," he replied. "A drink would be nice."

Following close behind, Foster couldn't help but take in the opulence and grandeur afforded to only a very few. It was certainly one of the finest homes in Mobile, and unfortunately one that would soon be owned by the bank. The creditors would come for their money, and even though Howard was good in the financial arena, there were limits to what he could do. He'd lost everything in the crash, and now it was just a matter of time before his house of cards came crumbling down and all of this disappeared. A few moments later, his thoughts quickly changed as they entered the dining room and Miss Bessie stopped in front of a beautiful ornate liquor cabinet.

"If'n you'd like ta jus help yourself Mista Siler," she said as she opened the doors. "I'll go an gets you some ice an be right back."

"Thank you Miss Bessie," he replied and picked up a tumbler. "That sounds great."

Gazing at the crystal decanters with golden nametags hanging from their necks, he read their labels and then grabbed the scotch.

Pulling the stopper, he poured his tumbler half full then lifted it to his nose and inhaled its aged aroma. Aaah yes, he exhaled with an approving sigh as he brought it to his lips and took a sip. It was probably the best that money could buy and for a short moment he savored in it taste, then swallowed just as Katherine's voice resonated from behind.

"Mr. Siler," she greeted with an extended hand as she entered the room. "Good evening."

"Good evening," he replied and took her hand.

"I must tell you how much I appreciate you taking time out of your busy schedule to come over like this, thank you."

"Well Mrs. Davenport," he replied, keeping his tone formal. "It's my pleasure." But before he could say anything else and tell her how lovely she looked, Miss Bessie returned with his ice.

"Here ya go Mista Siler," she said and held out the bowl.

"Thank you Miss Bessie," he replied as he took it and set it on the hutch.

"You're welcome. Oh, an Mrs. D, I gots supper all ready, so if'n you an Mista Siler is ready ta eat I can bring it on in?"

"Oh that sounds wonderful, but since it is so nice out I thought that we'd just have supper out on the porch if you don't mind."

"Oh yeass ma'am, I'll gets on it right away."

Stepping out onto the porch, Foster was once again impressed. A huge rectangular room filled with white wicker furniture and lush tropical plants, it spanned almost the entire side of the house. Light and airy with a lofty ceiling and giant screened windows, it also had two ceiling fans that provided a welcomed relief from the summers heat.

It was beautiful, but there was more, and as he continued to follow he was led to yet another room that jutted off of the corner at the far end. Octagonal in shape with an opened-beamed ceiling and hardwood floor, it had a large glass table centered neatly inside of it that matched the room and sat surrounded by eight wicker chairs. Immediately pulling one out for Katherine, Foster then took a seat across from her. Oversized and heavily cushioned, they were incredibly comfortable and made for the perfect dinning or lounging experience. A moment later, Miss Bessie set their plates heaping with food gently in front of them.

"There ya go's Mrs. D, Mista Siler, fresssh catfish. Mister Otis caught um yestaday. Now you jus lets me know if'n ya needs anything else okay, I'll be in the kitchen a cleanin up."

"Thank you Bessie," Katherine said as she picked up her fork and knife. "It smells wonderful."

"Amen to that," Foster agreed as he pulled a piece from one of the golden slabs and plopped it into his mouth.

To him fresh catfish was just about as good as it got, and as the taste of the perfectly cooked fish melted into his mouth and invaded his senses, he swallowed and then cried out. "Oh my God," he exclaimed as he snapped his eyes back open. "Miss Bessie, come back here."

"Ooh, yeass sur Mista Siler," she quickly returned with a worried look.

"You know, Otis told me you were just about the best cook in all of Mobile, but I gotta tell you," he began to shake his head. "After that fried chicken that I ate yesterday and now this here catfish, I have to disagree with him because I actually think you just may be the best cook in all of Alabama. In fact, I know so. I'll tell ya, in all my years, I don't believe I've ever had catfish quite like this."

Taken completely by surprise, the flustered woman took huge breath. "Oooh Mista Siiiler," she began with a lively laugh as she fanned her face. "For a second there, I thought that somethin wus wrong, but you shor knows how ta make a gal feel good that's for shor. An jus so's ya know, there's plenty more in the kitchen. So you jus holler if'n ya wants some more, okay."

"Oh I will," Foster assured as he picked up another piece and took a bite.

Dinner was fabulous and after they'd finished, Foster immediately began discussing his strategy to free her son even though his case was already a done deal. In part to maintain a professional facade in front of Miss Bessie, but also as a continued effort to ingratiate himself with the woman he lusted for. Dangling the carrot of hope in front of her, they talked at length, and as the evening drew on and Bessie departed, they finally retired to her bedroom.

A little nervous and hesitant without the alcohol, she feebly fought with her conscience but quickly lost the battle. He'd opened a door the night before she knew now she could never close. A door that deep down, she didn't want to close. She liked what they'd done and when she was naked, and he'd laid her on the bed she shared with her husband, she spread her legs and let him feast upon her with his tongue. Then rising above her, the brash young lawyer mounted her in a reckless and ravaged coupling and took his pleasures in another man's bed.

CHAPTER 13

WEDNESDAY MORNING WAS STILL QUITE pleasant, but the cool front that had rolled in with the storm Sunday night was beginning to wane. And as the day began in earnest, the late August heat and humidity slowly returned. Arriving early at his office, Foster blew in and went straight to his desk. "Dawn," he yelled. "Where's today's paper?"

"Right here," she said as she walked through his door and laid it on his desk. "And would you like a cup of coffee?"

"Yes please," he answered and picked up the paper.

Browsing the headlines, Foster read for a moment then began to smile at the bottom corner caption of the front page. *'Davenport Charges Skeptical in Light of New Evidence.'* Wow, what a great way to start the day. The wheels he'd put into motion on Monday with the prosecutor were finally rolling and with a quick call to him, and then to his favorite reporter ensuring that another release was in the order for Thursday's edition, he sat back in his chair. God he loved it when a plan came together, but even so he had plenty to do and with that he instantly turned his attention to Vicki. He was curious as if his hunch had been right and what she'd found out, but before he could yell, Dawn walked back in with his coffee.

"Here you go Foster," she said as she set the cup on his desk.

"Oh thanks Dawn," he replied. "Is Vicki in yet?"

"Yes sir, she just walked in the door."

"Good," he said as he picked up the paper again. "Get her and send her boney ass in here will you, I need to talk to her."

"Yes sir."

A minute later, Vicki appeared in the doorway. "Mornin Boss," she greeted with a cigarette in one hand and a cup of coffee in the other.

"Morning Vicki," he replied as he looked up from his paper and laid it to the side. "Come on in and close the door will you."

Approaching his desk Vicki couldn't help but smile for she knew what he wanted and she definitely had good news, really good news.

"Well," he asked. "Did you check on that ground like I asked?"

"I sure did," she replied as she took a seat in front of his desk. "Just like you asked... before I recorded anything."

"Annnd?" he gestured with a set of opened arms.

"Well, I'll tell ya boss, you're really not gonna believe this. I mean, what I found. In fact, I didn't either at first, so I kept digging as far back as I could go, you know, just to make sure."

"Aaah shiiit," he scrunched his face. "Some bank's got a lien on it, right?"

"Oh no, the properties free and clear, there isn't anything on it. I made sure of that on my first search, but boy I sure didn't expect to find this."

"Find this?" He cocked his head curiously. "What-a-ya mean?"

"Well, it seems you were right. It was a little bigger than two hundred acres, just like you thought."

"Yes I knew it," he said triumphantly. "So how much?" he asked as he rocked back in his chair and gloried in the fact that he was right.

Clearing her throat, Vicki smiled and dipped her head then peered over the top of her glasses. "Right about one thousand eight hundred acres," she drawled emphatically.

"Whaaat?" Foster stared as if he'd misunderstood. "What'd you just say?"

"I saiiid, one thousand and eight hundred acres bigger," she quickly repeated. "In other words boss, you just got yourself an extra eighteen hundred acres of ground to go along with your little two hundred acre deal."

"Eighteen hundred? Are you kidding?" He rocked forward in his chair.

"Nope," she smirked and shook her head. "In fact, I couldn't believe it either at first. But right there on those old abstracts, clear as a bell was two thousand not two hundred."

"Two thousand," he looked on with a bewildered gaze. "I, I don't understand... how?"

"Well, when I first picked up them old pages and looked at em, they had two hundred on the front-page just like it was suppose to. But something just didn't look right. I mean, you know how they file crap away down there at the recorder's office. Anyway, I got to lookin at it a little closer and that's when I noticed that it had a small crease in it right between the two zeros."

"Realllly?" His interest peaked.

"Yep, so I laid it back down and smoothed it out with my thumb and that's when your two hundred acres instantly became two thousand. And for the life of me," she shook her head and laughed. "I don't know how in the hell anyone could've ever missed or forgotten a damn zero, but boy they sure did. I guess since it was just worthless ol swampland, nobody cared. But," she took a breath. "Just to make sure, I spent all afternoon and followed the chain of title all the way back to the Civil War. Heck, I even went and saw Greg over at Hasty's Surveyin and had him follow the legal with me and then draw a rough map of the out-boundary. It took us a bit, but sure enough, after he was done and had figured it all up, he came up with two thousand too. Now as far as I can tell it hasn't affected the property, but thanks to that little crease in the paper, everyone thought it was just two hundred acres, including the Davenports, even after all these years.

"So boss," she finally finished with a contented sigh. "What-a-ya think? Nice surprise, huh."

"Yes it is," Foster nodded and smiled as he rocked back in his chair. "Yes it is," he repeated at the thought of his good fortune. "But Vicki," he suddenly asked and narrowed his eyes as he rocked back forward. "Did anyone down at the recorder's office know what you were doing?"

"Oh heavens nooo," she replied with a dismissive wave. "Heck, those dummies down there can't hardly tell north from south let alone read a damn legal description."

"Good," he chuckled. "Cause I'd really like to keep it that way and keep this kind of quiet if you don't mind."

"Oh yes sir, not a problem," she said as she rose from her chair and turned to leave.

"Good. Oh, and Vic," he called to her before she could take a step. "Just one more thing."

"Yeah boss?" she stopped and turned.

"That was really good work you did, thank you."

Beaming with a satisfied smile, Vicki turned and left.

Watching as she closed the door behind her, Foster sat for a moment thinking of the news he'd just received. His day couldn't have started any better, but even so it was far from over and without another thought he turned to the phone and picked the receiver. He had one more thing to do before he went and saw Bobbie Davenport, and that was to call his mother.

"Davenports, may I help you," the raspy drawl on the other end rang loudly.

"Miss Bessie?" Foster asked.

"Yeaass sur."

"Foster Siler here."

"Oo, ooh... Misssta Siler. How is you this mornin?"

"I... I'm just fine Miss Bessie, just fine thank you, but is Mrs. Davenport in? I need to speak with her if I may."

"Oh yeass sur, she's out on the screened in porch waterin the plants. Let me get her far you okay."

Cringing as she laid the phone down with a noisy clunk, Foster just shook his head and waited. A few moments later, Katherine's soft sensuous drawl resonated into the earpiece.

"Hello."

"Katherine?"

"Yes."

"Good morning, it's Foster."

"Well Mister Siler, what a pleasant surprise," she drawled. "Good mornin, and how may I help you?"

"Well, I was wondering if you got the Mobile Registry, you know, the morning paper?"

"Why yes, yes I do, why?"

"Because, there's something in it I want you to read."

"Whaaat?" she asked anxiously. "Is it bad?"

"No, it isn't bad, but... well, just get it and take a look at the front page okay."

"Okay, hold on just a second, it's laying right here."

A moment later, he heard her gasp and then slowly read the headlines. '*Davenport charges skeptical in light of new evidence,*' her voice seemed to rise with hope as she finished. "Oh Foster, what does that mean? What evidence? I thought they had Bobby cold?"

"They do, or should I say they did, until I discovered some irregularities in the girl's statement," he replied. "I was going to tell you last night, but I thought it still might be a little premature. But Katherine," he took a breath as if to prepare her. "I want you to understand something right now. Even though this is really good news, it still doesn't mean that Bobbie's out of the woods, or at least not yet. You do understand that, don't you?"

"Yesss, yes I do," she replied.

"Good, then just let me keep working on this and if I can put a few more pieces of this puzzle together correctly, I think I can still have your son out by Friday."

"Oh Foster," she sighed. "I just don't know what to say. You've given me such hope when no one else could. I do hope you know how truly grateful I am. I, I really don't think I could've survived another day if you weren't helping us."

"Well thank you Katherine, I appreciate that, but I'm just doing my job. Remember, you hired me to help your son and I'm going to do that the best I can."

"Well I must say, you're doing a most wonderful job, but when will you know more on Bobby?"

"Hopefully later this morning. I have a meeting with him, and as soon as I'm done with that, I have one with Cyrus. And after that, I should know a whole lot more on just where we stand."

"I see, and would you call me when you're done and fill me in. Pleeease. Or better yet, you could come over. Yes, that's iiiit. You could come over later, and we could talk."

"I don't know, it may be kind of late, you know, by the time I'm finished with my day and all."

"But I don't care," she pleaded. "I don't care how late it is. Maybe," she lowered her voice into an inviting whisper. "Maybe you could come over after Miss Bessie has gone for the evening. You know, after it gets dark an we could...?"

Closing his eyes, Foster rocked back in his chair, plopped his feet up onto his desk and smiled. He could tell by the underlying tone of her voice that it wasn't just her son she wanted to talk about, and that was perfectly fine with him.

"You could just park on the other side of the garage so no one would know and then walk around the house. I usually lock everything up after Miss Bessie leaves. But I can leave the door to the porch open and you could just come in there. You remember, where we ate supper, don't you?"

"Yes I remember… but where will you be?" he groaned into the receiver as he reached between his legs and adjusted himself. God, he couldn't believe that just her voice on the phone had this kind of effect on him, but it did.

"Why, I'll be waiting upstairs," she drawled. "You remember… just find the flickering light."

Slowly setting the phone back into its cradle, Foster exhaled and then shook his head. Wow, what a week it had been he thought as he reminisced. First, Monday with the boat ride and an incredible night in the cabin, followed by Tuesday, with supper and another evening of bliss. And now, with another invitation that left little doubt as to its outcome, he grinned with anticipation then rose from his desk and grabbed his coat. It was time to finally meet his client, but first he needed to make a stop at Crystal's Bakery.

It was something he'd done for years whenever he met with a client in jail, especially if it was in the morning. But in actuality, the donuts and pastries were never for them, no not at all. They were always for the underpaid staff that worked in the bottom of the jail-house. It was his way of showing his appreciation for he knew what it was like to be surprised with an occasional dozen or so of Crystal's hand picked favorites.

CHAPTER 14

CHESTER WAS DEAD TO THE world with his feet on the desk when Foster walked in and dropped the square white box onto the counter. "Wake up Chester," he boomed with a hearty laugh.

Flailing about as if he'd just been shot, the old deputy snapped out of his slumber and then jumped from his chair. "Goddamn you Foster," he cried out. "Jesus Chrissst, ya scart the plumb shit right out a me. What-n-the-hell are ya do'n sneakin up on somebody like that?"

Watching as Chester tried to regain his composure and stuff his heart back into his chest, Foster just laughed and shoved the box toward him. "Here, you old son-of-a-bitch, I brought you something. Now shut up and eat one."

Grinning as he eyed the box, Chester licked his lips then opened it up and reached inside. Roving his hand back and forth, he finally grabbed a heavily glazed apple fritter and pulled it from the box. "Damn Foster, thanks," he said and took a bite. "Oh man, are these from Crystal's?"

"Yes sir, and they're fresh too, right out of the oven. Ya like em?"

Nodding his head, Chester enthusiastically swallowed his bite and munched another, then turned his head and yelled for the others in the back room.

Quickly emerging from the other room to the sound of Chester's voice, two more officers and two secretaries walked up to the counter. Foster knew them all and smiled with a nod to the box as they approached. "I thought you guys might like a treat this morning since I had to come by," he said as he shoved the box toward them.

Eagerly digging inside, they each took a donut and started eating. Crystal's was the best in town and after a thank you from each, they offered Foster a cup of coffee.

"Yes, I'd like one very much," Foster said as he too finally reached inside and grabbed a donut.

"So who ya down here to see," Chester asked as he took his last bite and licked his fingers then reached for another.

"Well you ain't gonna believe it," Foster shook his head. "But I'm here to see the Davenport boy, and I guess," he paused and rolled his eyes. "To see if I can get his spoiled little ass out of jail."

"The who boy?" Chester choked as the others quickly perked up and stared. "The Davenport boy?"

"Yep," Foster replied nonchalantly. "You know, the usual did you do it and why, and are you innocent. You know, that type of stuff."

"An you're defendin him? I thought those people was broke."

"Well, this ought-a prove to be interestin," Frank, one of the other deputies chimed in with a hint of irony.

"Why's that?" Foster turned to the man.

"Cause he's Bobby Davenport, that's why," he replied as if Foster should've known. "I mean, haven't you ever met him before?"

"Nooo… no, I can't say that I have. Why, is he some sort of bogeyman or something?" He laughed and then looked to the others now staring.

"Oh no, he ain't no bogeyman," Frank shook his head. "But he shor is somethin I can tell ya that. See, I was the one that arrested him an brought him in last week, an I can tell ya right now that you're in for a real treat. But if you came here to see him, when you get done with that donut an that cup of coffee, well, you jus follow me. I'll be more than happy to take ya to him so the two of you can sit and talk," he chuckled and then took a bite.

It took only a few minutes to finish their coffee and donuts and as soon as they had, Frank took Foster to the cellblock. Unlocking the heavy door at the end of the corridor, the two stepped into the hallway that separated the dozen ten by ten cells then continued on until they came to the last one on the right. Pulling his key ring from his belt, Frank quickly found the right one then put it in the lock and called to the inmate to step back against the wall.

Watching as Frank opened the door, Foster could easily see that the boy was Katherine's son. A good-looking kid of about twenty, he had thick dark hair that'd been parted in the middle and pulled back in an unkempt fashion. Yet his facial features and hands were thin and he looked delicate, as if he'd never seen an honest hard days work in his life.

Stepping back as he was told, the young boy silently watched as the jailor entered and then pulled his cuffs from his belt. "Hold out your hands boy," he ordered.

Complying with a smirk, Bobby rolled his eyes toward Foster with a self-assured arrogance then uttered an indignant huff as the cuffs clicked around his wrist. To Foster it was easy to see that the boy had a chip on his shoulder, and it was also easy to see that he had no respect for the law.

"So just where ya takin me now dep-u-ty," the boy asked sarcastically. "Oooh, an who's the suit?"

"We're taking you outside for some privacy so you and I can talk," Foster answered before Frank could even open his mouth.

"An just who the fuck are you?" Bobby sneered.

"I'm your lawyer son," Foster turned and growled. "I'm Foster Siler," he added. "Your parents hired me to represent you in the hopes that I might find some magical way of getting your pathetic little ass out of the mess you're in. Now shut your goddamn mouth and let's go."

It was rare for the boy to remain silent, but just by the way in which Foster had barked his orders, and the fact that someone had even ordered him to do something, Bobby Davenport for once dutifully did as he was told. But just like everything else in his life, it didn't last long, for it just wasn't in his nature to keep his mouth shut. He was used to mouthing off whenever and to whomever he wanted, and before the three had even reached the main door, he opened it once again.

"Hey, I know who you are now," he crowed with a laugh. "You're that high priced lawyer my father has always talked about. The one that'll do anything to win an they say never loses. Oh yeah, I'vve heard of you all right. But how are ya gettin paid on this one mister lawyer?" He went on in a condescending tone. "You do know my stupid father lost everything we had in the crash don't ya? An hell, what he didn't lose he's already sold to hold off the creditors. That is," he laughed again. "Everything except my mother. So maybe you can collect from her. Shiiiit, she's still pretty enough she ought-a be worth something don't ya think?"

Shaking his head as they approached the outer door and Frank unlocked it, Foster couldn't help but think of just how much the kid needed to be set in his place. He'd taken all of the shit he was going to take, and the thought of decking him if he opened his mouth one more time, was growing by the second. It was just a thought, but no sooner had it entered his mind and Frank had turned his key, the kid did just that.

"So is that it counselor?" He sneered. "Is that how you're gettin paid? My mother?"

Turning back to Foster as he pushed the door open, Frank just shook his head and then stepped to the side. But Foster didn't move, he just stood were he was and looked to the ceiling then closed his eyes. He was completely incensed, and for a few fleeting moments he stood quietly until the sound of Frank's voice brought him back into reality.

"Foster," he asked curiously. "Are you okay?"

"Yeah Frank I'm fine," he exhaled with a heavy sigh and then held up his briefcase. "But could you do me a favor and hold this for a second?"

"Oh shor," he replied. "Don't mind at all."

Nodding as Frank took the case, Foster then slowly and calmly turned back to Bobby with a smart-ass grin still glued to his face. He really didn't like the kid, and the last remark that he'd made about his mother was just the excuse he needed to justify his actions. The boy needed to be set in his place and before he even realized it, Foster had made a fist and swung his arm. Dead on target, he connected just beneath the boy's right eye, and as his hardened knuckles embedded themselves into the tender flesh of Bobby's cheek, an incredibly loud smack resonated throughout the cellblock.

Tough and strong from years on the farm, Foster held nothing back and sent the surprised young boy sprawling across the floor with an agonizing groan. Wailing like a baby as he curled into a ball, Foster quickly pounced over him and yanked him from the floor then threw him against the bars of an empty cell. Instantly pinning him with a forearm across his neck, he gripped the bar beside his head and then crushed his arm into the boy's throat.

Grasping at Foster's arm as he choked and gasped for air, Bobby instantly turned to Frank and called for help. He was frantic, but Frank could've cared less and just shook his head then turned to Foster.

"Would ya like me to jus set this out here on the table while you finish up?" he asked.

"Oh sure Frank," Foster replied. "That'd be nice if you don't mind, thank you."

"Don't mind at all Mister Siler," he said with a glance to Bobby. "You an your client jus take all the time you need an come out whenever your done."

"Thank you Frank, but I really don't think this'll take long," he said as he turned back to Bobby with a snarling glare. "Now you better listen to me you little arrogant piece of shit," he growled as he pushed against the boy's throat. "You better realize something and you better realize it right now, you're in a lot of fucking trouble. And I mean a lot. Do you understand me?"

Nodding in wide-eyed fear, Foster quickly continued on. "Good, now understand this too. I'm not here to play around, you hear. Your parents have paid me to defend your sorry ass and to try and clear you of these charges. They want to help you, but for the life of me I can't imagine why anyone would want to do that after having the pleasure of knowing you for all of thirty seconds.

"Now you might think that you're pretty smart, but I can tell you this, if you ever talk to me like that again, I'll make sure Cyrus Buchanan gets his way with you and that you end up in the big house." He warned in a voice as chilling as his glare. "He really wants you, and right now I'm the only goddamn thing standing between your freedom and the next twenty years in the penitentiary. You do understand what I'm telling you, don't you Bobby boy? You do know what the big house is?" Nodding his head ever so slightly once again, Foster smiled then patted his cheek.

"Goood Bobby," he finally said as he eased the pressure against the boy's throat. "That's goood. Cause I'll guarantee you this, as pretty as you are, the sisters up there will have you in heels and a strapless in less than a week. Hell, I'll even send em a pretty new dress once a month just to keep things interesting. They'll dress you up and parade you around as their girl of the month, and then you'll really learn what it's like to be raped. Now, is that what you want?"

Releasing his grip as Bobby shook his head and his tears began to fall, Foster pulled his arm away and then lowered it to his side. Watching as the boy broke down and then slid to the floor, he quietly stood and stared as the reality of actually going to prison took its hold. He was frightened beyond any sense of the word, but after he'd finally settled, Foster reached for his hand and pulled him from the floor. Brushing the front of his chest with the palm of his hand, he straightened his jump suit and then placed his hand on his shoulder.

"Now," he finally said in a softer voice. "Do you still want me to represent you, or do you want me to leave your ass here?"

"No sir," Bobby cleared his throat. "I want you to represent me. Please."

"Okay then. Now wipe those tears off your face so those guys out there don't see you crying and let's go. We have a lot to go over if I'm going to get you out of here."

Nodding his head, Bobby wiped away his tears and then followed Foster out the door. Grabbing his briefcase from Frank mid room, the two continued on into one of the private rooms where they both took their seats at a small table.

"Okay," Foster sighed as he laid his pad of paper on the table and then reached for his pen. "Let's get started, shall we."

"Yes sir."

"Good, now why don't we start from the beginning, okay? Oh, and Bobby," Foster quickly added.

"Yes sir?" the boy instantly answered.

"Don't you even think of lying to me," he warned with an icy glare. "You understand me... ever."

"Yes sir," he replied with a nod. "I won't, I swear."

"Good, now tell me what happened. And don't leave anything out, because I have a meeting with the prosecutor after this and I'm hoping that I can persuade him to at least let you bond out."

They talked at length and after they'd finished, Bobby was escorted back to his cell and Foster was off to see the prosecutor. The meeting with Cyrus was cold but productive, and in less than an hour they'd created their headlines and news release for Thursday's edition of the newspaper. *'Prosecutor Considers Dropping all Charges, Trial Unlikely.'* Foster had learned from Bobby of the girl's past and he wanted to use it. It seemed she liked boys; lots and lots of boys, and with that new and incriminating information to help in their ongoing battle for public opinion, Cyrus picked up the phone and called the newspaper. Satisfied that everything was going as planned, Foster finally left with the reassurance that Bobby Davenport's release was still on schedule for late Friday morning.

Returning to his office, he worked on his statement to the press for Friday then left a little early and went home. He wanted to rest for he knew that his evening with Katherine was going to be a long one. She was insatiable, and as he lay on his bed and closed his eyes, he began to smile at the pleasures that awaited him.

Later that evening, he quietly pulled his car into Katherine's drive and parked on the other side of the garage as he was told. Sure, he'd already bedded her, but what he was doing now was different, and he was more than a little nervous. He was sneaking back into another man's house to enjoy his wife while he was away and that was dangerous no matter how you looked at it. But the thirty-five year old lawyer couldn't have stopped himself even if he'd tried, and as he stepped out of his car and cast his eyes toward the house, he smiled. A soft wavering glow in the corner windows of the second story was the only light emanating from inside the entire house. It was her bedroom, he was certain of it, and without another thought he quietly closed his door then anxiously headed around to the screened in porch.

Reaching for the door, he squeezed his hand tightly around the tarnished knob then closed his eyes and held his breath. A second later he sighed as the rusted mechanism turned and then clicked. It was unlocked just as she'd said it would be, and just like a thief in the night, he slowly pulled it open and slipped inside. It was dark, but with a hint of light from the moon he could see and he quickly made his way to the stairwell. Stopping at the bottom step, his heart pounding wildly at the unknown, he paused and took a long deep breath then boldly took a step and ascended the stairs. Reaching the top, he smiled at the thought of her words on the phone and the soft light radiating from within the room at the end of the hallway.

"Just find the flickering light," her voice echoed in his head. *"Just find the flickering liii..."*

It was all he needed, and without another thought, Foster, now drawn to the light like a moth to a flame, headed straight to her bedroom until he stood in her doorway. Bathed in the soft iridescent glow of a half dozen candles that had been placed around the room, the lady of the house lay naked on her side across a turned down bed with a glass of wine in her hand. There were no words spoken, but as he approached and stripped out of his clothes, she gulped what was left of her glass then rolled to her back and set it on the nightstand. She had abandoned every pretense she had, and as he knelt on the bed and stared down at her, Katherine smiled with a nefarious gleam to her eyes then slowly and sensuously spread her legs for her lover.

———◆———

It was way after two by the time an exhausted Foster finally dragged himself from Katherine's bed and headed home. She'd become insatiable in her newfound appetite, and he was certain that if he were to continue on a prolonged basis, that she just might kill him. But then he thought with a groan and a smile as he lay across his bed and closed his eyes. What a way to die.

Hours later, he woke to a bright beam of sunlight shinning through his window then rolled to his side and glanced at the clock. It was nine-thirty and he was late for work, and even though he wanted nothing more than to roll back over and close his eyes, he struggled from his bed and readied for work. An hour later, he huffed up the final steps to his office then strolled through the door and greeted Dawn.

"Foster," she asked in a concerned tone. "Are you okay? You look a little tired this mornin."

"Yeah I'm fine, I just didn't get enough sleep last night that's all, but I'm fine thanks. Oh, and do I have any messages?"

"Sure do," Dawn replied as she reached for her notes. "Aah let's see, the prosecutor called, and Mrs. Davenport. Oh, and she's called twice already, and then the newspaper, they called too."

"The newspaper?" Foster interrupted. "Where's the paper?"

"Right here," she said as she handed it to him. "And here are all of your messages too."

"Thanks Dawn," he said as he took the stack and headed to his office. Hanging his coat by the door, Foster dropped into his chair and plopped his feet up on his desk. Rifling through his messages, he quickly set them aside and grabbed the paper then popped it open and read the headlines. '*Prosecutor Considers Dropping all Charges, Trial Unlikely.*' It was perfect, and he pleased, but just as he began to read, he heard the phone ring and then Dawn call out for him.

"Foster," she hollered from the other room.

"Yesss," he answered as he looked up from his paper.

"I have Mrs. Davenport on the phone, can you take her call?"

"Yes, absolutely, just give me a second."

Pulling his feet from the desk, he threw the paper to the side then sat up in his chair. "I've got it Dawn," he yelled as he picked up the phone and put it to his ear. "Mrs. Davenport," he greeted cheerfully. "Good morning, I just got in and got your messages. What can I do for you?"

"Oh Foster, I'm so glad I was able to reach you. Have you read the paper this morning?" she asked excitedly. "I mean, did you see what they wrote? What does all of that mean? Is Bobby free?"

"Now just hold on a minute Katherine," he began in an attempt to soothe and slow her down at the same time. "First, Bobby's not free, or at least not yet. And remember, you're reading the newspaper not a judge's order. So I want you to take a second and try and calm down a little okay."

"Yesss."

"Good. Now listen, your son's case is very complicated, but I think I have some good news. And, well, if you have the time and can come into town sometime today, I'd be more than happy to go over everything with you."

"Oh my yes. I have to run some errands anyway and I can just stop by first if that's okay."

"That would be fine. Oh, and one more thing."

"Yes?"

"Well, this almost slipped my mind, but the other night after dinner when you so thoroughly distracted me, I forgot to get the title to your boat. And I was wondering if you would be so kind as to bring that along with you when you come to town."

"Well, I reckon I could since you asked so nicely. Just let me dig it up and I'll see you in about an hour or so."

An hour and a half later, Katherine gracefully walked into Foster's office just as Vicki and Dawn were leaving for lunch.

"May I help you?" Dawn asked as she approached her counter.

"Why yes, yes you may," she replied cordially. "I'm Katherine Davenport, and I'm here to see Mr. Siler. I called earlier."

"Oh, yes ma'am," Dawn replied as she rose from her chair. "I believe he's expecting you. Give me just a second and I'll let him know that you're here, okay."

"Yes, thank you," she replied as Dawn turned and left.

A few moments later, Foster appeared in his doorway. "Mrs. Davenport," he greeted as he stepped toward her. "Please come in," he said with an extended arm to his office.

Taking a seat in one of the plush leather chairs in front of his desk, Katherine was quickly joined by Foster after he shut the door.

"Now," he said as he sat next to her and then covered her hand with his. "About Bobby and the article you read in the paper this morning."

"Oh yesss, my baby," she sighed. "How's he doing, is he okay?"

"Yes, Bobby's fine, but he does have a black eye."

"A what? A black eye, but how, what happened?" she questioned anxiously.

"Now don't get all riled up there, he's just fine."

"But what happen?" she pleaded.

"Well, I'm not really sure of all the details, but from what I was told, it seems that some of the other inmates had been giving him a hard time about being a spoiled little rich kid. And after just so much, I think he finally had his fill, decked one of the guys and they all got into a big fight. But he's fine and you don't have anything to worry, because." He squeezed her hand. "I have another meeting with Cyrus this afternoon and if it goes as I hope, I think I could have Bobby out tomorrow morning. See, after really looking and digging into the girl's testimony, we found some pretty compelling evidence that disputes her claim against your son. And just possibly mind you, just possibly, I might get Cyrus to dismiss your case and drop all of the charges. And if I can get him to do that, well then, what you have is no trial. No nothing. It's finished and done with, and everybody just goes home."

"Oh Fossster," she gasped. "Tomorrow morning? No trial, no nothing, are you sure?"

"Yes ma'am," he reassured. "If Cyrus drops the charges."

"Oh my," she smiled. "I just don't know what to say. That is such wonderful news, when can Howard and I pick him up?"

"Well, I'm not quite sure on the exact time just yet, but hopefully around noon. I should know more later today after I talk with Cyrus. And after that, I'll let you know, how's that?"

"Yes, that would be great because I am supposed to call Howard later this afternoon and then I can tell him the good news. He's coming back tomorrow and maybe if he isn't too late, he'll be here when Bobby gets out. But now," she suddenly stared with a dispirited expression. "Now, I won't be able to see you anymore."

Sensing her discontent, Foster quickly reached up and slipped his fingers beneath her chin. "You miss me already, don't you?" he said as she blushed and turned away.

Pulling her face back to his, he stared into her eyes for just a moment then dipped his head and kissed her. He could feel her shaking her head as he tasted the sweetness of her mouth and he knew he was right.

"Yesss," she finally whispered into his mouth, her lips still lightly touching his. "I do, I miss you already. Since Monday I've been nothing but a wreck when you're not around, and all I do is think of you. I want to see you again, one last time. Please."

"I don't know Katherine," he replied with a reluctant sigh. "I know you said that Howard is due back on Friday, but what if he decides to come home early, you know, and surprise you."

"But I really don't think that he would," she argued. "He's having too much fun without me."

"Well, that's a mighty big thing to consider, because I for one, really don't want him coming home to find me in his bed with his wife. Do you?"

Shaking her head, Katherine sat quietly for a second then began to smile. "I know," she suddenly perked up with another idea to get her way. "I could come over to your house, you know, after dark like you did last night annnd."

"Naaah, that won't work either," he shook his head. "I have too many nosey neighbors. Especially ol Mrs. Crawford."

Disappointed but determined, the woman stewed for a few seconds longer then suddenly looked up with yet another idea. "Well how about the boat?" she grinned. "We could stay on the boat. You know, at the marina where we keep it docked. There's never anyone there and it's perfect. Besides ever since we've owned it, I've often thought of what it would be like to make love in that little cabin. So I guess if you really want the title," she continued with an inviting tease. "You'll just have to come and get it later tonight."

"On the boat?" Foster laughed. "Are you serious?"

"Why of course silly, where else… say about dark thirty."

CHAPTER 15

———◆———

EARLY THE NEXT MORNING, FOSTER woke to the deep bellowing sound of a foghorn resonating across the water. Obviously coming from one of the giant sea going ships out in the bay, it blew long and loud twice more then stopped. Opening his eyes, he stirred ever so slowly and then looked around. It was still dark, but the breaking dawn was not far away and its advancing light made it easy to see. Carefully pulling his arm out from under Katherine's pillow, he quietly rolled to the edge of the bed with a delightful groan then gathered his clothes and began to dress.

Subconsciously sensing a disruption to her sleeping milieu, Katherine stirred with a heavy sigh and rolled to her side. Floating somewhere in-between the dream world and consciousness, she blindly grabbed for the covers and pulled them over her shoulders then curled into a ball. He was going to wake her and tell her goodbye but quickly changed his mind then finished dressing and wrote a note instead. Neatly folding it, he set it next to her purse then picked up the title and the bill of sale to the boat on the counter. Scanning the back for the proper signatures, he smiled and stuffed it into his pocket then ascended the steps and quietly left.

Later that morning, Foster stood with Frank in front of Bobby's cell and watched as he inserted the key into the lock. Turning the heavy steel mechanism with a click, he opened the door then took a step back and turned to Foster. "Well, there ya go Mister Siler," he drawled as he turned and started walking away. "He's all yourrrs."

Watching the guard as he walked away, Bobby quickly turned his gaze back to Foster and began to smile as if he'd known all along his parents would bail him out.

"Well Bobby," Foster began bluntly. "There it is. There's your door. That's what you've been praying for, and what I've been working on all week isn't it? I finally got the prosecutor to drop the charges, so as of now, you're a free man. But before you walk through it," he went on, but now in a different tone. "I want you to sit your ass back down on that bunk and listen to me because there's a few things that you and I need to discuss."

Dutifully doing as he was told, Bobby took his seat as Foster entered his cell and sat beside him. "Yes sir," he replied. "I'm listening."

"Good. Well, first I want to talk about that eye of yours," he began as he reached beneath Bobby's chin and turned his face to his. "That's quite a shiner you got there, and just so you know, your mother already knows about it too."

"What!" he jumped back up and then looked down at Foster. "How'd she find out?" he fretted.

"Because I told her, that's how. Now shut up and sit your ass back down."

"Oh yeah," he smirked as he took his seat. "I bet you caught hell over that didn't you."

"Well Bobby," Foster chuckled and shook his head. "Actually I didn't and I'll tell ya why. See, I told her that it was your cellmates that did it. You see, she thinks that they were in here giving you a hard time about being a spoiled little rich kid and you ended up getting into a fight with a couple of them. You know, trying to pro- tect your good name and all. And you see, that's exactly what you're going to tell your parents when you see them because I don't want them to hear any other version except that. You do understand what I'm telling you here, don't you?" he questioned with an icy stare that left little doubt as to its message.

Staring back into Foster's eyes, Bobby swallowed hard and then nodded his head. "Yes sir," he finally replied.

"Good, now the second thing I want to talk about is not so much as to why you were in here, but more importantly as to just how and why you're getting out. Now the bottom line is, is that you're as guilty as sin. You know it and I know it, the girl and her parents know it, and the prosecutor reeeally knows it. So I want you to understand something and you better listen real, real good. The prosecutor still has it out for you. He wants you and he wants you bad. You understand? Real bad."

Nodding as if he truly did, Foster quickly continued on. "Now I've used just about every favor and connection that I had in town to get your spoiled little ass out of here. So if you screw up, and you end up back in here again for any reason, I'll guarantee he'll try to reopen this case and hang your ass for good. And Bobby," he paused and stared. "There isn't a goddamn thing that I or anyone else will be able to do to stop it. You understand? This is a one-shot deal son."

"And why's that?" Bobby asked with a deep concern. "If they're letting me go."

"Well, it's kind of complicated, but unlike what they call double jeopardy, Cyrus can still come after you. You see, you haven't been to trial. And because of that, you can still be charged again, arrested and taken before a court. See, this isn't some sort of game where you keep getting to start over. And like I told you the other day, if you do end up going to the big house, there is no doubt in my mind that you will learn what it's like to be a woman. You do understand me, don't you?"

Nodding with a heavy sigh, the boy sat quietly for a moment then slowly turned to Foster. "So what-a I do now?" he asked quietly.

"Well," Foster finally said as he stood. "How about if we start with your clothes. Here," he said as he tossed a plain brown package onto the boy's lap. "And when you get changed, get your things and then let's get the hell out of here. Your mother and father are waiting for us outside."

Elated at the thought, Bobby tore out of his jumpsuit and hurriedly changed. A few minutes later, he walked through the doors of the county jail with Foster into the bright morning light. He was a free man, and with a hand to his forehead, he squinted against the sun in search of his parents. A second later, he spied them waiting at the bottom of the steps next to the car. He wanted to run but he didn't, he knew better. He stayed where he was until a nod from Foster gave him permission and he bolted from his side and bounded down the steps.

Watching as the three embraced, Foster stood for a moment then slowly descended the steps and joined them. Turning as he approached, Howard instantly reached out and extended his hand. "I don't know how to thank you Mr. Siler," he began as he took Foster's hand. "You really have no idea what this means to us. He's our only son now, and Katherine and I were certain that he was never going to get out, especially after what the prosecutor had told us."

"Well sometimes," Foster drawled. "The prosecutor doesn't always have all of the facts just right."

"Well still, in five days you've done what we were told would never happen. I don't know how you did it, but we're truly grateful. And now am I to understand that you not only got him out, but you also got his charges completely dropped and that now there won't even be a trial?"

"Yes sir, that's correct. No bond, no trial, no nothing... it's over."

"Well, Katherine did say you were quite the animal."

"Oh she did, did she?" Foster laughed with a quick yet discrete glance to Katherine. "Well, I don't know about animal," he replied modestly. "But there were a few late nights."

"Yes, and Bobby's free."

"Yes he is, but like I told him, and I'll tell you the same thing," he turned his voice serious. "Since he didn't go to trial, the prosecution could still bring these charges back up, you know, if he were to get into trouble again and he wanted to give your son a hard time. That's why it might not be a bad idea if he were to leave town, at least for a while. You do know what I'm saying, don't you?"

"Yes, I do actually," Howard sighed with a solemn glance to his son getting in the car. "I guess it's a good thing that I've taken this new job in New Orleans and we'll be moving shortly."

"Yes, I'm sure you're right," Foster agreed. "And by the way, congratulations, I know that work is hard to find right now. Oh, and also," he added and reached inside his suit coat. "Before you go, I need you to sign these for me if you could."

"What are these?" Howard asked as Foster pulled the papers from the inside his coat and then laid them on the hood of the car.

"Well, these are the title and the bill of sale to your boat, remember?"

"Oh yesss," Howard nodded as if he'd forgotten. "I guess we're not going to be needing it where we're going are we," he laughed as he grabbed his glasses then pulled his pen from his pocket and laid his hand on the hood of the car.

"And what about the house and two hundred acres up river?" he asked as he scribbled his signature and then handed the papers back.

"Already taken care of," Foster replied. "You had it in that trust, and because of that, all that was required was Katherine's signature. So I guess Mr. Davenport," he said as he extended his hand. "I believe our business is concluded."

"Well, once again Mr. Siler," Howard said with a grip to Foster's hand. "We thank you, and now we better be going," he glanced to his wife standing next to him then turned and walked to the other side of the car.

Howard was one for little patience or words and with only seconds to spare Katherine quickly stepped forward. She wanted to thank him as well but she also wanted to see him one last time, and so with a discrete and open hug, she quickly pulled her mouth to his ear and whispered her desires. "Do you have a screened in porch?"

"Yes, actually I do," he replied with a knowing grin.

"Good, then leave it unlocked and I'll wake you in the morning," she sighed as she released her hold and then stuck out her hand. "And again Mr. Siler," she said in a loud clear voice. "Like my husband just said, we do thank you for all you've done." A second later she stepped back to the car, and with one last knowing look to Foster as he opened her door, she gracefully slid into her seat and took her place with her husband.

Closing the door as she settled in, Foster stepped back to the curb and stuffed his hands into his pockets then exhaled with a heavy sigh. It had been a hell of a week, and as the car pulled away and made its way down the street, he wondered if he would really see her again? Would she really show up like she said, or was it just wishful thinking on both of their parts? She sounded serious, but could she get away with her husband here? Watching as the car finally turned the corner and disappeared, he smiled with that final thought then turned and headed back to his office.

—◆—

The sun was just beginning to crest the horizon when Katherine, true to her word, quietly slipped inside the door of Foster's screened in porch. A few moments later, her heart pounding wildly, her throat so dry she couldn't speak if she wanted to, she entered his house and quietly closed the door. Removing her shoes, she looked around then silently but aimlessly continued.

She had no idea as to where his bedroom was, but led by intuition, she headed straight for the stairs. Placing one hand on the rail and a foot on the first step, she looked up to the top but then suddenly hesitated. She was nervous and strangely reluctant, yet even so she took a breath and continued on. A few moments later, she reached the top to find a door at the end of the hallway that had been left slightly ajar.

She knew it was his bedroom, it had to be, and she knew, or at least hoped, that she would find him still sleeping. Smiling at the thought, even though there were voices telling her to run, she boldly stepped forward. And as she slowly and quietly crept toward his door, her heart began to pound like it never had before. Stopping just a foot away, she closed her eyes and took another deep breath. A week ago this would've been unthinkable, but now it was all she could think of and with the gentle brush of her palm against the door, she exhaled and then slowly pushed it open.

Smiling at the sight of Foster still in bed, she immediately began to undress as she crept towards him. He was sound asleep on his back, with nothing more than a thin white sheet covering his waist and the top half of one leg. Breathing deep and steady, he had a pillow pulled over his head with an arm draped across the top.

Stopping just as she reached his bed, she stared down and then smiled at the sight of his manhood clearly defined beneath the shear silky linens. It was what she'd come for, and as a heated flush rose from within and swept through her, she boldly reached behind and unclasped her bra. Dropping to the floor without a sound, she quickly removed the last of her clothes and then stood beside his bed. Heaving with desire, yet still just a little unsure, she paused and took a breath to settle her nerves. But Foster had introduced and awakened in her the raw unbridled pleasures of guilt-free sex like she'd never known and as a result, she'd developed an appetite and a craving for it. In short, she was addicted, and with her desires now driving her actions, the sultry dark haired beauty gently knelt on the bed.

Slowly pulling the sheet from his body, she slithered over the top of his lean muscular torso as if in a daze. Feeling his body and his sex as they both awakened and stirred to life beneath her, she then slowly and sensuously lowered herself onto him. Taking him into the depths of her smoldering loins, she gently pulled the pillow from his face and smothered his mouth with hers.

It wasn't until noon that the two finally stood in his doorway for what they both knew was their final goodbye. Looking down the drive to her car, Katherine finally turned back and cleared her throat. "Well, I guess this is it," she began in a saddened voice. "But before I go, I want you to know just how much you mean to me and how truly special you really are. And how much I appreciate what all you did for us too. But now that we're moving to New Orleans, I guess I won't get to see you anymore. But maybe after we get settled," she quickly added. "I could write. I mean, that is, if it's okay? And who knows, maybe someday if you ever visit New Orleans, we could meet and I could? Well, you know," she smiled coyly. "Be your tour guide for the day... or night?"

"I would like that," he replied. "Very much, and I mean it," he added as he stared into her eyes then reached up and brushed her cheek with the back of his fingers. "And who knows," he said as he rolled his hand and cupped her chin. "Maybe your husband will be gone again."

Gaining a knowing smile, Katherine stared for just a second then tiptoed and brought her lips to his. She wanted him to know just how much their moments together had meant, and with all of the feeling in her heart, she kissed him deep and passionately. Savoring in what she was sure was their last embrace; she finally released her hold and lowered her head then turned away.

Watching as she slowly walked to her car at the end of his drive, Foster couldn't help but think of their week together. And even though he wanted to say something, he didn't. He just stood and watched until she stopped at the car and opened the door then looked back with a glassy-eyed gaze. A moment later, the beautiful Katherine Davenport shifted her eyes and descended into her car. She was leaving, and as she drove away and disappeared behind a billowing cloud of dust, he wondered if he would ever see her again.

CHAPTER 16

WAKING THE NEXT MORNING, FOSTER rolled onto his back then stretched and yawned. He ached like never before but as he slowly relaxed his muscles he couldn't help but smile. His week with Katherine had really taken its toll and it was a chore just to pull his ass out of bed. And even though he hadn't eaten very well, or had what he considered a decent night's sleep, he wasn't complaining. In fact, he was still grinning. How could he not? But now it was Sunday and he was hungry, really hungry. His belly was growling like a bear, and even though he wasn't meeting anyone, he rose from bed and began to dress. He needed food and Connie's Diner was calling to him.

Stepping out into the morning air, he smiled and took a big deep breath then headed to his car. Dropping behind the wheel, he pulled from his drive and then headed into town. Ten minutes later as he neared the diner, he suddenly began to think of the beautiful young girl he'd seen last week. The one at the counter that he'd tried to follow. Who was she, he wondered? And what's more, where did she come from and where did she go? They were perplexing questions that seem to haunt his thoughts until he'd turned onto the street in front of the diner. Catching a waft of early morning breakfast, he quickly found a parking spot and shut down his car. It was time to eat, and without a moment's hesitation, he exited his car and crossed the street.

Entering the diner, Foster nodded to Connie behind the counter, said his good mornings to a few of the people he knew and headed straight for his table. A moment later, Connie was at his side with a pot of coffee. She really hated waiting on him, but he was a regular and times were hard. And to her, every penny and every person counted, including him.

"Good mornin Foster," she said cordially. "Coffee, it's fresh?" she asked and held up the pot.

"Morning Connie, and yes please," he replied and turned his cup over then slid it to the edge.

"Are we havin guest this mornin," she inquired as she poured. "Or are we alone?"

"We're alone," he said. "And I'm starving too, so if you don't mind, could you bring me a menu."

"Sure can," she replied as she topped his cup. "Let me fetch ya one an I'll be right back."

Pouring a shot of cream into his coffee, Foster stirred it and took a sip just as she returned with his menu. "Just let me know when you're ready," she said as she laid it on the table.

Nodding his head, he swallowed his brew and thanked her, then picked up the menu. Gazing intently at the selections inside he debated over a few of his favorites then folded it and laid it to the side just as the door to the diner dinged.

To Foster it was an unnecessary distraction and he couldn't have cared less as to who came or went, but for some strange reason, something on this particular occasion caused him to look up. Why, he really wasn't sure. Maybe it was just plain ol curiosity kicking in. Or maybe it was the soft sweet drawl of a young girl's voice resonating above the noise and chatter as she greeted Connie. A voice he was certain he'd heard before. Either way, he froze and then smiled with an almost boyish delight at the sight of the same beautiful young girl that he'd seen last week casually walking back into the diner.

Dressed just as she'd been last Sunday, yet in clothes that had been cleaned and mended, she was fresh and rested-looking and smiled radiantly as she entered. Her thick auburn hair that'd hung wet and wild a week ago, was now neatly combed and pulled back into a ponytail that hung just past her shoulders. And although she appeared temporarily poised in between the metamorphic stages of adolescence and that of a mature young woman, Foster could clearly see that it was just a matter of time before her youthful appearance, exploded into a woman of devastating beauty.

Completely mesmerized and instantly smitten, he watched as she crossed the room to Connie and took a seat at the counter. Greeted as if she were a long lost friend, he watched for a few moments longer as the two idly conversed and Connie handed her a menu. It was his second chance, and with the most salacious of thoughts, he slid his chair back from the table, reached for one of the upside down cups and slowly stood. It'd been a whole week since he'd seen her, but she was back and with that Foster took aim and set his predatory sights straight on the young girl.

Taking his empty cup, he casually sauntered across the room with the confidence of an apex predator closing in on its quarry. Catching an immediate scowl from Connie as he approached, he quickly took one of the stools three places down from the girl and set his cup on the counter.

"Oh Connie," he called nonchalantly. "Could I have another shot of coffee please? Just about halfway if you don't mind," he added with a smirk as he turned his attention to the girl.

Connie knew what he'd done by leaving his cup on the table and it infuriated her to no end. And in an effort to warn the young girl and stop his advances before he could ruin another life, she quickly reached for the coffee pot then turned to make her stand. She knew exactly what she was going to say, but before she could intercede, the unconscionable lawyer had already caught the young girl's gaze. A second later, and as fate would have it, a call from a table now ready to order thwarted her hopes and she let them be.

"Well good morning young lady," Foster greeted with a cheerful drawl.

She'd noticed him approach the counter and even take his seat, but even so she hadn't expected him to speak to her. She was just a kid, and for a fleeting moment Willie thought he was speaking to someone else. But he wasn't, he was talking to her, and although she was a bit intimidated, she cleared her throat and mustered a reply.

"Good mornin," she smiled then blushed, uncertain of what to say next as an immediate and over-powering schoolgirl attraction consumed her. He was so handsome and well dressed, and exuded a kind of confidence she'd never seen in anyone before, not even from Mr. Johnson.

"Now if I'm not mistaken," he said with a curious tilt to his head. "Didn't I see you in here last Sunday?"

"Yes sur," Willie nodded as he scooted another stool closer. "I... I'd jus gotten into town, so I'm kind-a new here."

"Just gotten into town and you're new here," he repeated.

"Yes sur," Willie replied.

Staring in silence as he digested what she'd said, Foster began to salivate at the thoughts now reeling in his mind. She was new, she was young, and from what else he could surmise, she was all alone. His day was getting better by the minute and he smiled at his good fortune, but now he needed to find out who she was and where she was staying. Was she from a broken home or a runaway? He wondered then thought not. She really didn't look like a girl who would run from much of anything, but just like a witness in a trial, all of his questions would soon be answered for if Foster Siler was anything, he was a master at extracting information.

"Well then, I guess if no one has said it already. Welcome to Mobile. I'm Foster," he drawled politely as he extended his hand. "Foster Siler."

Swiveling her stool to face him straight on, Willie swallowed nervously then reached out and took his hand. "Thank you kindly, I'm Willie," she said. "Willie Mae Dawson."

Reeling as if a gentle electric current had suddenly flowed between them when they touched, Foster paused and caught his breath for there was more to the girl than just her stunning good looks that he found alluring. "Well, Miss Willie," he finally said as he quickly harbored his feelings. "It is certainly my pleasure. So tell me," he asked as he dropped her hand. "Where're you from? Are you moving here, or just visiting?"

He had to know if she had family, and especially over-protective parents. He was guessing and hoping that she had none. He'd seen a lot of tragedy and misfortune since the beginning of the depression and his summation of her situation was that she was another casualty of the times. A victim of fate, another lost soul who'd gotten caught in the turmoil and uncontrolled repercussions of an economy that'd gone so terribly wrong.

Taking a breath, Willie lowered her head at the thought of how and why she'd come to be there. Somewhat saddened, she swallowed hard then slowly looked back up. "Well, I ain't really shor now," she answered with an air of uncertainty. "But I'm from up north around Hale County, an when I left home last week an hopped the train, I thought I was go'n to New Orleens. See, I was go'n there to get an edjucation like I'd promised my momma, but on a axadent I ended up here. An since I ain't got much money, I really need ta get a job before I can keep go'n. But I've been lookin all week an nobody al hire me. They all say there ain't no work. So now I don't know what I'm gonna do," she trailed off and then lowered her head again.

"A job and an education, huh," Foster sighed as if he were pondering some great question. "So you are staying here?"

"Yes sur," Willie replied and raised her head. "I'm stayin at Miss Shelda's boardin house. Or at least I am until I can get ta New Orleens."

Digesting her words with a skill he'd honed from years of reading and questioning people, Foster could instantly sense the underlying sadness that seemed to envelope her. And he had also picked up on the past tense promise to her mother, surmising that there was definitely more to that too.

"So you need a job and you wanna get an education," he repeated in a concerned voice.

"Yes sur," she nodded.

"Well good for you, because those are both very important. But you know what's really important right now?" he continued, changing his tone in an attempt to lighten her mood.

"What's that?" Willie asked.

"Food," Foster replied. "Come on, let's get something to eat. I'm starving, how about you?"

Nodding excitedly, Willie's eyes lit up, but just as quickly as they had, her expression changed at the thought of how another breakfast like she'd had before would cost another dollar. "Oooh Mister Siler," she murmured politely. "Iii... I can't."

"What?" he said as he looked on. "I thought you were hungry?"

"I am, but its jus that Iiii," she stopped then went on. "Well, I need to save my money so I--."

"Oh yes you can," he interrupted as he rose from his stool and held out his hand. "Cause I'm buying your breakfast, now come on."

"Oh Mister Siler," Willie protested and shook her head. "That shor is awful nice of you, bu... but I jus couldn't."

"Nonsense," Foster insisted with a gentle tug to her sleeve. "You just said you were hungry right?"

"Yes, but."

"Well no buts," he persisted with another tug. "Come on. Besides," he added and leaned toward her. "I wanna talk to you. Didn't you just say that you were looking for a job?"

Sliding from her stool just as Connie returned, Foster turned to the woman with a victorious smirk. He'd wanted to get the girl away before she could return and disrupt his plans, and he did.

"Oh Connie," he began with a sanctimonious ring to his voice. "I'm so glad your back. I'd like to order please, if you don't mind. You see this young lady and I were just talking and she's decided to join me for breakfast this morning," he clapped his hands together.

"Now we're both starving, so if you don't mind, I think we'd like the steak and eggs with toast and fried potatoes. What-a you think Willie?" Nodding her head enthusiastically, Foster smiled and then turned back to the woman. "So why don't you ask Bill back there to dig out two of his best rib-eyes and rustle us up some grub, okay."

"Yes sir," she replied in a defeated tone as she scribbled onto a ticket. "An just how would you like your steaks?"

"Medium rare," Foster grinned. "And over easy on the eggs, okay. Oh, and I almost forgot, add a double order of potatoes to mine and a large glass of milk for the young lady. Actually, and now that I think about it, why don't you make that two glasses of milk will you, that sounds good. And make sure they're cold too, I hate warm milk. Oh, and one more thing," he added with an insolent smile as he turned and began walking toward his table. "As soon as you get a chance, bring me another cup of coffee would you please. I think the one on my table is probably cold by now."

Turning back to the kitchen as he walked away, Connie shook her head with a disgruntled huff and called to the cook. "Billll," she yelled as she laid the ticket with the rest of the orders. "Two steak an eggs medium rare. An they're for Foster, he wants two of your best."

Taking their seats across from each other the two quietly stared as Connie scurried toward them with a pot of coffee and a glass of milk. Setting the milk in front of Willie, she smiled amicably, then poured a new cup of coffee for Foster. "You're food will be out in just a few minutes an I'll bring your other glass of milk with it, okay."

Nodding politely as she left, Foster instantly turned his attention back to Willie. He had her in his clutches, but before he actually began with his inquisition he decided to wait until Connie returned with their tray of food.

Gasping as she laid their steaming plates in front of them a few minutes later, Willie stared for a second in wide-eyed awe then looked to Foster. "What is it?" she asked, as it's incredible aroma wafted into her sinuses.

"That's your steak Willie," Foster replied as he immediately cut into his own. "The best piece of meat you can get from an animal with four legs, go ahead... try it."

Grabbing her fork and knife, Willie quickly cut her steak and stuck the tender piece of beef into her mouth. "Oh my Lorrrd," she mumbled and closed her eyes then tilted her head upward and began to chew.

"Good... isn't it," he asked as she swallowed.

Nodding with a grin, Willie quickly cut another piece and stuck it in her mouth as Foster did the same. They were both hungry and for a while they ate in quiet, but after they'd devoured almost half of their plates he casually began to question her. He wanted to know everything about her, and just like a witness in a deposition, he meticulously began to extract the information he desired.

"Sooo," he began as he picked up his coffee and took a sip. "Did I really hear you right when you said that you'd hopped a train last week and thought you were going to New Orleans?"

"Yes sur," she replied and nodded as she swallowed her bite.

"But why were you going to New Orleans," he asked. "What's there?"

"Well," she began in a somber voice. "I... I promised my momma before she died that I'd go to a big city an get an edjucation. Jus like she wanted me to," her mood and expression changing as she went on. "An New Orleens was the only big city I could think of. An when I got on that train, I jus thought I was go'n there, but on a axadent I ended up here. An now I don't what to do," she finished then bit her bottom lip in an attempt to suppress the tears that'd begun to well.

"Well, I'm truly sorry to hear that. But what about your father?" Foster pried. "Where's he?"

"I ain't never had one," she sneered bluntly. "Or at least not no real one. Jus my stepdad, an he was mean. He use ta beat an hurt my momma all the time," she paused and looked down at her food. "But he's dead too."

"Well, what about your brothers or sisters?"

Silently shaking her head, Willie answered without looking up.

Confused, Foster took a breath then gently pressed on. "So did you choose New Orleans because your mother had friends or relatives there?"

Shaking her head once more, the young girl slowly looked back up in dismay. "I don't have no one there," her voice began to falter as the heartache within her came flooding back.

Willie was strong, but she was as alone and as lonely as anyone could get, and as the reality of that fact truly set in, she gently laid her fork on her plate and turned toward the street. "I don't have no one no where," she finished and lowered her head then coughed between tightly closed lips and began to cry.

To Foster it was awkward, sitting there as she wept, but he understood and was deeply moved for he too had lost both of his parents and he knew how she was suffering. It was one of the main reasons he'd stayed in Mobile and had never gone back to Tennessee. And even though her situation was one of heartbreaking sadness, he delighted in the fact with a twisted and demented sort of joy for now he knew she was truly alone. She was a hardship case and was vulnerable, and he smiled at the thought of his good fortune. He would take her and isolate her, and then ever so slowly, he would make her his.

"Willie," he finally said. "Are you okay?"

Nodding her head ever so slightly, she sniffled and wiped her tears then apologized.

"It's okay," Foster went on in an attempt to console her. "I know exactly how you feel. I lost both of my parents years ago and it still hurts when I think of it. But listen to me," he placed his elbows on the table and leaned toward her. "You have to go on, you hear... you must," he emphasized. "I know that it seems hard right now and maybe even impossible, but you have to do it. Besides, I'm going to help you now."

"You are?" she drawled as if she couldn't believe his words.

"Yes ma'am," he replied.

"But how?"

"Well, you did say that you were looking for work, didn't you?"

"Oh, yes sur," she answered and nodded.

"Well, I guess this must be your lucky day because I've been looking for someone to help me with a house I just bought up river. You know painting and cleaning up, taking care of the place while I'm away... that sort of stuff. It's up river quite a ways and you'd be all alone during the week. And it's a lot of work too, hard work. So you think you could handle some of those things for me?"

"You mean a real job?" her eyes widened.

"Yes ma'am, that's exactly what I mean... you interested?"

"Oh, yes sur Mister Siler," she grinned great big. "I... I'd be the best worker you ever had."

"You sure?" he raised his eyebrows. "Remember, it's a lot of work and I'll expect a lot out of you."

Unwavering, Willie instantly nodded her head with another enthusiastic grin. "Oh yes sur, I'm shor. I worked on a cotton farm ever since I was little an I'm used to hard work."

"Now remember, this is up river quite a ways and you'd be all alone. All during the week, all by yourself," he reiterated. "You won't get scared will you?"

"Oh no sur," Willie replied and shook her head. "I ain't afraid of nothin."

"Are you sure?" He dipped his head and stared.

Nodding her head once again, Foster smiled, for he knew now that she truly wanted to please.

"Well good then," he said and then extended his hand across the table. "Consider yourself hired young lady." Taking his hand, Willie beamed excitedly. "Now I'll start you out at thirty cents a day and not a penny more okay."

"Yes sur. An thank you. I promise I won't never disappoint you, not ever."

"I'm sure you won't Willie," he replied as they shook, his mind reeling as to just how she would or wouldn't disappoint him.

"So when do you want me to start? I can start today if you'd like. Or tamorrow," she added hopefully.

"No Willie, I'm sorry but I won't be able to have things ready until Wednesday. Until I can reschedule some appointments so I can take off work and come and get you. Then we'll get my boat and head up river, how's that sound?"

"Take off work? You mean you can jus take off when ever you want?" she asked in awe. "What kind-a job do you have that you can do that? Won't your boss get mad at you?"

"Nooo," Foster replied with a chuckle. "See, I'm an attorney."

"A whaaat?" she drawled and scrunched her face.

"A lawyer," he chuckled again.

"You're a lawyer?" she gasped.

"Yes ma'am," he nodded.

It was at that very instant that Willie's schoolgirl crush exploded into a full-blown fantasy. She'd always dreamed of being the wife of a doctor or lawyer and now here he was sitting right across from her. She thought of how lucky she was and for a few fleeting moments, she sat in a dreamy daze and gazed at the handsome older man. The room seemed to go silent and to her nothing else mattered except for him. She was completely smitten, but all too quickly her fantasy vanished as Foster quietly began to explain his plans for Wednesday and when he would pick her up.

She understood everything and couldn't have been happier, and by the time he had finished they'd stuffed the last bites of food into their mouths. Wiping their plates clean with their toast, they washed it all down with the last of their milk just as Connie arrived.

"Well," she asked as she refilled Foster's coffee cup. "How was everything?"

"Excellent," Foster replied as he wiped his mouth and then slid his plate to the edge of the table. "Just excellent. I'm stuffed. My compliments to Bill, tell him those steaks were perfect."

"I'll be sure an tell him," she nodded. "He'll appreciate that. An how about you sugar, what'd you think?"

Looking up, aglow with her good news, Willie couldn't wait to tell the world. "Miss Connie," she blurted happily. "I have a job."

Somewhat confused, Connie stared for just a second then slowly rolled her head back to Foster. "Well, I can only imagine," she said with an obvious disdain as she locked eyes with the man in a heated glare.

Her message of contempt toward him was clear and he knew it, but Foster didn't care, for like a snake in the grass, he'd already ensnared his prey and the girl was his. And now, unable to resist the chance of taunting her, he slid his chair back from the table then crossed one leg over the other and took a sip from his coffee.

"That's right Connie," he mocked with a condescending sneer as he set his cup back down. "You see, this here young lady has been looking for work all week. And as fate would have it, it just so happens that I have also been looking for someone to help me. You know, temporarily with a house I just bought. Can you imagine that? I mean the odds... why it's unbelievable. I'll tell you, someone from up above must have surely been lookin down upon us this morning, don't ya think?" He glanced to the ceiling then lowered and shook his head in a gesture of disbelief. "I like to think of it as divine intervention," he continued as he regained her gaze. "So here we are, isn't that nice? I just love being able to help people when they're in such dire need, don't you?" He sighed and glanced to Willie then returned his gaze to Connie with another smirk. "I mean iiit... it just gives you such a spiritual and uplifting feeling," he took a breath then paused as if he'd just been enlightened from above. "You know, kind of like, well," he sighed again. "Almost as if you were doing the Lords work himself, don't ya think?"

Quietly glaring as his cynical and religious overtones burned into her ears, Connie stared with an ever-growing contempt. She knew that he was as far from doing the Lord's work as the Antichrist, yet she also knew that there was nothing she could do to help the girl. He had her, and he wasn't going to give her up.

"You're nowhere near do'n the Lords work Foster Siler," she said vehemently. "An you know it," she added as she reached down and took their plates then turned to Willie. "An young lady, if you ever need any help, an I mean anything, you just come an see me okay."

"Yes ma'am," Willie nodded with a confused expression.

"Good, an don't you never forget it either, ya hear."

"Yes ma'am," she answered politely. "I won't."

Somewhat satisfied, Connie turned to Foster and laid the bill on the table then left without another word. She'd made her point as best she could and as she sauntered away, Willie leaned forward and questioned her newfound savior. "Does she not like you Mister Siler?"

"Well," Foster chuckled and shook his head. "To be right truthful with you... not really."

"But why not?"

"Well, it's kind of a long story," he said as he grabbed the bill. "And I'll tell you all about it some day, but for now let me go and pay for our breakfast." Nodding her head, Foster rose from his chair. "Good, then give me a minute and when I get back, we'll be on our way."

Casually approaching the counter, Foster stopped and laid the bill and his money in front of Connie. Snatching both with the swipe of her hand and a sullen glare, she punched the register and opened the drawer. Quickly counting his change, she slapped it onto the counter with a disgruntled smack. "Leave this one alone Foster," she demanded as she held her hand over the top of his money. "She's too young an you know it. There're plenty of others."

It was her final stand in an attempt to dissuade him and they both knew it. But Foster wasn't about to budge, and with a casual glance to her hand, he quickly calculated his change, then shrugged his shoulders and looked back to his table. "Not this time Connie," he said with an icy finality. "Not this time," he repeated as he slowly turned back and met her glaring gaze. A moment later, and with a smile as smug as his attitude, he exhaled with an arrogant humph and turned away. "Enjoy your morning Connie," he said as he walked back to his table.

Watching as he slowly crossed the room, Connie wondered if he'd forgotten his money or left it as a tip? Surely not, it was a dollar fifty and more than she made in three days of hard work. She wanted to say something, but she didn't. And then she wondered if it was just his arrogant way of trying to buy her silence? She didn't know and it gnawed on her heavily. His money was tainted as far as she was concerned, but just the same, it was money and times were hard. And as she watched him graciously extend his hand to the smiling young girl, she swallowed her pride and slid the dollar and two coins from the counter, then stuffed them into her pocket.

Looking back just as he and Willie reached the door, Foster paused until he'd caught Connie's gaze. He knew she would be glaring in her oh so judge-mental of ways, and with a final victorious smirk that he had the girl and was leaving with her; he turned back to the door and pulled it open.

Staring back from behind the counter, Connie could only watch as the two stepped through the door and then descend the steps outside. Certain that the memory of this young girl and who she was now with, would some day come back to haunt her.

Walking across the street to his car, Willie grinned with a euphoric giddiness that she'd never felt before. It was sunny, she was completely stuffed with more food than she'd ever had in her belly at one time, and she had a job. It just didn't get any better than that, and as Foster opened the door and she slid into his car, she couldn't help but think of her good fortune. She'd stopped at the diner just by chance and now here she was, being driven back to her place by a man who was not only her new boss, but one whom she now felt a warm and growing attraction to.

Settling in behind the wheel, Foster started the car then turned to the beaming young girl. "Well young lady," he grinned. "Which way?"

Twisting in her seat, Willie looked through her opened window then pointed down the street. "That way," she said excitedly.

Shifting into reverse, Foster backed from their parking spot then dropped into first. "Annnd," he dipped his head with a curious look.

"Go three roads down an then go to the right."

"Yes ma'ammm," he answered then smashed on the gas.

Accelerating down the street, Foster glanced at Willie like a young boy on a new date. She was smiling with excitement and it pleased him, but as they passed the diner something inside suddenly caught his attention. And although it was only a fleeting glimpse and was hard to see against the reflective glare of the morning sun, he instantly recognized the silhouette standing next to his table. An all too familiar figure who'd served him breakfast almost every Sunday since he had arrived in Mobile. Smiling within himself, he gloated in the fact that the woman who despised him with so much disdain, was still watching… even as they sped away.

The ride to Shelda's boarding house was exhilarating, but way too short as far as Willie was concerned. It seemed as if it had taken forever last Sunday, but after what seemed to be only a few short minutes, she was looking at the front door. She wanted to continue and stay with the man next to her for fear he would vanish and never return. Or that she would suddenly wake only to realize that her entire morning had been nothing but a dream. Her anxiety grew, and in her sudden state of worry the lustrous glow she'd just had began to fade like the dying flame of a candle, drowning in the excesses of its own paraffin pool.

Pulling alongside the curb, Foster finally brought the car to a stop, paused for a second, then reached down and shut off the engine. "Well Willie," he declared as he reclined back into the seat and draped his arm across the back. "Here we are."

Clearing her throat, Willie looked at the place she'd called home for the last seven days, and then slowly turned back to Foster. "Yes sur, this is it," she finally replied. "I… I guess that means ya need to get go'n, don't ya?"

"Yes ma'am," he said. "I still have some things to attend to, so I really need to be on my way."

It was easy to see that she was reluctant to leave yet still he was concerned that she might not believe he would come back to get her. Or that someone else would come along in his absence, and that she would go with them to somewhere else.

"But remember," he continued with an extended hand as if to reconfirm their deal and reassure her. "I'll be back on Wednesday, three days from now, right at twelve and I want you ready to leave okay." Grasping her four fingers with his right, he rolled her hand then gently covered the top with his left. "Wednesday at noon, okay," he reiterated as he pulled it toward him and then shook it in the most comforting of ways.

Gaining an immediate smile as well as a reassuring nod, Willie took solace in Foster's touch then turned and reached for the door handle. "I'll be ready an waitin," she chirped as she stepped out of the car.

"Good, then I'll see you Wednesday."

Starting his car, Foster smiled once again at the girl then slowly pulled away. A few moments later as he slowed for the intersection at the end of her street, he glanced into his mirror and caught her still standing on the curb, waving with her arm high above her head. Sticking his arm out just as he turned the corner, Foster waved once then disappeared from sight.

It had been a great morning, and now with the promise of yet another new young girl to pluck at his leisure, life for the thirty-five year old lawyer just couldn't get any better. His belly full, but now with his sleep-deprived body screaming for a reprieve, he had only one thing on his mind before his afternoon dinner date, and that was to go back home and get some much-needed rest.

Undressing down to his tee shirt and boxers, he lay across his bed with a heavy sigh then pulled a pillow from under the bedspread and draped it over his face. And even though his mind continued to whirl with thoughts of the new young girl, his body's need for rest ultimately prevailed. Moments later, Foster exhaled a long drawn-out breath and then dropped into a deep heavy sleep.

CHAPTER 17

———◆———

IT WASN'T UNTIL MID AFTERNOON that Foster finally stirred back to life. Checking the time he stretched and yawned then rolled to the edge of his bed and rose. At least now he could function again and he still had plenty of time to get ready before he was expected at the home of Judge Robert and Martha McAlister. A name that was not only known, but also revered by all in Mobile society, and one he hoped in the not to distant future, to call his in-laws. Their Sunday afternoon dinners over the past few months had become a ritual as his relationship with Melinda had grown.

The youngest of three daughters, she was their baby girl and the last one still at home. A little spoiled and a little over protected, her mother doted on her heavily. But at twenty-four, and in society's eyes, it was time for her to marry. They had dated for a little over a year now and recently it had turned serious, or at least in Melinda's eyes it had. Maybe it was because he'd finally succeeded in bedding her and had taken her virginity. He really didn't know, but whatever it was, it was shortly after that, that the McAlister women had developed a single-minded attitude toward him.

She was in love, and although he really wasn't, he still liked her. She was attractive, in fact very attractive, and even though she lacked what he thought was just good common sense, she was funny and smart and well educated. They got along well and genuinely had fun when they were together. In short she was the prefect match, but in reality, Foster considered their relationship as just another step in his climb up the ladder. For the McAlister's, by all acceptable standards, were blue bloods and everyone knew it.

He'd begun his career as a lawyer, but now Robert McAlister was one of most prominent and influential federal judges in the nation. And as such, his base of power and circle of friends was to say the least, without question. He was intelligent and held a wealth of knowledge that few men possessed. Foster knew it, and he knew that there was much he could learn from the man, both in and out of the courtroom. He sat in a very privileged position, but he also knew, as did many others that the judge was not a man to be trifled with.

And so it began that with each and every visit, Judge McAlister would intercept the young man before the women ever knew he was there and the two would abscond into the lavish confines of his library. Often discussing the law over a couple of drinks of his best-aged scotch and a fine Cuban cigar, they would sometimes spar over the most recent decisions that had been handed down by the courts in precedent-setting cases.

Foster would challenge the judge's position for not only did he possess a cunning insight into the law, he argued a damn fine case. And that was something that Judge McAlister not only respected, but thoroughly enjoyed. Foster was smart, and the aging adjudicator quickly picked up on the young maverick's hidden potential.

Stopping only after the women had found and then drug them to the table, the two seemed to bond a little more each time. Relaxing after dinner with a snifter of brandy and the rest of their cigars, the judge would slowly turn their talks back to politics and then to Foster's possible future in them. Senator Siler or Governor Siler, he would often say. And what a great first lady his daughter would make. Growing more and more in its appeal each and every time they discussed it, Foster, for the first time in his life, actually began to imagine a future in politics.

Pulling up to the huge palatial mansion set magnificently atop a high rolling hill, Foster slowly brought his car to a stop and looked around. Surrounded by ancient oaks keeping the summer's heat at bay, the white two-story home with its massive front porch and columns was impressive. Stepping from his car, he sauntered toward the porch and climbed the short set of steps to the door then pulled on the heavy cord to the doorbell.

Resonating from inside with a deep solid tone, he smiled then turned with his hands in his pockets and surveyed his surroundings. Enviously gazing across hundreds of acres of pristine pastures, he could see that Judge McAlister had certainly done well for himself. Neatly fenced and manicured, there were barns and living quarters for their help with hundreds of cattle grazing lazily in the fields. Yes, the man had made it that was for sure, and someday he too hoped to have a place just like this. It was a lofty dream, and for a few short moments he continued to stare and dream until the door finally opened behind him.

"Oh Mesieur Siler," the lady beamed delightedly. "Comes right on in, it's so good to see's you again."

"Thank you Monique," he replied as he stepped into the foyer. "It's good to see you too," he added but then froze and rolled his eyes. "Oh my Lord Monique," he said as he raised his head and inhaled. "What in heaven's name is that smell?"

"Vhy shat is your supper," she replied proudly. "A twelve pound Prime Rib Roas. Zhe Sjudge had vone of his cattle buschered las week so ve could havs it today. Jus for you!"

Monique was the McAlister's cook and house servant, and although she was light in color and had many of the features of a white woman, she was considered black and she knew her place. Born to a young white American model and a black African dignitary while living in France, she'd spent the first fifteen years of her life growing up in Paris. And even though her mother and father had never married, she still enjoyed and was afforded the finest in education available through the diplomatic core as well as extensive travel throughout Europe.

Returning to America after the sad and untimely death of her mother's lover, the two finally settled in New Orleans where she lived happily for the next ten years until her mother died. After that and at the age of twenty-five, she moved to Mobile in search of work and a new life. Arrested and wrongly accused of a crime she didn't commit, it was the ambitious but sympathetic Judge McAlister that she finally stood before in the courtroom.

Middle-aged, yet still very attractive, she had an air about her and a soft-spoken demeanor that Foster liked, especially her accent.

A sophisticated and pleasant blend of southern dialect mixed with the beauty of her native tongue. Obviously well educated, she was articulate and pleasant, and had been with the McAlister's for the last fifteen years.

Eternally grateful for how he'd helped her all those years ago, her intense and steadfast loyalty to the Judge was without question. But Foster often thought that she was also the man's mistress, for he'd noticed her on more than one occasion discreetly yet affectionately doting on him, especially when not in the presence of Mrs. McAlister or Melinda.

"It smells jus vonderful... oui?" she asked as she closed the door and then leaned toward him. "An you knows, ve shor did miss you las veek. Especially zhe Sjudge an Miss Melindsa!"

"Well, I certainly," he began only to stop and turned to the gruff heavy drawl that came from the far end of the foyer.

"Well young man," the Judge's commanding tone resonated from the double doors of the library. "It's about time you rescued me from this confounded sea of females."

"Judge!" Foster exclaimed as he began walking toward him. "It's good to see you sir."

"You too son," the judge replied with an extended hand. "But dammit Foster," he quickly insisted as they shook. "How many times do I have to tell you to call me Robert when you're here. You know how it is; here I'm Robert. In public or the courtroom, I'm Judge McAlister, so remember that next time will ya. Now come on before the women find out you're here," he finished and placed his hand on Foster's shoulder then turned toward his library. "You look thirsty."

The size and lavishness of the Judge's library was almost unheard of and true to its intent and design, it served as an intimidating presence to all who entered. Some eighteen feet wide and twenty-eight feet long, with a large fireplace centered on the outside wall, it occupied a sizeable corner of the homes first level. Finished by the finest craftsmen that Mobile had to offer, their work was second to none and stood as a testament to their extraordinary skills.

Entering through a double set of wooden and glass doors onto a pegged and planked hardwood floor, one stood almost center within the room. To the left sat the Judge's massive hand-carved desk with a thick high backed leather chair that sat directly behind it. And surrounding it on all three sides was custom ornate cabinetry and shelving containing his books and pictures and mementos. To the right and at the far end, two giant windows sat a foot from the inside corner, creating a cozy sitting and reading area. Almost twice as wide as they were tall, they began about three feet from the floor and stopped just short of the ten-foot high ceilings. Affording a splendid view of his sprawling estate, they also provided a soothing and much needed light throughout the room. And waiting beneath the massive panes of glass for whoever would use them, two over-sized stuffed leather chairs sat separated by a simple oblong table.

"So tell me," the Judge asked. "Just how've you been?"

"Busy sir," Foster sighed. "Very busy."

"And so I've heard," he turned to Foster with a knowing smile. "Now that wouldn't be because of that Davenport boy now would it?"

"Well," Foster grinned and shook his head. "Actually it is. Or was, I should say."

"Well, I have to tell you, that was really something you pulled off if I don't say so myself. Hell, the word I had was that it was an open and shut case and that Bobby Davenport was really going to do some time on this one. And then all of a sudden," he shook his head. "I wake up and read in the paper that Cyrus Buchanan was dropping the charges and that you're the boy's damn attorney. I'll tell ya, when I read that it really got me to wondering. I don't know how in the hell you did it, but you've sure got a lot of people in town guessing and talking, including me," he laughed then turned toward the custom made liquor cabinet that sat against the wall.

"And I must say, I sure didn't see ol Cyrus lettin go of that one, nooo sir," he shook his head again as he grabbed a couple of tumblers from the shelf. "Especially after that... that little ordeal that him and Katherine had. You remember that, don't you?" he laughed again. "When those two tangled at the mayor's inauguration party," he finished as he threw several chunks of ice into each one then reached for one of the crystal decanters.

"Yes sir," Foster chuckled along with him. "Who could forget that?"

"Well I always thought I had a pretty good insight as to what went on behind the scenes if you know what I mean. But when you pulled that little rabbit out of the hat last week, the only thing I could think of, was one, he really wasn't guilty, or two, you must have been holding some really nice cards."

"Well sir," Foster replied with a modest grin. "Just between me and you, they really weren't that good, but Cyrus didn't know that."

Smiling, Judge McAlister stared for a second and then handed Foster his drink. "Well son, just remember this," he narrowed his eyes and tempered his voice with a deep concern. "You wounded him pretty bad. And I know what kind of person he is and the group that he runs with, so take it from me and watch your back."

"That I will sir... thank you."

"Good, now let's have a seat, shall we."

Crossing the room to the windows, the two men casually took their seats. Swirling his ice in his glass as he settled into his chair, Foster slowly brought the heavy tumbler to his nose and inhaled the malted mixture's aroma. A second later he brought the glass to his lips then closed his eyes and took a sip. Holding the liquor in his mouth for just a few seconds, he savored in its taste and its mild but pleasant burn, then swallowed and exhaled with a satisfied aaah.

"Well son," the Judge asked as he looked on. "What-a-you think? Damn good isn't it?"

Turning toward the man with a grin, Foster held up his glass. "Mother's milk sir," he said with an affectionate smile. "Mother's milk."

"Good, I'm glad you like it cause I sure played hell getting it. You know, with all this damn prohibition crap and all. Came all the way from Aberdeen, Scotland. It's called Chivas, and it's aged twelve years before they even bottle it. Can you believe that? Anyway, after I tried it I had to have some for myself so I went and got me a dozen cases. But now," he chuckled and shook his head. "Now I owe favors to people all the way back to England."

"Well sir," Foster said as he held up his glass. "I think that this is just about the finest scotch I've ever had."

"I agree, but I still think it's missing something?"

"Missing something?" Foster curiously tilted his glass as if the answer was somehow inside. "And what would that be?"

"One of these," the Judge exclaimed.

Raising his head Foster smiled at the sight of the Judge's hand. "Aaaah yes," he agreed with a nod as he immediately reached for one of the cigars. "How could I've forgotten?"

Striking a match, the Judge lit Foster's first and then his own.

"Cuban?" Foster asked as he repeatedly puffed to ensure a good light.

"Nothing but," the Judge answered proudly as he too did the same.

Foster knew the answer before he had asked, but even so in the company of Judge McAlister it was the polite thing to do and he knew it. Then pulling hard on his cigar, he reclined back into his chair, titled his head toward the ceiling and held his breath. Savoring in the richness of the tobacco, he let the nicotine laden smoke work its magic, then slowly exhaled high into the air. "Aaah yessss," he smiled and nodded. "That isss nice. Thank you sir."

Relaxing in the comfort of their chairs, the two enjoyed their smokes and leisurely sipped their drinks as they quietly talked. Mostly about the economy and the effects that it was having on the country, how long it would continue and how fortunate they both had been. And of how if Foster were a Senator or Governor, how he could help institute and bring about change. They also talked of the Davenports and of how in only a few short days their lives had been ruined. It was a first-hand example of the misery that was yet to come for many more, for the depression had only just begun. Pouring a second drink, the two men continued on with their discussion until they heard Melinda calling for her father from a far off room.

"Ought oooh," the Judge cringed as he pulled on his cigar and shook his head. "We're in trouble now son."

"No sir," Foster chuckled and rolled his eyes toward the man. "That would be you sir... you're in trouble."

Acknowledging what he'd said to be true, Judge McAlister nodded with a grin, exhaled his smoke high into the air and then slowly turned back to Foster. "Aaah yesss," he replied with a subtle, yet victorious ring to his voice. "That very well may be, but that's only because she doesn't know you're here yet, just wait."

Both men knew that they should've told Melinda he was here, but what the hell, they were men and they were enjoying themselves. And to them, that was all that mattered. Grimacing at the sound of her footsteps and her insistent calling, they both began to laugh knowing that they would soon pay the price for their silence.

"Daddy," they heard her call again but a little louder and closer.

"I think she's in the dinning room," the Judge said as he turned his head and closed his eyes.

"Daddy, where are you? Supper's almost ready."

"Yep," he nodded and smiled. "Now I'm certain of it. Get ready son, we're next."

"Monique," Melinda asked in a frustrated tone. "Have you seen my father?"

She was setting the table for dinner, but before she could clear her throat to speak, the young mistress of the house had scurried right past her and out the other side of the room. She was talking and rambling on, but to whom Monique really wasn't sure.

"Supper's almost ready and I can't find Daddy. And Foster's not here either," her voice faded into the maze of the other rooms. "And everything's just going to be ruined."

Quietly listening, Monique smiled with the last plate still in her hand and patiently waited for what she knew was coming next. A few moments later and true to her intuition, she heard Melinda squeal from inside the library.

"Daddy! Foster?" she cried as she barged through the double doors of the library to find the two men sitting in the chairs. Waving her arms as if she were clearing the air, the exasperated girl stomped straight toward the windows and threw them open, Then turning back to Foster and her father, she instantly dropped into a diatribe. Ranting and raving as to why no one had told her that Foster was here, and smoking in the house. She went on for several more moments until she'd ran out of breath. "Well?" she declared as she planted her hands on her hips.

Grinning at his daughter, Judge McAlister took a short sip of his drink then turned to Foster who was pulling on his cigar. Looking at one another as if one were politely waiting for the other to speak but then didn't, they finally shrugged their shoulders and looked back up to Melinda.

"Well what?" They both said in unison as they began to laugh.

They were antagonizing her and she knew it, and now incensed by their uncaring actions, Melinda stomped her foot and stormed from the room.

Grimacing as the door slammed behind her, the two men continued to chuckle until the sound of Melinda calling for her mother resonated back through the doors. "Well son," the Judge said as he took one long last pull on his cigar and then snuffed the remaining half of his stogie into the ashtray. "I guess that means dinner's ready. What-a-you think?"

"I do believe you're right sir," Foster replied with a nod as he did the same.

Rising from their chairs, the two men crossed the room to the bar, downed what was left of their drinks and then left the library. But their journey to the table didn't last long before they saw Mrs. McAlister marching straight toward them. A few years younger than the Judge, the former debutante and mother of three had aged well over the years and played her role as a Judge's wife with a demure and dignified grace. She was everything she was suppose to be, but as they met in the hallway, it quickly became clear that she had no qualms in asserting her role within their household.

"Roberrrrt," she called as if to imply that that's enough with Melinda, and dinner is ready so get your ass in here. "What is the meaning of this?" she asked only to change her tone as she gazed beyond him. "Well hello Foster," she smiled and stepped past her husband to give him a hug. "It's so good to see you again," she added with a squeeze. "You know, we sure did miss you last week."

"Yes ma'am," Foster replied as they separated and she held him at arms length. "And I missed being here too."

"Well, I'm glad to hear that, and I'm glad you're back too. Now come on," she said as she spun and hooked her arm in his. "Supper's ready."

Escorting the two men into the formal dinning room, she quickly excused herself to find Melinda and Monique. "Now you two just have a seat and I'll be right back."

Pulling a chair from the end of the table, Judge McAlister took his usual seat at the head while Foster took his to the right and centered within the long section. A short moment later, and before the two could actually get settled, Martha returned with Monique and Melinda.

Following one behind the other with a steaming bowl of food in each hand, they watched with salivating grins as Melinda, the last to enter, walked in with the main course of their banquet. A golden brown prime rib-roast that'd been cooked to absolute perfection. Encrusted in a thick crispy coating of its own natural juices, it was without a doubt a true testament as to her culinary skills.

Beaming proudly as she set the white oversized deep-dished platter on the table, she stepped back as if she'd just finished the final act in a play and then spread her arms.

"Oooh Melinda," Foster grinned as he leaned toward the roast and inhaled its wafting aroma.

"You've outdone yourself this time baby," her father said proudly.

"Daddy," she said as she pulled a butcher knife from the side of the platter and presented it to her father. "Would you like to do the honors?"

Dinner was a feast fit for a king with conversations that floated from politics and the economy, to cattle, to even some playful ribbing about marriage and grandchildren. Afterwards, a leisurely stroll to the barn in an effort to walk off their meal afforded Melinda and Foster some time to themselves. A half-hour later, after viewing her new quarter horse and a little hanky panky in the hayloft, they returned to the house. Later, and along with the setting sun, a light dessert of sherbert on the porch for the women and a snifter of brandy and the rest of their cigars for the men ended their evening.

It had been a wonderful day and as he drove back home, Foster couldn't help but think of Melinda and her blue-blooded pedigree status, and just what it would mean if they were to marry. A moment later, his thoughts fondly shifted to Katherine Davenport and his still sore stomach muscles, a constant reminder of her insatiable appetite. Then with a broadening smile, they drifted to the young girl who he'd just met and the intoxicating allure of her sultry untouched innocence. Aaah yes, what a week it had been, and tomorrow it would start all over again. And with that thought rolling in his mind, he turned onto Spring Hill Road, flipped on his headlights and drove into the dusky light.

Pulling into his driveway some twenty minutes later, Foster shut off his engine and then his headlights. Completely stuffed for the second time in one day, he hauled his ass from the car and made his way into the house then quickly headed to his bedroom. Readied for bed in minutes, he finally crawled between the sheets and dropped his head onto a pillow.

A soft breeze blowing through his windows brought a much welcomed coolness and comfort to the room. It felt great, but as he lay and stared at the ceiling, waiting for sleep to overtake him, his mind continued to whirl like that of a spinning top slowly decelerating. And of all the thoughts still reeling in his head, the one he kept returning to was his visit with the judge in his library and to the sound of his voice. Why, he really wasn't sure, but he did.

'*That's right son,*' the man's gravely growl whispered in his head. '*Senator Siler... has kind of a nice ring to it doesn't it?*'

Subconsciously nodding his head, he listened as it continued to resonate deep within his cerebral core. '*You should think about it, think about it, think about it...*' He was, and as the lingering voice finally faded and disappeared, he smiled and closed his eyes then rolled to his side.

———•———

CHAPTER 18

EARLY MONDAY MORNING FOSTER ROSE and headed straight to his office. He wanted to comprise a list for Otis of the things that Willie would need to begin working. Closing his eyes, he pulled from the foggy remnants of his memory of almost a week ago. A push mower and a sickle, yes. Oh, and an axe, and wire brushes and putty knives. What else? He concentrated. Aah yes, a hammer and nails, and a saw and a ladder. His list went on and on. A shovel and a rake.

Thirty minutes later and right at nine, both Vicki and Dawn came strolling in gibbering with laughter. "Mornin boss," they both greeted in unison.

"Morning ladies," he greeted and glanced up from his list. "Did we have a good weekend?"

"Oh yes sir," Dawn chirped.

"You bet boss," Vicki added.

"Well good, I'm glad to hear that. Now here's what we have for today."

A few moments later they all settled down into their daily grind until Otis humbly walked through the door. "Yesss?" Dawn asked with a wary gaze as she looked up from her typewriter.

Quickly pulling his hat from his head, Otis lowered it to his waist and then slowly stepped forward. "Ye, yes ma'am," he stuttered as he shifted his eyes between the floor and the lower portion of her face. "I, I's here ta see Mister Siler."

"Oh you are now, are you," she replied haughtily. "Well I'm sorry, but Mister Siler doesn't represent negroes. You obviously have the wrong place," she snipped. "But I'm sure if you just turn on around and head on down the street, you'll find someone that can help you. So go on now and be about your way before I call the police, ya hear."

Otis certainly didn't want any trouble with the law, and for a few fleeting moments he just stood where he was unsure of what to do until he finally summoned the courage to speak again. "But I's suppose ta be here at ten o'clock. He said so."

"Who said so?" Dawn glared.

"Mister Siler," he answered emphatically with another step to the counter.

"Oh he diiiid?"

"Yes ma'am," Otis quickly nodded. "He told me ta be here right at ten, I swear!"

Staring at the man with a questionable gaze, Dawn finally rose from her seat. "Well, we'll just see about this," she replied. "Oh, and let me tell ya... ya best not be lyin ya hear," she pointed with a pompous and threatening scowl. "Cause ya know you can be arrested for lyin in a law office, don't you? Just like that," she snapped her fingers and deepened her glare.

"No ma'am. I, I mean yes ma'am," Otis's eyes widened in fear. "But I swear I ain't lyin, honest."

"Well then," she finally said after a moment of thought. "I guess the least I could do is check just to make sure. But you'd better not be lyin to me," she warned with another finger pointed gesture as if to assert her authority. "Or else... ya hear!"

"Yes ma'am." Otis nodded and twisted his hat in his hands.

"Good then you just have a seat over there," she motioned to the chairs against the outer wall as she walked from behind the counter. "And I'll be right back. Oooh," she stopped and turned back to the man. "And don't you move either or I'll have you arrested you hear."

"Now I gotta tell ya Mister Jim, when that little gal got up an told me that I could be arrested for lyin in a law office, well shiiiit, I didn't know what to think or do, an to tell ya the truth, I almost turned around an left cause I sure as hell didn't wanna go to jail. No sireee. But I was certain that Foster had told me ten o'clock, an since I had a wife an a little boy ta feed an needed a job, I took a seat jus like she told me to an waited while she scurried off down hall to his office."

Knocking as she opened the door, Dawn entered and quietly called to her boss. "Foster?"

"Yessss Dawn," he answered without looking up. "What is it?"

"Aah, I really don't know how to say this, but there's a negro out here wantin you to represent him. I told him to go away, but he's insistin you told him to come here. Do you want me to call the police and have him arrested?"

Glancing up from his work, Foster looked at her and then cocked his head. "Whaaat?" he asked as if he'd not heard correctly.

"I said there's a negro outside," she whispered in an urgent tone. "And he's wantin to see you. I think he wants you to represent him."

"Otis!" Foster exclaimed as if he'd forgotten. "Please, send him in will you."

"But he's a negro," Dawn gasped.

"Yes I know, and he works for me now, so send him in."

"He works for you?" Her eyes widened.

"Yes."

"Realllly?"

"Yesss, now send him in."

"Bu, but when'd you get a negro? I didn't know you were even lookin for one."

"Dawn!" Foster growled with an exasperated glare.

"Yes sir, I'm sorry," she hurried with a flustered apology. "I'll send him right in."

Walking back into the reception area, Otis quickly caught Dawn's steely gaze. "Well," she said as she crossed the room and then stopped in front of him. "I've spoken with Mister Siler," her tone still resonating with an aloft superiority. "And it seems as if he does have a few minutes to spare."

"Oh thank you Miss...aah," Otis sighed with relief.

"That would be Dawn. And you would be?" she raised her eyebrows like a schoolmarm.

"I'm Otis," he answered as he rose from his chair. "Otis Brown."

"Well there Mister Brown, if you'd like to follow me, I'll show you to Mister Siler's office."

Following as he was told, Dawn took him to Foster's door. "Mister Siler, your ten o'clock is here."

Scribbling one last note on his list, Foster hurriedly finished and then looked up. "Otis," he finally said as he rocked back in his chair. "It's good to see you again, come on in."

"Will there be anything else?" Dawn quickly asked.

"No Dawn, that'll be all thank you. Oh, but do close the door for me, would you."

"Yes sir."

Rising from his chair as Otis crossed the room, Foster extended an arm toward the chairs in front of his desk. "Otis have a seat," his said. "I have a lot that I want to go over with you this morning."

"Yes sur, thank you. Oh, an Mister Siler," he added as he slowly took his seat.

"Yes?"

"I wants ya ta know that I was here right at ten o'clock jus like you told me ta be."

"You were, were you?"

"Yes sur."

"Well good Otis, that's good, because I not only like punctuality, I insist on it."

"Pun-cho what sur?" he asked with a contorted face.

Foster knew that the man before him wasn't a scholar, but even so he couldn't help but shake his head and wonder. "Punct-u-ality Otis," he chuckled beneath his breath. "That means being on time. I really like people to be on time, it's very important to me."

"Oh, yes sur, I see now. Well I's always on time, always. You can jus ask Mrs. D if'n you wants."

"I believe you Otis," he assured as he took the seat next to him and handed him his list. "Now see what you think of this will you. It's a list of all of the things I think we need to start working on the house up river. Tell me if there's anything else we might need. Oh, and just so you know, I'll start you out at fifty cents a day and not a penny more. Payday is on Friday and you can pick up your money from Dawn at the desk out front okay."

"Yes sur," Otis replied as he stared at the list, only to sigh a moment later and drop it to his lap.

"What's wrong?" Foster instantly asked. "Did I miss something?"

"No sur," he replied. "Well, I mean, I really don't know."

"What-a-ya mean you don't know?" Foster pried.

"Well, it's jus that," he paused and shook his head with an embarrassed expression then handed the paper back to Foster. "That I can't read. I's sorry Mister Siler, but I aint never learnt how. I can do a whole lot of things, but one of the things that I can't do is read... or writes."

"Well then," Foster replied as he reclined back into his chair. "I guess that kind of changes a few things now doesn't it?"

"Yes sur," Otis replied in obvious disappointment. "I guess that means you don't want me workin for ya after all."

"Whoa whoa whoa," Foster laughed. "I said it changes a few things, but now that I know that you can't," he said as he rose from his chair. "Let's go, we have some shopping to do."

"Yes sur," Otis exhaled in relief. "But where's we go'n?"

"Jack's Hardware, where else," Foster replied as he looked down at his newest employee. "Oh, but you do know how to drive don't you?"

"Oh yes sur, I can drive good."

"Good, then let's go."

Walking out into the foyer Foster stopped at Dawn's desk. "Dawn this is Otis, he's going to be working for me now and if he calls or needs anything, I want you to let me know right away, okay."

"Yes sir," she answered with a glance to Otis and then back to Foster. "So are you leaving?"

"Yes ma'am, we're headed to Jack's Hardware," he replied as they headed out the door. "I'll be back in a couple of hours."

Foster had been getting his supplies from Jack's since the day he had arrived in Mobile, and over the course of the years he had become quite good friends with the manager. An older fellow of sorts with a great sense of humor and a boisterous laugh, he had a white haired crew cut along with wire rim glasses set to the tip of his nose. He'd managed the store for years, but what he really liked was fishing. And with the exploits of his latest catch often preceding any purchase, Foster always found a way to haggle over prices as they laughed and joked.

"An that's pretty much how an when I started workin for Foster Siler," Otis finished.

"Well, at least you had a job," Jim replied as he reached into his cooler and pulled an oversized sandwich along with a bag of chips from within. Neatly wrapped in wax paper, he carefully unfolded it and took one half then handed the other to Otis.

"Oh no Mister Jim," Otis shook his head and held out his hand. "That's quite all right, I'm fine."

"No no, dammit, I insist, eat. My wife made it, there's plenty. It's huge, see. Now go on. Besides you can't stop now, shiiit I need to hear the rest of this. Ooh, an one more thing, stop callin me Mister Jim will ya. Shit Otis, it's 1972... besides, it really makes me feel old."

Staring for just a second, Otis finally relented and took the sandwich then smiled and took a bite. Layered with a generous portion of ham, a couple of slices of Swiss cheese, lettuce, tomato and red onion. It had all been lovingly placed between two thin slices of fresh rye bread, and was truly nothing less than a work of art.

Throwing the opened bag of chips between them, the two men casually ate their lunch in quiet as the auction rambled on at a frantic pace. A few minutes later and after they'd finished, Jim stuffed everything back into the empty bag of chips, opened the cooler and pulled two more beers from the bottom. Handing yet another one to Otis, he reclined back against the side of the boat, wiped his mouth with the back of his hand and grinned. "Now, where were we?" he asked like a child in the middle of a fairytale.

Chuckling and shaking his head as he took the beer, Otis popped its top then looked to the sky as he once again recalled the past and slowly drifted back to the year of 1930. "Aah yess, I remember now," he nodded and smiled as he lowered his head. "We'd jus walked out into that reception area, an after he had a talk with that little gal sittin behind the counter, we was out the door an headed to his house. Then once we got there, I followed him in his old pickup to the hardware store. An that's when I met the manager of the store an a man that became one of my best fishin pals for the next ten years; all the way up until the day him an his wife moved out of state."

Pulling into the front of the store, Foster slid from his car then met Otis as he pulled into the spot next to him. "Otis, you stay here till I come and get you okay."

"Yes sur," he replied as Foster turned and walked to the door then disappeared inside.

"Hey you ol son-of-a-bitch you," he hollered down the isle.

Spinning around to the familiar voice, the aging storekeeper smiled brightly. "Well well wellll, Foster Siler," he boomed back. "Where in tar-nation have you been hidin? Hell, I gave you up for dead weeks ago," he laughed as he met and took Foster's hand. "How've ya been my friend?"

"Good," Foster replied. "And busy."

"Well, I wish I could say the same," Guy shook his head in dismay. "But I'll tell ya, business is slow. Ain't nobody buyin nothin with the economy the way it is. But," he sighed. "We'll get by somehow, we always do."

"Well, maybe I can help you out a little," Foster said with a grin. "I just bought an old house up river a ways and I'm wanting to do some work on it. And I'm gonna need a whole bunch of stuff."

Delighted by the news, Guy smiled again and then puffed out his chest. "Well you certainly came to the right place. What-a-you need to get started?"

Pulling his list from his pocket, Foster handed it to Guy and the two men began shopping. Isle after isle, they picked over tools and haggled over prices until the counter was overflowing with an array of items. Tallying the total, Foster signed his ticket and then stepped to the door. "Hang on a second Guy, I need to get some help here," he said as he yelled to Otis with a wave. "You don't mind if he comes in do you?"

Curiously looking over his shoulder and out the door, Guy smiled in surprise. "No not at all as long as he's with you, but when'd you get a negro?" he asked. "Hell, I didn't know you was even lookin for one."

"Well I wasn't actually," Foster chuckled. "He just kind of came along with a little deal that I put together last week, and so now here I am. Or should I say, here we are." They both laughed.

"Well, is he a good one? You know, a keeper?" Guy asked, studying the man as he approached.

"Yeah, he is actually. In fact, I kind of like him."

Entering the store, Otis immediately pulled his hat from his head and looked at Foster. "Yes sur, Mister Siler."

"Otis, come here. I want you to meet someone."

"Yes sur," he said stepping forward. "Otis, this here is Mr. Winters. He's the general manager of the store and the man I always deal with here."

Humbly stepping forward, Otis clutched his hat and nodded his head. "I's pleased ta meet ya Mister Winters, I'm Otis... Otis Brown."

"You too Otis, you too."

"Guy," Foster said. "I'd like for Otis to be able to get most of the things I need over the next couple of months if it's okay with you."

"Sure Foster, no problem at all. All he has to do is use the back entrance on the side over there. You know, for the colored, an just ring the bell. An if you wanna run an account an have him sign for everything, that's fine with me too. Your credit's good here, you know that."

"Aaah thanks my friend, I really appreciate that. Now Otis," he turned toward the man. "Let's get this stuff in the truck."

It took only a few minutes for the three men to haul everything from the counter to the truck and as soon as they'd finished, Foster thanked Guy once again and then turned to Otis. "Otis," he said as he did a final check of the load. "I want you to take this stuff over to the marina and load it all on the boat. And if I'm not there by the time you finish, I want you to just wait for me okay."

"Yes sur boss."

"I have to stop at the grocery store and then I'll be right there." Then, with a friendly goodbye to Guy, the two were off in separate directions. A half hour later, Foster finally pulled his car into the marina parking lot. A short walk down the pier found Otis in the back of the boat busily arranging the tools onboard.

"How we doing Otis?" Foster hollered as he approached.

"Good boss, good," he replied. "I jus about got everything on board."

"Good, then here, take this." Stretching his arms outward, Otis reached over the side of the boat and took the heavy box of canned and packaged goods. "Just set it on the table down below and then come with me. I want you to help me with the rest of this food."

"Yes sur, boss."

Several trips later, they finally had everything on board. "Okay Otis," Foster said as he set the last box down. "You'll have to finish up here by yourself cause I've got to get back to work. Now I want you to organize everything real neat and when you're done, close the boat up and then go back to my house. Then when you get there, I want you to go around to the side shed and get the push mower and rake. Cut the grass and clean everything up, and I think that should pretty much finish out your day. I may even make it home before you leave, but don't count on it."

"Yes sur," he replied as Foster stepped off the boat. "An so where you wants me tomorrow?"

Abruptly stopping, Foster turned then paused in a moment in thought. "Aaah, why don't you just come by the house around eight and bang on the door. I'll be getting ready for work and we'll get you started," he finished then turned back around.

"I'll be there boss," he replied as the man walked away.

Later that afternoon, Foster returned home to find Otis still working and his once shabby yard now a neatly manicured lawn. "Otis, you're still here," he beamed from the car as he shut it down.

"Yes sur boss, but I'm almost done an then I really needs to be on my way if'n it's okay. It's gettin kind of late and I gots me a real long walk to get home."

"Well, it sure looks good," he said, grabbing his briefcase from the seat. "You've done a fine job."

"Thank you," Otis replied.

"So just where is it you live that you have so far to go?" he asked as he closed the door and began walking toward the house.

"On the south side, out on Halls Mill Road," he replied.

"The south side? Jesus Otis, that's almost ten miles from here. Hell, it'll be pitch dark by the time you get home."

"Yes sur, but I aint got much choice."

"Well," Foster said as he abruptly stopped and turned to the man. "Why don't you just go ahead and pick everything up now. We can finish all of this tomorrow, okay. I'm gonna go in and change, and when I come back, how about if I just take you home tonight. How's that sound?"

"Oh, yes sur boss," Otis replied enthusiastically. "That sounds great. I'll clean up right away."

Returning a short while later to a waiting Otis, the two climbed into Foster's car and after a twenty-minute drive, he dropped him off in front of a rambled old shack. "Now I'll see you at eight, right?"

"Oh, yes sur, I'll be there right on time, I promise," he said as he closed the car door and then turned to his pregnant wife and three year old son standing in the doorway.

Driving away, Foster watched Otis in his mirror. A loving kiss from his wife and an affectionate hug from his son made him smile.

Right at eight the next morning, Otis rattled Foster's front door with a heavy knock. "Morning Otis," Foster said as he opened the door and greeted the man. "You made it, come on in."

"Mornin boss," he replied and stepped inside. "An yes sur, it was a long walk, but I made it."

"Well good, I'm glad, I really am. Now follow me, I have some things I want to go over with you." Returning to the kitchen, Foster poured a cup of coffee then turned to Otis. "Coffee?" he asked with the pot still in his hand.

"Oh yes sur, I mean, if'n it's okay."

"It's okay," Foster chuckled. "Now have a seat."

Reviewing his list while they drank their brew, Foster repeated it until Otis had memorized it. Finish here at the house and then take the pickup to Jack's for a few more things. Then head to the marina and clean and finish loading the boat. After that, gas it up so it's ready to go, and when you get that all done, come by the office. Reciting it one last time just to be sure, the two men downed their coffee then rose and headed out the door.

Completing his duties one right after the other, Otis finished early that afternoon then drove to Foster's office like he was told. Quietly entering, he pulled his hat from his head then stopped and stared at the two women behind the counter. Bent at her waist, Vicki stood behind Dawn sitting in front of her typewriter. Looking over her shoulder, the two were concentrating on a letter and were unaware that Otis was even there until he cleared his throat.

"Oh I'm sorry," Vicki said as she turned and looked up. "We didn't hear you," she added but then suddenly stopped and pushed her glasses back onto her nose. "Aaah, I think you have the wrong place," she said in a stern voice. "Mister Siler doesn't represent negroes."

Glancing up, Dawn smiled at the sight of Foster's newest employee. "Oh no Vicki, that's Otis. He works for Foster now."

"Whaaat?" She scrunched her face and turned back. "He works for Foster? Really?"

"Yep."

"You're kiddin?"

"Oh no."

"And just when'd he get a negro?" she asked, her voice resonating her surprise.

"Well, I'm not really sure, but I think it was yesterday while you were at school."

"Well I'll be damned. Heck, I didn't know he was even lookin for one did you?"

"Nope," Dawn shook her head innocently. "I didn't have a clue, but he got him one yesterday, see. There he is. His name's Otis, Otis Brown," she said as she turned her gaze toward him. "And Otis, this here is Miss Vicki. She's Mister Siler's paralegal, and in case you don't know what that is, that's a great big fancy word for a real smart secretary."

Stepping forward with his eyes slightly lowered, Otis nodded politely. "I's pleased ta meet ya Miss Vicki."

"Well you too Otis," she said, gauging the man with a critical eye.

"Otis," Dawn interrupted. "Did you need something?"

"Oh yes ma'am," he began with another step toward them. "Mister Siler told me ta come here after I was all done with my work. So here I am."

"Well Mister Siler is on the phone right now, but just as soon as he's done, I'll let him know that you're here okay."

"Yes ma'am. Thank you."

"So just have a seat over there and make yourself comfortable."

Five minutes later, Otis was in Foster's office and after he'd reviewed his day's work, Foster rocked back in his chair and slipped his hands behind his head. The man, from what all he could tell, had turned out to be an honest hard worker and one that clearly appreciated his job. "Otis," he finally said. "I've been thinking. You know that walk that you have to get from your home to here?"

"Yes sur."

"Well that's really something, and I know you've got to be tired by the time you get here so I'm gonna do something that I don't usually do and let you take the truck home tonight. See, that way, you'll have a way to get back here in the morning and you won't be so tired."

"You mean it boss?"

"I sure do. Why, you're not going to run off with it are you?" He chuckled.

"Oooh, no sur."

"Well good, then go ahead and take it. But just remember it isn't for running around. It's to go home and come back in only, right?"

"Oh, yes sur."

"Good. In fact," he suddenly added as if he were contemplating another thought. "Why don't you just start using it from now on? You know, to come back and forth in and do my running."

"Ye… yes sur, are ya certain boss?"

"Yeah yeah, I'm certain. Hell, the damn thing just sits in the yard, so somebody might as well use it. Just don't wreck it hear."

"Oh, thank you boss," Otis beamed. "An I won't, I promise."

"Good, now get on out of here and enjoy the rest of your day with that wife and boy of yours cause tomorrow we're going to take the boat up river and we'll more an likely spend the night."

"Yes sur," he grinned and rose from his chair.

"Good, then I'll see you in the morning."

A half hour later Foster finally put the finishing touches on his closing arguments for Friday afternoon's court case. Content that his argument was certain to win a verdict, his thoughts soon drifted to the beautiful young girl that he'd left waiting at the boarding house. God this was going to be fun, he thought. She was so young and innocent, yet so incredibly beautiful. He smiled at the promise of things to come but suddenly, and as if the forces of uncertainty had just taken hold, he panicked at the thought that she might not be there. His heart raced, and his mind whirled. She had to be; surely she would wait two days, wouldn't she? After all, he was Foster Siler. And then he thought of Connie. Oh my God! What if she'd known where she was staying and had gone to her? She could and would ruin everything, for deep down, she still blamed him for the death of her niece.

Unable to shake his thoughts, that somehow she would find and persuade the girl not to go with him, he rose from his desk. He had to see Willie and make sure she would still be there tomorrow. Nothing else mattered, and with that single thought consuming his mind, Foster grabbed his suit coat and headed out the door. Dropping into his car, he started the engine then backed from his spot and took off down the street. Several minutes later he turned down the street to the boarding house to find Willie still there, working in the yard with an older woman.

Slowing as he approached, Foster prepared to honk but then froze in a moment of disbelief. Oh my God, he cringed as the blood instantly drained from his head. How could he have been so blind, so stupid? Why hadn't it registered? Why hadn't he picked up on it? He was a lawyer for Christ's sakes and this was inexcusable. Hell, she'd even told him, '*Shelda's boardin house.*' He shook his head, and with their backs still to the street, he pressed on the gas and slowly passed.

Now what was he going to do? Did the woman know? He shuddered in dismay as he drove to the end of the street. Had Willie told her about him and what they were doing? His blood pressure rose, and then dropped at his own stupidity. He shook his head once again as he tried to devise a plan, for the woman next to Willie hated and despised him even more than Connie. And for good reason too, she was Connie's older sister Shelda. The mother of a girl he'd once dated and bedded years ago. A girl, who in a sad emotional breakdown over her unwed pregnancy, had tragically taken her own life. Distraught and unable to cope with her troubles, she had, while everyone else was at church one Sunday morning, hung herself from the rafters of their family barn.

It was a senseless death, but ever since the two women had blamed him. Insisting openly that he was the father of her unborn baby and that had he done the right thing and married her, she would still be alive. But it was a contrived story, for Shelda had known that her daughter was pregnant long before she'd even been with Foster. She'd done it along with Connie in an attempt to secure a better life for her daughter and Foster knew it. He even argued against them, for if there was one thing that he knew, it was that Betsy Burns laid down easy, and in the course of her short young life, there had been many a men who'd known her.

Slowly driving once around the block, Foster finally returned from the other end of the street then pulled to the side three houses down and parked behind another car. Wiping the palms of his hands on his pants, he waited and watched until Shelda suddenly turned and handed Willie her rake then went inside. It was the break he'd been waiting for, and without a second's hesitation he started his car and pulled down the street. Stopping in front of the house he leaned out of his window and called to Willie in a hushed but urgent voice.

"Oh Mister Siler," she turned, then dropped her rake and trotted to his car. "What are you do'n here?" she asked excitedly. "I thought you were gonna pick me up tamorrow."

Smiling at those few simple words, Foster knew in an instant that she knew nothing, but still he played his game and led her on. "Well Willie, I am," he reassured. "But I just wanted to come by and tell you that I have to pick you up a little earlier than what we'd talked about."

"You do?"

"Yes, about ten o'clock if that's okay."

"Oh shor, that's jus fine. But is everything okay?"

"Oh, heavens yes," he nodded and smiled. "Everything's just fine."

"Well okay then, I'll jus tell Miss Shelda when she comes back out that I'll be leavin in the mornin an I'll be ready."

It was most certainly the right thing to do, but not what Foster wanted to hear and with a feigned expression of shock he rolled his eyes and began to shake his head. "Oh no Willie," he cringed. "You can't, I mean, I really don't think that I would if I were you."

"You wouldn't?" She lowered her voice and leaned inside the car a little more.

"Oh nooo."

"But why not?"

"Well," Foster began with a cautionary glance behind her. "You do know that I'm a lawyer, right?"

"Yes sur."

"Well, I've heard that when this Shelda lady finds that out some-one is leaving, she goes and charges them for an extra day. Can you believe that?" Watching as her eyes widened, Foster knew that he was on the right track. "And then if you don't pay her, she has the police come and arrest you and throw in jail."

Gasping at the news, Willie raised her head from inside the car and then slowly turned toward the house. "Well, that ain't right. Heck, I shorly ain't gonna say nothin to her now. Shoot, that'll cost me another thirty cents."

"Good Willie, that's good," he said as he started his car. "Cause I'd sure hate to have to come and get you out-a that ol nasty jail. Now I've got to run okay. So you just keep quiet and I'll pick you up right here at ten okay."

"Yes sur," she said as she stepped back from the car and he began to roll. "I'll see you at ten."

CHAPTER 19

WEDNESDAY MORNING BROUGHT OTIS KNOCKING on Foster's door right at eight. After a cup of coffee and some instructions, the two men headed out on their separate ways. Otis, now with some money from Foster, was off to the icehouse for a couple of blocks of ice and then on to the boat. Foster, in an effort to organize today and tomorrow for the girls, headed straight to his office. A half hour later, Dawn and Vicki came strolling in and for the next forty-five minutes he worked with them and gave them their workload for the next two days. Shortly after that, he changed into his work clothes and bid them farewell. "See you girls on Thursday," he said as he headed out the door.

Crossing the street to his car, he looked to the sky and spread his arms then twirled and embraced the day. God, it was beautiful, and with a nice gentle breeze from the north, it just couldn't get any better, especially for the end of August. He felt great, and as he opened his door and slid behind the wheel, he grinned in anticipation for in just a few minutes he would have Willie beside him.

Turning onto her street, Foster smiled with relief at the sight of Willie standing on the sidewalk. Yes, she was waiting just like she'd said, but before he could even make it half way down her street, he saw her turn and glance back toward the front door. Oh my God, he cringed and inhaled a breath. Was Shelda there? Did she know? Was she coming out?

Tooting his horn as he approached, he gained her attention then quickly pulled to a stop in the middle of the street. Looking out through the passenger window, he hollered and then gestured with his hand. "Come on Willie," he said hastily. "Let's go!"

Gleefully responding, Willie grabbed her sack from the sidewalk and bounded toward the vehicle. Hopping into his car, she threw her sack between them and closed her door then turned to Foster. "Let's go," she said enthusiastically.

"Yes ma'am," Foster replied and stomped on the gas.

Speeding away as if they'd just robbed a bank, Willie thrilled in the excitement of her new and unknown destiny. Squealing around the first corner, Foster slowed slightly then turned to the smiling young girl. "Well," he asked. "Did that Shelda lady give ya a hard time this morning?"

"Oh nooo," Willie waved her hand in a dismissive gesture. "She's still sleepin, or should I say still in bed. She had a visitor last night if'n you know what I mean. An they stayed up real late an got real drunk. So when I got up this mornin I made shor I was real quiet. An after I got all packed, I went on down stairs an got me some break-fast an then jus left."

Raising his head ever so slightly, Foster smiled to himself then pressed back down on the gas. Her words were music to his ears, for now he knew with an almost absolute certainty that no one knew where she was going, or for that matter, who she had gone with. She was his now, and by the end of the day he would have her quietly tucked away up river.

Ten minutes later, the two pulled into the municipal wharf and parked. Exiting the car, Willie slowly looked around while Foster opened the trunk. She was in awe, for never in her life had she dreamed that any-thing like this existed. It was amazing, but after a moment she grabbed her shoulder sack from the seat and went to the back with Foster.

"Here Willie, take this," he said, handing her a box of canned goods. "I'll get this other one and then Otis can come back and get the rest of this stuff."

"Otis? Who's Otis," she asked.

"Otis," he said as he bent down and pulled the other box from the trunk. "Is my captain. Come on, you'll meet him in just a minute."

"A captin, what's a captin?"

Chuckling at what was clearly an innocent question, Foster just shook his head and started walking. "Aaah Willie," he replied with a glance to the sky. "You most certainly are a precious one aren't you, but let me explain. A captain you see is a person that drives and takes care of the boat. And Otis is my captain."

"So is he the one who's gonna take us up river?" she asked as she dutifully followed.

"Yes ma'am, just as soon as we get things loaded and get on our way."

"Oh good, this'll be fun. So where's your boat?"

"Right there," Foster replied with a nod. "That white one with the little row boat on top."

"Oh my lordy," Willie gasped as she slowed her walk and then stopped along side the boat. "This is your boat?"

"Yes ma'am," he replied as he set his box down. "You like it?"

"Oh heavens yes. It... it's beautiful."

Grabbing the stern line as she stood with her box in her arms, Foster pulled the boat toward them and then turned back to Willie. "Well then, just wait until you see the inside," he added as he turned back and called to Otis.

"Otis, we're here!"

"Yes sur boss," Otis hollered from inside. "Be right there."

A few seconds later, he appeared in the stern. "Here, grab that box will ya," Foster grunted with another tug to the line and a nod toward Willie.

"Yes sur," he said as he reached out and took the box then turned and set it down.

"Now Willie," Foster said as he grabbed her hand and motioned with his head. "It's your turn, let's jump on board."

Doing as she was told, Willie stepped on the edge and then dropped into the stern. Jumping onto the pier with the boat still close, Otis quickly grabbed the other box then returned and set it with the other. Releasing the line as soon as Otis was onboard, Foster stepped onboard and joined them.

"Otis," he said as he dropped between them. "This is Willie, Miss Willie Mae Dawson. She's going to be staying at the house for a while to work on it. And Willie, this is Otis. He's our captain. He's the one who's gonna see that we get up and down the river okay."

Quickly removing his hat, Otis nodded and smiled. "I's pleased ta meet ya Miss Willie."

"You too Mister Otis," she drawled and extended her hand.

"So wait a minute," Jim interrupted. "Was that the first time you met her? This Willie gal?"

"Yes sir," Otis fondly replied. "I remember I'd jus come out of the cabin here when I saw her. She was holdin a box of food that Foster had told me to grab. Now at first I thought that she was jus helpin out an that it was jus me an Foster that was runnin all that stuff up river. But after she'd jumped on board an he introduced us, I knew right then an there that that wasn't the case. An even though I had no idea as to who she was or where he'd found her, I kind of knew right off that he wasn't jus puttin her up there to work on that house."

"Okay Otis, are we all ready?"

"Yes sur boss," he replied. "I got everything ready jus like you wanted."

"Good, then all we need to do is finish loading and we're off. There're a couple of small boxes still in the trunk and some clothes in the back seat. Grab them and then lock everything up."

"Yes sur boss, I'll go an get em right now."

"So Willie," he said as Otis jumped off the boat. "Would you like to see the inside?"

Nodding excitedly, Willie followed as Foster stepped toward the cabin. Ducking beneath the doorway, he dropped into the salon then turned and reached for her hand as she did the same. Standing next to him between the two sofas, he released his grip then watched as she quietly looked around.

A few moments later, the young girl from Hale County slowly and silently began making her way through the cabin. Lightly grazing the walls and panels with the tips of her fingers as if to let the boat know she was there, she stopped with the most wondrous of smiles and turned back to Foster.

"Go on," he nodded for her to continue.

Slowly turning back, Willie proceeded to explore. Opening drawers and cabinet doors, then softly closing them, she continued on until she stood center in the galley and stopped. Then spinning to the door behind her, she curiously looked up and down and then slowly pulled it open. "Aah!" she cried out. "It's a, a...," she turned to Foster with a perplexed expression.

"Yes Willie, it's a toilet," he quickly assisted.

"In a boat?"

"Yes ma'am, in a boat."

"Oh my lordy," she drawled with a heavy breath. "We didn't even have one in our house, an you have one in your boat."

"Yes ma'am," he grinned. "I mean, you do kind of need one when you're out here."

Looking back into the tiny room, Willie gazed at the white porcelain apparatus then finally closed the door and turned back to Foster. "But how's it work," she asked and scrunched her face. "It aint got no hole. Where's everything go?"

"It's a marine toilet Willie," he chuckled and shook his head. "I'll show you how it works later."

"Well, who in the heck ever thought of that?" she queried curiously. "That shor is somethin."

"Yes it is," Foster chuckled again. "Now come on, let me show you the rest."

Taking the two steps up into the pilothouse, Willie followed Foster into the area where Otis did his job. Surrounded on three sides by large panes of glass affording great visibility, smaller ones to the rear were set up high overlooking the roof of the salon. A glass door on each side allowed easy access to and from, and on the forward wall, was a center console with a large wooden ships wheel and a small cluster of gauges. Directly behind that, sat a tall wooden chair.

Gravitating straight toward console, Willie grabbed the spokes of the wheel with both of her hands then rocked back and forth as if she were steering. "Is this where Mister Otis drives the boat?" she asked with a glance to Foster.

"Sure is," he replied.

"Well do you think I could drive it sometime? I mean, you think he'd let me?"

"I'm sure if you asked him he would."

"Oh wow," she smiled as she returned her gaze out front and continued to rock the wheel. "I'd like that." She was having fun but there was still more to see, and with a curious glance to where Foster was standing she suddenly stopped. "But what's down there?"

"Where?"

"There," she pointed at the steps leading down.

"Oh, that's the front. It's for sleeping if you stay out all night."

"For sleepin, can I look?"

"Sure Willie," he said as he stepped back. "Help yourself."

Curiously descending into the lower cabin, Foster couldn't help but smile as her astonished voice rolled up from below. "Oh my Lord. It's a bed! You have a bed in your boat! An closets an drawers for you clothes."

"Yes I do," he answered as he descended the steps and joined her. "You like it?"

"Oooh my," she nodded as she curiously stepped toward another door and then pulled it open. "Whaaat?" she cried out. "Another one. You have two toilets? Oh my gosh, I never dreamed..." Her voice trailed off as she gently closed the door and then turned her attention back to the bed. Slowly brushing her hand across the bed-spread, she finally turned back to Foster. "So if this is for sleepin, do you think I could sleep here some night?" she asked dreamily.

"Sure Willie," he replied as he stepped toward her. "If that's what you'd like. Heck, I'll even tuck you in if you want," he teased.

Gaining an instant smile, Willie suddenly blushed and looked away for although young and naive, she knew what he'd meant. Yet even so, she liked the idea of him tucking her in. It appealed to her immensely, and made her feel warm and safe inside. And although she wanted nothing more than to say something grown up, she didn't, for in her moment of fluster, she knew neither how nor what to say. And now uncertain of what to do, she awkwardly dropped her gaze to the floor and cleared her throat then shuffled her feet.

The silence that followed, although not more than a couple of seconds, was unbearable and seemed to Willie as if it went on for-ever. That was, until it was finally broken by the sound of Otis land-ing in the stern. "I'm back boss," they heard him holler.

Sighing with relief, Willie finally turned back to Foster only to be greeted with a grin as though nothing had transpired. "Good Otis," he turned and yelled. "Be right there," he added as he turned back to Willie. "Now come on," he said. "Let's go help Otis so we can get the hell out of here."

Stacking the boxes and clothes inside, Foster and Willie then jumped onto the pier and untied the boat as Otis started the engine. Pulling it to one side, they threw the lines onboard and held it steady until the engine had warmed and Otis stuck his head out of the doorway. "Okay boss," he hollered. "I's all ready."

"Okay Willie," Foster yelled. "Push the boat from the edge and jump onboard."

Quickly joining Otis up front, the two watched from behind as he held the wheel steady until the stern of the boat had cleared the end of the pier. Then turning it hard to starboard, he eased the throttle forward and the three on board slowly made their way out of the channel and toward the open harbor.

Stepping forward, Willie took a spot next to Otis and watched as the sights and scenery unfolded before her. She was enthralled, and as they proceeded out and into the open waters of the harbor, she began to tiptoe up and down and sing. Ooo, ooo, oooh, I'm in-a bo-ooat." She sang and bobbed her head. "I'm in-a bo-ooat."

Her lyrics were simple, yet before she could sing another verse, Otis suddenly reached up and pulled back on the throttle.

"What's wrong Mister Otis?" she asked, glancing first to his hand on the silver lever and then to his face with a serious gaze directed straight out front. "Why are you stoppin?"

"That's why Miss Willie," he said and nodded toward the open waters of the bow.

"Oooh my Lord," she exclaimed as she bolted out of the door and onto the bow. "It's a, aaa," she stuttered as she made her way to the tip.

"A freighter Willie," Foster yelled from the doorway as she steadied herself against the rail and stared. "It's a freighter."

Cutting in front of them less than four hundred feet away, Willie watched in amazement as the massive five hundred foot long steel hulk slowly passed. Billowing a thick cloud of smoke from its stack high above the water and with ribbons of rust stains dripping from its aged and weathered beaten sides, the once majestic iron lady blasted her horns with a long farewell and made for the open sea.

"Now when ol Willie first looked up an saw that freighter I thought she was gonna fall right over, I'll tell ya you should've seen the look on her face," Otis chuckled. "Her eyes got about as big around as silver dollars an her expression, well, it was jus priceless. But what was really funny was when that big ol ship blasted its horns cause she sure as hell wasn't expectin that.

"Yes sir, when it did that, I thought she was gonna jump right off that bow into the water it scared her so bad. Heck, it was so loud, it even startled me," he laughed at the thought of her reaction then took a sip of his beer. "Anyway after it'd finally passed an was downstream from us, I pushed the throttle forward an crossed her waves then turned the wheel an headed up river."

"But Willie was absolutely mesmerized, an jus as soon as it was behind us, she made her way to the stern an continued to watch it until it'd disappeared. Then, an only after it was gone an she was satisfied that she couldn't see it any longer, she came back up front an joined us. I guess she never realized that anything like that even existed. In fact, it seemed like jus about everything she saw that day was new to her. I'll tell ya, an I really didn't know it at the time, but I guess her whole existence an way of life was jus about as far removed from the modern world as you could of gotten. Anyway, after she came back up she started jabberin an askin questions like you couldn't believe."

A little disappointed that she couldn't see the ship any longer, Willie finally scampered back through the salon and returned to the pilothouse. "Did you see that Mister Otis... Mister Siler?" she asked, turning from one to the other in breathless excitement. "What kind of boat was that? It was huge. Do you know where it was go'n? Oh lordy, I never dreamed there was somethin like that."

"Well Miss Willie," Otis chimed in before she could continue. "That was a freighter, an more-n likely it was headed on down to South America or somewhere."

"South America," she scrunched her face. "Where's that?"

"That's about two thousand miles south of here," Foster interjected. "Across the Gulf of Mexico."

"The Gulf of Mexico? What's that?"

Looking to each other, Foster and Otis just shook their heads. They knew that it was going to be a very long ride but even so Foster tried his best to explain, and after a short and simple lesson in geography that really didn't interest her, Willie set about exploring the boat. Returning to the stern a short time later, she found Foster relaxing in one of the Adirondack chairs and joined him.

"What's ya do'n Mister Siler?" she asked as she plopped down beside him.

"I'm proof-reading a brief for a case I have on Friday," he replied. "It's important to be ready when I go into court."

"Oh, I see," she quipped as if she understood. "An are ya done?"

Sensing her boredom, Foster slipped the papers back into his folder and then laid it on the table. "Yes, I'm done," he replied. "Now tell me, how do you like your boat ride so far?"

"Oh my gosh, it's jus wonderful," she beamed. "I never knew that they made things like this cause where I'm from we didn't have nothin like this."

"An where's that? I think you told me but I forgot."

"Hale County ramember, it's way up north. Heck, it took me a whole day an night ta get here on the train. An the only thing that we had up there was cotton fields. That's where me an my, my momma worked," she suddenly quit talking and looked away. "In the fields afor she died," she finished and then dropped her head. A second later, she pulled herself from her chair and walked to the edge of the boat then folded her arms tightly across her chest.

Gazing at the girl from his chair, Foster watched as she then quietly began to cry. He knew she was hurting and for a few minutes he let her grieve then rose and stepped behind her. "Willie are you okay?" he asked as he gently touched her shoulder.

Turning with a stream of tears running down her face, Willie instantly fell into his arms. "I miss my momma," she coughed and sobbed into his chest. Her grief had returned full force and although she barely knew him, she found a soothing calm in his comforting embrace that seemed to slowly replace it. As if the divine feathery wings of an angel had just wrapped themselves around her and were now pulling the heartache and pain from within her as they held her sorrow at bay.

"I know Willie, I know," he murmured and swayed in an effort to console her. "But you're going to be all right, trust me, I promise. Right?"

Looking up into his eyes, Willie stared for a moment then took in a breath and nodded her head. And although she was slightly embarrassed, she seemed to sense that somehow and in someway he spoke the truth. Why, she didn't know, but she did.

"Good," he said as he brushed her tears away and then changed the subject. "Now, how about if we go and fix ourselves a couple of cokes. How's that sound?"

"A couple of what?" she asked with a sniffle.

"A couple of cokes. You know, a soda."

"Nooo," she shook her head.

"You've never had a soda before?" Foster raised his eyebrows.

"No sur," she shook her head again. "I mean, I've heard of it, but I ain't never had one. Jus water from our well an sometimes milk from one of Mister Johnson's cows, but that weren't very often."

"Well then young lady," he smiled great big. "Come with me, cause you're in for a treat."

Following Foster straight to the galley, Willie watched as he searched the cabinets until he had finally found what he was looking for. "Ah ha, there we are," he said as he pulled the six-pack of bottles from the shelf. "And right here," he looked into the next cabinet. "Are our glasses."

Pulling three down, he set them on the counter then turned in search of a bottle opener and an ice pick. Rummaging through several of the drawers, he finally found them both then turned back to Willie. "Now," he said as held up the ice pick and set the opener on the counter. "Let's see if we can get us some ice, okay."

"Some what?" She cocked her head.

"Some ice," he repeated. Did she just not hear him, or did she really not know what ice was? Surely not, it was ice. Everyone knew what ice was yet as he turned back around and opened the icebox he was instantly proven wrong.

"An what's that?" she asked as he began to chip away at the block. "I aint never had one of them before either."

It was only the simple fact that she was so genuinely sincere that kept Foster from laughing and with that he reached into the bin, grabbed a small clear chunk and turned to Willie. "Here Willie," he nodded and held out his hand. "Ice."

Reaching out, Willie took the chunk in absolute wonder. "It's cold!"

"Yes, that's what ice is. It's frozen water. Now put it in your mouth."

"It's water?" She stared in surprise at the glistening piece in her palm.

"Yes Willie, it's water," he laughed. "Now put it in your mouth before it melts."

Doing as she was told, Willie quickly popped it into her mouth and began to suck and crunch on the chunk until it was gone and her mouth was frozen. "Wow, that was cold," her eyes sparkled in wonder.

"Sure is," he chuckled as he popped the tops on three of the bottles and poured their glasses full. "Now here you go," he turned back and handed her one of the glasses. "Try this."

Still bubbling and fizzing, she listened in wide-eyed amazement then lifted the glass to her nose. "It tickles," she giggled and then looked to Foster.

"Yes, I guess it does," he agreed. "Now go on... try it."

Once again doing as she was told, Willie slowly brought the effervescent drink to her lips and took a sip. Beaming with delight as the flavor invaded her senses, she glanced to Foster then put the glass back to her mouth and took three big gulps. Setting it back down on the counter, she wiped her mouth with the back of her hand and then smiled with a great big grin. It was unlike anything she'd ever had before, but almost instantly she widened her eyes and looked to her chest then emitted a long loud belch.

"Oh my," she laughed in both surprise and embarrassment as she put her hand to her mouth. "I don't know wherrre?"

"It's okay Willie, it's just the carbonation."

"The whaaat?" She scrunched her eyes.

"The carba... oh never mind," he chuckled and waved his hand.

Shaking his head, Foster just reached for the other glass then turned back to Willie and handed it to her. "Here, take this to Mister Otis will you, and then join me in the back okay."

"Yes sur," she answered excitedly as she leaned toward him. "But does he know what a coke is?"

"I'm sure he does," Foster laughed. "But still, I think he'll be surprised."

Smiling brightly, Willie turned toward the pilothouse then called out to the man above. "Mister Oootis, I have a suprise far you."

Watching as the exuberant young girl disappeared up the steps, Foster just smiled then picked up his soda and headed to the stern. Relaxing in the comfort of his chair, he gazed at the slow passing landscape and sipped his drink then watched as the Louisville and Nashville barreled along the river's edge blasting its horns on its way into Mobile. It was a sight he remembered vividly, and with the steady sputtering of the motor clearing his mind, his thoughts soon drifted back to just over a week ago when he'd sat right here with Katherine Davenport. A few moments later and along with the passing of the train, they quickly turned to the beautiful young girl still up front, so all alone and naive, so uneducated, and so very, very unprotected.

She was his now as far as he was concerned, like a rancher's prized thoroughbred filly that'd been found running wild and free in the high mountain meadows, all alone without its mother. That under a twist of unforeseen, but yet very fortunate circumstances had unwittingly been captured and was now being brought to his stable. And just like the wild and free-spirited young filly she resembled, he would take his time and nurture her. As much time as was needed until she trusted him and surrendered her will then allowed herself to be mounted. It would be one of his finest conquest, and with that last simple thought rolling through his mind, Foster took another sip and closed his eyes. Smiling as he envisioned the future and basked under the late morning sun, he savored in his dream world until the sound of Willie's voice brought him back into reality.

"Mister Siler," she called excitedly as she walked through the doorway. "Did you see that train? That was the one I rode on, I'm shor. Oh, an guess what? Mister Otis let me drive the boat!"

"Good Willie," Foster opened his eyes and smiled. "Was it fun?"

"Oh my, yes sur," she nodded. "But after awhile, he said I should get on back here to you. That you'd probably think I might-a fallen over the side."

"Well not quite yet," he laughed. "But I was beginning to wonder. Ooh, and by the way," he said and cocked his head. "You can swim, can't you?"

"Oh, yes sur, I can swim good."

"Good, now why don't you join me and have a seat."

Plopping beside him once again, Willie tilted her glass skyward and gulped the last of her soda then set it on the arm of her chair. "That shor was good," she grinned.

"Well good Willie, I'm glad you enjoyed it. It's a nice drink, isn't it?"

"Yes sur, I ain't never had nothin like that before... ever. Thank you."

"Well, you're quite welcome."

A moment later Foster looked over as she picked up her glass and rattled her ice then put it to her lips. Tilting it skyward once again, he watched as she sucked on what little liquid had melted then slipped a chunk of ice into her mouth.

"So would you like another one?" he asked as she crunched on the cube.

"Oh my gosh," she replied excitedly. "Yes sur, I mean if it's okay," she added politely.

"It's okay," he assured. "Go on, help yourself if you want."

"Yes sur," she said as she sprang from her chair only to suddenly stop and turn back. "Oh, Mister Siler."

"Yes."

"Should I make one for Mister Otis too?"

"No Willie, I think Mister Otis is just fine for right now."

"Yes sur," she said and turned.

Disappearing below, Willie returned a few minutes later with a glass full of ice and an unopened bottle of soda. Taking her seat, she set her glass on the arm of the chair and then turned to Foster. "I forgot how you did it," she said with a shrug as she held up the bottle and opener.

Shaking his head with a smile, Foster casually leaned toward her and then reached for her hands. "Here Willie," he said as he gently took her hands in his. "Let me help you."

Glancing dreamily into his eyes as he concentrated on his task, she caught her breath then quickly averted them back to the bottle. He was touching her and she liked it, and as his hands covered hers in a strong caress, her heart began to flutter.

"First you put it on top like this. Then hook it under the edge and pull up. See… juuust like that."

Smiling as the bottle released its pressurization, Willie slowly raised her head and returned her gaze back to his eyes. She felt drawn toward him in ways she'd never felt before and wanted her moment to continue, but he was finished and had released her hands. Staring eye to eye for just a moment longer, she swallowed hard then bashfully blinked and looked away. She was smitten, and that's all there was to it.

Sensing her discomfort, Foster settled back into his chair as if nothing had transpired then grabbed his papers from the table. And although he secretly delighted in her response, he could see that she needed a moment to compose herself. Picking up where he'd left off, he began to read until he noticed Willie through his peripheral vision as she began to pour her soda.

"Not so fast. It'll..." he tried to warn as the bubbling cola over-flowed onto the arm of the chair and onto the floor.

"Oooh Mister Siler, I'm sorry," she said anxiously. "I didn't know it'd do that."

"That's okay," he chuckled. "It's just soda, it'll clean up," he assured as he rose from his chair and then ducked through the door-way. "Just let me get a towel," he hollered as he disappeared below.

Returning a few moments later, they quickly cleaned up their mess then settled back into the relaxing comfort of their chairs. It was a beautiful day, and as they motored up river and basked in the sun, Foster worked on his brief while Willie sipped on her soda. She was in heaven, and with twelve-mile island now far behind them, she had all but forgotten where she was until the boat suddenly slowed and blew its horn.

"What's wrong?" she asked as she sat up and looked around.

"Oh it's just the trestle for the Louisville and Nashville," Foster answered. "You know, the train. We have to signal it so they can turn the tracks and let us through."

Standing up in wide-eyed wonderment, Willie grinned then watched as the giant mechanical bridge slowly began to turn. "Wowww," she said as they passed beneath it. "How much farther now?"

"Just around the next bend, about another fifteen minutes. Why, are you getting anxious?"

"Anksish?" she turned and cocked her head.

"Yes, anxious," he laughed. "I mean excited."

"Oh heck yeah," she replied as if she suddenly understood. "I can't wait ta see your house," she added as she walked to the side of the boat and looked across the river. "But can I go watch Mister Otis drive again?"

"Sure Willie," he replied. "If that's what you want, that'll be fine."

Grabbing her coke, Willie disappeared through the doorway and left Foster to his own. Fifteen minutes later and just as Otis slowed the boat again, she came scurrying back through the door.

"Mister Siler, we're here," she exclaimed excitedly.

"Yes ma'am," he replied as he looked up from his papers. "I guess we are, aren't we."

Jumping to the side, Willie leaned over the edge and looked forward. "Oh an look, I can see the dock thing," she announced. "An your house too. Is this where I'm gonna be stayin an workin?"

"Yes ma'am, this is it."

Reducing his speed as they approached the pier, Otis veered toward shore and began making his question mark turn. Hitting reverse as they pulled along its edge, he kicked the stern sideways then immediately went to neutral. Bumping slightly as it settled and stopped, Foster grabbed Willie's hand and ushered her to the side. "Come on Willie," he said as they stepped onto the pier. "And go grab the front so it doesn't float away."

Doing as she was told, Willie quickly ran to the front and grabbed the rail. "I got it Mister Siler," she called as Otis stepped out of the door and onto the pier.

Holding two long lines, he promptly secured the front and then the stern. Checking his knots one last time, he stepped back inside and shut off the engine. A moment later he stuck his head back out of the door and looked to Foster standing on the pier. "Now what boss?"

"Let's get everything unloaded and set on the pier first," he answered. "I'm going to show Willie the house and we'll figure out what to do with it when we get back."

"Yes sur boss."

"So you guys finally made it up to the house," Jim asked.

"Yep," Otis nodded. "An jus as soon as we were tied an ol Foster had told me what he wanted done, he turned an grabbed Willie an the two of them started walkin down that pier. I remember he was talkin to her real smooth an casual like with one hand on her shoulder an the other pointin up toward the house. Now like I said before, I kind-of knew he wasn't jus puttin her up there to work on the house an as the two of them walked off of that pier, all I can remember thinkin an hopin was that he jus treated her nice an was good to her. Cause I'll tell ya, I liked her right from the very start."

CHAPTER 20

THE HOUSE, ALTHOUGH NOTHING MORE than a little river cabin that Howard Davenport had used for hunting and fishing, was still four times larger than what Willie had grown up in and had been furnished with an array of creature comforts.

"Mister Otis," Willie called as they returned, her eyes sparkling with excitement. "You should see the house, its huge! An it has beds, big beds. An fernachur, an a kitchen with a sink in the counter with a pump for water right there. An it even has a room with a big tub for taken baths! An Mister Siler says that this is where I'm gonna stay an work. That my job is ta take care of it an fix it up."

"Yes ma'am, Miss Willie," Otis replied. "I knows… it shorly is nice ain't it."

"Oh my lordy, it's jus wonderful," she sighed then turned and gazed dreamily at the house. "An when I'm done," she continued adamantly. "It'll be the prettiest house on the river."

"I'm sure it will Willie," Foster assured with a laugh. "But ain't nothing gonna get done if we don't get this stuff up to the house first. So let's grab some of these tools and get going."

Doing as he said, Otis and Willie followed Foster to the house, set their items outside and then returned to the boat. Making trip after trip under the afternoon sun, they hauled their wares to the house until they had the pier completely empty.

"What's next boss?" Otis asked as he leaned the lawn mower handle against the side of the house.

"Aah, let's see Otis," Foster paused and rubbed his forehead. "Why don't you grab that axe we brought and see if you can scrounge up some wood for a fire? I saw a pit under that big shade tree by the house. It had some blocks around it with a grate on top. Stack it there will you, then clean that pit out and make us a fire. Oh, and make a pretty good one too, I'm going to need a good bed of coals."

"Yes sur boss," he replied with a grin at the thought of the two chickens that Foster had put in the icebox. "I know right where ya means."

"And Willie," he said as he placed his hand on her shoulder. "You remember all those boxes of food that we put in the boat don't you?"

"Yes sur," she nodded.

"Well I need you to bring em all up here, okay."

Nodding her head once again, she was off. Retrieving box after box, Foster stocked and cleaned while Willie delivered until she'd emptied the boat. That was all but the giant block of ice still wrapped in burlap on the floor of the boat and the icebox full of cold goods.

"I think that's all Mister Siler," Willie said as she set the last box on the counter and then brushed her hands in a clapping motion.

"Good Willie, now why don't you help me finish cleaning this ol icebox and then we'll get the rest of the cold food when we're done."

Dutifully grabbing a rag, Willie went right to work. A few minutes later they finished their task and were off to the boat.

"Grab that empty box will you," Foster said to as they headed out the door.

Glancing to Otis as they made their way down through the yard, Foster smiled at the blazing fire and pile of wood he already had. "Looks good Otis," he said as they passed. "But come with us now, I want you to help with this block of ice."

"Yes sur," Otis replied as he threw another stick into the fire and then joined in behind them.

Once in the boat Foster opened the icebox and began transferring its contents to Willie's box. Filling it with everything except the half dozen beers in the bottom, he then pulled out a covered pan and set it on the counter.

"Ah aaah," he declared delightedly. "Dinner!"

"What is it?" Willie asked.

"Yard bird," Foster grinned.

"Yard what?" she scrunched her face.

"Yard bird, Miss Wille," Otis laughed at the look on her face. "You know, buc buc buc."

"Oh yeaaah," she beamed. "You mean chicken. Well, I like chicken."

"Good Willie," Foster chuckled and shook his head. "Cause that's what we're having for dinner. Now here take this," he said as he handed her the box of cold goods. "And Otis," he turned and pointed. "Grab that block of ice and let's go."

Returning to the house, Foster filled the icebox with their ice and cold goods then grabbed the two chickens he'd brought, cut them in half and seasoned them. "Otis," he said as he picked up his pan and headed out to the pit. "You and Willie shuck that corn, then smear some butter on em and bring em out to the fire okay."

"Yes sur boss," he answered as Foster stepped through the door.

From the stoking of the fire to the final results of his culinary efforts, Foster liked just about everything that there was to grilling. It reminded him of his days as a youth on his family's farm, when the colored folks that worked for them would help when they butchered a hog or a cow. Often times receiving the ribs or some other part of the animal as sort of a bonus for helping, they would then take it to their homemade pits and cook it outside.

Using a metal grate that'd been set on concrete blocks over a bed of coals, they would begin the long slow cooking process as they turned their meats again and again and lovingly coated them in a thick spicy glaze. And as they did, the incredible aroma of their food wafting through the air would always call to him and he'd stop and watch. Sampling tidbits here and there, he always marveled at how they'd brought about such wonderful flavors. The old men called it barbecue-in. Why, he really had no idea, they just did. So that's what he called it.

Rummaging through the pile of wood Otis had stacked, Foster picked out a poke stick and then proceeded to spread the coals. Content with the fire, he laid the heavy wire grate on top of the pit then took a seat on one of the empty blocks and threw the chicken on top of the grate. To him, grilling was a work of art and he took immense pride in what he'd learned from the old black men on their farm. A few minutes later, Otis and Willie showed up with their platter of corn.

"Where you want this stuff Mister Siler?" Willie asked as they approached.

"Right here Willie," he pointed to the ground. "Just put it here for now."

"But ain't ya gonna cook it?"

"Sure," Foster replied as he turned the chicken. "I'm going to cook it on the grill here after the chicken is done. See, corn only takes a few minutes on a hot fire."

"Oooh I see," she said. "Well, I ain't never had corn on the grill afor. An I ain't never had chicken on the grill afor either. Heck," she shrugged her shoulders. "I ain't never had nothin cooked on a grill, we always cooked our food on a stove in the house."

"Well Willie," he replied. "Then this afternoon you're in for a treat. Cause I'll tell ya, there isn't anything better than yard bird cooked on the grill. Ain't that right Otis?" He glanced up to the man.

"Ooh, yes sur boss," Otis agreed with a grin.

"See, even Otis agrees," he laughed.

Looking on with an anticipating grin, Willie took a seat on the block next to him and then watched as he arranged and prepared to flip the chicken once again. "Can I do it?" she asked as he reached for one of the birds.

"Sure Willie. But here, let me show you how first."

Flipping one over and then sliding it to a new spot on the grill, Foster positioned the chicken until he had it in just the right spot then handed her the utensils. "See how I did that? Now you try it."

Nodding with a smile, Willie leaned forward with the barbecue fork and knife then proceeded to do just as she was shown. Carefully watching as she flipped and moved the three other pieces, Foster finally rose and took a spot away from the smoke.

Stretching out across the ground, he propped himself up onto one elbow and continued to oversee her progress. "You're doing good," he praised. "But keep em turned so they don't burn."

"Yes sur," she replied, her attention focused solely on her task. "I won't let em burn."

"Good, now Otis," he glanced back up to the man still standing.

"Yes sur boss."

"You remember all of those bottles we put on the ice in the boat this morning, don't you?"

"Oh yes sur," he replied.

"Good, then why don't you go on down and get us a couple. Oh, and while you're at it, get Willie another coke and a glass of ice too."

"Yes sur boss," he said as he turned and headed toward the pier.

"So you guys were just havin a good ol fashion barbecue right there? Jim shook his head.

"Yep, an right after I got back with them two beers an Willie's coke, ol Foster surprised the hell right out of me."

"What-a-ya mean?" Jim asked.

"Well," Otis began as if he still couldn't believe it. "No sooner than I'd turned around to take a seat, than there he was handin me one of those beers back that he'd jus opened."

"Really?"

"Yep. I'll tell ya, he was full of surprises. I mean, there I was drinkin a beer with a white man who was not only my boss, but who was also cookin for me. But jus like when he'd given me that plate of food on the boat, he didn't think nothin of it. In fact, he always was real good to me.

"Anyway, the three of us sat their drinkin an cookin, an after a couple of more trips to the boat, an the chicken an the corn was done, we sat around that fire an ate until we jus about popped. I'll tell ya, ol Willie ate like she had a bottomless pit an by the time she was done, she was an absolute mess. I mean, she had chicken an corn smeared all over her face, but that little gal couldn't of been happier. Then, an not too awfully long after we'd gotten everything all cleaned up, Foster took Willie an went inside to go to bed."

"We'll see you in the morning Otis," Foster said as he stood and then turned to Willie. "Come on Willie, let's go and clean ourselves up for bed."

"Yes sur," she said as she rose from her block and began to follow.

"Oh an Otis," Foster stopped and turned back. "If you want the rest of those beers just help yourself, I'm not going to drink em."

"Yes sur boss, thank you."

"An that's pretty much how our first night on the river ended. Those two went in the house an I headed on down to the boat to drink a few more of them beers an do some fishin before it got to dark. I remember it was real nice out,

but even so them damn fish weren't bitten an after jus a couple of beers an no luck, I grabbed me a blanket an stretched out on the sofa."

Entering the cabin, Foster quickly lit four lamps and then placed them around the house. It was time for bed and after a quick search through his overnight bag he pulled out his toothbrush and powder. Walking to the kitchen sink he proceeded to pump the handle and brush his teeth to a very curious onlooker.

"Is that a reel toothbrush Mister Siler?" Willie asked as he scrubbed away.

"Ah-huh," he mumbled as he bent and spit into the sink then pumped the handle and rinsed his mouth. "Don't you have one?" he asked as he stood and wiped his mouth.

"Oh, no sur," she shook her head. "We couldn't never afford nothin like that."

"You couldn't?" he asked with a curious gaze. "Well you do know it's really important to take care of your teeth, don't you? Come here."

"Oh yes sur," she answered as she stepped toward him. "My momma would cut me splinters of wood an had me rinse my mouth out after every time we ate. She always told me I had a pretty smile an that I should take care of my teeth as best as I could."

"That's good," he said as he slipped a hand beneath her chin. "Now smile for me," he asked with a gentle tug upwards.

Gazing into his eyes, Willie suddenly blushed but did as he asked. He was touching her, and almost instantly her mind began to wonder. Did he like her or was he just being nice?

"Well Willie, I'm afraid to tell you, but I think your mother was wrong. You don't have a pretty smile you have a beautiful smile. But you do need to brush your teeth, so here."

Turning back to the sink, Foster applied the powdery mixture to his toothbrush then turned and handed it to her. Stepping behind her, he then instructed her in how to brush her teeth. A few moments later, she spit and rinsed her mouth into the sink only to suddenly stop at the sight of blood.

"It's okay," he assured calmly. "That's just your gums bleeding. They're not used to being brushed, but that'll change. Now turn around and let me see."

Doing as she was told, she smiled so Foster could see.

"Good. Now come on and let's get ready for bed, we have a long day tomorrow."

Quickly washing their faces, Foster blew out the kitchen lamp and then showed Willie to her room. "Well, here you are," he said as he stepped to the side. "This is your room from now on."

She'd seen it earlier of course, and although it was simple by Davenport standards, to Willie the furnishings were an unheard of luxury. "This is my room," she drawled. "Where I'm gonna sleep?"

"Yes ma'am," he answered.

"Oh my," she went on as she walked to the bed and sat on its edge. "I... I don't know what to say."

"Well you don't have to say anything," he replied as he stepped toward her and slipped a hand beneath her chin. "Just get a good night's rest," he added as he lifted it with the tips of his fingers and stared into her eyes.

Smiling with a quickened heart, Willie sucked her breath then reached up and encircled his fingers with hers. She could feel her attraction growing by the second, and it wasn't just his handsome good looks or the fact that he was rich and a lawyer. He was kind and nice to her at a time when so many things in her world seemed so cruel and mean.

To Foster it was a sign that it was just a matter of time before this woman-child was his. She would come to him just like he wanted, and with that final thought he dropped his hand and turned away. "And I'll see you in the morning," he finished.

Lying in their beds in opposite rooms, sleep eluded them both with thoughts of the other. Tossing and turning in the darkness, Willie's mind ran wild then took flight like an untamed horse she could no longer control. Venturing into the lush green pastures of a fantasy driven lifestyle, she glowed in a euphoric dream like state. The wife of a lawyer... yes! With kids and a car, and a big white house with pillars in front. She smiled to herself in the dark, her mind and body reeling with the ardent desires of a young adolescent woman in the throws of love.

But the thirty-five year old lawyer's were completely different. It had been just over a week since he'd shared the bed he was in with Katherine, and it seemed as if her scent was still there. Or was it? He inhaled deep. Was it his imagination or just his wishful thinking? He rolled to rid his mind of her but it only changed to that of the sultry untouched beauty lying so close. It was almost more than he could endure. His groin ached with the dull and burning desire of need and lust, tormenting his mind and his body. He wanted her in the worst of ways but knew he should wait. He punched his pillow in frustration then tossed and turned as he agonized over his thoughts.

That night, sleep for the both of them, was long in coming.

———◆———

CHAPTER 21

WAKING EARLY THE NEXT MORNING, Foster quietly gathered some wood from outside then built a fire in the kitchen stove and started a pot of coffee. To him it wasn't just a luxury, it was his elixir to life and a must have each and every morning. A few minutes later, he set a pan full of bacon on the stove and poured his first cup just as he Willie emerged from her bedroom.

"Good mornin," she greeted with a sleepy yawn.

"Morning Willie," he turned and took a sip. "Would you like some breakfast? I've got some bacon and eggs here I'm going to cook up."

"Oh my," she replied at the wafting smell of bacon. "Shor... but can I help?"

"No I've got it, but why don't you go down to the boat and get Otis, okay."

Doing as she was asked, Willie scampered away then returned about ten minutes later. "Mister Otis said he'd be right up."

"Good, now here," he said and handed her a plate. "Let's eat on the porch, shall we."

Taking her plate, Willie went outside and was soon joined by Foster. Quietly eating their breakfast, they watched as Otis finally emerged from the boat and then make his way to the house.

"Mornin boss," he said as he approached.

"Morning Otis," Foster replied. "Come on in and have a seat. I've got a plate of bacon and eggs on the stove if you're hungry."

"Yes sur boss," he said as he entered. "Thank you."

"Willie, go in and get Otis's plate, will you. Oh, and be careful it'll be hot."

"Yes sur," she replied as she rose and went inside.

Taking his seat, Otis waited patiently until Willie returned. "Here ya go Mister Otis," she said as she set his plate in front of him.

"Thank you, Miss Willie," Otis grinned as he picked up his fork and knife.

"Now Willie," Foster said as he slid his plate toward her. "Let's go an clean up the kitchen."

Returning inside, Willie put a pot of water on the stove then turned to find Foster brushing his teeth at the sink. Watching until he'd finished, she smiled when he turned and handed her the tooth-brush. "After every meal," he implied as if it was now her turn.

Vigorously brushing without any assistance, Willie rinsed her mouth and sucked her breath then handed the toothbrush back. Grinning as if she had something on her mind, she quickly turned and went to her room. "Mister Siler," she said as she returned and held up a fist.

"Yes?"

"Would you do somethin for me when you go back to town?"

"Sure Willie," he answered with a curious glance to her hand. "What is it?"

"Here," she said with a nod to her fist. "I want you to buy some-thin for me."

"And what's that?" he asked as he reached beneath her hand.

"A toothbrush an some of that powder stuff," she replied as she dropped the coin into his palm.

Taken by surprise, Foster stared at the twenty-five cent piece lying in the palm of his hand for just a moment then quickly reached back and grabbed her hand. "No Willie," he said as he rolled it over and returned her money then curled her fingers back over the coin. "You keep your money and I'll bring you a toothbrush when I come back. I promise, and you don't need to pay me either. It'll be my gift, okay."

"Oh nooo Mister Siler," she argued as she attempted to return the coin. "I... I jus couldn't."

"Yes, you can," he insisted. "I told you, it's my gift. Now let's fin-ish this kitchen," he added as he curled her fingers back around the coin. "And then when we're done here, I want to go over some things I want done around the house while I'm gone."

Dutifully doing as she was told, Willie set the coin on the counter and started cleaning the kitchen. Shortly after they were finished, Foster took her outside and began going over what he wanted done. Cut the grass and clear the brush from around the house. Cut and stack wood for the stove then start scraping the house so they could repaint it. The list went on but soon they'd finished and he was ready to leave. It was getting late, and he needed to get back. Returning inside as Otis and Willie readied the boat, he gathered his things but as he grabbed his toothbrush and powder from the counter, he suddenly stopped and then set them back down. Smiling at the thought of how surprised Willie would be, he turned and stepped back outside then headed to the pier.

"I's ready anytime you are boss," Otis yelled from the pilothouse as he approached.

"Good Otis," Foster replied. "Let's get going, I've got a busy afternoon," he said, throwing his bag into the stern. "And Willie," he added as he undid the stern and jumped in the back. "Untie the bow line for us will you."

Drifting away from the pier along with the current, Otis waited until the boat had cleared the edge then engaged the engine. "Now remember," Foster yelled over the sputtering exhaust as they pulled away. "I won't be back until Saturday okay."

"I know," she replied. "Don't worry, I'll be fine."

"Good, then we'll see you in a couple of days. Oh, and Willie," he yelled again as their distance increased. "I left you a present on the counter."

"A whaaat?" she asked with a hand to her ear.

"A present. On the counter!" he shouted and pointed toward the house.

Turning toward the house, Willie stared for a moment then looked back to the boat. "What is it?" she yelled with a hand to her ear again.

"You'll just have to see when you get there," he yelled back in a voice she could hardly hear.

She wanted to run right up and see what it was but she didn't, she stood on the pier and watched as the boat steadily motored away. A couple of minutes later, she waved with her arm high above her head just before it rounded the first bend in the tributary. Watching and waiting, she smiled at the sight of Foster in the stern waving back just as they disappeared. They were gone, and for a few short moments Willie gazed at the tranquil waterway, her thoughts slowly and quietly drifting like that of the current until she glanced toward the house, smiled great big and bolted down the pier.

Slowly making their way back down and out of the tributary, Otis skillfully navigated the narrow twisting waterway while Foster took a seat and relaxed in the stern. He was really enjoying the boat and was glad he'd taken the Davenport case. But no sooner had he settled into his chair than he sat back up to a sudden splashing and commotion on the river's bank.

What was that, he wondered as he curiously stood and surveyed the muddy bank. Gazing intently at the shore, he finally found its source then watched with a wary interest as a couple of very large gators, not more than a hundred feet away, wrestled over a bloated carcass. A small deer or stray calf perhaps, but what kind of animal he wasn't really sure. A second later, he shivered at the thought of Willie now all alone. He'd never warned her about the dangers of the river. Did she know? They were far enough away right now, but they could move closer. Then turning his gaze back up stream toward the house, he stared with a worried expression stretched tight across his face. An hour later, the two finally pulled into the marina and docked then quickly secured the boat.

"So where's you want me tomorrow boss," Otis asked as he closed the door in the stern and then stepped onto the pier.

"Ah let's see," Foster said, rubbing his chin. "Why don't you just take tomorrow off but be here at nine on Saturday and have the boat ready to go. I want to go back up to the house and do some work and make sure Willie is okay. Oh, and bring some clothes with you cause we'll be spending the night again and we won't come back until Sunday."

"Yes sur boss, I'll see's you on Saturday then. Do you want me ta drive the pickup home again?"

"Sure Otis," Foster said as they began walking off of the pier. "But remember, it's just for back and forth from work. Oh, and another thing, what we're doing up river ain't nobody else's business either, understand?"

"Oh yes sur," Otis assured. "I won't say nothin ta nobody."

A few moments later, the two men got into their vehicles and then went their separate ways. Shortly after that, Foster found himself ascending the stairs to his office until he had reached the top and then stepped inside.

"Oh, you're back," Dawn greeted him cheerfully. "Good afternoon."

"Afternoon Dawn, did we get everything done?"

"Yes sir," she answered proudly. "Everything's done and ready to go, just like you asked. And Vicki's done too. It's all on your desk with your mail. Oh, and opposing council called and they want you to call them as soon as you get in. I think they're scared and want to settle before you go to court tomorrow."

"Oh realllly?"

"Yes sir, and they sounded real anxious too."

"Good," he grinned. "They should be."

———◆———

It was close to three before Foster called opposing council. No deal; their offer was bullshit and he would see them in court tomorrow morning. Later that afternoon, as he continued with the last of his preparations for trial, he heard the phone ring and Dawn pleasantly answer. A moment later she knocked lightly on his opened door.

"Foster, I have Mrs. Davenport on the phone. Can you take her call?"

"Sure Dawn, thanks."

Leaning back in his chair, Foster grinned then put his feet on the desk and picked up the receiver. "Mrs. Davenport," he answered in a professional tone. "Good afternoon. How may I help you? Is everything okay? Bobby?"

"Yes yes, everything's just fine thank you."

"Good, good, I'm glad to hear that. Well then... how can I help you?"

It was a question she couldn't answer for Katherine hadn't called for help or advice, and now just a little unsure of what to say. As to why she really called, she fell silent.

"Katherine?" Foster called after a moment.

"Oh yes... I'm sorry," she began again. "I really don't know... well, maybe I shouldn't have called," she said and then stopped.

"No no," Foster quickly assured. "It's okay, tell me." He probed in hopes that she'd called for something other than a legal issue.

It was exactly what she needed to hear, and with a heavy sigh she slowly began. "Well yesterday they finally called Howard to start his new job, and this morning he and Bobby left on the train for New Orleans. And now since I'm all alone in this big ol house, and all of our so-called friends have suddenly become too busy for me. Well," her voice softened. "I thought that you might like to have dinner with me again? Say tomorrow night?"

Rocking back in his chair a little farther, Foster couldn't help but smile for he knew what dinner really meant. But this time he had to decline for he already had a date with Melinda, and that he wouldn't break even for Katherine. "Oh I'm sorry, I can't. I already have plans for Friday. But maybe..." he lingered on the word as if he were thinking. "Oh never mind," he suddenly dismissed his thoughts. "I, I just couldn't."

"Whaaat?" she asked. "Tell me."

"Well, I was just thinking that maybe I could still come by after-wards, you know, later on in the evening. But," he paused. "It'd prob-ably be way to late and you'd already be asleep."

"Oh no. No, that would be just fine," she answered with an invit-ing anxiousness. "I don't mind at all really," her refined drawl oozed with a seductive overtone. "We could drink a glass of wine or some-thing. You knooow."

He knew what that something meant all right, and almost instantly he could feel the blood in his groin stir. "Well, I guess since you are all alone," he groaned beneath his breath. "The least I could do is come by and check on you. You know, just to make sure you're okay and all. But it may be kind of late, are you sure?"

"Oh Foster," she sighed. "Thank you. And yes, yes I am. I just feel so much better knowing that you'll come by. You can park by the garage again and I'll leave the door to the porch unlocked. And if you don't mind, I'll just wait for you upstairs. You remember where to find me... don't you?"

He did, and for the rest of the afternoon, as he poured over his case, the vision of her lying naked in bed waiting for him haunted his thoughts. He tried to work on his opening statement he would deliver in the morning, but it was just too much. His mind was frazzled, and after another hour of torture, he called it quits and headed home.

———◆———

The next day Foster was in court at ten, and after a long and brutal battle, he and Vicki emerged from the halls of justice around mid afternoon. They were beat but victorious, and as they ascended the steps to his office with their boxes of evidence, Foster's energy seemed to quickly wane.

"Dammit Vicki," he groaned as they started in on the second set. "We've got to get on the ground floor. These damn things will kill you."

"Yes sir, but you like it up top remember. And besides, it's good exercise. You said so yourself."

"I did?"

"Yep."

"Well, I've just changed my mind."

Huffing and puffing, they finally reached the top and entered then plopped the two heavy boxes onto the counter. "Well," Dawn stood and clasped her hands together. "Did we win?"

"We sure did," Vicki beamed as she set Foster's briefcase on the counter. "Foster slayed those big ol city boys from New Orleans like it was nothin."

"Oh, I'm so glad," Dawn clapped her hands. "Congratulations. So are we gonna celebrate?"

"You bet," Foster answered as he walked into his office. "Grab us some coffee cups from the back and come on in."

Grabbing the bottle he kept hidden in the bottom of his desk drawer, he poured a healthy shot into each cup and then raised his mug. Following his actions, the girls lifted theirs and then toasted to their victory. Clacking their cups together, they tilted them to their lips and drank.

"Oh my God!" Dawn coughed and grabbed her throat then bolted from the room. "Aaugh! That's disgusting," her voice faded into the back. "You guys are sick."

Laughing together, Vicki and Foster listened as she carried on. A few moments later, they looked up to see her standing in the doorway with a glass of water in her hand. "What?" Foster asked as he and Vicki tried to stifle their laughter. "Don't you like whiskey?"

"No, I don't," she cringed. "That stuff's terrible. I don't know how you guys can even drink it?"

Chuckling at her displeasure, Vicki and Foster just shook their heads. "You were great boss," Vicki said then winced as she downed her cup and slammed it on the desk. "But I really do need to go if you don't mind. I need to get the kids."

"Not at all Vic, but before you go, thanks. You know I couldn't have done it without your help. I hope you realize that. I really don't know what I'd do without you," he sighed.

"Thanks, boss."

"Well it's the truth and you know it. In fact, we all need to get out of here. It's been a long day."

Heading home, Foster detoured to the general store and then to Jack's Hardware. He wanted to buy a few simple things for Willie. A toothbrush and a hairbrush, some soap and shampoo, and a shotgun to protect herself from the gators he'd seen. Around five, he finally made it home and took a short but much needed nap then showered and headed to Melinda's.

A nice dinner and a movie finally ended with her just a bit disappointed and back home a little before twelve. He feigned being overly tired from his trial, and after a heartfelt apology, he left with a kiss and a promise to be back early on Sunday. They would go riding like she wanted he told her, but tonight she'd just have to wait. Besides, if things went as he planned, it wouldn't be long before he'd be spending every night with her. But Katherine was another issue. Her time in Mobile was limited and soon she'd be gone. And with only that on his mind, he set off for her house.

Pulling into her drive, he parked in the shadows next to the garage just like before and quietly closed his door. Gazing up toward her bedroom, he smiled at the soft but definite glow in the window. It was all he needed to see, and like a thief in the night, he quietly made his way into the house and up the stairs then down the hallway until he stood in her doorway.

A large single candle in a beautiful ornate holder sat on the dresser in front of the mirror, it's flame providing a soft flickering glow throughout the room. On the nightstand, a half empty bottle of wine and two glasses sat, and beneath the hand-quilted covers of the oversized bed, the beautiful dark haired mistress of the house quietly slept. She said she'd be waiting, and with an ever-growing smile as he entered, Foster silently crossed the room and blew out the candle.

He'd awakened in her a ravenous appetite he could scarcely believe, and like that of an animal with a newfound hunger, craving and thirsting, she'd begun to feed on the decadence of her growing immorality. Gorging herself on the licentious pleasures of her own lust, she feasted until the burning desires within her had been satiated and he could give no more. Yet still, and even though it was late into the night, it was only after he'd promised to return that she allowed him to leave and he found his way home. Her new candle burning in its holder would be her signal that all was clear as she slipped naked beneath the covers and waited.

CHAPTER 22

RISING THE NEXT MORNING TO the beaming rays of light streaming through the parted curtains, Foster rolled to his back and rubbed his eyes. Surely it couldn't be morning already, could it? He looked at the clock on his dresser and groaned then rolled back over and covered his head with a pillow. Just a few minutes more was all he needed, but with thoughts of Willie waiting for him up river looming in the back of his mind, he drug his ass from the bed and headed to the shower.

Shortly after nine, Foster finally made it to the marina. His stop at the icehouse for a couple of blocks had delayed him slightly, but Otis was there and ready to go. He liked him and was glad he'd kept him on, and as he made his way to the boat with a brand new twelve-gauge in one hand and two boxes of shells in the other, he could see him busily wiping down the morning's dew.

"Mornin boss," Otis hollered from the back of the boat.

"Morning Otis," Foster replied in a groggy voice. "Here, take this," he said as he stopped and held out the gun. "Are we ready to go?" he asked as he stepped onto the edge of the boat and then jumped into the stern

"Yes sur boss," Otis answered with a wary look to the gun. "I cleaned an checked everything real good an even warmed up the motor. An I's ready anytime you are."

"Good Otis, that's good," he chuckled at the look on Otis's face. "And if you're wondering what the gun's for, it's for Willie. I saw a couple a gators when we came back the other day and I don't want her having any problems. They were just a little too close for comfort, if you know what I mean."

"Oh yes sur, I knows exactly what you mean," he nodded. "So where's you want me ta put it?"

"Aaah, just lay it on the sofa for now and then come with me. I've got some food and a couple of blocks of ice still in the car."

"Yes sur boss, but is you okay?" he asked with a genuine concern. "You looks a little tired."

"Oh yeah, I'm fine," he answered with a light-hearted chuckle. "I just didn't get enough sleep. I had a client last night who really needed my help. You know, one of those that you just couldn't say no to," he smiled to himself.

"Well, that shor was awful nice of you. I mean, to go an help someone like that after you'd already worked all day an all. I shor hope they was grateful."

"Oh they were," he chuckled again as he thought of his night. "They were."

"Well maybe you can take a nap on the way up an get some rest. That should make ya feel better."

"You know Otis, that sounds like a great idea, and I think I just might do that. Now, come on."

Stocking the boat with their provisions, the two soon had everything onboard and were on their way up river. Retiring to one of the sofas in the rear once they'd cleared the harbor, Foster was amazed at how quickly his mind seemed to clear. He thought of Katherine and what she'd said about how all of her worries just seemed to disappear when she was out here. She was right, and now with the steady drone of the motor lulling him into the relaxing depths of the dream world, Foster closed his eyes and was soon fast asleep.

Waking just over an hour later to the sudden change of the motor's steady drone, he rose and looked around. A second later, Otis reduced the throttle once again and he felt the boat slow even more as they started to round the last bend in the channel. Barely clearing the limbs of the cypress that jutted out low and over the water, he curiously stepped into the stern, leaned to the side and looked through the tangled web of hanging branches.

There was the pier, and in the middle of the yard he could see Willie. She had her back to them and was cutting the grass. Watching as she made a pass then turn and start again, he saw her suddenly stop as they emerged out from behind the tree. Waving with her arm up high in response to Otis blowing the boat's horn, she instantly dropped the mower's handle and then hurried toward the pier.

Waiting impatiently as they slowly approached and pulled along side, Willie anxiously bounced on the balls of her feet. She was happy to see them and it showed, but still he'd worried about her while he was gone, and it wasn't just the gators that'd concerned him. He knew she'd just lost her mother, and now here she was, totally isolated from all human contact except for him and Otis. She had to be lonely, but from the look and the smile on her face, her spirits seemed high and he was glad.

"Good mornin," she beamed brightly as Otis went to reverse. "You're back!"

"Morning Willie," Foster drawled over the noise of motor. "Did ya miss us?"

"I shor did. I'll tell ya, this shor as heck aint like be'n in town."

"No it isn't," he laughed. "But here, catch this," he said, throwing a line just as Otis stepped out of the side door and jumped onto the pier.

Pulling hard on the heavy boat, she found a pylon, looped the line and began to secure the stern as Otis quickly grabbed the bow and did the same.

"Mornin Mister Otis," she piped happily.

"Mornin Miss Willie," he replied as he approached to check her knots. "Did ya get it tied okay?"

"Yes sur, see," she stepped back so he could inspect her work.

Now about the biggest thing that Willie had ever tied, were the strings on the opened end of a cotton sack and it showed. Her knot, or attempted knot, was a tangled mess.

"Aaah that ain't gonna hold nothin Miss Willie," Otis chuckled. "Specially the boat. Here, let me show you how," he said as he undid the line and retied her knot. "See, like this," he finished with a tug to the line. "Cause we shor don't want Mister Siler's boat a floatin down river now do we."

"Oh nooo," Willie agreed and shook her head. "He wouldn't like that at all."

"Mister Siler wouldn't like what?" Foster quipped as he returned to the stern to hear Willie and Otis talking.

"Oh," Willie jumped and then turned with a smile as bright as the morning. "Your boat," she answered and stepped toward him. "You know, if it got loose an floated away."

"Nah, I don't think he'd like that at all," he jested as he stared up into her eyes.

Gazing back, Willie suddenly found herself without words. He was staring at her and she was glad, and wanted nothing more than to hug him, but she refrained in a moment of uncertainty and became quiet. Staring until Otis had stepped back into the boat to shut off the motor.

"But," he finally said as he held out his hand. "Now that we've got this boat all tied, how about if we get it unloaded." Nodding her head enthusiastically, Willie took his hand and jumped into stern. "Oh, and I almost forgot," he added as she landed. "I brought you a few things I think you'll like."

"You did?"

"Yes ma'am."

"What are they?" she asked excitedly.

"Well, you'll just have to see. Just a second."

Stepping through the doorway Foster dropped inside then returned a moment later with a brown paper sack. "Here you go Willie," he said as he handed her the bag. "Take a seat."

Grinning brightly, Willie quickly took a seat and stared at the bag.

"Go on," he encouraged as he took the chair beside her. "Open it."

"What is it?" she asked again as she shuffled her feet.

"You'll just have to see. Now go on."

Slowly opening the bag, Willie looked inside and then reached into the bottom. "Oh loook, a toothbrush," she exclaimed and held it up then turned to Foster. "I've been brushin after every time I ate, see," she smiled and showed her teeth then reached back into the bag.

"Good Willie, they look nice."

"An what's this," she asked as she pulled an unfamiliar bottle from the bottom.

"That's shampoo, and a brush for your hair. And there's a couple of bars of soap in there too."

"Sham what?" she asked.

"Shampoo," he laughed. "Go ahead and open it."

Opening the bottle, Willie closed her eyes and put it to her nose then inhaled its fragrant aroma. "It smells pretty," she said as she turned back to him.

"Yes, it's supposed to. And your soap does too."

"Oooh Mister Siler," she shook her head. "I jus don't know what ta say. Thank you. Nobody's ever bought me nothin before."

"Well, you don't have to say anything Willie," he replied. "Just use those things and make yourself prettier than you already are."

Blushing ever so lightly, Willie smiled then slowly returned the items to the bag just as Otis appeared in the doorway.

"What now boss?" he asked.

"Well first," Foster said as he pulled himself from his chair. "Let's get that ice up to the house before it melts any more than it already has. And Willie, you grab that box of food down there."

"Yes sur," she replied as she rose from her chair. "An boy am I ever glad you brought more ice."

"Oh you are?" Foster replied. "And why's that?"

"Cause, it's almost all gone."

"It's almost gone?" He turned back with a surprised expression. "Really?"

"A huh."

"But that was a twenty pound block of ice."

"Yes sur, I know. Or I knew it was big. But it's almost gone, I swear."

"It isss?" He raised his eyebrows and then glanced to Otis. "And just where'd it go?"

Gazing at him as if she were now in trouble, Willie quickly glanced to Otis and then back to Foster. "I... I ate it," she mumbled with a guiltily expression.

"You what?" Foster cocked his head and scrunched his face.

"I ate it," she repeated in a voice that seemed to suddenly grow lower.

"You ate it?" he repeated as if he couldn't believe it. "A twenty-pound block of ice. In two days?" he looked to Otis as they both began to laugh.

"Ah huh," she nodded with a sheepish expression. "I'm sorry, but I jus ain't never had ice before."

"An that is pretty much how our mornin started," Otis laughed as he fondly recalled the moment. "I'll tell ya, you should've seen the look on ol Foster's face when she told him she'd eaten all that ice. It was absolutely priceless."

"So she actually ate the whole block?" Jim began to laugh as well.

"Yep," Otis nodded. "I guess while we was away, she'd taken an ice pick to it an by the time we got back she didn't have enough to put in a glass of ice tea. Now at first, I really didn't know what to think, an neither did Foster really. I remember he jus kind-a stood there for a second with this look on his face as if ta say, how in the hell could you eat a twenty-pound block in two days. But hell, you couldn't be mad at Willie. Shiiit, she didn't know no better.

"Anyway, after we had our laugh an he'd explained to her how the ice was really for the icebox to keep everything cold, we jus started grabbing stuff an carryin it up to the house an not another word was said about it. An then, as soon as we got everything unloaded, Willie went back to cuttin the grass an me an Foster started cuttin wood an cleanin up the big stuff that she couldn't move. Then right around noon we took lunch, an while we was eatin ol Foster had a real long talk with Willie about the gators in the river. I remember he was real worried about her an wanted her to know jus how dangerous they were an how careful she had to be when she was down by the water. An so right after lunch, well, that's when he had me get the shotgun from the boat.

"See, he wanted to teach her how to shoot, an jus as soon as I got up there the three of us went back down to the river bank an started stickin branches in the mud so we could stick some of them beer an coke bottles on em from the other day. Then right after that, we went back up into the yard, an after he gave her a little safety lesson, he blew off a couple bottles an then handed that big ol gun to Willie. Now she said that she'd shot a gun before, but I really don't think that she understood jus how big a twelve-gauge shotgun was. An that's when we really had a good laugh."

Chambering a shell, Foster turned and gave the gun to Willie. "Okay Willie, now turn sideways and hold it tight against your shoulder."

"It's heavy."

"I know, but hold it up and aim it like I showed you, okay. And remember, keep it pulled tight against your shoulder."

"Like this," she asked as she leveled the gun and took aim.

"Yes ma'am," he said as he stepped to the side and dropped behind her. "Now spread your feet apart a little and then squeeze the..."

But Willie had quit listening once she'd leveled the gun, and before Foster could finish she eagerly pulled the trigger with a 'Boom' and flew backwards onto her ass. To both of the men it was funny as hell, but still Foster reacted instantly and with a deep concern. "Are you okay?" he asked as he jumped to her side and reached for the gun then started laughing.

"Aaaugh," she groaned as she rolled and rubbed her shoulder. "That shor did kick, but yeah I'm fine," she assured in an attempt to ease his concern.

"Ya sure?" he pried as he pull her from the ground and continued to laugh.

"Oh yeah," she nodded as she brushed herself off and began to laugh. "Shoot, I'm tougher-n woodpecker lips," she boasted. "But can I shoot it again?"

"Sure Willie," Foster replied as he handed her the gun. "But what was it you just said?" he asked with a chuckle. "You're tougher than what?"

"Woodpecker lips," she exclaimed.

"Woodpecker lips?" he repeated and raised his eyebrows.

"Yes sur, you know," she emphasized and pursed her lips.

"Yes, I know, but Willie," he chuckled again, but now as if to inform her of the obvious. "Woodpeckers don't have lips."

"Oh I know," she scoffed. "But if they did they shor would be tough don't ya think?"

Pausing for just a moment, Foster finally shook his head and laughed. "Well, I never really thought of it that way, but yeah, I guess you're right."

"So can I shoot it again?"

"Sure, but this time remember to spread your feet, okay. Like this, see."

Watching and then emulating his stance, Willie chambered another shell and brought the gun to her shoulder. Taking a deep breath, she pulled it tight and steadied her aim then slowly pulled the trigger. This time she was ready for the recoil and bore her weight against it just as he'd shown her. Rocking to the jarring force of the weapon, she saw the bottle explode a split second later.

"I hit it, I hit it," she squealed as she twirled to Foster and Otis.

"You shor did Miss Willie," Otis cheered.

"Good shot," Foster quickly added as he ducked and then pushed the barrel of the gun away.

"Can I shoot it again?" Willie beamed as she looked at Foster and then the targets. "Please."

"Sure Willie," he replied. "Shoot em all, that's what they're there for. But this time," he nodded toward the water. "Let's try and keep the gun pointed that way okay."

Nodding with a grin, Willie blasted bottle after bottle until she'd emptied the gun. Watching as Foster reloaded it and Otis stuck new bottles back on the limbs, she resumed her blasting until Foster took them to the water's edge for a different kind of practice. He wanted to shoot what was left of their bottles in the air, and after a brief explanation of what he wanted he had Otis walk out to the end of the pier. Throwing them one at a time as far and as high as he could, Foster blasted the first two without a miss then handed the gun to Willie. "Okay, now did you see how I did that?"

"Yep," Willie nodded and readied the gun.

"Good, now just holler at Otis when you're ready okay. And remember to follow the bottle."

Taking her stance, the budding young Annie Oakley hollered at Otis then followed the twirling brown bottle on its arc toward the water. Hitting long before she was ready, she blasted it in the water in a burst of aggravation then hollered at Otis once again. This time, she shattered her bottle just off of the surface with a rain of glass sprinkling down onto the tranquil waters.

Squealing with delight, Willie called to Otis again and blasted another. She seemed to be a natural, and for the next ten minutes, Otis threw bottles as high and as far as he could. She was having fun and it showed, but all too quickly they'd emptied a box of shells. And now with her shoulder beginning to sore and Otis's arm worn out, they finally called it quits.

"That was good Willie," Foster praised as they walked off the pier. "You did good. Now let's go and clean the gun."

"Yes sur," she replied.

"Oh, and Otis," he stopped and turned his head over his shoulder. "While I'm helping Willie, why don't you clean that pit out and fill it with wood so we can light us a fire later."

"Yes sur boss," he answered.

"Thank you Mister Otis," Willie piped over her shoulder as they hit the grass and separated.

"You's quite welcome Miss Willie," he replied as he headed off to his duties and they headed to the screened in porch.

Spreading the newspaper he'd brought along across the table, Foster gently laid the gun down and took a seat. "Now you know," he said as he began to disassemble the firearm. "That it's really important to clean your gun after you shoot it, don't you?" He added and then glanced back up to find Willie staring at the newspaper as if she were engrossed in an article.

"Oh, so what-a-ya reading?" he asked nonchalantly.

Breaking her concentration, Willie raised her head with a self-conscious look. "Oh nothin really," she fidgeted then smiled as if trying to sound casual.

Her tone and demeanor spoke volumes and Foster instantly took note. He could sense that something was amiss, and that she wasn't quite telling the truth. "Well, it sure looks to me like there's something there," he said as he leaned toward her and looked at the page. "Here, that looks interesting," he said and pointed to the headlines. "Tell me what that says while I clean the gun."

But Willie couldn't read, and with an embarrassed look she rose from her chair and looked outside. "Oh look," she feigned. "I think Mister Otis needs some help."

She wanted to leave and avoid the obvious, but before she could take a step, Foster reached out and grabbed her arm. "Hold on a second Willie," he said as he caught her gaze. "Stay, and sit back down. Please," he softened his voice as he gently confronted her. "You can't read can you?"

It was at that very instant that Willie felt another wave of embarrassment consume her. He was so smart and now she felt so stupid. "No sur," she admitted as she took her seat and lowered her head. "I ain't never had no schoolin an nobody'd teach me," she went on. "An even though I wanted to learn, an tried, it didn't work. I guess that's cause I'm too stupid like my step dad always said I was," she raised her head and gazed out the window then sighed and turned back to

Foster. "So I guess that means ya don't want someone like me workin for you now."

"No Willie," Foster quickly replied. "No, that's not true. It's okay, because one, you're not stupid, and don't ever let anyone tell you that, you hear. Not ever. And two, they're a lot of people who can't read. Heck, even Otis can't read. Did you know that?" Curling her lips ever so slightly, Willie smiled and shook her head. "So don't worry about it, okay. Besides if you'd really like to learn, I can teach you. How's that sound?"

Nodding her head with another smile, Willie slowly turned her gaze back to the paper. "I'd like that," she replied gratefully. "So could you bring me some readin books ta learn with?"

"Sure Willie, I can bring you lots of books. But why don't we just start right now."

Sliding his finger beneath the words, Foster started at the top with the date. "Sep-tem-ber third 1930," he began, slowly sounding out the words as he went.

"September third?" Willie repeated excitedly. "Are you shor? Oh my Lord!"

"Yes ma'am," he laughed. "I'm sure. Why?"

"Cause it's almost my birthday."

"It is? And when's that?"

"Yes sur, on September leventh."

"Well then," he stared with a curious grin. "Tell me, just how old are you going to be next week? No wait," he held up his hand as if to stop. "Let me guess. Aaah nineteen, right?"

Shaking her head, Willie smiled coyly.

"Twenty?" He cocked his head.

Shaking her head once again, she lifted her hand and turned her thumb down.

"Eighteen?" he guessed as she shook her head with her thumb still down.

"Seventeen?" he guessed again in a voice a pitch higher.

Rolling her eyes, she smiled mischievously and then shook her head once more.

"Sixteeeen?" he slowed and lowered his voice with a growing uneasiness.

Looking on with a devilish grin, Willie said nothing and just stared as if to say guess once more.

Surely not, he thought. She couldn't be? A second later, and as if he really didn't want to know, he took a breath and guessed one last time. "Fiff--teeeen?" he finally drew out the word.

Nodding her head with an elated smile, Willie clasped her hands together then stood and went to the balls of her feet. "I was born September 11 1915," she said excitedly as she counted her fingers. "An that'll make me fifteen this birthday," she finished then looked back to Foster.

Staring in disbelief, the thirty-five-year old lawyer just cringed. Jesus she was young, even by his standards. And worse still, was that she wasn't even fifteen yet! She was fourteen, going on fifteen, and she still had a week to go. They were twenty years apart to be exact. He reeled at the revelation, yet even so he didn't care, for she was as beautiful as any girl he'd ever seen and he was determined to have her. He had to have her, and even though he was more than a little surprised, Foster was a master at hiding his expressions and acted as if her age was of little concern. It was a skill he'd developed and perfected in the courtrooms. He wanted her to think of herself as a young lady that was all grown up and ready for womanhood. Not some little girl who was still in the confusing and awkward stages of adolescence. And even though he felt a small twinge of guilt envelope him, he remembered that neither he nor she answered to anyone. She had no one.

"Well Willie, I guess we'll just have to celebrate your birthday next weekend then, won't we?" Smiling with a nod, Foster continued on. "Good, now how about if you sit back down and we finish cleaning this gun."

Doing as she was told, Willie took a seat then watched as Foster disassembled and cleaned the weapon. Carefully explaining weapon safety as he did, and how she should always shoot to kill. He went on to explain how at night, she should always keep it by her bed with the magazine fully loaded when they were gone. "Now you do understand all of that, right?" he asked as he finished.

Nodding her head, Foster smiled and then handed her the gun. "Good, now here. Let's see if you can put it back together for me."

Studying the pieces for just a few moments, Willie slowly yet methodically pieced the brand new Browning twelve-gauge back together until she'd completed her task and had it in working order. Standing up, she worked the action several times then leveled the gun and took aim out the window. Pulling the trigger, she smiled at the sound of its click then turned back to Foster. "There," she beamed and held out the gun. "How's that?"

"Good," he answered and shook his head.

Her powers of observation were stunning. She'd watched him take it apart only once, and rather quickly at that. And yet she possessed the ability to reassemble it without a hitch the very first time. Almost as if she'd done it before, dozens of times. She was surprisingly sharp, and he could clearly see that the young girl before him possessed much, much more than just beauty. "Very good," he added, reaching up to take the gun. "Now let me see."

Carefully inspecting it, he worked the action then held it up and pulled the trigger. It was perfect, and he was impressed. "Well, I guess now we can go help Otis, what-a-you think?"

"Yes sur, I think he'd like that."

Returning outside they found Otis just as he was finishing with the pit. "Looks good Otis," Foster complimented. "Now go ahead and light it so it can burn down then come and help me."

"Yes sur boss," he replied.

Picking up where she'd left off, Willie finished her grass while Foster and Otis worked around the house. Later, and after the fire had burned down, Foster buried five potatoes wrapped in foil into the bottom edge of the coals. An hour after that, he prepared the three large steaks he'd brought along and threw them on the grill. Dinner was delicious, and the whole baked potato thing with the salt and pepper and butter was a new experience for Willie. She's never seen a potato cooked in such a way, but the steak was something she remembered, and once again she ate as if she had a bottomless pit.

Shortly after dinner and the beautiful sunset that'd followed, their long eventful day finally came to a close. The glowing orange ball had dropped below the horizon and the dusky light that remained slowly began to wane and give way to the night. And even though it was a beautiful evening and still a little early, Foster was tired and ready for bed. Downing what was left of his beer, he grabbed Willie's hand and said good night to Otis then retired to the house.

Stepping inside, they quickly readied for bed and for the first time in her life, Willie brushed her teeth with her very own toothbrush. Finishing her task, she spit into the sink and began to pump the handle to rinse her mouth. "Ah ah aah," Foster said in a parental way. "Don't forget your tongue."

Smiling and nodding as if she'd forgotten, she stuck out her tongue and did just as she was told. Swishing and rinsing her mouth after she'd finished; she banged her toothbrush against the side of the sink and laid it on the counter then turned to Foster. "Good?" she asked as she sucked in a breath and smiled.

Stepping toward her, Foster reached up and took her chin between his thumb and forefinger. "Very nice," he said as he scrutinized her smile then shifted his gaze to her eyes. He wanted nothing more than to kiss her right then and there, hard and passionately, and then to drag her into the bedroom. But he didn't, for he was determined to wait until she came to him. Until the budding desires within her drove her into his arms and she wanted to be taken. Until she dared to cross the threshold that would lead her into the world of womanhood. It was all he wanted, but before another thought could enter his mind, Willie stepped forward and wrapped her arms around him.

"Thank you for be'n so nice to me," she mumbled as she nuzzled her head into his chest and squeezed him.

Touched by her humbled act of appreciation, Foster dropped his arms around her with a shameless smile. So this is what a toothbrush gets, he thought as he pulled her tight.

Glowing with giddiness as the strength of his arms tightened around her. One on the small of her back and the other on the back of her head, Willie closed her eyes and savored in the moment. Was this love? Did he like her? Was this what it felt like? Her heart quickened then pounded wildly as a sudden warmth seemed to surge from the depths of her inner core. Yes, it had to be… it felt too good. Consumed by its essence, she took a deep breath then looked dreamily up into his eyes.

Unable to resist just a little forwardness, Foster gently took her head in both of his hands then bent ever so slightly and kissed her on the forehead. A heated flush drew across her face and her mind reeled. Yes, he did like her. She was certain of it. Her heart raced and fluttered once again.

"Well Willie," he finally said. "You don't have to thank me. But you are welcome. Now, how about if we wash ourselves up and get some sleep."

Nodding her head, she cleared her throat and then finally released her hold. Yes, he'd kissed her! Her schoolgirl crush exploded again. That night, sleep once again was hard for the both of them.

The next morning Foster rose early and made breakfast. The left over steak and potatoes topped with a couple of eggs made for a tasty surprise, and after they'd eaten they worked around the yard until mid morning. There was a lot to do yet even so, Foster really needed to leave. He needed to spend a little more time with Melinda, but even more than that, he wanted to talk to her father. He'd been thinking of what the Judge had said last Sunday and it intrigued him greatly.

Senator Siler, the man's commanding voice kept repeating itself in his head. It was a title that resonated well and he wanted to discuss it further. Especially with visions of Washington and the White House occupying his thoughts. The pinnacle of power after all, was most certainly a lofty and alluring goal. An hour later and right around eleven, they said their goodbyes and left Willie standing on the pier as they pulled away.

"Now remember," Foster hollered from the stern. "When you're out here working, you keep that gun with you and watch the water when you're in the yard too. Remember what I told you about those gators. They're sneaky... and you shoot to kill, you hear!"

"Yes sur, I ramember. Don't worry, ain't no gator gonna get me!"

"That's my girl," he commended. "Oh and remember," he raised his voice as their distance increased. "Otis will be back on Tuesday to check on you and Thursday too. And then I'll see you Saturday."

"See you then," she shouted back and waved with her arm high above her head.

Standing on the pier, Willie watched until they rounded the bend and disappeared behind the big tree. Settling into his chair as Otis increased their speed, Foster closed his eyes and emptied his mind only to have it instantly filled with the vision of the two large gators he'd seen the last time they'd left. Oh my God, he thought as he sat up and glanced toward the shore. This was it, wasn't it? This was where he'd seen them, he was certain of it. Scanning the shoreline he saw nothing, but curiosity had the best of him and even increased as they continued downstream. Where were they, he wondered as he stood and looked to the other side? They were here somewhere; they had to be.

Scouring the opposite shore, he searched the muddy walls and inlets that were partially hidden by the grasses and reeds growing from the shallow bottom. The vegetation was thick, but after only a few moments, he spotted the same two reptiles he'd seen the other day. Basking in the sun at the water's edge, the two behemoths laid almost undetectable in the sawgrass. Damn they were big, he thought. Much bigger than he had remembered. Twelve footers at least, or maybe even bigger. And then he thought of Willie. He'd really worried about her the last time they'd left, but now, and after the way she had handled that shotgun, he dismissed all concerns. Looking behind the boat, he smiled as he recalled her parting words. They would do well to stay put now he thought.

It was a little after twelve by the time the two men pulled into the marina and secured the boat. Checking the lines one last time, they finally headed to the parking lot.

"Is we all done for the day boss?" Otis asked as they walked off the pier.

"Yeah, Otis we're done. So just go on home and enjoy the rest of the day with that wife and little boy of yours. In fact, why don't you just take tomorrow off too."

"Are ya shor boss? I can work if ya needs me to."

"Nah that won't be necessary, but I do want you to take the boat back up first thing on Tuesday and check on Willie for me okay. I know she's got that gun and all now, but still I'd like you to check on her. Now I can trust you to do that can't I?"

"Oh yes sur, I won't let ya down. I knows how much Miss Willie means to ya. An I'll make shor she's okay an don't need nothin too."

"Good. Then that should put you up there around nine or so and while you're up there you can help her around the house too.

But I want you back early okay... mid afternoon. And when you get back, I want you to come by my office and check in with me."

"Yes sur boss. Is there anything else?"

"Nah, that's all."

"Ya shor? I could take her another block of ice if ya wants," he jested with a grin.

A little surprised at his wit, Foster just chuckled and shook his head. "Naaah Otis, I think Miss Willie's had just about enough ice for a while. Now let's get out of here."

"Yes sur boss, then I'll see you on Tuesday."

CHAPTER 23

———◆———

As SOON AS HE WAS home Foster took a relaxing shower then laid across his bed for a nap. A half hour later he woke and dressed then headed to what'd become a Sunday afternoon ritual with his fiancé and future in-laws. A ritual he was actually looking forward to, that would include another scotch and cigar with the Judge, and then hopefully some conversation as to what they'd talked of last week and of the decision he'd come to make.

Pulling the cord to the doorbell, it wasn't but a few moments before the door swung open to the sight of the olive skinned beauty. "Oh Mesieur Siler," Monique greeted in her honey mixed dialect and smile to match. "You sure are heres early. Please please, comes on in," she continued with her ever-endearing and gracious formality. "I vill get Miss Melindsa for you an lets her know shat you're here already. She'll be so surprised. I shinks she is in zhe kitchen helping her mother."

Dropping his head in a humorous yet hopeless denial of the attraction he felt for her, Foster could only shake it back and forth for she was without a doubt unlike any woman he'd ever met before. A stunning mix of intelligence and beauty stemming from a black and white gene pool, she was attractive and worldly and had a mysterious aura about her that intrigued him greatly. But above all, he loved her accent. A smooth yet sophisticated blend of her native language mixed with a light southern drawl she'd acquired over the years. It melted him every time and she knew it, and as often was the case, she would use it and tease him when he visited. When she would open the door upon his arrival, and in their fleeting moments alone, discreetly yet provocatively glance toward him and speak in French then slowly and seductively roll her eyes. It was a game she liked to play, and it drove him nuts.

"Oh, no no Monique, please," he whispered and pulled on her arm as she started to turn. "Just hold on a second. I don't want to bother her if she's busy," he continued as he quickly glanced toward the kitchen and then back to her. "Or at least not just yet. See, what I'd really like to do is to visit with the Judge for a few minutes first. That is, if he's in and he isn't busy."

"Oh oui, Mesieur Siler," she smiled and then turned. "Jus comes with me. I believes he's still in zhe library working. An I bet shat he'd be more than happy to sees you."

Knocking softly, she pushed on the double doors and found the Judge busily working at his desk. "Mesieur Sjudge," she called.

Glancing up from his papers, Judge McAlister smiled and then leaned back in his chair. "Foster," he called out delightedly as he removed his glasses and laid them on the desk. "You're sure here early. Come on in son," he gestured with a wave as he pushed back his chair and stood.

"See," Monique quietly jested to Foster as he passed. "I tolds yooou."

Approaching the man he hoped would be his next son in law, Judge McAlister quickly averted his eyes to his housekeeper and stepped toward her. "Mo," he asked as he discreetly reached behind and rubbed the small of her back. "Do the women know he's here yet?

"Oh nooo Mesieur," she grinned demurely and shook her head. "Mesieur Siler vanted to come straight here first. Ans to tell you the truth, I don't shink Miss Melindsa even heard zhe doorbell. Or for shat matter, is even looking for his car yet."

"Well good," the Judge replied. "At least we can have one drink to ourselves before we're interrupted. But I think we need some ice. So, why don't you see if you can slip into the kitchen and bring us some back? Oh, and if the women ask what you're doing, tell them. Aaah, tell them that you're just getting it for when Foster comes like I asked."

"We Mesieur," she replied with a knowing glance as she turned and left.

"Now son, come on and let's relax, I've had just about enough work for one day."

"Well sir, I really didn't mean to bother you if you're still busy. It's just that I've been doing some thinking about our conversation last week, and I thought that I could come over a little early and talk with you. But if you need to finish, I could go and pester the women for a while."

"Nonsense dammit," he replied gruffly. "I wouldn't hear of it. Besides it's time for a drink don't you think?" He continued with a glance to the clock on the mantle.

"Well," Foster chuckled in agreement. "Yes sir, I do believe it is."

Standing in front of the liquor cabinet, Judge McAlister reached for a couple of heavy tumblers and set them on the counter then grabbed one of the hand-etched crystal decanters from the back. "Another Chivas?" He turned and asked as if he already knew the answer.

"Yes sir," Foster answered and nodded.

Pouring their drinks, the Judge reached into the ice bucket and grabbed a few chunks left from yesterday's ice and splashed them into their glasses. "It ain't much but it should do until Mo gets back," he said as he turned and handed one to Foster then raised his glass. "Cheers, young man."

"Cheers, sir," Foster repeated and touched his glass to the Judge's. "That really is the best."

"Yes it is, now come on and let's have a seat."

Turning toward the chairs, they crossed the room and took their seats then settled into the comfort of the thick plush leather. "Now tell me," the Judge said after another quick sip. "What's on your mind? You look a little preoccupied."

"Well sir, like I said, I've been doing some thinking about our conversation last week and what you said," he paused and took a breath. "Actually, I've been thinking a lot about what you said."

"And what was that?"

Taking another quick sip, Foster pulled himself to the edge of his chair and then cleared his throat. Silently staring into the bottom of his glass, he paused as if he were searching for the proper words then raised his head and looked straight into the Judge's steely gray eyes. "Sir," he finally said. "I want to be the next U. S. Senator from Alabama."

Smiling as if the words themselves had brought new meaning to his day, Robert McAlister stared with an almost parental pride for he truly considered Foster the son he never had. A creature of the same making whose only commitment in life was to that of his own unyielding quest for wealth and power. Wealth and power that the aging and influential adjudicator had and could wield, to aid and assist the young up and coming lawyer. To open the hidden political doors normally closed to all others as he strived to join the exclusive circle of men who comprised the definitive pinnacle of power as a United States Senator. "And so you shall," the Judge replied and raised his glass. "And so you shall," he repeated as he took a sip and then gently set his glass on the table. "But now," he smiled and rolled his eyes. "You need a wife. You do know that, don't you?"

"Yes sir," Foster nodded and chuckled. "I know. But I was thinking that... well, she doesn't know it yet, but I thought that I would ask for Melinda's hand sometime before Christmas. I mean, that is with your permission of course. See, I was figuring that maybe a spring wedding early next year would be good. You know, to kind of coincide with the beginning of the campaign. And who knows," he grinned wryly. "Maybe we could even get some favorable press coverage out of it."

"Yes, yes," the judge exclaimed as he sat forward in his chair. "Excellent idea to both of them. Damn Foster, I'd be proud to call you my son-in-law. And see, you're already thinking like a politician. Why hell, we could invite everyone from the Governor on down. And use it as an informal way of introducing you to some very influential people. People who you'll need to meet and get to know. Yes sir," he finally drawled as he relaxed back into the comfort of his chair. "You most certainly have been thinking about this. Haven't you?"

"Yes sir," Foster nodded. "And to be honest, quite a lot actually. I'm ready for it; I can feel it. I want to be Alabama's next Senator," he went on with an elevated zeal. "I'm ready. And I can win," he finished with a determined expression etched into his brow. "I know I can."

Digesting his words in a short but quiet moment, the Judge took a deep relaxing breath then slowly began to smile. "Well son, this certainly is wonderful news. I'll tell you, you sure know how to make a man happy, and proud. And to tell you the truth, a lot of other people too. The party's been looking for a suitable candidate for quite sometime to run against Crandell in next year's election. That self-serving son-of-a-bitch has been in office long enough and needs to go, and that's why I've been bugging you for so long. We need someone who can beat his sorry ass, who's new and young, and fresh and bold. Someone who's smart, yet with the working-class values of middle America that the people can relate to and that's you. You're just the man. You come from that stock.

"And I'll tell you," he continued and pointed his finger. "Harlen Crandell doesn't. He doesn't relate to the people or for that matter, even his other colleague's. He's a goddamn idiot and everyone in Washington knows it. Hell, every economic proposal he's ever taken to the Senate floor he's screwed up and the companies and the jobs have ended up in some other state. Hell, he even screwed up the bonds for the new state docks they just finished a couple years ago. But a lot of good it did to put them in because we still don't have any shipping business to speak of. It all seems to be going to New Orleans for some reason. And we have one of the nicest ports in the country now.

"Yes sir, what we need is someone who is going to fight and win," he said as he poked his finger on the table between them. "Someone who can stimulate the economy of this state... and Mobile. You know, from the federal level. And that's you son," he finished emphatically. "Now," he said as he rocked forward once again. "I believe that this calls for a cigar."

Rising from his chair, Judge McAlister crossed the room to his desk and then returned with two of his finest. "Here you go son," he said as he extended a hand with one of the cigars.

Reaching up, Foster took the stogie and then pulled the brown cylindrical roll beneath his nose. "Aaaah yes," he smiled as he inhaled it's aroma. "Thank you. Oh and sir," he suddenly added as if he'd forgotten something. "There is one more little thing I'd like to ask if it's okay?"

"Sure Foster, what's that?" the Judge replied as he picked up the matchbox from the table.

"Well, if you don't mind, I'd really like to keep this marriage thing just between us for now."

Gazing down at the young lawyer, the old Judge just smiled and opened the box. "Not a problem son," he chuckled as he pulled a thick wooden match from within. "You just pop the question to

Melinda whenever you're damn good an ready. And in the mean time, I'll make some calls and start knocking on some doors. We've got a lot of work to do you and I, and it's gonna be tough. But before you know it," he smiled again as he drug the match across the striker. "People will be addressing you as Senator Siler, trust me."

Instantly blazing to life in a miniature sulfuric explosion, he bent and lit Foster's cigar first and then his own. Puffing repeatedly to ensure a good light, he finally pulled the cigar from his lips and blew out the match then tossed the charred remains into the ashtray and took his seat. Settling back into his chair, he took another puff and picked up his glass just as the doors opened behind him and Monique entered with a bowl of ice.

Quickly crossing the room, she stopped beside the Judge then bent with her tongs and began dropping ice into his glass. Pulling on his cigar as if nothing was amiss, Foster couldn't help but notice as the Judge's hand suddenly dropped off the side of his chair and then ran up the back of Monique's leg. Jumping ever so slightly, she smiled coyly and glanced to Foster then blushed and quickly returned to her task. She knew he was watching, but even so she didn't move and allowed the Judge's hand the unbridled access he so desired until she was done.

He'd been right about her, she was his mistress. And although her submissive demeanor surprised him, she stood back up as if nothing had happened and then looked to Foster. "Mesieur Siler," she said as she lifted her tongs. "Ice?"

"Please Monique," he said and pushed his glass to the edge of the table. "If you don't mind."

Stepping closer with a provocative smile tugging at her lips, Monique gave a subtle glance to his hand then stared into his eyes as she filled his glass. As if to say that he too could do the same if he liked. She was teasing him and he wanted nothing more than to run it up under her dress. But she was the Judge's property, and that was a line that even Foster dared not cross. It just wasn't worth it. A few chunks later and before he knew it, his glass was full and the ever-dutiful house-servant had turned away and returned to the liquor hutch.

Dumping her bowl into the ice bucket, she then grabbed the decanter of Scotch and returned to the two men. "Mesieur Sjudge,

Mesieur Siler?" she said as she held up the decanter. "Would you likes a refill?"

Holding their tumblers up, Monique poured a shot into each then returned to the liquor hutch. A moment later, she opened the windows for some much needed air and then turned back to the Judge. "Will zheir be anyshing else Mesieur Sjudge?" she asked in a dutiful tone.

"No Mo, we're fine for now," he answered with a smoke-filled breath. "That'll be all thank you."

"Oui Mesieur," she replied and excused herself.

Closing the doors behind her, the two men quickly picked up where they'd stopped when she'd entered. The Judge was still elated, and as they smoked their cigars and sipped their drinks, he laid out the platform upon which they would base and run their campaign. An economic recovery plan that would stimulate growth and bring desperately needed jobs back into the state for the people.

Assured that Foster's thoughts paralleled his own, he continued on with the grueling riggers that would come with the year-long campaign that lay ahead. How much the time he would have to spend away from his home and practice, and the obligations that would come with it. The fundraisers he would have to attend and the money that would come from the influential donors. The favors he'd owe to various political big shots and the special interest groups he would have to deal with.

"Well son," the Judge finally said as he pulled on his cigar and reclined back into his chair. "I think that's just about it. So what a ya think?" he asked as he blew his smoke into the air and then picked up his drink. "You still interested?"

"Absolutely sir," Foster answered without hesitation.

"Good, then there's only one more thing left to do if either of us has any hope of making it through the rest of the day alive," he added as he tilted his tumbler and drained his drink.

"And what's that sir?" Foster looked on with a curious gaze.

"Well," the Judge chuckled as he dropped his glass back to the table and then wiped his mouth with the back of his hand. "That'd be for you to find your new bride-to-be before she finds you here again. I'll tell you, them damn women railed on me for two whole days after you left last Sunday. Hell, I thought I never was going to hear the end of it!" They both laughed.

"A point well taken sir," Foster nodded as he rose from his chair.

"And besides," the Judge quickly added as he did the same. "I've still got this case that I've got to finish up for tomorrow if you don't mind."

"Oh no sir, not at all. I think it's time I found Melinda anyway. She wanted me to go for a ride with her before supper and I promised her that I would, so that'll make her happy."

"Well good, then the two of you can ride out and check the southern fence line for me. I've been missing some cattle lately and I think I might have a break in it somewhere. Tell Melinda about it. She'll know where to look," he finished and then held up his cigar. "Now why don't we save the rest of these for later and we'll talk some more after dinner."

Taking one last puff, Foster snuffed the remaining portion of his cigar into the ashtray then downed what was left of his drink and cast his eyes back to the Judge. "Sir," he finally said with an extended hand. "I want to thank you for what you're doing. And I want you to know that I won't disappoint you," he emphasized. "Or the party."

"Well I ain't done nothing yet," he said and took his hand. "But you are welcome," he added as he reached up with his other hand and placed it on Foster's shoulder. "And I know you won't disappoint us either," he added with an air of pride as they shook. "Now go on and find that daughter of mine before she finds out you're already here and starts railin on us again."

"Yes sir."

Quietly making his way through the house, Foster followed the noise emanating from the kitchen as the women chatted and worked. Melinda and Monique were jabbering in French and giggling like sisters, and Mrs. McAlister was snipping at her daughter to pay more attention to her pie dough. "A little more flour there Miss Shortcake," he heard her say.

Stopping just outside, he listened for a short moment then slowly and silently stepped through the doorway. Surprised and just a little overwhelmed, he stood for a second and marveled at the sight before him for in all of his visits, he'd never been in the McAlister's kitchen. And he certainly had never seen anything like it.

A large rectangular room with ten-foot ceilings, it had a row of windows from the counters up that stretched across the entire outside wall allowing for air and light. Below them, a double set of sinks occupied most of the counter space with Monique standing at one of them washing dishes while she talked with Melinda in a language he didn't understand.

On the far wall, opposite of where he stood, sat two large black iron stoves trimmed in a dull silver metal separated by four feet of counter space that made for a convenient workspace. Cluttered with several large spoons and a half dozen canisters, it had an opened faced wall cabinet directly above it that held dozens of jars of herbs and spices.

To his right sat two modern day electric refrigerators with an assortment of cupboards and pantries filling the walls next to them. And in the center of everything, was a large four by six-foot butcher's block that served as their workstation. Above it, an oblong iron rack just a little smaller in size hung from the ceiling with an array of pots and pans dangling from easily reached hooks. Equipped with every modern convenience and device that one could imagine, it was a cook's ultimate playground and was truly something to see.

Finding Melinda with her back to him, Foster grinned mischievously then quietly began to sneak up behind her. She was humming pleasantly while she talked with Monique and busily rolled out her dough on the butcher's block. Her mother, peeling potatoes across from her, began to speak but stopped at the sight of Foster's finger to his lips. Gazing at him for just a second, Martha just smiled and lowered her head then watched as he quickly stepped up behind her daughter.

"Gotcha," he yelled as he stomped his foot and dug his fingers into her rib cage.

Jumping in fright, Melinda squealed and dropped her rolling pin then instantly spun to face her attacker. "Foster," she yelled in an exasperated yet playful tone. "Don't do that! You just scared the heck out of me!"

Patting her chest in an attempt to catch her breath, she stared into his eyes then smiled and stepped toward him. Opening her arms to give him a hug, she suddenly stopped and widened her eyes then backed away and held his shoulders at arms length. She could smell the liquor on his breath and cigar smoke in his clothes and hair, and she knew in an instant that he'd been with her father.

"Okay Mister Siler," she began like a schoolmarm as she plopped her hands on her hips. "So just when did you get here?" she asked as she turned to Monique washing dishes. "I didn't hear the doorbell, did you Monique?"

"Oh no ma'am, I zid not hear anyshing. Maybe Mesieur Sjudge lets him in. Oui?" she said with an inconspicuous glance and wink to Foster.

"So you've been with daddy already, haven't you?" Melinda turned back and scowled.

Taking his cue from Monique, Foster quickly recited his version of how he arrived. He knew he'd been caught and that the telltale signs of alcohol and tobacco were too overwhelming. "Well to tell you the truth," he drawled with a humorous grin then raised his hands as if he'd just surrendered. "Yes I have. He was working in the library when I rang the doorbell and when nobody answered it he was kind enough to let me in. Now I'd come to get you, but we got to talking and before I knew it he'd dragged me into his library. Anyway one thing led to the other, but just as soon as we were done," he grinned. "He directed me right here, right to where all you pretty ladies were."

"Well, wasn't that just nice of him," Melinda snipped. "Now I know why he wanted the ice so early. To entertain you while we were in here working and slaving away. And did he make you drink and smoke too?" She went on in a tizzy. "And just what are you doing here so early anyway? I don't have any makeup on and my hair's a mess. And supper isn't for another two hours." She feigned her displeasure then crossed her arms.

"Well, don't you remember?" he smiled and spread his arms. "You said last week that you wanted to go riding right? So here I am, let's go. Besides," he grabbed her around the waist and pulled her tight. "You look just fine and your daddy wants us to check the southern fence line. He thinks some of his cattle are getting out."

"Oh Foster," Melinda cringed with a regrettable sweetness. "I can't, I promised him that I'd make him an apple pie for supper. And I've just started rollin out the dough."

"Melinda honey," her mother quickly interceded. "If you and Foster want to go for a ride and your daddy needs that southern fence line checked, then you just go ahead and go. There's plenty of time before supper and I think that Monique and I are quite capable of finishing up here just fine without you. Besides," she raised her eyebrows. "You've been wantin to ride that new horse of yours all week. Now it's a beautiful day. So go on an get out of here."

"Are you sure Momma?" Melinda drawled with a questionable gaze. "I really did promise daddy that I'd make him one of my pies."

"Now I already told you that Monique and I could handle this just fine," she frowned and then pointed toward the door. "Now quit your frettin and go. Besides if you don't, I'm gonna take that handsome young man you're standin next to and go ridin myself," she smiled and winked.

Beaming brightly, Melinda quickly wiped her hands then pulled the apron from around her waist. Rounding the butcher's block, she kissed her mother on the cheek then turned and headed for the door. "We'll be back in a couple of hours okay," she said excitedly as she grabbed Foster's hand.

"Well just be careful, ya hear. And don't be too late either."

But there was no answer; there was only the sound of laughter as the two headed out the door and disappeared.

That afternoon at the McAlister's turned out to be one of the most gratifying days that Foster could remember. His visit with the Judge when he first arrived had turned out to be so much more than he had expected. The start of a long and fruitful relationship that was also a career changing decision. A decision that caused him to once again relish in the prospects of his future, for not since his days in law school had he truly felt so alive and invigorated.

And then there was his ride with Melinda, which turned out to be a most enjoyable time. It seemed as if he were suddenly seeing her in a different light, in her natural state without the perfect hair and makeup as she rode atop her new chestnut gelding. And for the first time, he truly began to see the hidden beauty that lurked deep within her. Not the prissy little debutante she'd always appeared to be, but a strong willed young woman who was confident and in command of her mount. And had it not been for the fact that they were on a time sensitive mission to check the fence for her father, he probably could've talked her out of her dress. That was, if he'd really tried.

It was a secluded grassy area, flat and still in the sun on the curve of a small babbling creek, where they'd stopped to let the horses drink. But between her protest and the fact that they had yet to find the break in the fence, along with her promise to visit on Monday, he reluctantly ceased with his advances. Besides, they would do well to find the break if there was one, for he knew what it meant to lose animals. It was expensive, and it would most certainly please the Judge if they could close it.

Shortly after that, they came upon the break where a large limb from a tree that'd been struck by lightning had dropped straight on top of the fence. Snapping the top two strands of wire, it sent the third deep into the ground beneath it. It was an open invitation to the lush green pastures on the other side, and clearly visible in the dirt next to it was the telltale signs of hoof prints leading to them. How many cattle had gone through they didn't know, but after a few minutes of piling brush and broken limbs they had the new gateway blocked. Satisfied that it would serve until the Judge's farm hands could retrieve his cattle and repair it the next day, they mounted their horses and headed back.

Shortly after their return, there was supper. A delicious fried chicken dinner with all of the trimmings that finally ended in what the Judge most certainly thought was an apple pie that'd been lovingly made by his daughter. Nobody said a word, and as soon as they'd finished dessert, a snifter of brandy and the rest of their cigars on the porch finished their evening.

Yes, it had truly been a fantastic day. Yet as he drove back home, Foster couldn't help but think of his life and just how mundane it had become, and of how restless he'd become. He was thirty-five and had basically gone as far as one could really go in Mobile, especially with an economy that'd just come to a standstill. He felt stuck but he wanted more and always had, for in the back of his mind he'd always thought he was destined for greater things. Things other than just being a great trial lawyer. And then he thought of his talk with the Judge in the library when he'd first arrived, and then of the one later on the porch after dinner. Of how together they would open the doors into the sordid world of politics, and of how the actions he was about to take would carry him on a journey he never could have foreseen. It was the opportunity of a lifetime and he knew it. And as he finally pulled into his drive and turned out his lights, he wondered as to where it all would really take him.

CHAPTER 24

MONDAY MORNING FOSTER STROLLED INTO his office just after nine. After a cup of coffee and a few quick phone calls, he called Vicki into his office. He'd been thinking of how taken Willie had been with her toothbrush and shampoo, and of how she'd hugged him the night before in gratitude. He'd never imagined that the simple little gifts he'd given her would've had such an effect on her, but they did and it intrigued him. She was impressionable, and now with her birthday coming up that weekend, it was the perfect opportunity to buy her some more gifts. Gifts that she would need like clothes and shoes and girly things.

"Yes sir boss," she said as she took a seat with her pen and pad.

"Vicki," Foster began somewhat awkwardly. "I have sort of a problem that I need your help with. Oh, and you won't need that," he pointed to her tablet.

Looking up from her pad, Vicki pushed her glasses back onto her nose then set her pen and paper on the edge of his desk and cocked her head. "Is everything okay boss?"

"Yeah yeah," he replied with a dismissive wave. "Everything's fine, thanks. But like I said, I do have a little matter that I could use your help on. That is, if you don't mind?"

"Sure boss, I don't mind at all. Just name it, you know that. But what's wrong?" she pried. "You look a little troubled there."

"Well, I don't know if I've ever told you about my sister and her husband up in Tennessee."

"No, no you haven't. Why, are they in trouble? Do they need legal help?"

"No they don't need legal help, but they are in trouble. See, just like everybody else in this damn depression, they've fallen on some pretty hard times," he said and shook his head. "In fact, they've lost just about everything they had. The bank came and took it all last week, the house, the farm... everything."

"Aaah, that's terrible."

"Yes it is. It's really sad, especially since they have so many children. Hell at last count, I think they had seven or eight in all, and they're all young too. And now they can't even feed em all."

"Oh boss... that is sad."

"Yes it is," he nodded then turned his gaze out the window. "It really is."

"Well, what are they going to do? I mean, you just can't let all those little kids go hungry like that. It ain't right."

"I know, and that's why they've asked me if I could help them out."

"But how, what in the heck do they want you to do? Send them money?"

"No," he shook his head and laughed. "They've asked me to take in one of their children for a while, their oldest daughter actually. You know, to stay and live here in Mobile with me until they can get through these God awful times."

"Their oldest daughter? And what'd you tell em? Are ya gonna do it?"

"I already have."

"You have?"

"Yep, she got here Saturday."

"Aaah boss, that's so nice of you. Ya know, I just don't get it?"

"Get what?"

"Where everybody in town seems to think you're such an ass. Cause I'll tell ya, as far as I'm concerned, I think you're a saint. And you're sure gonna have a place in heaven for this one."

"Oh I ammm... am I," he raised his eyebrows. "Well, let's not get too carried away here with this whole benevolent thing and keep this to ourselves, okay. "I mean, the less people know, the better off my reputation as an ass will remain right?" he grinned.

"Yes sir," she snickered and scooted to the edge of her seat. "So just how can I help? What-a-ya want me to do?"

"Well," he sighed. "I need you to do some shopping for me. To buy her some clothes and some of those girly things that she'll need."

"She doesn't have any clothes?"

"Not really. I mean, you should've seen her when she got here and got off the train. She was just filthy. She had on these overalls that looked like they hadn't been washed in months, and a pair of worn out work boots with holes in the sides and the bottoms. It was just terrible, and sad. And what little she'd brought with her wasn't much better. All of it rolled up in a homemade shoulder sack. I'll tell ya, she just doesn't have anything to wear. And I know you have girls, right?"

"Yes sir, two of em," she beamed proudly. "Sixteen and twelve."

"Good, then you'll know what she needs and what to get. And since we're kind of slow this week, I was thinking that maybe you could take off a couple of afternoons early. Of course, on the clock that is. See, I'm just not very good at all that girly stuff. And quite frankly," he lowered his voice and leaned toward her. "I find it just a little embarrassing."

"Sure boss," Vicki giggled at his discomfort. "I'd be happy to. So where is she, at your house? You want me to pick her up there or do you wanna bring her here?"

"Oh nooo, she's not staying at my house."

"She isn't?"

"Oh heavens no," he said and shook his head. "I took her up river to the Davenport's house. She's going to be staying and working for me up there. You know, fixing it up and all. See, even though the place was nice, it still needs a lot of work."

"Whaaat?" Vicki stood and raised her voice. "Foster Siler, are you serious? That's mean. You just can't put a little girl up there all alone. All by herself," she argued with a scowling gaze. "She's probably scared half to death."

"Sure I can," he replied as if it were no big deal. "You don't need to worry about this little gal Vic. She's just fine; she's tough and smart. And besides, you remember Otis, don't you?"

"Sure I do. He's your new negro you got last week."

"Well... kind of," he chuckled and shook his head. "Anyway, he's going to be checking on her every Tuesday and Thursday for me just to make sure she's okay."

"Well, that still doesn't make it right!"

"I know, I know, but she's fine really," he assured. "Trust me. I wouldn't leave her up there if I thought anything could happen."

Looking down at her boss, Vicki, still just a little perturbed, shook her head and then slowly took her seat. "Well then mister smarty britches, just how in the hell am I supposed to buy her clothes? Ya know a body would be kind of handy."

"Yes yes, I know," Foster said as he threw up his hands and then rocked back in his chair. "But you'll just have to do without one for now."

"Oh good grief," she sighed and shook her head. "Then just tell me how old and how big is she."

"Ah she's fifteen, I think. And she's, aaaah. Well, she's just about your size actually. But maybe just a little bigger up here," he placed his hands over his chest and then snickered.

Instantly gaining a disenchanted scowl, Vicki sat forward with a huff. "All right buddy, you don't have to rub it in. I know what you're tryin to say. So how much do you wanna spend an just what kind of clothes do you want me to buy?"

Later that afternoon, Vicki took advantage of Fosters' request and left early. She didn't have to get everything, but she wanted to make a good start. Besides she was getting paid to shop, and that was something every woman enjoyed. Some money along with another reminder to keep mum and she was out the door. Finishing out his afternoon, Foster couldn't help but drift with his thoughts to Melinda and her promise. She'd said four thirty, and with a glance to the clock he exhaled with an agonizing sigh. He had an hour to go.

———————

It was hitting close to five before Melinda finally pulled into his driveway. She was late but it didn't matter and within minutes Foster had her in bed. It seemed that once she'd given herself over to him and the pleasures of sex, she was his. She liked what they did, and each time they made love, she seemed to slip a little deeper under his control. She would do anything he asked, for it was without question that she loved him and wanted desperately to marry him. He was smart, successful and dashingly handsome. The ultimate catch in not only her eyes, but in the eyes of many others as well. Especially her mother and father, who approved of him immensely. Yet for some reason he hadn't asked, even after dating for almost a year. And now at twenty-four, it began to weigh heavily on her mind. Her clock was ticking and it certainly didn't help that most of her friends were now married, some with children already. She wondered if something was wrong with her.

They ate a light supper and talked. They laughed, and drank some wine. She gave herself to him again, passionately and completely, as if she were attempting to prove she could be a good wife. This is what married women did for their husbands to please them. What more could he want from her? She'd given him everything, or so she thought. They rested, and then around nine, she finally dressed and left for home.

Rising with the sun, Foster ate a quick breakfast then decided on a whim to meet Otis at the boat. He wanted to make sure he showed up on time and would make it up river okay. Driving to the marina, he waited until eight then watched as his newest employee pulled into the parking lot. Pleased but not surprised, he drove up beside him just as Otis had shut down his truck.

"Mornin boss," Otis greeted as he opened his door and stepped outside. "Are ya go'n with me?"

"Morning Otis," Foster replied as he too stepped from his car. "And naaah I can't. I just wanted to make sure that you got out of here okay and to remind you to stop by my office when you got back."

"Oh yes sur, I won't forget."

"Good, and I also wanted to give you this," he said as he held up his arms. "To give to Willie."

Reaching up, Otis grabbed the two six packs of coke. "Oh yes sur. Miss Willie'l shorly like this," he said as he looked at one and then the other. "I'll give em to her jus as soon as I get there."

"Good Otis, you do that. But listen, she's going to want to drink them all right away, but you tell her I said only two a day, okay. And preferably in the afternoon," he raised his eyebrows. "I don't want her drinking all of these in two days like she did that block of ice if you know what I mean," he added as they both began to laugh.

Ten minutes later, Foster stood on the edge of the pier and watched as his boat slowly disappeared into the bay. He was really glad that he'd taken the Davenport case and he marveled at how the last two weeks had unfolded. There was the house and the boat and Katherine, and now Willie. And he was glad that he'd kept Otis on too. He had a comforting sense about the man and for some reason he trusted him completely. Maybe it was that Otis seemed genuinely and almost instantaneously loyal. He really didn't know, but he was glad that he was checking on Willie. And as the boat finally faded from sight, he turned back to his car and headed to work.

Later that morning, Vicki struggled up the steps and into Foster's office. Dropping her two bags in front of his desk, she grabbed a cup of coffee from the back then returned and plopped into a chair. Lighting a cigarette, she took a pull then blew her smoke to the ceiling and looked at Foster. "Mornin boss," she said as she pushed her glasses back up her nose. "Wanna see what I bought?"

As it turned out, Vicki proved to be a most frugal shopper. It seemed that the years she had spent shopping for her daughters had honed her skills to a perfection and she'd really stretched the twenty dollars that Foster had given her. And even though she'd bought mostly working clothes for boys, boots, pants, and socks and shirts, she also bought a few girly things. Some new underpants and a nice hairbrush, things like that. Things that girls really wanted and liked, and other than guessing on the shoe size, everything else as she so eloquently insinuated, should be a prefect fit.

"It looks great Vic," Foster said as he looked over the pile of clothes. "But I still have one more favor to ask if you don't mind."

———◆———

Gazing vigilantly forward, Otis finally spied the pier through the branches of the big tree hanging out over the water. Rounding the bend in the tributary, and now only a hundred yards away, he gradually pulled back on the throttle and blew the boat's horn. A few seconds later, he smiled and watched as Willie sprinted across the grass and then down the pier. She was fleet and fast, and even though they'd only been gone a day, he could tell she was excited to see the boat. Beaming brightly, she called to him as he began his turn into the pier. "Mornin Mister Otis," she piped happily.

"Mornin Miss Willie," he yelled back through the opened door as he threw the boat into reverse. "Catch me, can ya."

"Now that was the first time that I went back up river by myself. I remember it real well too cause jus as soon as we got the boat all tied up, I gave Willie those two six packs of coke. An jus like ol Foster had predicted," he shook his head. "She wanted to drink em all right then an there. An she would have too, but I stopped her an told her what he'd said about how she was only suppose to have two of em a day, an preferably in the afternoon."

"An so what'd she think of that?" Jim asked.

"Well," Otis chuckled. "She didn't like it. In fact, she didn't like it at all, but she took em on up to the house anyway an shortly after that we started workin. I remember we were scrapin paint off the house when after about a couple of hours, ol Willie jus up an disappeared. Now at first I didn't think much of it, but after a little while I started ta wonder where she'd run off to when all of a sudden I heard her callin my name. She called me Mister Otis back then," he paused as he fondly recalled the sound of her voice. "An to tell ya the truth, I kind of liked that cause back then there wasn't nobody that called me Mister, specially a white girl. It jus wasn't done, but Willie, well she was different.

"Anyway, I walked on around the house to see what was wrong, an that's when I got the surprise of my life cause right there at the picnic table was Willie. An right in front of her was two plates of food an two cokes sittin right next to each other. It was lunch that she'd made for the both of us."

It was close to three by the time Otis returned and made his way up to Foster's office. Politely removing his hat as he entered, he took a nervous step toward the counter and then waited until Dawn looked up. "Well, hello Otis," she greeted.

"Good afternoon Miss Dawn," he replied, somewhat surprised at her tone. "I, I's here ta see--."

"Yes yes, I know," she interrupted. "Mister Siler told me you'd be comin in, so just have a seat and I'll let him know that you're here."

"Yes ma'am," he replied as he turned and took one of the chairs along the wall. "Thank you."

A couple minutes later Otis was in Foster's office discussing his trip and Willie's status. "And did she like the coke?" Foster asked with a grin.

"Oh yes sur," Otis replied. "An jus like you said, she wanted to drink em right then an there. But I told her she couldn't cause you said so."

"An what'd she say to that?"

"Well boss," he grinned and shook his head. "She didn't like it. In fact, she didn't like that at all."

Rocking back in his chair, Foster laughed and listened as Otis recounted his day with Willie. About ten minutes later, the young black man finally finished and rose from his chair. "Oh and Otis," Foster said as the man stood. "Grab another block of ice and take it with you when you go back on Thursday. And when you get back, I want you to check back in with me again."

"Yes sur," he said as he left.

Satisfied that Willie was fine, Foster soon turned his thoughts to Katherine and for the rest of the day she occupied his mind until he quietly pulled along side her garage and shut off his lights. It was a beautiful night, and as he stepped from his car and looked up, he smiled at the soft glow radiating from her bedroom window. It was the only light on in the house, and with a deep breath he quietly closed his door and headed toward the front porch.

They'd developed a carnal relationship over the last two weeks and in the process they'd dropped all discretion for tonight he would brazenly use the front door. The nervousness and guarded caution that he'd felt and used in his earlier visits had waned. Disappearing with each successive visit until it had metamorphosed into a self-assured arrogance and then into a reckless abandon. Her husband was gone and as far as he was concerned, she was his to use for as long as he wanted. It was that simple.

——◆——

Wednesday morning came with an unexpected and excited call from the Judge. It seemed that the calls he'd made on Monday, had generated a great deal of interest. More so than what he'd really expected. There were men visiting from out of town who wanted to meet him. Important men, who were connected both politically and professionally, and the Judge was having lunch with them later today. They talked briefly of its significance, and with the opportunity at hand, Foster quickly cancelled the rest of his day.

Around twelve-thirty, he found himself sitting at a private table with the Judge and six other men in a small upscale place downtown. Some of whom he recognized by name and some he didn't. An eclectic yet cohesive group, that'd been brought together by a common bond. A bond that was actually twofold in its propose. One, they were united in their efforts to find a suitable candidate who believed in the basic principles of capitalism. Which now seemed to center around him. And two, was their clear and obvious disdain for the incumbent.

Their discussion as they ate was direct and to the point. They were men of business and obvious power, captains of industry who were struggling in the hardest of times and had little time or need for chit-chat. They wanted to know Foster's thoughts on the economy and the various possibilities of bringing new companies into the state. Answering a barrage of questions as they ate, Foster sparred and danced with the men like a seasoned politician. He was a natural and Judge McAlister, who'd been quietly watching, beamed delightedly.

Gaining a number of smiles and nods, they finally finished with a discrete round of drinks from the back and cigars from the Judge. To Senator Siler, they quietly toasted. And so it was, that in a single meeting, the wheels of Foster's political future were quietly set into motion.

The next day he awoke to an overcast sky but that aside, Foster was still he grinning like a kid on Christmas morning. He was euphoric, yet as he rose from bed he wondered. Did they really like him as well as he thought? Could he do it? Could he win against such a long seated opponent? Stepping into his bathroom he turned on the water and then whipped up a lather in his cup.

"Well ol buddy, what-a-ya-think?" he raised his eyebrows and stared at his reflection. "That Crandell ain't so tough," he smirked and puffed out his chest toward the mirror. "Shit, you can whip his ass any day of the week, and that Senate floor ain't so scary either. Heck, it ain't no different than a big ol courtroom, right?" He nodded with a grin, then wiped the steam from the mirror and began shaving. "You're just changing directions a little, that's all."

A few moments later, he finished with a contented sigh and wiped his face clean. Smiling into the mirror, he reflected on all of the questions rolling through his mind, and as his grin slowly dissipated into a confident stare, he decided he already knew the answers.

Stepping outside, Foster looked to the sky. It'd darkened somewhat and looked like rain, yet it remained dry. And then he thought of Otis, who by now should be on his way up river. He dropped into his car and headed toward the marina. He wanted to check and make sure he'd gotten away. The slip was empty. He looked to the bay and then his watch. It was eight thirty and Otis was gone.

Later that afternoon he returned and reported back in. It was right around three and Foster couldn't have been happier with his newest employee for true to his word, he was if anything, punctual. His trip was good and Willie was in good spirits he said. And even though she was out of ice, which hardly surprised him, she still had six cokes left. They both laughed. Foster gave him Friday off then made arrangements to meet at nine on Saturday at the marina.

It was close to six by the time he made it home and could finally clear his mind. The what ifs and the unknowns of political life had been a constant concern and had drained his energy. He was tired, but now it was time to think of something else. To think of the beautiful woman who would soon be lying in her bed beneath the covers, naked, waiting for him to arrive.

Pouring a drink he stood and stared through the dirty panes of his bedroom window, watching as the sun slowly disappeared below the horizon. A silver lining shown briefly on one of the far off cumulus clouds then quickly disappeared. He smiled. His head was finally clearing with new and more pleasant thoughts replacing his concerns of earlier. He showered and then lay across his bed and waited. Patiently, like the high lord of the underworld, for the impending cloak of darkness that would conceal his movements before venturing out.

They'd decided on Tuesdays and Thursdays. It worked perfect for the both of them. After sunset she would open a bottle of wine then bathe and perfume herself and retire to her bedroom. Lighting a large single candle, she would place it in front of the mirror on the dresser then crawl between the covers and wait for him to come. To take her at his will, and in any way he desired. It would be the only light on in the house and she would continue to light it she told him, until the house had sold and she'd joined her husband in New Orleans.

Friday morning on his way to work, Foster detoured and made a stop at Crystal's Bakery. He wanted to get Willie a cake for her birthday. His bet was that she'd probably never had one before and that she would react with undying gratitude. Besides, what kid didn't like cake? Browsing their selections while he picked out some donuts for the girls, he finally settled on a small chocolate cake with chocolate icing to pick up on Saturday morning.

The donuts turned out to be a real surprise, and as they ate and gabbed and drank their coffee, Vicki retrieved the small stack of books she'd brought and gave them to Foster. "Here ya go boss," she said as she plopped the stack on his desk. "These are some of the books my kids had when they were little. They're used, but they're still in good shape an you can just have em."

Reaching for the stack, Foster pulled it toward him. "Thanks Vic," he replied as he picked one from the top and opened it up. A second later, he nodded and smiled. They were perfect and he was delighted, the writing was big and there were colored pictures on every page.

Finishing their donuts and coffee, the three finally set about working and trudged through the day. Later that evening, another date with Melinda followed by a roll between the sheets finished it on a high note. Her heart was his yet even so, after he'd dropped her off and drove back home, he couldn't help but think of Willie.

CHAPTER 25

———◆———

THE NEXT MORNING FOSTER AND Otis loaded the boat with groceries and supplies to restock the cabin. All of the items that Vicki had bought, including the books, were now all wrapped in plain brown paper. Certain that Willie wouldn't venture up front, Foster put them in the forward cabin on the bed along with the cake from Crystal's Bakery. They were surprises for her birthday, and after several more trips to the car, they were ready.

"Is that it boss?" Otis asked as he jumped into the stern with the last box.

"Not quite," Foster turned and grinned. "I still have one more thing we need to get."

"What's that boss?"

"A boat."

"A boat?" Otis repeated with a curious gaze. "Really... what kind-a boat?"

"A little fishin boat with one of those new outboard motors on the back. You know, the one with the handle so you can steer it. Come on, it's right down here at the end of the pier," he gestured with his hand and began walking. "I bought it earlier this week for Willie."

Twenty minutes later the two finally headed out of the harbor and turned up river. The little craft they'd secured to the stern followed some forty feet behind and even though it slowed their speed, Foster didn't mind.

"An that's pretty much how we started up river. I remember Foster was all excited cause it was Willie's birthday an he was gonna surprise her. You

282

know, with a few simple gifts. He said that it was the nice thing to do an all since she didn't have no family.

"Anyway, the go'n was kind of slow cause of that little fishin boat, but we finally made it up there an jus as soon as we rounded the last bend an cleared that big tree that stuck out over the water, ol Foster reached up an blew the horn."

"Think she'll be surprised?" Foster asked as he released the knotted rope and then watched as the object of his desires came sprinting across the grass.

"Oh yes sur," Otis replied. "I think she'll be real suprised.

Pulling alongside the pier, Otis hit reverse and brought the boat to a stop then immediately went to neutral. And just as she'd done the last time they had arrived, Willie stood on the pier, bouncing on the balls of her feet waiting to catch a line. "Good mornin Mister Siler, hey Mister Otis!" she yelled happily. "What's that?"

"Morning Willie," Foster drawled as he coiled a line to throw. "And what's what?" he teased.

"That," she said and pointed. "That little boat, with the thing on it."

"Oh that," he laughed. "Why that's you're new fishing boat. And that little thing on the back as you so eloquently put it, is a motor so you don't have to paddle it," he grinned and threw the line.

"For meee?" she beamed as she caught the flailing mass. "An it makes it go… like the big boat?" she asked, tying the line to the pylon just as Otis jumped onto the pier and did the same up front.

"Yes ma'am," he laughed. "It makes it go, just like the big boat."

Standing on the pier with a grin from ear to ear, Willie stared at the little craft for just a second then jumped into the boat beside Foster. Glancing toward the boat and then to him, then back to the boat again, she wrapped her arms around him and gave him a big warm hug.

"Oh thank you," she said. "Can I see it closer?"

"Sure Willie."

Releasing her hold she quickly turned and began pulling on the line until the boat bumped against the stern and she jumped over the side. Carefully stepping to the back, she took a seat then grabbed the handle to the motor. "Can we go for a ride?" she asked as she swiveled the motor back and forth.

"Sure Willie," Foster laughed and shook his head. "Just as soon as we get unloaded, we'll go for a spin. I'll even have Otis teach you how to make it go. How's that?"

Grinning excitedly, the young girl was out of the boat just as fast as she'd gotten in and without a moment's hesitation began carrying supplies to the house. She wanted to drive the little boat in the worst of ways and just as soon as they'd finished and had everything stocked, she returned to the pier with Otis and set about pulling it to shore. A quick little lesson from him on how to start it and make it go, and then a warning about the dangers of the spinning propeller, and she was ready.

Pushing her away from the shore, she turned the throttle to the little motor and was on her way. Standing at the water's edge, Foster and Otis watched while Willie sped up and down the tributary. She was having the time of her life and for almost ten minutes she churned up the waters, circling and turning first one way and then another until her little motor suddenly stopped.

It seemed that no one had bothered to check the fuel and after a few minutes of pulling on the cord, it dawned on Otis and he yelled at the frustrated girl to paddle in. That afternoon, they did very little work but to Foster it didn't matter for in the back of his mind he wanted to make sure she had plenty to do while he was away. It was important to keep her busy and make her feel as if she were helping and needed for as long as was possible. It was part of a plan he'd devised in an effort to seduce and bed her, for there was nothing more that he liked than the hunt and the stalking of a new quarry, and then ultimately the spoils of his success. They had fun but the day soon passed, and after a dinner that was fit for a king and a bit of stargazing, they all went to bed.

———◆———

Early the next morning, Foster quietly rose from his bed and slipped into the kitchen. He'd wanted to surprise, or more accurately, to seduce Willie for her birthday. He'd remembered her reaction to the toothbrush, and knew that the cake and gifts would take him far. How far he really wasn't sure, but she was young and naive, and very very impressionable. And with the breaking dawn now providing just enough light to see, he retrieved the cake and her gifts that he'd hidden in the cabinets while she was boating. As far as he could discern, she suspected nothing and with an ever-growing smile he lit the candles and picked up the cake then turned and headed to her bedroom.

Waking to the soft knock and the creak of her door, Willie groggily opened her eyes to the sight of Foster holding a cake with fifteen candles burning brightly in the dim morning light. Propping herself up onto one elbow, she wiped the sleep from her eyes and then smiled. She was completely surprised, and as he entered into a terrible rendition of happy birthday and began walking toward her, she began to giggle.

Foster was a terrible singer and he knew it, but still he continued on as he crossed the room and took a seat on the edge of her bed. Finishing with the cake on his lap, Willie silently stared at the candles, their flickering flames radiating and bathing her face in a soft angelic glow. It was a surprise unlike anything she'd ever had before and she wanted to cry, for no one other than her mother had ever shown her such kindness. But here was this handsome older man, who she was so deeply attracted to and who'd already given her so much, sitting on the edge of her bed with a cake. He had remembered. He did care about her. Her heart swelled to an almost unbearable level.

"Now make a wish," he said softly. "And blow out your candles."

Hesitating for a second, Willie stared deep into Foster's eyes as if she were trying to send a message. A stare that was unwavering and lascivious in nature, as if to say that she was all grown up now and ready to become a woman. That was enhanced to an even greater degree by the iridescent glow reflecting in her eyes. Then shifting them to the burning candles, she propped herself up just a little more, rolled to her side and took a big deep breath. A second later, she extinguished the tiny blue and yellow flames in a billowing plume of smoke.

"Well Happy Birthday Willie," Foster said as she lay back down. "And did you make a wish?"

Nodding her head, Willie just smiled and stared at the man she'd come to care so much for. She felt a little more at ease without the glaring light from the candles, and as her eyes slowly readjusted to the dim morning light, she could clearly see him staring back. And even though she felt a little self-conscious, she felt warm and safe and special under his gaze. She liked it, and now for some reason, she felt a little older and all grown up.

She wondered if he'd seen and read the message in her eyes. She felt as if he had, but she was still unsure of what to do. She knew what she wanted and had wished for, yet even so she was anxious and reluctant to act. She wanted to kiss him like a married woman. Like a married woman would kiss her husband. Like she'd seen her mother and stepfather do when she was younger and in happier times. But he was her boss and she didn't dare, she would get fired and she needed her job.

The seconds seemed like minutes, and as she fidgeted and agonized with a nervous uncertainty, she watched as he carefully leaned forward and set the cake on the nightstand. Pushing it from the edge, he then casually turned back, placed his hand on the other side of her hips and gazed down at her. This was it she thought as her heart began to pound, she was supposed to say something; he was waiting. Something grown-up. But what? "Is that a real cake?" she finally blurted.

She'd said it with all of the innocence in the world, but before the words had even escaped her mouth she cringed with regret and quickly turned away. God Willie, how stupid could you be. Of course it was real. Why in the heck would he bring you a cake that wasn't real?

"Yes ma'am," Foster chuckled as he glanced at the cake and then back to her. "A chocolate cake with chocolate icing," he drawled in an effort to ease her anxiety. "Direct from Crystal's Bakery."

Rising back to her elbows, Willie turned and stared at the cake, its candles still emanating wispy trails of smoke into the air like miniature chimneys. "What kind?" she asked as she cocked her head and scrunched her face. "A cho-ca-whaaaat?"

Chuckling and shaking his head, Foster sat for a moment and wondered if everything was so completely new to her? Had she really been that sheltered? She was one of the most beautiful young women he'd ever met and appeared to be highly intelligent, yet she knew so little about common everyday items. And then he thought of who she was and where she'd come from. An orphaned and isolated sharecropper with no education. A sad and harsh existence, especially in the eyes of society and one that really wasn't much better than that of the slaves of the 1800's.

"Chocolate, Willie," he answered kindly. "It'sss... well, it's really really good. I had it made at Crystal's Bakery, just for you. For your birthday."

"A real store bought cake?" She gasped. "An you had it made for me. Oooh Mister Siler," she continued in a grateful tone as she looked at him and then the cake. "I ain't never had a cho-ca-let before," she said as she turned back. "What's it taste like?"

"Well it's chocolate," he said as he casually reached for the cake and pulled out a candle. "It's good, and since you've never had it before, how about if we just change that right now."

Nodding her head, Willie sat up with both hands behind her and watched as he dipped the tiny wax stick into the icing. Smearing and twirling it across the top until he had a nice large glob rolled onto the end, Foster finally turned back to Willie. "Here ya go," he said as he brought the ball of frosting to her lips. "Now close your eyes and open."

Closing her eyes with an anticipating grin, Willie parted her lips and waited until she felt the thin waxy stick with its ball of frosting lightly touch her lips. Taking the candle in like a straw, she gently sucked and pulled the soft creamy mixture into her mouth and across her tongue. A second later, she opened her eyes in wide-eyed wonderment. "Oh my," she gasped with a great big grin. "I ain't never had nothin like that before."

"See, I told you it was good, didn't I?"

Nodding with yet another smile, Willie watched as Foster took the candle and coated it once again. Closing her eyes, she parted her lips and waited until she felt the tip and took the light creamy mixture into her mouth. Savoring in its flavor for just a moment, she finally swallowed then stared as if she were searching for something to say. Until, and in what was nothing more than a simple act of appreciation, she leaned toward him and hugged him. "Thank you for be'n so nice to me," she mumbled as she laid her head on his shoulder and nuzzled her face into his neck.

Quickly responding, Foster encircled his arms and pulled her tight. Yes, he thought as she melted into his chest, this was what he'd been waiting for, his opening that would lead into the next stage of his seduction. A seduction that would play upon her emotions of love and trust until he could manipulate and control them at will. He was thirty-five and definitely knew what to do when it came to women. Not some adolescent boy who was awkwardly stumbling into uncharted territory. He knew what to say and how to say it, and how to judge and read her reactions. And he knew how and where to touch her, especially in places that would give her pleasure and build desires. Desires that he hoped would grow with an ever-increasing intensity. That would drive her into his arms and then ultimately into his bed.

Reaching from behind, he gently pulled her hair away from her shoulder and then cradled the back of her head with his hand. Holding her gently, he lowered his head and then tenderly kissed her neck just below her ear. A second later, she felt his breath on her ear, hot and moist, and then his lips and teeth as he gently nibbled and pulled at her earlobe. Inhaling sharply, Willie trembled and moaned then clutched his shirt in her hands and tightened her hold around his back. Smiling once again, but in the most salacious of ways, Foster returned her squeeze and then brought his lips to her cheek as he boldly and shamelessly continued.

Closing her eyes as a euphoric rush invaded her body, Willie felt as if she were in a dream. She was delirious and confused, and afraid, but still she wanted him to continue. It was her wish, and now it was coming true, until, and to her chagrin, it ended when he suddenly stopped and pulled back. Opening her eyes as if she'd done something wrong, Willie dropped her hands back to the bed for support and then cleared her throat. She wanted to say something but couldn't, she was at a loss for words and could only think of what he'd just done and what was hopefully about to come.

Would he kiss her again... on the lips? Like a married woman? She silently prayed then swallowed and watched as he slowly leaned toward the cake and dipped a finger into the icing. "Would you like some more?" he whispered as he brought his hand to her mouth.

Instantly nodding her head once again, Willie closed her eyes and parted her lips. A second later, she felt the tip of his finger trace lightly across her lips as he coated and smeared them in a thin layer of frosting. She was in heaven, and as she slowly licked her lips she began to wonder if she would suddenly wake and find it all a dream. She hoped not, but still she fretted until she opened her eyes to the sound of his voice as he leaned to gather another taste.

"More?" he simply asked as he dipped his finger into the icing again.

Brought to her mouth before she could answer, Willie suddenly and surprisingly reached up and took his hand then held his gaze. She wanted him to see her as a woman who was unafraid, and as she continued to stare she brazenly leaned forward and took his finger into her mouth. Sucking and licking, she slowly cleaned the icing from it as if it were her own.

It was an act she enjoyed, but no sooner than she'd finished and it had slid from her mouth, she batted her eyes and turned away as if she'd done something she shouldn't have. She wanted to take back what she'd done but she couldn't, she could only sit and wonder if she'd been to forward and gone to far until Foster reached beneath her chin and turned her back.

Swallowing nervously, Willie tried to look away again but he held her gaze and then slowly leaned toward her. He was going to kiss her and she knew it, and as he moved ever closer, she clenched the bed sheets with both of her fist and closed her eyes. A second later, she felt his breath and then the softness of his lips on hers as he slowly and sensuously kissed the outer folds of her mouth. Lingering and testing with a tender caution.

To Willie, it was the most magical of moments. As if a thousand tiny butterflies had just landed on her at once, tingling her skin with the fluttering of their wings. Reeling with an erotic and ecstatic pleasure that she could hardly endure, she twisted the bed sheets into knots as she tightened her grip. She wanted to breath but couldn't, she was frozen in a state of euphoria. It was her wish come true, but all to soon Foster broke their kiss and pulled back to gauge her reaction.

Her comfort level was growing and he could sense it, and although her eyes were heavily glazed and her nostrils flared with each and every breath, she seemed undaunted. She liked what he'd done, and before she knew it she felt his lips again, gently and tenderly, then full and rapturously as he pressed against her with an increasing fervor. Closing her eyes, she blindly brought her hands to his shoulders. Yes, he was kissing her... like a married woman!

A heated rush of pleasure instantly swept throughout her, almost narcotic like in its effect. As if a hundred tiny candles had just been lit deep in the pit of her stomach, transmuting their warmth into a dampened heat that seemed to well like a giant wave from the depths of her loins, fueling and driving her passion. She remembered her bath at the pool before she'd left home and the pleasures she had experienced. Her breast hardened and ached to be touched. And now with those very same feelings and desires driving her actions, the fifteen-year old birthday girl wrapped her arms around him and parted her lips, then melted into his mouth.

She was passionate, yet even so Foster knew to take it slow. He knew she'd never been kissed before, and could feel her body trembling as he began to feed on her innocence. A few moments later, and after what seemed like an eternity, they finally broke and took a much-needed breath. Willie was glowing and in a dream world as she laid back down and stared up at Foster. "You kissed me," she drawled with the sweetest and most radiant of smiles.

"Yes... I did," he replied. "Did you like it?"

Biting her lower lip, Willie looked into his eyes then answered with the nod and a devilish grin. "Can we do it agin?"

Chuckling beneath his breath, Foster just shook his head and stretched out beside her then lowered his face to hers. She was a quick learner, and was soon kissing like a grown woman while he cagily began to touch and caress her in places that would build her desires yet not offend or frighten her. Playing and plucking at her body like a concert pianist, he worked on her in the most salacious of ways but still he kept it clean. He wanted to build her desires until she came to him. It was what he wanted most, and with the way she was responding, he knew that it wouldn't be long.

A short time later, Willie slowly opened her gifts one by one. Her new shirts, pants, and shoes were the finest things she'd ever owned, but what she coveted the most were the books he'd brought. She was overwhelmed with a thankfulness she could barely express, and was joyous almost to the point of tears. "Oooh Mister Siler," she said in a quiet voice as she stared at the books in her lap. "I, I jus don't know what to say. Nobody's ever done nothin like this for me before an I," she stopped and raised her head, then brushed a tear from her cheek.

"Well Willie, you don't have to say anything," he said. "It's your birthday and those are my gifts to you. It's that simple," he added as he reached up and pinched the tip of her chin. "But from now on," he smiled and raised his eyebrows. "Why don't you just call me Foster, huh? I think after what we just did, we can leave the Mister part off now don't you?"

"Yes sur," she nodded and drawled with a shameless grin.

A few moments later, Willie cut and ate her very first piece of chocolate cake. Consuming it in minutes, she washed it all down with a cold glass of milk and quickly cut another while Foster ate his with a cup of coffee. She was ecstatic and marveled at the new taste of chocolate. "Can Mister Otis have a piece too?" she asked.

"Sure Willie," he chuckled. "If that's what you want. It's your birthday."

"Good," Willie replied. "Cause he's nice to me an helps me a lot when he comes up."

"He does?"

"Ah huh," she nodded.

"Well, then let's cut him a great big piece, cause I think Mister Otis would really enjoy that, don't you."

To Foster, Willie had a gentle kindness toward other people that touched him deeply. Colored or not it made no difference, and that was a quality that sat highly within him. A few minutes later, and after she'd dressed in her new clothes, she cut a large piece of cake and poured a glass of milk, then headed out the door.

"Now ol Foster had said that he wanted to surprise her an from the look on her face an the sound of her voice when she came walkin down that pier, I guess he must of really succeeded. I remember I was fishin right off of the end, you know, jus kind-a waitin for the two of them to wake an start stirrin when I turned to the sound of her singin an callin out my name long an slow." 'Missster Ooootis... I brought you a surpri-iiiise,' *he imitated. "An there she was, all dressed up in her new clothes an grinnin from ear to ear with a glass a milk in one hand an a great big piece of chocolate cake in the other. I'll tell ya she sure was happy, an jus as soon as she got next to me, she plopped down with this big shit eatin grin on her face an said here! I remember she was absolutely glowin an almost ready to bust. An that's when she told me that it was her birthday an that Foster had surprised her.*

"*Really, an so how old was she?*"

"*Fifteen,*" *Otis replied as if he still couldn't believe it.* "*I remember when she told me, an how I damn near choked an fell off of that pier.*"

"*Fifteeeen?*" *Jim repeated and cringed.* "*You're kiddin?*"

"*Oh nooo,*" *Otis shook his head.*

"*Really?*"

"*Yes sir, although she didn't look like no fifteen year old that I ever knew,*" *he chuckled.*

"*An so how old was your boss, this Foster guy?*"

"*Aaah, I think,*" *Otis looked to the sky.* "*He was around thirty-five if I remember right.*"

"*Jesus, what a dog,*" *Jim rolled his eyes and shook his head.*

"*Dog,*" *Otis scoffed with a laugh.* "*Shit he was way worse than a dog. Anyway, I didn't waste no time diggin into that cake, an while I sat there an ate ol Willie told me about all the stuff that Foster had bought her for her birthday. Oh, an when she started callin him Foster instead of Mister Siler, well, I knew right then an there that somethin was up. But the thing that I remember the most was how excited she was about those little books that he'd given her. I'll tell ya, she wanted to learn how to read worse than anyone I'd ever seen. Then, an jus as I finished that cake an downed my milk, well, that's when ol Foster came walkin on down with a cup of coffee an joined us.*

"*He was real laid back that mornin, an after he sat down an we'd chit chatted a bit about the fishin an how they wasn't bitten to good, he told me to jus keep on tryin cause we wasn't gonna do any work on account that it was Willie's birthday.*

"*An that's pretty much how we spent the mornin, with me fishin an cleanin the boat while I waited for somethin to bite an the two of them up on the porch, with Foster given Willie her very first readin an written lesson. Yes sir, we didn't do a lick of work which suited all of us jus fine. Anyway, by the time we finally left I had a bucket with a few nice catfish an ol Willie was already startin to read her first little words. I'll tell ya Jim,*" *he paused and stared.* "*That girl wasn't jus pretty, no sir, she was smart too... damn smart.*"

CHAPTER 26

———◆———

WITHOUT MUCH OF A BREAKFAST other than their chocolate cake, the three ate an early lunch then Foster and Otis prepared to leave. Standing in the stern as they rounded the bend with the big tree he waved a final goodbye to Willie and left her to her own. He felt good about his progress and smiled at the fact that it was overly and abundantly clear she liked the act of kissing.

He remembered their last kiss in the house before he left and knew that it wouldn't take long to break down any barriers she might have that would impede her in coming to him. He would have her, he was certain of it, and soon. He took a chair in the stern and relaxed. Otis's bucket of fish setting tight in the corner, stirred lazily as they moved and jostled amongst themselves in search of an escape from their oxygen deprived environment. Smiling, he then turned his gaze to the passing shore and caught a glimpse of an all too familiar sight.

There they were again, the two largest inhabitants of the river lying on the muddy bank, basking in the late morning sun. And although they were now a little closer to the house, he still didn't worry. Willie had a gun and she knew how to use it. A moment later, he closed his eyes and drifted with his thoughts as to how his week was starting all over again, and in the most routine of fashions.

Later that afternoon, it would be dinner with his future in-laws along with some serious discussion and planning with the Judge. Monday after work it would be another visit from Melinda. Tuesday's and Thursday's, Otis would take the boat and check on Willie then report back in. And on each of those days after dark, he would make his illicit visit to the Davenport household.

They had a good thing going, but he knew, as did she, that their time was limited. That it wouldn't be long before the bank came and took the house and she moved to New Orleans. It was just a matter of time, and so he made it a point to take advantage of what little was left. Staying late into the night, he would leave an exhausted man. On Friday it would be another date with Melinda, most likely a dinner and a movie. And then on Saturday morning, he and Otis would head back up river.

"Now if I remember right, it was the Thursday after Willie's birthday, that I'd made my second trip up that week. We'd worked pretty hard all mornin scrapin paint an had gotten a lot done when we finally decided to call it quits an take lunch. Willie had made us a couple of really nice sandwiches an jus as soon as we sat down at that picnic table, she opened up one of those little books that Foster had given her an started lookin at the pictures while we ate. Then, an jus as soon as we'd finished, she smiled great big an started readin to me."

"I'll tell ya, she sure was proud that she could read, even if it was jus a few simple words. An then she asked me if I wanted ta learn. Now at first I thought she was kiddin an started laughin, but then, an before I knew it, that little gal started given me my very first readin an writin lesson. Actually, the first of many to come."

"So wait a minute," Jim seemed surprised. "You mean you didn't know how to read?"

"Oh heck no," Otis shook his head. "Or at least not back then I didn't."

"An how old were you?"

"I was twenty-five," he replied. "Now at first it was kind of embarrassin an all, but there wasn't no one else around so I let her point an read to me jus like Foster had done for her. I remember we sat there until we'd gone through that whole book an after that, we got up an went back to work. Then about an hour later, I decided to jus take off an head on back, an since there was still plenty of daylight left, Willie told me that she was gonna go for a ride in her new boat. To go explorin as she put it," he chuckled as he recalled her words. "An jus as soon as I'd pulled away she headed back up to the house to get her shotgun."

Grabbing her shotgun and a small container of water from the house, Willie returned to her boat and after checking her gas like she'd been taught, she gave her little motor a couple of pulls and was off. Sputtering away from the pier, she turned the boat north and headed up river.

He'd been paddling and floating for a day and a half in an effort to reach Mobile, and although the small wooden boat that he'd stolen served as his transportation, it provided little comfort. Exhausted from the pain that still coursed through his leg and shoulder, and the sleepless night that he'd spent along the shore, he tiredly paddled on. Unshaven, filthy dirty, and unbelievably hungry, every exposed part of his body was welted with mosquito bites from his night on the river. In short, he was just plain miserable, yet as he floated on he could sense that he was getting close.

The river had widened and slowed and was looking more and more like the delta with each passing mile. He looked to the afternoon sun; now beginning to drop in the sky then dug his paddle into the water and renewed his efforts. A sharp bolt of pain instantly shot through his shoulder but another night on the banks of the river was not an option. The mosquitos would drive him insane, and with that he continued on.

Minutes passed like hours, but with the lack of food and water, and the pain in his shoulder all taking their toll, his energy and spirits quickly waned. It was just too much; he could paddle no more and needed to rest. Grimacing as he laid across the seat, the tired man exhaled with a heavy sigh and closed his eyes. It was peaceful, and as he drifted along with the current, he began to wander with his thoughts. Aimlessly conjuring memories from the past until he suddenly snapped his eyes back open at the thought of his brother and best friend, and of just how lucky he was to have actually survived the whole ordeal. And then he raged inside with a boiling anger at what'd happened. Someday he swore, he would get revenge, but for now he was too tired to think. A few minutes later, he closed his eyes again and drifted off to sleep.

Motoring upstream for the very first time, Willie was all eyes as she made her way up the twisting tributary. Carefully checking her landmarks as she went, just like Otis had told her, it wasn't more than five minutes into her journey when she came to a cross roads in the waterway. Slowing slightly in a fleeting moment of uncertainty, she contemplated her choices then turned to the left and gave her little motor the gas.

The time that'd elapsed was uncertain, but it was the gentle bump of his boat against a fallen tree jutting out into the water that had awakened him. Quickly sitting up, he looked around only to find that he'd floated into what was clearly a smaller branch of the river. It was a swirling eddy on the bend beneath his boat that'd pulled him to the outer side of the curve, allowing for the current of the tributary to then pull him away.

Was it just an island he was going around, or a fork in the river that led to a stagnant dead end? He looked around some more but found no answers, only the sight of the main river as he slowly drifted away. He grabbed at a tree branch hanging out over the water but missed then picked up his paddle and drove it into the water. An excruciating pain shot through his shoulder and he doubled over. He had to get back to the main river or risk getting lost and spending another night in hell. He tried again but the tributary had narrowed and the current had quickened. His shoulder throbbed in agony and he was going nowhere. He turned and looked downstream with a sullen gaze, then set the paddle on his lap with a disgruntled sigh and resigned himself to a river that was now controlling his fate.

The tributary, although only half the width of the river, still seemed to be moving at a reasonable rate. Taking comfort in that fact, the man relaxed with hopes that somehow and in someway it would lead back to the river. An hour later into his new route, he rounded a bend in the waterway with a fork to his right. And although it was open and wide, he quickly surmised that it went nowhere and floated on. The waterway was becoming a maze and he took note, carefully watching his course.

A half-hour after that, he rounded a bend and spied a home with a pier. Quickly standing, he put his hand to his forehead to block the sun and smiled. It was civilization, a home on the water, and neatly cared for. He'd made it. Surely there was someone there who would help a poor hungry grifter? He paddled his boat to the left, gazing at the house as he approached the end of the pier. A few moments later, he grabbed hold of the giant finger and then cautiously surveyed his surroundings.

"Hellooo," he yelled, then waited and listened. "Anybody home?"

Releasing his hold on the pylon, he drifted to the downstream side of the pier and began working his way toward shore. Pulling himself along its edge, he stopped midway then looked to the house and called again. "Hellooo," his voice rang out again. "Anybody home?"

Still with no answer, he reached for the line in his boat and tied it to the pylon. Watching in the most vigilant of ways, he studied the house with shifting eyes then crawled from his boat up onto the pier. Standing with the help of a homemade cane, he took a step toward the house and began limping down the wooden walkway.

"Hellooo," he hollered yet again as he stopped at the edge of the grass. "Anybody home?"

A few seconds later and still with no answer, he proceeded with a guarded caution and stepped onto the freshly cut lawn. This was someone's home that was cared for, and he knew that at any second, he could be looking down the barrel of a gun. It was a daunting thought, yet even so he continued on, his pain and hunger driving his actions until he reached the front door.

Knocking hard as he looked around, he called out again then slowly reached up and twisted the knob. Pushing the door open, he called out yet again with just his head inside and listened. There wasn't a sound, and with that he quietly slipped inside. His goal was simple, to eat and drink as much as he could and take what ever he could carry before the owners got back. Quickly moving to the kitchen he began to look for food. Gorging himself on almost everything he could find, he then began to ransack the house. Looking for anything of value he could take, the man suddenly stopped and inhaled a sharpened breath. Frozen by a sound that was emanating from outside, he turned his head and listened then rushed to the window.

An instant later, he cringed at the sight of a small boat headed straight toward the pier. He was caught. His heart raced, he had to get away. People on the river shot you for things like this. He scrambled in a confused and frantic manner at what to do and where to go then looked back out of the window once more. Gazing intently as the boat slowed and approached the pier, he narrowed his eyes and stared then suddenly gasped in disbelief. A second later, he ceased to breathe completely. It was her... the girl from the train. He was certain of it, and as he continued to stare his mind began to reel as it instantly flashed back to that fateful night.

Jack Mosley was the only thug from train who'd survived. He remembered crawling and making his way back up onto the tracks then calling and looking for his brother and Lester in the dark. But they never answered; there was only the quiet and the distant rumblings of a far off thunderstorm. He was hurt, but even so he managed to make it to the next town. A week and a half later, and after he'd recuperated enough to walk, he went back in search of them.

He remembered returning to the spot where he'd landed, and then searching the tracks. And then the sickening sights forever implanted in his mind when he finally found them. First his brother's scattered remains lying in the muddy flats beneath the bridge. A body, that had been ripped and dismembered into indiscernible pieces, identifiable now only from the tattered remains of his clothes. He remembered the thrashing noises of gators feeding ravenously on something below the night he'd crossed and a sickening and sinking feeling quickly enveloped him. And then his best friend Lester, whose skeletal remains he finally found tightly coiled in a barbed wire prison. No doubt eaten alive by the creatures of the night, he then became food for the vultures and insects that followed. Picked almost clean to the bone over the days that'd passed, he vomited at the sight.

Distraught and all alone, the embittered man slowly sank to his knees between the steel rails. His brother and friend were dead, and in a moment of sorrow and rage, he looked to the sky and swore a sobbing oath of revenge. "I'll find em for ya, I swear. An when I do I'll kill that fuckin nigger, I promise. An I'll fine his little white whore too, I swear I will. An when I do, I'll kill her too."

Still gazing through the window, Jack anxiously watched as Willie slowed and pulled along side the pier then stopped and tied her boat. She would soon be his, and he smiled with a malevolent grin at his good fortune. He would have his revenge, but first he would have his fun. Yes, that was it; he would have his fun and then kill her like he'd promised. Or maybe he would use her for a couple of days while he rested and ate her food, then kill her and take her boat when he left. Yes, he smiled again as he wiped the drool from his mouth and licked his lips. He would use her for his brother and his friend, and then he would find out where her nigger was.

Checking her knots like Otis had taught her, Willie jumped onto the pier and crossed to the other side. Was someone visiting from up river, she wondered as she looked at the other boat. How nice and exciting! Otis had said there were other people nearby, and now here they were. Smiling at the thought, she turned toward the house and raised her hands to her mouth. "Hellooo," she called out and then waited. Listening for an answer that never came, she turned to the water and stared out across its surface. Surely they hadn't fallen in and drown? Looking back to the house just a little confused, she stared for a moment then turned back to the water a second time.

"Hellooo," she curiously called out as she scanned the surface. Listening again to an answer that still didn't come, Willie shrugged her shoulders and began walking down the pier. Glancing to her boat just to make sure it was tied, she looked at her shotgun lying on the seat and suddenly slowed.

Should I take it, she wondered? Naah, she scoffed at the thought. You don't need that thing. It was for gators, ramember. Besides, Otis had always said that people on the river were friendly. An you shor don't wanna scare off or offend your first visitor that's for shor. Smiling at the thought of meeting someone new, she turned back to the house and resumed walking then called out once more as she hit the grass.

Taking a position against the wall and to the hinged side of the door, Jack waited like a spider on the edge of its web. She was coming, and in a few short moments he would have her. He labored to breathe and his heart pounded. She was getting closer, and even though his mouth had turned a pasty dry, he smiled and licked his lips. A moment later, the doorknob turned with a rusty squeak and door slowly opened. "Hellooo," Willie called out as she stepped inside. "Anybody here?"

It was the last thing she uttered before Jack Mosley jumped from behind the door and grabbed her around the throat. "Ramember me, you little bitch?" he yelled as he slammed her against the wall.

Caught completely off guard, Willie screamed at the top of her lungs then instantly grabbed for the man's arm. Gripping it with all of her strength, she tried to pull free but his obsessive rage had made him strong and he pinned her hard against the wall. Then, with one hand around her throat and the other on the front of her shirt, he pushed and lifted her into the air. Choking as the balls of her feet left the floor, Willie struggled in a valiant fight for her life.

"Where's your big buck nigger now?" he snarled through rotten teeth and breath to match. "He shor can't protect ya now can he?" he added with a sadistic smile.

Horrified and unable to answer over the crushing hold that he had on her throat, Willie could only struggle and gasp for air. He was going to kill her and she knew it. She could see it in his eyes that were sunken and filled with hate. That were black from a broken nose, and that were wild and crazy like those of an animal gone rabid. But why, what'd she done? She tried to think but couldn't, until, and in a horrifying moment of revelation, she remembered her train ride.

"Now you listen ta me you little whore. You an me's got some unfinished business an some fun ta have. Like we was sapose to on the train," he said maliciously. "Afor your nigger got in the way. Ramember?" But then he flinched and grimaced in a pain, and Willie instantly picked up on it. His shoulder still hurt from his fall, and throwing and holding her against the wall had strained it to its breaking point. It was a sign of weakness, and in the fleeting second that he tried to refocus, Willie's survival mode immediately kicked in. Seizing upon the moment in an adrenaline induced action, she brought her leg up in a powerful kick to his crotch.

She was strong from years on the farm, and with her adrenaline glands feeding her body with its magic elixir; Willie kicked with an unbelievable force. Connecting with her foot to his groin, the man screamed in agony and released his hold then dropped to his knees and doubled over. Free from his grasp, Willie leapt past his body and bolted out the door as he flailed his arms and threatened to kill her. Running as fast as she could, she hit the pier and jumped in her boat. She had to get away, and in an instant she had the pull cord wrapped around the motor.

Frantically pulling, the little motor sputtered and coughed but failed to start. Quickly wrapping the cord, she tried again. But the motor still didn't start, and with the look of terror etched into her face, Willie quickly wrapped the cord once more. Pulling with all of her strength, it sputtered and came to life but then suddenly coughed and died. Panic stricken, she quickly checked her motor then looked up to the sound of the man yelling as he headed toward her with a knife in his hand. He could hardly walk much less run, yet even so he reached the pier all too quickly and was soon upon her.

But Willie wasn't about to become his victim, and without a second's hesitation she grabbed her shotgun and chambered a shell then spun to meet her attacker. Leveling and locking her gun into her shoulder, she pointed it straight at his chest with the confidence of a seasoned lawman.

It was a sight that instantly stopped the man, and for a few fleeting moments Jack Mosley quietly stared straight into the barrel of the twelve-gauge shotgun. A second later, he looked into her eyes and felt a sick and sinking feeling settle deep in his gut. The short and shiny butcher knife that he'd held so tightly and defiantly a second ago now dangled loosely in one hand. "Hel, helll there little girl," he stuttered with an apologetic laugh. "I, I ditn't mean nothin," he added. "Heck I, I was jus funnin you... you know that."

His voice was sincere but his eyes were wild and crazy, and Willie wasn't buying it, and without another thought, she lowered her head and sighted her gun. There wasn't a sound, and for a few short seconds the two stood in a stalemate until their eerie silence was broken by the clear and unmistakable click of her safety as she slid the tiny lever to fire. He knew the sound all too well and swallowed hard, yet even so he tightened his hold on his knife and took a short step to test her bluff.

"I'll blow you straight to hell if you take another step Mister," Willie threatened as her hands twitched and tightened around her weapon. "You hear me, you son-of-a-bitch?"

He did hear her, and he knew she was serious, but even so Jack couldn't help himself for he was now controlled by force more powerful than his own will. An overpowering and fanatical rage for revenge that just wouldn't allow it. It was all he wanted, and without another thought he lunged toward her and called her bluff. But Willie wasn't bluffing, and she pulled the trigger at point blank range without hesitation. A millisecond later, to Jack, it was as if time itself had suddenly slowed. He saw the gun explode in a fiery blast, with its shock wave and ear-shattering boom that instantly followed. And then he felt the red hot lead from the double-aught buck rip into his body, mutilating his left shoulder as it blew him upwards and backwards into the air. A heavy expanse of air gushed from his lungs and before he knew it he'd landed on the other side of the pier, rolled with a groan and fell off its edge into the water. A second later he surfaced, screaming and gasping for air as an excruciating pain coursed through his body. His bad shoulder ached unbelievably, and his good shoulder, or what was left of it, was now useless. Bleeding profusely, his arm now limp at his side, he cried out for help as he thrashed and struggled to stay afloat.

Jumping onto the pier, Willie warily watched as he made his way to the back of his boat and grabbed at its edge. He was hurt and desperate and pleading for help, yet even so she just stood and stared with a cold uncaring gaze. She wanted to blow him straight to hell and finish it, and to never worry about him again. It was what she wanted, and without another thought she chambered another shell, stepped to the edge of the pier and then drew down on top of him.

Hearing the action to her weapon, Jack quickly looked up and into the barrel of her gun then past it and into her eyes. Eyes that were now as chilling and unforgiving as any he'd ever seen. Green crystalline orbs unflinching and blazing with hatred. She was going to kill him and he knew it; he could tell by the way her nostrils flared with each and every breath, and her hand as it opened and closed around the pump of the gun in an involuntary reaction to the adrenaline coursing through her.

Now certain of his impending doom, he immediately began to beg for mercy as Willie listened and decided his fate. A fate that they both knew she could change with the twitch of her finger. A second later she turned to the line that was tied to the pylon. She'd decided not to kill him, but she wasn't going to save him either, and with another ear shattering blast from her gun, she severed the twisted strand of hemp and watched it drop into the water.

His fate was sealed and he knew it, and as he and the boat slowly drifted away from the pier, Jack began to curse and scream his revenge. Watching as he clung onto the back and struggled to get in, Willie could see the blood as it gushed from his wound. Pumping from his body with each and every attempt to pull himself into the boat, he left a trail of red that pooled and followed in the water close behind. He was helpless, and before he knew it, he was in the middle of the tributary and headed downstream.

Relaxing as his distance increased, Willie finally lowered her gun. The current had grabbed him, and as he continued on and slowly approached the bend with the big tree, she saw him drift to the outside of the curve and to shore where he could stand.

Reeling in pain and weak from the loss of blood, Jack sighed with relief at the touch of the muddy bottom. Yes he thought, at least now he could get into the boat and stop his bleeding. He had to, for he knew that he wouldn't last much longer in the water. Pushing hard in chest deep water, his feet sank deep into the gooey mixture of delta mud and his first attempt ended in failure.

Screaming in agony, he struggled to free himself and make his way closer to shore. His life depended on it, but unknowingly it was already far too late. For between the commotion and the smell of blood gushing from his wound, he'd gained the unwanted attention of the two resident reptiles. Hunters of the murky depths that'd been quietly sunning in the sawgrass just at the water's edge. Twelve-foot long killing and eating machines, whose predatory skills had been honed to perfection over millions of years of evolution. Always on the lookout for an easy meal, the large carnivorous pair quietly slipped into the water and beneath its surface without a sound.

Exhausted, Jack slowly pulled himself closer to shore where he could finally lean against the transom and roll into the boat. Yes he'd made it, but before he could act and save himself, he was suddenly and violently jerked back down into the water. Caught between the crushing jaws of one of the scaly skinned creatures, he screamed in horror and pain as the bones just below his knees splintered into pieces and the gator tore at his limbs. His mind went wild and he tried in frantic desperation to hold onto the boat. Clutching and clawing at the thick wooden planks with his arms draped over the side, he fought for his life.

But Jack was no match against the powerful reptile and was easily ripped away with a violent twist into the water. Thrashing wildly in an attempt to sever his limbs, the shallow waters boiled and turned red with his impending death. Flung from side to side like that of a rag doll in the mouth of a dog, he screamed in horror and begged to God. But God wasn't answering, and Jack Mosley was now nothing more than a living dead man. And as the second gator joined in on the carnage and sank its teeth into his shoulder, his blood curdling screams that had echoed upstream, quickly faded as they tore at his flesh and began to feed.

Standing on the pier, Willie watched and listened, quietly and without emotion to the man's final cry for help. An indiscernible and gurgling plea that finally ceased completely as the two behemoths ripped him apart and disappeared beneath the surface. She knew it was over for him, yet even so she watched. She watched as the water where they'd been, that'd boiled so violently just a moment ago and ran red with his blood, quickly calmed and cleared... and then she listened.

But there was only quiet now, a haunting silence, and the sight of his boat lazily drifting with the current. Spinning idly in half circles as it gently touched the shore and then continued on, floating ever farther until it finally disappeared behind the big tree and around the bend. She'd just watched a man die, but to Willie it was a fitting end and without another thought she lowered her head and turned then quietly walked off the pier. He would bother her no more.

———◆———

CHAPTER 27

Returning from the head up front, the two men took their respective places back in the stern now ready for another cold one. Reaching into the cooler, Jim pulled out two more beers and then handed one to Otis. He was completely enthralled, and although the sun was starting to drop in the sky and the auction was beginning to slow, he quickly popped the top to his can and then reclined back against the hull. "Okay," he sighed and took a sip. "Where were we?"

Looking at Jim, Otis took a quick slug from his beer and then picked up where he'd left off. "It was that next Saturday after Willie's birthday," he began slowly. "That we took off an headed back up river. I remember it real well too cause right as we was go'n out of the harbor, well, that's when ol Foster came up an asked me if I could teach him how to drive."

"Really? You mean he didn't even know how to drive his own boat?" Jim asked.

"Yep," Otis nodded. "Not a clue."

"So what'd you do?"

"Well," Otis replied. "I got out-a the way an let em have it. I remember we'd jus come up on this big ol freighter headin out to sea when he took the wheel."

"Here ya go boss, now jus add a little more gas an turn up this a way some," Otis instructed from the side as they approached the ship. "We wanna have jus a little more speed so we can hit them waves straight on so they don't rock us over."

Rising up onto the crest of the first wave Foster did just as Otis had said then rode its downward slope until they'd plowed headlong into the bottom of the second. "Four-footers," Otis hollered as they buried the bow and spray went up and over everywhere.

Gripping the wheel with both of his hands, Foster bent at his knees then whooped like a cowboy as they rose and fell between the giant rollers. Whooping with each and every one, he continued his rodeo ride until they'd finally passed with a boat that was soaked from bow to stern.

"Goddamn that was fun," he howled as he quickly looked around for more waves.

"Yes sur boss," Otis agreed then pointed up river. "But we need to go that way if'n you wants ta see Miss Willie."

Turning the wheel in the direction that Otis had pointed, Foster just smiled then looked behind and gazed at the ship they'd just passed. Its name, *The Alexandria,* emblazoned on the stern, suddenly gained his attention and with a curious expression pulling at his face, he cocked his head and turned to Otis. "Otis," he said. "Answer me a question will you."

"Yes sur boss, I'll shorly try," he replied. "What is it?"

"Well every time we come out here and I see one of those big ships coming or going, I've noticed that they all have names on the back of em. And I was just kind of wondering, why in the hell they all do that?"

"Well boss, I think it's got to do with them a loadin an unloadin over at the docks. You know, so they know's which boats to work on. Or, at least I think that's why they do it."

"But what about the other boats at the wharf, you know the smaller ones like this? They all have names. Or a lot of them do. Why is that?"

"Well," Otis shrugged. "I rightly don't know boss."

Staring out front, Foster thought for a second then turned back with a perplexed expression. "Well how come this boat doesn't have a name?"

"Well now," Otis began with a grin that he just couldn't contain. "That's kind of a different story. In fact, that goes all the way back to the day when ol Mister Davenport bought this. See he wanted to name it one thing while Mrs. D, well, she wanted to name it somethin else. Anyway, every time they went out it seemed like they argued about it until one day they got in the biggest fight you ever seen, an that's how it got the name it's got right now."

"And what's that?" Foster asked.

"Nut-in," Otis replied with a shit-eating grin. "Miss Nut-in. Or at least that's what Mrs. D called it after they was done fightin… an so, that's what I called it."

Gazing at Otis for just a second, Foster mentally pictured Howard and Katherine Davenport arguing over a silly name then broke into a quiet chuckle. "Well I think that we need a name, don't you? I mean, I gotta have a name right?"

"Oh yes sur boss, it shorly would be nice. So whats you wanna call it?"

"I don't know," he replied with a shrug and another grin. "But I want one," he added as he turned his attention back driving then reached up and pushed on the throttle.

"Now I think that not havin a name on his boat really bothered him. I don't know why, but it did. Anyway, after we'd passed that freighter, we both started tryin to think of a name to put on the back. Sayin this one an then that one, an then makin faces an laughin then shaken our heads. But jus like ol Mr. an Mrs. Davenport, we jus couldn't think of none either. An then, before either one of us knew it, we were go'n around the little bend in the waterway jus before the cabin."

Rounding the bend with the big tree, Foster reached up and pulled on the knotted rope. He'd driven the entire way but was still reluctant to dock. Stepping to the side, he gave Otis the wheel and went to the stern then watched as Willie raced from around the house and across the grass then trotted down the pier. A small wave of euphoria enveloped him. He'd missed her more than he cared to admit, and it had only been a week.

"Hey," she yelled, bouncing on the balls of her feet with a great big grin.

"Mornin Willie," Foster greeted as he threw her his line. "Ya doing okay?"

"Oh, yes sur, I'm jus fine. But I shor did miss ya'al," she replied as she stepped to the pylon and wrapped the rope as Otis had shown her.

"Well, we missed you too," he drawled as he opened his arms for a hug.

Tying her knot in record time, Willie stared for just a second then jumped into the boat and into his warm embrace. She'd missed him too.

Their weekend that morning began in the most relaxing of ways with little to no work being done around the house. Piddling and inspecting, Foster looked everything over, then made a list of some other things he wanted done. He told her how pleased he was, and how good things looked, and that they were just going to relax for the weekend. His plan was to slow her progress and maintain the illusion that she was really needed. He told her to help Otis with the boat, then retired to the porch to work on his campaign.

Walking down onto the pier, Willie caught Otis just as he was stepping off the boat. "Hey Mister Otis, Foster told me ta come an help you," she grinned. "So what's ya do'n?"

Holding a roll of heavy line in his hand, Otis looked to Willie just as she stopped. "I'm gonna make us a trotline so we can catch us some fish," he said excitedly. "But first we needs to string it across the water," he pointed to the other bank.

"A trotline?" she asked. "What's a trotline?"

"Come on," he said as he began walking. "An I'll show ya, but we needs your boat."

Watching from the porch, Foster smiled as the two labored against the current and strung the heavy line across the tributary. It took both of them to do the job, but working together and using the new little boat, they finally accomplished their task. Willie was having fun, and as they slowly made their way back across, they set and baited their hooks then returned to shore with anticipating smiles.

Pulling the boat up onto the grass, they tied it to a stake and then returned to the cruiser. The boat was a mess after Foster's roller coaster ride, but with a couple of buckets and some rags from below, the two began cleaning the brightly varnished woodwork and glass. To Otis it was a labor of love, but so was fishing, and as they cleaned both he and Willie kept a vigilant eye on the four floating jugs tied to his line. Their goal was simple, to catch enough for supper, and just as they'd hoped, later that afternoon, Willie watched in complete fascination as Otis threw two ten pounders up onto the pier.

"What kind are they," she asked as she gazed at the slimy-skinned creatures flopping on the board.

"Them's catfish Miss Willie," Otis replied. "Best eatin fish in the river, jus wait till ya taste em."

"Catfish?" she queried and cocked her head. "Oh, I seeee," she gushed with a grin. "It's cause they have them little whisker things, jus like a kitty."

Chuckling to himself, Otis just picked up his knife and cut into the fish. Filleting the monsters from the deep, he quickly finished and then threw the thick slabs of meat into a bucket of ice water.

That evening for supper, the three dined on fresh fish grilled over an open fire and fried potatoes. And as the sun hung on the horizon, painting the sky with its crimson rays, they stuffed themselves into misery. Washing their meal down with a couple of beers and a coke, they continued to pick at the white flakey fillets even after they were full. It was a wonderful meal, and Willie marveled at the fact that you could actually catch something from the water so easily and then eat it. She'd watched Otis carefully that afternoon as he caught and prepared the fish, and then Foster as he tenderly and lovingly grilled the fillets, even talking to them as if they were babies when he turned them. She laughed, they all laughed, and when they were done and had finished eating, her love for fishing was forever engrained into her soul.

Downing the rest of her coke, Willie rose from her seat and gathered their plates then went into the house. She was dirty after her day with Otis, and now that she smelled of smoke she wanted to take a bath while it was still light. She felt amorous, and wanted to be clean and to smell pretty, and to be kissed again in the worst of ways. She felt all grown up when she did, but then wondered if it was just a onetime thing? If he'd done it just because it'd been her birthday? She hoped not. She did her dishes quickly then pulled the pots of boiling water from the stove and dumped them into the tub.

A couple more beers by the fire with Otis and the two men finally retired as well. It was getting dark and as Foster entered the house he lit a lamp and then called out for Willie.

"I'm in here," she answered in an alluring voice from her room.

Smiling with the most salacious of thoughts, Foster quickly washed his face and brushed his teeth then gently knocked on her door. Pushing it open, he smiled again at the sight before him bathed in the soft light from her lamp. Truly a vision of innocence, she sat on the edge of her bed brushing the last of her tangles from her hair. Looking up as he crossed the room, Willie swallowed nervously then set her brush on the nightstand. He was coming to her just liked she'd hoped, and as he stopped in front of her and blew out her lamp, she knew that her dreams and desires were about to come true.

They kissed until the desires within them both had become unbearable. Foster raged at the thought of what lie beneath the thin cotton fabric of her panties, and he pushed her barriers until she wanted to scream. She was fiery and passionate, and even though she'd begun to grind herself against him, he could tell she was reluctant. But why he wondered as he pressed his thigh between her legs and slipped a hand inside her gown. Was it morals, or was she scared? She certainly didn't seem or act as if she were afraid. He kissed her again and caressed her breasts. Pointed and firm, they heaved under his touch as she squirmed beneath him, wanting and yearning yet holding herself back, then mumbling how she loved him.

Alert as ever, Foster instantly cued in and picked up on her words. It was the key that would unlock the door as to her yet untouched treasures and he knew it, he was certain of it. And now he knew exactly what to do. He'd been working on her physically and progressing well, but had forgotten all about the emotional and mental side of the whole equation. It was a mistake, but one he would instantly correct as he brought his mouth to her ear and told her how much she meant to him. And then, of how he'd never felt this way about any other woman before.

Reeling at his words, she kissed him deep and passionately. Yes, he did love her! He pushed again, yet still she clung onto the virtues that had been instilled in her. Values she'd learned from a mistake her mother had made years ago, of giving herself to a man before she was married. A man who didn't love her, and who quickly disappeared after the ensuing pregnancy that followed. Willie had never forgotten her words.

Sensing she would need more time, he sighed in frustration then eased his advances. He'd pushed her far enough for one night, and as much as he hated to, he began to relent. Maybe next weekend he thought and then hoped. He wanted her in the worst of ways and even though he ached and throbbed with the desires of a teenage boy, he was determined to make her come to him. His pride and arrogance wouldn't have it any other way. And so, and as frustrating as it was, he kissed her one last time and then tenderly tucked her in.

Lying in bed, sleep eluded him and for most of the night he laid in restless agony, tormented by the dull and constant yearning between his legs. Until, and in a groggy haze early the next morning, he awoke to the smell of coffee and the creaking of his bed. Opening his eyes, he smiled at the sight of Willie taking a seat on the edge of his bed. She'd come to him and was smiling, and in her carefully cupped hands was a fresh full cup of his favorite morning elixir.

"Good mornin," she beamed in a dreamy drawl.

Taking the cup, Foster took a short sip and then carefully set it on the nightstand. "Morning," he replied as she sensuously crawled over the top of him. "Did you miss me already?" he teased as she slowly slithered into his arms. Nodding her head with a wanton smile, Willie lowered her face to his and smothered him with a kiss as he lay beneath the sheets.

She could tell he was naked and it excited her, and as she straddled and kissed him she slowly began to rock and press against him. Yes, he thought with a growing excitement. Had she changed her mind? Had the promiscuous side of her desires finally prevailed? Had her unyielding will and resistance eroded that much during the night? He smiled at the thought then rolled her to his side and boldly reached between her legs. Maybe she too had spent the night in agony.

He felt the smooth cotton fabric of her panties, then gently stroked and brushed the softness of her curls lying just beneath them. He felt her shudder and then gasp, and then her arms as they pulled at his shoulders. She liked the way he touched her, and in an act without shame, she relaxed and parted her legs ever so slightly. A second later, she called out his name and then brought her mouth to his.

They kissed with a heated abandon, and in her hazy moment of passion, Foster cagily slipped his fingers beneath the folds of her waistband. It was without question what she wanted, but almost instantly, Willie stiffened and grabbed at his wrist. Staring deep into his eyes with an expression of anxiety, she reflected back to his words of last night. Of how he felt about her and how he needed her, and how much she meant to him. She thought of them and then the words of her mother. A fleeting moment of silence passed between them, of indecision and of apprehension. Of doubt and then sincerity, until she slowly relaxed her hold and closed her eyes then pressed on his hand. It was her answer, and he acted instantly.

Pushing into the soft tangled mat of her triangle, he felt the dampened heat of her arousal as he entangled his fingers into her curls and beyond. Whimpering with a ragged breath, she felt her heart jump and then raced like that of a humming bird's. He was touching and rubbing her in the most private of places. Her magical place of pleasure that only she'd touched in this way before. She held her breath then bit her lip to stifle a moan.

A small twinge of guilt ran through her at the thought of how she was forsaking her mother's words. She felt remorseful, but still she didn't stop him. She couldn't, and as his finger slowly slipped pass her soft golden curls and into the secret depths of her silkiness, she exhaled with a heavy moan then kissed him deep and rolled her hips. Giving herself over to the erotic sensations now consuming her, the young fifteen year old whimpered and then groaned in blissful agony.

It was close to an hour before Foster once again could take no more. She'd cried out more than once under his manipulations and that pleased him. And he knew that he probably could've gone all the way, especially after he'd worked her into such a euphoric state. But now it was daylight, and he was sure that Otis was stirring outside. Besides, it would've been in haste and that was not how he wanted it. He wanted her comfortable, and for her first time to be romantic and special, and so with a great reluctance the two finally rose. Willie was glowing with giddiness and totally in love. Foster was frustrated with a cold cup of coffee and about to go home.

They ate a light breakfast then spent the rest of the morning with another reading and writing lesson while Otis happily ran his trotline. It was cloudy and looked like rain but none had fallen. He showed Willie how to spell and write her name, *Willie Mae Dawson*, then watched as she practiced again and again. He was surprised and pleased at how swiftly she'd progressed and could see that she was gifted and smart. She'd mastered the alphabet with a dazzling speed and he knew that she would need more books next week to keep her mind working at or near its potential. Besides, it would slow her work on the house and help pass the time while he was away.

They finished their lessons and just before noon he stood in the stern and waved goodbye. "I'll see you on Saturday, okay. Oh, and keep an eye out for those gators, I saw them when we came up and it looks like they're getting closer."

"I will," she said as they pulled away.

She'd never said a word about what'd happened to her, and as they rounded the bend with the big tree, Foster gave her a final wave then turned and headed up front. He would drive them home.

"So you guys would just go up an visit and then leave Willie up there?" Jim asked. "Every time?"

"Yep, an to tell ya the truth, I think she was actually gettin used to it. Anyway, it wasn't but a few moments after we'd rounded that first bend when ol Foster came up an asked if he could drive again."

"Really?"

"Yep, an jus as soon as he took a hold of that wheel, well, that's when he started talkin about namin the boat all over again. I remember we started in jus like we'd done on our way up an continued on all the way down river until we jus couldn't think of nothin no more. I'll tell ya, nothin seemed to fit, an I mean nothin. Then, an jus before we got to the marina, I remember we turned an cut in right behind another one of those big ol freighters leavin the docks.

"The tugs had jus pulled away from her an she was jus startin to move, so we passed right off her stern. Foster was still drivin an I was standin in the doorway watchin an pointin jus to make sure he didn't hit none a them tugs. An that's when I jus so happened to look up on the back of that big ol ship. An even though I couldn't read, somethin right then an there told me that all those scrambled up letters was makin some sort of ladies name. Now for the life of me I don't know why, but it did. An then I remember thinkin of Willie."

"Go this way boss," Otis pointed toward the wharf as they fell in behind the slow moving freighter. Gazing up at the stern as they passed, he stared at a name he couldn't read yet still in the back of his mind he sensed that it was a woman's name. He was certain of it, and with a great big grin he turned to Foster. "Boss!" he called excitedly.

"Yeah Otis?" Foster answered, his gaze still fixed vigilantly forward.

"I gots a name that I think you'll like."

"Oh you do, do you?" he queried as he continued to concentrate out front.

"Yes sur, I was jus thinkin that. Well, why don't you call it the *Miss Willie?*" he said proudly. "She'd shorly like that I bet."

Turning to the man in the doorway, Foster quietly stared as if he were on to something. "The *Miss Willie,*" he repeated and turned to the stern then stared as if he were trying to envision the name on the transom. A second later, he began to smile as if he'd just been enlightened. "Oh my God, Otis," he said as he turned back to Otis.

"Yes sur?"

"You're a genius," he praised excitedly. "A goddamn genius I tell ya."

"Yes sur boss, if'n you say so," Otis puffed out his chest and smiled, but then cocked his head with an uncertain look. "But boss?"

"Yeah Otis."

"I know that you probably means good an all, but aaah… what's a genius?"

"A genius Otis," he laughed. "You know… a smart person. You just gave me the name."

"But I thoughts that you didn't like it," he replied as he quickly changed his expression.

"Only half Otis…. ooonly half. We'll call it the *Willie Mae.* See, that's her first and middle name. What-a ya think?"

Looking to the transom as if he were envisioning the name, Otis paused for a moment then turned back to Foster. "I like it boss," he said as he slowly repeated her name and then looked back to the stern. "Ya think Miss Willie'l like it?"

"Yes I do," Foster replied. "Yes I dooo."

"An that's pretty much how this ol boat got its name," Otis paused and stared at the transom.

"So you really did help name it, huh?" Jim seemed a little surprised.

"Yep," Otis replied as he turned back. "An it's the only one she's ever had."

———◆———

CHAPTER 28

DINNER AT THE MCALISTERS, AS usual, was excellent. Shortly afterwards, the Judge and Foster retired to the front porch and the comfort of the large wicker chairs with a snifter of brandy and the rest of their cigars. The Judge was excited with news from the party. Word had spread and there were people who wanted to meet him.

"Now I've set up a meeting with them in Montgomery for Tuesday," the Judge drawled casually. "The head of the party wants to meet you. Think you can clear your schedule?"

"Absolutely," Foster replied without a second's hesitation.

"Good," the Judge smiled and then downed his brandy.

———◆———

Monday morning Foster arrived at work with a box of donuts from Crystal's Bakery. It was time to enlighten the girls as to his plans. They were the ones closest to him and really needed to know. Besides if he did run, he would need their help and support during his campaign.

They squealed with delight then looked saddened and dismayed as if maybe they'd just lost their jobs. "It's okay Dawn," Foster reassured. "If we do this, you and Vicki will be in charge of my campaign headquarters right here until the election. And then if I'm... I mean, when I'm elected, we'll turn this into one of my state offices and the two you can run it for me."

"Ya got my vote boss," Vicki said as she sipped her coffee and then pulled on her cigarette.

"Me too," Dawn chirped gleefully.

"Thank you both, now listen I have some things I need to go over with you."

He told the girls he was leaving and wouldn't be back until late Thursday. He told Vicki of his niece and how smart she was, and how she could really use some more books. He quietly found a painter to paint the back of the boat, scheduled him for Friday morning and then went in search of Otis. He was going to be gone for three days and he wanted to make sure that Otis knew and would check on Willie. It was his day off, but Foster knew where he lived. A poor section on the south side out on Hall Mills Road, where he met his wife and son for the first time.

Returning to his office later that afternoon, he sat at his desk and stared out through the windows. He could see the water out on the bay, and soon his mind began drifting to Willie and of how she'd come to him the other morning. He remembered how beautiful she'd looked as she lay beneath him, the taut and youthful tone of her body, the fragrance of her hair and the softness of her lips. And then the strength of her arms as they pulled on his shoulders and the stifled moans of pleasure she emitted as her long lean muscular torso quivered beneath his manipulations. He closed his eyes and smiled. And then he thought of the long week ahead with the Judge. He looked at the phone and picked up the receiver. A moment later he heard the soft sophisticated drawl of Katherine Davenport's voice on the other end. She was surprised but delighted to hear from him.

———◆———

Tuesday morning Foster met the Judge on the platform right at eight. He was a little nervous, but excited and definitely ready. Melinda had driven her father but had also come to wish Foster luck. A round of kisses and hugs as a final goodbye, and the two men boarded a private first class car on the Louisville and Nashville. Departing the station right at eight-thirty, the train finally began on its trip north to the city of Montgomery. A few minutes later they crossed the trestle at Chickasaw Creek, and as they rolled along the western banks of the river and left the city behind, Foster settled into the lavish comfort of their first-class accommodations.

Gazing out of his window, he stared at the serene and placid waters as they barreled along the river's edge. Waters, that he'd actually come to know quite well. It was picturesque, but then and much to his surprise, an all too familiar sight suddenly caught his eye and he sat back up. The timing was perfect and was almost as if he'd orchestrated it himself. He'd wondered and had even worried, but now there it was. There was Otis on his way to see Willie, and his mind suddenly eased.

The boat looked great as it cut through the water with a perfectly mirrored reflection of its clean white hull and varnished topside shimmering off the glass-smooth surface. Following just behind it, a giant vee of multiple waves began at the bow then rolled like extended logs from the stern and slowly spread from shore to shore until they lazily lapped at the muddy banks. And adding to the final scene as they passed was the morning sun hidden behind a thick sky of scattered clouds, showering the landscape with a giant halo of beaming rays. Golden shafts of radiant light, skewering the ground like divine spears that'd been thrown from above.

It was a beautiful sight, and he smiled within. Otis was a good man, and he was glad he'd kept him on. And he was also glad to have finally met his wife and small son. He knew that Otis liked Willie, and was relieved that he was on his way to see her. A moment later he saw an arm wave from the cabin door of the boat and then the sound of the train's loud shrill whistle. He smiled again then thought of Katherine and of how she loved to wave at the trains until they blew their whistles. He was glad he'd seen her last night, and was pleased when she told him her candle would burn again on Thursday until he returned and blew it out.

The old black steward brought in their coffee and pastries on a cart draped in fine white linen. He served them with elegance, and when Foster finally cast his eyes back out to the river, his boat was gone.

"So you actually got the train to blow its whistle?" Jim chuckled.

"Yeah, I guess I did," Otis laughed as he thought back. "I was jus up from Chickasaw Creek, on my way to see Willie when it came barrelin by. Anyway after it disappeared, I went back to driven, an that's when I started thinkin of jus how lucky I was. You know, workin for Foster, an boatin up an down the

river like I was. I tell ya, I sure had it good back then, or at least a lot better than a lot-a other folks did. An then I began to wonder as to jus when all of his craziness would end. When he'd finally get tired of the boat an Willie. Or spendin so much money on that damn house an jus say the hell with it all. But he never did, an even though things began to change, we still kept go'n up river.

"Anyway, I finally made it up there an after we'd gotten the boat all tied an had finished goofin off, we set about workin an scrapin paint. Now normally ol Willie was pretty carefree, but that mornin I noticed that everywhere she went she took her shotgun an kept glancin out at the river as if she was lookin for somethin.

"Now at first I thought that it was cause she'd seen them two gators right around the bend an was being real careful. So I finally asked her while we was eatin lunch, an that's when she told me all about what'd happened. Of how this man had come an tried to hurt her, an how she'd shot him, an then of how them two big ol gators ended up finishin him off.

"She told me in secret, an when she finished she made me promise not to ever tell Foster cause she was worried that he'd send her back to town an she needed ta work. An like she said, there wasn't no work in town for her. Or at least not any kind of respectable work that was. I tell ya, even though she was jus fifteen, she was one tough little gal. So I kept her secret jus like she asked an never said a word anyone... that is, until now."

"Now you keep that shotgun close by ya hear," Otis yelled from inside the pilothouse as he began drifting away from the pier.

"Always," Willie beamed with a glance toward shore. "See," she gestured with a nod to her gun leaning against the first pylon.

Looking through the doorway, Otis just shook his head and then put the boat into gear. "Good, then I'll see you on Thursday," he hollered as he pushed the throttle forward.

Instantly sputtering to life, Willie watched as the murky waters beneath the stern churned into a boiling caldron and then the boat as it slowly pulled away. She watched until it hit the bend in the tributary then listened as the three short blasts from its horn emanated and echoed up the channel. It was Otis's final goodbye before he disappeared behind the big tree. A moment later, she raised her hand from her side and waved. "Bye," she said in a quiet voice as she turned to shore.

Other than Duncan, she'd never really known a black person before and the stories she'd always heard of the negro kind were nothing in the way that he was. He was kind and polite, and was always there to help. They talked and laughed when they worked together, and she liked him immensely. He was her friend, and in her short and sheltered life, he was the only one she'd ever had.

Stopping at the pylon she bent and grabbed her gun, cradled it confidently under her arm and then slowly turned back to the water with a vigilant gaze. A small gust of wind whispered through the air and then settled across the water, rippling the surface into a million tiny waves. It was quiet now that Otis was gone, almost too quiet. Looking in both directions with a guarded uneasiness, she stared intently and listened then finally turned and continued on to the house. It was time to read.

———◆———

It was late and she was asleep by the time he bent and blew out her candle. And as he looked down at her lying naked beneath the covers, he couldn't help but smile at what he considered to be a most fitting end to his journey. His trip to Montgomery had been an unbelievable success but now it was time to take his pleasures. Slipping beneath the sheets, it wasn't until late in the morning when he finally left the dark haired beauty.

Friday morning he was running on borrowed energy, but even so he met the painter at nine and after a few simple sketches, he gave the go ahead to start. It would cover almost the entire back of the boat, and he could have it done by the afternoon. Foster was pleased and headed to his office with a stop at Crystal's Bakery. The girls were waiting for the news, and now that it was certain, he wanted to officially announce it and celebrate.

They were elated to say the least, and squealed with delight then laughed and danced in a euphoric celebration. They ate their pastries and drank their coffee, then besieged him with an endless barrage of questions. They picked up the phone and in a mock rehearsal of what they hoped would come, answered with exaggerated voices.

"Senator Siler's office... may I help yooou?" They laughed.

"Oh no, I'mmm sorry, but the Senator will be in Washington all this week. Yes, that's right, he has meetings with the President."

They laughed again; Foster shook his head and joined in with them. A short while later, and after they'd all settled, the two women stood, and with warm congratulatory hugs, promised their boss complete and unwavering support.

CHAPTER 29

BY THE TIME FOSTER HAD made it to the marina, Otis was already there and had the boat ready to go. "Mornin boss, ja have a good trip?" he asked as Foster approached.

"Morning Otis, and yes, I did actually. Thank you. I had a wonderful trip. And ya know what started it out the best?"

"What's that boss?" He stopped his wiping and raised his head.

"Was when I saw you heading up river."

"You saw me?" Otis grinned.

"Yep, you were just up from Chickasaw Creek, motoring right up the middle when I looked out my window and saw you. I'll tell ya, what a pretty sight."

"So you was on the train that passed me the other day?"

"Sure was," Foster nodded.

"An so did you see me wave?" He grinned again. "When the train blowed it's whistle?"

"Sure did," Foster drawled.

Reflecting back to that moment, Otis quietly stared for just a few seconds and then changed the subject. "Well boss," he finally said. "I got jus about everything all cleaned an ready ta go whenever you's ready."

"Good Otis, that's good. So tell me, what'd ya think of the back?"

"The back? The back a what boss?"

"That back," he repeated and pointed to the stern. "The back of the boat. You mean you haven't seen it yet?"

"Oh no sur," he cocked his head. "Why, what's wrong? Is it broke?"

"No it's not broke," Foster laughed. "I had it painted yesterday. Come look, I put Willie's name on it just like we talked. Remember?"

Jumping to the pier, Otis walked to the stern. "Oooh boss, Miss Willie al shorly like that. So is that how you make her name in writin for real?"

"Yes," Foster replied with a quiet softness. "That's how you make her name," he added as he then pronounced and spelled it out.

"Yes sur boss, the *Willie Mae*." Otis repeated. "I like it. I like it a lot."

That morning Foster drove again while Otis cleaned on the boat, but when they finally hit the bend with the big tree and he reached up to pull on the knotted rope, he hesitated.

"You ain't gonna blow the horn boss?" Otis asked.

"Not today, Otis. I want to surprise her this time. I wanna see how long it takes her to see her name on the back. What-a-ya think? Think she'll notice it?"

"Oh, yes sur boss, I think she'll see it right off."

"You do?"

"Oh, yes sur. An I bet she'll be plenty suprised too, don't you?"

"Yeah," he turned and smiled. "I guess I do actually."

Foster knew that she would be surprised, but what he didn't know was whether or not she would fall for his ploy. Would naming the boat after her work as he hoped? Surely she would see how much he cared and give herself over. She had to, but just in case and as an added measure, he had the gifts that he'd bought in Montgomery. Smiling as they approached the pier, he stepped back from the wheel and gestured to Otis. "Here you go Otis, you dock it okay. I'm going to the back."

Taking the helm, Otis slowed the boat while Foster made his way to the stern and looked around. Willie was nowhere in sight, and as they began their turn and pulled along side to tie, he smiled at the fact that he'd achieved his goal. He really wanted to see the look on her face when she saw her name, and just as soon as they were tied, he stepped back onto the boat and blew the horn.

Breaking the quiet of the morning with three long blasts from the brass-belled tube on top, Willie stopped her scraping with the snap of her head and smiled. Yes, they were back, and in an instant she jumped from her ladder and darted from around the house. Foster was back, and her heart raced with an overjoyed happiness. She'd missed him terribly.

Racing across the yard, she was surprised to find that the boat was already tied and that Foster was standing in the back with his arms spread wide as if he were waiting for her embrace. Had he missed her too, she hoped as she slowed. She'd thought of nothing but him and what they'd done all week, and it was torture waiting for his return. She wanted to kiss him again and more, but before another thought could enter her head, she suddenly stopped just before the pier and stared.

"Oh my Lord," she gasped as she placed her hands to her mouth and then read the words on the boat. It was her name, in big black letters, out-lined and bordered in red and gold. She knew it because Foster had taught her how to spell and write it, and she'd practiced all week, perfecting her penmanship until she could connect her letters with flawless flowing lines. And now it was on the back of his boat. He did love her; she was convinced of it. Her heart jumped and she reeled with joy.

"Well, what-a-ya think?" Foster hollered with a glance down at her name and then back to her.

She'd seen it all right, just like Otis had said she would. But Willie just stared with her hands to her mouth unable to answer. Was she dreaming? A moment later she dropped her hands and slowly shuffled forward. One small step followed by another and then another, until her heart-warming grin turned into an uncontrolled smile and she bolted down the pier.

"So ol Willie was really surprised, huh?" Jim asked.

"Oh yeah, she was surprised all right." Otis chuckled.

"An so what'd she do?"

"Well, when she first saw us she jus froze an stood there in the grass with her hands on her mouth. Then, about a second or two later, she dropped em an with a great big grin stretchin from ear to ear, came runnin down onto the pier a squeelin an a jabberin somethin about it be'n her name. She was all excited, an jus as soon as she got to the back of the boat she stopped an then jus kind-a stood there. I think she was readin her name again up close jus ta make sure. I remember Foster was standin right here with his hands on his hips," he pointed. "Grinnin at Willie, when all of a sudden she jumped right at em. Actually," he laughed and corrected himself. "Lunged is more like it."

"You mean from the pier?" Jim asked with a wide-eyed gaze.

"Yep," Otis laughed again. "From the pier. Now I really don't think that he was expectin her to do that, an for a second I thought that the both of em was gonna go right over the side into the water."

"Really?"

"Oh yeah, an it was funny as hell too, cause ol Foster was do'n everything he could to keep from go'n overboard. An Willie, well, she had her arms an legs wrapped around him so tight I thought she was gonna cut him in half. Anyway, I guess puttin her name on it must of really done somethin to her cause there wasn't nooo doubt that she was absolutely love struck. An that was jus what Foster had wanted."

"Willieee," Foster croaked as he gasped for air and regained his balance. "Let me breath."

Dropping her legs to the floor she stared dreamily up into his eyes but kept her arms around his neck. "You put my name on your boat?"

"Yes, I did. Do you like it?"

Smiling with a nod, she lowered her arms and then wrapped them around his torso. "I jus don't know what ta say," she replied as she laid her head in his chest. "I, I jus never dreamed that," she tried to pick her words. "That--"

"Willie," Foster interrupted. "You don't have to say anything, you know that."

"But why'd you do it?"

"Do whaaat?" he teased.

"Put my name on your boat?" she smacked his chest with the flat of her hand.

"Well, you are my girl, aren't you?" he drawled with a grin as he pulled her tight.

Nodding her head with a glowing smile, she gently laid her cheek against his chest. "Yes," she mumbled and squeezed until she saw Otis step into view.

"Mister Otis," she squealed as she left Foster's arms and stepped to the stern. "Did you see the back of the boat?"

"I shor did Miss Willie," he replied. "That's your name on there. Do you like it?"

"Oh my lordy, heavens yes," she piped with a glance back up to her friend. "I love it! I jus can't believe it," she said as she turned back to Foster. "I love you," she cooed as she laid her head in his chest and squeezed him.

Feeling her arms as they tightened around him once again, Foster smiled to himself. It had worked, and even better than he'd thought. He could feel it in her body and sense it in the tone of her voice. She would come to him tonight, he was certain of it, yet as an added measure he would dole out the gifts he'd brought like tidbits of sugar to a filly.

First he would give her the four little books that Vicki had gotten this afternoon, then, and some time before bed, the small bottle of perfume and the beautiful silver locket. Gifts he'd purchased while on his trip with the Judge. As added enticements to lure his wild and free spirited young mare into his bed. Where, and in the most long awaited of moments, she would surrender her will and allow herself to be mounted and ridden for the very first time.

"I love you too Willie," he whispered and returned her squeeze as his thoughts continued to revolve. This was what she wanted to hear and he knew it, and just as he'd surmised, her reaction to the three magical words was instant. A renewed strength to her arms as they tightened around his torso along with a big deep breath that seemed as if she were trying to inhale the very essence of the words themselves. He smiled once more. Later he would use them again, but only if needed and sparingly, to ignite the smoldering desires that lay deep within her. "Now," he began as they finally relaxed and separated. "How about we get this boat unloaded before Otis there goes to sleep on us."

Nodding, Willie turned and glanced at Otis then grabbed a box from the floor.

"So there I was grabbin boxes while Willie handed em to me, an as soon as we got everything off the boat an onto the pier, we started packin it all up to the house. I remember every time she walked past the stern, she'd slow down jus a little then glance back an giggle. I guess she was checkin to make sure her name was still on there an wasn't gonna fall off or somethin. I tell ya, she was funny, an me an Foster both had a pretty good laugh at that.

"Anyway, jus as soon as we'd gotten everything up an all packed away, ol Foster decided that he wanted ta go boatin again. Now that kind of surprised me cause we'd jus gotten there, but that's what he wanted to do so right off we headed back down to the boat. Willie was all excited cause she'd only ridden

in it once an she didn't waste no time in untyin it an jumpin on board. Then, an jus as soon as we pulled away, well, that's when Foster started askin me how well I knew the river on up cause that's the way he wanted ta go. He said that he wanted ta check to see if he could find his property lines. Heck, he even had a great big map with lines on it showin him where to look."

"Now back then, I actually knew that part of the river pretty good, an for quite a-ways on up too. Even past where his map ended, cause the Davenport's really liked go'n up that way, specially Howard. See, he had a real fondness for shootin snappin turtles off a logs while they was sunnin. I remember he use sit up there on the bow with his high-powered rifle like he was some kind of big ol game hunter while we motored up stream. He called it target practicin an sport. I jus called it turtle blastin. An Mrs. D, well, she jus called it disgustin.

"Now as best I can recall, he wasn't much of a shot an rarely hit any of em, but I'll tell ya, that sure didn't keep him from blastin. No sireee. An I'll tell ya another thing too," he laughed and shook his head. "It used ta jus drive ol Mrs. D plumb crazy."

"Really?"

"Oh yeah, in fact onetime I remember to the point where," he started to laugh again as he recalled the day then paused to regain his composure. "Well, we were out one afternoon when I guess she'd had jus about enough of that big ol loud gun an of him a killin all them poor little turtles. An that's when she came stompin up through the cabin from the back jus a stormin mad an blew right past me an out onto the bow. An then, right after she yelled his name real loud, she lit into him an started yellin an tellin him how if he didn't put that goddamn gun down an stop killin turtles she was gonna take it away from em an shove it up his fat ass," he laughed.

"You're kiddin?" Jim laughed as he envisioned the scene.

"Oh hell nooo. I tell ya, she really railed on him. Then, an after she was all done, she came back inside, looked at me an smiled, then headed right on back to the stern jus as fast as she'd come up. Now I was do'n everything I could do jus to keep a straight face, I really was, but when I looked back out on the bow an saw Howard sittin there like a little kid that'd jus been scolded an told that he couldn't play with his gun no more, well... that's when I finally couldn't take it no more."

"Damn, I bet that was funny," Jim shook his head.

"Oh it was," Otis assured. "An ol Howard, well, he never did blast turtles after that. Anyway, we pulled away from the pier an headed right up that *little tributary. Foster was up front with me an his map, an it wasn't too long before he started pointin an askin me if I recognize this an that an if I knew where all these places were. An Willie, well, I'm not really sure where she was," he chuckled. "But I think she was in the back, lookin over the stern at her name."*

Laughing, Jim downed what was left of his beer then crushed his can and threw it into the corner with the others. Clanging nosily as it bounced off the hull and into the pile, he shook his head then looked to the sky. The sun now mid way on its afternoon descent, had just disappeared behind a thick bank of clouds granting a temporary reprieve from its burning rays. The auction that had bussed with so much activity earlier was now nothing more than a quiet group of people milling and ogling over their latest purchases. A second later he dropped his gaze back to Otis.

"So did ya find the property lines?" he asked as he opened the lid to the cooler and reached into the freezing water.

"Sure did," Otis replied as he downed his beer then crushed his can and threw it into the corner.

"The last two Otis," Jim drawled as he pulled the final pair from their icy confines and handed one to the man.

"Thank you," Otis said as he took the beer and continued. "But I'll tell ya I sure was beginnin to wonder there for a while."

"Why's that?"

"Well," he began as he popped his top. "After we left we made our way up through that little tributary until it connected back into the main river. An then when we hit it, we jus kept go'n up river while Foster checked his land marks until we'd gone at least a couple a miles.

"Now I was really beginnin ta think that he'd plumb lost his mind go'n that far, an I tried to tell him that too. But hell he wasn't listenin, in fact, I don't think he ever listened to anyone really. He jus looked at me with this shit eatin grin until I'd finished an that's when he explained to me all about the title to the property. You know, how for all them years it'd been mistakenly misread."

"Misread? What-a-ya mean?"

"Well, I remember he said somethin about a piece a paper with a fold in it hidin a zero, an how it wasn't two hundred acres like the Davenport's had always thought, but actually two thousand. An that all the ground in-between there an the house was his now. Anyway, an jus about the time he was done explainin it all, well, that's when he finally spotted the big ol white stake he'd been lookin for."

"There it is Otis," Foster called out as he stood in the doorway and gazed to the shore.

"Oh yeah, I see it too," Willie chimed in right behind him. "It's right there," she added and pointed out the glass. "See."

"Yes sur boss, I see's it. Ya wanna get closer?" He slowed and turned before Foster could answer.

Stepping out onto the bow with his map, Foster steadied himself then began checking the two against each other. Looking first at the map and then to the shore, he verified the property pin's location then smiled and turned to the other shore. "Now, let's go over there," he hollered and pointed. "The other pin should be almost straight across."

Turning the wheel, Otis took the boat to the other shore then slowed as they approached the bank. A few minutes later they found the other pin.

"Now up until that time, I had no idea that the Davenports had that much property. An ta be right honest with ya, I don't think that Howard did either. Heck, in all the years that I'd work for him we never went lookin for his property lines like ol Foster did. But right after we found that other pin, he came back in with a great big smile, rolled up his map an told me to jus keep on a go'n up river. That he wanted to do a little more boatin as he called it. An with that, he grabbed Willie an the two of them went to the back."

Taking their seats in the comfort of the Adirondack chairs, Willie closed her eyes with a relaxing sigh and quickly drifted off into her own little dream world. A dream world that was so far removed from the dry scorched fields of her earlier life that it seemed impossible. A dream world that'd put her right onto the pages of a magical fairy tale, where she was now the beautiful princess in a never-ending story. But this wasn't a fairy tale, it was real and she knew it. She was living it.

She felt privileged and special and radiant, and wished her mother could see her, riding in such a beautiful boat with a rich handsome lawyer. A man who loved and cared for her so much that he had named it after her. She envisioned the two of them standing on the pier looking at the stern while she read her name then receiving a proud motherly hug. And then turning to view the house with its built in pump for water right in the kitchen and a place for taking baths, and more food than she ever dreamed she could eat. Her heart swelled with pride and then sadness as she recalled her mother's face and then the sound of her voice. Sweet and gentle, yet hauntingly sad. She remembered how they'd giggled like sisters the day she had returned from the creek, counting the nicks and cuts from under her arms and on her legs after she'd shaven for the very first time. And then of how proud she was of her and how she'd gone and grown all up on her to be such a pretty girl.

They were some or her last and fondest memories, but along with them came the sudden return of her unbearable loss. She missed her terribly and swallowed hard to remove the growing lump in her throat. She knew she needed to change her thoughts before she cried, and in an attempt to remain strong, she opened her eyes and focused on the passing shore. A family of turtles dropping into the water from their sunbaked log drew a small but definite smile. Obviously startled by their presence as they passed, they submerged with a scurrying haste into the safety of their underwater world. A moment later, she cleared her throat and turned back to Foster basking in the sun. Reaching for his hand, she gave him a gentle squeeze, and with a contented smile, closed her eyes and returned to her enchanted world.

Responding to her touch, Foster smiled within himself then rolled his over and opened his palm in an inviting gesture. Yes he thought, everything was working just as he'd hoped, and as her fingers intertwined with his and she squeezed him once again, he couldn't help but think of the evening still to come. Would she give in to her desires and come to him? The blood in his groin stirred.

Relaxing in the sun, the two rode quietly until Foster finally rose from his chair and ducked into the cabin. He was thirsty, and a nice refreshing coke sounded like just the thing. Making three ice filled glasses, he stepped up into the pilothouse and gave one to Otis and told him to turn the boat around. He'd seen enough of the river and it was time to head back, and as he walked back through the cabin he grabbed the neatly wrapped package of books he'd hidden in the cabinet. Slipping them under his arm, he picked up the other two cokes and returned to the stern.

"Okay Willie," he announced as he stepped through the doorway. "Ya thirsty?"

"Oh myyy," she smiled and pulled herself forward. "A coke."

"Yes ma'am, with ice in it too," he teased. "Here."

Blushing at his remark, Willie reached up and took the glass. "Thank you."

"Well, you're quite welcome," he said as he took his seat then pulled the package from under his arm. "Oh, and here," he added as he set it on the arm of her chair. "I bought you a little surprise."

Her reaction was just as he'd predicted, and as surprise and excitement turned into a gracious humility, he knew he'd made a good choice. Willie loved her books, and even though these were a little more advanced and above her skill level, he knew she would conquer them quickly. Skimming through the pages of each one, he watched as she oooed and aawed at the pictures then picked out one and set the rest on the arm of her chair. Clearing her throat as she settled into her chair, Willie opened up her first Farmer John book and slowly began to read.

"The da... oog, cha, chaaa..." she stammered then turned to Foster with a questionable gaze.

"Chased," he assisted with a glance at the book. "The dog chased."

Nodding her head, she repeated the words with a renewed and heightened clarity. "The da-oog cha-ased the cat in... innn."

"Into the barn," he added softly.

Taking a breath, she reread the sentence once again and then turned back to Foster with a grin.

"That's right," he praised. "Now keep going, you're doing good."

Doing as she was told, Willie continued to read as they slowly made their way back down the river. Stumbling with the bigger and more complicated words, she would look to Foster for his ever-gentle assistance then sound them out and reread them. Willie was smart and with every new word she conquered, her confidence level grew.

Pulling the throttle back to idle, Otis dropped downstream just a ways from the pier then made his question mark turn back toward the pier. A touch to reverse brought the boat to a stop right along side the wooden structure and within a few moments they had it tied. They'd been out all afternoon and it was late, and now that it had clouded and looked like rain, Foster sent Otis to gather some wood and start a fire.

"Now Willie," Foster said as he jumped back into the boat and then ducked into the cabin.

"Come with me, I want to show you something before we go up."

"What is it?" she asked as she followed and ducked through the doorway.

Turning with a small cream-colored box tied in a golden string bow, he met her just as she stepped inside. "Here, I bought you a little something else."

"Aaah Foster," she gasped as he placed the little box in her hands. "Oooh," her voice softened. "What's this?"

"Well, you'll just have to open it now won't you," he replied and folded his arms.

Nodding her head, Willie stared at the box for a just second then pulled on the string and lifted the lid. Holding the small clear bottle of liquid in front of her, she stared with a radiant smile then looked to Foster with an inquisitive gaze. "Iiit, it's smellin water?"

"Yes Willie," he chuckled at her naiveté. "It's smellin water. Or as most people call it... perfume."

"Oh my," she returned her eyes to the bottle. "I ain't never had perfume before."

"Well here, let me show you," he said as he took the bottle from her hands. "Here you go," he invited as he twisted the cap off and brought it to her nose. "Now smell."

Inhaling deep, Willie smiled and then rolled her eyes.

"This is what all of the rich women in the city wear," he insinuated in hopes that his words would resonate their hidden meaning. "Do you like it?"

"Oh my yesss, it smells jus wonerful."

"Good, then would you like me to show you how to put it on?"

Nodding her head with a tight-lipped grin, Willie watched as he turned the bottle over onto the tip of his finger. "Now perfume is very expensive," he began as he brushed her hair away. "And very powerful too, so just a little behind the ears and neck is all you need, okay. First on one side," he said as he gently traced his finger from behind her ear and down the side of her neck. "And then on the other," he added with another dab to her other ear. "And sometimes," he finished with a wink and a smile. "After you've taken a bath, you can put a little in other places too. Oh and remember, more is not necessarily better. You never want to put on too much okay. Now let me see," he leaned forward and inhaled. "Aaah yes... perfect."

"Oooh Foster," she cooed. "I jus don't know what to say," she lowered her head and stared at the bottle then lifted her gaze back to his. "It's so nice, Iii," she suddenly stopped and tiptoed to the balls of her feet then squeezed him around his neck. "Thank you."

"Well you're quite welcome, but it's just a bottle of perfume. Nothing special."

"Well ta me it is, cause I ain't never had perfume before." she pressed herself against him. A second later they were kissing. Soft and passionately, then heated and hungry.

CHAPTER 30

———◆———

THE TIME THAT'D PASSED BEFORE they finally emerged from the boat was longer than either had thought, but Willie was all smiles and now certain of her feelings of love. She was utterly smitten, and as they slowly strolled toward shore, she couldn't help but stopped and turned then cast her eyes to the stern of the boat. "Willie Mae," she finally said with a far off dreamy gaze.

"Yes it is," Foster said as he dropped his arm across her shoulder and tugged her along. "But come on, I wanna cook before it rains."

Glancing up at the dark grey clouds, the two quickened their strides and hurried toward the house. Their bellies were growling, and with the likelihood of rain, they needed to hurry. A few moments later, while they were inside preparing their dinner for the grill, Willie built a fire in the stove and then set three large pots of water on top.

"I wanna take a bath after supper," she answered the unspoken question in Foster's eyes with an inviting smile.

Returning her smile, Foster stared for a second then tenderly brushed the side of her cheek with the back of his hand. "Good Willie," he drawled. "I like it when you smell pretty."

"Now by the time those two had finally made it back outside with the food, I had a pretty nice fire go'n an right away ol Foster settled in an started cookin. I guess he was jus as worried about the weather as me an Willie was cause he kept lookin up at the sky every so often. It'd darkened even more since we'd gotten back an you could tell that he really wanted ta get done before it rained. Not ta mention the fact that none of us had eatin anything since mornin an we was all starvin.

333

"Anyway, if I remember right, I think we had pork chops an green beans that night. Big ol thick ones ya know," he held up his hand and separated his thumb and finger. "Yes sir, ol Foster sure did like to cook on that grill, an to tell ya the truth he was pretty good at it too. Damn good, actually. But after a little bit he had Willie take over an he jus stretched out across the grass an relaxed. I guess he was determined to enjoy the day to the very end cause that's when he had me go an grab us a couple of beers an a coke from the boat. I'll tell ya, I sure did enjoy those times back then, sittin there with those two around the fire, eatin an drinkin," he sighed and then took a sip from his beer.

"Sounds like some pretty good times."

"Oooh they was," Otis replied. "They really was. Anyway, ol Willie tended to them pork chops jus like Foster had showed her while me an him sat there an drank our beer. I think she really liked cookin on that grill too, an jus as soon as she was done, we ate real quick cause it was beginnin to get dark too. I remember the smell of rain was real heavy in the air an we all knew that it was jus a matter of time before it started, an that's when Willie finally stood up an took our plates. She said that she was gonna go in an do the dishes an then take a bath cause she was dirty from scrapin paint all mornin. Then, an jus as soon as she did that, ol Foster sent me back down to get a couple more beers. He called it dessert, an when I got back, well, we jus stayed out there, drinkin an enjoyin what was left of the day. That was, until this great big ol flash of lightenin an crack of thunder jus across the tributary lit everything up an finally brought the rain.

"Now at first it was jus a couple of heavy drops here an there, but we knew it was comin cause you could hear it across the water. In fact, it was comin pretty fast so we both downed what was left of our beers then jumped up an started runnin. I remember Foster sayin somethin about seein me in the mornin, but I really wasn't payin much attention cause I was makin for the boat.

"Anyway, I made it down the pier an inside jus before it really hit an right quickly I made sure that everything was all buttoned up. You know, the doors an the hatches an all. An after that, well, I jus stretched out on one of those sofa's, an with the rain hittin the roof an my belly plum full a food, I went to sleep an didn't move until late the next mornin."

She soaked for a while in the warm sudsy water then slowly and carefully shaved her armpits and legs. Her dexterity had improved immensely, and after a short examination, she smiled at her skills. Yes, no cuts, and then she remembered what Foster had said in the

kitchen before they ate. *'I like it when you smell pretty,'* his voiced resonated with its subtle overtone.

Closing her eyes, she soaped her sponge then washed her body
and then her sex. It felt heated and wet with desire. She remembered
last weekend, and how he'd touched and caressed her, and had
made her quiver. She smiled then exhaled with a moan and slid a little deeper into the tub. She felt amorous and womanly, and wanted
nothing more than to be touched again by the man she loved. It
was her fantasy, but all too quickly it ended with a brilliant flash of
lightening and crack of thunder that broke her moment and finally
brought the rain. Pattering the roof and the ground with a billion
tiny droplets, it gave a pleasant and soothing sound to an otherwise
quiet moment. A few moments later, she heard the door and then
the sound of Foster's voice as he called out her name.

"I'm in here," she hollered as his footsteps approached. "I was jus
gettin out."

"Well take your time," he drawled and rolled his back to the
door. "There's no hurry. I'm just going to brush my teeth and then
jump in bed," he added and held up his last little gift. "But when
you're done, come on in. I have something that I want to show you,"
he finished as he stared at the silver locket, designed and embossed
in a beautiful filigree.

"Okay," she answered. "Jus give me a minute ta dry off an I'll be
right out."

Stepping from the tub, Willie dried herself before the mirror as
an array of thoughts began to run through her head. Would he kiss
and touch her again like he'd done last week? Her stomach knotted
and she heaved with a nervous breath of anticipation. Would he try
to love her? She wondered as she picked up the small glass bottle
from the counter and perfumed herself. A tiny dab behind her ears
and neck like he'd shown her, and then another between the curves
of her breast.

'This is what all of the rich women in the city wear,' she remembered
him saying as her hand lingered in a caressing manner, tweaking
her points until they'd swelled and the fiery flashes within her had
warmed her belly. Looking into the mirror, she smiled wantonly and
dropped her hand then reached for her nightgown and slipped it
on. Buttoning the front, she ran a brush through her hair and then

reached for her panties. Staring at the clean cotton garment folded neatly in her hands, she paused for a second then suddenly cast her eyes back to her reflection.

'*Whaaat?*' she asked with a guilty expression. '*Well, this is what you wanted, isn't it?*' The sound of her own voice suddenly resonated from within. '*It's what you've been thinkin about all week an you know it. Now put them back.*'

Somewhat confused, she looked at her panties then returned her gaze into the mirror as her mind began to whirl. A little frightened, she stared silently for a moment then listened as the voice in her head returned. '*Besides, you liked it when he touched you there, didn't you?*'

Slowly nodding her head as if in a daze, Willie suddenly felt a heated and overpowering wave of desire well from between her legs. Desires that she could no longer control; that had been built to an unbearable level and were now consuming her like never before. Buckling under the crushing surge of its onslaught, she took pause to steady herself against the counter then regained her gaze. '*An you want him to do it again, don't you?*' Her eyes narrowed, as the voice grew daringly stronger. '*Admit it... you know you do! An more!*' Her nostrils flared as the dampened heat between her legs rose to an insufferable level. '*You want him to love you, don't you? You want him to love you... like a married woman!*' "Yes!" she hissed with a ragged breath. "Yessss!"

It was exactly what she wanted and she knew it, but her war of wills wasn't over, and just as quickly as she'd confessed her desires, she snapped her eyes back open to the sound of her mother's voice as it too suddenly rose from within. '*No Willie,*' her voice battled back in an effort to re-instill the values and virtues of love and marriage. '*He doesn't love you.*'

'*But he does,*' Willie argued with a determined and defiant retort. '*He'd told her so. An he would take care of her. He already was.*'

Torn between the voices in her head and what she really wanted, Willie stared into the mirror with a glassy eyed gaze. She was afraid and nervous, but the heated desires within her far out weighed her trepidations. A moment later, and without another thought as to what it was she was about to do, she set her panties back on the counter then turned and reached for the door.

His door was half open, yet still Willie knocked and called his name.

"Come in Willie," Foster replied as he rolled to one elbow. "Please," he encouraged.

Smiling nervously, Willie pushed the door open and took a step but then suddenly stopped at the sight of Foster lying in bed with the sheet around his waist. Was he naked, she wondered anxiously, then hopefully as she stared at his lean muscular torso exposed and illuminated by the dim light of the lamp? Shuddering at the thought, she swallowed nervously and then slowly continued.

Approaching ever closer, Foster couldn't help but think of how she was coming to him just as he'd wanted. For weeks he had worked on her and now here she was, silently crossing the room like an angel that'd been sent from the heavens. A gift from the gods, that'd been divinely delivered in answer to his prayers. Yet still, and even though she stood at the very portal of womanhood, he knew that she still might not take that final step across its threshold. That doorway that once opened would lead her from the realm of innocence in which she lived into another from which she would never return. It concerned him deeply, but as she approached ever closer and he caught her gaze, he could clearly see by the look in her eyes that he need not worry. Smiling at the thought, he discreetly set the little white box with the locket back onto the nightstand.

Stopping just at the edge of his bed, Willie silently stared at the man she loved then cleared her throat and dropped her eyes to the floor. "Foster," she asked as if she were almost afraid to hear his answer. "Do you really love me?"

Somewhat surprised by her question, Foster took pause but then quickly regained his senses. He knew what she wanted and needed to hear for he'd been here before. She was giving him the keys in which to free her. That would liberate her from the virtues she was imprisoned by and the guilt of what it was she was about to do. She wanted to hear the enchanting phrase that meant so much. The three magical words that would finally unlock the gates as to her yet untouched treasures. It was all he needed to do and true to his nature, Foster delivered without hesitation.

"Oooh Willie," he feigned with a heartfelt breath. His eyes narrowing in an effort to devoid her of any and all doubt as to the sincerity of his feelings. His voice changing as if there was nothing else in the world that mattered more than his love for her. "Yes baby. You know I do, Iiii.

How could you even think?" He stopped and then raised his arm to take her hand, only to watch her retreat with a small step backwards.

Oh my God, had he blown it? Had he misread her? Was she changing her mind? He cringed at the thought and began to speak, but then stopped as she brought her hands to her chest and began to unbutton her gown. Watching as she slowly and methodically began with one and then another; he wet his lips in silent anticipation as she quietly proceeded, undoing the next two just as slowly. Until she'd exposed her chest and had gently slid it over her shoulders.

It seemed like minutes, but it was no more than a few seconds before she slowly let the gown slide to the top of her breast where she held it tight and then looked back with a smoldering glare. Was she teasing him or just nervous? He couldn't tell, nor now did he care. A second later, and with a heavy breath, she tilted her head upwards and closed her eyes then released her hold and let the gown fall. Dropping to the floor and around her feet like a waterfall, Willie for the first time in her life stood naked before a man. Her soul and body both bared in every sense of the word.

Catching his breath, Foster rose from his elbow as he tried to encompass her beauty, for she was as perfect and as beautiful as any woman he'd ever seen. Bathed under the dim light of the lamp, he could see her firm round breasts shimmering with a lustrous glow and the soft curves of her body highlighted and shadowed like the rolling hills of the plains before the morning sun. He could see the perfect vee of her sex, and her nostrils and chest as they flared and heaved with each and every breath. And then her eyes, heavily glazed with a smoldering desire as they finally opened and connected with his.

A long luminous flash of lightning illuminated the room, and for a split second she stood before him like a living statue, gloriously bathed in the flickering light from the heavens. His heart quickened and his mouth grew dry. He wanted to say something but he didn't, for he knew that it was a moment where words were not needed. A few seconds later, a loud rumbling roll of thunder broke their silence. Rattling the house itself, it slowly faded, leaving only the sound of the soft yet steady rain. It was the moment he'd been waiting for and with a tender and inviting gesture, he reached out once again. She was his now, and with a single graceful step toward him the sultry young virgin took his hand and joined him in bed.

Lying beside him, Foster slowly and tenderly began to undo the fears and doubts of what it was she was about to do. He'd deflowered more than one girl in his day and he knew to take it slow. And so, with everything he'd learned from all of the women he'd been with, he began to play her body like a piano. Caressing her in the most sensuous of ways, he preceded it seemed as if he could anticipate her needs and wants before she became aware of them. As if her body were his own. He kissed her passionately then nipped at her neck and worked his way to the taut pointed tips of her breast. He smelled her perfume as he took one into his mouth and smiled to himself. *'And other places too,'* he remembered telling her.

She felt his mouth, hot and wet, and then his teeth as they nipped and pulled. She trembled and held his head, whimpering wordless noises as he suckled first one and then the other. He was loving her, and it was everything she'd dreamed.

He reached down to the curve of her hip then slid his hand between her legs, caressing and brushing her matted curls. She remembered last Sunday and how he had touched her there and then made her quiver. They were feelings of pleasure and she liked them, and in a shameless shedding of her inhibitions, she parted her legs and welcomed his finger. Determined to inflame her desires until they had enslaved the very will of her body, he ever so slowly began to pleasure her.

Consumed with bliss and lost in the sensations flowing through her, Willie flattened her palms against the bed and gripped the sheets with a moan of incoherent pleasure. Giving herself over to the delight of his efforts, she strained numerous times toward the pinnacle of pleasure as he wickedly coaxed her to the brink again and again only to stop in a cruel and teasing kind of way. Torturing her until she cried out for him to continue, only to whimper and beg for him to stop moments later as her body convulsed into uncontrolled spasms.

Smiling as she descended from her state of euphoria, Foster could see in her eyes that his efforts had worked. And as she gently slipped her hand beneath the sheet and then sensuously ran it down the flat of his belly, a wishful thought flashed through his mind. Would she do it? Was she bold enough? He prayed and held his breath but then suddenly shuddered as she stopped and gained his gaze. It was another moment of doubt and he knew it, but with a gentle and reassuring touch to her hand, Willie continued on until she'd reach his hardened member and awkwardly began to explore. A second later, he felt her exhale and then moan as she encircled and squeezed him. Rolling his eyes with a groan, he shunted his hips toward her and kissed her passionately.

She'd often wondered what it would be like to touch a man, and now here she was holding him in the most sinful of ways. She could feel the raw and veiny hardness of his flesh pulsate with a life of its own as her fingers closed around him. It felt strange and foreign, and nothing like she'd imagined. She felt guilty and wanted to let go but she didn't, she couldn't, for the lustful desires that he'd built inside of her overruled any thoughts of stopping. She squeezed again.

Deliriously consumed by love and desire, she wanted nothing more than to be loved and to make love. To give herself to him openly and freely, and with that she abruptly withdrew her hand and brought it to his face. Softly caressing his cheek, she stared deep into his eyes for just a moment then swallowed and pulled on his shoulders. "Love me," she whispered as she closed her eyes. "Love me," her soft yet heated breath burnt into his ear. "Like a married woman."

Closing his eyes, Foster gave thanks to every god and deity that'd ever been worshiped. Yes, he'd done it. It was the moment he'd been waiting for and now he would have her. He would ride his young filly, and with a kiss as his answer, he rolled on top of her and slipped between her legs. Then with all of the passion in the world, he slowly and tenderly pushed into her. A moment later, he felt her tremble and stiffen as he passed the barrier of her innocence then cry out and moan. Gazing into her eyes, he paused with a tender concern as she relaxed and adjusted around him.

To Willie, it was everything she'd ever imagined and what she'd hoped and dreamed of for almost a month. Never in her life had she experienced so many feelings at once running through her. Of love and passion and desire. As if a soft glittering shower of lightening was now sweeping through out her, touching and tingling each and every one of her nerves in the most pleasurable of ways.

Deliciously and deliriously drugged into a state of euphoria, she savored in the moment. She was being loved like a married woman, and she reveled in the burning and unbridled heat now running through her. Fully aroused and lusting for more she called out his name then beckoned with her eyes and pulled on his shoulders. And as the primordial instincts within her body took over her actions, she lifted her legs and rocked her hips.

It was all he needed, and with that Foster slowly pushed himself into the oily depths of her inner sanctum. And as the youthful walls of her untouched innocence greedily gripped and squeezed him, he closed his eyes and then exhaled with a groan of muted pleasure. A euphoric bliss of ecstasy shot through him and his mind reeled. He thought back to the last time that he'd laid with a girl so young; so taut and lean, so fresh and so pure... so heavenly beautiful. He was nineteen.

———◆———

It was barely light when she quietly rose from the bed and slipped on her gown. Smiling with memories of her night, she carefully made her way to the kitchen and built a fire in the stove. A few moments later, she set the pot of coffee on the thick iron burner, took a seat at the table and then stared out through the rain soaked windows. It was gloomy and foggy with a light misty rain; yet somehow, deep inside, she felt radiant and warm as if it were bright and sunny.

She looked to the boat and the pier still shrouded in the wispy patches of the early morning mist. Vaporous reminders of the moisture-laden air hanging low over the land and water, eerily swirling and drifting about like silent ghostly spirits. Wandering with her mind as she replayed the night's events and the coffee brewed, she thought of her mother and what she would say then rubbed her belly and inhaled a long deep breath. She turned her head to the bedroom door and stared.

She felt older now, as if she were a grown up woman and the trivial things that little girls cared about no longer mattered. She'd given her love to a man and received his back; twice in fact, she smiled. And it had felt good and right, and not dirty and ugly. She was a woman now, she was in love, and she held her head up high. A few moments later, Willie rose and poured a cup of coffee then added the cream and sugar and turned to the bedroom door. She would love her man once more before he left.

"Now it'd rained pretty much on an off all night long an the next mornin when I got up, it was still rainin. Not real hard mind you, but one of those

drizzly kind that was jus enough ta keep things good an wet. So I jus kind of hung out inside the boat here an waited for Willie to come down an tell me that breakfast was ready. But she never came that mornin. No sirree... not that mornin she didn't," he chuckled and shook his head.

"Really, an why not?"

"Why not?" Otis raised his eyebrows and stared. "Have you not been listenin to me?"

"Oh yeaaah," Jim replied with a grin and a nod. "I get it now."

"Well I sure as hell hope so," Otis chuckled. *"Anyway, after the rain had quit an I still didn't see her, I jus grabbed me a couple a poles an a bucket an went to the end of the pier an started fishin. That ol rain had really stirred up the fish an right away I started catchin some real nice keepers. In fact, I'd pretty much forgotten all about breakfast until I heard Willie callin my name from behind me. An boy was she ever happy."*

"Hey Mister Otis," Willie hollered as she stepped onto the pier. "Morinin! What's ya do'n?"

"Mornin Miss Willie," Otis replied as he swiveled on his bucket and craned his neck to see. "I's fishin," he said excitedly. "An I'm a catchin the heck out of em too. Take a look!"

Stopping next to the bucket with her hands on her hips, Willie looked down at the swirling mass. "Oh wow, it's those catfish kind right?"

"Yes ma'am," Otis chuckled.

Staring for a moment longer, Willie finally raised her head and then looked back to Otis. "Mister Otis," she asked.

"Yes um."

"Can you teach me ta fish too? You know, like you do. So I can catch some on my own."

"Why shor I can, heck I'd be more'n happy ta teach ya. Maybe when I come back on up on Tuesday we can do it. Then we'll have all day, an I can teach ya how ta catch em, clean em, an cook em, all in one lesson. How's that sound?"

"Oh gosh, that sounds great," she beamed as she stared into the bucket. "Anyway, Foster sent me down ta see if you wanted some breakfast, he's cookin up some a bacon an eggs. Are ya hungry?"

"Oh, yes ma'am," he replied as he pulled in his pole.

"Now by the time we'd finished breakfast it was pretty late an ol Foster wanted to leave. But Willie wanted him ta give her another readin an writin lesson before we left so I jus went on back down an started fishin again. I remember I was still catchin the hell out of em an by the time they finally came back down, I had two big ol buckets full an was ready ta leave too. One for me, an one for my new fishin buddy Mr. Winters. Anyway, Foster was kind of in a hurry an jus as soon as I got the boat all started an untied, he gave Willie a big ol kiss then jumped in the back an we were on our way."

Standing in the back as they pulled away, Foster couldn't help but grin. "I'll see you next Saturday okay," he hollered over the noise of the motor. "And remember, don't forget to study and practice you're writing, hear? I'm gonna test you when I get back," he warned with a finger pointed smile.

"I will," she promised with a smile right back.

"Oh, and one more thing, I almost forgot. I left you a little present on the nightstand by the bed."

"You did?" she beamed with a glance to the house. "What is it?"

"You'll just have to see," he hollered with a wave as he turned and disappeared through the door.

Raising her hand with a heavy breath, Willie started to wave back but stopped. He was gone, but even so she uttered the word still in her throat. "Bye," she said softly.

Standing on the pier, she watched as the boat slowly made its way back down the tributary. Farther and farther until it had rounded the turn with the big tree hanging out over the water. It was a sight she'd become accustomed to, and as it slowly disappeared from sight and blew its horn, she turned toward the house. It would be a long week waiting for him to return and she missed him already. A second later, she bolted down the pier.

"Then right after we'd gone around that big tree an ol Foster had blowed the horn, he asked me to slide over so he could drive again. I remember he was smilin, an jus about as happy as I'd ever seen him. You know, like some big ol game hunter returnin from a successful hunt. Yes sirrr, it was pretty clear that he'd finally gotten what he was after an I guess he must of sensed that I knew it too cause that's when he finally, as he liked to say. Took me into his confidence."

"Otis?"

"Yes sur boss."

"We need to have a little talk. I need to tell you some things okay," Foster began as he applied more throttle. "Some things in confidence," he glanced toward the man then returned his gaze out front. "You do know what that means don't you?"

"Well kind of," Otis concentrated and scrunched his face. "I think it's," he began but then surrendered and shook his head. "No sur, I guess I don't boss... nots really."

Foster knew that Otis wasn't stupid, he was just uneducated, and without another thought he continued on. "Well its kind of like trust. You do know what that is right?" He glanced to him again.

"Oh yes sur," he replied and puffed out his chest. "It's kinds a like you trust me ta take the boat up river an check on Miss Willie for you right?"

"Well kind of, but not exactly. But that's a good start. See, confidence is kind of like a secret an..."

"Now when he first turned an told me that we needed ta have a talk, I jus knew that I'd done somethin wrong an was in trouble. But that wasn't the case at all, no sir," he laughed and took a sip from his beer.

"An so what'd he want?" Jim sat forward.

"Well," Otis replied as he thought back. "After he finally got done explainin what confidence was, an he was certain I understood, he started explainin how he was go'n to run for the United States Senate," he chuckled again and shook his head.

"Annnd," Jim urged with an ever-growing curiosity.

"Well, for the first few minutes as he rambled on I jus kind-a stood there with this real dumb look on my face, cause what was so funny. Was that back then," he paused and began to grin great big. "I didn't even know what a Senator was let alone how ya got ta be one." The two men laughed.

"Anyway, an after he finally got done explainin to me what a Senator was, he went on about all the things that was gonna start happenin an how he was really gonna need my help. About how he was go'n to have to start travelin a whole bunch because he was gonna be campaignin, an how he was really go'n to have to depend on me. You know, to keep things neat around his house, an to keep the boat all up an go'n, an most importantly, to keep an eye on Willie for him. To check on her an help her, an make sure she was okay an all. You could

tell he was really startin ta like her jus by the way he acted. An more I think, than what he really wanted to admit. Specially after that weekend.

"Then after that, well, that's when he started explainin about how there might be some people, you know, newspaper reporters an such, who would start comin around after they found out I worked for him an start askin all kinds of questions. He told me that they'd try an trick me in to sayin somethin about him an I was suppose to jus tell em I didn't know nothin. That I jus worked for him, an was hired to drive his boat an help him fix his house up river.

"Oh, an he also told me that if anybody ever asked me about Willie, or her name on the back of the boat, I was to jus play dumb. In fact, he told me real dumb. Like I didn't know nothin. I remember he made a real point of that. Anyway, he kept go'n over an over everything until he was sure I under-stood, an after he was all done, well, that's when I finally realized that things was really gonna start changin. An for all of us really."

"Now you do understand all of that, don't you?" Foster question after he'd finished. "You do understand how important this is to me, don't you?"

"Oooh yes sur," Otis gushed with a pledge of loyalty. "I won't lets ya down Mister Siler… ever, an I means it. You jus let me know what ya wants me ta do an I'll take care of it for ya. An I won't ever say nothin to nobody bout Miss Willie either. Honest!"

Turning back to Otis, Foster studied his expression as if he were about to cross examine a witness then smiled and placed his hand on the man's shoulder. "I know you won't Otis," he said as he turned his gaze back out front. "I know you won't."

Otis was a good man and Foster knew it, and with that worry out of the way he soon turned his thoughts to that of the Judge and their conversation that was yet to come. What promising news did he have, he wondered? Did they have the full support of the party? What would their next move be? When and where would they offi-cially make the announcement? What would he do with his cases? His mind reeled at the endless unknowns. A moment later, he turned toward the stern and stared. And now, what would he do with Willie?

CHAPTER 31

———•———

IT WAS LATE IN THE afternoon by the time he pulled the cord to the bell at the McAlister's home. A few moments later, Monique answered the door in her usual provocative manner. "Mesieur Siler," she greeted with a teasing smile. "Goods afternoon. Please, please, comes in. Zhe Sjudge is in zhe librarie'," she continued with a subtle yet lustful gaze that trailed her words. "Would you likes to sees him? Oui? Or would you likes to sees somesing else?" She traced her fingers across her chest and raised her eyebrows as if to taunt and test his loyalty to the Judge.

Pausing in what was clearly a loss of words, Foster could only smile and shake his head. God, he hated her. She'd gotten to him again and there wasn't a damn thing that he could do about it. "Please Monique," he finally answered and gestured with a hand toward the library. "If you don't mind."

A few moments later, he found himself sitting with the Judge in his library, a glass of scotch in one hand and a cigar in the other.

"Well son, you must have really impressed them," the Judge exclaimed as he struck a match and lit Foster's cigar. "Cause they're puttin their money on you... and a damn lot too," he said as he lit his too then extinguished the flame and tossed the charred remains into the ashtray. "I've talked to them twice already since we got back, and I'm telling you the whole goddamn party's behind you. They absolutely hate Crandell and think you're the man that can beat him. They like your style. You're smart and young and good-looking, and you're not afraid. And that's the combination they've been looking for." He pulled on his cigar then paused and looked down at the young lawyer. "So what-a-ya think?"

"That's great!" Foster grinned with a gleam to his eyes. "And I can," he added confidently.

"Can what?" the Judge cocked his head.

"Beat him, I can beat him."

"Oooh really," the Judge scoffed. "Well, let's not be so quick to wave the victory flag hear," he cautioned. "Or at least not just yet. I've seen more than one opponent get his nuts cut off and handed to him."

"Yes sir, I didn't mean to imply," Foster apologized.

"It's all right son," the Judge interjected. "I know you can beat him, it's just that we need to do it right you know," he stepped to the window then narrowed his eyes and cast his gaze outside.

"So what's next?" Foster asked as he sat forward in his chair.

"Well first," the Judge turned back and stared. "We register your ass and make it official, and we need to do it this week too. The sooner we get in this game and get your name out there the better. Then we need to figure out your campaign strategy, you know what you're gonna run on to convince the people that you're the right man for the job. The man that can change things for the better, and after that, we get the right people in place that can make things happen, and then we hit the newspapers. Hard. Locally at first, and then statewide. I have a friend who can help us with that," he paused and took a sip from his glass. "In fact, you might've heard of him. Have you ever heard the name Alexander Harkin?"

Scrunching his face, Foster thought for a moment and then shook his head. "No sir, I can't say that I have. Why, who is he? Is he someone important?"

"Well, let's just put it this way," the Judge chuckled. "Have you ever heard of the expression, don't ever get into a fight with a man who buys ink by the barrel?" He raised his eyebrows and waited.

Staring at the Judge as if he were deep in thought, Foster sat for just a second then suddenly widened his eyes. "Oh my God, that Harkin?" He elevated his voice and began to smile. "As in Harkin Publishing? The one who owns all of the big newspapers?"

"Yes sir," the Judge beamed proudly.

"And you know him?" Foster continued. "Personally? And he'll help us?"

"Yes sir, I know Al Harkin well, and he'll help us too," the Judge smiled. "He owes me in a real big way if you know what I mean, and it's time I collected. But still, we're the ones that'll have to find and dig for the dirt on Crandell. He'll print whatever we dig up, but we'll have to find it first. It's out there I tell ya, and there's plenty to be had too, you can bet your ass on it. But if I know Crandell, it's buried deep. And," he added with a knowing grin as he locked eyes with Foster. "We will get dirty. Real dirty."

"Well sir," Foster began with a nonchalant drawl and a smile to match. "I spent most of my life growing up on a farm. And I can tell ya right now," he added in a tone that seemed to clearly reflect his resolve. "I ain't afraid to get dirty."

Gazing at the young man for a just a moment, the Judge studied his expression then smiled with an approving nod. "That's good son, that's good. I knew the first time I met you that you were a fighter, and I've told everyone in the party that too. But remember, there's a hell of a difference between just finding it and then proving it if you know what I mean?" He gestured with his cigar hand as if to make his point, then turned his gaze back outside. "That's going to be the hard part. He's been in the Senate a long time and he knows the game and how to play it. And he has a lot of friends too, ones that'll come to his aid and try and protect him. Oh, and I almost forgot. He's really good at blaming others," he pulled on his cigar then exhaled into the glass with an agitated huff.

"In fact," he turned back to Foster. "Just take a look at the new state docks. You know, the ones the city built several years ago," his gravelly growl rose with a cynical anger. "Five hundred and forty acres of swampland a mile north of downtown and now one of the nicest goddamn ports in the country. Thirty-two piers and wharfs connected directly to the railroads and all of it just thirty-five miles from the Gulf. And all of it just sitting there, doing nothing. And why?" He took a breath and a sip then continued on.

"Oh, and let's not forget how we had to take that amendment before the voters twice before it finally passed. So we would have something! So the city would have something! And do you know why?" he asked but continued on before Foster could speak. "Because there was a campaign against it... to stop it. Rumor had it that Crandell was behind it the whole time but nobody could prove anything. Can you imagine that? A sitting U. S. Senator against the prosperity of his own goddamn state. Thaaat son-of-a-bitch!" he fumed.

"I remember he kept trying to convince everybody that New Orleans was such a better port and that it was too close for us to compete against. You know, and still survive with a ten million dollar bond to pay back. I'll tell you Foster, it seemed like that man tried everything he could to keep those docks from being built. And why was that? Hell, we had to fight that son-of-a-bitch every step of the way to get those bonds passed. But they finally did.

"Anyway, a lot a good it did cause they still don't have any kind of real business to speak of." He lowered his voice with a disgusted sigh. "Or at least that's what the boys down at the State Dock Commission tell me. But dammit Foster," he raised his voice back up. "Those new piers should be bringing in all kinds of boats from all over the world," he waved his arm in a big circle. "Even with this depression that we're in. And they aren't! And why? I'll tell ya, there's something going on and Crandell's behind it, I'm certain of it. It's almost as if he's deliberately trying to sabotage the shipping industry here. I can feel it, I tell ya. He's as crooked and corrupt as anyone I've ever seen in politics." He shook his head then turned his gaze back outside and pulled on his cigar.

"Anyway," he finished and then exhaled his smoke to the ceiling. "Whatever he's been doing, it's been working, and I've been told that if business doesn't pick up within the next year or so that the Commission will default on those bonds. And that son-of-a-bitch is already going around the state pointing his finger at people while he tells everyone I told you so."

Sensing the Judge's discontent, Foster rose from his chair then strolled to where he was standing. Gaining the man's eyes as he approached, he smiled then stopped and held up his glass. "Well sir," he drawled matter of factly then continued on with a humor and wit that was Foster at his best. "I guess we'll just have to get us a couple of shovels then won't we."

Gaining an instant smile that quickly turned into a light-hearted chuckle, Judge McAlister just shook his head and then raised his glass. "I guess you're right son," he agreed as they touched and then took their respective sips.

Swallowing the burning liquor, the Judge looked to the ceiling with a grin then pulled on his cigar. "Yes sirrr," he elevated his voice then exhaled high into the air again. "We'll need some shovels all right... and a couple of big ones too!"

Beaming with thoughts of the future, the Judge lowered his head then turned and placed his hand on Foster's shoulder. "Foster, my son," he began with a broadening smile as he stared into the eyes of his young apprentice. "In another year ol Harlen Crandell is gonna get the federal tit he's been sucking on for the last twelve years pulled right out of his mouth. Trust me," he nodded. "And then, he'll really have something to cry about. But enough of politics," he finished then turned and snuffed out his cigar. "I smell supper and I'm hungry. How about you?"

Dinner as always was superb, and a fantastic ending to a great weekend, but it was on his way home that Foster found himself more excited than he'd ever been before. It was his conversation with the Judge after dinner, and what was planned for the week ahead that really had him thinking. Another trip to Montgomery to register and formally announce his candidacy. And then there was the workload and cases he had pending and ready for trial that would need to be dealt with.

Cases that would now need to be doled out to other law firms and trusted colleagues. Some who would gladly take them just to see him go, and others who would do so in hopes of gaining a favor from a sitting U. S. Senator. Yes, Senator Siler, he thought. He smiled and imagined what life would be like in Washington. The city lights, the buzz of political life, the perks and privileges that came with the job, and the women. He drove on and then he thought of the beautiful young girl waiting for him up river. Willie. Yes, Willie. But what would he do with her?

———————

"Now I didn't see Foster again until that Tuesday after we'd gotten back an I was go'n back up to check on Willie for him. An that's when he met me at the boat. He told me he was gonna be gone again until Thursday but that on Friday mornin he wanted to see me in his office."

"An where'd he go?" Jim asked.

"To register or whatever it was, so he could run for the Senate. Anyway, that week went by pretty quick if I remember right cause about all me an Willie did was play an goof off. See, that was when I taught her how to fish an she began teachin me the A B C's. Heck, we didn't get nothin done that week. Then, an before I knew it, Friday came along an," he suddenly stopped and raised his head to the sound of the massive doors closing behind him.

"Well, I guess that's it for the auction," Jim laughed as the two enormous walls of steel finally came together with the clang of metal against metal. *"An that's it for the beer too,"* he added as he downed his beer and threw it into the pile of others.

"Yeah, I reckon you're right," Otis drawled as he too downed his beer and then threw it into the pile. *"Heck, I need to get go'n anyway. I've got a sister who lives here in New Orleans an I promised that I'd stop by an see her while I was here. Besides, if I know her, she's been cookin all afternoon an I sure as hell better not miss dinner. But it sure was nice of you to let me sit an visit. I'll tell ya,"* he sighed as he took another long last look around. *"I sure am gonna miss this ol girl. You make sure that you take real good care of her, hear."*

He'd said it as if he were completely unaffected by leaving, but as he gazed at the boat in a dream like state, Otis looked almost saddened. As if in some way, another treasured friend or possession in his life was being taken away. He'd been connected to it in someway or another since he was twenty-five, and now he was saying goodbye. A moment later, he slowly rose and stepped to the stern.

"Hey Otis," Jim called out with a groan as he picked himself from the floor. *"Hold on a second, I have a proposition for you."*

Turning back, Otis cocked his head. *"A proposition?"* he drawled and narrowed his eyes.

"Yeah, a proposition," Jim repeated.

"What-a-ya mean?"

"Well," Jim began. *"How'd you like to help me? You know, restore this ol girl,"* he stared excitedly. *"I mean, from the ground up, but with today's technology an bring it back to its former glory. What-a-ya say?"*

"Oooh I don't know," Otis replied. *"I really have a lot to do around the house."*

"Oh come on," Jim persisted. *"You know this ol boat better-n anyone, an to tell ya the truth I sure could use your help. Hell, the last boat I had took me five years to finish an almost ended in a divorce. So see, I need you. An besides, you've gotta finish your damn story. I mean, you just can't stop in the*

middle an leave me hangin," he added with a hopeful grin. "Shit, what in the hell happens to this Willie girl, an to... to that Foster guy?"

Chuckling at Jim's request, and not so much as what he'd said but how he'd said it, Otis stared at the man for a moment. Then quietly turning his gaze toward the salon, he gave the boat a long slow look. "Well," he sighed. "I reckon since they up an sold the church an I really ain't got a job no more. An ain't nobody exactly rushin out ta hire a 67 year old black man; I don't see why I couldn't help you out every now an then. I'd kind-a like that. Besides it'd get me out-of the house an give me somethin to do. An actually, it would be kind of nice to see her brought back to life. I'll tell ya, back in her day, she was jus about the prettiest thing on the river," he cast his eyes forward again.

"Good!" Jim exclaimed as he reached for the cardboard box sitting next to him. "Now here," he said as he tore off a flap then pulled a pen from his pocket and began to write. "Is my address an phone number. Now they're not go'n to be able to deliver the boat until next Saturday. Sometime around ten they said. An if you're not do'n anything next weekend, I sure could use your help settin it up."

Taking the cardboard from his hand, Otis stared for a second then reread the address and phone number. "That's right," Jim said with an extended hand. "Saturday? Around nine?" He raised his eyebrows and then cocked his head.

"Aaah what the hell," Otis chuckled and took the man's hand. "Saturday it is."

"Great," Jim whooped. "Now let's get out of here."

Quietly gathering their cans back into the cooler, the two men used the head one last time and then climbed out of the boat.

"Well I know one thing that we're gonna have to fix," Jim said as he glanced beneath the boat.

"Yes sir," Otis agreed. "Back in the old days there weren't no holding tanks, it jus all went in the river."

It had been a great day but now it was over, and after they'd crossed the parking lot, the two men shook hands one last time and then went their separate ways.

CHAPTER 32

———◆———

IT WAS JUST AFTER NINE by the time Otis pulled to the end of the street and stopped. Jim had said that it was an older neighborhood with modest homes set back away from the street. Gazing around he finally spied what appeared to be what his new friend had described. A plain and simple yellow brick home with a two-car garage setting way off the street on a flat oversized lot.

Looking to the left and away from the house, he saw the out building that Jim had talked about too. The one that they would work out of with a dozen adjustable jack-stands setting in front ready and waiting. All encompassed by a sea of grass, it was neat and clean and just as he'd said. Checking his piece of cardboard just to make sure, he stared for just a second and then turned into the long flat driveway. A few moments later, he knocked on the front door and was greeted by Jim's wife.

"Yesss?" The woman cocked her head as she wiped her hands on her apron.

"Mrs. Williams?" Otis drawled as he removed his hat. "I'm--."

"Ooh yesss," she interrupted. "Why, you must be Otis."

"Yes ma'am," Otis replied politely. "I--."

"Well I'm Meredith," she blurted and cut him short.

"Otis ma'am... Otis Brown, an it's my pleasure."

"Well the same here Otis, come on in, Jim's been expectin you. In fact, he's done nothin but talk about you an that silly ol boat all week, an some crazy ol story he said that you was tellin him. Must of really been a good one ta get that ol fart that excited," she laughed.

"Yes ma'am," Otis agreed as he stepped inside.

"Come on, he's in the kitchen makin another pot of coffee, an I just pulled a pan of banana nut bread out-a the oven. Would you like some?"

Lifting his head as he followed, Otis inhaled the wafting aroma of the freshly baked bread and then smiled. "Oh my my, if that's your bread I smell, I do believe I would. That is, if you don't mind."

Glancing back, she smiled then called to her husband as she turned the corner into the kitchen. "Jim honey, you're friend's here."

"Otis," he spun from the coffee pot and extended a hand. "Mornin, I'm glad you could make it; please, please have a seat," he gestured with his arm. "Would ya like some coffee?"

It wasn't until they'd eaten almost half the pan of bread before Jim and Otis finally turned to the sound of the tractor-trailer stopping out in the street. "She's here," Jim exclaimed as he leaned back in his chair and glanced out the window. Grinning like a couple of kids, the two men stood and downed their cups then dropped them to the table and headed out the door.

Setting the boat from the trailer onto the stands proved to be a little harder and took a little longer than what they'd all expected, but after a couple of hours they had her setting nicely right in front of the outbuilding.

"There, that ought-a hold her now don't ya think?" Jim said with a final tug to the chain around the stands.

"Yeah, I think that'll do it," Otis grunted as he did the same from the other side. "She looks real good from over here, an with that chain wrapped around those stands like that it ain't go'n nowhere that's for sure," he added as he rose from underneath and walked to the other side.

"Well," Otis began as he stood with Jim and stared at the boat. "We sure got our work cut out for us now. I don't think in all the years I've ever seen it look this bad."

"Well Otis," Jim finally sighed. "I can't tell ya how much I appreciate you comin over an helpin. Really, an I mean that. Thank you. But listen, before we get started, why don't we grab some lunch first, I'm hungry."

It was just over a half hour by the time the two finally returned with a stepladder and climbed back into the boat. Armed with an arsenal of tools, they slowly began the task of disassembling the boat. Beginning with the rails, cleats, and lights outside, they striped everything off that they could then quickly made their way inside.

"I guess we ought-a start with the drawers an doors first. What-a-ya think?" Jim suggested as they both surveyed the inside.

"*Sounds good to me,*" *Otis agreed. "We need to get rid of all this loose stuff anyway. Jus hand me that screwdriver an I'll start right here."*

Disassembling the boat a piece at a time they worked together for a short while longer until Jim mysteriously disappeared but then returned almost as fast as he'd left. Turning to the sound of a heavy thud coming from the stern, Otis just shook his head and smiled at the sight of Jim's cooler.

"*Okay Otis,*" *the big man grinned as he set an ice-cold can down in front of him. "Let's take a break, you look tired."*

Turning with the screwdriver in his hand, Otis dropped his head ever so slightly then peered over the top of his glasses. "Tired?" he repeated with a confused expression. "What-a-you mean tired? I ain't tired, heck I'm jus gettin started."

"*No no, you need to stop so you can pick up where you left off?*"

"*Left off?" Otis cocked his head and scrunched his brow. "Whatever are you talkin about? I've been takin these cabinet doors off the whole time you was gone."*

"*No nooo, I mean the story you were tellin me last week at the auction. You knooow... Willieee! An that lawyer fellow!"*

Peering over his glasses at his newfound friend, Otis couldn't help but smile then pick up the can and join him at the table. "I swear," he said as he shook his head and popped his top. "You're worse than a damn little kid with a bedtime story, but let me see... jus where was I?" He took a drink and removed his glasses. "Aaah yesss," he finally nodded as the memories deep from within came drifting back. "I remember now.

"*It was that Friday, after Foster had been gone all week an came back. Payday actually, when I was supposed to stop by his office an let him know how Willie was do'n. Now Vicki an Dawn, well, they really didn't like me gettin there when they was tryin to get things all up an go'n, so I think I got there somewhere about ten or so. I remember Dawn was sittin behind the counter an Vicki, she was standin there talkin to these two men in suits who seemed to be written down jus about everything she was sayin."*

"Mornin Otis," Dawn greeted with a glance from behind the counter.

"Mornin Miss Dawn," he replied as he closed the door and removed his hat. "I's here ta--."

"Yes yes, I know," she interrupted with a dismissive tone as she returned to her work. "Just have a seat an as soon as these gentlemen are done, Mister Siler will see you."

But no sooner had he turned to take his seat, than one of the reporters talking to Vicki turned his eyes toward Otis. "Sooo," the man asked with an inquisitive grin as he began to write. "Mister Siler represents negroes is that correct?"

"Nooo," Vicki huffed. "Mister Siler does not represent negroes. That's Otis, his caretaker."

"Aaah I see," said the other. "So he has a negro then? Well, how about that," he looked to his partner and raised his eyebrows. "And just how long has he had him, do you know?"

"Look gentlemen," she snapped with an agitated tone. "Mister Siler doesn't own a negro and he never has. Otis works for him. Now, if you'll just have a seat right over there." She pointed to the other seats by Otis. "He'll be with you in just a minute."

"Now jus as soon as those two fellers came over an sat down, they started talkin an askin me all kinds a questions real quiet like. You know, stuff about Foster."

"An what'd you tell em?" Jim asked.

"Well, right quick, I thought back to what he'd told me on the boat that last weekend an I didn't say a word to either one. But boy that sure didn't stop em, an they kept askin away real nosey like jus like he said they would. That was, until we all heard Foster's voice from across the room."

"Gentlemen, good morning," Foster said as he approached and extended a hand. "Thank you for coming," he continued, giving each one a firm and generous handshake as they rose. "I'm glad you could make it, please, please come on in," he gestured toward his office and began walking. "I know you have a lot of questions right now, but you'll have to excuse me. I've been gone all week and about ten minutes is all I can give you this morning. We can do more next week if you'd like," he added but then he suddenly stopped and turned back to Otis. "Oh and Otis, just sit tight. I'll be with you when we're done."

"Yes sur boss."

"Now true to his word, it was right about ten minutes later that he came walkin back out with them two reporters. I don't know what all he'd told em, but they was all laughin an carryin on about what a great story they was gonna write. I

remember they kept sayin what a fresh breath of air he was, an how it was about time that the state had some new blood. An after he posed for a couple a pictures by the flag in the corner, they all shook hands again an those two guys left.

"I'll tell ya Jim, sittin there watchin them while they talked an took those pictures, you could jus feel the energy in the room. Like somethin big an excitin was gonna happen. Yes sir, I think right from the start the newspapers took a likin to him, specially those two fellers. Then, an jus as soon as he'd closed the door behind em, he turned an looked down to me. I remember he was grinnin great big an had both hands on his hips."

"Okay Otis," Foster jerked his head toward his office and began walking. "It's your turn now."

"Yes sur boss," Otis replied as he sprang from his seat and hastily followed.

Passing the girls at the counter the two slipped into Foster's office and closed the door. Taking their seats, Foster instantly began with a round of questions. "So how's Willie? Is she okay?"

"Oh, yes sur boss, Miss Willie's jus fine. She's up there jus a scrapin an brushin away. Heck, she's got half the house done already an it won't be to awfully long before she'll be ready for paintin."

"Really?" Foster seemed surprised. "Already?"

"Yes sur, she's been a workin real hard. But she did want me ta ask you somethin if'n it's okay."

"Sure Otis, what's that?"

"Well, she said she was done with all them books that you'd given her an she wanted ta know if you could bring her some more when you come back up."

"So wait a minute," Jim interrupted. "He went from campaign mode to Willie just like that?"

"Yep," Otis laughed. "An jus as soon as I was done tellin him all about Willie, he went back into campaign mode again cause that's when it all started. Foster's campaign that is. It was right around the first week or so of October 1930 if I remember right," he continued, recalling the past as best he could. "Anyway, I don't think at the time any of us had any idea as to where his election was gonna take us, but I do remember we was all real excited, specially the girls. Oh! An right at the same time, well, that's when I became a one man sign shop."

"A sign shop?" Jim cocked his head. "What-a-ya mean?"

"You know," Otis replied as if he should've known. "For his election. He needed signs, so he sent me down to Jack's Hardware right after I left his office to get supplies an paint, an then take em to his house. Then, when I got there, he had me clear out the old garage an set up shop. An after that, well, it was gettin on into the afternoon so he jus sent me home.

"Now the next day, Saturday, we took off an went back up river to see Willie jus like regular. Foster had brought her some more little books jus like she'd asked, an after she ooed an awed over em an finished huggin on him, we set about an started workin. It was a good time that weekend, but I really didn't see a whole lot of em cause they jus kind of stayed in the house until we left on Sunday. An then on Monday, well, I jus went back to makin signs.

"I'll tell ya, I really don't know how many I made them first couple a months, but no matter if I was ahead or behind of what they wanted, he kept me go'n up river. Tuesdays an Thursdays jus like always. I'd deliver supplies an then help Willie with whatever chores she was do'n that day.

"At the time that was mostly scrapin the house an gettin it ready for paintin, but as the winter began to set in that kind-a changed into gatherin an cuttin wood too. I remember how she used to jus jabber away while we worked, an how she used to tell me over an over again how Foster was gonna marry her an move her back ta Mobile jus as soon as the house was done. Where she was gonna have kids an a car, an a big ol white house with pillars in front. She told me that that was her dream.

"Now I'd often wondered when she'd talk about that as to jus what all he was fillin her head with cause I kind-a knew how ol Foster was. I was hopin that she'd see how he was an realize what was go'n on, but she never did an I never said nothin to her either. Maybe I should have," he added with a hint of regret. "But I didn't, cause ta be right truthful with you, I needed my job. Heck, we both needed our jobs, cause like I said before, times was hard back then, real hard. An Willie, well, I reckon she knew it better'n anyone really.

"Anyway," he went on, his tone changing as he continued to recall the past. "Whenever we'd take our lunch, she'd give me another readin an written lesson. You know, written an sayin the alphabet, an then readin the words with the pictures. Jus like Foster had done for her. Now I wasn't exactly what you'd call the smartest student if you get my drift, but I was determined that I was gonna learn cause I was tired of not knowin what stuff said. You know, jus a simple sign in a store window or one on the road. It seemed pretty silly at the time, but nobody else in my family could read or write an Willie was real *patient with me. So, twice a week after lunch, we'd take about an hour or two an she'd help me with my studies.*

"Heck, she even gave me a piece a cardboard with the alphabet on it. She told me to set it by my wheel so I could study it on my way up an down the river until I knew all the letters by heart. I remember when she gave it to me," he smiled. *"An how she pointed her finger at me jus like an old schoolmarm, an then warned me on how she was gonna test me when I came back up."* He smiled again and then took a sip of beer. *"Yes sir, if it weren't for Willie, I still don't know if I could read."*

"Really?" Jim seemed genuinely surprised. "She taught you?"

"Yep," Otis nodded. "Anyway, right after I learned the alphabet, she started given me the readin books that Foster had given her when she first started. You know, to take home an study. An then whenever I'd come back up an we'd eat lunch, she'd make me read to her. At first I was jus horrible an couldn't make sense of nothin, but she was a bossy little thing an she made me keep workin an tryin until I started to get it. I think it was durin those first few months that Willie was up there, when she started helpin me, that her an I became so close. You know, kind-a like an older brother an a little sister'd have knowin that they only had each other in life. Hell, I don't think there wasn't nothin she wouldn't do to help ya if she could. An to her, it didn't matter one bit that I was black an she was white. No sir, not ta Willie it didn't, cause that's jus the way she was.

"Anyway," he went on. "On the weekends me an Foster would still go back up. Or at least most weekends that was. See, it was right about this time that he started missin some of his visits cause of his campaignin. He didn't want to but he was gettin real busy an there was times that he jus couldn't go so he'd send me up by myself for the day. Jus so Willie wouldn't be alone for so long. Heck, he even let me take my little boy Zareck with me on them trips. I think at the time he was about three or four an he jus loved go'n up river, you know helpin dad drive the boat.

"Now on them days, we didn't get nothin done except for a whole lot-a playin an fishin. I'll tell ya, him an Willie really hit it off an it wasn't too long before he was askin to go with me all the time. He really liked her cause she played with him an gave em cokes." He laughed.

"An so what'd Willie think when Foster started missing his visits?"

"Well, deep down, I think she felt as if he really didn't care for her anymore. Now she never said anything, but boy you could sure see it in her eyes an in the way she acted when she realized Foster wasn't on the boat. I'll

tell ya, I never will forget how sad she always looked, but then whenever he did make his next visit he'd always have somethin to cheer her back up an charm her with when we got there, you know, like clothes or jewelry or somethin."

"Oh, so he started buying her gifts to keep her happy," Jim scoffed. "An did it work?"

"Oh hell yes, an better'n you'd think. See, ol Willie really like those surprises, but the thing that I noticed more than anything, an what she really liked the most, was those damn books he kept bringin her. Bigger an thicker ones... with short little stories in em."

"Really?"

"Yep, it seemed she'd developed a real appetite for readin an had actually began to progress quite well on her own. But what I think she really liked about em was that they really helped her pass the time. You know, be'n up there all alone an all. Anyway, as the weeks slowly passed an October turned into late November, it seemed like we jus kept do'n less an less work with each visit. We had the house jus about ready for paintin but for some reason ol Foster jus couldn't pick out the right color an that's when I finally realized what he was actually do'n."

"Do'n?" Jim cocked his head. "What-a-ya mean?"

"You know... what he was do'n with Willie. Shiiit, he didn't give a damn about that house. He jus wanted to keep her up there as long as he could as his little plaything, which at the time suited me an her jus fine cause we was both gettin paid. I'll tell ya, he was really draggin that thing out. In fact, I remember a bunch of times if it was pretty out; we'd jus go cruisin way up into the delta, sometimes all afternoon. You know, explorin an checkin out all those tributaries to see where they led to. Hell, the three of us was nothin more than a bunch of kids with a great big boat havin a whole lot of fun. But I knew it wouldn't last, it jus couldn't."

"You mean him and Willie?" Jim asked.

"Yep."

"An so what happen?"

"Well, over the course of those first few months you could see that she had fallen in love. In fact, I'd say wildly in love. Specially after he adopted her."

"After he what?" Jim's voice instantly rose. "Adopted her? You've got to be kiddin?"

"No sir," Otis shook his head. "Or at least that's what he told her."

"But I don't understand. Why in the hell did he do that?"

"Well," Otis began after another sip. "If I remember right, I think it was cause she'd started given him a hard time about not be'n married an all like a proper woman. You know, considerin they was do'n what they was do'n. Anyway, I guess it was right about the end of November or so that it finally got to the point where she was actually gonna up an leave him an move back to town.

"Now ol Foster really had it good if ya know what I mean, but when Willie told him that she was actually gonna move back to town, well, I think that that was when he really started to panic. See, he was jus crazy over her an I think he would of done or told her jus about anything to keep her up river, an that's when he came up with that whole crazy idea of adoptin her."

"You've got to be kiddin," Jim rolled his eyes.

"Oh no," Otis shook his head. "See, he was real smooth an right off he told her that they couldn't get married cause she was still to young an that it was against the law. But ol Willie had become pretty stubborn over the whole ordeal an she wasn't havin nothin ta do with not be'n married. Somethin about a promise to her mother or somethin like that. Anyway, when ol Foster finally realized that that wasn't gonna work, he came back a week later an told her that he'd found a way around it all. A loophole in the law he called it, that would let them get adopted ta each other."

"A loophole in the law?" Jim scoffed. "An she actually bought that?"

"Well sure she did," Otis defended. "Heck, at the time Willie didn't know no different, an for that matter, neither did I really. Shit, we didn't know what adopted meant; we jus thought it was another fancy lawyerin word for be'n married. Besides, Foster had said it was. I remember he told her that it was jus like be'n married except that she couldn't never tell no one until she was older or they'd both get in real big trouble. Hell, he even went as far as to get her a little ring an have an official lookin piece of paper all typed up tellin her so. He called it a marry'n license or somethin like that."

"Good God, what a dog," Jim shook his head in disgust. "An he was runnin for the Senate."

"Yep," Ots grinned at his satirical tone. "He was runnin for the Senate. Anyway, whether he really did or didn't we didn't know, but after he put that ring on her finger in a little ceremony down by the water, ol Willie couldn't of been happier. She'd finally gotten what she'd wanted an after that, well, I guess that's when she started given ol Foster jus about everything he could handle," he shook his head with another grin. "Hell there was some days that the two of em wouldn't come out of that house until almost noon. I remember *a lot-a times he'd be draggin his ass like he didn't get a wink a sleep, but I also remember that he'd always be smilin.*

"Now normally when we left, he'd jus stretch out on one of them sofa's in the back an take a nap while I drove us back on home. An usually, we'd end up gettin home about one or so. But this one weekend I remember, I think it was right around the beginnin of December. Well, it was one of them Sunday's that we didn't end up leavin until kind of late in the afternoon. Now I don't know if it was cause Willie had kept him occupied all mornin or if he'd jus forgotten or what. But I do know this, that once they rolled out of that house an he realized what time it was he got in a real hurry. An that's when on the way back down river, I first learned about his other life."

"His other life?" Jim scrunched his face. "What in the hell ya mean, other life?"

Smiling as he took another drink from his beer, Otis sat for a second in silence, swallowed with a sigh and then answered with a smirk. "Wellll," he began matter of factly as he dipped his head and raised his eyebrows. "That'd be the one he had with the girl he was really gonna marry. An iiiit wasn't Willie."

"Let's go Otis," Foster hollered from the stern as Willie threw him the line. Turning the wheel to the left, Otis pushed the throttle forward and pulled away from the pier. A few moments later, he felt Foster's hand on his shoulder as he stepped up behind him. "Give it a little more gas Otis," he said as they headed down stream. "We need to hurry cause I'm running waaay late."

"Yes sur boss," Otis said with another push to the throttle. "Is you gots ta be somewhere soon?"

"Just Sunday dinner with my fiancée and future in-laws," he chuckled as they picked up speed and approached the first bend.

"Oh I see," Otis replied as if he understood. But he didn't really, he had no idea what a fiancé was and it instantly began to gnaw on him. He hated appearing stupid, especially in front of Foster, a man he looked up to and admired for his intelligence. He concentrated and tried to think as he turned the wheel and entered the bend in the tributary. He watched as Foster blew the horn then stepped to the door and waved a finally goodbye to Willie. He cocked his head deep in thought, but still there was nothing, just a hollow word that he could hardly repeat.

"What's wrong Otis?" Foster asked as he turned back and caught the man's expression.

"Well boss, I thoughts that I knowed what that word was but I guess I don't really."

"Knowed what word," he teased as stepped back inside and joined him.

"What a fi, fiii-onn-saay is," he stuttered in an attempt to repeat the word but then stopped.

"Fi-an-cee," Foster assisted with a lighthearted chuckle. "A fiancée is a girl you're engaged to and are going to marry, see."

"Oooh, I see now boss," he smiled and proudly repeated the word. "A fiiianceeee. So you gots ya a girl that you's gonna marry in Mobile?"

"Yeah I do," Foster replied without a thought.

"But I thoughts that you an Miss Willie was already...?" Otis turned his head and stared back up river. "Or at least, I mean you...?" his voice trailed off.

Staring at Otis, Foster knew in an instant that this was something that had to be explained and discussed, and then kept to himself. He could see the confusion pulling on Otis's face, and so once again he took the young man into his confidence.

"Otis, you remember when I told you I was going to be running for the Senate, don't you?"

"Oh, yes sur."

"And you remember how I explained what confidence was, don't ya?"

"Oh, yes sur, an I ain't never said nothin ta nobody bouts that, or bouts Miss Willie either."

"That's good Otis, that's good, I'm glad to hear that. But you need to listen now because I have something else that I want to explain to you, something very very important. You see..."

"Now it was right after we'd gone around that bend when ol Foster suddenly realized he'd let the cat out-a the bag. That I knew a whole lot more about his scrambled up life an what he was do'n than I really needed to know an now he had to deal with it. You know, to make sure that I didn't do or say nothin that'd get him in trouble. An that's when he began to explain everything to me, or at least a part of his other life that was. You know, how he was gonna get married to this Melinda girl in the spring, an how her father, or the Judge as he called em was gonna make him a Senator.

"Now at first I didn't know what to think cause I jus naturally thought that him an Willie was already married, specially after their little weddin in the grass that one day. But that wasn't the case at all, no sirree. Cause ol Foster, well, he had other plans, an as we went back down that river he kept go'n over everything again an again. Almost as if he was preparin me for a trial. I guess it was jus his way of makin sure there weren't no mistakes cause he was a lawyer an he knew the importance of keepin your story straight. An so, as we headed on back, he told me all about Miss Melinda an the Judge, an then of how I was never ever ever to say anything about Willie when they was around. Or, how I was never ever ta say anything to Willie either. He said he'd tell her when he thought the time was right.

"Now like I said before, I didn't always agree with what he did an this was one-a them times cause I knew if Willie ever found out it'd jus break her heart into a million pieces. Now he knew that I liked her, an after he saw the look on my face an saw that I really didn't care much for what he was do'n, well, that's when he stuck his finger in my face an gave me a real stern warnin. Actually threatened me was more like it, an as soon as he was done, well, that's when I first started to realized jus what a cold hearted son-of-a-bitch he really was.

"Anyway, the river that day was runnin faster than usual from all the heavy rains that'd fallen up north an we was makin real good time. In fact, with that an our added speed, it seemed like we were back at the wharf in no time. Now normally ol Foster'd always kind of help with the boat when we got back, you know, tyin it up an makin sure that it was all closed up real good. But that day, as soon as we docked, he was off the boat an headed down the pier. One of the last things I remember was him mumblin somethin about how he had a ring to put on that girl's finger an then somethin about seein me tomorrow at the garage."

CHAPTER 33

—◆—

PULLING UP TO THE HOUSE, Foster shut his car down and exhaled a heavy sigh of remorse, for not only was he late and in trouble, he'd also ruined his own plans. Plan's that he'd made weeks ago, to propose to her and ask for her hand in marriage. To live together for the rest of their lives as husband and wife, and to have kids and grow old together. He'd thought that they would go for a nice quiet ride before dinner and he would ask her then, in the most romantic of ways. But after Willie had pulled him back inside and caused him to be two hours late, he knew he needed a new plan. Maybe after dinner he thought, during dessert?

Knocking on the door with just a twinge of trepidation, Foster shuffled his feet with thoughts of what he'd say to Monique when she answered. His quick-witted rebuttal to her suggestive looks and innuendos that he'd use in their ongoing game of verbal foreplay. That would convey the hidden thoughts he secretly harbored for her. That someday he hoped, would cumulate into something more. But as the door slowly opened and the person behind it came into view, Foster suddenly caught his breath. "Me, Melinda," he stuttered in surprise.

"Oooh! Well well well," she snipped with a scowl. "If it isn't Mister Siler. Why how nice of you to finally show up. You do know you're only a couple of hours late don't you? And just where have we been? Oh, no no, wait, let me guess," she placed her hand to her forehead. "Aah, let's see. Oh, I knooow," she rolled her eyes and raised her voice. "We've been out playing on some stupid boat. Right? And just where and when did you get a boat, might I ask?"

Caught completely off guard, Foster stammered for just a second but then quickly collected his thoughts. He'd learned to hide surprise and then to change the subject whenever he'd been caught unprepared. It was a skill he'd developed in the courtrooms, and one that he'd become very good at. Perfecting and honing it, until it had evolved into an art form.

"Well no, not exactly. See, I was actually out getting you this," he reached into his pocket and then slowly withdrew a small square box.

Glancing down at the tiny container in his hands, Foster stared for a second then raised his eyes to meet Melinda's gaze. He could tell she knew what it was just by the way she had put a hand to her mouth to stifle her gasp and her eyes as they instantly welled with tears. "And," he continued in the most charming of drawls as he opened it up and exposed the ring. "I was just kind-of wondering if, well, if you really aren't doing anything for the next twenty or thirty years, that maybe you wouldn't mind spending it with me, as a Senator's wife? As my wife?"

Now Foster hadn't planned on proposing in quite this manner, but in its own unique and romantic way, it worked out great. It took Melinda less than half a second to enthusiastically lunge toward him and then melt into his arms. She'd been hoping and praying for months that he would ask and now here he was. The man who she loved more than anything in the world had just asked her to be a part of his life.

Separating after a long and soulful kiss, Melinda held up a trembling hand and gazed into his eyes. She was crying and her cheeks were wet with the tears of happiness. "So does this mean yes?" he asked as he gently slipped the glittering symbol of fidelity onto her finger.

Gazing at the eternal circle of silver encrusted with precious gems, Melinda could only nod her head and then lay it on his shoulder. He could feel the warmth of her heart and soul as her undying love radiated from within, and as she slowly settled and regained her composure, Foster glanced up to see the Judge standing in the foyer, staring and smiling.

"Thought you didn't like him anymore," he grumbled in his own dry brand of humor.

Instantly spinning to the sound of her father's gravelly drawl, Melinda wiped the tears from her cheeks and then rushed toward him. "Oh Daddy Daddy," she called excitedly. "Look, Foster just asked me to marry him," she exclaimed as she held up her hand and began to bounce on the balls of her feet. "Can you believe it? He wants to marry me. Is it okay? Look. See. Isn't it pretty? Oh please, please say yes... paa-leeease."

Taking a heavy breath, Judge McAlister stared with the stern expression then rubbed his chin as if deep in thought. "Well baby, I really don't know. See, I'm thinking that we just may have a conflict of interest here," he began as if he were actually deliberating a case that'd been brought before him. "But first, how about if we just take a big deep breath and calm ourselves down a little okay," he said as he placed his hands on her shoulders. "There, that's a little better.

"Now if I remember right, aren't you the same little gal that was just running around here yappin and crying about how you never ever wanted to see this... this irresponsible and inconsiderate Foster guy again? That you'd had it, and were done with him," he raised his eyebrows and teased. "I believe the words that you used were, I'm finished, correct? And now here you are less than fifteen minutes later wanting to spend the rest of your life with him? Now to me, and in a court of law, that would be a pretty compelling reversal of your earlier decision, and would actually lead one to really question the soundness of your judgment, don't ya think?"

Shaking her head yes, and then no, and then yes again, Melinda tried to answer as best she could but failed just like so many attorneys before her. She'd learned a long long time ago that you really didn't get very far arguing with a Federal Judge, whether he was your father or not.

"And besides, ya know the boy really ain't got much of a future in front of him. Maybe you ought-a wait another year or so just to be sure," he teased with a growing grin and a glance to Foster. "You know, to see if he amounts to anything and to see if you really wanna spend the rest of your life with someone like him."

"Daddy," Melinda scowled with a playful smack to the center of his chest. "Stop teasin, you know you like Foster. You told me so yourself... and Momma too," she insisted, only to look on and stare as if he really were serious. Her heart skipped a beat at the thought, for in all her life she'd never been able to really read her father, or to discern from his facial expressions or tone as to when he was teasing and when he wasn't. A second later, and with eyes beseeching his approval, she questioned him with a sheepish uncertainty. "But you do like him... don't you?"

Gazing into the eyes of his youngest daughter pleading for an answer. His baby girl that was all grown up and ready for a life of her own. Judge McAlister could clearly see the radiant glow in her face that this moment had brought. He knew she loved him and wanted his approval in the worst of ways, and in the end, to the gruff old adjudicator, that was all that really mattered. Then, placing his fingers beneath her chin, he tilted her head and held her gaze.

"Well," he began with a glance to Foster and then back to her. "Maybe just a little, so I guess if you're really sure," he took a breath. "Then you have my blessings. Now, why don't you go and tell your mother and show her that pretty little ring you just got while I take my new son-in-law here and have a drink to celebrate, okay."

"Oh Daddy," she gushed as she lunged and threw her arms around his neck. "Oh thank you thank you. I love you so much," she finished with a kiss to his cheek as she dropped back to her feet then turned and called for her mother.

Watching as she scurried away into the other room the two men laughed. "Well, congratulations son," the Judge said as he shook Foster hand. "And welcome to the family. Now come on, let's have that drink shall we."

"Yes sir, and thank you sir. I sure could use one."

But before the two men could even turn, Melinda was back. She simply adored her father, and with another hug and a kiss on the cheek, she thanked him once again then turned and scampered away just as fast as she had come. She was overwhelmed with joy, and as she disappeared into the other room they could hear her calling to her mother and Monique.

Laughing to the sound of squealing voices a moment later, the Judge slowly turned to Foster and placed his hand on his shoulder in a fatherly gesture. "Well son," he said as he turned to the library. "All I can say is that I sure am glad you finally got that done."

"You are?" Foster replied. "Why's that sir?"

"Good God," the Judge rolled his eyes and shook his head. "Have you ever tried to live with a twenty-four year old girl who thinks she's an old maid? Where most of her friends have already married and have started families?"

"No sir, I can't say that I have actually," he laughed. "But I think I get your point."

"Well good. Now come on and you can tell me why she's been stomping around here for the last two hours railin on your ass about some boat or something. What the hell is that all about?"

It'd been over ten years since the passing of his parents, but that evening at McAlister's, the empty void that they'd left behind seemed to disappear. He felt a renewed sense of contentment, for as he took his seat at the dinning room table as the newest son-in-law to join their household, Foster, for the first time in a very long time, felt as if he were part of a family once again. That he truly belonged, and was welcomed and appreciated. And as they talked and laughed and drank, dinner turned into more of a celebration. They made plans for the wedding. A huge wedding at the biggest church in Mobile Melinda insisted, with the Reverend Stone officiating. She stared at her ring and giggled. When asked of the boat, Foster explained how he'd gotten it from the Davenports in lieu of his fee and of how he'd been saving it as a surprise, as a wedding present.

Intrigued, Melinda and her mother insisted on going for a ride. It would be fun to go boating, they said. Later, another scotch and the rest of his cigar on the porch with the Judge finished his evening, and with a deep loving kiss from his new bride-to-be, Foster left for home.

"So whoa whoa whoooa. Let's just hold on a second here an let me get this straight," Jim held up his hands then sat forward in kind of a humored disbelief. "You're tellin me that this Foster, your old boss," he paused for a second as he collected his thoughts. "He named the boat after Willie, this little fifteen year old girl that he was seein on the weekends right?"

"Yep," Otis replied.

"That he tricked into thinkin that she was married so he could keep sleepin with her, right?"

"Yep."

"While at the same time he was supposed to be getting married to this other girl, this Melinda McAliss... or whatever her name was."

"Yes sir," Otis grinned. "That's exactly what I'm tellin ya. Melinda McAlister, Judge McAlister's youngest daughter. Like I said before, ol Foster had a real appetite for women, an without a doubt got more favors if ya know what I mean, than any other man I ever knew. In fact," he added with a chuckle. "If I was a gamblin man, I'd wager ta say that he was still seein ol Mrs. Davenport at the same time too. An I believe all the way up until she left for New Orleans."

"Really, the lady he got the boat from?"

"Yep, that's the one. Anyway, it was that very Monday, the day after we'd gotten back so late when I got to his garage to start makin signs that he came out an told me to go on down to the boat an start cleanin it an get it ready to go out. I remember I thought it was kind of strange cause we'd jus been up river an seen Willie, an now here we was go'n back out already. Anyway, I guess I must of looked real confused cause that's when he sat me down an started explainin everything to me real careful like. You know, how he'd told his fiancée all about the boat an the little huntin shack as he called it up river. An then of how her an her mother thought it would be fun to go for a ride.

"Now when he first started talkin an tellin me all that stuff, I really didn't know what to think cause it was jus the day before that he'd told me never ta say nothin to nobody. But after a little bit, an after he'd gone over everything a time or two, I finally had a pretty good idea as to what all was go'n on, an what he really wanted from me. Specially the part about keepin quiet about Willie. I remember he made a real point about that.

"So, I headed on down to the docks an started cleanin an gettin every-thing ready jus like he'd asked me, an it wasn't but an hour or so an they all showed up. I remember lookin up when I heard em all comin down the pier an seein Melinda an her mother for the first time. A woman I'd never met, an until the day before, never even knew existed.

"Now she was a pretty little thing all right, you know, long blonde hair an blue eyes, an if I ain't mistaken, I think right about my age too. But boy did she ever have an attitude. Oooh yeaaah. Shit, I don't think I'll ever forget the look on her face after they all finally stopped beside the boat," he laughed and shook his head.

"So this is it? This is my wedding present?" Melinda huffed as she plopped her hands on her hips and turned to Foster. "A boat?" she continued with a hint of cynicism. "Oh how lovely," her sarcasm grew as she walked around and assessed it. "You know, most girls get a home or jewelry, but me, oh nooo, Iiii get a boat," she finished then stopped at the stern and looked down at the name. "Willie Mae," she curled her nose and then turned to Foster. "Who's Willie Mae?"

Caught completely off guard, Foster hesitated for a second and then quickly turned to Otis with a panicked expression. It had never even dawned on him that she would ask about the name, but no sooner than she'd seen it, then that's exactly what she'd done.

"Well, I'm not really sure exactly," he finally replied, his eyes now pleading for help. "See, it was already on there when I got the boat, but maybe Otis knows."

Catching Foster's look of hopeless desperation, Otis instantly answered without even blinking an eye. "Oooh yes sur boss," he began. "Heck, I thoughts I told you all about that already. See, that was ol Mr. Davenport's grandmother, Willma Mae," he went on to a shocked but pleasantly surprised Foster. "But everyone called her Willie for short, or at least that's what I's told. Anyway, I guess him an his grandma must-a been real close cause he use ta talk about her all the time, an then when they got this ol boat here, he had her name painted on it... in memory of her."

"Now jus where in the hell I came up with that whole Davenport thing I rightly don't know," Otis chuckled and shook his head. "But I can tell ya this, it sure made ol Foster happy. Heck, I can still remember the look on his face when I first started in, an then him smilin an noddin his head when I finished. Yes sir, he was really happy all right. In fact, he even gave me a raise the next week cause of it." He laughed.

"Anyway, after we got all untied an headed out, well, that's when Foster told me to take us out into the bay. Now at first I thought that that was kind-a strange cause it was pretty windy an cool out, an I knew that it'd be pretty rough. An I told him that too, you know, that we should go up river an get out-a the wind. But he insisted on go'n out into the bay an that's when I saw the look in his eyes an realized jus what he was up too. Shiiit, he didn't want those ladies ta have a good time, no sir. So when we hit the mouth of the harbor, I turned the wheel an I did jus like he asked.

"Now Mrs. McAlister, she didn't seem ta mind at all that it was rough, an quite frankly, I think she actually enjoyed herself. In fact, she even drove

for a bit. But her daughter, well, I don't think there was nothin about boatin she liked. I don't know if it was cause she started feelin queasy or couldn't swim, or that if it was too cold an windy or jus what in the hell it was. But I do remember this, by the time we got back an got all tied up, I had the distinct impression that she wouldn't be do'n much boatin... an I really believe that that is exactly what ol Foster wanted."

It was mid afternoon by the time Foster finally made it back to his office. A quick run down with the girls as to his schedule for the week and he dropped behind his desk completely exhausted. He'd been on pins and needles for most of the day, but now it was over. Now Melinda had gone out on the boat and was happy. Gazing out of the windows, he thought back to how she'd questioned its name and then of how quickly Otis had seized upon the situation. Howard Davenport's grandmother, he smiled and shook his head as he replayed the man's intervention. What a story. Otis had really shown his loyalty in a way he'd never expected, and it pleased him to know that he truly had his back. He was glad that he'd kept him on and decided to give him a raise. Yes, a raise was definitely in order, and with that he closed his eyes and plopped his feet up on his desk then rocked back in his chair. Emptying his mind he quickly drifted off until his moment of peace was broken by the sound of the phone and then Dawn as she tapped on his door.

"Foster," she called. "I'm sorry to bother you, but it's Katherine Davenport. She said it was important. Can you take her call or do you want me to take a message? I told her I thought you were in the middle of something, but that I'd check."

"Oh no Dawn, that's fine, I can take it," he replied as he pulled his feet from his desk. "Thanks."

He'd missed his visits the last couple of weeks, and with a curious thought he cleared his throat and picked up the phone. "Mrs. Davenport, how are you?" he asked in a professional tone.

"Oooh Foster," she sighed. "To tell you the truth, I just don't know anymore."

"Really, is there something wrong?" he asked, clearly concerned. "Bobby's not in trouble again?"

"Oh no, Bobby's fine, but it's just that, well, I haven't seen much of anyone in weeks and to be right truthful with you, I feel lonely and almost as if I have been abandoned. Why even my own attorney has seemed to have forgotten where I live," she laughed, but at the underlying message she was trying to convey. A message that seemed to resonate her sadness at his waning visits.

"Well yes, I'm sorry that I've missed you the last couple of weeks, but I've been out of town trying to get my campaign started. I don't know if you've heard, but I'm making a run for the Senate against Harlen Crandell. It's a long shot, but I think I can beat him."

"Yes, yes. I just read about that in the paper over the weekend... congratulations. I know Harlen Crandell, and to be blunt with you, he's a pig. You're twice the man he is and I'm sure that once you get your name and your picture out to all those voters, you'll do just fine. I really think that the people are ready for a change."

"Well, thank you, I really appreciate that. That means a lot. Especially from you."

"Yes, well I just wish that I was going to be here to vote for you, but unfortunately my time here in Mobile has finally come to an end."

"It has?"

"Yes."

"So you're leaving? When? Where?"

"Saturday morning... for New Orleans."

"New Orleans?" he repeated.

"Yes, New Orleans," she laughed beneath her breath. "You remember, where my husband lives. See, the bank has finally foreclosed on the house and, well, I have until Friday to be out. But I was wondering if I might ask a small favor of you."

"Sure, just name it; you know I'll do anything to help you. Do you need money or...?"

"Oh no noo, I have plenty of that. See, over the last couple of weeks, I've sold just about every piece of jewelry I ever owned, and then just the other day I sold all of the furniture in the house too. Everything, and that's why I'm calling. I was wondering if you'd kept Otis on, you know, if he still worked for you?"

"Yes, yes he does. Why?"

"Well, the people that've bought the furniture are coming over on Friday morning to pick it up and they wanted to know if I had someone who could help them. You know, for just a half a day or so. Anyway, the only person I could even remotely think of was Otis, and I was wondering if he could help me. I'd be more than happy to pay him for his time."

"Well, I don't see why not," he replied. "You just let me know what time you want him, and don't worry about paying him, I'll take care of that."

"Oooh Foster, I just don't know how to thank you. You've been so kind to me when others have been so cruel that I... well, I want you to know that I'll never forget you, and that I'll always hold a special place for you in my heart."

"Well thank you Katherine, I really don't know what to say, I--."

"You don't have to say anything my friend," she interrupted. "I just wanted you to know that. But since I am going to New Orleans and I know I'll never see you again, I was wondering if," her voice softened but then resurged after a breath of courage. "Well, if you remembered the candle? And if, and I know that this is going to sound just shameful. But I was wondering if you would like me to light it again, say tomorrow night? You know... one last time."

Rocking back in his chair, Foster closed his eyes and smiled. He knew what she was implying, and just the promise of lying with her one last time thrilled him to no end. He felt the blood in his groin stir at just the thought of her waiting beneath the covers, naked and ready to be taken. Ready to give and receive pleasures with an ever-increasing hunger.

"Yes, I remember," he whispered into the receiver. "And yes, I do want you to light it," he lowered his voice even more. "But I want you to light tonight, you hear. I want you tonight Katherine," his words sizzled with the desire of his lust. "And tomorrow, and the next..."

"Now if I remember right, it was the same week that we'd given Melinda an her mother a ride an the day after I'd helped ol Mrs. Davenport move that Foster sent me back up to see Willie. It was a Saturday an one of them times that he couldn't make it again so he wrapped up a couple of books that he'd bought an told me to give em to her. He also reminded me not to say anything to her about Melinda. That I remember real well cause he pointed his finger at me again real serious like.

"Now like I said before, I really didn't like keepin somethin like that from her cause I knew that somehow or somewhere down the road, someone was gonna get hurt. An I had a real strong feelin that it was gonna be Willie when he broke her heart. But I kept my mouth shut an never said nothin hopin that somehow an in someway maybe things would all work out.

"Anyway, I think I made it up there around mid mornin or so an jus as soon as I did we set right in an started scrapin the last of the paint. I remember we worked for a bit but then took an early lunch cause we was both real hungry, an that's when I gave Willie them books. Now she always did get pretty excited when she got to open or unwrap somethin, an that day wasn't no different. But boy let me tell ya, when she finally finished tearin the paper away an then held them up for me to see, I thought I was gonna have a heart attack right there on the spot. I remember I--."

"Whoa whoa whoooa... heart attack?" Jim interrupted and laughed. "Why, what in the hell kind of books were they?"

"Well," Otis began. "They was kids books, but right there on the cover of one of them was a picture of this mean ol nasty witch an she was cookin these two little kids in a great big pot over an open fire. Now back then, shit like that scared the hell right out-a me an that's when I looked out across the tributary an started thinkin about all the stories that I'd always heard of the swamp witch that lived out in the delta."

"A swamp witch," Jim scoffed with another laugh. "Out in the delta?"

"Yes sir," Otis nodded. "Out they say, where no man had ever been or was willin to go. Deep in the shadowlands as they use to call em, where the creatures an the strange green reptiles grew. Some said that she was over a hundred years old. Others said she was even older than that, an that she was nothin more than the spirit of the livin dead, the ghost of a woman who was still searchin for her new-born baby. A baby they say, that'd been taken durin the night by the creatures of the swamp."

"Oh come on, you're kiddin," Jim laughed yet again.

"Oh hell nooo," Otis shook his head. "Really, it's true. In fact, it all started with a survey expedition sometime in the early 1800's that'd stopped an made camp for the night on the banks of the river. An if I ain't mistaken, I believe it wasn't to awfully far from where Willie was stayin. Anyway, the story goes that after pitchin their small tent an then puttin their infant baby to bed, this young bride an her husband then went to one of the boats for some private time alone. Fallin asleep after makin love under a full moon, the couple didn't wake until dawn the next mornin. Then realizing what they'd

*done, that they'd left their baby alone all night long, the woman an her hus-
band rushed back to their tent only to find that their child was gone."*

"Gone? Where'd it go?"

"It'd been taken through a hole that'd been ripped in the back of the tent."

"Really?" Jim raised his eyebrows.

*"Yep, or at least that's what I was always told. Anyway, they say that right
then an there that young girl snapped an completely lost her mind, an that she
then broke down in a way that no man had ever seen. That the screams that
came from her weren't human, an that if you listen real close on a calm quiet
mornin jus before sunrise, you can still hear em deep in the swamp.*

*"Now I guess the group started searchin right away but after a couple a
days an with no luck, they finally gave up an moved on down river. They
had to, but that young mother wouldn't have nothin to do with leavin cause
she was convinced that she could still hear her little baby cryin for her. She
kept tellin everyone she could, but nobody'd listen, specially after she'd broken down the way she had. Anyway, I guess the night before they left, an
unwillin to listen to anyone, includin her husband, she walked back out
into that swamp in search of her little baby an jus never returned. That's
why even to this day, when there's a full moon an it's real quiet out, people
on the river swear that they can still hear the sound of that little baby cryin
for its mother."*

"Look Mister Otis," Willie gleamed excitedly. "It's a book, about a
witch! See! Wa, Wa... anda the Witch," she read then looked to Otis.
"Want me to read it?"

"No," Otis answered abruptly.

"What?" she scrunched her face. "But why not?"

"Cause," he lowered his voice then turned and looked out across
the tributary. "There's a witch that lives out there somewheres. Deep
in the shadowlands they say. It's true, I tell ya," he emphasized as he
slowly turned back to Willie. "An I don't wants nothin ta do with no
witch."

"Well," Willie exclaimed as she opened the book and stared at
the pictures inside. "I ain't afraid of no witch. In fact," she continued
with a growing air of excitement. "I'm gonna get my shotgun an go
out an find her an catch her. An when I do, I'm gonna bring her
back here an then cook her an eat her, jus like she's do'n ta these
kids."

"So did she really go out an look for this witch?" Jim asked.

"Yep," Otis nodded and laughed. "I told her not to do it an not to go, that she'd end up jus like one of them little kids on the cover of that book or even worse. But she wasn't listenin, she jus kept starin at that picture with this real determined look that said, well, that said she was gonna go an do exactly what she wanted, an that was to go out an catch that witch."

CHAPTER 34

———◆———

SHE'D BEEN HUNTING FOR THE witch for just over two weeks, ever since
Otis had told her the story. One day at a time, searching the dead-
end tributaries and the stagnant gator filled reaches of the delta
with her ever-trusty shotgun. Looking for signs, until one day, and
not more than a mile or so from where she lived, Willie caught a
whiff of smoke carried on the midmorning breeze. It was a campfire
and she knew it, and with that she followed her nose until she finally
found herself at the beginning of a tributary she'd never explored.

A hidden offshoot that was naturally concealed by a thick cluster
of vines and water born trees about thirty feet in width. A foliage so
dense, that almost nothing could enter. But Willie was more determined now than ever, and with an ever-growing curiosity, she shut
down her motor and worked her way through to the other side.

There was something about this place and she knew it, she could
sense it, and as she broke into the clearing on the other side, she
stared in awe as if she'd just entered a different world. An underworld of sorts, a cavernous enclave shrouded and shadowed in a
ghostly dimness. Was this the witch's secret lair? Had she finally
found it? Her heart quickened, and her throat tightened and dried.
It was so spooky and unnerving.

Maybe it was the way the giant canopies of the ancient Cypress
had draped themselves out and over the water, blotting out the rays
of the morning sun, their huge limbs dripping with a thick moss that
hung like stalactites in a cave. Or maybe it was the morning's foggy
mist mixed with wispy trails of smoke that lingered and hung in the
air. Eerily floating about as if they had a life of their own. She didn't

know, and nor did she care for this was where the smoke was from, and with an undaunted resolve she restarted her motor and slowly continued on.

Meandering ever deeper into the swamp, into the quiet back-reaches of the brackish waters, Willie followed the waterway until she was forced once again to shut her motor down. Was this another dead end, she wondered? There had been so many. She thought of turning around but didn't. Maybe just a little farther, she thought as she raised her head and sniffed the air. Yes, the smoke was stronger and its source wasn't far away. Someone was back here, and with that she tilted her motor then stood and began pushing her boat with an oar against the muddy bottom.

There was little noise save but a small tree frog calling for a mate and her oar sliding against the side of the boat. The quiet was unnerving, but still she continued on until she'd made her way around the next bend. She could see that the ground had risen and was now dry and clear of undergrowth; no doubt a result of it shaded environment. And she could also see what were clearly the signs of human footprints right at the water's edge.

A shivering chill ran up her spine and her mind began to reel. Was this it, had she finally found her? Staring in disbelief, she suddenly snapped her head upwards to the screeching of a large black crow as it flew from its perch and then disappeared into the forested canopy. Its warning call fading into the dense foliage of the swamp until it had been swallowed completely and it had become eerily quiet once again. But as she turned and surveyed her surroundings, she could sense that something wasn't right. That there were eyes upon her, and that there was danger lurking nearby. It was a feeling deep in her senses, and as the hair on the back of her neck stood up and bristled, a shivering chill ran up her spine once again.

It was her body's own sense of survival telling her to leave and to get out of there, but Willie wasn't listening. She was determined to find the witch, and as her uneasiness grew she quietly laid her paddle down and grabbed her shotgun. Rising with the gun cradled in her arms, her heart pounding like a drum, she cautiously looked around and then chambered a shell. She was ready, but unknowingly and unfortunately, she had already come upon a large sleeping gator. Startled by the boat's invasion of its territory, along with the sudden noise from her gun as she readied her weapon, it instantly and viciously charged in a ferocious attack.

Lunging toward her with its jaws wide open, Willie knew instantly that she was in serious trouble. But she'd never forgotten what Foster had always said about shooting to kill, and as the hissing reptile quickly closed in, she drew down on it and fired at point blank range. Reeling in reaction to the double-aught buck as it tore into its flesh, the animal rolled violently then slammed its tail into the side of the boat. Unbalanced by the blow to the hull and the recoil of the gun, Willie lost her footing and fell. Hitting her head against the edge of the boat her world went dark and in the quiet that followed, she began drifting aimlessly in the swamp.

It was the sound of gunfire coming from just around the bend that'd startled her. A sound she had heard far to many times before in her life. A sound that'd haunted her for years and had given rise to the nightmares that wouldn't go away. Snapping her head up from her fire, she quickly rose from her knees then gazed out across the stagnant waters and into the dense forested surroundings. Turning ever so slowly with her head slightly cocked, she stared with a cautious eye, listening intently to the sounds of her world.

She'd ventured up into the delta almost ten years ago and not too long after she'd returned from the battlefields of Europe. From the killing fields of the Great War that'd taken the lives of so many young men whom she'd tried to save as a front line surgical nurse. A war that in its process, and in the course of its last two years, had traumatized and destroyed her will to live. Unable to cope with the horrors and the haunting nightmares of a war that wouldn't go away, the young nurse escaped from society into the solitude of the swamps to live out the rest of her days.

But somehow and in some strange way, death had eluded and cheated her. Inexplicably evading her until she'd metamorphosed into a creature of her own environment. A mysterious woman in flowing rags who walked in the shadowy back reaches of the swamp and was sometimes seen by passing boaters on the banks of the river. Who then, in the blink of an eye, would be gone the next time they glanced up, lending truth to the rumor and spreading fear that a witch truly did exist and live up in the delta.

Standing ever so quietly as the birds and animals that'd bolted in alarm slowly settled, Hadie Gerthrud Grossman continued to listen and stare at a world that'd now become eerily quiet. She hadn't seen or spoken to another person in years, and the thought of someone invading her territory frightened her immensely. Yet even so she grabbed her walking stick, and with a large degree of trepidation and guarded caution, she headed toward the water's edge. Toward the sound of the gunfire, and now the gentle rolling of a few small waves as they rounded the bend.

Staring as they lazily rolled across the glass smooth surface, the woman in rags then cast her eyes in the direction that they'd came. A second later she caught her breath at the sight of Willie's small boat drifting aimlessly on the placid waters. She wanted to run, but for some reason she didn't. She stood her ground and stared. Maybe it was that the only thing she could see was a foot resting on the center of the back seat and a hand that was bent at the wrist and draped over the edge. There'd been a gunshot, and now a person lay in the bottom of a boat.

Fearing the worst, Hadie instantly reacted as her instincts and training as a battlefield nurse kicked in. She had a natural desire to help anyone who'd been hurt, and as the boat slowly neared, she waded into the shallow waters then reached with her walking stick and pulled on its edge. Dragging it toward her, she finally spied the person lying inside. Sprawled like a shipwrecked victim across the seat, Willie laid in an unconscious state, blood oozing from a cut to her head.

It was getting late into the afternoon by the time Willie finally stirred and opened her eyes. Jerking in fright as if the gator was still charging, she inhaled a heavy breath only to realize that there was no gator and that there was no boat. She was inside of some shelter, lying on a bed of matted leaves and grass, covered with a tattered blanket. But where, she wondered. And how did she get here? What had happened? Was she dead? Was this heaven? What'd happened to the gator? Did she kill it, or did it eat her? Or, was this all just some sort of crazy dream?

She tried to think but her head was pounding and hurt like nothing she'd ever felt before. Reaching up, she gently touched the spot that hurt so bad. She could feel a bandage had been wrapped around her head, causing her to wonder even more. Someone had put it there, and now she was lying in their shelter. But who? A split second later, a shivering chill ran up her spine at the thought that she'd been caught by the witch. She tried to think again of what'd happened and how she had gotten here, but could only remember firing at the gator and then falling.

She exhaled her breath then focused her eyes on the roof of the shelter. Her vision was blurred but soon it cleared until the hodge-podge of materials and boards that kept the elements at bay came into view. She concentrated, then raised her head and looked past her feet to the outside. To the burning campfire with its yellow and blue flames rising out from the ground, licking and tasting the air as if they were the tongues of underworld serpents searching for prey. Then to the waters edge, not more than fifty feet away and her boat that'd been pulled onto shore. Yes her boat, she sighed in relief.

But still, who'd helped her, and how long had she been here? She could see that it was late in the day by the way the sun had pierced through the trees and penetrated into the darkened environ-ment. Shooting across the cavernous surroundings, she stared for a moment at the golden rays enhanced and highlighted by the smoke from the fire only to watch them fade with the passing of a cloud. A moment later she refocused her attention to the sound of footsteps that were now making their way through the brush. Approaching closer and closer, she knew that it was the witch.

Returning with an arm full of wood, Willie watched in horror as the woman with long blonde hair and a tattered and dirty dress dropped her pile of sticks by the fire then bent and stirred some-thing in a pot. She was everything that Otis had said she was and more; she was real. Shuddering at the thought, Willie, in a sudden epiphany, realized the worst of her fears. She'd made a terrible mis-take, and as her stomach knotted with a sick and sinking feeling, she turned a ghostly white. She thought of the story of the witch in the book, and how she'd captured and then cooked and eaten the chil-dren of the forest. Discarding and scattering theirs bones about the forest floor so that no one could ever find them. She looked at the pot by the fire and cringed. Her mind ran wild with fear.

It wasn't big enough for her to fit in, but the witch could cut her up. Yes, that is what she would do. She looked around for her shotgun, but it wasn't there. She felt empty and alone and wanted to vomit and to run, but was too weak and trapped. She wished she'd listened to Otis and had never left the house this morning. She thought of him and Foster, and how they would look for her but would never find her, no one would. She would die in the swamp all alone.

Horrified at her impending doom, now certain that she was about to be cut up and eaten, Willie cried out in fright. A cry that, and although was no more than an overly loud gasp, was one that she instantly regretted. But it was too late for regrets and she knew it, for it had just gained the witch's unwanted attention.

Looking out from the shelter, Willie watched as the woman in rags quickly looked up from her fire and stared. She could see her eyes, beady and small, glaring as if she were trying to cast a spell from afar. She tried to close her own and break it but for some reason she couldn't, she could only watch as the woman slowly turned and set down her spoon then picked up her walking stick.

She was coming to get her and she knew it. Her fire was ready, and now she had a tasty child to eat. She wondered what kind of magic she would use on her? She squirmed in frantic desperation like a worm in hot ashes as the witch ever so slowly drew closer. She had to do something and get away, but how and where? She tried to move, but was somehow frozen with fear. She watched the witch set her stick against the hut then bend at the waist and look in. It was the end and she knew it. Paralyzed with fright, her heart beating like a drum, Willie drew in a heavy breath then cried out with a frantic and frightened plea.

"Ooh God! Don't eat me! Pleeease," she begged as a sickening feeling enveloped her.

But the witch said nothing and just gazed at Willie, twisting and turning her head in a confused and curious manner. She'd been in the swamp a long long time and other than herself, Hadie Grossman hadn't heard or spoken a single word to another person in years. That was until after a short and awkward silence, she answered the young girl.

"Whaaaat?" she asked in raspy drawl.

"Don't eat meee," Willie repeated with another frightened plea. "Pleease, I don't wanna die. I, I…" she tried to catch her breath as she began to hyperventilate.

"Eat you?" Hadie croaked and then scowled at the thought. "I'm not going to eat you."

"You're not?" Willie's eyes instantly widened with relief.

"Oh heavens nooo," the woman chuckled. "Why on earth would I wanna eat you?"

"Ca, cause you're the witch."

"The whaaaat?"

"The witch," Willie repeated in a voice still laced with fear. "The swamp witch that everyone talks about... that, that eats the little kids of the forest."

Staring at Willie in a short but somber moment of silence, Hadie thought of what she had just said then looked at herself and thought of what she had become. At how she had changed, and of how her appearance after all these years could and would lend credence to the rumors that she was a witch.

Smiling, she then thought of one of her favorite fairy tales from the Brothers Grimm, the one of Hansel and Gretel and the witch that lived deep in the forest. She'd read their stories during the war and had remembered them well, and now here she was with this beautiful young girl sitting before her, frightened beyond belief, and from all indications thoroughly convinced that she was about to be eaten by a witch.

"Oh nooo my dear," Hadie shook her head with another raspy chuckle. "I'm jus a little old lady that lives out here in the swamp."

"You arrre?"

"Ah huh."

"For real?"

"Ah huh."

"An, an you don't eat little kids?"

"Noooo," she shook her head again. "I don't eat little kids."

"You dooon't?" Willie gushed with relief. "Bu, but then who are you?"

"Why I'm Hadie," the woman answered quite simply. "Hadie Grossman, an who might you be?"

"I, I'm Willie," she answered in a still shaky voice. "Willie Mae Dawson."

"Well there Miss Willie, it's my pleasure. Now tell me how's that head of yours? How do ya feel? Are you okay?" she asked as her eyes narrowed in on the bandage.

Touching the sore spot on her head with the tips of her fingers, Willie nodded and smiled. "Yeah, I think so, but my head hurts somethin awful. What happened?"

"Well, I'm not really sure, all I know is that I heard a gunshot an then just a little bit after that I found ya floatin. You were unconscious, layin in the bottom of your boat. It seems that you took a little spill and gashed your head open right there just below your hairline," she pointed to Willie's head. "Anyway, after I saw that you were hurt I brought you in here an stitched you up."

"You did whaaat?"

"I stitched you up."

"You stitched me up?" Willie scrunched her face.

"Ah huh, you know, sewed you back together, kind-a like you would a tear in a dress."

"A dress? You sewed me back together like a dress?" Willie gasped as she touched her forehead and then gazed into her eyes.

"Ah huh," Hadie drawled as if it were nothing. "I kept em real small too so you wouldn't have much of a scar on that pretty little head a yours. You sure gave yourself quite a cut there, but keep it clean an dry an you'll be jus fine in a couple a weeks."

To Willie, it was an unheard of thing and she knew that it was something only a witch could do.

Staring with a look that questioned what she'd done without any words, Hadie quickly seized upon the moment and explained just who she was and what she'd done until Willie finally relaxed.

"Now come on," she urged in a motherly way. "How abouts if we get us something to eat okay? You look hungry."

Helping her up, the two women shuffled toward the water and then settled by the campfire. "Ah yes," Hadie said as she carefully picked up one of the skewers of perfectly cooked meat. "Here try some," she said as she handed her stick to Willie.

"What is it?" Willie asked as she took the stick and brought it to her nose then looked to Hadie.

"Go onnn," Hadie gestured with her arm. "Try it... it's good."

Bringing it to her nose once again, Willie glanced to Hadie then closed her eyes and took a tiny nibble. Tasting and chewing, she savored in the flavor and texture of the meat then finally swallowed and opened her eyes in surprise.

"Good?" Hadie asked.

Nodding her head, Willie smiled back and quickly took another big bite. She hadn't eaten since morning and she was hungry. "Ah huh," she mumbled as she began to chew. "What is it?"

Now even though she'd been in the swamp for years, Hadie hadn't lost her sense of humor. And with just a little pent up orneriness, and the fact that she just couldn't resist having a little fun with her new visitor, she looked to Willie and narrowed her eyes. "It's that fat little boy I caught last week fishin down on the river bank," she quipped without missing a beat. "He's been a soakin for about four or five days right over there," she pointed behind her. "So he should be real good an tender. You like him?"

To Willie, there couldn't have been anything worse than the idea of eating a little boy. It was disgusting beyond belief, and in an immediate reaction to that very thought, she spit her mouthful of food back into the fire and then jumped to her feet. The woman had tricked her, she was a witch, and she did eat little kids. Coughing as if she were going to die, she wondered if she were next? She tried to think of what to do but couldn't, she could only hear the cackling of laughter.

"What's so funny," she turned and yelled at the woman rolling on the ground.

"You are," Hadie tried to reply between gasps of laughter. "I mean, you should've seen yourself," she said as she continued to laugh. "The look on your face when you thought you were eaten a fat little boy." She cackled some more. "Bu... but I'm sorry, I jus couldn't help myself, especially after you thought I was gonna eat you."

"What-a-you mean?" Willie demanded.

"I mean, that that ain't a little boy."

"It ain't?"

"Ooh heavens noooo," she chuckled and shook her head.

"Well then what is it?" Wille cocked her head and stared.

"It's gator," Hadie drawled in a scratchy voice as she took a bite. "You know," she smiled. "The one you shot this mornin. I found him shortly after I found you, but he was dead already. An thank the lord for that cause he was really startin to bother me. For a while there, I thought I was gonna have ta move, but you took care of that for me. Thank you. Now come on an sit back down."

That afternoon as the sun slowly set, the two women talked for the longest of time while they dined on fresh gator skewered on sticks and cooked over the open fire. To Willie, it was retribution for the cut above her eye, but to Hadie it was the ultimate and final victory in an ongoing battle for territorial control of her campsite. She'd won with Willie's help, and now the two were dinning on the most succulent parts of the scaly skinned creature.

Hadie really couldn't remember the last time she'd spoken to another person, or for that matter had even wanted too, but right from the start the old battlefield nurse took a liking to the innocent young girl and the two just jabbered away. They shared stories of how and why they had come to be where they were. They found a soothing comfort in each other's company, and as they continued to talk and the day came to a close, Willie reflected on how her mind had changed. Hadie wasn't a witch in any sense of the word; she was sweet and kind and smart and funny... and she liked her immensely.

The next morning the two women woke, and after a breakfast of fresh catfish on a stick, and after Hadie had carefully examined her stitches and redressed her wound, Willie climbed into her boat and said goodbye. She'd made her first new friend on the river and her name was Hadie Grossman, and with a promise to return next week, Willie slowly paddled away.

"So wait a minute, are you tellin me that this witch woman was actually real, an that Willie went out an found her?" Jim's tone reflected both his surprise and amazement.

"Yes sir," Otis drawled. *"In fact, it wasn't but a couple of weeks or so after I'd told her."*

"Really?"

"Yep," Otis shook his head in disbelief. *"I remember it was jus before Christmas when I'd gone back up that, well, there she was with this big ol bandage wrapped around her head."*

"A bandage?"

"Yep, at first I thought she was jus be'n silly, but then she unwrapped it an showed me this big ol cut she'd gotten on her forehead right here," he pointed above his right eye. *"Jus below her hairline that'd been all stitched up real nice like. Heck, I can still remember how proud she was when she showed*

it to me, smilin great big like it was some sort of badge of honor," he chuckled. "You know, her first battle scar so-ta-speak. An then how excited she got when she started tellin me all about this real spooky place that she'd gone to an how this gator had almost gotten her an then of how she'd fallen an hit her head an got knocked out. She said that that was how the witch had caught her."

"Really? Jim chuckled as he reached into the cooler and grabbed two more beers.

"Yep," Otis laughed and took one. "An then right after she told me all of that she started tellin me how this woman who'd found her floatin an sewed her head up while she was asleep really wasn't a witch at all but some sort of army nurse from a war in a country called Europe.

"Now at the time I'd never heard of it before, but she said it was a place somewhere all the way on the other side of the world. She said that the woman used to take care of the soldiers over there that'd been hurt on the battlefields an knew all about doctorin an sewin people up. An then," he postured as if to make another point. "That's when she tried ta get me to go with her, you know, to go an meet her. She said that she was real nice an we could jus jump in her boat an be there in no time, that she knew right where to go an that if we hurried we could even eat lunch with her. Swamp food, she called it. But I wasn't havin nothin to do with no swamp witch, or no swamp food! No sir, an I told her that too cause stuff like that back then, well, it jus scared the hell right out-a me.

"Now Willie really wanted me to go an really pressed her point, but after I finally got it through that thick skull of hers that we had work to do an I wasn't go'n ta see no witch, she finally gave up an we started unloadin the boat. Foster had finally picked out a color an I had the whole back of the boat filled with paint cans.

"Now she was all excited cause after all a that scrapin she'd done she was finally gettin to paint, an jus as soon as we had it all unloaded an I'd given her a little lesson in how to hold the brush an dip it in the can, we set about paintin. I remember I gave her a bucket an a brush an showed her where ta start an then I went an started right around the corner from her."

"But wait a minute," Jim interrupted with a curious gaze. "What color did you paint it?"

"Oh, white," Otis grinned. "The same color it was. Anyway, ol Willie couldn't of been happier cause she was finally paintin the house, but boy she sure wasn't any good I can tell ya that. In fact, by the time I checked on her about ten minutes later to see how she was do'n, she already had more paint on her than she did the house. Shiiit, she had it everywhere. In her hair an

on her face an arms, an all over the front of her clothes where she'd wiped her
hands. Yes sir, she was a real mess all right," he laughed and shook his head.

"That bad, huh?" Jim laughed.

"Yep. Anyway, after we finally quit laughin, an after we'd settled, I gave
her another little lesson an told her that she really needed to slow down a bit.
I guess I should of done that before we started really," he chuckled. "Anyway,
I showed her how to be a little more careful an not so messy, an after that we
went back to work, only this time I stayed on her side."

"Now she did a whole lot better then, but she still wasn't very good, an
after a couple of hours we cleaned up an took lunch. Actually, I cleaned
Willie up, which really took some time," he chuckled again. "Then, after we
finished eatin, she gave me another real long readin an writin lesson. Willie
was always real patient with me, but by the time we'd finished it was gettin on
into the afternoon an since it looked like rain, we jus closed everything up, an
after that I left an headed on back."

It was late in the afternoon by the time Otis had made it back to an
anxiously waiting Foster. He'd been gone all week and listened with
a curious smile as Otis told the story of Willie and the witch and the
cut on her head. Assured that she was fine, he then laughed when
told of how and what a fine painter she was. They both laughed.
He told Otis to take Friday off but to meet him at the marina on
Saturday morning. It'd been two full weeks since he'd seen his sultry
young plaything and he was really beginning to miss her. The rest
of the afternoon, or what was left of it, he tried to work, but it was
pointless for the story that Otis had told of Willie and the witch kept
replaying itself in his head. He smiled and shook his head at the
thought that she had actually gone out and found her.

But what about the cut above her eye? Yes, the cut, he began to
fret. Jesus, that's all he needed now, was for her to get sick over an
infection caused by some sort of voo-doo lady out in the swamp. He
looked at the clock on the wall; it was four. He sighed and closed his
folder. The hell with it all, it was late enough, besides he had a date
with Melinda that would surely end at his house. Then on Sunday,
it was the McAlister's Christmas dinner with the entire family, an
afternoon of food and drink where friends and relatives gathered
for a day of celebration. It was a festive event, and one he was looking
forward to again.

He smiled at the thought of last year and how after dating for just a couple of months and having met her parents only twice, Melinda had invited him to their dinner. How it was as they were eating, that he and the Judge had first sparred in a friendly but lively debate over a local court ruling that he thought had been wrongfully handed down.

He remembered how Melinda had kept patting his leg beneath the table in a discrete but concerted effort to quiet him, and then of even trying to change the subject. But the two men were having fun, and they continued their friendly battle until the Judge had smiled with a knowing nod as they drew into a stalemate and dessert was finally served. He liked the man immensely, and in another four months, he would call him his father-in-law. He called the girls and called it a day.

"Now on Saturday I met Foster at the marina jus like he told me an as soon as we'd loaded all our supplies, we jumped on board an headed up ta see Willie. Now normally he was always real relaxed, like he didn't have a care in the world. But that mornin he seemed jus a little anxious, like he was in a hurry to get there for some reason. He never said nothin, but deep down I think he was actually kind of worried about her, you know, that she'd been hurt an he really didn't know how bad. But jus as soon as we got there an Willie had finally finished huggin an kissin on him, he unwrapped her bandage so he could examine her cut. I remember him be'n real surprised an impressed when he did, an then countin the stitches real serious like. Twenty in all I think he said. An then right after that he started chucklin at all the white paint that she had splattered all over herself." He shook his head and grinned. *"Shiiit, she never did learn to paint really."*

"Anyway, that weekend ended up pretty much like all the rest if ya know what I mean. I remember he inspected her paintin an right after that, the two of them jus kind of disappeared inside the house. Hell, we never did pick up a brush, but I sure did a lot of fishin. Then on Sunday, an after we'd eaten breakfast, we headed back down river an left Willie to her own. I remember thinkin as we rounded the bend an disappeared behind that big tree that I hadn't even wished her a Merry Christmas. I tell ya, I really felt kind of bad at first, but then, an after I thought about it, I guess it really didn't matter much cause if the truth be known, I don't think she had any idea that it even was Christmas."

"*Not a clue, huh?*" *Jim seemed a little surprised.*

"*Nope, not really, or at least not that she let on. Anyway, the holidays passed an right after the first of the year, January of 1931, well, that's when ol Foster really began to put his campaign into high gear. I remember it real well too cause that's when he sat me down one day an had a real long talk with me. He told me that he was gonna be real real busy for the next five to six months an was gonna be gone a whole lot too, an that's when he gave me instructions that no matter what, I was to keep checkin on Willie for him. Tuesdays an Thursdays, jus like always, an if he wasn't there on Friday when I picked up my pay, I was ta jus go ahead an go up on Saturday. He said that he was really dependin on me an if I ever needed ta get ahold of him for some reason, that I was ta tell Miss Vicki an only Miss Vicki. An so, as we rolled into the new year, Foster hit the campaign trail an I kept an eye on Willie for him.*"

CHAPTER 35

CRISSCROSSING THE STATE BY RAIL Foster finally began on what was to become a long and grueling campaign for Harlen Crandell's seat in the U. S. Senate. Generating support and contributions along the way, he slowly began to build and assemble his political machine. A machine that would carry them all into battle as they waged war against Crandell for the next ten months.

Hitting town after town, talking to any and all who would listen, Foster gave speech after speech in an effort to spread his message and gather votes. At first it was discouraging with hardly anyone attending his speeches or rallies, but even so he persisted, and as he and his volunteer staff continued from town to town, the crowds began to grow. His word had begun to spread, and as it did more and more people came to listen. They wanted to see and hear what the young charismatic lawyer from Mobile had to say. Their excitement grew, and along with it, so did Foster's. They liked what they heard, and believed in his values and way of life. And they believed in his economic philosophy. A philosophy that was based on the merits of capitalism, that would help restore jobs to the desperately unemployed now struggling to survive in the midst of a depression.

The months slowly passed, and Foster continued on with a relentless tenacity, holding luncheons and giving speeches wherever he went. He met with the local politicians and business leaders in almost every town he visited, and he listened carefully to their concerns. He was gone for weeks at a time, but even so he continued to see Willie every chance he could, bringing her books and gifts from around the state whenever he returned. Arriving back home late on

Friday evenings, without Melinda's knowledge, he would often times stay on the boat at the marina then wait for Otis the next morning and head up river to see his young lover.

He knew that Willie missed him and wasn't completely happy, and that her heart pulled heavy and hard each and every time he left, yet even so, and for all of her loneliness, she never complained. She only asked where he'd been and when he was coming back, which he never really answered. He liked that about her, but still he could sense that she was beginning to grow restless and tired of being alone. Tired of him not being there every weekend like he used to be.

She'd been up river for over six months, and he knew that if he didn't keep his young filly feeling needed and wanted that he could lose her. That she could and would bound over the fence of his unattended corral and bolt into greener pastures where other stallions most certainly roamed. He thought of her often while he was away, even to the point of worrying. It gnawed on him knowing that he wasn't there to guard his precious young treasure. He'd always considered himself lucky to have found her first, and then to have enjoyed the fruits of her untouched innocence. But she was a spirited and stunning beauty, and he knew that it wouldn't take long for her to quickly gain the attention of another man if she did. And so in an attempt to keep her isolated and occupied as long as he could, he began to add things for her and Otis to do. He knew that it was wrong and that he would have to end their affair eventually; yet for some reason, and even though he himself was about to be married, he could not let go of the sultry young girl.

He felt tattered and torn in a way he'd never been before. But why? Was it because he was the only man to have ever had her and that he now considered her his possession? Or was it just the simple thought of her leaving him and then giving herself to another man after he'd educated her in the art of love that bothered him? He'd been with plenty of women in his life, yet for some reason he'd become addicted to her charms in a way an unlike any other woman he'd ever been with before. She haunted his thoughts during his long and boring train rides and the lonely nights when he would finally lay his head to sleep. He liked her far, far more than he cared to admit.

He let Melinda and her mother have complete control of the wedding. That was excluding the guest list, which he and the Judge handled personally. It was an opportune time to invite the press and all the right people. Powerful business and political types from the Governor on down who would all gather in one spot and in one afternoon. Where Foster could then meet and talk with them in an informal social setting. It was a great use of the occasion, and the Judge had called them all. Then in the first week of May, on a beautiful Saturday afternoon under shimmering blue sky's, Foster K. Siler and Melinda S. McAlister were joined together in holy matrimony by the Reverend R. L. Stone. Officiating in what was considered by all to be the biggest and most lavish wedding in all of Mobile's history, the Reverend Stone gave to the couple their eternal vows that they would live by for the rest of their lives.

Melinda was ecstatic for she had known him since she was a little girl. He'd even married her two older sisters, Marsha and Maryann years ago, and now that it was her turn, she wouldn't have it any other way. To her he was a dear man with a winning smile and a zest for life that equaled few she knew. Combined with that and the wonderful sense of humor that he had brought to their vows, the twenty-four year old daughter of Judge Robert and Martha McAlister couldn't have been happier.

Immediately after the wedding, the reception quickly turned into the who's who of introductions for the budding young politician. The Judge and Foster were in their element, and as they slowly made the rounds, Robert McAlister proudly introduced his newest son-in-law to all he knew. That was until Martha finally grabbed her husband and reminded him in a very specific way that it was his daughter's wedding and not a campaign rally.

———◆———

Returning from their honeymoon after a week of Florida's sun and sand, Foster quickly picked up where he'd left off. There was no time for idleness and he knew it, for he was behind in the polls and November would come all too quickly. He hit the campaign trail hard, and as spring rolled into summer and his commitments increased, his visits to Willie slowed even more. He was busier now than he'd ever been, and now that he was married, it had become harder and harder to get away. His concerns grew, and for good reason, for by summer, Willie had had enough.

She was lonely and felt completely neglected, and even though she and Hadie had become great friends, sharing and dining on just about every kind of fish and swamp animal they could catch, she needed more. The house was done and she'd become bored and restless and insisted on leaving. She told Foster she wanted to move back to Mobile and get an education like she'd promised her mother, and to live with him and take care of him like a wife should. But that was something that was not going to happen, it couldn't. Yet even so, the writing was on the wall and he knew he would have to relent soon. That he would have to act before she bolted from his corral into the open fields.

He envisioned her out wandering the streets of Mobile, then cringed at the endless scenarios it could create. Crandell and the press would have a field day if they found out about her. He pictured the headlines. *'Married Senatorial Candidate Keeps Secret Mistress.'* It would ruin him both personally and politically, and that was something he couldn't allow.

He stalled, at first making excuses and then promises, but found it harder and harder to appease her. He had really relied on her uneducated ignorance to keep things as they were, but was amazed at how quickly her insight had picked up on his tactics and had begun to question his motives. Probing questions, as if she could see through the very veil of his deception. She wasn't stupid by any means and he knew that he would have to be careful in how he manipulated her. But manipulate her he would, for even though she was of a precocious nature, he knew that she loved him. Then in July, during the height of his campaign, Foster quietly began his search for a place to move her.

"So I'm takin it that ol Willie finally had enough of livin up river?"

"Yep, an that's when we started lookin for a place to move her. It was right around the beginnin of that summer if I remember right, that she'd finally had enough of him not be'n there like he use to. I can remember how sad an lonely she'd become, an how they use to argue whenever he'd visit an how he use to try an stall an lead her on in his slick lawyerin way. Tellin her

how much he loved her an all an how he was tryin to find the perfect spot so she'd be happy.

"But Willie was as stubborn an as bullheaded as any little thing you'd ever seen an she argued right back until one day she actually up an told him that if he didn't move her back to town an do it real soon, that she'd do it herself. That she'd promised her momma that she'd get an education, an by God she was determined to do jus that. In fact, I can still remember her tellin him how if she had to get in her little boat an paddle it back to Mobile herself, she'd do it. An she could of too.

"Yes sir, she was determined all right. But hell, you couldn't hardly blame her really, shit she'd been up there for almost a year. Anyway, it was right after that that we started lookin real serious like for a place to move her. I remember him tellin me how he wanted somethin close, you know, somethin that he could still get to by water real easy, but yet at the same time still far enough away so that Willie jus couldn't up an go walkin into town. He knew that he couldn't have her do'n that an so did I really. Heck, I knew what his damn life was all about. I knew he couldn't have people knowin what he was do'n. An I'll tell ya somethin else too... so did ol Foster."

"So whoa whoa whoooa, let's just hold on a second here," Jim stopped the man with a curious grin. "I'm kind-a gettin the impression that Willie still didn't know that Foster was runnin for the Senate, or, that he'd gone out an gotten married right?"

"Not a clue," Otis shook his head. "Not a cluuue."

"An I'm guessin that she still thought that they were married too?"

"Yes sirrr."

"An you never told her any different?"

"Oh hell no. An to tell ya the truth, it really bothered me too, you know, knowin what he was do'n with her an all. But I never said nothin cause deep down I knew that he'd a fired me in an instant if I did. An ta be right truthful with ya, I needed my job. See, I was one of the lucky ones back then cause I did have a job, an a good one too. I mean, it was the Great Depression, an back then there wasn't no work anywhere... specially for an uneducated black man. So as much as it hurt, I kept my mouth shut an hoped for the best.

"Anyway, at first we looked all around Mobile, heck we even went as far down as the Fowl River but he couldn't find nothin that he liked an so that's when we started lookin on the other side of the bay. He knew that all those little towns over there was real real hard to get to by road so whenever he got

the chance, we'd scurry across the bay an run the shoreline searchin for a place for Willie.

"Now as it turned out, we'd been lookin on an off for a quite awhile when we was out one day an jus so happened to spot this little inlet right off the bay. It was a place called Devil's Hole, an if I remember right, I think it was somewhere between the towns of Daphne an Fairhope. Now why it was called that I rightly don't know, but jus as soon as we'd entered it an began to follow it inland, ol Foster began to grin an I knew right then an there that we'd found Willie's new home.

"Anyway, that's pretty much how we found it. Then, an jus a couple of weeks later, I think it was right around the first of September by then, he sent me up to get her an move her. To a little cabin that he'd rented about halfway up that little tributary. A pretty nice place actually, right on the water with a little pier to tie up to. Heck, it even had electric lights in it."

"But wait a minute," Jim cocked his head. "I thought she wanted ta go back to Mobile an get an education? You know, an live with Foster?"

"Oooh she did," Otis grinned. "Or at least she did until that slick talkin son-of-a-bitch convinced her otherwise."

"Convinced her otherwise? What-a-ya mean?"

"Well, with this crazy cock-a-mammie story he made up about how he needed her help with his poor old sick aunt that was lyin in some hospital bed witherin away."

"Whaaat?" Jim scoffed. "You mean he just made up some story so he could string her along?"

"Yes sir, that's exactly what he did, an it wasn't the first time either... orrr the last"

"You gotta be kiddin?"

"Oh nooo," Otis replied. "Ya see, ol Willie had a heart jus about as big as you could ever imagine an boy did he ever play on it. In fact, I can still remember the day she told me all about her, an how sad an worried she'd gotten jus thinkin about how that poor old woman was jus lyin in that hospital bed dyin. Jus like her mother had done not much more than a year ago. I remember we were eatin lunch one day about a week before she was supposed to leave when she started tellin me how Foster had been tryin to help his aunt but that he jus didn't know what he was gonna do cause of all a the doctor bills that she had. That the hospital wasn't gonna let her stay any longer unless they got some money an he jus knew that if she left that she'd probably die without the proper care.

"Now ol Foster was real smooth, an I guess after he finally had her feelin real sorry for him, well, that's when he started tellin her all about a house that she had on the other side of the bay. He told her that she'd told him to go ahead an sell it so they could pay her bills but that they had to fix it up first before they could. Anyway, I guess that that was when he finally asked Willie to help him because he jus couldn't bear the thought of losin his aunt an--."

"Whoa whoa whoooa... let's just hold on a second here again," Jim interrupted with another chuckle. "Are you tellin me that he actually went an rented a house all the way on the other side of the bay an then made up some kind of crazy story about how it was his dyin aunt's? An then convinced Willie that they had to fix it up so they could sell it in order to pay her doctor bills? So she wouldn't get kicked out of the hospital?" he raised his voice and stared with an incensed expression. "Are you really serious?"

"Yes sirrr, that's exactly what he told her," Otis nodded.

"An she believed him?"

"Yes sir, every word, jus like gospel."

"But why?"

"Well, it was simple, she loved him."

"Jesssus Chrissst," Jim shook his head then stared as if he still couldn't believe it. "At least tell me this... did the son-of-a-bitch even have an aunt?"

"Not one that I ever knew of," Otis drawled with a growing grin. "An I knew the man jus about as well as anyone."

"Goddamn what a snake," he shook his head once again then took a drink from his beer.

"Oh yeah, he was a snake all right. But hell, that wasn't even the half of it really."

"It wasn't?" Jim asked as if what more could you possibly add.

"Oh hell nooo. See, an I really didn't find this out until a few months later, but what he'd actually gone an done was to make a deal with the ol boy that owned the house."

"A deal, what-a-ya mean? I thought he rented it?"

"Oh he rented it all right," Otis chuckled. "He really did. But ya see, well, an even though the house was nice, an it really was, it still needed a lot of work. Anyway, I guess the ol boy that owned it had been wantin ta fix it up but couldn't cause he was an older feller. An then when Foster came along an asked about rentin it, well, I guess that's when the two of them got to talkin an before it was all over, they'd made a deal to trade paintin an fixin up the house in return for free rent."

"*Really?*"

"*Yep, an I'm sure you can jus guess who got to do all the work.*"

"*Oh my God,*" *Jim blurted and rolled his eyes.* "*You have got to be kiddin... Willie?*"

"*Yep,*" *Otis nodded as he took a sip from his beer.* "*Like I said before, he was crazy over that little gal an I think he would've said or done jus about anything to keep her as long as he could.*"

"*Unbelievable, but what the hell, I guess it really shouldn't come as too much of a surprise cause he was a damn lawyer wasn't he,*" *Jim snickered.* "*An shit, lawyer, politician; hell it don't make no difference, they all seem to crawl out from under the same kind of rock don't they,*" *he laughed.*

"*Pretty much,*" *Otis agreed as he joined in.*

"*An I'm taken it that you didn't say anything about that either, huh?*" *Jim asked.* "*I mean, what he was do'n with the house?*"

"*Oh nooo,*" *Otis shook his head and sighed.* "*No I didn't, but I'll tell ya, I sure wanted to. But like I jus said earlier,*" *he turned and stared out through the window then watched as the man across the street pulled a lawnmower from his shed.* "*I knew better cause I'd already been warned.*

"*Anyway,*" *he turned back after a moment of silence.* "*I'm not really sure as to jus what all else he told her or how much talkin he really had to do, but I do know this. That by the time he was done layin it on, he had poor ol Willie feelin jus terrible over this lady an had actually convinced her to go an help her. He told her where it was, you know, that it was jus on the other side of the bay an that it'd jus be for a few months or so, an that after she was done he'd move her back to town an put her in school jus like she wanted.*

"*Now after that, Willie was happy again. In fact, I can still remember how excited she was the day I pulled up to that pier cause she new that this time I'd come up ta get her an take her some place new. See, Foster had told her the weekend before an boy was she ever ready. Yes sir, by the time I got back up there on Tuesday she had that whole house all cleaned an boarded up, an had packed up everything she owned an had it all sittin on the end of the pier ready to go. Includin all her books.*

Shiiit, she'd even packed up some of her clothes an supplies an went an said goodbye to that damned ol swamp witch too. I guess they'd become pretty good friends over the months an she wanted to tell her that she was leavin," *he chuckled and shook his head.*

"*Anyway, we got everything loaded in pretty short order, includin her shotgun an all her books, an then right after that we jus kind-a stood there on the end of the pier an stared at the house. Willie had done jus what she said she'd do, an that was to make it the prettiest house on the river. But, it was time to move on an I think deep down everyone knew it. Then right after that, we jumped in the boat an cast off. I can still remember when we pulled away from the pier an how Willie stood in the back makin sure that her little fishin boat followed okay. An then of how she jus stayed back there, starin at the pier an the house as we headed downstream. Watchin all the way until we'd finally rounded the bend with that big tree hangin out over the water.*

"I think in a way she was really kind-a sad, you know, leavin after she'd worked for so long an hard, but that all changed when she finally came up front an joined me. I remember she was smilin an bouncin on the balls of her feet like she always did when she asked me if she could drive. Yes sir, she was excited all right, so I stepped to the side an let her take the wheel, an from that point on she drove all the way back down the river. Back down past Twelve Mile Island an Chickasaw Creek, an then on past the new state docks while I jus sat beside her an played my harmonica. All the way along the downtown waterfront to the bottom of Pinto Island where the river finally turned into the bay an we met one of those great big freighters comin back up into port. An then right after we passed it, we turned left an headed out into the wide open waters of the bay an to her new home.

"Now when ol Willie first saw all that water, I gotta tell ya she really started ta get antsy. I can still remember how big her eyes got an then her gettin this look on her face as we headed out across it. See, an even though she'd been on the river an around all that water, she'd never seen anything quite like it. But it was pretty calm out that day, an after a bit, she settled back down an we made our way over an down to the other side. She drove the whole way until we pulled into the mouth of that little tributary where I finally took over an after that, it wasn't but a few more minutes an we was pullin up to that little pier. It wasn't near as big or nice as the one up river, but it did okay, an after we got all tied up, we headed right on up to the house to check it out."

"So what'd she think of her new home? Did she like it?"

"Oh yeah," Otis chuckled. "She liked it all right, specially when she found out that it had e-lectric lights as she called em. Shiiit, I bet she must-a turned them damn things on an off a couple a dozen times before I finally got her to stop."

"Really?" Jim laughed.

"Oh yeah, see, I guess she'd never had anything quite like that before an found the whole idea of flipping a switch to make a light come on to be

a real fasinatin thing. Anyway, after I finally got her to quit playin with them, which took some do'n, we went back down an started unloadin the boat. Now we had a lot of stuff from that other house, you know tools an food, an all of Willie's stuff, an by the time we'd finished unloadin an had carried everything all up an had packed it all away, it was gettin way late into the afternoon.

"Now Foster knew it'd take all day to get her moved, an I think that that's why he told me to jus go ahead an stay the night. Besides, I think he really wanted me there that first night jus to make sure she'd be okay an all. Anyway, Willie ended up makin us a real nice dinner that night an by the time we was all done it was gettin dark so we jus went to bed. Then the next mornin, an pretty much right after breakfast, I left her standin on the pier an headed on back to report in jus like I always did.

"I remember when I got there an how worried he seemed until I told him that everything had gone okay an that Willie was happy. An then after that, after he relaxed a bit, well, that's when he told me to jus take Thursday off but that on Friday he wanted me to go to the marina about noon an get the boat ready. Then after I had it all cleaned an fueled, ta come to the office around three an get him. That we was go'n to spend both Friday an Saturday with Willie. He said that is was her birthday again an he wanted to surprise her an spend it with her in the new house."

It was early afternoon by the time Otis had made it back to the office and reported in. Foster was pleased to say the least, and even a little amused over the whole e-lectric light thing. But the day had been a long one with thoughts of Willie consuming his mind as he waited. He'd worried excessively about her the night before too, tossing and turning as he lay in bed next to his wife, almost to the point of sleeplessness. But now that he knew she was fine and everything was okay, he dismissed Otis with a thanks and then turned his thoughts to her upcoming birthday. She would be sixteen this weekend and he wanted to surprise her with a special gift.

He thought of the chocolate cake from Crystal's Bakery that he'd had made last year, and of Willie's reaction. Yes, another one was most certainly in order, but still he wanted something more, something special that'd show how much he still cared and make up for his times away. He stared blankly at the wall of books across the room; his mind wandering until he suddenly began to smile.

God Foster, he thought as his grin began to broaden. You're a genius. Yes, that was it; he would give her a book. But not just any book, he would pick one from his collection and he knew exactly which one. Willie loved to read; he knew that without question, but he also knew that she'd never read anything like this, for this was a book that was special. This was a book that he himself had read many times before, years ago, as a young boy while still in school. That depicted the lives and times of the people along the Mississippi just before the mid 1800s. An endearing and colorful tale of a young boy who befriends a runaway slave, and then of their drifting journey as the two embark on a homemade raft down the muddy river in search of freedom.

It was perfect and Willie would love it, he was certain of it. Her reading skills had developed over the last year to such a level that even though it was almost four hundred pages long, he knew she could handle it with ease. She was gifted and smart, and with a contented sigh, he rose from his chair and crossed the room.

Scanning the books amongst his collection of classics, he searched the titles until he spied the one he wanted then pulled the old but beautiful hardbound copy from its place. Blowing the dust from the top of its pages, he slowly turned it in his hands and studied its cover. Staring at the picture of the young boy standing in front of a fence with his hands buried deep in his pockets, he thought back to the first time he'd read it. He was ten and had absconded to the hayloft of their barn one rainy Saturday morning. Yes, he thought as he brushed the cover with the swipe of his hand and quietly read the title. *The Adventures of Huckleberry Finn,* by Mark Twain.

Smiling again as he envisioned Willie's reaction when she opened it, he clenched it in his hands then turned and walked back to his desk. Taking his seat, he then carefully wrapped it in a sheet of brown paper, smiled again and then placed it in the bottom drawer of his desk. Yes, it was perfect, and with that he called it a day and went home.

CHAPTER 36

———▪———

THURSDAY AT THE OFFICE FOSTER spent most of his day contriving a story that would allow him to leave for the entire weekend without suspicion. Later that evening over dinner, he told Melinda of a sudden campaign opportunity that had arisen in Montgomery. It was an unexpected invitation to speak before a group of voters and one that he had been trying and hoping to get. He feigned his sadness at leaving her alone once again and on such sudden notice, but as always Melinda was understanding and even supportive, for she knew without question what her role as a candidate's wife was. He said that he would just leave from the office and catch the afternoon train, but that he would be back by noon on Sunday and in plenty of time for dinner with her parents.

He knew their schedules by heart and had no problem reciting the departure and arrival times. He told her that Otis could take him to the station and then pick him up so she wouldn't have to bother. She knew that he used and depended on Otis for a lot of things, and liked the fact that he was using him. Besides, and in her eyes, that was what his kind were for. She made love to him that night and then again in the morning for good luck, and also she said, to hold him over until he returned. He ate a hearty breakfast then left around nine with a kiss at the door and headed to the office.

The day seemed to drag on with an excruciating monotony until, and right at three, Otis arrived to pick him up. It'd been a long and tiring week and he couldn't wait to get away. He told the girls that he was off to Montgomery and would see them on Monday when he got back. Then, and after some last minute instructions and permission to close an hour early, he headed out the door. He was finally free and in less than twenty minutes, he was on the boat and in his casual clothes. Untying just a few moments later, the two pulled from the slip and set a course for Willie.

"Now I don't know what it was exactly, but as soon as we got underway I could tell right off that it was gonna be a pretty good weekend. I think a part of it must of been when ol Foster came up from below as we was leavin the docks with two cold beers an then set one of em down right in front of me by the wheel. I remember lookin at him real surprised like, but he never said a word, he jus smiled an patted me on the shoulder an then walked over to the doorway with a great big grin.

"I guess he'd really been lookin forward to spendin the weekend with Willie in her new house, not to mention the fact that we was finally gettin to go some place new for a change. You know, somewhere other than up that damn river. Shit, I don't know how many trips we'd made, an we was both real tired of that, specially me," he laughed.

"Anyway, I can still remember him standin in the doorway with this grin on his face as we motored down river, sippin on his beer while he looked at everything until we came up on the new state docks. An then of him gettin this real serious look on his face as we slowly passed, like he was studyin em or somethin, until he finally turned back to me."

"They're empty?" Foster remarked with a curious look.

"Oh, yes sur boss," Otis replied as if it were the most common of things. "They's always empty."

"They are?"

"Oh, yes sur," he emphasized. "Heck, there's hardly any boats in em. Or at least not very often."

"Really?" Foster raised his eyebrows.

"Yes sur," Otis reiterated.

Taking a deep breath, Foster reflected on the man's words for a moment then turned and stared at the empty docks with an ever-increasing curiosity. He thought of what the Judge had always said about Crandell, and then of what it really meant to the people of Mobile. To the people who were not working because of his greed. It angered him, but still he wondered as they slowly passed and the docks faded into the distance, where were all the ships? Where had they all gone?

A little over an hour later, Foster finally reached up and pulled on the knotted roped then watched as the sultry young sixteen year old bolted from around the house.

Running down the yard and onto the pier she smiled at the sight of the boat and the man she loved standing in the doorway of the cabin. A few moments later, she had her arms wrapped tightly around him in a loving embrace.

"Now like I jus said a bit ago, I could tell that it was gonna be a pretty good weekend cause jus as soon as Willie had finished huggin an kissin on him, he had us go up an make a fire pit. See, he'd brought a whole mess of food, an as he put it, he jus wanted to relax an take it easy cause it was Willie's birthday. It was kind of strange though, you know, be'n in a different place an all, but ol Willie seemed happy again an I think that that was all that Foster really cared about. In fact, I knew it was cause he'd been really worried about her. Anyway, after our fire burned down, he cooked us a real nice dinner an after we'd eaten an it'd gotten dark, him an Willie jus got up an went to bed."

Waking early the next morning, Foster carefully pulled his arm from beneath Willie's pillow then quietly rose and slipped on his boxers. He wanted to surprise her just as he'd done last year, and with the breaking dawn now providing just enough light to see, he made his way into the kitchen and retrieved the cake and book he had hidden in the pantry. Carefully arranging the candles on top, he quickly lit them, then slipped the book beneath his arm and walked back into their room.

Willie was still asleep when he entered, but as soon as the off-key minstrel dropped into another rendition of happy birthday, she lazily opened her eyes and smiled at the sight of him and the cake topped with burning candles. It was her birthday again, and she hadn't even known it. But Foster had remembered, and he did because he loved her and cared for her, she knew that now.

Sitting up as he stepped toward her, she quickly brushed the hair from her face then plopped her hands behind her and began to giggle. For Foster was a terrible singer and they both knew it, and in the one year that'd passed, he hadn't gotten any better. Yet even so, he continued on to Willie's delight and slowly crossed the room until he stood at the edge of the bed.

Looking down at the auburn-haired beauty, the flickering flames bathing her face and chest in a soft angelic glow, he finally finished and then took a seat. "Morning Willie," he greeted and held up the cake. "And happy birthday."

"Aaaah Foster," she drawled in the sweetest of voices. "Is it my birthday again? Already?"

"Yes ma'am," he replied. "You're sixteen now, sooo happpy birthday."

"An you got me another cake? Again?"

"Yes ma'am, a chocolate cake with chocolate icing. Just like last year. Remember? Now go on, make a wish and blow out your candles."

Pausing in thought, Willie stared deep into Foster's eyes as if she were trying to send a message. A message that would let him know just how much she loved and cared for him, and how grateful she was for all he'd done. And then of her wish, that she could finish the house and it would sell so they could finally be together. It was what she wanted more than anything else in the world, and with a great big smile and a breath to match, she blew out her candles.

It had started with just a simple kiss, but by the time they'd finished and cut their first piece of cake, an hour had passed and they'd eaten most of the icing from its top. Stripped away a finger swipe at a time, they'd fed it to each other in the most decadent of ways. Willie was in heaven, and as soon as they'd finished their cake, Foster gave her his gift. Smiling as she held it in her hands, she could tell that the item within the plain brown paper was a book. A second later, she ripped it open and held it before her. Thick and heavy, she stared at the cover then slowly read the title.

"The Aa… aad, ve, vennnn," she stammered and then looked to Foster for help.

"The Adventures," he quickly aided.

"The Ad-ven-tures," she repeated proudly. "Of Huc.. al.. ba.. bary Finn." She broke down the word and then sounded it out just as she'd been taught her.

"That's right," he complimented. "The Adventure's of Huckleberry Finn, by Mark Twain. It's a story about this young boy named Huck Finn who floats down the Mississippi River on a raft and helps this runaway slave named Jim."

"A runaway what?" she asked and scrunched her face.

"A slave, you know," he replied as if she'd not heard correctly.

"A slave?" she drawled inquisitively.

It was apparent just by her expression that she had no idea as to what he was talking about. That in her short and sheltered life she'd probably never heard of such a thing as a slave or slavery. But to Foster it was important that she knew the truth about such things, and so he carefully explained the history of slavery and the Civil War.

"An Mister Otis ain't your slave?" she probed after he had finished.

"Nooo," he shook his head with a light-hearted chuckle. "Mister Otis ain't my slave, he works for me and I pay him remember."

"Oh yeah, that's right, I forgot. So then can I give him another piece a cake, like I did last year?"

"Sure Willie," he said as he stretched out on the bed. "I think Mister Otis would enjoy that."

Rising from the bed, Willie quietly dressed then picked up her cake and book and went into the kitchen. Cutting a piece, she then poured a glass of milk, grabbed her book and headed out the door. Rolling to his side as the screen door slapped behind her and the house became quiet, Foster found the comfort of his pillow then yawned and closed his eyes.

"Now by the time Willie finally came down from the house, I'd already been fishin for quite a while. See, I'd learned a long time ago not to even bother with waitin on them two an had gotten to where I jus pretty much did whatever I wanted until one of em finally showed up. Most of the times that was Willie, an that mornin proved ta be no different than any other.

"Anyway, I remember when she came walkin down the pier, she was singin an callin out my name with a great big piece of chocolate cake in one hand an a glass a milk in the other, jus like she'd done the year before. She was real happy, an jus as soon as she handed me that cake an milk, she plopped down right next to me on the edge of the pier. An then right after she got herself all settled, well, that's when she showed me what ol Foster had given her for her birthday."

"Look Mister Otis," Willie gushed as she took her seat beside him. "Look what Foster gave me for my birthday. It's a book called the Ad-ven-tures of Huc-al-bary Finn, by Mark Twain. Seee." She held it out so he could see. "An look how big it is. Heck, it'll take me forever ta read it," she said, her dangling legs now swinging back and forth at the knees in an excited manner.

"Well that shorly is nice Miss Willie, but what's a big ol book like that all abouts? It don't have no witch in it, does it?" He raised his eyebrows.

"Nooo," she laughed. "Foster says it's about this boy who goes down the Mis-a-sippi River on a raft an helps this man who's a runaway slave," she replied then turned with a curious expression. "Did I live on the Mis-a-sippi?" she asked.

"Oh no," Otis shook his head. "You lived on the Mobile, heck the Mis-a-sippi is all the ways over in New Orleens."

"Oh I see," she shrugged her shoulders. "Anyways," she said as she turned back to her book and stared at the cover. "Is'n this jus swell? I'm gonna read it right now."

"Now right after she'd finished showin me her book, she turned around an laid across the pier then opened it up an started readin jus like she'd said. I'll tell ya, I don't think ol Foster could of gotten her anything else in the world that she'd a liked better than that damn book. Yes sir, she was jus beamin over it, an I had no doubt that she wouldn't stop until she was done. So while she laid there an read, I started in on that cake, an jus as soon as I was done, I went back to fishin. Then about an hour later, ol Foster came walkin down an joined us. I remember one of the first things he always use to do was ask me how the fishin was an that mornin wasn't no different."

"Really, an how was it?"

"Oh hell, it was terrible. Shit, I don't think there was any fish in that little tributary, an I told him that too. I remember we both laughed an jus as soon as we were done, well, that's when he looked at me real serious like an then told me that what we ought-a do is jus get the boat an go out in the bay.

"Now in all the days that I'd known him, I'd never once seen him pick up a pole, but jus as soon as he said it we loaded up an then spent most of the day out on the water trollin up an down the shore. Now even though we didn't catch but a few, we had a lot-a fun. Then when we came back in, he made us a real nice dinner on the grill again, an by the time we'd eaten it was gettin dark so we jus got up an went to bed. Yes sir, we didn't do nothin that whole weekend. But ol Foster had to get back, an jus as soon as we was done eaten breakfast the next mornin, we packed up, an after a long goodbye to Willie,

got in the boat an left her standin on the pier. An that was pretty much how we spent her sixteenth birthday."

He'd told Melinda he would be back by noon on Sunday and for once in their relationship he had every intention of fulfilling his promise. Why he wasn't sure, but something inside of him kept telling him to get back early. Maybe it was a feeling he had that she just might try and surprise him. He knew the train schedules by heart, and knew that the Sunday morning express from Montgomery arrived at ten thirty. He wanted no chance of being late and of getting caught if she did.

Waving a final wave to Willie as they rounded the first bend, he turned his chair toward the stern and took a seat under the early morning sun. It was a beautiful morning, and as Otis slowly headed out into the wide-open waters of the bay, he began to wonder as to just how long he could keep her. He knew deep down that it couldn't continue for long, especially if he were to win the election. But what would he do with her? He pondered his options until they'd reached the docks and he'd turned his thoughts to his wife and the station.

CHAPTER 37

———◆———

THE WEEK AFTER WILLIE'S BIRTHDAY Foster finally took a much-needed break from his on-the-road campaigning and began to prepare for his upcoming debate in Montgomery. He had agreed on a date in mid October that would pit him against his arrogant and overly confident opponent. He'd worked hard over the last nine months and had gained substantially in the polls, but still he was behind, and now he was about to battle the man in a one on one debate. It would be tough and he knew he needed something extra, something that would give him the edge when they finally met.

The week drew on, but Friday finally came and along with it so did a sky of dark gray clouds that seemed to have settled right over the city. A gloomy day with a light but steady rain that made the job of staying inside just a little easier. Settling in with his first cup of coffee, he dove back into Crandell's record looking for dirt, searching for anything that could derail the man's train back to Washington. He had to find that piece of evidence, that something, that anything, that would link Crandell to the corruption that everyone talked of.

He worked hard into the afternoon, yet found nothing but conjectures and unsubstantiated claims. Gossip and rumors that'd circulated for years, but certainly nothing he could use. He was frustrated and tired, fatigued and brain dead to the point where he could think no more. He needed to rest and he knew it, and with that he set his feet on top of his desk then closed his eyes and rocked back in his chair. Aaah yes, he thought, just a few short minutes and I'll be as good as new. A moment later, he emptied his mind and with a long deep breath, drifted off into the dream world.

But like all good things, it didn't last very long before a knock on his door and then the sound of Dawn's voice calling his name brought him back into the world of reality. He wasn't sure of just how much time had passed, but he could tell he felt better. Opening his eyes, he glanced at the clock on the wall and then to Dawn standing in the doorway as she called his name again. God, a half hour, how nice.

"Foster... are you awake?"

"Yeah Dawn," he finally replied with a yawn as he pulled his feet from his desk and rubbed his eyes. "What's up?"

"Well, I'm sorry to bother you but there's a lady out here that says she really needs to see you. In fact, she's insisting. She said she came all the way from Montgomery. Now I already checked your schedule to see if she had an appointment, but I couldn't find anything. I thought maybe Vicki had forgotten to write it down, so I asked her if she'd made one and she said no.

"Anyway, I told her that you weren't taking any new clients and all cause of your election an that normally you don't see people without an appointment but that I would check. I asked her what it was in reference to, but she wouldn't tell me. She just said that she had something you really needed to see and that it was very important that she talk to you immediately." She paused and then waited.

"A lady?" He rubbed his chin. "All the way from Montgomery?"

"Yes sir."

"And did you get her name?"

"Yes sir," she glanced at her note pad. "A Miss Suzanne Schubert."

"And she wouldn't say what it was about?" he asked as he drew his eyebrows together.

"No sir," Dawn shook her head and shrugged. "She just said that it was really really important that she see you right away. Do you want me to tell her you're busy and to come back another time?"

Gazing at Dawn with a growing curiosity, Foster thought for a moment and then began to smile. He wasn't quite sure as to just why or what it was, but there was something intriguing about the lady from Montgomery and her request to see him that'd suddenly grabbed his interest. Who was she he wondered, and what did she want? What was so important to have made her travel so far just to see him? An old girlfriend perhaps that he couldn't remember? God he hoped not. Or someone he'd met on the campaign trail he couldn't remember? "No Dawn," he finally drawled as he sat forward in his chair. "Why don't we go ahead and see what she wants. Go ahead and bring her in will you."

"Yes sir," she replied as she turned and disappeared.

A moment later, Dawn returned with the lady, and as they walked into his office Foster began to smile, for there was no doubt that he had a weakness for good-looking women. Tall and slender and smartly dressed, she was a perfect example of everything he liked. And as she confidently crossed the room with a folder held tight to her chest, he couldn't help but cast his eyes to her fingers curled tightly around its edge then smile again and push his chair from his desk.

Standing as they approached, he came from behind his desk and greeted the lady in a polite and professional manner then offered her a chair and dismissed Dawn. Gazing upon her as she took her seat then gracefully crossed her legs and smoothed her skirt, he stared for just a second then stepped back behind his desk and took his chair. She was definitely in a class by herself, and with a last subtle glance to her left hand as she laid the folder on her lap; he rocked back in his chair and cleared his throat.

"Now, Mrs. Schubert," Foster began. "My secretary said that it was really important you see me. So, how is it that I might help you today?"

"It's Miss," she raised her head and corrected, her honey smooth voice evoking both a refined and educated blend of southern charm. "Miss Schubert," her eyes lingering with his as she drew her lips into a knowing smile. "And it's not so much in how you can help me Mr. Siler," she continued confidently. "But how I might be able to help you."

"Help me?" he chuckled beneath breath.

"Yes sir. Help you."

"In what way?"

"Why with your election," she answered matter of factly.

"My election?" he repeated and cocked his head.

"Yes sir," she replied.

"Well, that's mighty nice of you and all, but I'm not really sure that I understand. Are you wanting to become a volunteer? Is that it?"

"Oh heavens nooo," she laughed with a dismissive wave.

"Then what, because to be quite honest, I'm really kind of confused here, so if you don't mind." He opened his arms in a gesture as if to proceed.

"Yes, I'm sorry, you're absolutely right. How very unprofessional of me, but please if I might have just another moment of your time to continue?" Nodding with another open handed gestured the lady from Montgomery quickly continued. "Thank you. Well, to put it bluntly, I have come here to help you in your struggle to dethrone the great Harlen Crandell."

"Oh you have, have you?" He chuckled again.

"Yes, I have," she replied with a serious gaze.

"And just how are you proposing to do that, wave some sort of magic wand or something?"

"Well no, not exactly, but close. See, and although you are probably unaware of this, I've been watching the progress of your campaign with a great deal of interest, and as you well know you are still behind in the polls. You know it and I know it, and so does Crandell. Now I know that you've probably tried an done just about everything you could think of to close that gap, but the simple facts are, are that you're still behind and if you do not do something to change that, and something soon, I can almost guarantee that in November you'll lose the election."

"And your point is?"

"My point is Mr. Siler, is that I can change all of that for you and put you ahead almost instantly."

"Oh you can, can you?" He raised his eyebrows.

"Yesss, I can," she defended.

"And just how do you intend to do that?"

"With this," she said and held up her folder stuffed with papers.

"And what's that?" He rocked forward and narrowed his eyes into a wary gaze.

"Well, let's just say shall we, that if this information were to actually get out and get into the right hands and become public knowledge, I really believe that Senator Crandell, after all of the ethical and criminal charges had been brought against him that is, could quite possibly spend the next ten years or so in a federal prison." She finished. "Nowww do I have your interest?"

It was at that very moment that Foster's mind took off and began to whirl. Could it be, he thought? Could this really be the dirt that he'd been searching for? The gritty proof of Crandell's corruption that had eluded him for the last nine months? His smoking gun? But who was she, and why was she doing this, and why had she waited until now? He looked to her with burning curiosity then smiled and cleared his throat.

"Yes ma'am," he replied and nodded. "That you most certainly do, but before we proceed any further, I do need to ask you a few questions if you don't mind."

"No sir," she grinned. "I don't mind at all."

"Good, well first I need to know just who you are, and exactly how it is that you came by all of this? I mean, if it is what I think it is. And second, why me, why am I the beneficiary of such benevolent generosity? What is it that you are looking for precisely?"

"Well, first of all Mr. Siler, let me assure you that all of the documents that I hold here in my hand were not in any way stolen or derived by any other ill-gotten means."

"Yes, well then just how is it that you happened to of come by, or should I say managed to acquire all of thisss... this information if you don't mind?"

"Well you see, that's where the interesting part comes in."

"Annnd," he tilted his head and raised his eyebrows.

"Yes, well let me see if I can explain," she took a breath and slowly re-crossed her legs. "See, it all actually started about six years ago, right after I'd graduated from college. I was twenty-three at the time, and that's when I first met him at one of his campaign rallies."

"Who?"

"Why Harlen Crandell, that's who," she replied as if he should've known. "It was so exciting being in the presence of an actual Senator. I was young and wanted so badly to make an impression. Anyway, it was right after the rally that he came back over to me and we started talking. He said that he'd just found out that I'd graduated from college and congratulated me. He was so interesting and wanted to know everything about me, and after we talked for a bit, well, that's when he finally told me that if he won his re-election he could really use another person on his staff just like me. He said that I was perfect, and just what he'd been looking for in a new assistant that he'd been thinking of adding to his staff in Washington. You know, someone who was pretty and smart and well educated, and who could project his new image to the public.

"Now I'm sure you can just imagine my excitement, because here was this man that I'd just met, and a Senator at that, offering me a job. It was a girl's dream. Now he did tell me that I'd have to work a year or so here in Alabama until I learned how everything worked, but that just as soon as I did, he would take me to Washington. And then right after that, well, that's when he asked me if I wanted to help, you know, as a volunteer on his campaign staff until the election.

"Now naturally I couldn't believe my good fortune, so like any young ambitious girl, I jumped at the chance and worked all summer for him. For free of course, and then right after the election and true to his word, he hired me. Now for the first six months or so everything was just great. Harlen was always so nice and thoughtful, helping me and all whenever I needed it, taking me to lunch and of course, always talking about my future in Washington and his plans for me. It was just great and I couldn't have been happier, but after awhile, all of that began to change, and rather quickly I might add. In fact, it finally got to the point where it was so uncomfortable and so bad that I really thought of quitting."

"Uncomfortable?" Foster repeated curiously. "What-a-you mean exactly?"

"Well, let's just put it this way shall we. Harlen Crandell is nothing more than a pig, and as soon as he realized that I wasn't going to sleep with him, and I mean under any circumstances, it seemed like he just up an forgot all about the promises he'd made to take me to Washington. Yes sir, I went from being his favorite girl in the office to one of, shall we say," she chuckled and waved her hand. "Well, I'm sure you get the point. Anyway, it wasn't too long after all that, and I guess as some form of punishment or something, that he stuck me back in the mail room of his Montgomery office opening all the mail that came in. Right in the middle of all this disgusting heat and humidity that he knew I just absolutely detested.

"He knew I'd hate it, and I think he thought that I'd just up and quit but I didn't. I just kept opening the mail like I was told. And actually, it really wasn't so bad after that because I didn't have to deal with him anymore. And then after the depression hit an all, well, it just didn't make sense to quit. You know, a single girl giving up a good-paying job. So I stayed on and kept opening the mail and filing everything just like I was suppose to.

"See, my job Mr. Siler, was to open all the mail and read through it, then sort it and file it and deliver it to whoever and wherever it needed to go. Now at first I didn't pay much attention to what was in all those envelopes because I'm sure you can just imagine how much mail a Senator gets. But after awhile I began to notice all of these letters and correspondence from different companies and businesses from around the state protesting how they were being forced to deal with the shipping companies and the port authorities all the way over in New Orleans.

"Now have you ever wondered why the new state docks here in Mobile have languished for the last three years and have never had very much business? Or ever wondered where all the ships were? The ones that were suppose to come after they'd built all those docks, but then didn't."

"Yes, I have actually," Foster answered, his curiosity and excitement growing by the second.

"Well, I know the answers," Suzanne grinned. "I know the where, annnd I know the why. See, it seems that our illustrious Senator has been on the take... and for quite sometime."

"I knew it," Foster blurted and smacked his desk as if he'd just been vindicated. "I knew the son-of-a-bitch was crooked."

"Oh he's crooked all right," she assured. "And as far as I can determine, I think it all really started about four or five years ago when the city here of Mobile was trying to build the new state docks. Actually, or more accurately if you will, it began when they tried to pass the bonds to finance them, and that's when he got all hooked up with a bunch of crooked business types from the port authority down in New Orleans.

"See, those guys over there, well, they really didn't want you guys over here to have a nicer port than they did because they knew that eventually it would hurt their businesses. Anyway, and I'm not sure exactly how they did it, but they got ahold of Crandell and right off started wining and dining the hell out of him. Now from everything I can gather, it didn't take very much or very long before they had him stuffed in their pockets and he began pressuring companies from here into selling and steering their business to the port in New Orleans in lieu of some very generous kickbacks."

"And you have proof?" Foster's eyes widened.

"Yes sir," she smiled and held up her folder again. "All right here in a nice little bundle. See, I know the who, what, where and when, on almost every single deal that he's been involved in over the last four years. Now I'm sure he must of thought that I was just another empty-headed plaything wrapped in pretty paper, but I can assure you that I'm not. In fact, I think it would be pretty safe to say that I know more about the man and his crooked dealings than he does himself. Including, if you will, some very interesting and questionable points on how he even tried to sabotage the bond issues on the docks before they were built.

"So now, you know the whole story. Or at least that part of it, that is. And now, Mr. Siler," she paused and took a breath. "As to precisely why I am here and what I want. Well, as you can plainly see, I am really quite disgruntled and that is why I've come here today, to make a deal with you."

"A deal?"

"Yes sir, a deal. You did say that you wanted to know why you were chosen to be the beneficiary of such benevolent generosity, didn't you? Well, this is it. All of this information here in this folder, that not only implicates, but proves what Crandell and his business partners have been doing for the last five years. Everything you need to bury his fat ass and assure your certain victory in November for what I want in return."

"And what's that?" he asked pointedly.

"A position," she replied without hesitation. "On your staff in Washington. Or shall I say, just to be a bit clearer, one as your new personal assistant, along with a small housing and clothing allowance," she smiled with a touch of optimism. "You know, so that a girl might afford to live in the manner and custom in which she has always desired."

Gazing at the woman, Foster sat for a second contemplating her request in kind of a mystified daze. Just a half hour ago he'd been agonizing over how to defeat Crandell. What he would say at the debate and what his next plan of attack was going to be. He'd been worried for quite some time, but now here was this woman laying the golden goose right at his feet, for if what she was saying were true, it would destroy Crandell. He was stunned at his good fortune, but he was also wary like a hunter approaching a fresh kill.

She seemed to have come out of nowhere. Magically appearing as if she'd descended from above, like some sort of angelic savior in what seemed to be his most desperate hour. Was this a setup or a trap that Crandell had orchestrated just before the debate to divert his attention and trip him up? He wondered and continued to stare for a moment longer, and then it hit him; he could see it deep in her eyes. It was neither. Nor was it blackmail. She could've gotten that without him, and they both knew it. No sir, it was revenge. Pure and simple revenge, he was certain of it. She'd been dealt an unfair blow and yet had managed to not only persevere, but to seize upon an opportunity. She'd compiled all of this evidence on her own, and, he surmised after further thought, without anyone else knowing about it, especially Crandell.

She'd clearly thought it out, and now that she had her royal flush, she intended to lay it down and use it against the man who'd treated her so unfairly. A man whom she'd come to vehemently despise and whom she would now extract her revenge upon in a way in which would hurt him most. He liked that about her. In fact, he liked it a lot, for in a subtle kind of way she reminded him of himself.

She was smart and resourceful, with a creative and calculating insight. And on top of that, she was very, very attractive. He imagined them together in Washington, then smiled wryly and cleared his throat. "Well, Miss Schubert," he drawled as he leaned toward her and extended his hands across the desk. "Let's see what you've got."

CHAPTER 38

———◆———

Robert McAlister couldn't have been happier to have received Foster's call. It was delightful news, but even so he urged a bit of caution. He knew how Crandell worked, and she could just be the bait for one of his traps. He asked if the woman could stay the night and meet again in the morning for breakfast. He wanted to meet her and hear her story, and to review the so-called information she had brought as well.

Early the next morning, the Judge and Foster met Suzanne in the restaurant of the Battle House Hotel. It was an opulent and quiet place set just off the lobby floor with good food and a great view of the river. Taking their seats at a table with a large window overlooking the water, they ordered their food then watched as a beautiful wooden cruiser with a clean white hull slowly made its way down the river. It was a comforting sight, and Foster smiled to himself knowing that Otis was on his way to help Willie.

Eating as they talked, the Judge listened as the young woman from Montgomery began to explain just how she'd come by all of her information. Reviewing the contents of her folder as she continued to speak, the aging adjudicator analyzed it like evidence in a courtroom and saw that it was not only detailed and organized, but also very very compelling.

Shaking his head as she finished, he sat for a moment in quiet contemplation. He'd always thought that Crandell was crooked, but had no idea as to the extent in which the man had really gone. He was appalled and angry, yet elated at the fact that his insight had been right and that they would now take him down. That they would drop him to his knees, and then in a long awaited ceremony, cut off his head. He was impressed to say the least, and with a contented sigh he closed the folder and looked back at the woman.

She was sharp and attractive, and on top of that, she could think on her own, a combination that would work well for Foster in Washington. But the game of politics was a nasty one and he knew it, and in a moment of caution, he caught her gaze and stared deep into her soft brown eyes. A piercing gaze that left little doubt as to what he was looking for as he tried to discern her true intentions. That tiny hint of deception or untruth that would betray and reveal her hidden agenda. It was a skill he'd developed from years on the bench and one he'd certainly mastered. But in them he saw none, only a young ambitious woman who'd been unduly wronged, and who was now seizing upon an opportunity and extracting her revenge. Certain of her intentions, he turned to Foster and nodded.

Solidifying their deal, the three toasted with a fresh round of coffee and began making their plans. The Judge insisted Suzanne move to Mobile as soon as possible to help prepare for the upcoming debate. They had less than a month and she would be needed as they poured through the evidence she'd compiled. They would put her up at the hotel until the election and pay her expenses.

He knew that Crandell was as devious and as crooked as they came, and that they had just three weeks to verify as quietly as possible all of the information and evidence she'd given them. To plan and to lay the groundwork that would ensnare the unsuspecting Senator in a tangled web of his own making. A web of lies and deceit, and of greed and corruption, that would prove how he'd used his position and betrayed the people for his own personal gain. They discussed and negotiated a number of items that she wanted, and even though she didn't get them all, there was one thing that was certain. That when Foster K. Siler was finally elected as Alabama's new Senator in November, in January Miss Suzanne Schubert would accompany him to Washington as his new personal assistant.

"Now as it turned out, it was that next Saturday, a week after Willie's birthday, that Foster sent me back down to see her again. I'd already been down an seen her twice that week but he couldn't make it that day so he sent me on

*down by myself once again. He said he had some sort of real important meetin
with the Judge an some lady that I'd never heard of before an couldn't go.*

*"Anyway, I think I ended up gettin there around mid mornin or so, an
after we got all-a her supplies unloaded an packed away, we set about workin
an started scrapin paint. Now Willie was workin real hard cause she had it
in her head that jus as soon as she was done with the house an it'd sold, she
was gonna move to Mobile an get her an education like she'd promised her
momma. But for some reason, somethin that mornin jus didn't seem right."*

"What-a-ya mean?" Jim asked.

*"Well," Otis continued. "Usually she was jus about as close as you could
get to be'n an endless chatterbox, but that mornin she was actually kind of
quiet, you know, like she really had somethin on her mind. You could tell jus
by the way she was actin, like somethin was really botherin an eatin on her.
At first I thought that she was jus mad at Foster cause he didn't come again,
but as it turned out, that wasn't the case at all."*

"So what was the problem?"

*"Well," Otis grinned. "It was right around noon when she up an disap-
peared. Which wasn't real unusual cause she still liked makin our lunches,
an then jus a short while later, she was callin my name to come an eat."*

"Mister Otis," Willie called to her friend just as she'd done for almost
a year. "Lunch timmme."

Dropping his wire brush, Otis quickly stepped down off of his
ladder and walked around the corner. It had been a long morning
and he was hungry, and just as soon as he took his seat across from
Willie, he picked up his sandwich and took a bite. She'd always taken
such pride in making their lunches and that day was no different,
and as he began to chew he watched as she picked up her sandwich
to take a bite but then suddenly stop and set it back down.

"Mister Otis," she began as if she were deep in thought. "Do... do
people ever call you a nigger?"

"A whaaat?" Otis mumbled with a mouthful of food.

"A nigger," she repeated in a serious yet inquisitive kind of way.
"You know?"

Staring with a surprised and confused expression pulling on his
face, Otis swallowed his food then stammered in search of an answer
to a question he couldn't believe he'd just been asked. For not one
white person that he'd ever known had ever asked such a thing. It

just wasn't done, especially from a young white girl. But Otis knew Willie for who and what she was and he answered with the truth.

"Sa… sometimes they does Miss Willie," he replied sadly. "Bu… but why do you wants ta know somethin like that?"

"Well, you remember this book that Foster gave me for my birthday, don't you?" She held it up.

"Oh, yes um," he nodded.

"Well, I know you ain't read it an all, but you see it's a story about this boy named Huckleberry Finn, an in it he helps this black man who was a run away slave. You know, that's a black person that's owned by a white person. Foster told me they use to do that a long time ago until they had this great big war an all the people from up north came down an fought against all the people in the south so they could free all a the black people. He said that it was called the Civil War, an that after it was over, they made it aganst the law for a white person to own a black person. Did you know that?" She finished but then continued on before he could answer. "He said that it wasn't right for one person to own another, an that under the eyes of God all men are made equal an that on the inside everyone's blood is red. Even black peoples," she added but then stopped and cocked her head with a curious gaze. "Is that true, is your blood really red too?"

"Oooh yes um," Otis assured.

"For real?" she asked, her tone still lingering with doubt. "Jus like mine?"

"Oh yes um," he instantly reaffirmed.

Content that what Foster had told her was true, Willie stared for just a second then continued on. "Anyways, this black man in the story was runnin away cause a this mean old lady was gonna sell him and in it everybody called him a nigger. I remember my stepdad use ta call people that when he was drunk, but I never knowed what it really meant until now. You know, that it was an ugly name for a black man. Then, after I got done the other day readin, I thought about it a whole lot an I decided that I really didn't like it. That it ain't a very nice word, an I was jus wonderin if anybody ever called you one, or if Foster ever called you one cause of you be'n black an all?"

Pausing in thought, Otis took a moment to reflect upon what Willie had just said, and of what it really meant. She was sincere and he knew it, for even though they lived in a world still divided by race, he was sitting across from a girl who was truly unfettered by the barriers of color or the attitudes of racial bigotry. He liked that about her and was proud to call her his friend.

"Ooh nooo Miss Willie," he assured her. "Mister Siler ain't never called me that, he always calls me Otis," he added, only to pause as he remembered back to the day that they'd named the boat. "Cept once he did call me a genius."

"A whaaat?" Willie scrunched her nose.

"So that's what she was all worried about?" Jim asked, somewhat surprised yet slightly amused. "Was if people called you the N word?"

"Yes sir," Otis drawled as he took another sip. "That, an the fact that she wanted me ta know that she didn't like it," he added with a chuckle. "An I mean not at all."

"Really?"

"Oooh heavens yes," he assured and then took a sip. "Anyway, jus as soon as I got done explainin to her what a genius was, we went back to talkin about why a lot of white people used that word when they was talkin or referrin ta black folks. See, you gotta remember, ol Willie had lived a pretty sheltered life up until she'd met Foster, you know, growin up out in the middle of nowhere, pickin cotton on some gods-forsaken sharecropper's plot. An ta be right truthful with ya, I'm not too sure if she even knew a black person before she got ta Mobile. Anyway, I don't think she knew what it really meant until she'd read that book, an after that, well, I guess that's when she decided that she didn't want nobody callin me that ever, specially Foster."

"Oh she did, did she?"

"Yes sir. See, Willie had developed this real motherly instinct about her, an if I'm not mistaken, I think that that might of been the day that she became my self-appointed guardian," he laughed. "Anyway, we finished our lunch an after we was done we jus sat there at that little picnic table on the deck an talked about that book. I'll tell ya, I can still remember how excited I got listenin to her while she told me all about Huck an his adventures down the Mississippi. At the time, that was the most amazin story I'd ever heard, an then when she was finished, she told me that as soon as my readin got a little better that she'd give it to me so I could read it too."

"An did you?" Jim asked.

"Oh yeah," Otis drawled as he fondly reflected back. "Many times. First by myself, an then to my wife an children. An then later on in the years, even to my grandchildren. In fact, I still have the very copy she gave me.

"Anyway, after she finished, we went back to work scrapin paint. Or at least we tried. See, the both of us was already real tired of do'n that an it didn't take but jus the mention of fishin for us to drop our tools an head on down to the pier. Now ol Willie had become quite the little angler by then, but still the fishin wasn't nothin like it was up river so we jus kind of passed the afternoon talkin an be'n lazy. We both knew that Foster wouldn't care if we took some time off, an then around three or so I finally packed up an headed back on home.

"I can still remember leavin her standin on the pier wavin goodbye an then thinkin as I drove out across the bay of all the things that she'd said to me that day. Of how she wanted to know if my blood was red like hers, an of how she'd thought that it jus wasn't right for one person to look down upon another, or treat em bad jus because the color of his skin was different than theirs... orrr to call them names either.

"Yes sirrr," he smiled. "I guess that book must of really opened up her eyes in a way that I never could've imagined cause here it was 1931 an here was this little white girl all worried about what someone was gonna call a poor ol uneducated black man. Now back then, that was really somethin. An hell, to be right truthful with ya, in the eyes of most people, she wasn't considered much more than white trash herself. You know, be'n a sharecropper an all. Anyway, I finally made it back home an for the rest of that weekend, all I could do was think of what Willie had told me."

———◆———

By Wednesday of that week Suzanne had arrived back in Mobile on the afternoon train. It had taken her less than three days to pack everything she owned into the confines of five large suitcases and return. She'd told everyone at work of her ailing mother and how she urgently needed to leave, and as she stepped from train at the Mobile station, she waved with an exuberant smile at Foster and Otis waiting to greet her.

"So is that the lady that's gonna help you boss?" Otis asked with a glance to his boss and then back to the lady waving two cars down.

"Sure is," Foster replied as he waved back. "Come on," he added as he headed toward her and slowly made his way through the crowd of exiting passengers.

"Suzanne, welcome back," he greeted as he took her hand. "I trust you had a pleasant journey?"

"Oh my yes," she drawled. "I just love trains, and everything was just fine."

"And the people at your office? They?" He raised his eyebrows.

"Not a thing," she said with a devious twinkle to her eyes. "They all think I left to go back home and take care of my mother. She is quite ill, you know."

Smiling back, Foster just stared for a moment then turned and placed his hand on the small of her back. "Good, that's good," he chuckled along with a gentle nudge. "I like that. Now, let's see if we can't get your luggage and get you to the hotel so you can rest. We have a wonderful room on the top floor that's waiting just for you."

"Now that was the very first time that I met Miss Suzanne Schubert an jus as soon as I saw her steppin onto the platform an then saw the way she was lookin at Foster after they'd greeted each other, I started to get a real sneakin suspicion that that little gal was gonna be do'n a whole lot more than jus helpin him with his campaign."

"Ooooh," Jim raised his eyebrows. "An why's that?"

"Well, I may have been black, but I sure as hell wasn't blind," he chuckled. "An shiiit... I already knew how ol Foster was." They both laughed. "Anyway, we made our way to the baggage car an got all her luggage, an jus as soon as we got it all loaded, we headed to the hotel. Foster had a real nice room on the top floor, an jus as soon as we got there the two of them went up an left me an one of the porters to bring up all of the luggage."

Unlocking the door, Foster pushed it open then stepped aside and allowed Suzanne to enter first. Following on her heels while she took in the room, he quickly made his way past her to the over-sized window and drew the curtains. "Well, what-a-ya think?" he asked as she approached.

"Oh my," she gasped as she gazed out across the river and watched as a lone large freighter slowly made its way toward the bay. "It's just lovely," she turned back and stared. "But this is so much more than I, I..." her voice trailed off.

"Than you expected?" he finished.

"Yes," she answered. "I just don't know what to say or, or how to thank you."

"Well, you don't have to say anything, or for that matter, thank me either. It is I who should be thanking you. You're the one who found the dirt on Crandell and then put this together."

"Yes, I guess I did, didn't Iiii," she smiled and then stared in sort of a dreamy haze. Her mind whirling with thoughts of what life would be like with him in Washington. "And now, here I am."

"Yes, here you are," Foster said as he stepped toward her and took her hands. Lifting them up he brought them together with a gentle squeeze and stared deep into her eyes. He wanted to tell her a number of things but before he could utter another word, Otis and the porter broke their moment with a knock on the door.

———◆———

By nine the next morning, Foster and his unlikely ally were already preparing for the debate. Suzanne was meticulous, and had organized everything in a clear and concise manner, a methodical progression of each and every crooked deal that Crandell had made. Foster was amazed as to the extent at which the man had gone, and as their morning slowly passed, and more and more of what he'd done and to whom he'd done it to came into light, he smiled with an ever-growing fervor.

Working tirelessly into the afternoon, they reviewed and studied, then checked and verified every single deal. They tied up the phone for hours and even enlisted the help of Vicki and Dawn. Foster was brilliant and a master at leading witnesses into answering questions without being asked, and now they would use this information to formulate his questions. Questions that he would use in the debate to get their answers on record as to the failures of the new state docks.

They worked closely together for days on end, and with each successive week that passed, Suzanne's attraction toward Foster seemed to grow. Even after she'd met Melinda. She hadn't planned on it, but it did. She knew it was wrong, and had even tried to reason with her conscience, arguing with herself over how he was a married man, but it wasn't listening. Foster was smart and handsome, and everything that she'd ever looked for in a man. She was falling for him, and the longer they worked together, the stronger her feelings became.

She was amazed at how easily he could manipulate a conversation, changing a question into an answer or an answer into a question whenever he wanted. She wondered if it was his mind or his rugged good looks that had attracted her. That'd caused her to feel like she'd never felt before. They dueled and flirted whenever they were alone, and at the end of the day, when she had finally laid her head to sleep, she would dream of a life with him in Washington as his assistant and then hopefully, as something much, much more.

Befriended by an ever-gracious Melinda, she often ate dinner at their house but kept her feelings for Foster repressed and hidden deep inside. Melinda suspected nothing and even insisted that she join them on Sundays for dinner at her parents, where Foster and the Judge would spar in a mock debate. They had fun while Foster honed his skills and the time finally came.

———◆———

The debate was a draw as far as the press was concerned, but to Foster and the Judge and Suzanne it went just as they'd planned. Foster was in his element, and with every opportunity, he took the overly confident and unsuspecting Senator down the road of entrapment. Twisting his answers back into questions, he easily achieved his objective as the man defended and professed what his position and roll had been in the building of the new state docks. The trap had been sprung and Crandell didn't even know it. It was a mistake he would realize all too late, and one he would quickly regret as the papers began to call.

It took less than a week after the debate before some of the top reporters at Harkin Publishing began receiving information as to Crandell's corruption. Of the deals he'd orchestrated and what he'd done to the people of his own state. Fed anonymously, yet in a meticulous and calculated manner, they quickly picked up on the stories and began to investigate. Digging relentlessly, they tore into the man's past, and as they did, the world around him began to unravel and implode in a manner and speed in which he never could've imagined.

Attacking like sharks with more and more joining in, the news soon turned into a feeding frenzy with almost every reporter in the state vying to uncover the worst of his transgressions. It was of the likes and magnitude of which nobody had ever seen before. The people had been betrayed, and now they were mad. They wanted answers. The reporters tore at the man's reputation until the waters had turned red with the blood of his deception and the voters had turned in disgust.

They watched as he tried first to dodge the accusations, and then to defend himself. But he failed at both, and soon he was sinking in the very pool of quicksand he'd made for others. Seizing upon the opportunity, the Judge and Foster used every chance they could to give speeches and interviews, sermons on the ethical qualities of how a U. S. Senator was to represent all of the people and not just himself or the interest of big businesses.

They watched as Crandell's popularity disappeared almost overnight, then screamed at the top of their lungs for the people of Alabama to demand justice. The Senate Ethic's Committee immediately called for an investigation then later on for his resignation. The wheels of his demise were rolling but by the time of the election it'd become a moot point, for the voters of the state had overwhelmingly ruled on his fate.

The victory was a landslide, and the newspapers ran with the results before all of the votes had even been counted. The press seemed to love Foster and showered him with praise, citing many of his qualities and his feverish desire to return those desperately needed jobs back to the state. Back to the people who needed them now more than ever.

It had been a long hard race, but in the end it was the simple truth that'd prevailed. Stripped of his position and political power, Harlen Crandell's twelve-year reign in the United States Senate was finally over. Disgraced over some of the most blatant and corrupt charges to have ever been brought against a sitting Senator, he quickly disappeared from the public light.

CHAPTER 39

———•———

THE VICTORY CELEBRATION AT THE McAlister's home had been slated for two, but by twelve thirty when Foster, Melinda and Suzanne had arrived, there were already a hundred cars parked throughout the grounds and more were coming. The Judge had always said that if Foster won, that they'd celebrate in a grand style, and now here they were. It seemed as if he'd invited everyone he knew, and every-one who had been invited, was coming.

There was the Mayor, along with many other politicians and businessmen from around the state who'd worked behind the scenes and had donated so graciously to his campaign. And then the press and campaign staff who'd worked so long and hard over the months, along with many of their friends and relatives who'd supported him from the start. Even the Governor and his wife had come to give a rousing and congratulatory speech.

It was a beautiful sunny afternoon with bright blue skies and puffy white clouds. The atmosphere was festive and alive and excit-ing, and people were everywhere. The Judge had butchered two of his finest cattle just for the occasion, and as the three stepped from the car, they all drew into smiles as the wafting aroma of beef roast-ing over an open pit of hardwood, drifted from behind the house on the warm gentle breeze.

Looking around as they made their way to the house, they could see a large banner that had been stretched from the corner of the porch to a tree. It read 'Congratulations Senator Siler' and hung over the walkway where all who were arriving were being directed to by one of the many servants. A parade of people migrating toward the back of the house. A few moments later, and after a couple of congratulatory handshakes, Foster and the girls climbed the steps to the porch and were met at the door by Monique and the Judge.

A round of hugs and kisses came first, but as soon as that was over, the Judge instructed Monique to take the girls and help Mrs. McAlister. He told Melinda he wanted to talk to Foster for a moment in private, and that they would join them out back with everyone else when they were finished.

"Come on Foster," the Judge said as he placed his hand on Foster's shoulder and then turned toward his library. "I know it's a little early, but I thought since we're celebrating your victory that we'd have a short drink and talk for a bit before we joined the party. What-a-ya say?"

"Sounds great, sir," Foster agreed. "I could use a drink actually."

Stepping through the double doors, the two men headed straight to the liquor hutch, poured them-selves a couple of scotches and then made their way to the two large chairs by the windows. Gazing outside as he took his seat, Foster smiled at what seemed to be an endless procession of people and cars. He'd won, and they were coming to see him, all of them. He was their Senator now, and he reveled at the fact that he would soon be on his way to Washington as their representative. A second later, he turned as the Judge approached and then stopped by his chair.

"Well son," the man beamed as he held up his glass and then tossed the front page of the weekend paper onto Foster's lap. "Congratulations, you're on your way to Washington."

"Thank you sir," Foster replied with a glance at the headlines and then to the Judge as he raised his glass.

Clinking their heavy tumblers together, the two men took their respective sips. Then with a smile and a twinkle to his eyes, the Judge continued on in what could only be described as a colorful yet accurate summation of the institution and circle of men that Foster would soon be joining.

"Yes sirrrr," he began with a robust yet humored tone. "You are now a member of one the most corrupt organizations in the world, and that my son is the United States Senate. Which, if you are not aware of already," he continued on with a finger pointed grin. "Is nothing more than a cesspool of thieves, liars and whores, who as individuals, not all mind you but many, will do anything to seek re-election and enhance their lives all at the expense of the people of this great country."

"Well sir," Foster chuckled and then replied with his own brand of wit. "I didn't realize that I'd just joined such an exclusive club."

"Exclusive?" The Judge laughed. "Shiiiit, who said anything about being exclusive," he retorted and laughed again. "Haven't you ever heard of the House of Representatives? You know Congress?" He raised his eyebrows. "Hell, they're just as bad if not worse. Yes sir, that whole bunch up there in Washington is without a doubt the crookedest dirtiest lot of self-serving sons-of-bitches I've ever had the pleasure of meeting. Trust me when I tell ya, there is always someone cooking something up behind somebody's closed doors. Remember that and watch you're back, ya hear."

"Yes sir, that I will."

"Now, there's something else that I wanna talk to you about," he continued as he finally took his seat. "And this comes from all that Crandell nonsense we just went through. When you get to Washington, you're going to get a lot of so-called business deals or opportunities shall we say, that will seem to of just come your way. Now, most often the people that bring you these deals are going to want something in return, which is usually your vote on some bill in one way or another.

"Now I'm not saying that you can't take advantage of some of them here and there, but don't ever do it at the expense of the people. Don't ever become the very thing you just tried so hard to beat." He paused and took a sip then regained Foster's eyes. "I want you to promise me that okay. Don't ever betray the people that put you into office."

Looking at the Judge, Foster stared for just a second then shifted his gaze outside and watched as the very people the man was speaking of walked beneath the banner with his name. Reflecting on what he'd just said, it was the sight of the people that truly brought his words to heart and in a flash he thought of everything that Crandell had done. Of how he'd betrayed the people with all of his crooked deals and destroyed their faith. And then he thought of the core values and principles that he and the Judge both shared, and of how he would rather die than disappoint this man he respected above all others. A second later, he returned his eyes back to the Judge. "I won't sir," he vowed with a heartfelt assurance and a steady gaze. "I promise. Ever."

Gaining an instant smile, the Judge stared for just a second then relaxed his demeanor and sat back in his chair. "Good, I'm glad to hear that cause we've already got too many of them son-of-a-bitches up there that seemed to have forgotten who they work for. Now, there's one more thing and this is important," he added with a nonchalant drawl as he reached across the table and pulled two fresh cigars from the box between them. "And you probably ought to do this just as soon as you can, and most definitely before you get sworn in in January."

"And what's that sir?"

"Go to Washington, before Congress takes its Christmas recess," he paused then struck his match.

"Washington, why's that sir?" Foster asked as he bent to the flame and pulled on his cigar.

"Well, even though you're only a Freshman Senator and most of the boys up on the hill think that you should be seen and not heard, you still need to learn and understand the rules of protocol that they work by. You know, all that parliamentarian crap that they like to use on the floor. Especially if you're going to challenge someone, you know, just like you would in a courtroom. It's essential ya hear, that is unless you want your head handed to you on a silver platter in front of everybody in the chamber." He laughed as he brought the lingering flame to his own cigar.

"Yes sir, I see what you're saying," Foster answered and exhaled his smoke high into the air. "But all the way to Washington just to learn protocol? Isn't there some sort of rulebook or something?"

"Yeah yeah, there's a rulebook all right, but forget that goddamn thing," he scoffed with a grin then snuffed the match and discarded it into the ashtray. "I've got something that's a whole lot better than that, and that's why I want you to go." He tilted his head toward the ceiling and exhaled a heavy plume of smoke.

"Oh really," Foster raised his eyebrows. "And what's that?"

"A tutor," the Judge replied simply.

"A tutor?" Foster repeated.

"Yep, a tutor," the Judge smiled. "See, there's a Senator up in Missouri that I know, a good friend actually, who is probably one of the smartest people in the whole Senate with regards to all of their silly rules and regulations. Hell, she has to be, being the only woman in a room full of men," he chuckled at the thought then pulled on his cigar and shook his head. "You know how they like to do things. So I want you to get a hold of her just as soon as you get to Washington."

"Yes sir, buuu... but did you just say woman?" He cocked his head.

"That's right," the Judge smiled again. "A woman. You surprised?"

"Well," Foster stared with a surprised expression. "Yesss... yes I am actually. See, I thought that, well, I guess I was just under the impression that the Senate was all men."

"It was," the Judge quipped. "Or at least it was until the Governor of Missouri appointed her."

"Appointed her?"

"Yep," he grinned. "See, her husband use to be one of the Senators from there, but he died while he still had two years left in office. He was a good man and was actually one of the leading voices on the floor that helped push the confirmation of my federal judgeship through years ago. Anyway, under the law, whenever there's a vacancy by a Senator for whatever reason, the Governor of that state can then appoint whoever he chooses to fill that position until the next election. And that's exactly what happened, right after the funeral. The Governor, who was a good friend of theirs, went and appointed her to her husband's position."

"Wow, the first woman Senator?"

"Well, not exactly, that privilege belongs to some eighty seven year old gal over in Georgia who served for just one day. And that was actually some years back. But she does hold the distinction of being the first woman to go on after her term had expired and win re-election all by herself. The first woman to become a United States Senator by a vote of the people, now that was something.

"Anyway, when she first went to Washington after she was appointed I guess it wasn't too awfully bad. There were a few ruffled feathers here and there, but on the whole I think everyone was pretty civil and respectful cause a lot-a those boys liked her husband. They let a lot of things slide when she was on the floor, but when she decided she was gonna run for re-election and then actually won.

Well, that's when a lot of those boys that'd been bitten their tongues and being so cordial for so long all of a sudden changed their tune."

"Really, why was that?"

"Well, I guess they just didn't want a woman to be in what they considered an all male club, and that's when they got it in their heads that they were gonna run her out of town."

"Really?" Foster narrowed his eyes.

"Oh yeaaah. Remember what I just told you about that whole lot being nothing but a cesspool?"

"Yes sir," he nodded and grinned.

"Well son," the Judge drawled with a growing smile. "That's politics in Washington. Now most if not all of it came from the opposite party, you know, the mud slinging and all. It seemed as if all of a sudden, after they'd gone back into session, that she couldn't do nothing right on the floor without one of those arrogant asses jumping all over her. It was as if she'd returned to the lion's den, but instead of being welcomed back, they attacked her. I think that there might of been about twenty of em or so that'd ganged up and did their damnedest to make her quit. But she didn't; she hung in there until they took their summer recess and that's when she called me."

"Called you, why?"

"Well one, we were good friends and she trusted me, and two, she wanted someone who was on the outside of the Senate yet still knew enough about how they worked on the inside to help and advise her, and that was me. Anyway, if I remember right, I think it was back in the summer of 26 when she came down and stayed with me and Martha, and that's when I helped her. You know, to interpret their rules and make sense of the way they liked to do things so to speak. After all," he raised his eyebrows and grinned. "I am a Federal Judge."

"Aaah yes, I see your point," Foster nodded as if he'd just been enlightened. "Who better than a Federal Judge to interpret the rule of law for you."

"Exactly," the Judge emphasized as he pulled on his cigar. "And that's just what she wanted too. She wanted to know exactly what each and every one of them meant and how they where used so those pompous jackasses back in Washington couldn't trip her up anymore. And boy let me tell you... was she ever determined.

"Anyway, we worked and studied for about a month or so I think it was, you know, practicing and rehearsing just like you would with a witness before a trial. Going over each and every one of those rules again and again until she knew em inside and out and was able to recite just about all of em by heart. Yes sir," he chuckled and shook his head. "By the time she left and went back to Washington, she knew those rules better-n a preacher's favorite Sunday sermon.

"So," he then added with a gesture from his cigar hand. "When it comes to protocol, or as those boys in the Senate like to call it, 'their parliamentarian procedures,' she really knows what she's talking about. And from everything I've heard that has come out of Washington over the last couple of years, she has no trouble at all barking at em like a barnyard dog when they get in her way.

"Yes sir," he continued with a lighthearted chuckle. "She's a feisty ol gal that's for sure, and she ain't afraid to mix it up with any of em, and so now they just pretty much leave her alone."

"Well sir, she sure sounds like someone I can learn a great deal from."

"Oooh that you can," the Judge assured. "And that's precisely why I want you to get a hold of her just as soon as you get to Washington. See, she has the experience now, where I don't."

"So she'll help me?"

"Absolutely, and hell, if you play your cards right, she might even get you a seat on a couple of the lower level committees. You know, to get your feet wet."

"Great," Foster beamed. "I can't wait to meet her. So tell me," he asked with a curious gaze. "Who is this lady? What's her name?"

Smiling to himself as if he were slowly pulling the name from the depths of his cerebral core, the Judge paused for a second then returned his gaze to Foster's. "Sellers," he answered with an obvious pride to his gravelly growl. "Senator Sellers. Adell. And when you get there," he added with an unusual yet genuine smile of affection. "You tell her that Robert McAlister said hello."

"Yes sir," Foster replied. "That I will."

"Good, now come on. You've got a whole lot a people waiting that wanna congratulate you."

For most of the people in attendance that day, it'd been weeks and weeks since they'd seen him yet even so everyone was there to celebrate his victory. Everyone who'd helped in some way or another and who'd been a part in his struggle to gain his seat. There were his friends and family, and the volunteers. There were business associates and colleagues, and as he and the Judge emerged from the rear of the house and his presence became known, the crowd of almost four hundred erupted into a rousing applause. They were thrilled to see the man they'd all voted for and were placing so much hope in. And after a short and gracious speech from the steps of the porch, profoundly thanking each and everyone who had come, the newly elected Senator descended into the crowd of well wishers with Melinda and Suzanne at his sides.

Greeting the people in a whirlwind of congratulatory handshakes and brief conversations, the three slowly made their way through the crowd. Melinda and Suzanne were both brilliant in helping Foster from the pitfalls of memory loss as they did, whispering the names of people he could not recall as they would approach, ensuring that each and every person they talked with felt a warm and personal connection to the man they'd voted for.

Forty-five minutes later, the trio finally returned to their tables and joined the Governor and the rest of their family. It was a joyous occasion with a jubilant crowd, the waiters served the food, the music played and the speeches were made. Some were brief and some were long, but each and everyone that was made were based on the hope of a brighter and better future. The celebration continued, but as the afternoon sun began to drop and the crowds began to disperse, the Judge and Foster escaped back into the quiet of the library.

"Well son, you belong to the people now. So what-a-you think?" the judge asked as he handed a tumbler to Foster. "Just how was your first day of public life?"

Taking the glass as he took his seat, Foster smiled then yawned. "Well sir, it was great, but to be honest with you, it was tiring, very tiring."

"Yes, I can see that," the Judge grinned as if he already knew then held up his glass. "It shows; you look tired. Hell, actually you look like shit." They both laughed and then sipped their drinks.

"Yes sir, and just between me and you, I kind of feel that way too." They laughed again.

"Well, you've got every right to be," the Judge replied. "That campaign was a real meat-grinder and would of torn the hell out of anybody. Shit son, I'm not sure if you really realize it, but you just did twelve rounds with a real heavyweight. And that was something a lot of people said you couldn't do. But damned if you didn't... and ya whipped him too. Yes sirrrr," he grinned great big. "It might of taken you awhile, but in the end you knocked his arrogant ass right out and I'm proud of you. Damn proud, and I want you to know that," he added then turned and stepped to the windows.

"Anyway, all that's over and behind us now so it's time to relax," he continued as he took another sip and stared out at the cars, his eyes fixed into a steady gaze as if he were pondering some great question. "In fact," he turned back. "I think it's time that you took a little break. You know, took some time off and got some rest before you go to Washington. Maybe go somewhere and get away for awhile," he finished and took another sip then continued on with an elevated zeal. "Hell, I know, why don't you go up to that little huntin cabin you said you got from the Davenports. You know, and hide out for a few days... do some huntin and fishin. Clear your head and relax. Shit, after what you've just been through, you deserve it. In fact, you ought-a just take the whole week off cause starting in January," he beamed proudly. "You've got a brand new job. Oh," he quickly added as if he'd forgotten something. "You do still have that, don't you?"

"The cabin?" Foster queried.

"Yeah."

"Oh, yes sir."

"And you still have that negro fellow with you too, don't you? You know, the one Melinda said you got with the boat?"

"You mean Otis? Oh, yes sir."

"Good, well then take him with you so you're not all alone. You know, just for safety's sake and all. I'll feel a whole lot better knowing that you're up there with someone else."

"Yes sir, that sounds great. I tell ya, I really could use a break about now," Foster admitted then paused and stared into his glass as if he were trying to collect his thoughts. As if his mind had suddenly diverted toward something else. To something he had been thinking of for quite some time. "But sir," he began as he looked back up and regained the Judges eyes. "There's something I'd like you to know."

"What's that son?"

"Well, it's about my new job actually. See, I've been thinking, and it's just occurred to me that I've never really had a chance to thank you for everything you've done."

"What-a-ya mean?" he asked warmly.

"Well, I know how hard you worked behind the scenes and I just want you to know how much I appreciate it, and that I couldn't have done any of this without you're help and support. In fact, I owe it all to you really, and I... well, I just wanted you to know that and to thank you."

"Ah nonsense," the Judge quickly asserted with a hearty rejection of what he knew was the truth. "Shit, all I did was knock on a few doors and make a few phone calls then sit back and watch. Hell son, it was you. You're the one who did it," he insisted. "Well, you and that little gal from Montgomery who brought you that folder full of goodies," he grinned and shook his head. "And damn lucky for us that she did or this election could of turned out a whole lot different than what it did, you know what I mean? Shit, we could both be sitting here sulking instead of celebrating." They both laughed.

"Yes sir, she did help, didn't she."

"Yes she did," the Judge agreed with a smile still pulling at his lips. "And I watched her today, working that crowd for you. She's good, really good, and she'll be a tremendous asset to you in Washington. And speaking of Washington," he quickly added. "There's something else that I need to talk to you about. Something I've noticed, that's kind of been on my mind for awhile."

"And what's that sir," Foster asked.

"Well, it's about Suzanne," he replied in a concerned voice.

"Suzanne?" Foster repeated. "Has she done something wrong?"

"Well no, not exactly. Or at least not yet," the Judge drawled with a heavy sigh. "And hell, who knows," he waved his hand as if it were no big deal. "It may be nothing more than these old eyes playing tricks on me, but I've seen the way she looks at you sometimes. You know, when she thinks no one else is looking. And I can tell you this," he paused and stared with a piercing gaze. "I know what that look means."

Caught somewhat off guard by the Judge's revelation, Foster feigned complete surprise but kept his composure and continued to listen. He wanted to refute the man's assessment but didn't dare for he knew that there was very little that made it past the eyes of Robert McAlister. The man was right, and Suzanne Schubert's lingering looks and mannerisms, however subtle they may have been, had definitely caught his attention. But the Judge was no saint by any sense of the word and Foster knew it, and as the man began to dwell into the complex issues of what the social and political life in Washington was like, he listened. He listened to the Judge's concerns and then to the consequences of what a scandal or an embarrassment could bring to the family by such reckless behavior.

He heeded his advice and warnings, then smiled wryly as the man continued on and explained how men of wealth and power were privileged and entitled to certain things that others were not. To certain pleasures that were theirs for the taking. Discreet pleasures, that befitted their positions and fulfilled their needs, but that were to be kept hushed and hidden behind closed doors, where they were to remain in secret and never spoken of. They talked at length, and by the time they'd finally finished and were ready to leave, the crowds were gone and the sun was on the horizon.

By the time Foster and Melinda had made it home, they were running on fumes and wanted nothing more than to sleep. Their year long campaign that had culminated into the day's events, had finally caught up with them and taken its toll. From beginning to end, they had worked without a break, but now it was over and behind them. The election was over and he'd won, and as Foster laid his head on his pillow and closed his eyes he began to think of how his life had changed. Of how less than a year ago he was just another lawyer trying to carve out a living in the midst of an economy that'd gone so horribly wrong. And now here he was, a United States Senator on his way to Washington.

He thought of all the things that he and the Judge had talked about that afternoon, and of the expectations that were now on his shoulders. He thought of what life would be like in Washington, the big city with all of its people and lights, the energy and politics... and then Suzanne. He opened his eyes for a fleeting moment and gazed at Melinda already asleep, then closed them with a heavy sigh and rolled to his back. He was exhausted, yet sleep eluded him. He listened to the sound of his wife's steady breathing, and then to the clock on the wall as the minutes slowly ticked by. He rolled to his side in an effort to shut down his mind, but it continued to drift until the haunting vision of the beautiful young girl waiting for him on the other side of the bay suddenly appeared.

It had been weeks since he'd seen her and it was only through Otis that he knew of her status and well-being. He thought of the year that'd passed, that they'd spent together and smiled. He liked and cared for her immensely, but even so, he knew now that it was truly over and that he could no longer keep her. He was a Senator now, and would soon be on his way to Washington. But how would he tell her, and most importantly, what would he do with her? He exhaled a long and worried breath, then thought of the conversation he'd had at the party with his friend Tom Portman. Yes, that was it.... but would it work after their incredible loss?

CHAPTER 40

———◆———

"Sooo," Jim drawled as he pulled two more beers from the cooler. "That ol son-of-bitch actually became a Senator didn't he?"

"Oooh yeaah... he became a Senator all right," Otis replied with a chuckle as he reached for one of the cans. "An I'll tell ya somethin else too," he quickly added, as he looked first at the can and then back to Jim.

"What's that?" Jim replied as if he were waiting for the rest of his story.

"That if you don't stop pullin them beers out-a the cooler like that, we're gonna end up gettin drunk an then we ain't gonna get nothin done."

Chuckling together, the two men reflected upon what they knew was the truth, but even so, and with an almost simultaneous precision, they popped their tops and tipped their cans.

"Oh well," Jim surmised after a quick but sizeable gulp. "That don't matter none cause the way I see it, we've already done enough work for one day. Heck, just look, we got the boat all set an all the hardware an lights off on the outside, an hell," he sighed then looked around. "We even got half the insides here taken apart. So see, it ain't gonna hurt none to take a little break an drink a few beers. Besides, you gotta finish this damn story you've been tellin.

"Sooo," he grinned. "Tell me. What'd he do with poor ol Willie? He didn't jus dump her an leave her in Mobile did he?" He probed with a disdainful look then instantly continued before Otis could answer. "Oh... an what about you?" He raised his eyebrows. "What happened to you? You didn't lose your job did you?"

"Well," Otis drawled as he slowly dropped back into his story. "As it turned out, nooo I didn't. At first I thought that maybe I had cause I knew that he was gonna be go'n to Washinton real soon. An I knew that when he did that he sure as hell didn't need no boat, an if he didn't need no boat he *sure as hell didn't need me either. So to tell ya the truth, I actually started ta get pretty worried, an that's when I started thinkin that it was all over for me an that it was probably jus a matter of time before he let me go an sent me on my way. But as it turned out, that wasn't the case at all, no sir."*

"Really?" Jim looked on curiously. "Why's that?"

"Well, I guess it all boiled down to the simple fact that over the course of that year that we'd been go'n back an forth to see Willie, ol Foster had gotten to where he really enjoyed that boatin stuff as he used to call it. An so, as it turned out, he ended up keepin both the boat an me. Besides, he never did learn to drive this thing right. Hell, I can still remember the time he took it out by himself once an how he damn near tore the whole bow off when he brought it back an tried to dock it. I'll tell ya, he really did a number on it, but I got it all fixed an after that, well, he never did take it out again."

"He really screwed it up, huh?"

"Oh yeah," Otis laughed. "Hell, we had to pull it out-a the water an everything. Took me damn near two months to fix it," he laughed again. "Anyway, an even though my job did change a little after the election, an I started do'n a whole lot of other things for him, one of the things that did stay the same was me takin care of this ol boat an his little house up river. Every week, whether we used her or not, I'd go down to the marina an--."

"But wai wai waaait," Jim interrupted and narrowed his eyes. "What about Willie, what'd he do with her?"

"Well," Otis began with a heavy sigh. "That was a whole different story. An a pretty sad one too, cause I kind-a knew that as far as ol Foster was concerned, it was finally over for em. That he'd be go'n to Washinton pretty soon an that when he did, he wouldn't be able to take care of her no more. That he'd be forced to do somethin with her. An even though he really liked her, an I really believe he did, he wasn't about to jeopardize his marriage or his brand new career as a Senator for some sixteen-year-old girl. No sir, that was somethin that jus wasn't go'n to happen.

"Now of course Willie didn't know all this yet, but I sure did. I knew what he was all about. I knew that all of his promises wouldn't mean a thing when the time came, an that he'd jus discard her like some used up ol mop. But the one thing that I didn't know, an that really bothered me the most, was jus how or when he was gonna tell her, an most importantly, jus what he was gonna do with her when he did. Now that really worried me, an it worried me a lot, cause I really liked Willie an I didn't wanna see her get hurt. But I'll tell ya, that sure didn't happen."

"*So he did dump her, didn't he?*" *Jim rolled his eyes in disgust.*

"*Oh yeah,*" *Otis drawled with another sigh.* "*He dumped her all right, although it didn't quite happen like I thought it would. You know, the how or the when an where.*"

"*It didn't?*"

"*Oh no. See, as best I can recall, I think it was right after they'd had that great big celebration out at the McAlisters that him an I went back across the bay an saw her. It was a Monday, which really surprised me cause that was suppose to be my day off, but I'll be damned if he didn't drive all the way across town that mornin jus to get me.*"

"*So the two of you went an saw her?*"

"*Oh yeah,*" *Otis nodded.* "*Now although we didn't get away until later that afternoon, you know, until we'd gotten all of our food an ice loaded, but yeah, we went an saw her. In fact, we ended up spendin about three or four days with her. Had a hell of a time too, eatin an fishin.*"

"*So is that when he finally told her?*" *Jim probed again.*

"*Actually,*" *Otis shook his head.* "*No, it wasn't. At first I thought that maybe he would, you know, that maybe he'd at least tell her somethin. That he was leavin an wouldn't be able to take care of her anymore or somethin, but as it turned out, he never said a word to her. He jus led her on about how good of a job she was do'n on the house an how he really thought that he had someone who was gonna buy it. An that jus as soon as they did he was gonna move her back to Mobile where she could go to school an get an education. Jus like she'd promised her momma.*"

"*Now when he told her that an she realized she was finally gonna be movin back to town, she got all excited. But when she told me, I really didn't know what to think an was jus about as confused as confused could get, cause here he was about ready ta leave an go ta Washinton, an yet at the same time he was tellin poor ol Willie how he was gonna move her back to Mobile.*"

"*Now to me, an as hard as I tried to figure it all out, that jus didn't make sense. But ol Foster was real smart, an if I'd learned anything from workin an be'n around him over the course of that first year, it was that if he was tellin her that, I knew that he already had somethin else up his sleeve. That secretly, he knew exactly what he was gonna do with her, an that when he did, he was gonna break her heart into a million pieces.*"

"*An you still didn't tell her?*"

"*Oooh nooo,*" *Otis shook his head again.* "*I'll tell ya I felt real bad about it too, you know, knowin how he was do'n her like he was do'n. Lyin an toyin* with her an then leadin her on an given her hope when there really wasn't none. But ya know what," he added as if he were now trying to justify his actions of the past. "When I look back an think about it, it was the beginnin of the depression, an how ever much I really did or didn't care for how he was treatin her, Willie was happy an cared for, an was without a doubt livin life a whole lot better than what she ever had before. In fact, I don't believe that I've ever seen a girl so in love with someone as much as she was with Foster. Yes sir, she loved that man more than you could ever imagine, an I don't mean jus puppy love either.

"See, he'd come into her life at a point an time when she'd needed someone the most. She'd jus lost her mother an was all alone an heartbroken when he found her an scooped her up. Then in his slick lawyerin ways he worked on her until he'd managed to turn her life completely around, until he'd become everything to her. He was her friend an father figure an teacher, an then later on, her lover. He gave her hope an made her smile, but still that didn't make what he was do'n to her right an the longer it went on, the more an more I disliked it."

"So what happened? I mean, what'd he end up do'n?"

"Well," Otis replied. "Past him tellin her that he thought he had someone who was finally gonna buy the house an that jus as soon as it sold he was gonna move her back to town... nothin."

"Nothin?" Jim blurted. "You gotta be kiddin? All of that an he never told that poor little gal the truth? About anything?" His voice rose along with his sense of disbelief. "Tha... that he was married an, an that he was a Senator... an was gonna be go'n to Washington."

"Oh hell nooo," Otis replied as if it were a silly question. "See, an even though I didn't know it at the time, that whole trip was nothin more than for him to enjoy her one last time before he broke off their affair."

"Whaaat?" Jim blurted again. "Just so he could enjoy her one last time? Are you serious? Jesssus Chrissst, what a snake! But what the hell," he went on with an incensed breath and in what was a clear an obvious disdain for the man's profession. "He was a lawyer right?"

"Ooh yeaaah," Otis nodded. "He was a lawyer all right... an then," he added with his own dry humor. "He became a Senator." They both laughed.

"Anyway, if I remember right, I think it'd been close to several weeks since the two of em had seen each other, so to be right truthful with ya, I didn't see a whole hell of a lot of em if ya know what I mean. Willie had really missed *him, an I think if they weren't up in that little cabin rollin around between the sheets, ol Foster was sleepin cause he was jus about as worn out as you could get from all that campaignin he'd done. I'll tell ya, an this is somethin that a lot of people didn't realized, but that man had worked real hard to win that election an by the time it was all over, it really showed. In fact, I had actually worried about him at times, so to me, if he wanted to sleep all day, well, that was jus fine cause as far as I was concerned, he deserved it.*

"Then after about the third or forth day, an I ain't really sure which anymore, an after I'd caught what fish I could catch an the two of them had finally gotten their fill of each other, we packed up one bright sunny mornin an left. Jus like that."

"Really?" Jim quizzed.

"Yep," Otis reiterated. "Heck, I can still remember ol Foster standin on the pier with Willie while we got ready to leave. We had everything all loaded an I'd already started the boat an had jus stepped back out to untie it when I over heard em talkin an then him tellin her how he had to go away on business again. Now at first she looked kind of sad an all, but that seemed to change pretty quick when he assured her that it was jus for a little bit, an that jus as soon as he got back he'd come an see her again. An that hopefully he'd have good news about the house an then take her back to Mobile so she could go to school like she wanted.

"Now by then Willie was smilin again, but I hnew he was lyin, an even though I still hadn't figured out jus how or what he was gonna do with her, I knew that he was still lyin. Lyin jus like he always did... all the way up to the very moment we left her standin on the pier that mornin."

"Well ya know why that was don't ya," Jim retorted with an obvious cynicism then answered before Otis could even open his mouth. "It's cause he was practicin."

"Practicin?" Otis repeated and cocked his head. "Practicin for what?"

"For be'n a Senator," Jim smirked as if he should've known. "Shiit, that's all them sons-a-bitches do isn-it?" They both laughed again.

"Anyway," Otis continued on. "I finally got the lines all undone an had jus stepped inside an was gettin ready to pull away when I thought that I'd better check an make sure ol Foster had gotten onboard. I remember I stepped to the doorway an poked my head back out an was jus about ready to holler when I saw him an Willie kissin."

"Now in the whole year that he'd been seein her I'd never seen him do that before, you know, on the pier like that. Oh sure, I'd seen em kiss before, but

never like that. Not like… like some sailor who was about to leave his wife on some long long journey. Now right off I thought that that was kind of strange, but jus as I was tryin to sort out all them thoughts runnin through my head, you know, of why he was do'n what he was do'n. I noticed that I was startin to float away from the pier an that's when I finally hollered at him."

"Boss," Otis called out with a humored sense of urgency. "The winds got me. You's better hurry."

Turning his head, Foster could see that the boat was drifting away. Caught by a gentle gust of wind that'd swept across the water, it was already two feet from the pier and getting further by the second. He needed to act, and in a final and hasty goodbye, he cupped Willie's face in his hands, kissed her one last time, then spun and jumped into the stern. "I'm good to go Otis," he hollered through the doorway as he regained his balance and then turned back to Willie.

"Yes sur boss," came his echoed reply that was quickly followed by the sputtering exhaust.

"Now, I'll see you just as soon as I get back okay," Foster promised over the noise as they pulled away and the boat pushed forward. "And keep your finger crossed too," he added as he held up his hand and crossed his fingers.

"I will," Willie replied as she did the same.

He was leaving and she would miss him, and in what had clearly become a subconscious act, she reached up with her other hand and took hold of the beautiful silver locket hanging from around her neck. The one he'd given her the first time they'd made love. As if it were possessed with some sort of magical powers that could span any distance or time and keep them together when they were apart. A second later, she went to the balls of her feet and waved. "I love you," she hollered with another smile as the boat sped away.

"Now jus as soon as ol Foster had landed in the back an hollered, I hit the throttle an pointed the boat down that little tributary. Then, an jus as soon as I was sure we was go'n straight an wasn't gonna hit nothin, I stepped to the doorway so I could wave to Willie jus like I always did. I remember lookin back an seein Foster; he was still in the back with his hands in his pockets jus lookin at her as we pulled away, an Willie, well, she was standin on the pier with a great big smile an a hand high above her head wavin.

"I can still remember clear as a bell her tellin him how she loved him, an then right after that her glancin toward me an tellin me goodbye. Now I hollered right back, but Foster, well, he never said a word, he jus blew her a kiss an stared a bit longer, then turned around an came up front. Now it was right about that point, after I'd jus seen him do that, an how he'd kissed her on the pier, that I remember thinkin an then gettin this feelin that somethin jus wasn't right."

"What-a-ya mean?"

"Well, like I told ya earlier," Otis drawled with touch of finality. "I'd already suspected that as far as Foster was concerned, their relationship was gettin real close to be'n over an that whatever plans he had for Willie, he'd already set into motion. But in all my wildest dreams would I of ever thought that when we pulled away an left her standin on the pier that mornin, that that would be the last time that they'd see each other for four years."

"What?" Jim scoffed. "Four years?"

"Yes sir," Otis nodded. "Four years."

"An so that's how he dumped her, huh? He just left her standin on the pier an motored away?" His voice rose in disgust. "Just like that? An he never said a word to her?"

"Well," Otis replied and sipped his beer. "To be right truthful with ya... yep, that's jus pretty much how it happened. Now Willie didn't know it yet, an for that matter neither did I really, but in answer to your question, yep, that's pretty much how it happened.

"Anyway, we made our way back out of that little tributary an jus as soon as we hit the inlet to the bay I stepped to the side so Foster could take the wheel. See, he still liked drivin every once in a while, but for some reason he didn't feel like it that mornin. I think if I remember right, he said somethin about it be'n to borin or somethin an that he was jus gonna go to the back. He said he wanted to relax an catch the mornin sun, an with that, he turned around an went to the stern."

Spinning his chair toward the stern, Foster took his seat and then plopped his feet up on the transom. It was a wonderful morning and even though it was mid-November and the sun's radiant strength had diminished, it felt good to relax and bask under the warmth of its gentle rays. It always felt good on the boat, and as they made their way out into the placid waters of the bay, he stared at the inlet to the tributary and smiled. He'd just spent some of the most relaxing days that he'd had in a long, long time. No one bothering or pulling at him to go here or there, or wanting this or that; no one that was except for Willie and her youthful charms.

He was glad that the Judge had insisted on taking some time off, and he'd gotten to see and enjoy her one last time. And now as he settled into his chair and they headed toward home, it was just the steady drone of the motor and a few noisy gulls following close behind. It was peaceful, and as they began on their way across the bay he closed his eyes and began to think of Willie and of how and what it was he was about to do.

He'd thought long and hard on it over the last couple of weeks, and had even tried to figure out a way to keep her, but in the end it was not to be. And even though he'd considered what the Judge had told him after the party, a sixteen-year-old mistress was most certainly not what he had in mind, and it was most certainly not something that a newly elected Senator took with him to Washington. Things had changed over the course of their year together and he knew that Willie not only deserved but wanted and needed more, more than what he could or was now willing to give. It was time, and he knew it. Time to end their yearlong affair and to call his friend just as soon as he got back.

They'd first met years ago, just after he'd moved to town and set up shop. A highly contentious courtroom battle that left the young and cocky Foster defeated to the older and more experienced lawyer along with a stinging little lesson in humility. It was a lesson that hurt, yet even so, and despite their ten-year age difference, the two men took an instant liking to each other and soon became close friends. Growing closer as the years slowly passed until Tom had become like brother. A brother Foster never had, and a trusted friend he could confide in. In fact, he was the only one he trusted. He thought of what they'd talked about at the celebration. Of how he and his wife had still been looking for help; live-in domestic help, to assist her with the chores on their small farm while he fulfilled his duties as one of the new circuit judges for the five surrounding counties. White help, that wasn't afraid to work, that could live with them and perform many of the menial tasks.

He remembered telling Tom of a young girl he knew, an orphan who'd done work for him in the past. She was perfect he'd told him, a good worker, who would have no problems at all earning her keep. Tom had seemed interested, even excited after Foster's little pitch and said to call him next week. He thought of it some more, yes, they were perfect for each other, she would be safe and cared for, and they would gain a great little worker. But would it work?

He wondered, then thought of their only child, a beautiful young girl of only seventeen who in many ways reminded him of Willie. Unofficially her adopted uncle, he remembered watching her through the years as she'd grown from a little girl into a happy go lucky teenager only to be struck down by tuberculosis in the prime of her youth.

He remembered her lingering sickness and the desperation of her parents as they tried to save her from the horrible disease. And then as the months slowly passed and it maliciously pulled the life from her body. It was the late fall of 28 when it had struck, a chronic cough with chills and a fever that soon turned deadly and by the spring of 29, Rebecca Portman was gone.

It was a crushing blow to everyone. He remembered the funeral and how they had all grieved, and then of how he'd tried to console and help his friend through those terrible, terrible times. Times that still brought forth some of the most heart wrenching and painful memories that he had... the loss of an innocent child. He shook his head and snapped his eyes open in an attempt to rid his mind of the memories but it didn't work, they were too entrenched and too powerful.

He looked around and sighed then instantly returned to the past as he remembered months later, during that summer when he would visit and how depressed and empty Tom had said his wife still was. They'd been left with nothing but a dark and empty hole that seemed to have no bottom. Their daughter's presence no longer filled the house, nor did the sound of her voice or laughter. It was a haunting quiet that tortured Elizabeth on a daily basis. The joy in her life was gone, and in a state of grief-filled depression, that fall, she failed to return to her beloved teaching job.

He thought of it some more, and then he thought of Willie. He knew that she could never replace or fill the void that'd been left by one's only child, but maybe there was a chance. Maybe there was hope. They'd each suffered an incredible loss, and in their own quiet kind of way, still grieved deep in their hearts. He thought for a while longer and then smiled. Yesss, just maybe... maybe it would actually work. A few moments later, as the tiny inlet to Willie's home slowly faded from view, Foster closed his eyes once again and then turned his thoughts to Washington. Yes, Washington he thought as he conjured the image into his head. The city and the people, the lights, and of course, his beautiful assistant who was already there waiting for him.

CHAPTER 41

———————◆———————

EVEN THOUGH HE WAS SCRUFFY and smelt of smoke with a three day old beard, Melinda was over-joyed to finally have her husband back and not the least bit disappointed that he hadn't made a kill. She'd missed him like any young wife and that night for dinner, she made a delicious pot roast with potatoes and carrots, and when they were finished, she took him to bed.

The next morning, Foster arrived at the office right at nine. The girls and Otis were already moving furniture and filing cabinets so the carpenters could work. The remodeling of his office was going just as planned even though everything seemed a mess. A quick run down with the workers and he headed to the back with Vicki and Dawn. He had a stack of calls to catch up on and two of the first on his list were to his friend Tom and then to the local bank.

———————◆———————

It was a quaint little diner down on Main Street, a place that they both liked and frequented where they'd decided to meet. Tom had arrived first and had taken the liberty of ordering two ice teas and two Friday afternoon specials. A hearty helping of meatloaf with mash potatoes and green beans that would easily carry them the rest of the day. A few moments later and right at noon, Foster arrived, spotted Tom by the windows and headed toward him.

"Well well wellll, Judge Portman," Foster jested as he approached. "Fancy meetin you here."

"Why Senator Siler… I'll beee," Tom drawled as he quickly turned from the window to his friend. "I must say, this is most certainly an unexpected surprise, but please please, have a seat won't you? I was just about to have lunch and would be delighted if you'd join me," he extended a hand toward the empty chair across from him.

Tom Portman was a good man with an impeccable reputation. A hometown boy, who'd returned to Mobile right after college, married his high school sweetheart and then built a solid and successful law practice. Tall and slender with an unassuming and easy-going demeanor, he was wickedly smart and could easily turn the tables in any argument and against any foe, including Foster.

Taking his seat, Foster reached for his tea then held it up and stared at his friend. "Well Tom ol buddy," he began as their laughter subsided. "We did it. You are now the new Circuit Judge and I'm a Senator. So what-a-ya think of that?"

"It's great my friend," Tom beamed and clinked his glass with Foster's then took a sip. "Just great! Although I sure never thought I'd see the day that somebody'd actually unseat ol Harlen Crandell," he shook his head and set his glass back down. "I'll tell ya, that was a real long-shot you pulled off there, but I'll be damned if you didn't do it and beat his ass. Yes sir, you whipped him all right, and Liz and I are both real proud of you. Heck, everybody in town is proud of you."

"Well thanks Tom," Foster replied. "That really means a lot, especially coming from you, and I want you to know that, but there's something that Iii," he suddenly quit speaking and took another sip of his tea, then turned and stared out the window.

"But there's what?" Tom probed. "What's up?" he asked then waited only to watch as Foster just stared out the window as if he were trying to collect his thoughts. "Hey man," Tom pried again. "Come on, what's up? I've known you for a long time, and certainly long enough to tell when something's on your mind so let's have it. What in the hell was so damn important that we had to meet in person huh? And don't tell me that it was just so we could sit here and look at each other's sorry asses while we eat. You've got something on your mind, I can tell. Now cough it up."

"Well," Foster finally began after a long and reluctant sigh. His voice now hushed as he turned back and glanced around the room just to ensure no one was listening. "I kind of need your help."

"Help," Tom whispered curiously. "What-a-ya mean help? What kind-a help? Hell, the elections over, and if I remember right, I believe you won," he chuckled.

"Yeah yeah, I know, but see I've got this…" he paused and sighed again then continued on as if he were giving a forced confession. "Well, you remember when we talked at the party don't you, and you told me that you and Liz were still looking for help."

"Sure I do, why?" Tom grinned.

"Well," Foster continued as he looked around once again then lowered his voice even more. "You remember me telling you about that little gal that I knew don't you? You know, the one that'd done some work for me?" He paused with the look of remorse pulling at his face. A look that he tried to conceal but couldn't.

Staring at Foster, Tom could tell just by his expression and the tone of his voice that there was a whole lot more about this girl than what he'd been told at the party. And that once again in Foster's wild and reckless ways, he'd probably crossed the line and done the unthinkable.

"Oooh noooo," he exhaled and rolled his eyes. "Don't tell me. You aren't, are you? Not again?" He shunted toward Foster and then instantly locked eyes in a duel for the truth.

Staring at each other in a fleeting moment of silence, Tom gazed deep into Foster's eyes then finally sat back and exhaled an exasperated breath. "Oh my God, you are aren't you? Goddammit Foster!" he hushed from between clenched teeth in an effort to keep his voice as low as possible. "Don't you ever learn? Wasn't that Betsy Burns episode that you went through a couple a years ago enough? Didn't you learn anything from that you dumb bastard! Jesus Christ, you just got married and just got elected to the United States Senate, and now you're telling me that you've been having an affair!" He shook his head. "And just how long has this been going on?"

"Oooh," Foster finally answered in a voice that was barely audible. "About a year."

"A year!" Tom repeated. "Are you serious? Are you out of your ever lovin mind?" He turned his gaze toward the window and stared outside in an attempt to regain his composure, only to snap it back a second later and continue on with his tirade. His voice now a little louder than what was really needed or should've been.

"Good God, do you realize that if the press ever finds out about this you're finished! That your illustrious career as a Senator would be over just like that," he snapped his fingers. "Shit, I can see the headlines already, *'Senator Siler keeps Secret Mistress.'* Oh, or how bout this one? *'Senator Siler's other Woman.'* Oh yeah, that'd be a good one too wouldn't it, right on the front page of every Goddamn newspaper in the state. In great big bold letters for everyone to see. Oh, and let's not forget about the rain of crap that your wife and father-in-law would undoubtedly unleash upon your sorry ass when they found out." He fumed. "Have you even thought about that?"

Gaining the curious stares from a few of the tables across the room, the two men paused, smiled warmly at the other patrons, then quickly resumed in much quieter voices. "I know, I know," Foster lowered his head. "It sounds really bad, but I swear it's over. Really, I swear."

"Yeah right!" Tom scoffed.

"No really, you gotta believe me."

"Believe you, why in the hell should I believe you?" he snapped then continued on in a hushed but hostile whisper. "Did you forget that I was the best man at your wedding, and that I stood right next to you while you recited your vows. You know, the ones that you gave to that other woman called your wife. Where I believe, and if I'm not mistaken, you promised to cherish and forsake all others. Remember that? Oh, and let's not forget about the faithful part either, shall we." He rolled his eyes then glared with disdain.

"Yes, yes I know," Foster admitted. "I know it sounds really bad, but you see I've changed," he insisted as he tried to defend himself. "And I've amended my ways."

"Amended your ways?" Tom repeated with a contemptuous laugh. "Really?"

"Yes really."

"Bullshit, you're a lying dog and you know it."

"No nooo, really I have!" Foster insisted. "I sweaaar! Just ask Melinda; she'll tell you. See, we've been going to church," he declared proudly. "You know on Sundays, almost every week now. Heck, I already know most of the prayers and a lot of the hymns, and last week I even got to sing with the choir. So see! Oh, and the Reverend Stone says that, well, he says that I'm making real good progress and that pretty soon I'll be--."

"Church?" Tom scoffed with a chuckle. "You're kidding right?"

"Oh nooo," Foster assured with the straightest of faces. "Seriously."

Looking up to the ceiling, Tom took in a heavy breath then shook his head in disbelief. "Oh my God," he exhaled as he dropped his gaze back to his friend. "I don't believe this. When in the hell did you start going to church? Jesus Foster, I've known you for over ten years now and the only time I can ever remember seeing you even close to a church was at your own damn wedding. And now you're telling me that you've been going on a regular basis. God, you're such a hypocrite."

"No no, you see... it's my salvation," Foster insisted.

"Salvation?" Tom challenged beneath his breath. "Salvation my dying ass. Let me tell you something my sorely misguided friend," he began with a finger pointed gesture between them that instantly turned into a repeated poking on top of the table. "It's gonna take a whole lot more than a damn church and a few Sunday sermons from the Reverend Stone to pry open the pearly gates and grant you salvation. Oh yeaah," he rolled his eyes. "And you can count on that. And I don't care how much fire and brimstone he pulls down out of the heavens and showers on top of your sorry ass.

"Shit, going to church ain't gonna help or change your ways none," he laughed with a cynical humor. "You're way past that point. Besides who in the hell are you trying to kid anyway? You did it for the votes. You know it and I know it, so please, if you don't mind, just take and shovel all that sanctimonious bullshit somewhere else okay," he gestured with a dismissive wave. "I'll tell ya, the more I think about it the more I think ol Liz was right."

"Right?" Foster's interest suddenly rose at the mention of Tom's wife. "Right about what? What'd she say?" he pried. "Tell me!"

Smiling, Tom, for just a moment, took pleasure in the simple fact that Foster now sat across from him in a state of uneasiness. It was a rare event, but occasionally it did happen. He knew that Foster actually cared for Liz and what she thought, and after his short little moment of discomfort, he leaned toward his friend and whispered. "That you're nothing but a man whore, and that the only way you're ever gonna change or amend your ways, is if they cut off that thing that's hanging down between your legs."

"Oh dear Lord... Liz said that?" Foster feigned with a frightened gasp as he glanced down to his lap and then back to Tom. "Surely she didn't?" His eyes widened. "Not Big Jim and the Twins."

Staring at his friend, Tom tried to maintain the seriousness of his demeanor but couldn't and began to laugh. There was no doubt that no matter what the situation was, Foster was always able to find a bit of humor in it, and today was no different. It was just the way he was, and with sort of a defeated sigh, Tom slowly sat back in his chair then turned and smiled at the waitress arriving with their food.

Both of the men were hungry, and just as soon as the woman had left, they dug into their food and continued on with their conversation. At first Foster was reluctant, but as they ate and his anxiety eased, Tom was able to learn more and more until he knew almost everything there was about the young girl from Hale County. Of her harsh and tragic life she had endured while growing up, and of how she'd come to Mobile. And of how Foster had come to find her in Connie's Diner, and then of how he'd put her up river in the old Davenport house.

He was shocked, and for a moment could only stare in disbelief. They were the best of friends, and yet he couldn't believe that he'd never heard of her before, or that Foster'd kept their yearlong affair such a secret. He listened carefully to everything Foster said and by the time they'd finished eating, the newly elected Judge for Mobile County had heard enough. The magnitude of Foster's problems were staggering, and with a long deep breath, Tom laid his fork and knife onto his empty plate and slowly pushed it away. Digesting his meal as well as his thoughts, he wiped his mouth and threw his napkin onto his platter, then settled back into his chair and glanced around the room. There were still other diners close by, but after a brief assessment as to their desires to listen in, he cleared his throat and leaned toward his friend.

"Okay, so let me get this straight," he began with a huff. "You've been having this affair with this little gal and now that you're on your way to Washington and it's over, you want me to take her off your hands, right? And so now I guess I'm just supposed to take her home with me, is that it?" He stared with a questionable gaze. "Now just how in the hell do you propose I do that, huh? Please, if you don't mind, and would be so kind as to enlighten me, I am just dying to know."

"Well," Foster replied. "You did say that you were still looking for help didn't you? And that the farm was a getting to be a little more than what Liz could handle?"

"Yes, yes I did. But do you think for one minute that I can just go home and waltz through the door with this girl and say hey Liz, look what I found, someone to help you. Oh, and by the way, just in case you're wondering, this is Foster's sixteen-year-old mistress that he's been having an affair with for the last year. I hired her cause he's going to Washington and can't take care of her anymore, and he wants me to keep an eye on her so she doesn't go around town talking or telling all kinds of crazy stories about him. So she's gonna be staying with us now, okay.

"Now do you really think for one minute that I can do that? Huh? Seriously?" He scowled and shook his head. "Good God man, think about it; Liz ain't exactly stupid you know. She knows how you are with the women. Shit, I just can't go walking home with some… some strange girl without her asking a million questions. Hell, you know that, so get real will you. And God forbid if she were to find out that you were having an affair with her right after you got married. Jesus! Then what in the hell would I tell her."

"I know, I know," Foster finally replied after a reflective pause. "It's asking a lot, but she's a great little worker, and heck, she never complains… ever! Hell, she's perfect. Really. She's sweet and nice and--."

"I don't know Foster," Tom interrupted, his words dripping with the lingering doubts that he now felt. "I really don't know. It's all just so much," he sighed and shook his head. "Besides, I think Liz has just about given up trying to find someone anyway."

"But you gotta help me," Foster appealed to the weaker side of Tom's compassion. "I can't take care of her anymore and you're the only one I can trust with this. I can't go anywhere else and you know it, so I'm asking. Please. Besides, in all the years that we've known each other, I've never asked you for anything… ever, but I'm asking you now. As a friend for me, but mostly for her, she's an orphan." He finished and sighed.

Gazing at his friend in a moment of silence, Tom slowly digested the sincerity and desperation of his plea. He was right, in all the years that they'd known each other, Foster had never asked for anything. Nothing except for his friendship, and then later on, a brotherly love that seemed to of sprung forth and develop between them. But now here he was, asking not so much for himself, but for a young orphaned girl. A girl he'd never met, but who he was now, mysteriously and curiously drawn to. He thought of it some more, and then shook his head in a confused and frustrated manner.

"But why dammit? What's so damn special about this little gal anyway?" He stared with a curious gaze. "Why do you care so much? This ain't your usual self. Hell, the Foster I use to know would've already of dumped her back on the streets where he had found her and been gone. So come on pal, let's have it, what's really going on here? She isn't pregnant is she?"

"Oh God no," Foster gushed with relief.

"Then what?" Tom pried again and then waited. "What's sooo?" he continued to pry but then suddenly paused and began to smile. "Oh my God, you like her, don't you?" He probed like an older brother then watched for a reaction. "That's it, you do!" he grinned as the truth slowly unveiled itself in Foster's expression. "You actually like her, don't you?"

"Whaaat," Foster scoffed with a fabricated chuckle. "Are you crazy? Me? Oh heck no, I'm just worried about her that's all. See, I just... well, I just want to help her," he stammered. "She has no one, and I mean that literally. No one. No mother or father or family, no one but herself, and I'd really like to see that she doesn't end up out on the streets again. That's all. Heck you know how times are right now. They're not good and I'd just like to see that she gets half a chance in life. She's never had that before and she deserves it."

Staring at Foster in a moment of silence, Tom finally exhaled a long defeated sigh and shook his head. "You know," he began with a chuckle. "For the love of God, I really don't know why I do some of the things I do for you, and I'm sure that some day this'll probably all come back to bite me in the ass, but if it'll really help, I'll go ahead and take her. But remember," he instantly added with a stern finger pointed warning. "It's just temporary you hear, and if she's trouble, or ain't the little worker that you say she is... or if Liz doesn't like her, she's down the road. Understand!"

"Oh yes, yes, absolutely," Foster nodded.

"Okay then," Tom sighed. "I'll see if I can't find a way to keep her through the winter, or at least until we can find a suitable orphanage or a nice family who might want to take her in. Which is probably going to be pretty damn hard considering the times we're in. But after that, when that happens... she's gone. Agreed?"

"Agreed!" Foster repeated.

"Oh, and there's something else too," he continued with a glaring afterthought and another finger pointed gesture. "I don't want you anywhere around while she's staying with us either, is that clear. Your little tryst with this girl or whatever in the hell it was is over and I mean it, you hear. You're a United States Senator for Christ's sakes and it's time that you started acting like one, understand!"

"Yes! Yes! You're right, never again. I swear. Oh God Tom, thank you, thank you," Foster gushed with his undying gratitude. "I just don't know what to say. I truly owe you for this one."

"Oh yeah," Tom drawled with a snicker. "You owe me all right. In fact, I believe," he added with a smile tugging at his lips. "That I just may have collected the first I. O. U. from Senator Siler."

"Yes, yes you did." Foster instantly added. "And I won't forget it either. I'll tell you, you may be a circuit judge right now but in the future if there's ever an opening for a position on the Federal bench and it's in the southern district and I'm still a Senator, I can assure you that your name will most certainly be at the top of that list."

"Well that all sounds real nice, but I sure ain't gonna hold my breath on that one cause your father-in-law isn't ever gonna retire. Shit, that crusty ol goat'll die before he ever gives up his judgeship." Tom chuckled.

"Yeah, I know what you mean," Foster grinned. "But still, I'll never forget this and I mean it."

"Well, like I said, that's all real nice and I appreciate it, I really do, and I won't forget it either believe me. But for right now we need to figure out just how in the hell we're gonna pull off this little charade and then hopefully put this whole messy affair that you got yourself into behind you. Cause I'll tell you something my little wayward friend," he paused with an icy gaze in another finger pointed moment. "If you don't, I can assure you that this whole great big happy world of yours will come to a screeching halt, and I mean real quick. You do understand that, don't you?"

Answering with a simple nod, Tom smiled then dropped his hand and continued on. "Good, then I want you think about it over the weekend and in the mean time, I'll try and figure out just what-in-the-hell I'm gonna tell Liz," he shook his head as if it were a moment he would surely dread. "And then on Monday, let's see if we can't get back together again and wrap this all up. Oh, and one more thing," he added with a smile as stood and pushed in his chair. "Thanks for lunch."

Foster's appointment with Gordan DeWeese, the new ambitious president of Mobile Savings, was for one thirty. Gordan had been given the reins from his predecessor just over a year ago in a move by the board to try and salvage by whatever means as many of their failed mortgages as he could. It was desperate times that called for desperate measures, and as they themselves faltered under the crushing surge of a failing economy, DeWeese was determined to save the bank.

The house had gone into foreclosure just over a year ago and had been sitting empty with hardly any lookers, and absolutely no offers. A magnificent manor that in its own subtle way had left an indelible mark on him right after he'd seen it the very first time. A house that for almost a year he'd dreamed of owning, and that now, if things went as he hoped, would soon be calling his home.

He'd been watching and waiting, and knew that the bank had already dropped its price three times in an attempt to attract a buyer. But there were none to be had, for the depression had hit hard in the Mobile area. They wanted desperately to get it off of their books and he knew it, yet still he inquired with a casual indifference. He was a United States Senator with a guaranteed salary for the next six years and he knew that the bank wanted his business.

It took almost a half hour of hard but friendly negotiating and two more favorable price reductions before the two men were able to come to an agreement and strike a deal that pleased them both. The bank, to their great relief, got a bad mortgage off of their books. And at just less than half of its market value, with nothing down and no payments until after the first of the year, Foster got a great deal and became the new owner of the Davenport's old house.

CHAPTER 42

MELINDA WAS COMPLETELY CONFUSED AND just a little flustered on
Saturday morning when just after breakfast her husband playfully
ushered her into the car and blindfolded her. The twenty-minute
drive that they then took soon turned into the most torturous of
rides as she began to giggle and laugh then beg to know where they
were going. But Foster held his tongue and only teased until he'd
stopped in front of the house and helped Melinda from the car.
Leading her by the hand until they stood in just the right spot, he
stepped behind her and then pulled the blindfold from around her
eyes.

"Surprise!" he exclaimed as he placed his hands on her shoulders.

Standing in the driveway, Melinda stared for a moment and said
nothing. She saw the big red bow on the door yet still it didn't register until she turned back to Foster and saw the look on his face. She
hadn't a clue that he was even thinking of such a thing, and with a
squeal of disbelief, she wrapped her arms around him and began
to cry. Just a year ago she'd begun to think of herself as a failure. A
twenty-four year old who seemed destined to grow into an old maid
that no one wanted. But now here she was, living in an enchanted
and magical world. A make believe life, where she was the beautiful
princess in a fairytale. She had it all it seemed, a wonderful marriage
to a loving husband who was now a United States Senator... and now
a big new house in which to raise her family.

It was more than any dream she'd ever dreamed, and as they
opened the door and stepped into the foyer, she twirled in slow
motion with her head to the ceiling. She was ecstatic and grinning,

and even though she'd grown up in a house that was very much like this, this one was hers.

They toured the lower level first, meandering from room to room until they had looked in every room there was. There were pull bells in all of the important ones, each with its own unique ring. It was a system that had served quite well for years to summon the help. She pulled them all as they toured, then listened intently to see if their sound would resonate from the servant's quarters.

Returning to the foyer and the grand circular staircase, Melinda paused and quietly looked around the massive vestibule. She felt like a kid on Christmas morning, and as her eyes curiously roamed and then attached themselves to the beautiful ornate banister that led upstairs, she began to grin. A second later, she turned back to Foster and stared as if to ask permission.

"Go on," he nodded with an extended hand as the haunting sound of Katherine's voice suddenly resonated in his head. *'You remember,'* her soft sophisticated drawl echoed like that of some ghostly spirit as he followed behind his wife. *'Just find the flickering light.'* He did remember, and as they slowly ascended the steps, he thought of the past and the many times that he'd climbed them. A few moments later they were at the top, and after a quick look around, they turned toward the bedrooms.

Proceeding down the hallway, they slowly went from room to room until they had finally stepped through the doors of the master suite. Occupying a sizeable corner of the home's upper level, it had ten foot ceilings and large walk in closets. Designed for comfort, with its very own over-sized bath-room and octagonal sitting room that extended out and over the screened in porch, it was wrapped in windows and was light and bright, and clearly a testament as to the opulent lifestyle that the Davenport's had once lived. Gasping in awe, Melinda could only smile as she looked around until an object on the floor beneath one of the windows suddenly caught her attention.

"Oh look," she raised her hand and pointed. "A candle, over there on the floor beneath that window. See. I bet the movers must of forgotten it when they packed," she surmised as she quickly headed toward it. "What-a-you think?"

"Well," Foster drawled as he stepped to the center of the room. "I'm not really sure, but I guess they could have. Hell, you know how the hired help is these days," he added as Melinda bent and picked up the candle.

"Look," she exclaimed and then turned with her newfound treasure. "Isn't this beautiful?" she gushed as she held it up and then slowly stepped towards him. "I can't believe they forgot it!"

Staring at his wife as she cradled the large melted candle in its beautiful holder, Foster's mind instantly flashed back through the many months of memories. Memories that he wouldn't trade or change for anything in the world. Memories of the many many times that he'd slipped into this very room late at night, and had blown out the very candle his wife was now holding. A candle that had been lit again and again just for him, by the beautiful matriarch of the home as a signal that she was ready and waiting for her lover to arrive. A lover, who like a thief in the night would enter into her private sanctuary and then extinguish the flame. Who would then under the very cloak of darkness that he'd just created, slip quietly between the sheets and lay with her.

It was the only thing that'd been left in the house... the only thing, and it caused him to instantly wonder as to why only it had been left behind. Had it been forgotten as it truly seemed, or had it been intentionally left as some sort of sign or message for the next owner to find? His thoughts raced as he tried to dissect and discern over a million equations that were now running through his head. He pondered the reasons as his wife approached, but then suddenly remembered a conversation he'd once had with Katherine.

It was just a day or two before she'd left for New Orleans, and one of the last times that they had seen each other. She was sad and had been crying at how she'd lost everything. The furniture was all being sold the next day and on Saturday the bank was taking the house. They talked for the longest of times and then made deep and passionate love. Afterwards, he tried to console her, telling her of how he'd always dreamed of buying their house and that if he ever became a Senator, he would do just that. And that when he did, that at least she would know that the house was in good hands. He'd meant it in jest, but even so, he remembered her reaction, a gracious and heartfelt smile that was quickly followed by a long and soulful kiss.

At first he scoffed at the notion. No way Foster, you're crazy. A second later, he began to rethink and even second-guess himself.

But what if she really did? He questioned again. What if she really had left it as some sort of message? A message to him with the hope, that it would somehow and in someway, find him. As a reminder and a keepsake of the moments that they'd both shared, and that said goodbye for the final time in her own unique and unspoken way.

Surely not he tried to reason... how could she have possibly known. He'd been joking about some thing that was almost a year away and uncertain at that. He thought of her again, her voice and her smile, and then the smell of her perfume. He inhaled a breath as if he were trying to catch her scent still lingering in the air and smiled. It was almost as if she'd just been in the room. His mind reeled until his wife had stopped in front of him and he gazed lovingly into her eyes.

"Oooh my baby... yes it is," he agreed as he gently reached up and placed his hands over hers. "It really is," he added as if a closer look had suddenly revealed more than what he had expected.

Watching as Foster carefully examined the holder, Melinda thought for a second then shifted her eyes to her husband's. "Well," she began with sort of a hesitant drawl. "I know that this is probably Mrs. Davenport's and all, and I know that she'd probably like to have it back, but," she paused as if she were thinking. "I'd really like to keep it if you think it would be okay. You know, for us," she grinned with a wanton twinkle to her eyes. "Here in our new bedroom."

"Well, I don't see why not," Foster replied wryly. "I'm sure that Mrs. Davenport isn't gonna miss some silly ol candle holder that's been sitting here ever since she left. Besides," he raised his eyebrows as if to insinuate the obvious. "It was here in the house when we bought it, wasn't it?"

Smiling with a sigh, Melinda slowly turned and took the candle back to the window. Carefully placing it on the floor where she'd picked it up, she returned to Foster and thanked him with a kiss. There was no doubt that he loved his wife, but still, as he stood in the center of the room with his arms around her, he couldn't help but stare at the candle and think of the past.

———◆———

"Now if I remember right I think it was the followin Monday after we'd gotten back from seein Willie for the last time that ol Foster had me back in his office

workin. I think he really wanted to get the biggest part of all that remodelin done before he left for Washinton an had even been helpin us when right at noon he stopped an put on his jacket an left.

"I remember him tellin Vicki as he headed out the door that he had some kind of meetin or somethin with some new Judge that'd jus gotten elected. Then, about an hour later, an not to awfully long after we'd gone back to work, he came walkin back in. Now ol Foster was always full of surprises, an that day wasn't no different than any other cause jus as soon as he did, he came an got me an told me to get all a my tools an the truck an then to follow him over to the Davenport house."

"The Davenport house?" Jim looked on curiously. "You mean the people he got the boat from?"

"Yep, them's the ones."

"Well what in the hell did he drag you over there for?"

"Well," Otis replied. "He bought it, an I guess he got a hell of a deal on it too cause the damn thing had been sittin for over a year by then. Anyway, he had a whole lot-a stuff that he wanted to fix up an get done on it before he an Melinda moved in. I remember it had a whole bunch of crap that was wrong with it, you know, leaks in the roof an lose steps an rails, an plaster that was fallin off. But ol Foster seemed pretty unfazed by it all an jus told me that what he really wanted was for me to try an have everything done in time so that he could move in before Christmas.

"Anyway, after we'd finally gone through everything that he wanted done, well, that's when he took me back outside an sat me down on the steps of the front porch an started talkin about his new job. Now I already knew he was a Senator, an that he was real important, but I sure as hell didn't know what one of em did that was for sure. But ol Foster always seemed ta have a pretty good reason for everything he did an for the next ten minutes or so I jus sat there an listened while he explained to me what his job was all about. An it was right there on the steps of his new home, that afternoon, that I learned jus what a United States Senator was, an did. Hell, I even learned where Washinton D.C. was," he chuckled.

"Anyway, it was right after my little lesson in politics when he told me that he was gonna be leavin later on in the week. That he had to go to Washinton for a few weeks an that when he did he wanted me to go an get Willie for him. He told me to go on Friday an to get everything she had loaded up but to jus go ahead an spend the night. Then on Saturday mornin, bring her an all of her stuff back to town, includin that little fishin boat. He told

me to tell her that he had to go away on business, but that he'd finally sold the house. He said that he'd found her a real good job too with this real nice man an lady who was gonna help her an take care of her till he got back, an for me not to worry about her. That the man was a Judge an good friend of his, an that he an his wife had a small farm jus on the outskirts of town an really needed help. He said that it was perfect for Willie. Now right off I knew that ol Willie was gonna be jus as excited as you could ever imagine. Heck, I was even excited until it suddenly dawned on me an it all began to make sense."

"What made sense?" Jim instantly asked.

"Foster," Otis replied. "An not so much what he was gettin ready to do, but more importantly, how he was gettin ready to do it. See, he was finally dumpin her an had planned to have me do it all while he was gone to Washinton."

"Whaaat?" Jim looked on as if he couldn't believe it. "He had you do it? Are you serious?"

"Yes sir, although it didn't appear quite like that on the outside, but yep, that's exactly how it happened. He'd planned it all, jus like he did everything. Jus so he wouldn't have to deal with it."

"Goddammit, I knew it," Jim exclaimed with an incensed finger pointed gesture. "See, that's just like a chicken shit politician to have someone else do their dirty work. God Otis, so what'd you do?"

"Well, I knew that all this was gonna have to happen at some point in time, but I sure as hell didn't think that it was gonna involve me. Anyway, that was on a Monday, an for the rest of the week I was pretty much a wreck. I tell ya, I felt jus terrible, an all I could think about was Willie an what he was gettin ready to do. An then I thought of all the things that I could try an do to help or warn her, but in the end I decided against em cause none of em would of worked really, an to be right truthful with you, about all it'd a done was got me fired.

"So then I started thinkin that maybe this really wasn't such a bad thing after all. You know, that maybe go'n to these other people could actually be a good thing. See, I knew that he really liked Willie, an I knew or at least hoped that he wouldn't jus send her off with anyone, an that kind of gave me a little comfort, but still I worried about her. I worried about her all that week while I worked on his house, frettin an thinkin of jus what she was gonna do when she finally figured everything out. But it didn't do no good, an before I knew it Friday mornin had rolled around an I was helpin Foster an Melinda load up all his luggage so I could drive him to the train station. See, he was finally go'n to Washinton to learn how to be a Senator.

"I remember he was pretty excited about the whole thing too, an right after that big ol locomotive blew its whistle an the conductor yelled out all aboard. Well, that's when he gave Melinda a kiss, an with one last finger pointed reminder at me not to forget to move all those things that we'd talked about, ol Foster jumped onboard jus as that train started to roll.

"Now I knew exactly what he meant jus as soon as he'd said it, an so right after he was gone, I went an did jus like he'd told me. I had the boat all ready to go an jus as soon as I got to the marina, I took off back across the bay one last time to move all the things that we'd talked about. To get Willie, an then bring her back here to Mobile jus like she'd always wanted... to her new life.

"Anyway, by the time I finally made it across the bay an had rounded the last bend in that little tributary, I was really startin to get nervous cause I wasn't sure if I could really go through with it all. I was all torn up, but jus as soon as that little house came into view, I blew the horn to let Willie know that I was there. I remember she was up on the porch paintin an as soon as she heard me she turned an waved great big, jumped off of her ladder, an by the time I got to the pier, was standin there waitin to catch me.

"It had been a whole week since I'd seen her last, an jus as soon as we had the boat all tied up, I started tellin her all about the good news. All of it right there on the pier. All one great big giant lie, jus like Foster'd told me to tell her. Of how he'd finally sold the house, an how grateful he was to her for helpin him save his poor ol dyin aunt. Now, she was real proud of that," he laughed. "An then, of how he'd also found her a job an a place to stay with this real nice man an lady who was gonna help her until he got back an could come an get her. Yes sir, I told her all of it, an when I was done, about the only thing that wasn't a lie was the fact that I really had come to take her back to Mobile. Now, at first she jus kind of stood there with this real strange look on her face until it--."

"Whoa whoa whoooa," Jim interrupted. "Damn Otis, didn't ya feel jus a little bad?" he asked then stared as if he were searching for some semblance of guilt. "You know... lyin to her like that?"

"Well," Otis sighed. "At first I thought I would, an that I'd feel jus terrible, you know, cause I was lyin to someone who I really cared about. But to be right truthful with you, the more an more that I thought about it while I crossed the bay that day, the more I kept comin back to the conclusion that this was probably the best thing that ever could've happened to her.

"See, there was absolutely nothin but no good that was gonna come out-a their relationship an I'd finally come to realize that. An even though Willie

was wildly in love, there was no way that Foster was go'n to give up any part of his new life for some sixteen year old uneducated sharecropper. No sir, that was somethin that was jus not go'n ta happen. Now I didn't know what all was in store for her, you know, go'n to live with these new people an all an that kind of worried me. But what I did know was that here was a chance for Willie to finally get away from Foster. To get out from under his influence an then to hopefully go an live a normal life with a real nice couple that was willin to take her in an care of her.

"Now back then, back in the depression, that was really somethin to take someone in cause times was real lean an hard an another mouth to feed wasn't exactly what anybody was lookin for. So the way I started to look at it all was that Willie was actually pretty lucky cause she could of jus as easily ended up back out on the streets again. The only thing that I kept thinkin an hopin though, was that these people were as nice as Foster had said.

"Anyway, like I was jus sayin, at first ol Willie jus kind of stood there with this real funny look on her face until it dawned on her that she was finally leavin an that's when she got jus as excited as you could ever imagine. I remember she started do'n this little happy dance an then started gigglin an jabberin an askin me questions so fast I was forgettin what she asked before I could even answer.

"Yes sir, she was really happy all right, an jus as soon as she'd settled, we went on up to the house an put all a her paintin stuff away then started collectin all her things an loadin the boat. Then right after breakfast the next mornin, we tied the little fishin boat to the stern and took off back out across the bay. Back to Mobile."

"So then what happened? You know, when you guys got back?"

"Well, we ended up gettin back right about noon an jus like Foster had said he would, his friend was there waitin for us. We'd jus finished tyin up an was in the back wiping everything down when he came walkin down the pier real casual like an then stopped right by the boat."

"Afternoon," Tom greeted to the two standing in the stern.

"Afternoon," Willie and Otis both replied.

As soon as Willie had turned, Tom understood why his friend had strayed. He'd always thought in the back of his mind that Foster had been exaggerating, but as he gazed upon her he could see that he hadn't, for she was as beautiful as any young girl he'd ever seen, even in her boots and paint stained overalls. Surprised in a way in which he hadn't expected, he paused for a second then caught the young girl's gaze.

"And you must be Willie?" he asked.

"Yes sur," Willie replied as she stepped towards him. "I'm Willie, Willie Mae Dawson."

"Well there Miss Willie," he drawled and then casually extended his hand. "I'm Tom, Tom Portman, and I guess I'm gonna be your new boss for awhile."

"Oooh yes sur," she beamed excitedly. "You must be the man that Mister Siler said I'd be workin an stayin with till he gets back an can come an get me. He's workin in some place called Washinton, it's real, real far from here."

"Yesss, yes I know," he agreed as a myriad of thoughts filled his head. Thoughts of just how truly ingenuous she sounded, but yet at the same time was still ready and unafraid to embrace her future. A future that somewhere down the road, he was almost certain held the promise of disappointment and heartache. He couldn't believe that he'd allowed Foster to talk him into doing this but now here he was. He thought of telling her the truth, right then and there, and having it all out in the open but then decided against it. He reasoned that he'd made a promise, and that as of now there was little good that would be gained from it. Then shaking his head as if to deny what it was he was about to do, he cleared his throat. "Well let's get your things and get going shall we. It's a ways back to the farm and we have lots to do before supper, hear."

"Yes sur," Willie replied as she stepped through the doorway get her things.

"Now all the way up until that point I'd been pretty worried cause I'd never met this Tom fellow before, but jus as soon as he started talkin I knew I didn't need to worry about a thing."

"Really? Why's that?"

"Well, to tell ya the truth," Otis sighed. "I really don't know why other than the fact that he was real easy go'n an was nice to Willie. Anyway, we got all her stuff an books loaded up in the back of his truck an jus as soon as we had she turned an looked at me real funny like. Then, an before I knew it, she'd jumped up to the side of the truck, reached into her bag with all her

books an pulled out the one that Foster had jus given her for her birthday, The Adventures of Huckleberry Finn.*"*

"Here ya go Mister Otis," Willie smiled and brushed the cover then held it out. "This is in case I don't get ta see ya for a while."

"Bu... but Miss Willie," Otis stammered. "That's the book that you jus got for your birthday. I can't take that."

"I know," she drawled with another smile. "But I want you ta have it anyway, so I'm givin it to you. See, I've already read it two times, so now it's your turn. Besides, I want you ta have it. An I want ya ta read it. For me."

It took a few moments of arguing for Otis to truly accept her gift, but after he had and Willie was satisfied, she hugged him goodbye in a warm and open display of affection. A moment later, she released her hold and with a smile and a gentle pat to his chest, she slowly turned and then opened the door to the truck.

"So that's how you ended up with the book an how she ended up with those other people, huh?"

"Yep," Otis nodded.

"An she wasn't afraid or worried, or upset or nothin like that?"

"Nope, not in the least bit... or at least not that I could tell. I sure thought she would've been but she wasn't. In fact, if I remember right, it was pretty much the opposite."

"Opposite? What-a-ya mean? Wasn't she gettin dumped?"

"Yep, but she didn't know that... or at least not then she didn't. See, she still had it in that little head of hers that ol Foster was gonna come an get her, you know, jus as soon as he was all done workin in Washinton. Besides, she was all excited cause she was finally gettin ta go somewhere new. See, you gotta remember, she'd been on that river all alone for over a year by then an boy let me tell ya, was she ever ready for somethin new."

"Oooh yeaah," Jim nodded. "I guess I really didn't think of it that way. So then what happened?"

"Well," Otis continued on after a quick sip from his beer. "They got in the truck, an after she'd closed the door she told me that she'd see me jus as soon Foster had come an got her. Now I knew that that was never gonna happen, but still I never said nothin. I kind of felt bad about it too," he sighed.

"Specially after she'd jus given me her book. Then, an jus as soon as she was done talkin, that ol Tom fellar started the truck an they took off.

"I remember watchin as they pulled away an then seein Willie turn an wave through the back window. She was smilin an seemed happy, an that kind-a gave me a little comfort. But then I remember thinkin of what I'd jus done," he added as if he still regretted his actions. "An as they pulled out-a the parkin lot an onto the road, I really began to wonder if I'd ever see her again."

The twenty minute ride to the farm seemed to pass in the blink of an eye for Willie. Tom used the time to explain many of the reasons as to why she was there and what was expected of her while she was with them. Willie listened carefully, and although she was disappointed that Foster wouldn't be back for some time, she understood, and before she knew it he was slowing the truck to turn.

"Well, here we are," Tom finally said as he turned onto the long dirt drive to their house.

"This is your farm?" Willie asked as she gazed out across the fields. "Where I'm gonna be workin an stayin?" she grinned as she glanced from side to side.

"Yes ma'am," Tom replied, pointing with his finger first out one side and then the other. "All this on both sides, see. All the way over to those other houses... way over there."

"Wow, that's really big."

"Ah, not really, it's just a hundred and fifty acres, but it's just about more than me and Liz can handle anymore. Especially with my new job, that's why we decided to hire you," he added as he shifted gears and stepped back on the gas.

"Oh, an look," she gushed. "You have horses an cows. An look, they're followin us," she giggled.

"Yes ma'am," Tom chuckled and shook his head. "We have horses and cows. And they're following us because they see my truck heading back to the house and they think that it's feeding time. See, up there," he pointed down the road and then shifted into second.

Looking out front to where he'd pointed, Willie stared in awe at the white two-story farmhouse and barn sitting amongst a cluster of giant trees. There was no doubt that the home was nice, but to Willie, as they drew closer and the house grew in size, it seemed like a mansion.

"That's your house?" she asked with a glance to him and then back out.

"Yes ma'am."

"Where I'm gonna be stayin?"

"Yes ma'am. Why is something wrong?" he teased.

"Oooh no sur," she replied. "It's jus that ain't never been in a house like that before."

"Well," Tom replied as he turned the wheel. "You will be in a few moments."

Looking back out as Tom turned into the driveway and scattered the chickens, Willie saw the front door open and then a woman, slim and casually dressed emerge from within. Staring as she stepped out onto the porch and made her way to the edge of the steps, Willie suddenly felt a bit of anxiety rise form within. Why, she wasn't sure. Maybe it was because she was the first woman other than Hadie that she'd seen in over a year, or maybe it was the fact that she reminded her of her mother.

"Is that your wife?" she asked.

"Yes ma'am," Tom answered. "That's Mrs. Portman. The real boss, if ya really want to know." He joked. "And that mix breeded mut over there barking and wagging his tail next to her is Rex."

"She's pretty," Willie said as they pulled to a stop.

"Yes she is," Tom agreed as he turned off the truck and then stared at his wife through the plume of dust now settling around them. "And now that we're here," he added with somewhat of an uncertain breath. "I think we should go and meet her don't you?"

"Yes sur," Willie replied with a tug to the door handle.

Walking around to Willie's side of the truck, Tom placed his hand on her shoulder then looked back up to his wife. "Liz honey," he said with a glance to Willie and then back to his wife, his mind reeling with the hope that she would like and accept the young girl into their home. "This is Willie, Miss Willie Mae Dawson."

Slowly stepping from the porch, Elizabeth quietly gazed at the young girl for just a moment then smiled cordially and extended her hand. "Well, hello there young lady," she drawled with a gentle kindness. "I'm Mrs. Portman."

"Yes ma'am," Willie replied as she took the ladies hand. "I... I'm Willie, an want ya ta know jus how truly grateful I am to ya for helpin me, an for givin me a chance ta work." But then Willie suddenly stopped speaking and caught her breath. Why, she wasn't quite sure, but there was something about the woman's touch that caused a feeling to rise from within her. A feeling she'd not felt in over a year. A soothing and comforting sense that could only come from a bond that'd been forged between a mother and daughter. A feeling and a warmth that until now, she'd not realize she had missed. She thought of her mother again.

"Well," Elizabeth smiled at the unexpected graciousness that'd sprung forth from the young girl. "You're quite welcome. Buuut... you do know that a farm as big as this is a lot of work, don't you?"

"Ooh yes ma'am," Willie nodded. "I know, but I'm a good worker, you'll see. I promise. I growed up on a cotton farm an I'm use ta work hard."

"Well, I'm glad to hear that," she smiled again. "But before we get started, why don't we eat first." She raised her eyebrows. "We can't start working on an empty stomach now can we?"

"No ma'am," Willie replied.

"Good, then come on," she said as she placed her hand on Willie's shoulder and turned. "I've made us a real nice lunch, and when we're done and after we've gotten you all settled in," she stopped and stared. "I'll show you all around the farm."

It was at that moment and for the first time in years, watching as the two women talked, that Tom saw in the eyes of his wife a sudden glint of light. A brightness that seemed to have come out of nowhere and instantly catch his attention. It was subtle and brief, but still it was there. He could tell, and as he opened the door and then followed behind them, he began to wonder.

Was this girl in some strange and mysterious way God's answer to his long awaited and desperate prayers? Had her parents been taken from her just so she could end up here? Could she, just by the virtue of her presence possess the healing qualities that the love of his life needed to overcome her debilitating sadness? He shook his head. Liz hadn't been the same since the death of their daughter, neither of them had really, but still he wondered with a kind of uncertain hope. A second later, and with a heavy sigh as he crossed the threshold, he turned and closed the door.

CHAPTER 43

———◆———

It was mid-afternoon by the time the train finally pulled into the Grand Terminal at Union Station and stopped for the last time. After two days of traveling, Foster was more than ready to get out of his rolling tin can as he'd come to call his railcar. Looking out of his window, he grinned at the sight before him for never in his life had he seen anything like it. It was amazing, and seemed as if they'd designed it straight from the pages of the history books. A recreation on an unimaginable scale, as if to symbolize and pay homage to an architecture that'd long since passed. He had seen it in books before but never in real life, and now it was as if he'd suddenly gone back in time. Back to an era in ancient Greece and Rome, where ionic columns rose from a vast concourse of white marble floors to support a barreled ceiling ninety-five feet high, and where chiseled inscriptions and allegorical sculptures marked its neoclassical façade.

Staring in awe as the train slowly crawled to its final stop, he marveled for a few moments longer then quickly turned his thoughts to Suzanne and began to look for her amongst the sea of travelers. She'd said she would be there, but there were so many people swarming about, he wasn't sure he would find her. He narrowed his eyes and scanned the faces as they went by hoping to see her until he spotted her standing by the edge of the platform checking each and every car as it slowly passed. Catching his breath, Foster smiled then knocked on the window and waved. A second later, he saw her smile and her eyes light up as she turned and began to follow his car.

A warm and professional greeting soon turned into a cab ride to a fairly new and elegant hotel not far from the Capital. The

Hay-Adams, which catered to the uppity and political types where Suzanne had reserved a room. Proudly registering under his new official title as Senator Siler, they were soon escorted to a one-bedroom suite on the top floor. The accommodations were lavish to say the least, and after the porter had set his bags in the bedroom and then pulled the curtains to a breathtaking view of 1600 Pennsylvania Avenue, he took his tip and left.

It took only a few moments after he'd closed the door for the newly elected Senator and his assistant to fall into each other's arms and then locked together in a heated embrace. Their desires for each other had been built to a breaking point over the last few weeks, and even though he was her boss and was married, and she knew that what she was about to do was wrong, she didn't care. He'd given her everything she'd ever wanted and now here they were, all alone in a hotel room in one of the most exciting cities in the world. It was a moment she'd longed and waited for, and one she was now determined to seize. She felt alive and bold and reckless, and as the uncontrolled and burning desires within her took hold of her actions, the lustful and hungry side of Suzanne Schubert quickly began to show. She'd not been with a man in a long long time, and as the dampened heat in her loins welled into the pit of her stomach, defeating any and all remaining remnants of self-control; the ambitious young girl from Montgomery Alabama, that afternoon in a suite on the top floor of the Hay-Adams hotel, abandoned every moral principle that she had ever lived by.

———◄►———

Foster's appointment with Senator Sellers was for ten and as soon as he entered her office, he was greeted by a lovely young intern. "Good morning," she said as he closed the door behind him and turned. "May I help you?"

"Why yes ma'am," he drawled with a dashing smile as he crossed the room and approached her desk. "I'm Senator Siler, and I have an appointment with Senator Sellers."

"Oh yes sir," the young girl acknowledged with a quick glance to her calendar. "I believe she's expecting you," she added, blushing that her eyes had lingered with his just a little longer than they should have. "Please, if you'll just have a seat," she said as she rose from her chair.

Crossing the room, the young girl knocked softly on the door and then opened it. A second later, and after an exchange of mumbled voices, he saw her open it wide and then turn. "Senator," she called with an inviting arm gesture.

Rising from his chair, Foster crossed the room and followed the young girl into the office. "Ma'am," she announced as they entered. "Senator Siler."

"Thank you Debbie," Adell nodded as if to dismiss her and close the door. "So you're Robert McAlister's son-in-law?" She beamed with a protracted gaze as she rose from behind her desk.

"Yes ma'am," Foster replied with an extended hand and a step toward her. "I'm Foster, Foster Siler. And I want you to know just how much I appreciate you taking the time to meet with me."

"Oh nonsense," she jested and took his hand. "It's my pleasure, besides how could I ever refuse a request from Robert McAlister after everything he's done for me," she laughed. "But I must confess before we go any farther that the real reason I wanted to meet you was to be the first to congratulate the man who took down Harlen Crandell. God, he was such a prick," she shook her head. "And a crook too, as I'm sure you're well aware of."

"Yes ma'am," Foster chuckled. "That I was."

"Anyway, I don't think you realize it, but you're quite the talk on the hill right now. Word was that you didn't stand a snowball's chance in hell against him, but boy you sure proved everyone wrong didn't you." She smiled great big. "That was quite the little rabbit you pulled out of the hat there."

"Yes ma'am," Foster humbly agreed. "The Judge and I worked on that for quite awhile."

"Yes, I can see that. And lucky for the people of Alabama that you did. So tell me, speaking of Alabama, just how is my old friend down there in Mobile?"

"He's fine and well ma'am, thank you for asking. And he sends his regards too."

"Well good, that's good. I'm glad to hear that," she sighed. "Robert is such a dear. But come now," she turned and gestured toward the two large chairs in front of her desk. "Let's have a seat and talk, shall we."

Adell was everything that the Judge had said and more, and Foster could tell in an instant as to why he'd spoken so highly of her. Small in stature yet saddled with a spirited intellect and a dry yet wonderful sense of humor, she was kind and sweet and gracious, and had welcomed him into her office with open arms. There was an instant and mutual liking, and they talked for over an hour before he finally left with an invitation to return on Tuesday. Another visit that soon turned into his daily lessons.

Adell was patient, but above all she was an excellent teacher and under her tutelage, Foster learned the ways of the Senate and its parliamentary procedures with an amazing speed. The days passed quickly into weeks and by the time he was scheduled to return home, the two had become good friends and he'd forged what was to be his first true alliance in Washington. The day before he left, he visited her one last time.

"Well my friend," Adell began proudly. "You've learned well and I want you to know that there's no doubt in my mind that you'll make a fine Senator. You'll do the people of Alabama proud, and I mean that too."

"Yes ma'am, thank you. That means a lot and I really appreciate it, especially coming from you."

"Oh don't mention it. But listen, the real reason I asked you here today was that there's something that a few of my colleagues and I have been thinking about and it's something that we'd like you to consider while you're gone."

"Yes ma'am, and what's that?"

"Taking a chair on one of our committees."

"Committees?" Foster question excitedly.

"Yes committees, I'm sure you're aware of the importance of sitting on one of these aren't you?"

"Oh yes ma'am."

"Good, because there's a seat on the Merchant Marine and Fisheries Committee that needs to be filled and... well, I know it isn't much or it doesn't sound like much, but it's a good start for a freshman Senator and I'm sure that somewhere down the road it'll lead to bigger and better things. So when you come back and get all sworn in, I'd like to see that you get put on it right away."

"Yes ma'am," Foster grinned. "That sounds great. But I do have one question if you don't mind."

"Oh heavens no, not at all. What's on your mind?"

"Well," he cocked his head and stared with a perplexed expression. "Just what exactly does this committee do?"

"Dooo?" Adell paused and then laughed. "I have absolutely no idea. But I do know this," she quickly added as she continued on in a more serious tone. "For some reason, ol Harlen Crandell seemed to have a great deal of interest in it and was actually trying to get one of his cronies to sit on it. Now exactly why, well, that seems to be the million-dollar question that nobody's been able to answer yet. But he's gone now and since the balance of power has changed with the elections, a few of my colleagues and I would like for you to fill that spot. Sooo," she smiled. "You interested?"

The first few days for Elizabeth proved to be the hardest, for in many ways Willie was very much like her own daughter, and even though it had been over two years since her death, the voice and the laughter of another young girl filling the house was almost more than she could bear. She felt guilty and torn, haunted by the thought that in some strange way she was forsaking her daughter's memory.

She struggled with her feelings, and even though she wanted nothing more than to help the young orphaned girl, she had her doubts as to whether or not she could truly cope and continue on. It was hard for her, especially at night when she laid her head to sleep. But as the days slowly rolled from one to the other, her feelings, if only but a little, seemed to gradually ease.

She remembered how anxiously she'd waited the afternoon that Tom had brought her home, and then of how the three of them had eaten lunch in the kitchen parlor and became acquainted. And although appalled at what she considered to be quite possibly the worst table manners she'd ever seen, there was something about the young girl she liked. Something that seemed to touch her heart and make her smile. That she'd not felt in a long long time. That seemed to lift her spirit and give her a renewed and growing sense of purpose. Her heart and soul had been so empty for so long, but now here was this young girl, all alone and in desperate need of help, filling it with the joy of life.

They worked together closely and much to her delight, Willie proved to be just what she'd said she was, a great little worker. She was also inquisitive, displaying during the first few days, a delightful sense of wonder for each and every new discovery she'd made, especially the inside flushing toilet and the refrigerator that kept things cold without any ice. There were also the horses, the simple gathering of eggs and the milking of their cows, things she had never done before. She even played with Rex their dog, a pet she'd never had. She learned the farm well, and as the days slowly turned into weeks, the barriers and walls that Elizabeth Portman had erected around her heart gradually began to crumble.

It was Willie's sweet and gentle disposition that at first opened the door, but the longer they worked and talked, and the more Elizabeth learned of her horrific and tragic past, the more she began to open and warm to her endearing ways. It was one of the very last things that she had ever expected. To be touched in such a powerful way as if to even think or imagine that her grief could be lifted. But it was, and it was becoming lighter everyday, she could feel it in her heart and soul as her motherly instincts gradually returned to take control of her emotions.

Willie had been sent to them for a reason, and now with a renewed and almost divine purpose to her life, Elizabeth became determined to help her for as long as she could. But still in the back of her mind, she kept reminding herself that it was just temporary, that it was just until spring or until Tom could find a suitable family or orphanage that could take her in.

As for Willie, it was only natural to find herself genuinely drawn towards the older woman. It had been just over a year since the death her mother and now, here was this lady whom she deeply admired, nurturing and helping her. She liked her immensely, and she liked being and working with her. And although Mrs. Portman was somewhat older than her mother, she found a soothing comfort in her kind and caring ways. But even so, she thought of the man she loved every day, gazing at the cars that would sometimes pass on the road, wondering with an ever-increasing anxiousness as the days slowly turned into weeks, if one of them would finally turn to come and get her.

He'd been away for almost three weeks and as he rolled into Mobile on the afternoon train and crossed the trestle at Chickasaw Creek, he gazed across the river and then thought of Willie. It had been almost a month since he'd last seen her and her well being weighed heavily on his mind. He'd talked to Tom only once since he'd left and that was the following Monday after Willie had arrived. He'd wanted to make sure that things had gone okay, but now he wondered with an almost parental concern as to how she was doing and if she liked her new home? Were they comfortable with her and did they get along? And... did she still look for him to come and get her?

He wanted desperately to know and to see her, but he knew that he couldn't, for his friend had made that abundantly clear. A few minutes later, the train slowed and then finally came to a stop. Looking out through the glass, he smiled at the sight of Melinda and Otis waiting then rose from his seat. A loving kiss and a hug from Melinda, along with news that Otis had finished the house and that she'd already moved in, brought another smile. It was good to be home.

The next day, just a few days before Christmas, Foster had lunch with Tom. They talked at length of Willie, of how she was doing and if he'd found a home for her yet. Tom assured him that things couldn't be better. In fact he said, he thought that Willie was probably the best thing that ever could of happened to him and Liz, and that he'd actually slowed his efforts to find her a home. There was something about her, he added, that seemed to be bringing the joy of life back to his wife. He shook his head in disbelief then thanked his friend. Foster was pleased and took a great comfort in knowing that Willie was happy and cared for, and wanted nothing more than to tell his friend to say hello. But he didn't, for deep down he knew better. Their time was over and he knew it.

A few days later, Christmas came with the warm exchange of gift giving and passed. And as the days quickly rolled into the end of the year and 1932 came into view, Foster and Melinda, along with the

Judge and Mrs. McAlister, boarded a private car on the Louisville and Nashville and headed to Washington for his inauguration.

The weather was terrible with a snowstorm the night before that seemed to paralyze the city, but even so the opening day ceremonies for the newly elected Senators began at ten. It was a bitterly cold and gloomy morning, which quickly turned into a long and grueling day but in the end and when it was finally over, Foster stood proud as Alabama's newest Senator in the photo shoot.

Dinner that evening turned into a festive celebration with Adell and Suzanne joining in. It carried on into the night far later than it really should have, but still the very next day, an excited yet foggy headed Foster rose to embrace his world as a freshman Senator.

"Basically," Suzanne began as she started at the top of her list. "You'll be going in for coffee with the democratic minority leader then after that you'll have breakfast with the majority leader. Oh, and then after that you'll have some talks on orientation, you know, how to get a phone and get around, where the cafeteria is… mundane stuff like that. Then there's a speech from Senator Dryden on the institutional protocol of how to act when you're on the floor. Oh, and I've already been told that it's real long and real boring so be prepared," she rolled her eyes and laughed. "And when all of that's over, then last, you have an appointment with Senator Sellers. I think they're going to put you on that committee they were talking about. You know that Merchant Marine thing."

Staring up from behind his new desk, Foster smiled.

———◆———

By the onset of spring, which seemed as if it had come early that year, Elizabeth and Willie had become quite close. It was the heartache and grief that each had suffered and shared that had brought them so closely and so quickly together. A lost daughter and a lost mother each replaced by the other in a strange twist of fate. A new emotional bond, that in its own unique way, seemed to bring a sort of mending quality to each of them. The filling of an emptiness in their hearts, that gave them each a kind of solace that only they understood.

They worked hard at preparing and planting a huge garden that was filled with vegetables, most of which Willie had never seen or even heard of before. Lettuce and tomatoes and carrots and squash, they even had strawberries. She'd never planted anything in her life that she could eat before, just cotton, and she found a wondrous joy in the fact that these little plants that she was sticking into the ground would soon yield a food that would fill her belly.

But soon they were finished and by the time they had hung up their hoes, it'd become abundantly clear to Elizabeth as to just how sheltered Willie's existence had been, and just how uneducated she really was. She knew that Willie could read, and surprising well considering all things. But even so it troubled her immensely that a girl who was as pretty and as smart as what she seemed, was in such a way. It was obvious that her level of education was far below those from her own age group, and with each and every passing day Elizabeth grew more and more concerned about the girl's future.

She wanted to help, but it had been so long since she'd taught, she wasn't sure. She wasn't even sure if Willie wanted help for that matter. But the nurturing instincts that lay deep inside were growing and it wasn't long before, and with an almost unconscious effort, she'd begun to help. She could see that Willie was rough, actually very rough, and although polite, it was clear that she lacked the skills and social graces that were expected and needed in society, especially from a young lady.

At first she taught Willie table manners and corrected her English, then, and in an even greater sign of affection, she began to teach her the ways of a proper young woman. In the evenings after her bath and before bed, they would play, combing and curling her hair into different styles. They laughed and giggled and grew closer, and before she knew it, and by the beginning of summer, Elizabeth Portman's desire to teach, a desire she'd lost over two and half years ago, had returned.

Pulling her books from their shelves, the once former schoolteacher rose to the challenge with a steadfast determination to educate Willie in all of the basics. It was an arduous undertaking with chores early in the morning followed by lessons of reading and writing and arithmetic until noon. After lunch, and after another hour or so of chores, the two would return to the dining room table where Elizabeth would test her pupil on her morning's lesson. Then before dinner, Willie would finish the afternoon with an hour of piano practice.

It was clear that she wanted to learn, and Elizabeth delighted in the rapid progress of her young student. Willie was amazingly gifted, with a grasp and a thirst for knowledge that exceeded anything she'd ever seen in her twenty years of teaching. She advanced her lessons and within weeks her new pupil began jumping grades. Advancing rapidly in both school and music, she continued to study into the summer delighting not only in each and every new discovery she learned, but also in the fact that she was finally getting her education, just like she'd promised her mother.

By then Elizabeth had come to adore Willie in many ways. She was polite and thoughtful, and had become such a joy in her life that without even realizing it, she had begun to treat her more and more like her daughter than the hired help she actually was. Even to the point of pulling old clothes and shoes from Rebecca's closet for Willie to wear. Most of which fit almost perfectly. The ones that didn't, they altered and sewed together.

To Tom, it was an amazing transformation, watching as his wife returned back into the woman she once was. It was the unintended gift that'd come from a favor he'd done for a friend. There was joy and laughter once again in their house and without informing his wife, he ceased all attempts to find a home for Willie.

They had even begun attending church together, again something that Willie had never done. She met their priest Father Ruggeri and learned prayers and hymns, and became acquainted with the other people that the Portmans knew. There were young boys that would stare with dreamy-eyed gazes then quickly turn away when she looked back. She found them to be funny; Liz did too, but with the guarded instincts of a knowing mother. Especially when it came to the young sandy-haired Danny Mitchell who lived just a couple of farms away. A boy who didn't look away.

Her life had changed in a way she never could have dreamed of with a whole new world that seemed to be opening up to her everyday. She loved it and she loved the Portmans, but even as happy as she was, she never stopped thinking of Foster. He'd promised to come and get her, and even though it had been six months, she still raised her head and looked to the road whenever a car would pass. Stopping whatever it was she was doing, she would catch her breath and then stare with the anxious hope that it would turn. That it was him, finally coming to get her. But the cars never turned, and with each and every one that passed, her hopes and heart seemed to sink a little more. Diminishing in the face of reality, until she'd begun to think that he would never come at all. Until the fateful day finally came when she accepted the fact that he truly was... never coming.

At first she was sad and hurt, and then she became confused. Lost and torn in an emotional way, unable to understand how or why someone who'd professed their love could do such a thing. He'd meant everything to her, but now he was gone. She inquired with Tom but he knew nothing, or so he said. Her heart ached in a way she'd never thought possible and soon she became despondent, doing her chores and studies in an almost hypnotic like way. Shortly after that, her heartache turned to anger and then to hate, until one night as she readied for bed, she pulled from her treasured collection of keepsakes, her marryin paper that he'd given her.

She remembered the day they'd stood in the grass and how happy she had been, and then the sound of his voice as she read its words. *'I Foster K. Siler do hereby adopt Miss Willie Mae Dawson as my lawfully wedded wife to have an to...'* But all to quickly her dream world of yesterday began to fade, and as the grim reality of the truth quickly reclaimed its hold, Willie lost her battle to suppress her tears. She hated him now more than ever, and in a determined effort to end the hold he had on her, she held up the paper to tear it in half. It was her defining moment, but in the fleeting seconds before she pulled, her door squeaked open and she suddenly stopped.

"Willie honey," Liz said as she pushed her door open and entered. "It's time for bed," she added only to suddenly stop at the sight of Willie setting on the edge of her bed crying. "Willie?" she asked as she quickly crossed the room. "What's wrong honey?" she probed as she took a seat and draped an arm across her shoulder. "Are you okay?"

But Willie didn't answer; she just stared at the paper on her lap and wept. Glancing down with a curious concern, Liz studied the paper for just a moment then looked back to Willie. She'd suspected for some time that something had been gnawing at her. Something that she'd tried to pull from on several occasions but failed. She wondered if the paper on her lap was it? "Come on Willie," she coaxed again as she gently rubbed her back. "Tell Miss Liz what's wrong, okay?"

It was all that Willie needed to finally open up, and with a face streaming with tears, she turned to the woman, stared for just a moment then slowly looked back down at the paper. "He told me it was jus like being married, except I couldn't tell no one or I'd get in trouble," she sobbed with a heaving gasp. "An he told me that he loved me an that he'd come back an get me, but he lied," she added as she laid her head into the comfort of Elizabeth's embrace. "He ain't never comin back."

It had been building for months and for the next couple of minutes, Elizabeth listened as Willie, in a moment of heartbreak and sorrow, cried her heart out. She'd always known Foster as a womanizer, but keeping her for a year while he played on her innocence and then tricked into thinking that they were married by pretending to adopt her was just too far. Even for him. She was appalled and incensed at the extent of his deception, and after Willie had settled she tried to explain. But the young girl refused to believe her. Arguing that it wasn't true. That she had her marry-in paper right there and that he wouldn't do that. That he loved her and she knew it. But Elizabeth persisted, and all to soon Willie came to realize that it was Foster who'd lied from the start, and that there was no such thing as adopting someone in marriage. Besides, Liz finally added with a heartfelt reluctance, he was already married to another woman.

It was the final blow to an already fragile heart that reeled Willie in a way in which she hadn't expected. She wanted to die as the illusions of a love she'd once held so dearly instantly disappeared and an overwhelming sense of betrayal enveloped her. She felt sick and nauseated, and wanted nothing more than to end the hurt and escape from the emptiness consuming her. But there was no relief from what she suffered, and the hurt didn't end, and after Liz had tenderly tucked her in and said good night, the sad young girl, all alone and with a broken heart, quietly cried herself to sleep.

The days that followed her heartbreaking revelation proved to be the hardest, but with each and every one that slowly passed, Willie seemed to heal a little more. She'd come to despise Foster for what he'd done, and soon her daily thoughts of the man she once loved, that'd consumed her every waking minute for months, began to wane. He'd deceived and betrayed her in the most unforgiving of ways, and in doing so, he'd lost her love.

CHAPTER 44

BY JULY'S END, IT SEEMED as if Willie had returned to a semblance of
her old self. She no longer cared or thought of Foster and thrived
on her lessons with Miss Liz and church. It was Father Ruggeri and
all of the people she got to meet and talk to on those days that she
enjoyed the most. And although she really didn't understand as to
why they had to sit, kneel and stand so many times in one hour,
she always looked forward to her Sunday mornings. When, after the
animals had been fed and watered, she and Liz would dress in their
Sunday best and get ready for church.

But sometimes it just wasn't in God's will for two women to get ready
on time, and just as it had been so many times in the past, they were late
again. It was a habit that drove Tom crazy, and with a determined to
make up time he turned onto the main road leading into town and hit
the gas. A half-mile down the road they zoomed past two men on horses
and thirty or so men off the side of the road clearing ditches. Dressed in
dirty white jump suits with giant black Ps on their backs, they all looked
the same except for one. And even though she'd caught just a glimpse
of him when they'd passed, Willie knew it was him.

"Stop!" Willie cried out.

"Whaaat?" Tom pulled his foot from the accelerator and jerked
his head to the rear.

"Stoppp," she instantly repeated. "That's my friend!"

"Your friend," he chuckled as he looked around in a state of confusion. "Where?"

"There," Willie turned and pointed out the back through their
plume of dust. "Workin on the side of the road!"

"Working on the side of the road?" Tom repeated with a bewildered glance to his wife.

"Yes, right back there. He's my friend," Willie repeated again. "An I wanna say hi. Pleeease."

"Willie, we can't stop here," he scoffed.

"But why not?" she frowned. "That was my friend. You have to."

"Well, for one we're late for church, and two--,"

"Willie," Elizabeth interrupted as she turned to the back. "Surely you must be mistaken?"

"No, it's him, I saw him, I'm certain. He told me that he'd come here to find work an he did, see!"

"But Willie honey, if that is your friend, you should know that he isn't working there because he wants to. He's working there because he's on a chain gang."

"A what?"

"A chain gang," she repeated. "See, those men back there are prisoners and the men on horses with the shotguns are the guards."

"Prisoners?"

"Yes, prisoners. You know."

"Yes I know, but he couldn't be. Mister Duncan wouldn't hurt no one."

"Well, I'm sorry to say, but if your friend as you wish to call him, is on that chain gang, I can assure you that he has in some way broken the law and that is why he is there. See, that's why we have laws and courts, so we can punished those who are bad or would want to hurt us."

"But he wouldn't do nothin bad, or hurt no one, I know him."

"You know him?" She raised her eyebrows. "And just how is it you know this man?"

"He saved my life," she answered as she lowered her head and the men disappeared.

There was a somber quiet that quickly followed until Tom finally sighed and then glanced into the mirror. "Willie," he said in an attempt to appease her. "I'll tell you what, how about if we stop on our way back after church, okay? I can assure you those men aren't going very far, and then we'll have a little more time to deal with it, okay?"

"Okay," she answered and smiled. "But you promise?"

Glancing back into the mirror, he caught Willie's gaze then nodded and pressed on the gas. "Yes, I promise."

The hour long service and the conversations that came afterwards proved excruciating for Willie, but just as soon as they'd left the church, Tom drove back just as he'd promised. But the men and guards they'd seen earlier were gone, and with them so was her friend. Distraught that he was no longer there, yet still certain that the man she'd seen was her friend, Willie insisted that they drive the other roads. An hour later, and after searching every back road there was, they returned to the farm. Willie was disappointed and that night at supper, she ate her dinner with a quiet somberness.

"Come on Willie," Elizabeth encouraged. "Eat your supper, aren't you hungry?"

"No ma'am, I mean, not really," she replied as she continued to dabble at her food.

"But you love meat loaf, it's your favorite."

"I know, except tonight I'm jus not very hungry for some reason."

It was clear to both Tom and Elizabeth as to what was bothering Willie, but still they were confused as to just how to handle the situation. Pausing in thought, Liz finally looked to her husband then raised her eyebrows and dipped her head if to say that it was now his turn. Taking his que with a reluctant nod, Tom took a sip from his tea then wiped his mouth and cleared his throat.

"Willie?"

"Yes sur," she answered and looked up from her plate.

"Can I ask you something?"

"Yes sur," she nodded.

"You seem just a little preoccupied there. Now that wouldn't be because you're still worried about your friend, would it?"

"Yes sur, I think."

"Well, I can certainly understand that, but can I explain something to you."

"Yes sur," she nodded again.

"Good, now you know that I'm a judge right?"

"Yes sur."

"And you know that part of my job as a judge is to put bad people in jail. People that have broken the law, right?"

"Yes sur."

"Good, now your friend has obviously--."

"But Mister Duncan didn't do nothin," she interrupted in his defense. "I know he didn't! An he shouldn't be there!"

"Willie," Tom raised his voice and inhaled an aggravated breath. "If your friend is there, he's there for a reason! He has either hurt someone or he has done something wrong, it's that simple. Now, as I was getting ready to say, he has obviously had a fair trial and has been found guilty."

"Nooo!" she cried out and rose from her chair. "He didn't hurt no one, an he didn't do nothin wrong either. I know he didn't. He couldn't!" A second later, the defiant young girl pushed her chair from the table and rushed to her room.

Gazing at each other across the table, Tom and Elizabeth could only shake their heads and exhale with heavy sighs. They were lost at what to do, but before they could say a word and much to their surprise, Willie returned just as fast as she'd left then sat back down with a jar full of money.

"Willie?" Elizabeth queried with a confused expression. But Willie didn't answer, she just looked at Tom and slowly pushed her jar towards him.

"What's this?" He narrowed his eyes and cocked his head.

"It's my money that I've been savin... all of it."

"But what?" he drew out his voice.

"You said you was a lawyer before you was a judge, so there. I want you to take it an help my friend. He saved my life, an if he's in trouble, I wanna help him."

Taking a heavy breath, Tom looked first at the jar and then to his wife. He was looking for help, but found only a simple shrug of her shoulders and with that he slowly looked back to Willie. "And you're willing to give me all of this to help your negro friend?"

"Yes sur," she nodded. "It's all I got, but it's over a hundred dollars. An if that ain't enough, I can do extra chores for you."

It was at that very moment that Tom suddenly realized just how much her friend really meant to her. Touched not only by her convictions but by her actions, or her stubbornness really, he stared at the jar for just a moment longer then pushed it back to Willie. "I'll tell you what," he sighed. "You just keep your money. And if you really feel that strongly about it, I'll try and meet with the prosecuting attorney in the morning and see if I can't at least find out why your friend is in jail. But there's no promises ya hear," he pointed his finger. Gaining the smile and nod that he thought he would, Tom reached down and picked up his fork. "Good, now let's finish your supper before it gets any colder than what it already is."

The very next day and just as he'd promised, Tom Portman walked into Cyrus Buchanan's office. "Well," Delores greeted as he walk through the door. "Good mornin Judge."

"Morning Delores," he greeted as he approached her desk. "How are you today?"

"Oh heck, I'm jus fine thank you. An you?"

"Great," Tom replied.

"Well good, an I guess you're here to see Cyrus?"

"Yes ma'am," he grinned. "He is in, isn't he?"

"Oh yes sir, jus go right on in," she waved her hand. "Heck, he ain't do'n nothin."

Stepping through the door with a knock, Tom found Cyrus sitting behind his desk and quickly gained his attention. "Morning Cyrus."

"Well well," Cyrus greeted as he looked up. "Mornin Tom, come on it," he added as he stood and extended his hand. "It's been awhile. Please, have a seat won't you."

"Thank you Cyrus," Tom said as he shook the man's hand and then settled into his chair.

"So tell me, what the heck brings you out so early?"

"Well," Tom began as if he didn't quite know where to start. "I'm actually looking for someone, someone who I think you might have here in the county jail."

"A prisoner?"

"Yeah, I think so."

"Well shit Tom," Cyrus laughed. "We've got lots of them. Does he have a name?"

"Yeah he does. It's Duncan Haywood. You don't remember him by any chance, do you?"

"Duuucan Haywooood," Cyrus repeated as if he were trying to recall the name, only to shake his head and then look back to Tom. "Boy Tom, I sure am sorry, but I just don't recall no Duncan Haywood," he said as he continued to shake his head. "But if he's in jail, I can sure get him for you pretty quick. Why, what'd he do?"

"Well," Tom chuckled. "I'm not really sure to be right truthful with you, and that's what I'm trying to find out. He's a black man if that helps you any... a great big black man."

"A great big black man you say?" Cyrus repeated and cocked his head. "Like a great big giiiiant black man?"

"Yeaaah," Tom nodded. "Do you know him?"

"Well, you know, now that you said that, I think I do know who you're talkin about. Yeah, as matter of fact, I'm certain of it," he added, proud that he'd remembered. "Hell, we put that ol boy away sometime last fall if I remember right."

"You did?"

"Yep."

"So what'd he do?"

"Do?"

"Yeah," Tom insisted. "You know, what kind of crime did he commit?"

"Crime?" Cyrus chuckled. "Aaah to be right truthful with ya, I'm not really sure, but I think the official charge by the time we got to court was vagrancy."

"Vagrancy?"

"Yeah, I'm pretty sure that's what it was. Hell, we couldn't get him on anything else, an shit, I had to have something to put him away on," he chuckled again.

"Put him away...why? What was he doing?"

"Well, to put it bluntly, he was scarin people."

"Scaring people? What-a you mean?"

"Well, just what I said, he was scarin people... shit, all over town."

"How?"

"Goddamn Tom, have you not ever seen this boy?"

"No, I can't say that I have. Why?"

"Well let's jus say that he is without a doubt the biggest goddamn nigger that you'll ever see."

"Whaaat?" Tom stammered in disbelief. "What'd you just say?"

"You heard me, I said he's big. Reeeeal big."

"So wait a minute," Tom took an incensed breath. "Are you actually telling me that you arrested and convicted a man on trumped up vagrancy charges and then incarcerated him just because he was big and black and people were afraid of him? Is that what I'm hearing?"

"Wellll, yeah, I guess," Cyrus replied. "If you really wanna put it that a way."

"Put it that way? Meee?" Tom's sense of outrage rose. "Are you out of your goddamn mind? Jesus Christ Cyrus, do you have any idea as to just how many counts of prosecutorial misconduct you've violated?" He paused for a breath then instantly continued. "Shit, I ought-a get up right now and call the Attorney General and have charges filed against you."

"Ah come on Tom. Hell, it ain't nothin to go and get all riled up about," Cyrus argued in defense of what he'd done. "Shit, he's just a big ol dumb nigger. Heck, he don't know no better. And besides, who in the hell cares."

"Well, that he very well may be, but let me tell you, he's still a man and in case you've forgotten, he's still entitled to due process and equal justice under the law. And as far as who cares, well, let's just say that I do now. Now," he said as he rose from his chair and pointed his finger on top of Cyrus's desk. "Here's what I want, and I want it to happen today!"

That evening at dinner Willie was ecstatic to learn she'd been right about her friend and that he'd be freed the next day so he could go back home. "Thank you Mister Tom, I'm truly grateful."

"Well Willie, you're quite welcome, but you don't have to thank me, all I did was correct an injustice that should've never of happened in the first place. You're the one who really deserves the thanks, especially from Mister Haywood."

"Oh no sur, Mister Duncan doesn't never have to thank me for nothin, not ever. Not after what he did for me."

"Well, that very well may be, but still, he'll have his chance cause tomorrow morning were going to meet him at the train station."

"Really?" Willie smiled in surprise.

"Yep, he's going back home and I told him that we'd meet him there so you could visit for a bit and say goodbye before he left. That is, if you still want to see your friend?"

"Oooh yes sur," she nodded with another smile. "What time?"

"Ten o'clock, which still gives you plenty of time to get all your chores done and still get to the station so you can visit before he leaves."

It had quickly turned into a contentious fight, but in the end it was Tom's threats to take Cyrus before the State Board of Inquiry that'd prevailed and persuaded him to finally do as he was told. He absolutely hated the fact that he was being forced to help a black man, but the very next day and just as he'd been instructed, he had Duncan Haywood at the train station dressed in brand new overalls and boots, along with twenty-five dollars cash, a sack full of food and a bona-fide ticket all the way back home. All of which were the compliments of the prosecuting attorney of Mobile County.

Accompanied by two armed deputies just to ensure that things went smoothly and he got on the train without an incident, Duncan waited. And although he was required to ride in the baggage car, he couldn't have been happier. But the reunion between he and Willie was not to happen, for on the way into town Tom hit a pothole and blew a front tire. It was a harrowing moment, and even though they'd changed it as hastily as they could, by the time they'd pulled into the parking lot and stopped, the train was already leaving.

"Noo," Willie cried as she jumped from the car and ran toward the rolling train. Watching in hopes of seeing her friend, she stared at each and every car until she finally spied him sitting against the far side of an open boxcar. Yelling his name along with a great big wave, she tried to gain his attention, but the rumbling of the train and the distance was too great, and her words never reached his ears.

It was a disheartening moment, for she'd wanted desperately to see and visit with him, and to give him her little present, an envelope with his name and five one dollar bills in it so he could eat. And even though she stood and watched with watery eyes as the train slowly rolled away, she was glad that he was finally returning home to his family. Then with a final wave to a man who couldn't see her and didn't know she was even there, she turned to Tom and hugged him then began to cry.

CHAPTER 45

———◆———

THERE WASN'T A THING THAT Foster didn't like about Washington. The city and its energy, the constant buzz of political life, and of course, his very attractive aide, Miss Suzanne Schubert. A woman who he now shared his bed with on a regular basis. But it was his appointment to what he considered as the not so glamorous Merchant Marine and Fisheries Committee that proved to be what he relished the most.

It was early that spring that he'd been given the task of drafting the language for the new change in policy. The request had come directly from the White House. Hoover had been looking for ways to revitalize and stimulate the growth of the shipping industry and in doing so he asked for a new construction and operational program that would help subsidize the high cost of doing business. Direct cash payments from the Federal Government to qualified companies seeking to buy and build new ships and then operate them in the world of international commerce. Ships that were desperately needed for the country, that could compete on a global scale and in such a depressed market.

Working tirelessly as one of the leading architects of the bill, Foster soon came to realize not only the government's desire and need for a Merchant Marine fleet, but also the unprecedented opportunity that was now at hand. Ships that were heavily subsidized by the federal government, free money for private enterprises, how interesting.

He thought of the docks back in Mobile and of all the ships he'd seen coming and going on his journeys to see Willie. His mind began to wander, but just as quickly as he envisioned himself at the helm of one of his own ships, he dismissed it. He was a United States Senator for Christ's sake and hadn't even been on the ocean, besides he couldn't even drive the *Willie Mae* without wrecking it.

A few months later, and just shortly after the bill had passed, one of the first applications to come before the Commission was from the former Senator Harlen Crandell. He'd heard rumors of the man's intentions after politics and now here they were, all confirmed. It seemed that just shortly before the election, Crandell and his business partners had purchased a five hundred foot-long freighter. He knew that the administration had been planning to draft a new bill and push it through Congress, and in his arrogance he'd made a hasty purchase with every intent of subsidizing their ship just as soon as it had passed.

Anticipating what they believed would be a quick and favorable approval from the Shipping Board, Crandell and his partners never could've imagined that the man who'd taken his seat now sat on the very committee that controlled the board... and their fate. Viewed with what was clearly a great deal of disdain, Foster quickly stalled the approval process to a snails pace. Bogged down in what had quickly become one of the most tangled webs of bureaucratic red tape that he'd ever seen, Crandell and his partners soon found their application rejected again and again. In part out of revenge for the vicious and slanderous campaign attacks that Foster had endured during the election, but also for the pure and simple fact that a golden opportunity had just been laid down in front of him. He knew that Crandell and his partners could never hold on without their subsidy. They'd paid way too much for their ship, and without the government's assistance, they could never compete and survive in such a depressed and competitive market. He'd found his boat, and now if everything played out as planned, it was just a matter of time. But still in the back of his mind, he wondered as to what would he ship? He needed something to ship.

Later that summer, the junior Senator called on the Continental Paper Company, a national leader in the growing paper products industry. He'd heard they were wanting to build a new plant and that they'd considered other cities, but with Mobile's location, abundant supply of water and wood that was suitable for manufacturing, it looked to be the best. Yet even so, their talks with the mayor and the city council had stalled and they were ready to move on.

Assessing the significance of their proposal and what it could actually mean to the local economy, Foster worked tirelessly to regain their business. They talked for weeks, but still the company was reluctant, they needed and wanted more to make the move and build their plant. They talked of tax breaks and then of a subsidy upon completion of their plant. It was the final enticement needed to lure them back to Mobile. A one hundred thousand dollar subsidy to be raised by the local Chamber of Commerce and businesses who stood to gain from their coming.

The people joined together and after a successful campaign headed by Foster, the deal was made. A few weeks later, along with the promise of five hundred new jobs for the community, the company broke ground in a much-publicized ceremony. It was a win win for everyone, but especially for Foster. The new company would need trees on an unprecedented scale, and with his untouched old growth forest lying just north of their plant, he quickly made a deal with the board of directors to harvest half of his acreage.

By the fall of that year, 1932, and with the success of Continental Paper now behind him, the ambitious young Senator set his sights on an even larger company, American Aluminum. With the demand for aluminum on the rise in the country, the company had been looking for a place to build a new bauxite refinery. A state of the art plant that could turn bauxite ore into alumina for the smelters up north. A plant that had a multitude of requirements, including a good geographical location along with a good port facility and a cheap supply of labor.

It'd taken some time, but before the end of the year, Foster had finally struck another home run for the people of Mobile. Again working tirelessly with the local business and civic leaders, he finally convinced the board of directors to sign a ninety-nine year lease on one of the new state docks and along with it, purchase the adjoining seventy-five acres to build a four million dollar plant.

It was a deal that instantly brought a national attention to the city and its new port facility, and as soon it had closed, construction began with another ground-breaking ceremony covered in almost every paper there was. Forging a strong relationship with the men on the board during the process in which he had worked so long on, Foster soon learned of their impending plans to bring shipments of bauxite up from Latin America. Shortly after that, he orchestrated another deal with them and quietly secured the rights to deliver their ore. His timing couldn't have been better for he had almost a year in which to secure a ship. A ship he was certain he would take from Crandell and his partners.

———◆———

It was a small school with mixed grades not far from the farm where Elizabeth had enrolled Willie. She wanted to develop Willie's social skills with her peers, and to continue her education in a different environment. And although it was hard at first, Willie, under Elizabeth's tutelage, excelled at her studies and by the spring of 33 had made it through her first year of school.

But even so, Elizabeth wanted more for the incredibly gifted and beautiful seventeen year old. She could see her potential and she wanted her to have every advantage in life there was. And now that Willie was of the appropriate age, she enrolled her in Miss Winfields. A finishing school for up and coming debutantes, that offered a six-week course during the summer.

"But I don't wanna go Miss Liz. It's summer an I just got out of school," Willie whined in protest. "An I'm tired of readin an writin an do'n homework, an I just wanna ride my horse. Pleeease."

"I know, I know," Elizabeth replied as she set her bucket of water down and then wiped her brow. "But if you keep on riding poor ol Cricket the way you've been doing I'm afraid you're gonna wear his little hoofs right off of him," she laughed. "Besides, I'm pretty sure that little Danny Mitchell will be just fine without the presence of your company every single day."

"Whooo?" Willie feigned with the most innocent of expressions.

"Danny Mitchell," Elizabeth repeated with a knowing gaze. "You knooow... that cute young boy that you go and see every time you take off and go riding," she teased. "I've seen the way he looks at you at church. And if I'm not mistaken, I'd say he's just about as sweet on you as he can get isn't he?" She raised her eyebrows and waited.

"Wellll," Willie blushed and smiled then dropped her gaze and kicked a clump of dirt. "He isss kind-a cute."

"Yes he isss," Liz agreed. "And he's all boy, too," she added and pointed her finger. "And young boys have a way of talking young girls into doing things that they shouldn't. So I want you to promise me right now that you'll stay out of them haylofts, ya hear. That's no place for a proper young lady."

"Yes ma'am," Willie sighed and kicked the clump of dirt again. "Iiii promise."

"Good, now back to this school business. See, at Miss Winfield's there are no books and there is no homework."

"Well then, if there ain't no books, then why do ya need to go?"

"Aren't!" Elizabeth instantly corrected. "If there aren't any books."

"Yes ma'am, I'm sorry, I forgot."

"Well, you go to learn how to eat and sit, and walk and talk and just all kinds of things that make you a lady."

"But I already know how to walk an talk an--."

"Well this is different," Elizabeth interrupted. "And Miss Winfield's is the best. Besides, you'll have fun and you'll get to meet other girls from all over the city.

"But."

"No buts, hear. It's all ready settled. I enrolled you two weeks ago and you start next Monday. Now let's get these tomato plants watered and when you're done, make sure you pull all the little suckers off like I showed you, okay."

"Yes ma'am," Willie drawled with a defeated sigh.

A week later and just as Elizabeth had wanted, Willie walked through the doors of Miss Winfield's School for Young Ladies. And just as the doctors had predicted to Foster and Melinda last fall, their newborn son, Robert Randal Siler entered into the world at the Mobile County Hospital. It was a jubilant and exciting time for Foster, for along with the birth of his son, the plans that he'd worked on and set into motion over a year ago were finally coming together. He'd already secured the contract with American Aluminum to begin bringing bauxite up from Latin America upon completion of their plant, and now with his final payment from Continental Paper for his trees, he had his seed money in which to get his ship. Everything that he'd been working on was complete. The pieces were in place, and now he even knew where to go. He'd been watching, closely and calmly like a predator ready to strike.

It had been almost two years since Crandell and his cronies had purchased their boat and they were struggling to survive. Business was slow and Crandell had relied far to heavily on his status and clout as a means of gaining his much-needed subsidy and all the business they would need. But over the years the once powerful Senator had made more enemies than friends, and almost instantly after the election, his status and influence had evaporated.

His reputation had been ruined in the scandal and he could no longer strong-arm and bully his way into deals, or toss about political favors like pieces of candy. People met with him and were cordial, but did little to help. Some even made a point to distance themselves. He called in favors from the past and discounted their rates in an attempt to save their business, but to no avail. His world was crumbling, and with each and every attempt for that crucial government subsidy, Foster thwarted their progress, ensuring that they continued toward a slow yet certain financial death.

It wasn't exactly common knowledge, but Foster knew through their application that it was a bank in New Orleans that held their mortgage. First Southern and Savings. He'd even called expressing an interest in the ship that did nothing but sit in port most of the time. It was all that the board needed to make their decision and call in their note late that summer of 33. His tactics had worked, and just after they had foreclosed on Crandell's ship, and just four months before the new bauxite plant was to open, Foster made plans to visit New Orleans.

CHAPTER 46

———◆———

THE INSPECTION OF THE SHIP, along with his meeting of its captain, the thirty one year old Ralston DuPree' proved to be exactly what Foster had hoped it would be. The ship, *The Eastern Star*, was sound and had just undergone a number of upgrades. The captain, although a little younger than what he'd imagined, seemed professional, intelligent and confident, and had a crew that was more than ready to make for the sea. They were mariners and they'd been at port long enough.

He told them of Crandell's demise and of his intent to buy the ship, and then of his contracts with American Aluminum to begin bringing bauxite up from Latin America on a regular basis. They all agreed to come on board and were elated to know that once again they'd have work. And although they would be working at reduced wages and would port out of Mobile, they still promised their new boss timely and worry-free deliveries. An easy run they said, straight down into the Gulf with a right turn through the Panama Canal, then a left on the other side and down the coast in gentle seas.

Later that same afternoon, Foster strolled through the doors of First Southern and Savings of New Orleans. His day so far had been a success, and as he stopped in front of the reception desk, he was instantly greeted by a lovely young lady. "Yes sir, may I help you?"

"Yes ma'am," Foster drawled. "I'm Senator Siler, and I'm here to see Henry Fletcher."

"Oh yes sir," she replied. "Mr. Fletcher's been expecting you. Please, if you'd like to have a seat," she continued as she rose from her chair. "I'll let him know that you're here."

"Yes ma'am. Thank you."

His wait was short for no sooner than the girl had disappeared, than he was turning to the sound of a man exuberantly calling his name. "Senator Siler?"

"Yes sir," Foster stood and extended his hand as he approached.

"Henry Fletcher here. I must say, it is certainly a pleasure to finally meet you."

"Yes sir, and you too. I've been looking forward to this for some time."

"Well good, then come with me won't you. Oh and Betty," the man suddenly stopped and turned back. "Could you be so kind as to let Mr. Sinclair and Mr. Cummings know that Senator Siler is here. I'd like for them to join us if they could."

"Yes sir, I'll get them right away."

Henry Fletcher's office occupied a sizable corner of the banks second floor with windows on both outer walls that afforded a view of the tree-lined streets below. As soon as they were inside, he re-arranged the chairs in front of his desk and offered Foster a seat then took his place behind his desk. A moment later, the two men he'd spoken of entered the room and joined them. They were the boards ranking members, and after a round of introductions, they too took their seats next to Foster.

"Now Senator," Henry began. "Just how is it that we might be of service to you?"

"Well gentlemen," Foster replied with a glance to the two men beside him and then to Henry behind his desk. "As I mentioned in my phone call several weeks ago, I am here because I have an interest in a boat that you have. Or, if I may be a little more precise, the one that you just repossessed from Harlen Crandell. *The Eastern Star.*"

Gaining a smile from all three, Foster paused for just a second then continued on. He knew that they didn't want to carry a high priced ship on their books, and their reactions, however subtle they may have been, confirmed it. "Now, if we can come to what I'd like to call, a mutually acceptable agreement, I'd like to purchase this boat. That is, if it is still available? And, the price is right."

Gaining another round of smiles, Jasper Cummings cleared his throat then sat forward in his chair. He was the chairman of the board and what he said mattered. "Well, that sounds wonderful Senator," he began then looked to Henry behind his desk. "Henry, just what-a we need to get out of this mess and get this goddamn thing off of our books?"

"I believe," Henry replied as he opened the folder and studied his papers. "It's right at two hundred and thirty-five thousand... and some change."

"Well gentlemen," Foster began as if he'd just wasted their time. "I'm truly sorry, but I'm afraid that is far more than I'd bargained on. See, I was thinking more along the lines of two hundred."

"Two hundred?" Morgan Sinclair scoffed. "Come on Senator, the boat's worth two fifty and you know it. Especially with all of the upgrades that've been done to it."

"Well, that's probably true Mr. Sinclair, but only if you have someone who is willing to pay it. And with the economy the way that it is, I don't see a whole lot of people walking around with two hundred grand in their pocket."

"And you do?" He raised his eyebrows and stared.

"Well, not exactly. But I do have the financing."

"You have the financing?" He narrowed his eyes in a skeptical way.

"Yes sir."

"And what crazy bank did this?"

"The Federal Government," Foster smiled.

"The Federal Government?" Sinclair repeated as if he'd not heard correctly.

"Yes sir, the Federal Government," Foster reiterated along with another smile. "See, and I know that you're probably not aware of this yet, but there's a whole bunch of people back in Washington that've gotten it in their heads that the Federal Government is the only one who can revitalize this god-awful economy we're in. Now the good thing is, is that they think the only way that they can do this is by spending the hard earned money of the American tax payers in ways and in amounts that well," he shook his head and smiled. "That you just can't possible imagine.

"Now last year, I was put on a committee that rewrote a new bill for the shipping industry. See, President Hoover, before he was voted out, had been wanting to replace the older and slower ships from World War I that we use in our merchant marine fleet. Now even though this was done under his administration, it passed with over-whelming bi partisan support and was not only endorsed, but embraced by our new President, Mr. Roosevelt himself. Who, by the way, just loves the idea of a newer and stronger merchant marine fleet for the country. Now you're probably wondering just what in the hell does all of this have to do with us? Well gentlemen, let me explain if I may."

This was his moment and he knew it, and for the next ten minutes the men listened as Foster laid out his proposal in a friendly and per-suasive way. At first they scoffed at his idea, but the young Senator was convincing, showing first his exclusive contracts with American Aluminum then of how he could manipulate and fast-track the system, ensuring that within sixty days of the sale and transfer of the ship to Siler Shipping, that they'd have their money. All of it he told them, the courtesy of the Federal Government. Their interest peaked and soon they came to realize that there was not only merit to his ideas, but profits as well... and large ones. But still, there was a reluctance amongst them and Foster could sense it.

"Well Senator," Morgan began with a heavy breath. "Your little gov-ernment subsidy sounds all fine and rosy in a perfect world, but with all do respect I do have a couple of questions that I'd like to ask if you don't mind."

"No sir, not at all."

"Well one, what you're really proposing, isn't that breaking the law?"

"No sir," Foster answered without hesitation. "Not at all, although it could be seen by some as bending it, it is certainly not breaking it. And you gentlemen, and your bank, would in no way be tied to any of the things that I do."

"Okay, I can accept that, but tell me. If we do decide to go along with your proposal, what's to keep your application from getting tan-gled up in committee? You know, like Crandell's did?"

"Well Mr. Sinclair, I can certainly understand your reluctance, especially after what he has put you through. But let me assure you in no uncertain terms, that that will not happen to us."

"And why's that?"

"Because I not only was one of the leading architects that drafted the language for the bill, I also sit on the committee that oversees and controls the shipping board."

Gazing at the young Senator, Morgan Sinclair stared for just a moment then began to smile. "So it was you all along, wasn't it? You killed it?"

"Killed it… killed what sir?" Foster asked innocently.

"Crandell's application. He kept telling us for almost a year that he was going to get it approved, but it never happened. And now we know why, don't we," he finished as if he'd just solved some great riddle.

"Please, Mr. Sinclair," Foster feigned as if he'd just been offended. "Such a harsh accusation."

"But it's the truth and you know it," Morgan pressed.

"Well," Foster replied in defense of his actions. "You can look at Mr. Crandell's inability to get his subsidy any which way you'd like, but the way I prefer to see it was that he and his associates were just unable to meet the stringent requirements of the government. You know, the safeguards that'd been put in place to ensure that the hard earned money of the American tax payers was used in the proper way."

"Well, the son-of-a-bitch certainly got what he deserved, but still, I just don't know," he shook his head. "See, we didn't become the largest bank here in New Orleans by making one bad loan after the next, and since we actually made this one under pressure, what we'd really like to do is just get our money back and go on down the road."

"Then do my deal." Foster insisted. "I have everything in place! Everything, and I guarantee that within sixty days you'll have your money."

He'd given it his best and with that he sat back in his chair, took in a heavy breath and waited. It was a big decision, and for a few short moments he watched as the three men looked back and forth between each other and contemplated his proposal. There were no words spoken, but yet he knew that they were communicating. Conversing in a silent language with their eyes until the two sitting beside him gave Henry the subtlest of nods and the deal was made.

"Well Senator," Henry exclaimed with an elated smile. "Congratulations, you've just bought yourself a boat. We would be delighted to do business with you... annnd the Federal Government. Now, let's see if we can't work out all of the details, shall we."

By the time Foster had exited the bank he'd gotten almost everything he had wanted including an unexpected invitation to dinner and a night on the town. The men he'd met with had quickly picked up on the creative young Senator's grasp of capitalism, and saw in him a new and valued customer. A customer with the potential of bringing future business to their bank, big business, that was backed by the government. They were elated, and so with every intent in the world to wine and dine him in a way he never could've imagined, they made plans to show him their city's nightlife.

———◆———

First it was a five star dinner at Rafi'ls, an amazing combination of French and Creole cuisine that was unlike anything he'd ever had before. Shortly after that, it was a tour of the French Quarter that led the four men into one of the most exclusive and elegant brothels in town. A place where some of the most beautiful women in the city came to ply their charms and cater to the affluent in the most discrete yet decadent of ways. A sanctuary of ill repute that'd been set off of the beaten path, where the quest for pleasures had no limits.

The big man at the door knew the bankers well and as soon as they entered, a scantily clad young girl greeted them in the parlor with a tray of champagne. It was an old but beautiful Victorian manor, meticulously remodeled and lavishly decorated with the finest of everything that money could buy. A place that'd been created just for the wealthy, and as he looked around and took in the room, Foster smiled and then lifted his glass to take a sip. But before the bubbly even touched his lips, he stopped and narrowed his eyes as if he'd just seen a ghost from the past.

At first he wasn't sure, but as he continued to stare from across the room, he knew without question that it was her. Standing with a group of well-dressed businessmen, talking and laughing as if she hadn't a care in the world. Still as beautiful as ever, he could see her face and her smile, and then her eyes as she casually looked up to see who had entered.

She knew the men well and thought nothing of them being there, until she spotted Foster and a surprised gleam filled her hazy blues as they narrowed in and then lock with his. She'd not seen him in almost three years, and for a few fleeting moments she could only stare in a state of uncertainty. She felt embarrassed and ashamed that she'd been caught by someone who she cared a great deal for in a place she really shouldn't be. But there was no escaping the obvious, and after just a few moments, and in what appeared to be a polite and gracious exit, she excused herself and casually crossed the room.

He'd often wondered what'd happened to her and now he knew. And as she crossed the room and came toward them, he saw a knowing smile pull at her lips. Yet somehow, and deep down, he could still see a sort of sadness to it. As if the failures in her life had finally caught up with her and had begun to eat and chip away at her hardened exterior, gnawing and chiseling at her until all that remained was what stood before him. He thought of the many times that they'd spent together and smiled, then wondered how it was she had ended up here. He cleared his throat to greet her, but before he could say a word she was talking and acting as if she'd never seen him before.

"Gentlemen, good evening," she drawled with a radiant smile as she gave each of them a glance but then settled with her eyes on Foster. "And Hennnry, what a pleasant surprise, and how nice of you to visit again. But tell me, pleeease," she rolled her eyes in the most flirtatious of ways. "Just who is your new friend here? I don't believe that I've ever seen him here before, have I?"

"No ma'am," Henry answered. "I don't believe you have, but please allow me, if I may. Katherine, this is Senator Foster Siler, a new and very special client of ours. And Foster, this here is Miss Katherine Davenport, the lady in charge of this here fine establishment, and without a doubt one of the most beautiful women that we have here in our fine city."

Blushing at his compliment, yet still pretending as if they'd never met, Katherine took a small step forward and with the subtlest of winks, extended her hand. "Well Senator," she began as she stared into his eyes and shook his hand. "I must say that this is most certainly an unexpected pleasure, how nice to make your acquaintance."

"Yes ma'am, but I do believe," he said as he gently pulled her hand to his lips. "That the pleasure is all mine."

Smiling as yet another light blush swept across her face, Katherine turned to Henry. "Oooh my, Henry," she drawled with a laugh. "Not only is your new friend here divinely handsome, he is charming as well. So I must ask, where ever did you find him?"

"Well," Henry answered amidst a rise of chuckles. "Actually, he found us. But in answer to your question, I believe Mobile."

"Mobile?" She feigned her surprise. "Surely you jest?"

"No ma'am," he shook his head.

"Well I'll be, what a small world it truly is. Why that's where I'm from, but yet I don't believe that we've ever met before... have we?" She smiled.

"No ma'am," Foster answered as he joined in her game of charades. "I don't believe that we have actually, but I'm sure we must know some of the same people. Mobile isn't that big."

"Yes, yesss," Katherine's eyes lit up. "I'm sure you're right, and now that you mentioned it I would just love to," she went on but then she suddenly stopped and dismissed herself with the wave of her hand. "Oh never mind," she apologized. "I'm sorry, I just couldn't."

"Oh no," Foster encouraged. "Love to what, ma'am?"

"Well," she sighed. "I know that you have obviously come here for other reasons, and that you are probably going to think that this is incredibly rude and selfish of me, but I was wondering if you might spare just a few moments to sit and chat. I do miss Mobile so, and I would just love to hear about everything that has been going on since I left. That is... if you don't mind?"

"Oh, no ma'am," Foster replied with a knowing smile. "I don't mind at all, in fact, I'd be delighted to talk with you."

"Really?"

"Absolutely."

"Oh how wonderful," she said. "I must say you have no idea as to how truly happy that makes me. Now Henry," she turned back to her friend. "Why don't I see if I can't find some special ladies for you gentlemen. And then, if you don't mind, I'm going to abscond with your new friend here for just a little while, you know, to catch up on all the latest."

"Well, I don't know Katherine," he teased. "I've heard some stories about you."

"Henry!" she cried out as if he'd offended her virtue then laughed. "Let's not start telling tales."

"Well okay," he relented. "But only if you promise to bring him back in one piece."

Gaining another round of chuckles, a slightly embarrassed Katherine just shook her head then turned and surveyed the room. A second later, she spied the girl she was looking for talking with the bartender.

"Charlotte," she called with a beckoning wave over the mixed drone of a half dozen conversations.

Turning to the sound of her madam, the pretty young brunette quickly crossed the room and then stopped. "Yes ma'am?"

"Charlotte, you remember Mr. Fletcher here don't you?"

"Oh, yes ma'am," she smiled coyly.

"Well good, because I'd like you to take him and these fine gentlemen that are with him, and go and find Sally and Rachael. And then I want you girls to see to it that they get whatever it is they want for just as long as they want it, okay."

"Oooh yes ma'am," she nodded with yet another smile. "I can certainly do that."

"Yesss, I thought you could," she replied and then turned back to the men. "That is if that's okay with you gentlemen?" she jested as she glanced from one to the next. "And now Senator," she said as she turned back to Foster. "I guess that leaves just you and me now," she continued on as she slipped her arm in his. "So shall we?"

A moment later, and with the promise to see them the next day, Foster left with the dark-haired beauty and headed toward the stairs. It was awkward at first with little or no words from either, but just as soon as they'd reached the steps and were out of hearing range, Katherine stopped and turned.

"Oh Foster," she began. "I do hope you're not upset that I acted as if I didn't know you, but I thought it best to keep things--."

"No nooo," he interrupted. "I don't mind at all, but what are you?" He cocked his head and narrowed his eyes.

"What am I doing here?" she finished his question with a dismissive laugh.

"Yes."

Pausing in thought, Katherine just shook her head with a heavy sigh then grabbed the banister of the grand circular staircase and took a step. "Well it's kind of a long story... but you!" she exclaimed in an attempt to change the subject. "Look at you, you're a United States Senator now, just like you said. And I know you don't know this, but I read about you all the time in the paper. I'm so proud of you and everything that you've done for Mobile."

"Yes, thank you, but still, what are you doing here?"

"Oh yesss, that." she paused again after just a few steps. "Well, like I just said it's kind of a long story," she began as if she were confessing her sins. "But after Howard died, or should I say, killed himself. You did know he died, didn't you?"

"Yes, I read about it in the paper last year, I'm truly sorry, Howard was a good man."

"Yes, he really was actually," she lowered her head in a moment of reverence but then turned and continued with her steps. "But even so, he just couldn't get over the fact that we'd lost everything, and after he lost his last job, well, that's when I found him. It was just horrible, then, and if things couldn't get any worse, Bobby left me not too long after that and took off for California. I was just devastated and just about as alone and destitute as one could get. I didn't have anything anymore, nothing to pay the rent with or buy groceries with, nothing."

"But why didn't you call me? I could've helped you. You know that."

"I know," she sighed. "But by then I was determined to make it on my own so I went out and got a job as a waitress in a little café, actually not to far from here really. It was the first real job that I'd ever had and to be right truthful with you, I hated it," she laughed and shook her head. "But it bought the groceries and paid the rent, so I kept working. Every day, until one afternoon about a year ago, the two owners of this place came in for lunch. They were older gentlemen, nice and polite and well dressed, and seemed genuinely surprised to find someone like me working there. They told me that they couldn't believe that a woman who was as beautiful and sophisticated as I was, was providing such menial services," she laughed again then turned at the top of the steps and proceeded with a casual stroll down the hall.

"Anyway, it was slow that day and I was kind-of flirting with them, you know, trying to get a good tip, when we got to talking and before I knew it, they were offering me a job. They said that I was just what they'd been looking for in a new madam for their brothel. A fresh new face, yet someone who was cultured and refined, who had class and knew how to mingle and interact with the wealthy.

"Now, although I was actually quite flattered, I'm sure you can just imagine how embarrassed I was as well, and of course I scoffed at their offer. Me running a house of ill repute, how silly, and I told them that too. But they were insistent and didn't wanna take no for an answer, and that's when they began offering me money, easy money, and lots of it. And all I had to do was run their little business for them," she stopped and smiled then pulled a key from the cuff of her sleeve.

"Well, here we are," she said as she unlocked her door and stepped inside.

"Yes we are," Foster agreed as he followed and closed the door behind them. "Nice," he said as he looked around and took in the opulence of the suite. "And big."

"Yes it is… they treat me very well here. Anyway," she continued on as she made her way toward the sitting area. "They finally finished their lunch and when they got up to leave, they very politely asked me if I'd at least think about their offer and that if I had any doubts or questions as to what it was they were wanting me to do, that maybe I could pay them a visit so I could see for myself. Now I was still working on that tip, so I told them that I'd at least think about it. Of course I was joking when I did, but after they'd left and I'd gone back to clear the table, well, that's when I found a brand new twenty-dollar bill lying beneath a piece of paper with their names on it and an address that simply said nine p. m. Saturday. It was more money than I made in two weeks of hard work," she finished and sighed. "And so now you know."

"Know?" Foster queried as he stared. "Know what?"

"What I'm doing here, and that I'm a…" she began but then stopped and turned away.

"That you're what?" He slipped his fingers beneath her chin and turned her back. "Tell me, it's okay, really."

Torn by the truth of what she really was and what she wanted to say, Katherine hesitated then drew in another heavy breath. "Well, let's just say that I've changed, and that I'm not quite the same woman you use to know."

"Oooh," he raised his eyebrows. "And just what kind of woman are you now?"

Staring deep into his eyes, Katherine paused for just a moment then began to shake her head. "A whore," she finally admitted as an overwhelming blanket of shame enveloped her. "I'm a whore," she repeated and turned away, unable now to even look at the man she cared so much for.

She felt as if she'd just bared her soul in the ultimate of confessions, and without another word she crossed the room to her dresser, certain that she would hear the door close behind him. That he would leave without a word and never come back. But he didn't, he stayed. He could see and sense her shame, and wanted nothing more than to hold her and to comfort her, and to tell her that it was okay. That in their own unique and simple kind of way, they were both creatures of the same making and that it didn't matter. But he didn't, he just watched as she quietly stood in front of the mirror with her head slightly lowered, gazing at the reflection of her sad yet beautiful face that was staring back. A face that clearly conveyed her desires for him to stay.

A few seconds later, she shifted her gaze as if something had just caught her attention and reached for the small silver snuffbox setting to the side. Opening its lid, she cleared her throat then dipped a tiny spoon into a pile of fluffy white powder and brought it to her nose. Sniffing hard, she inhaled a generous helping then returned the spoon and did it once more. Closing the lid with a snap, she set the box back down and then turned with a glassy eyed stare.

"What's that?" Foster asked curiously.

"It, it's called cocaine," she replied with what was clearly a manufactured smile.

"Cocaine?"

"Yesss. My, my doctor prescribed it after Howard died last year," she continued with sort of a dismissive nervousness, as if she were trying to justify its use and seek his approval. "They say it's suppose to help cure your worries and make you feel better," she added.

"Never heard of it. Does it work?"

"Yes, I believe it does actually. Oooh, and it does other things to you too," she smiled nefariously and picked up the box. "Would you like some?"

"No thanks," he declined. "But I could use a drink if you don't mind," he added and held up his tall-stemmed glass. "This champagne isss."

"Oh yes, how rude of me. Scotch, right?" she asked as she set the box back down and then nonchalantly pulled on the heavy cord hanging next to the wall.

"Yes please, if you don't mind."

Turning to her liquor hutch, Katherine made Foster a drink then turned and handed it to him just as a knock sounded at the door and a well-dressed elderly black man stepped inside.

"Yes ma'am," he greeted as he entered.

"James," Katherine drawled. "I'd like you to find Lillian for me, okay. Tell her that I need to see her right away, will you?"

"Yes ma'am," the man replied with a nod as he turned to leave. "Will that be all ma'am?"

"Yes James, thank you."

Closing the door behind him, it wasn't long before it opened again and a lovely young blonde of about twenty-five, dressed in heels and a shear silk robe that hung to the floor, entered the room. He could clearly see that she was naked beneath it, and although she was demure and passive looking, he knew that it was just an illusion. There was more to this girl than what met the eye, he was certain of it. And with an unconcerned glance from her as she crossed the room toward Katherine, he watched with a curious fascination.

Stopping in front of her a second later, the girl was greeted with a smile and then a gentle caress to her cheek. They were quiet and said nothing, but in the fleeting seconds that followed, he could see that they were communicating. Speaking to each other with their eyes in a short and silent moment until Katherine finally turned and grabbed the elegant silver box from the dresser. It was clear that it was what the girl wanted, and with the snap of its lid, Katherine dipped the tiny spoon into the powder and brought it to the girl's nose. Disappearing with a heavy sniff, she carefully did it again then snapped the lid closed and set the box back on the dresser.

But the girl seemed greedy, like a small child still looking for another cookie after she'd just been given one. Her actions said it all, and after pleading with her eyes in what was clearly a display of unspoken insistence, Katherine finally relented and then dipped into the powder once again. Sniffing twice more, the young girl smiled with a satisfied nod then turned and acknowledged Foster.

"Lillian," Katherine whispered in a seductive drawl as she slipped behind her. "I'd like you to meet a very special friend of mine."

Staring, the girl said nothing and just laid her head against Katherine's shoulder as her hands slowly encircled her waist and then slipped beneath her gown. Closing her eyes with a pleasurable sigh as they found her breasts, she turned and tilted her head then reached up with her arms and sought out her madam's lips. Blindly pulling on Katherine's face until she'd found her mouth with hers, the two women kissed in a heated embrace. A few seconds later they parted, and as Katherine slowly and seductively untied the young girl's sash and pulled on the folds of her robe, they stared at Foster with a wanton lust.

There was no doubt that she was truly a vision with full firm breast and creamy white skin, and that she seemed to glory and delight in being exposed. At being displayed in a raw and open manner for him to view and examine like some sort of slave that he would soon be using. Then, and as if she were presenting the ultimate of sacrificial gifts to some great king, their eyes still lock with his, Katherine reached up and gently slipped the robe from the girl's shoulders.

Falling to the floor without a sound, Lillian stood before Foster in all her naked glory, her taut firm breast heaving to the gentle touch of Katherine's hand as she reached up from behind and caressed one and then the other. Her legs bending and spreading ever so slightly in anticipation as the other, now on the flat of her belly, slowly slid toward the top of her sex.

Responding to her touch as she worked her way down the inside of her thigh, Lillian moaned then lifted her leg as Katherine ever so slowly and sensuously began to trace her fingers back up, teasing and caressing her until they'd reached and had become lost in the downy tuft of her matted curls. A playground of soft golden tangles where they lingered and danced, pulling at the silken strands until she felt the slippery folds of her womanhood begin to part. Until, and along with a rigid reaction and a sharp yet pleasured gasp, she welcomed her middle finger deep into her inner sanctum.

It was exactly what she'd wanted; he could tell just by the way she writhed and undulated her hips. He could also tell that Katherine was in charge as she quickly quieted the girl's cries with her lips in another deep and heated embrace. She hadn't given her permission to cry out, or at least not yet she hadn't that was plain to see. And as she broke her kiss and looked back to Foster, she stared in the most defiant of ways, her eyes smoldering and heavily glazed with a predatory hunger he'd never seen before. She was right, she had changed; the Katherine that he'd once known was all but gone.

"Come closer," she demanded in a husky whisper as she pulled her hand from the girl and held it up. "See," she continued. Her finger glistening in the light as she brought it to his mouth and grazed it across his lips, leaving a pellucid and gelatinous reminder of what was soon to come. "Isn't that what you want?" she asked in a bewitching drawl as she then brought her hand to the girl's mouth. "Isn't that what you really crave?"

Overwhelmed as the heady scent of the girl's sex mixed with her perfume pervaded his senses, Foster could only nod his head as if he'd been induced into a trance. She was right and he knew it. They both knew it.

"Yes, I thought sooo," she added as he licked his lips. "And so does she... seeee," she smiled salaciously as she grabbed the girl's head from behind and pulled.

Greedily taking Katherine's finger into her mouth, the young girl quickly began to feed on the delights of her own nectar. Sucking and licking until her madam's long slender finger had been pulled from her mouth and replaced by her lips in another kiss. As to say that it was now time. That it was time to feed, for it was clear that she'd developed a taste and an appetite for the delicacies of the softer flesh.

To Foster, it was almost more than he could bear, watching as the two women continued, for never in his life had he ever been in a situation so perverse yet so erotic. His mind whirled as the heated desires within him ignited like gasoline, consuming any and all misgivings as to what was about to happen. It was as wild as anything he'd ever imagined, and in a flash he threw off his coat and loosened his tie then stepped forward and took one of the girl's creamy white orbs into his mouth.

Moaning as his teeth closed over her nipple, she writhed as he took one and then the other while Katherine pulled on her arms from behind and held her tight. A second later he felt a hand clutch the back of his head and then pull him hard against the girl's breast. It was Katherine asserting her dominance in a role she seemed to not only enjoy, but one she would play most of the night as she began to direct and guide his actions.

His mind ran wild with thoughts as to just how far she'd truly fallen from the pedestal of purity she had once occupied. She'd had so much just five years ago; a loving husband and family, money and social status. But now the once wealthy and socially prominent housewife was gone. She'd lost it all it seemed, but most of all, she'd lost her dignity. She no longer cared what people thought or said, and in doing so she'd come to find another life.

Lured by the temptation of easy money and completely unfettered by the moral restraints of a puritan society in which she lived, she'd taken the job and entered into the dark and seedy depths of a forbidden world. A world of drugs and alcohol, and sin and carnal pleasures. Excesses of a lifestyle that had no boundaries and from which most, once they'd entered, never returned. A world where the dreams of far too many, all too often and all too quickly, had a way of becoming nightmares.

A place that she'd willingly embraced and in which she now lived and thrived as she gradually descended deeper and deeper into the ever-darkening abyss. Growing and molting until she'd meta-morphosed and then re-emerged as the creature she now was. A creature of the night; a seductress and a temptress who could easily lure and entice the best of men. A place that Foster was more than ever, willing to enter.

She let him suckle for only a moment before placing her hands on the girl's shoulders and sending her to her knees. The action was clearly implied, and as she obediently dropped between them, Katherine reached up and pulled on Foster's tie until her lips were touching his.

It had been almost three years since he had last tasted the sweetness of her mouth, but he remembered it well. He remembered her passion and sensuality, and as they dueled in a heated embrace, he felt the girl's hands on his buckle as she began to undo his belt. An instant later, he felt his button and then his zipper being undone, and then her hands as they found and freed him with the caressing promise of much much more to come. His knees weakened and his mind whirled in disbelief. Was this really happening, he thought? A second later, he closed his eyes and groaned in a state of pleasured agony as she found him with her mouth then greedily took him and began to suckle. Hot and wet and slow... then deep and hungry.

His thoughts were answered without a word, and so it was, that in the private sanctuary of Katherine's room, the young Senator from Alabama descended into a world of illicit and decadent pleasures so perverse and immoral he never could have imagined. Powered by the strange white powder, the young submissive and Katherine quickly proved to be a combination that was almost more than he could endure. Insatiable in their appetites for him and each other, they feasted like heathens at the table of depravity.

Gorging themselves like gluttons at a never-ending banquet of decadence, yet unable to get their fill, they descended as the night wore on into the ever-deepening abyss of moral turpitude and carnal pleasures. It was a feast without limits, and before they'd finished and the sun had risen the next day, the two women had pulled from him his seed, more times than he'd ever thought possible.

The next morning when Foster finally woke, the room was still dark but he knew it was late. He could tell by the light of the day as it spilled out from behind the heavily curtained windows. And although he could barely think let alone move, he was smiling, for behind the pain and the foggy haze of the night was a memory he knew he would never forget. A memory, that now and in the worst of ways, he wanted to relive. But it was not to be, for as bad as he wanted to stay he had to leave; he had papers to sign at the bank and then a train to catch back home later that afternoon.

Stretching with a giant drawn out yawn, he rolled to his side and gazed at the two women lying next to him. Yes, he thought with a sigh of relief, they were finally asleep. Both of them dead to the world, sprawled beneath the covers like a couple of shipwrecked victims that'd been washed ashore. Shaking his head, he slowly rolled to the edge of the bed and rose.

Humorously gathering his clothes that'd been strewn about the room in their hasty removal, he quietly dressed and then headed for the bathroom. He was moving slower than he had in a long long time, but a hot wet towel to his face seemed to help shake off the night's haze. A few moments later, he returned and took a seat back on the edge of the bed. Looking down, he could see that the women had stirred and that Katherine, although still lying face up with Lillian snuggled tightly into her side, had raised one of her arms and draped it over her forehead. A move that had pulled the sheet and exposed one of her breast.

Staring for just a moment, he thought of waking her to say good-bye, but she was deep in the throws of sleep and he decided against it. He would just leave and avoid the hassle of a long good-bye, but before he rose and in an act that he just couldn't resist, he drew his fingers in a gentle caress around the fullness of her breast and then playfully tweaked her nipple.

He was looking for a reaction and he got it as she stirred to life with an unconscious smile that pulled at her lips and then her eyes as they blinked open in an unfocused and almost comatose gaze. "Staaay," she whispered as she reached out with her hand. Gently taking it in his, Foster smiled and began to speak. He wanted to thank her and tell her how he had to leave, but before he could say a word, she had closed her eyes and had drifted back into her dream world. She was out, but still as he gazed upon her, he said his good-byes in the only way he knew. Then, with a long and tender heart-felt kiss to her hand, he gently laid it by her side, covered her with her sheet and rose from the bed.

Crossing the room, he stopped at the door with his hand on the knob then turned and looked back one last time. It had been one hell of a night and most certainly one he would never forget, but now with thoughts of business replacing his memories of the last ten hours, he shook his head then turned and opened the door. He had papers to sign and a deal to close, and with that in mind he stepped into the hallway, gave a long final glance to the dark-haired beauty and quietly closed the door.

———————◆———————

CHAPTER 47

"SO YOU'RE TELLIN ME THAT this ol Foster actually went to New Orleans an bought him a ship?" Jim surmised as he set two more beers on the table. "Just like that," he raised his eyebrows with a dubious gaze. "Right in the middle of the depression?"

"Yes sirrr," Otis nodded as he reached for one of the cans. "Jus like that."

"Really?"

"Oh hell yesss," he assured as he popped the top and then took a slug. "In fact, if I remember right, it wasn't but a few days after he'd gotten back from New Orleans that he came an got me. I think I was workin on his house or something. Anyway, he wanted to watch it come in so we went an got the boat an then headed out into the bay, right out into the middle of them shippin lanes.

"Now ol Foster was pretty excited. In fact, he was more excited than I'd seen him in a long time an before we was even below Pinto Island he was up there on the bow jus like some little kid lookin for his new toy. Then, an jus as soon as we'd dropped into the bay, he spotted it less than a half mile away, steamin straight for us."

"There it is Otis!" Foster whooped and pointed then turned back to the man behind the wheel. "See? It's here!" he exclaimed. "Son-of-a-bitch, it's here!"

"Oh yes sur boss, I sees it. So that's your new boat?"

"Yep, The Eastern Star, five hundred feet of floating steel. What-a-ya think?" His eyes twinkled with pride. "Ain't she a beauty?"

"Oh yes sur, she shorly is. But what is you gonna do with somethin like that boss?"

"Ship stuff," he answered and then waved to some of the deck hands as the massive hulk slowly steamed by. "Ship stuff, all over the world," he added as he turned and looked through the glass. "Now come on, let's follow it."

"Now jus as soon as we met up with that boat, we fell right in behind it an came up the other side then followed it all the way in until the tugs finally took a hold of it. I'll tell ya, he sure was havin fun up there on the bow hollerin an pointin like some sort of general makin sure that we was go'n the right way. Then, an jus as soon as those tugs had grabbed a hold of her, we headed right back to the marina, got all tied up an got in the car, then drove straight over to the docks to meet em. I remember they was jus tyin up when we got there so we had to wait a bit until they got that big ol walkway up to the side of the boat. See, Foster wanted to talk with that captain an take another look at his boat an jus as soon as those boys on the pier had that walkway all secured, he told me to follow him an we started up that ramp.

"Now normally someone like me would of been told to jus wait by the car cause back then, back in 1933, a black man didn't have no business taggin along with a white man. Specially if he was someone who was as important as Foster. But as strange as it may sound, I think he really wanted me to see that boat. I have no idea as to why, but he did, he was jus like that sometimes. He always did treat me good. Anyway, for me it turned out to be a whole lot-a fun cause I'd never been on a big ship before, an while he walked an talked with that captain, I got to look all around.

"Then when he was finally all done lookin at the boat an had given that captain his orders to sail down to South America, well, that's when he took me over to this great big metal warehouse that was right there on the pier. He wanted to take a small corner of it an make a couple of little offices out of it for his new shippin company, an after about a half hour or so of go'n over everything that he wanted, I had enough work to keep me busy for the next couple a months.

"Now at the time, it really didn't seem like much, you know, a couple of offices in the corner of a great big warehouse an a single ship. But let me tell ya somethin, ol Foster had plans an they were big ones, an in all of my wildest dreams would I of ever imagined that from the humble beginnins of those two little office's an that one ship, that he'd build Siler Shippin into one of the biggest shippin companies in the world."

"Really?" Jim sat forward. "One of the biggest in the world?"

"Yes sir, in fact by the end of World War II, he not only owned that but also one of the biggest ship buildin companies in the nation too. Yes sir, he'd gone an built himself a real honest-to-God empire an by the end of the war he'd become one of the most powerful an wealthiest men in the country."

"An you still worked for him?"

"Oh yeah," Otis nodded. "In fact, I worked for im all the way up until he died."

"Really?"

"Yep, he was--."

"But wai wai wait, an just hold on a second," Jim stopped him. "That all sounds real interestin an all, but what I really wanna know is, is what about Willie? What in the heck had she been do'n all that time? Was she still with those people that you took her to? You know, that Tom feller an his wife... oooh what the hell, I forget her name."

"Elizabeth," Otis interjected.

"Yeah, Elizabeth. Was she still with them?"

"Well, as far as I knew she was," he scrunched his face as if deep in thought. "An if I recall correctly, I believe that it was right about the same time that ol Foster was gettin his ship that Willie was in her last week of finishin school."

"Finishin school?" Jim repeated with a surprised look.

"Yes sir," Otis drawled matter of factly. "Finishin school. See, that ol Mrs. Portman had really taken a liken to her an I guess she'd got it in her head that she was gonna turn her into a real proper young lady. Anyway, it was that same summer of 33 when..."

There were only eighteen girls in Miss Winfield's summer session that year, and by the last weeks of school Willie had become friends with all of them except two. Daphney DeWeese, the daughter of Gordan DeWeese, the new bank president for Mobile Savings, and Angela Posey, the daughter of Frank Posey, the three-term mayor for the city of Mobile. They were an inseparable pair, and had snubbed and made fun of her from the very beginning, mostly because she was so much prettier than they were and she was popular with the other girls, but also because they'd learned that she'd come from such humble beginnings. A sharecropper they'd teased and ridiculed, how unworthy. But all of that changed one Friday afternoon when Willie, in an unintended moment, overheard the two girls talking and crying in the bathroom.

It was just after school had been dismissed and most of the other girls had gone, when Willie, who was already in the bathroom, heard the door fly open and someone rush in. A second later, she heard the sound of running water and then a person vomit into one of the sinks. Concentrating, she listened closely in an attempt to discern the voice of the girl on the other side of the barrier as she moaned and groaned beneath her breath. She seemed to be terribly ill, but before Willie could rise and exit her stall to help, she heard the door opened again and another person rush in. A second later, and in what was clearly a desperate and emotional plea, she heard a voice that she knew all to well.

"Oh God, Angela," Daphney cried out. "What am I going to do?"

"Well, maybe you're just late, you know," Angela surmised in an effort to comfort her friend.

"No, I'm not! This is my second month and I still haven't had it! I'm pregnant, I know it, I can feel it! Besides, I've just thrown up for the fiftieth time.

"Well, maybe..."

"No Angela, there are no maybes. I'm pregnant; an I'm going to have a baby! Jesus, can't you understand that?"

"Well then have it," Angela replied as if it were no big deal. "Get the boy, whoever he is, an get married. Of course you'll need to have a great big wedding an all so everyone in town will know that you are truly in love an ready to start your own little family... an then just have it."

"I can't."

"You can't? Why not, can't you figure out who it was ya little hussy," she retorted and giggled.

"Shut up Angela, you don't have any room to talk," Daphney instantly shot back with a scathing glare. "You're still the biggest slut in Mobile an you know it. Besides, I've only been with one boy this summer, an so yes, I know who it is."

"Oh really?" Angela smirked and rolled her eyes. "Just one? How very unusual. Do I know him?"

Gaining another scathing glare, Angela finally stopped and changed her tone. "Okay, okay, I'm sorry, but if that really is the case, then there you have it, it's easy," she plopped her hands on her hips as if she'd just magically solved all of her friends' problems.

"What-a-you mean it's easy? Did you forget that I'm pregnant?"

"No I didn't, but if there really has been only one boy as you so righteously claim. Oh, an by the way, an jus so you know, I really don't believe you, then there can only be one father right. So it's actually quite simple. You tell him an then get married. See," she declared.

"No Angela, you don't understand. I told you I can't, I just can't."

"Sure you can. You just go and tell him that he's the father and to step up and do the right thing."

"Nooo Goddammit," she growled with yet another glare. "You're not listenin. I cannn't."

"But why not?"

"Because."

"Because why? Who's the father Daphney?" she asked and then waited.

But Daphney didn't answer; she just turned and then gazed at their reflections in the mirror until Angela's eyes suddenly widened and she brought a hand to her mouth. "Oh my God," she blurted with a burst of zeal. "I don't believe it! That's it! He's already married isn't he?" She smiled as if she'd just solved some great mystery. "You've been havin an affair with a married man an that's why you can't say anything, an that's why I didn't know about it either, right? Oooh, how wicked. God Daphney, you're such a little whore. Now tell me, does his wife know yet?"

"No, Angela," she shook her head. "He's not a married man."

"Oooh really," Angela replied with a disappointed sigh. "Well then who is he?" She continued to probe. "Come on Daph, tell me, I know you're scared but I'm your best friend remember. We grew up together, so let's have it. Tell me who he is, an give me one good reason why you can't marry this boy, whoever he is?"

Gazing at her friend's reflection for just a second longer, Daphney finally turned back and stared through watery eyes. They were like sisters and had been through everything together, and she wanted nothing more than to tell her, but try as she may, she could not find the words. "I cannn't," she cried and shook her head then turned away.

It was the look on Daphney's face when she turned away that gave Angela pause. A look that said there was something more to her secret, than just a baby. That there was something dark and sinister that accompanied it, and it was scaring her like nothing before. Daphney was distraught beyond any sense of the word, and now it was beginning to scare her as well. But even so, she pressed the issue and called her name.

"Daphney," she began with a growing sense of trepidation. "Come on now girrrl, you're really startin to scare me, hear. What've you done? You need to tell meee," she stared. "Whooo's the father Daphney? An whyyy can't you marry this boy?"

Slowly turning back in a ghostly gaze, Daphney could only stare at her friend as the tears of shame and regret began to run down her cheeks. Insane with the desire to be taken in the most forbidden of ways, by a man whom she should never have been with, the seventeen-year-old blonde had done the unthinkable. Driven by a lust she couldn't control, she had repeatedly crossed the line in the hayloft of a barn and now the consequences of her actions, was growing inside of her. His seed had taken root, and with a heavy breath, the distraught young girl finally broke down and confessed. "Because he's black," she sobbed and lowered her head into her hands.

Staggering backwards as her eyes widened from disbelief to horror, Angela could only stare in silence and shake her head. Her friend was in serious, serious trouble, for in the eyes of society, there was no greater sin.

"Oh my God Daphney," she gasped and began to cry as she opened her arms to embrace her. "Ooh baby... oh nooo," she went on in a voice quivering with fear. "If your daddy ever finds out about this an what you've done, he'll hurt you. He will, Daphney, he'll hurt you bad. I know he will. You've ruined his name an he won't let this go without punishing you. You know it an I know it. An you know he'll kill that boy too... an I don't mean figuratively either. He hates negroes, an he'll find him whoever he is, an when he does, he'll hang him from the first tree he can find."

"I know, I know," Daphney sobbed in heaving gasps. "Oh God Angela, what am I going to do?"

Hugging her friend, Angela tried her best to console her, but there was none to be had. There was only the pain of knowing that she'd done a terrible wrong, and that the worst of what she was about to face was still to come. That when people found out, she would be branded a whore and without question an innocent young man would die.

"I know," Angela finally exclaimed as she stepped back and wiped her tears. "We'll just find some one to give you an abortion. You know an..."

"Oh God Angela, really! I know you mean well an all, but sometimes you really amaze me."

"Whaaat?" She frowned at what she perceived as an undeserved insult. "It's a great idea."

"Oh really? An just where am I suppose to go, huh? Think about it. Do you have any idea as to just how many people in this town know us? Or did you forget that your dad's the mayor and my dad's the president of Mobile Savings. So please, tell me, just where in the hell would we go?"

Daphney was right and deep down Angela knew it. They were trapped just by the fact of who they were. There wasn't anyone they could turn to, nor was there anywhere in town that they could go where someone wouldn't know them and say something, or even worst, want money to keep quiet once they found out. But there was a baby of color growing in Daphney's belly and all to soon she would run out of time. And as the stark and dim reality of their situation took hold, the two girls hugged once again and began to cry.

A few minutes later and after they'd finally settled, Daphney and Angela left the bathroom as if they hadn't a care in the world. They were in denial, but all to quickly their carefree charade came to an end when they heard the unmistakable sound of the bathroom door as it closed yet again behind them. They'd never even thought to check any of the stalls, but as soon as they turned and gazed at the person standing by the door, they realized their mistake. They could tell just by the look on her face that she knew and that they'd been overheard. That the very secret that they had so desperately needed to keep had already been compromised. That Daphney's fate was now in the hands of a girl whom for the last four weeks they'd snubbed and made fun of.

Cringing as the blood drained from her face, Daphney stared in horror. She felt sick all over again, for she knew that if Willie were to say anything to anyone, word would spread like an out of control fire and in a flash, her life as she knew it would be over.

"Oooh Willie," she called. "What a surprise. Angela an I were just talkin when... well, all of a sudden here you are." She laughed and flipped her hair. "So just where'd you come from?"

"Who me?" Willie replied with a smug indifference. "Well, I was right in there," she glanced toward the door and stared then turned back. "I can't believe you didn't see me?"

"Oh," Daphney feigned as she placed her hand upon her chest. "I see, well then, I guess you must have overheard us teasin an funnin each other then," she laughed again, but now with a nervousness that wasn't there before. "Isn't that right, Ange?"

"Oh absolutely," Angela chimed in. "Heck, you know how we are," she laughed. "Always kiddin."

"Oh really," Willie replied. "Teasin? Well, to me it sounded like you was in trouble."

"Trouble?" Daphney laughed. "Oh, how funny. Why whatever gave you such a silly idea as that?"

"Because I heard you Daphney," she retorted with an emphatic glare. "I heard you both! So don't pretend that you're all goody goody! An don't lie to me either cause I know you're secret. I heard you cryin, an I know that you're pregnant," she took a breath and then finished in what they all knew was the heart-wrenching truth. "An I know that you're go'n to have a negro baby."

Her words cut like a knife, but it was the truth and in an instant Daphney's eyes welled with tears. "Oh God Willie, please," she choked as she began to cry and plead for Willie's silence. "Pleeease, you can't say anything to anybody. You don't understand what I've done... an what it means," she lowered her head and began to sob. "They'll hurt me..."

They'd been mean to her since they'd met and she resented them both, yet even so as she watched Daphney cry, Willie felt a wave of compassion slowly envelope her. Daphney was in serious trouble, and she knew all to well the horrors that awaited her if people were to learn of her secret. A young unmarried white girl who'd willingly laid with a black man, and who now had his baby growing in her belly was as unforgivable and as bad as it got in a white southern society.

Daphney was a wreck but after she'd finally settled the three girls talked in a quiet huddle. "Okay okay, I won't," Willie finally promised. "I won't say nothin to nobody I promise." But before she could say another word, she turned to the sound of a horn from outside and stared through the doors at the end of the hall. "But I have to go now my ride is here," she said as she began to walk away.

"You promise," Daphney called out as Willie approached the doors.

Turning back with her hand on the door, Willie stared at the two girls standing in the dim light of the hall, their faces still etched with fear, then with a simple nod, she turned and pushed it open.

It was hard to forget what she'd heard in the bathroom, and for most of the weekend it was all she could think of. Replaying their conversation again and again in her mind, Willie remembered the desperation and terror that was in their voices, and then of Angela's idea to just get an abortion. It was a word she'd never heard before and knew not what it meant so just as Miss Liz had shown her, she looked it up in the dictionary. She thought of its meaning and then of Daphney, and then of her friend up river.

She knew that Daphney had nowhere to turn, and now she wanted to help. She thought of it carefully and by the following Monday when she'd stepped through the doors of Miss Winfield's for their final week of school, Willie had conceived a plan. A bold and uncertain gamble that would involve two of the people in her life she considered friends. A gamble that would only work if one, she could find and convince Otis to take them up river, and two, if she could then find and convince Hadie to help them. It had been almost two years since she'd seen Otis and even longer since she'd seen Hadie, so she knew that the chances of even finding them and then getting up there and back without getting caught were slim. The odds of success were against them, yet even so Daphney was in trouble, and deep down, Willie knew that it was the only hope she had.

CHAPTER 48

"*Now like I was sayin, it was the summer of 1933. Actually, an if I remember correctly, I think it was right around the later part of August that I was down workin on the boat one mornin when ol Willie out-a the clear blue jus showed up an surprised me.*"

"*Willie?*" *Jim repeated curiously.*

"*Yep,*" *Otis nodded.* "*It was a Saturday an ol Foster had jus taken off for Washinton earlier that week an I knew he wouldn't be back till Thanksgivin so I went on down to work on the motor. You know, oil an filters an plugs... stuff like that.*

"*Anyway, I guess she'd been lookin for me for some time when she finally remembered that the best place to really find me was at the marina cause I used to go down there sometimes on the weekends an work on the boat. Now I hadn't seen her since the day that I'd brought her back to Mobile, but boy jus as soon as I heard her voice callin my name from outside the boat, I knew it was her. An even though it had changed jus a little, there was only one person in the whole world that'd ever called me Mister Otis an that was Willie, an when I stood up an looked through the glass I couldn't believe my eyes.*

"*I'll tell ya Jim, in jus two years that little gal had turned into such an incredible young lady it was hard to believe. I mean, she'd always been jus as beautiful as you could ever imagine, but with her hair all fixed up an that pretty little dress that she was wearin, well, she looked jus absolutely priceless. Anyway, jus as soon as she finished squeezin an huggin on me we started talkin about all of the things she'd been do'n an how she was finally gettin her education jus like she'd promised her momma. An then after that, we started carryin on an reminisin about the good ol days.*

"We talked about everything, includin Foster. You could tell that she still kind of cared for him, specially when she realized that her name was still on the boat. But I guess after two whole years of never hearin from him, she'd come to terms with it. Anyway, after we were all done, well, that's when she started tellin me about a little friend of hers that was in trouble an needed help. An when I say trouble, I mean trouble."

"Really?" Jim instantly quizzed. "What-a-ya mean, what kind of trouble?

"Well," Otis replied matter of factly. "The kind that back then... could of gotten ya killed."

"Killed?" Jim's eyes widened.

"Yep, killed! You know, like hung from the end of a rope till you're dead type killed."

"Hung?" Jim cringed. "Jesus what in the hell she do... kill somebody?"

"Nooo," Otis chuckled and shook his head. "Not exactly, but boy in the eyes of society she may as well of. See, I guess this little gal that Willie knew, well, her daddy was some kind of big shot banker or somethin in town an owned thousands an thousands of acres of farm ground. Most of which I think he'd actually acquired, or should I say took from people who couldn't pay their mortgages.

"Anyway, the story that I got from her was that this girl's daddy had jus acquired another new farm earlier that year an wanted to fix it up so he sent this young black man that worked for him out there to start clearin an fencin some of them old fields. Now from what all I was told, I guess this piece of ground was a real isolated piece clear out on the other side of everything that he owned, but it had a little shack an a barn on it, so that boy jus stayed out there. All by himself, all summer, clearin an fencin the ground jus like he was told until he'd run out of food an supplies an have to come back in. I think that was about every two weeks or so, an after he'd spent the night an got everything that he needed, he'd load up his mule the next day an go back out.

"Anyway, I guess it was durin the course of that summer that this little friend of Willie's, Daphney was her name, had gotten to where she'd started go'n out about every four or five days to check on this boy's progress for her daddy. See, she had horses an jus loved to ride, so he got to where he jus started sendin her out so he didn't have to go anymore. It was prefect really, she had a place to ride to an got to help her daddy, an he didn't have to go anywhere.

"Now I'm not exactly sure as to jus how it all started really, but from everything that I could piece together from what Willie an her other little *friend Angela had told me, I think that this Daphney had gone out one day right around the beginnin of summer to check on this young man for her daddy. Now I was told that normally she'd jus go straight to the fields where she knew he was suppose to be workin, check on him an see if there was anything that he needed an then leave. But I guess on that particular day it was real hot so instead of go'n there first she started lookin for this little pond that was suppose to be out there so she could give her horse a drink.*

"Well, an again from what all I was told, I guess she finally found it but when she did she also found that young man swimmin in it... buck-naked. Now I really don't think that he knew she was there, an she sure as hell didn't announce her presence I know that. An I ain't real sure as to jus how long she sat there an watched him without him knowin it either. But I can sure tell ya this. Accordin to Willie an that other little gal Angela, seein that young boy naked must of really done somethin to her. See, he was a man if you get my drift, a full-grown man an not some teenage boy.

"Anyway, to make a long story real short, it was right after she'd sat there an watched him swim that she seemed to of developed a real desire for him. Now I guess she was jus about as reckless as they came, an it wasn't long before that little snow white blonde had lured that young buck into the hayloft of the ol barn out there. Then, an in the heat of that summer, they got ta do'n things that they really shouldn't of been a do'n. Yes sir, they was really playin with fire them two, an then before either one of em knew it... she was pregnant with his baby."

"Oh my God," Jim widened his eyes. "You really weren't kiddin, were you?"

"Oh hell nooo," Otis scoffed. "Not in the least bit."

"Then you were right. She really was in trouble, wasn't she?"

"Oooh hell yes," Otis replied as if it were an understatement. "She was in big trouble, an I mean real big trouble, an she knew it too, an she was scared. It was the south an it was 1933, an she was a young single white girl that was pregnant with a black man's baby. An let me tell ya, back then, it jus didn't get any worse than that.

"Anyway, I ain't really sure as to jus what all they would of done to her had all the facts really been known. I don't think that they would of actually up an killed her, but I'm sure it wouldn't of been very pretty. But as far as that young black man was concerned, well, it didn't matter how or which way you looked at it, for him... that was a hangin offense, pure an simple. Yes sir, if that girl's daddy would've ever found out, they would of caught that poor boy

an after they'd beat him half to death, an before he could've actually up an died on em, they'd of hung him from the first tree they could've found an not one word would of ever been said bout it."

"Jesus," Jim shook his head. "I can remember them days when I was a boy. There sure was a lot-a hate back then wasn't there?"

"Yes there wasss," Otis agreed as they both reflected on the past.

"But I don't understand," Jim cocked his head. "What'd Willie want with you? I mean, what in the hell they think you were gonna do?"

"Well," Otis chuckled. "That's the interestin part. See, ol Willie an her two friends, well, I guess they'd gotten together an concocted a little plan an it all revolved around me."

"You... why you?"

"Well shit that was simple," Otis grinned. "I had the boat an they wanted me to take em up river."

"Up river?" Jim repeated and narrowed his eyes. "What-n the hell for?"

"To find the swamp witch."

"The whaaat?"

"The swamp witch. You know, Willie's friend. The one that'd stitched her head all up."

"Oh yeaaah, I remember," Jim nodded. "But what'd they want with her?"

"Well at first I wasn't quite sure, but then I remembered Willie tellin me how that ol swamp woman was actually some kind of old army nurse from the war. Anyway, I guess by about the time they'd finally found me, that little Daphney gal was gettin pretty desperate an they'd gotten it in their heads that this woman could give her an abortion without anyone knowin about it. Shiiit they had it all planned out, but the more an more I learned as to what it was that they was actually wantin me to do, the harder an harder I kept shaken my head.

"See, I didn't wanna have nothin to do with taken three young white girls up river to see no swamp witch, no sir. Specially to do what they was wantin to do. Shit, if someone would of found out about it, or if somethin would of happened or went wrong, why they'd of hung my ass right along with that other boy's an not even blinked an eye. Besides, it'd been almost two whole years since Willie had seen her, an we didn't know if she was even alive let alone willin to help. But that damned Willie was jus about as stubborn an persuasive as you could ever imagine, an after about an hour or so of pleadin an arguin, she finally talked me into go'n along with their little scheme. Hell, I still ain't sure how she did it, but she did." He smiled and shook his head.

"An so that next Friday, the three of them went to the marina right after school an snuck on the boat an waited for me. See, they'd each told their parents that they were stayin the weekend at the others house an with that they were pretty much free till Sunday. Then, after I finished work that day, I headed on down to the marina an got on the boat. An so there I was, Otis Brown, a black man with three young white girls in Foster's boat, gettin ready to take it up river without him knowin nothin about it to see some swamp witch so one of em could have an abortion. Now it jus didn't get any worse than that, an to be right truthful with ya, I don't believe that I'd ever been as scared as I was that afternoon when we took off.

"I can still remember when we pulled out-a that slip with that little fishin boat behind us an how I kept tryin to think of all the excuses an reasons that I could for do'n what I was do'n. I thought that it would make me feel a little better, you know, if I could somehow justify that what I was do'n was right. But I'll tell ya," he sighed and shook his head. "For every good reason that I thought of, there was a bad one right behind it, an as I turned up river an those three girls came up front an joined me, I jus started hopin an prayin that nothin bad happened an that we didn't get caught."

"Damn Otis," Jim shook his head. "So you actually went an took those girls up river?"

"Yep," Otis sighed. "I sure did."

"An so what happen?"

"Well, like I said, we'd jus turned up river when Willie an them other two girl's came up front an joined me. Now in all my years of livin I don't believe that I'd ever seen a person as scared as that little Daphney was as we headed up river. She'd really gone an gottin herself into a terrible mess, an to tell ya the truth, I really wasn't so sure that we weren't gonna make it worse. I tell ya, I had a real bad feelin about the whole thing if you know what I mean.

"Anyway, other than the storm that was startin to roll in, there wasn't a whole lot to talk about which made for a pretty long ride. But we finally made it up to the cabin an jus as soon as we did, an had gotten ourselves all tied up, ol Willie grabbed her shotgun an jumped in her boat. Then with a promise to be right back, she fired up that little motor an took off to find that witch.

"I remember we all stood on the pier an watched until she'd disappeared around the last bend jus up from the pier. Now I knew that she knew those waters like the back of her hand, but still I was real worried about her cause by the time she'd left it was startin to get dark an that storm was really beginnin to move in. Anyway, after she was gone, the three of us walked on up to *the house, gathered us a bunch of wood an then built a fire in the stove. Then after that, I got all the lamps filled an lit, made sure that they had plenty of water an then walked on back down to the boat."*

"So what happen, did she find her?" Jim asked.

"Oh yeah, she found her all right," Otis chuckled.

"An she brought her back?"

"Oooh yeah, she brought her back too. Although by the time she did it was completely dark an we was all jus worried sick cause she'd been gone so long, but yeah, she finally made it back all right. An let me tell ya it was jus in the nick of time too cause that ol storm had finally made it there an boy was it ever gettin ready to cut loose. Yes sir, that ol wind had whipped up an the temperature had dropped an that whole sky was jus dancin with lightnin. Now their wasn't any rain yet, but let me tell ya, it sure was flickerin an grumblin like you couldn't believe.

"Anyway, I remember I was right here in the cabin when I finally heard the little motor on Willie's boat comin back jus as fast as she could tryin to beat that storm. She had that thing wide open an jus as soon as I heard it I jumped up an looked out the window right there."

"There?" Jim looked up with his eyes.

"Yep, she had jus turned in right before the pier. An then without even slowin down, she ran that little boat right up into the grass. Now like I jus said, we was all jus worried sick cause she'd been gone so long, so when I finally saw her boat I didn't even think about what I was do'n an hopped right on out onto the stern so I could see better. I was gonna holler at her cause I thought that she might of needed some help or somethin pullin that boat up but she'd run it up enough I knew I didn't need to do that. So, I jus kind-of stood there like a big ol dumb ass while they climbed out until I thought that I ought a at least make sure everything was okay. You know. Anyway, jus as I got ready to yell, well, that's right when this great big ol long flickerin flash of lightnin lit everything up like you couldn't believe. An that's when I finally saw her... standin there in this long tattered dress that was blowin in the wind with this blanket or whatever the hell you wanna call it pulled over her head an around her shoulders."

"Saw her... saw who?" Jim asked.

"The Witch!" Otis exclaimed as if he should've known. "Who else? An she was starin right at me!"

"Really?" Jim teased with a grin that quickly grew into a lighthearted chuckle. "The wiiiitch?"

"As God as my witness, I swear," Otis raised his hand. "It was real strange too cause she'd jus taken a few steps up into the grass, but then had stopped for some reason an turned right at the very instant that that lightnin had hit." His expression and voice both reflecting the moment in which he'd seen her. "Like she'd conjured it up herself cause she already knew that I was standin there an she wanted to see me in the light.

"Now I know that this is go'n to sound real stupid, but I swear to God in the few seconds that we could see each other it felt as if I'd been completely paralyzed an that every drop of blood in my body was drainin right out of the bottom of my feet. I tell ya, I had a chill run through me like you couldn't believe cause I jus knew that she was do'n everything she could to suck the life right out-a me an take my soul. See, that's what witches do to you so you can't resist em an I knew that, an I also knew that there wasn't a damn thing in the world I could do to stop her.

"Yes sir, right then an there, I thought I was a real goner cause I jus knew that at any second she was gonna turn me into a zombie an that when she was all done with that little Daphney girl up at the house, all she had to do was come back down an get me. That I'd jus be sittin there in the back of the boat waitin for her an wouldn't have any idea as to what was happenin while she jus loaded me up an then took me back to her little witches den out there in the swamp."

"So what'd you do?" Jim asked as he tried to stifle his laughter.

"Well goddamn, what in the hell do you think I did? As soon as that flash of lightnin quit flickerin an she couldn't see me anymore, which broke her hold on me, an then that God awful rumble of thunder that'd followed it went away, I jumped right back inside here jus as fast as I could an closed the door an locked it. Actually, I locked all three doors an the hatches too, an this is right where I stayed all night long, right here." He glanced around the cabin.

"See, back then there was some of them witches that'd developed a real fondness for black people an I knew it, specially for strong young males cause they liked to use em in a lot of their potions an voo-doo stuff. But there wasn't no way in hell that I was gonna let one get me... nooo sireee. Anyway, right after I got everything all locked up, I got me a blanket an settled in on one of those little sofas right back there." He gestured with his head toward the stern.

"Now I was probably jus about as scared as I'd ever been in my whole life. An I don't know why I did it or jus what in the hell I thought it was gonna do for me, but I remember pullin that cover all the way up over my chin until jus the tip of my nose an my eyes was stickin out an then tryin to go to sleep.

But that sure as hell didn't happen I can tell ya that, in fact, I don't believe I slept a wink that whole night cause every time a flash of lightnin would light everything up, I jus knew that I was gonna look up an see that ol witch standin there at the door tryin ta get in. So..."

By the time Otis had finished Jim was in stitches and rolling with laughter. "Oh God Otis, please, you've gotta stop, I can't it take anymore," he pleaded as he wiped the tears from his eyes and tried to catch his breath. "Oh shiiit, now that's funny."

"Well it sure wasn't funny at the time," Otis stared as if he'd failed to see Jim's humor.

"Okay okay," Jim cleared his throat in an attempt to compose himself. "So what happen the next mornin? Obviously the witch didn't get you," he snickered.

"Nooo, the witch didn't get me," Otis frowned and shook his head. "Anyway the next thing I knew, it was daylight, the rain had stopped an I could hear Willie's little fishin boat. I remember it real well too cause as soon as I woke up, I began to panic cause I jus knew that I'd screwed up."

"Ooh really?" Jim grinned and rolled his eyes, certain that he was in for yet another of Otis's amusing exploits.

"Oh yeaaah, shit, the very second I opened my eyes I started gaspin an scramblin for that blanket cause like a complete dumb ass I'd gone an let myself go to sleep an in do'n so, I'd let that witch get to me," he chuckled and shook his head again. "Yes sir, I guess I was havin one hell of a dream, but I finally came to my senses an after I looked all around an then kind of touched an patted myself jus to make sure that I was really alive, I jumped up an looked out the window right there," he looked up with his eyes. "An that's when I saw Willie an that ol swamp witch in her boat, headin back up that tributary. An boy let me tell ya, was I ever relieved. Yes sir, she was gone an I was still alive, an just as soon as they'd disappeared around that first bend I let out a great big ol gush of air an collapsed right back down on the sofa."

Chuckling and shaking his head, Jim took a moment but then finally regained his composure. "So that was it?" he asked as if the woman should have done more. "She just came an gave that little gal an abortion an then left... just like that?"

"Yep, pretty much."

"Well didn't she come back an check on her? You know, to make sure she was okay an all?"

"Nope, which if ya really wanna know the truth, didn't bother me in the least bit."

"But damn Otis, what about that poor little Daphney gal... jeeees, she just up an left her?"

"Well, I wouldn't say that she jus up an left her really, I mean, she did stay an watch over her all night. But I guess after it had gotten light an she knew that that Daphney was gonna be okay, she jus told em what all to expect an what all to do an after that, I guess she asked Willie to take her back home. Anyway, it must have been about a couple of hours or so before Willie finally came motorin back. I remember I was out on the end of the pier fishin when she pulled up with a great big smile an shut off her motor."

"Hey Mister Otis," Willie said as her boat bumped into the pier. "Mornin."

"Mornin Miss Willie," he replied as he grabbed her line and helped her tie. "It's about time you got back, I saw ya leave, but where the heck you been? I was startin ta get all worried about you."

"You were... really? Well, I've been with Hadie. After I took her back, I stayed an drank some swamp tea with her while she tried on all those dresses an those workin shoes we brought her. Why, were you worried that she'd eaten me or something?" she teased and laughed.

"Nooo!" he denied with a scowl as he helped her from the boat.

It was a lie and Willie knew it, for she knew that Otis was still deathly afraid of the witch as he called her and with a lighthearted banter, unable to resist a little fun, she continued to tease him. "Well I think you were. In fact, I think you were all worried that she was gonna come back here an get you too. You know that witches really like black people. In fact, she was askin me all about you, an now that she knows where you are, wellll." She rolled her eyes.

"Miss Willie!" Otis huffed then turned away and sat on his bucket. "That ain't funny now, ya hear. Not one bit, an you needs to stop talkin like that. An I'm serious."

"Okay okay, I'mmm sorry," she giggled. "Heck, I was just funnin you, but I promise I won't talk about her anymore okay. So what's ya do'n?"

"I'm fishin, an I'm slayin em too... look!" He turned and proudly pulled a stringer of four large catfish from the water.

"Oh wow, those are nice. Heck, we can eat em for lunch, can't we?"

"Yes ma'am, in fact, all we needs to do is catch a few more an we'll have enough for everybody. We can grill em on the fire pit like we use to."

"Oh yeaaah, that sounds great," she replied then turned and looked toward the house. "But can me an Angela help? You know, an fish with you? Hadie said that Daphney was suppose to just rest so we really don't have nothin to do."

"Why shor you can, I got plenty of worms, an there's two more poles in the boat. Go an get her."

"So that was pretty much how we ended up spendin the day, Daphney rested while me an Willie an that Angela girl fished. I remember we caught the hell out of em too, an then later on, we grilled an ate almost everything we'd caught. I'll tell ya, I never dreamed that three girls could eat so much." He chuckled. "Anyway, after dinner an after it got dark, we all went to bed an then bright an early Sunday mornin, we got up an headed on back. I remember it was real pretty out an by then that Daphney was feelin a whole lot better so them girls all went up front an rode on the bow. Now let me tell ya, the mood go'n back was sure a whole lot different than the one go'n up but I was still jus as nervous as you could ever imagine."

"Why's that, you just said that that Daphney girl was okay an that the witch didn't get you." Jim chuckled, unable to resist the chance of giving Otis one last little jab.

"Yes I did," Otis shook his head as if he never should've told Jim of the witch. "But see, we still hadn't made it back yet. An to be right truthful with ya, the closer we got to that damn marina the worse I got cause I jus knew that somehow, somebody'd seen us an found out what we'd done an all of them parents were gonna be standin there at the pier waitin with the police to take me away."

"An was there?"

"Nope," he grinned. "In fact, there wasn't nobody there except for a couple of people that worked around the docks. I remember I waved to em when we was pullin in but everyone was so use to me an this ol boat comin an go'n all the time that they never even gave us another look. They jus waved an kept on about their business an that's when I finally started to think that we'd done it. That we'd actually made it back without gettin caught an nobody'd died.

Then, an jus as soon as I got us all docked an tied up, I jumped back inside an said goodbye to Willie an them other two girls.

"See, the plan was for me to leave first an then after I was gone an the coast was clear, they would leave. I remember Willie gave me a great big hug an a kiss on the cheek with the promise to come an see me jus as soon as she could, an them other two girls, well, they couldn't hardly thank me enough, specially that Daphney girl. Anyway, as you can jus imagine, I couldn't wait to get away an jus as soon as I could I was out the door there an down the pier."

"Unbelievable," Jim drawled and shook his head. "An nobody ever found out, huh?"

"Nope, that there was a secret that jus five people in the whole world ever knew about. An after we got back, I don't think that a one of us ever spoke of it again. Or at least that was, until now."

There was a short moment of quiet between the two men as they reflected upon the story that Otis had just told. For the most part, it'd been funny, but even so they both knew the price that they all could've paid as a result of their actions. The attitudes and mindset of most people back then would not have had it any other way.

"An ol Foster, he never found out about it either?" Jim asked and took a sip.

"Nope," Otis shook his head. "Cause if I recall correctly, about the only thing that he was concerned with was findin another ship to buy."

"Really... another ship?"

"Yep, an let me tell ya, it was the only thing that he had on his mind. An shit, I wasn't even done with them offices yet."

"Really?"

"Oh heck yeah. In fact, by the spring of 34, he had four of em already."

"Four? Really?"

"Well sure, remember? I told you that he'd built one of the biggest shippin companies in the world, don't you."

"Yeah, but ya didn't say anything about him do'n it overnight. Good God, how in the hell he do it? I mean, I know he was a Senator an all, but Jesus Christ you just don't go out an start buyin ships just like that. Not in the middle of the Depression. Where in the hell was he gettin his money?"

"Well, I ain't really sure as to jus how he did it or where he got his money. All I remember was that every time he bought one of em an it would come into port for the first time, me an him'd go out an greet em. Or at least that's what *we did for the first ten or twelve that he bought. I'll tell ya, I can still remember him standin there on the bow every time we did too, smilin great big as if he'd jus won some sort of high stakes poker game or somethin an then askin me what I thought. 'So what-a-ya think, Otis? He'd holler an spread his arms then look up at his ship. 'Compliments of the Federal Government.' He'd say, then turn back an look at me."*

"Compliments of the Government?" Jim scrunched his face. "What in the hell he mean by that?"

"Well," Otis chuckled. "I guess that's how he was buyin them ships."

"What? Through the Government?"

"Yep, the good ol Federal Government."

"But how?"

"Well, an even though he was kind enough to try an explain it to me one day, it was so far over my head I didn't understand none of it really so to be right truthful with you, I really ain't sure as to jus how he did it or how it all worked. All I knew, was that he was gettin lots an lots of money from the government an it wasn't to awfully long after I'd gottin them offices all finished that he took off on a real buyin spree."

CHAPTER 49

By the late fall of 1933 Foster's name within the Senate and the city of Mobile had become a force synonymous with hard work and success. He was a deal maker and a good one, and he understood and played the political games in Washington well. He forged relationships and did favors for all the right people, but it was his grasp on the capitalistic needs and desires of companies that wanted to grow that served him the best. He was creative, and through his efforts, he'd brought a number of businesses, both large and small into the city. And although Siler Shipping was considered to be one of the smallest and had but a few employees, he was proud that it was amongst them. His first ship *The Eastern Star,* had been making a trip almost every other week to South America, but with American Aluminum's almost instant demand for more bauxite to fill their growing production needs, it wasn't enough.

They'd pushed their plant to its capacity almost from the start and they needed more ore to fulfill their requirements. Quickly responding to the board's request, the young Senator contacted Henry Fletcher, orchestrated another deal with his bank, and by February of 34 had happily fulfilled their needs with the addition of another freighter.

That same month, the call also came in from Continental Paper. Their plant was finally on line and they would soon be in need of a shipping company that could transport their finished products to Canada for further processing. He knew the men on the board well and by the spring of that year, had added two more ships to his growing fleet. A month later, and in what was purely a stroke of luck in a chance encounter with the Postmaster General, he secured the very lucrative and highly sought after mail contracts for the U. S. Postal Service's new routes in their southern district.

But there was a huge difference between just buying the ships and then running them, and as Foster divided his time between his Senatorial duties and his fledgling shipping company, he soon found himself busier than he'd ever been in his life. The world of shipping was not quite as simple as what he had thought it would be, and even though he'd brought Vicki in from the beginning to help oversee and run things, the demands and amount of work that was involved to keep six ships up and going was monumental to say the least.

There were so many things about them and the business that he didn't know and understand; he wondered what in the hell he'd gotten himself into. He grew tired and irritable, and had even thought of selling, but it just wasn't in his nature to quit; besides, they were already turning a profit. But even so, he knew that if he were to grow and continue any further than what he had, that he needed help and he needed it from someone who knew the industry. Someone who knew and understood the ships and the men, and the ways of the open seas.

"So by the summer of 34?" Jim cocked his head. "He already had six ships?"

"Yep," Otis nodded and then took a sip from his beer. "Two of em was runnin down to South America for that aluminum company, two of em was runnin up north to Canada for that paper company, an two of em was runnin mail for the Postal Service."

"Well, he sure didn't waste no time did he?" Jim chuckled.

"Foster? Oh hell no. But I gotta tell ya, even though he was one of the smartest men that I ever knew an could go out an find an buy them ships like nobody else you'd ever seen, he didn't know a damn thing about the shippin business."

"Really?" Jim chuckled again. "But I thought you just said that he'd built one of the biggest shippin companies in the world?"

"Oh he did," Otis assured. "But boy, it sure didn't start out that-a-way, I can tell ya that."

"Really?"

"Oh hell yes. See, ol Foster had gone out an jumped right into do'n somethin that he didn't know nothin about, an I mean nothin. An let me tell ya, it didn't take him very long before he realized that he needed help."

"So what'd he do?"

"Well, if I remember correctly, he'd started lookin for someone right off the bat, but it wasn't until around June or July of that year that he finally found his man. I remember I'd jus picked him up at the train station one afternoon an had taken him over to his offices at the pier when his pride an joy the Eastern Star, jus so happened to be pullin in."

His search had continued into the summer with an array of potential candidates, good and highly qualified businessmen who could easily fill the spot, but there always seemed to be something that held him back. A gut instinct that he couldn't quite pin down until one day late in June, when he stood on the pier and watched as his first ship, *The Eastern Star,* along with its captain Ralston DuPree', pulled into dock. They'd just unloaded earlier that day at American Aluminum and now here they were, happy to be home with a few days off while they re-provisioned and refueled for another journey back down south at week's end.

The son of French and Russian immigrants, Ralston had certainly proven himself to be a fine and competent sea captain with over a dozen trips to South America. He was a mariner of the highest degree with a completely unblemished record, and it had all begun years ago when he and his parents had left Europe and come to America.

He was ten, and it was the first time that he'd ever seen the ocean. Bubbling with excitement and curiosity, it wasn't but a half day before he began to explore the ship. Opening almost every door he could, he went from bow to stern and from level to level until he'd met almost every single member of the crew there was, including the captain. He was in awe, and by the time they'd reached New York, the sea's mystic and magic had grabbed him in a way he never could've imagined.

For years it was all he could think of until his sixteenth birthday, when he finally said goodbye to his parents and left home, joined the merchant marines, and soon found himself in Hong Kong. It was a love affair that spanned the next fifteen years and took him to ports of call all over the globe as he steadily rose through the ranks. Beginning as an able bodied seaman, he grew up tough, but still he worked hard and kept his nose clean, learning each and every position that there was until the day had come when he'd finally achieved the rank of captain.

But Foster had always sensed from day one that there was more to the man than just someone who was destined to spend his life at sea. He was different from the other captains and it showed; there was drive and ambition in him, and a restlessness that said he wanted more out of life. He knew that feeling well, and as he gazed up at the black steel hulk floating towards the pier and then to the man with the thin short beard standing just outside of the pilothouse, it hit him.

His search was over, he'd found his man and of all things, he already worked for him. Ralston was perfect, he was smart and confident and respected by his crew, but most importantly he knew every-thing that there was about the ships and the ways of life on the open seas. Medium in stature yet ruggedly handsome, he was looking down with his hands on the rail, vigilantly watching, ensuring that the men on deck and the line handlers on the pier did their jobs and secured the ship. It was one of his final duties as a captain before leaving the boat and stepping ashore.

A moment later, he spotted his boss standing on the pier with his hands in his pockets. A subtle nod and a casual salute quickly generated a wave back along with a hand gesture to come to the office. Thirty minutes later, the two were eating lunch at the Battle-House Hotel. Their discussion was all business and by the time they'd finished, Ralston had pledged his loyalty and gladly accepted Foster's offer. It was the opportunity of a lifetime and he knew it, especially in the grips of a depression. Four days later he made one last trip to South America to watch and train his replacement and upon his return, Ralston Alexander DuPree', under the watchful eyes of Foster, took the helm of Siler Shipping as its new vice president.

"An so that's who he finally picked, huh? This Ralston DuPree' dude."

"Yep," Otis nodded. "The captain of his very first boat."

"Well, I guess that makes sense really if ya think about it," he surmised. "You know, him be'n a captain an all, an knowin how all that shippin stuff works."

"Oh it did, in fact, probably better than anyone had ever imagined. See, that ol Ralston was a real pit bull an jus as soon as he took over, ol Foster took off like nothin I've ever seen."

"*What-a-ya mean?*"

"*Well, at first it was jus buyin them ships again, one right after the other which made me so busy I didn't have time to do hardly nothin.*"

"*You... why you?*"

"*Well first, it was addin on to those damn offices that I'd jus finished so they could have more room. An then, if I wasn't workin on that, me an Foster was out on the boat lookin at all the abandoned dry docks.*"

"*Dry docks?*"

"*Yep, dry docks. I remember it was right around the early fall of that year; he'd bought a boat that needed some work done to it. Ralston had told him that he wouldn't send it out to sea until it was done cause it wasn't safe. Anyway, the depression had hit the shipyards here in Mobile pretty hard an after a few years there wasn't but a couple of em left that could do the work.*

"*Now these guys, well, they really had everybody over a barrel an they knew it. An it wasn't long before they started turnin the screws to jus about everyone who walked through their doors, includin Foster. Yes sir, every time he took a boat in to get somethin done, it seemed like it kept taken longer an longer, an their prices kept gettin higher an higher. Shit, they was screwin everybody. Anyway, he was already pretty aggravated cause his boat had been in the yard so long an he was losin money, but boy when he got back from a quick little trip to Washinton an found out that it was still in them docks... well,*" Otis chuckled. "*That man went absolutely plum nuts.*

"*I remember Ralston had gone an picked him up at the airport an jus as soon as they got back, they went inside. I was workin in the back on that remodel an it wasn't more than a couple of minutes before I overheard him yellin at some guy on the phone. Actually, he was screamin at him if ya wanna know the truth, an let me tell ya, I swear to God if he could of reached through that phone an gotten a hold of that ol boy on the other end, he'd a strangled his ass right there on the spot. Yes sir, they was really yellin at each other from the sound of it, but after another minute or two I guess them ol boys down there at the shipyard must of told Foster that if he didn't like their prices or the way they was do'n things that he could jus stick it up his ass an take his boat somewhere else.*

"*Now let me tell ya, that really pissed him off, an if there was one thing that I'd learned over the years that I'd worked for him, it was that you did not want to piss off Foster Siler. No sir, no how an no way, an I don't care who you was.*"

"*Really,*" Jim raised his eyebrows.

"Oh hell yes. Shiiit, that man was the most coldhearted, ruthless son-of-a-bitch that I'd ever met, an if you crossed him, well, you could damn well bet that he was gonna come after you one way or another. An let me tell ya, that was an absolute certainty."

"Damn," Jim shook his head. "So what'd he end up do'n?"

"Well, one of the first things he did after he slammed that phone down was to let out a string of cuss words an then yell for me."

"You? What in the hell he want with you? You didn't do nothin."

"Oh I know, he jus wanted me to get the boat."

"The boat? What in the hell he want with the boat?"

"Well," Otis chuckled as he thought back. "That was the afternoon that me an him an Ralston went out an started lookin at all the dry docks an shipyards that was all closed up. See, it was way easier to go by boat so we took off an drove that whole river right in front of town, all the way from Chickasaw Creek down to Sand Island an then all the way back up again. I'll tell ya, we looked at everything until we finally found this great big track on the northern part of Pinto Island. There was this old shipyard that was already out there with a twelve-thousand an an eight-thousand-ton dry dock that also had outfitting wharves an a whole bunch of other shops on it too. Now he really like that piece an wanted to walk it, but by then it was gettin late so we jus went on home. Then, the next mornin, we met down at the boat so we could go back out again. I remember I was gettin it ready when he came walkin down the pier an then jus stopped right behind it an looked down at the stern."

"Have you seen her?" Foster asked as he raised his eyes from the transom.

"Seen who boss?" Otis replied and cocked his head.

"Willie," he said as he dropped his gaze back to the stern and stared.

Looking at Foster, Otis thought for just a second of all the things he could say, but in the end he knew better than to lie. "Yes sur boss," he replied somewhat nervously. "Sh, she comes an sees me every once an awhile an brings me books."

"She does?" Foster seemed surprised.

"Yes sur, she wanted me ta keep readin, so whenever she comes into town for that Mrs. Portman, she brings me a new book ta read an then helps me with my readin an writin. But I can tell her not ta come no more if'n that's what ya wants," he finished in hopes that Foster wouldn't be mad.

"No no, that's okay," Foster assured with another glance to the transom. "I know that you and Willie are friends, and if she wants to visit and bring you books, and it makes her happy, well, that's okay. Besides, you should learn to read."

"Are ya shor boss?" Otis smiled with a relieved expression.

"Yeah, I'm sure," he smiled back. "Just tell her that I..." he began but then suddenly stopped with another quick glance to the transom. "Just tell her that I said hello, if you would."

"Oh, yes sur boss, I can certainly do that."

"Good, now come on, I wanna take another look at that Pinto Island ground and walk it before I make my offer."

"An that was all he said about her," Otis sighed.

"Really?" Jim seemed surprised.

"Yep."

"So Willie did come by an see you, just like she said she would?"

"Yeah she did actually," Otis nodded as he fondly recalled her visits. "It was rare cause she was still in school an I was so busy tryin ta take care of everything that Foster had me do'n, but yeah, every once in a while she'd catch me down at the boat. See, she really wanted me to keep on readin, so after she'd learned to drive that ol farm truck the Portmans had, she got to where whenever she got the chance to come into town, she'd come by an bring me another new book to read. We'd talk an visit an if I wasn't there, she'd jus leave it up there by the wheel for me to find with a little note on it. Sometimes she'd even leave me a little bag of cookies or somethin she'd baked that mornin. I tell ya, I really enjoyed gettin them. In fact, I even got to where I started lookin for em," he laughed.

"An Foster... he didn't care?" Jim asked.

"Nope, not a bit. He knew that Willie an I was friends. Besides, he still liked her, an even though he'd never talked about her until that day, you could tell. You could see it in his eyes whenever he'd look at the back of the boat. But he was a Senator an was married, an after that mornin, he never said another word about her."

"But wait a minute, I thought you told me earlier that they ended up gettin back together?"

"Oh they did, but heck that wasn't for another year or so if I remember right. See Willie, she'd spent most of that summer practicin an learnin how

to be a lady at that finishin school, an after that, after summer, she up an went back to another year of schoolin, that fall of 34. I'll tell ya, that ol Mrs. Portman was really lookin out for her, an it showed too. Heck, every time I saw her it seemed like she got prettier an smarter. An ol Foster, well, about the only thing he was concerned with at the time was business an politics... an tryin to find a way to buy that damn shipyard so he had a place to work on all of those ships that he was buyin."

———————

By the middle of November, Foster had ten ships and had developed a rare sentimental attachment to the business of merchant marine shipping where the profits were not the end but the means by which to construct a maritime empire that would encircle the globe. He had a vision for the company that was unlike any of his competitors and through his political connections, he rapidly extended routes into Puerto Rico, the West Indies and then across the Atlantic to Liverpool and Manchester.

He finished his offices and quickly expanded into the shore side activities of stevedoring, the loading and unloading of cargo. He surrounded himself with the brightest and the best he could find and imposed a policy of plowing the profits back into the company rather than wasteful spending. Ralston ruled beneath him with unquestionable loyalty and an iron fist, instilling into the company a military type discipline and restructuring operations while Foster finalized plans for the acquisition of all the abandoned and bankrupt dry docks on Pinto Island.

Gordan DeWeese the president of Mobile Savings couldn't have been happier to see Foster Siler walk through his door again. Still intent on saving the bank and making it grow in the midst of the depression, he listened with a keen and excited interest as the Senator told of the Navy's interest then laid out his plans to buy and resurrect the floundering shipyards.

It was without question a bold and gutsy move, but his reputation as a creative and successful deal-maker had preceded him, and Gordan DeWeese wanted his bank to be a part of whatever it was the charismatic Senator was doing. A few days later, the board returned with a unanimous vote to fund his venture. Then in the first week of December, in a much celebrated and publicized ribbon cutting, Siler Shipbuilding went into business and pulled their first ship, a U S Navy Frigate, into its docks.

"So he got this all put together just in time to give himself a little Christmas present huh?" Jim chuckled and shook his head.

"Yep, if you call a buyin a shipyard a little Christmas present," Otis grinned. "That's exactly what he did. An what was so damn funny about it was, was that the only reason he bought it was cause someone had tried to screw him an it had pissed him off. Well, that an he was hell bent on runnin em out of business too."

"Now that's just about the craziest goddamn thing that I've ever heard," Jim scoffed. "I mean, Jesus, the guy buys a shipyard cause someone pissed him off?"

"Oh I know," Otis chuckled. "But that was Foster, he did it, he really did, an I watched him. An as it turned out, it wasn't jus a Christmas present for him, it was a Christmas present for a whole lot a people who didn't have work too. People that wanted to work, an needed to work.

"See somehow, an I couldn't even begin to tell you as to how or when he did it, but he'd gone out an secured these contracts from the Navy to start repairin all of their ships in the Gulf. In fact, by the time they had that big ol ribbon cuttin ceremony they already had one of their smaller warships sittin there. I'll tell ya, it was a hell of a deal an there was people everywhere, an jus as soon as ol Foster had cut that ribbon an the band started playin, they began pullin that boat in to work on it."

"An you were there?"

"Yep, right there in the middle of it."

"Boy, he sure didn't screw around did he?"

"Oh hell no. In fact, by the time Christmas had rolled around, he already had two more ships there an almost two hundred men workin for him. An let me tell ya, every single one of em was jus tickled to death to have a job again an boy did they ever show it."

"Really, how do you mean?"

"Well, if I recall correctly, I think it all started with one of the foremen really. It was about four or five days before Christmas an I guess this guy's wife was so overwhelmed that he finally had a job again that she went an made Foster a great big ol plate of cookies an fudge jus to thank him. Vicki told me that when she brought it in an dropped it off there at the office down

on the pier that she was actually cryin, an that she must of told her a hundred times to please make sure that Mr. Siler got them, an to be sure an tell him how grateful they were for everything that he was do'n.

"Now the rest of them workers, well, I guess they must of all felt pretty much the same way cause after word got out an kind of spread around, it wasn't but a couple of days or so before that whole front office looked like a damn bakery."

"A whaaat?"

"A bakery. You know, pies an cakes an stuff," he emphasized. "See, there wasn't a man there that wanted to be the only one that didn't get Mr. Siler somethin for Christmas, an by the end of that week I swear that every one of em must of gone home an had their wives bake somethin for him. Yes sir, when I walked into them offices that Friday mornin to finish the last of my paintin, I don't believe that I've ever seen so many pies, cakes, cookies an fudge in all my life. In fact, that whole damn office was filled to where you couldn't hardly set nothin down nowhere."

"Really?"

"Oh hell yes, an let me tell ya it was a real humblin thing to see too cause times was still real hard an most of them people didn't have two cents to rub together. Yet here they were, givin whatever they had to say thank you in the only way they knew how... or could. See Foster, without even knowin it, had given em hope an a piece of their dignity back in a time when there wasn't any to be had, an they loved him for it. Everybody loved him, an everywhere we went it was the same. I saw it, cause I was drivin him an Melinda around town that whole holiday season."

CHAPTER 50

━━━◆━━━

IT WAS A CELEBRATORY TIME of the year for everyone, but even more so for Foster and Melinda. They'd become the toast of the town, the dashing Senator who'd done so much for the city and his beautiful wife, attending almost every social event there was. But the holiday season soon passed and by mid January of 1935, the news of Siler Shipping and Siler Shipbuilding had begun to resonate throughout the industry. He'd done and acquired more in a shorter period of time than anyone had ever seen, but in his quest to grow and unbeknownst to him, he'd finally gained the unwanted attention of a New Orleans Steamship Company.

The Lucass Brothers Steamship Line whose ultimate objective in business was to acquire a virtual monopoly over all of the shipping in the Gulf. They were modern day pirates and they were ruthless, corporate raiders who were good at destroying and running other companies out of business. But their new president, the former Senator Harlen Crandell, wanted more.

Blinded not only by greed, but by hatred, he wanted revenge for what Foster had taken from him and then put him through, and now with the opportunity at hand, he was determined to destroy him. But neither he nor the men on the board that he served could've ever imagined that when they went after Foster and his ten ships, that in less than a year, and in what would be hailed as one of the most unprecedented business moves ever seen, Foster would control them all.

The battle had begun over a simple bidding war that they themselves had created, a quiet campaign of letters and then visits to all of Foster's clients, claiming that they were being over charged and that if they were to switch companies, they could save them money and provide better service. Their plan was simple, to cut Foster's rates and take his business until he was financially dead, then take his ships and raise their rates back up.

They'd done it before a number of times, they were good at it, and they knew the process well. Crandell had just taken their company public several months earlier, and now with loads of cash in with which to wage war, the Lucass Brothers Steamship Line prepared a battle plan and came after the unsuspecting Senator.

Taken by surprise, it was only his ironclad contracts that saved him from their first attack. After that, they quickly moved to Washington, an arena that Crandell knew well, and launched a full-scale assault. They threw money at everyone in an effort to undermined and change the political alliances that Foster had forged on the Commission as well as with the Secretary of Navy and Transportation.

The months passed and the battle escalated with lies and deceit that had no limits as they tried to secretly hinder and block Foster at every opportunity. Crandell knew how to play the game and he wanted Foster's head on a platter. They were vicious and vindictive, but Foster Siler was far from lying down for anyone, especially for Harlen Crandell and the goons that he worked for. And even though they'd pinned his back to the wall, he fought back with a tenacious perseverance.

At first it seemed hopeless, they were well funded and well run and they out gunned him at every turn. He had only a year left on his contracts with American Aluminum and Continental Paper, and he knew if he were to lose those that the game would be over and he'd be finished. But their plan had a flaw, for in their arrogance and their blinded quest for total domination, they'd left their back door open. It was something that Foster instantly picked up on, and in a game of where winner takes all, he quietly made plans to slip inside.

There was no time to waste, and with that he hastily scheduled trip to see Henry Fletcher. They'd done ten ships together by then, and all had gone through without a hitch. In fact, it'd become almost routine; a phone call, followed by papers in the mail and then a money transfer. Their relationship over the last year had been built on the merits of trust and solid deal making, but this time the Senator from Alabama needed more, he needed to see Henry in person. A week later, and even though he'd been expecting him, the mild-mannered banker seemed surprised to look up and see his secretary enter into his office with Foster. Immediately rising from behind his desk, he smiled and greeted him mid room.

"Foster it's been too long," he said and extended his hand. "How've you been my friend?"

"Yes it has Henry," Foster agreed as they shook. "Yes it has. And I've been just fine, thank you."

"Well please, please, come on in and have a seat. Ooh, and can I get you anything before Betty slips away? Coffee, tea?" he asked as he looked between him and his secretary waiting at the door.

"No no, I'm fine, but thanks." He took a chair in front of Henry's desk

"You sure?"

"Yes, thank you."

"Well then, I guess that'll be all Betty, thanks," he said, dismissing the woman at the door.

"Yes sir," she replied. "Just let me know if you need anything."

A second later, Henry took his seat behind his desk. "So how's Washington? I hear lots of good news about you and all of the things that you've done for Mobile. In fact," he pointed his finger. "We could use someone like you over here in Louisiana. You know how to get things done and I know plenty of people that'd put a lot of money behind you if you ever decided that you wanted to live here in New Orleans."

"Well thanks Henry," Foster chuckled. "That's very flattering, but I have to say that for right now, Mobile's my home."

"Yeah, I thought so, but it sure doesn't hurt to ask," he added as they both began to laugh.

But Foster hadn't come all the way from Mobile to chit-chat and Henry knew it, and with that he quickly changed the subject. "So just how is everything?" he asked guardedly. "The other day on the phone you sounded as if something was pretty pressing and now here you are. What's up, you in some sort of trouble or something?" he asked and then raised his eyebrows.

"Well Henry," Foster hesitated as if he wasn't quite sure where to start. "To be real blunt with you, yes I am. In fact, it's pretty big trouble actually. I've got someone here in New Orleans whose trying to put me out of business."

"Well, for what its worth, we've already heard."

"You have?" Foster seemed surprised.

"Yep, it seems your old friend Harlen Crandell is out to get you."

"So you know what they're trying to do?"

"Oh yeaaah, we know," he nodded. "I guess he really didn't like it when you took that boat away from him, and now that he works for the Lucass Brothers, well, let's just say that he's back to pullin the same ol crap that he use to. In fact," his voice rose as he leaned toward him with his arms on his desk. "Can you believe that that son-of-a-bitch actually had the goddamn unmitigated gall to come in here and threaten us? To tell us that if we kept doing business with your company that they were going to let it be known so to speak, around town and to all their customers that we were on difficult times and about to go under, and that they should move their accounts before it was too late?" He exhaled with an incensed breath. "Can you believe that?"

"Well, that's Crandell," Foster grinned.

"Oh yeah," Henry agreed. "So what are you going to do? You know you can't compete against them boys, shit, they'll bleed you like a stuck pig and then skin you before you're dead."

"Yes, I know, but I have a plan."

"A plan?" Henry scoffed. "What, you gonna just waltz on over to their office's while you're here and shoot his ass?" He laughed.

"Well," Foster chuckled. "That really doesn't sound like too bad of an idea, but in answer to your question, no, I have something else in mind. Something better. Something much much better."

"Oh really," Henry perked up. "And just what in the hell would that be?"

"I'm going to take them over."

"Take them over?" he scoffed.

"Yes," Foster repeated. "But I need your help."

"Are you serious? Jesus Foster, I've seen the Lucass Brothers go after and destroy more people that've tried to get into the shipping business than I can count, and if you haven't noticed my friend, you're about to be their next victim. And now you're sitting here telling me that you're going to go after them, and take them over? Are you feeling okay? Please tell me, just how in the hell do you propose to do that?"

"Well, I'm not sure if you're aware of this yet, but several months back Crandell took them public and when he did, they issued right about sixty percent of their company's stock on the exchange."

"Annnd?" Henry narrowed his eyes in a curious manner.

"I wanna buy it... all of it. Slowly and quietly... very, very quietly. Until I have, as they say in the industry... controlling interest."

"Buy it! Are you serious? Goddamn Foster, do you know how big their company is? They've got twenty-six ships, how in the hell do you propose to do that? Besides, you know and I know that just as soon as they get wind of what you're doing the game is gonna be over."

"It's twenty-eight. They have twenty-eight ships," he corrected and then proceeded with all of the confidence in the world. "And to be quite honest with you, they won't have a clue that it's happening until it's too late."

"Oh really, and why's that?"

"Because over the last several weeks, I've created twenty-eight different corporations in twenty-eight different states all with the sole intent of keeping my name out of it. You know, kind of one company for each ship," he smiled. "Now of course, all of this hinges on money, lots and lots of money. And that my friend, is why I'm here."

"And I suppose that you wanna borrow this money and use your ten ships as collateral, huh?"

"Well, those and my new shipyard on Pinto Island, and of course the stock certificates as well. Oh, and I also have two thousand acres of swamp land just north of the city that I'd throw in for good measures if you want."

"Swamp lannnd," Henry scoffed and waved his hand. "Keep it, I've got enough damn ground on my books right now." But then the mild manner banker quit talking, took off his glasses and slid his tablet to the side. "You do know how risky this is don't you?" he sighed.

"Yes."

"And that this whole crazy scheme of yours could backfire and you could lose everything you've got. Including your Senate seat."

"Yes, I know, but I don't have a choice. It's either this or a slow and certain death, because in a year, most of the contracts that I have with my customers will expire and when that happens, the Lucass Brothers will cut their rates and it's all over for me. But I do have one thing in my favor."

"And what's that?" Henry stared curiously.

"Well, Crandell and his bosses think that they're already hurting me."

"And are they?"

"No, or at least not yet they aren't. But that's what they believe and that's exactly what I want them to believe. See, I want them to think that they're squeezing the life right out of me and that my time is limited. Very limited. In fact, you're going to let word get out that I came here looking for money to try and hang on for another year. That I was desperate, and even though I'd pleaded with you, your board turned me down. Now if I know Crandell, it won't be very long before he hears about it and begins to gloat, and after that, they'll try and turn up the heat even more."

"And why am I going to do that?" Henry asked.

"Because if they think that I'm without funding, then they'll think that they've wounded me in a financial sense. Now that's exactly what I want them to think because then they'll relax and the last thing in the world that they would ever expect or imagine is for me to try and come after them. I mean, come on... who in their right mind would be crazy enough to even try such a thing?" He smiled as if he could already see the future unfolding. "See, they'll be focused on one thing and one thing only, and that's trying to destroy me just as fast as they can. They're already spending money in Washington like a drunken sailor and as long as I'm still in business, they won't give a shit who's buying their stock."

Rocking back in his chair after Foster had finished, Henry quietly contemplated everything he had just heard. He'd never seen nor heard of anyone doing what Foster had just proposed, but after just a few moments, he began to smile and shake his head. "You know, as far fetched and as crazy as this whole thing sounds, it really could work, couldn't it."

"It will work," Foster assured. "And just as soon as I have controlling interest and they have their first shareholder's meeting," he paused with a resolute glare. "I'll walk in and fire them all."

There was really no love between Henry Fletcher and Harlen Crandell, or the Lucass Brothers for that matter. They were bullies in every sense of the word, used to getting whatever they wanted by whatever means it took, but this time they'd run into a formidable foe, and Foster's final words made Henry smile.

"You know, when Jasper and Morgan found out that the Lucass Brothers actually had Crandell come in and threatened us, they weren't very happy. In fact, they got down right mad. They don't like those two boys, never have, and if they believe in your plan," he paused and smiled. "You just might get your money. But even so, this'll still have to go before the full board. You do know that?"

"Yes, but when can you do it? This afternoon?" Foster insinuated with a grin.

"No, it's way to late for that, but I can sure have everybody together in the morning. How's that?"

The two men talked for a while longer as Foster explained the details of his proposal. He wanted Henry to understand exactly how everything would work and how the bank would get their money back. How just as soon as he'd replaced the board he'd destroy their company by sliding the entire debt of his stock purchase onto their books and then force the sale of all their ships to pay it back.

A fire sale, direct to Siler Shipping. It was without question one of the most brilliant and gutsiest buyouts that Henry had ever seen and it made him smile. Then rising with the assurances that he would have an answer in the morning, the mild manner banker walked Foster to the door.

"Well my friend, I'd sure like to take you out to dinner tonight, but unfortunately my wife already has me obligated."

"Oh hell Henry, don't worry about it, I kind of had plans to go and see an old friend tonight anyway, someone who I haven't seen in a while. But maybe next time."

"Well, it would be my pleasure, you enjoy your evening and we'll talk in the morning then."

A two-dollar tip to the big man outside opened the door without a second's hesitation, and as soon as he'd stepped inside he was greeted by a lovely young brunette. "Champagne?" she asked as she held up her tray, only to suddenly stop and smile. "Ooh hey," she drawled in the sweetest of voices. "Iiii remember you. You're the one who came in with Henry last year an then spent the night with Miss Kat, aren't you? I'm Charlotte."

"Well," Foster smiled as he took the glass, somewhat embarrassed that she'd actually remembered him. "Yes, I guess I am."

"Well, how about that. You know, you shor was the talk around here for a real long spell."

"Oh I was, was I? Why's that?"

"Cause you spent the whole night with Miss Kat upstairs in her private quarters, an she ain't never done that with no one before. Ever."

"Oh really?" Foster seemed surprised.

"Oh yes sir, an boy was she ever happy that next day. I shor don't know what you did to her while you were here, but after you left she was happier than I'd seen her in a long long time."

"Really?" he replied again as he thought back to that night.

"Oh heck yeah, in fact, she smiled for days. I think that deep down she kind of looked for you to come walkin back in some day... but you never did. Anyway, we use to all tease her an ask her what you'd done to her to make her smile like that, but she never would tell us. She would just smile an blush, an tell us that you was just a tall cool drink of water... but that your glass never ran empty."

"Oh she did, did she," he blushed at the fact that he'd been talked of in such a way. "Well, I guess I'll just have to speak to her about that now won't I," he added as he took a sip from his glass. "So, where is she? She is in, isn't she?"

"Miss Kat?" The girl's smile instantly disappeared.

"Yes, Katherine. You know, the lady we were just talking about."

"You, you mean, you don't know?" She turned and then stared at the portrait on the wall. "Miss Kat passed away last year. Just before Christmas. We was all real sad too, specially Lillian."

"What?" Foster's voice and expression instantly changed. "She, she died?" he stammered as he tried to regain his composure. "Wha, what happened?"

"Well, we're not really shor, but the doctor said he thought that she took to much of that cocaine medicine that she'd been taken an that her heart just up an stopped one night."

The news came as a shock and for a few fleeting moments, Foster could only stand and stare at the painting as a mix of emotions welled from the depths of his insides. She'd been so much more than just a lover, and now she was gone. Gone forever and gone without a goodbye. He felt saddened and dazed, and now unsure of just what to say, he glanced back at the girl and stared for just a moment then turned and crossed the room to where the portrait hung.

It was a large and beautiful painting in honor of one of the most beautiful woman he'd ever known. He thought of her life and of everything that she'd once had, and then of everything she had lost. He thought of the very first time they'd met at Connie's Diner, and then of their boat ride up river and the first time they'd made love. He smiled then thought of the night he'd spent here. Then reaching up, he gently touched the thin golden plate engraved in old world calligraphy and with a heartfelt sadness, quietly read her name. *'Katherine Louise Davenport.'*

She was gone and he would miss her, but she was at peace now, and with a raised glass in honor and in memory of her life, he gulped his champagne and said his goodbyes in the only way he knew how. A second later, he turned back to the girl and gently set his glass on her tray.

"You know, you really don't have to rush off if you don't want," she drawled invitingly. "I mean, if you don't wanna be alone, we are kind-a slow, an I could take the rest of the night off if you'd like. Of course at no charge, an we could..." her words trailed off as if she'd sensed his answer before he could say it.

He could clearly see that she meant no disrespect, and that she was without a doubt as beautiful and as desirable as they came, and that under any other circumstances, he would've leapt at her offer. But tonight, Foster would honor the dark-haired beauty in a way in which he never had before, and with the most gracious of smiles and then the tenderest of kisses to her cheek, he declined her offer. He would sleep alone tonight, and with a long last look at the beautiful portrait hanging on the wall, he said goodbye for the very last time then turned toward the door and quietly walked away.

———◆———

CHAPTER 51

ALTHOUGH HIS TRIP TO NEW Orleans was a success and he'd gotten almost everything he had wanted from Henry and his bank, the unexpected news of Katherine's death had turned it bittersweet. He'd actually hoped to see her again, and even though he had secured the financing he had so desperately sought, the pain of losing someone who he had actually come to care for, seemed to overshadow it and follow him home.

Katherine was gone, and as his plane touched down and then taxied onto the tarmac, he looked out of his window to see Otis waiting patiently by the car. He'd hired him because of her and the boat, and after all of these years, he still worked for him. He was a trusted employee and he was glad that he had. He thought of the first time that they had all gone up river, and as the plane slowly rolled to a stop and shut down its motor, he looked at the man walking towards him and smiled.

Pulling two more beers from the cooler, Jim set them on the table and then shook his head. "So ol Katherine Davenport died?" His voice seemed to resonate his surprise.

"Yeah she did," Otis sighed as he took one of the cans and then popped its top. "I think it was sometime jus before Christmas of 1934, but I didn't actually find out about it until Foster had gotten back from New Orleans. It was late spring of 35, I'd jus picked him up at the airport an was drivin him back to the offices to see Ralston when he told me. I remember I was real sad too cause I really liked her. She was a good lady. In fact, if the truth be known, I

think even ol Foster was a little upset cause deep down, I think that he really liked her too. Anyway, she was gone, but boy had she ever started somethin."

"Started something? What-a-ya mean?"

"Well, jus think about it. Heck, the only reason he even had this damn boat was cause of her an it was because of that that he got in to do'n all the things he started do'n."

"How do ya mean?" Jim scrunched his face.

"You know, first me an Willie... an then all of them ships an the shipyards. Yes sir, if it wasn't for this here boat," Otis sighed and looked around. "Even me an you wouldn't be here," he laughed and then took a slug from his beer.

"Ya know," Jim surmised as he popped his top. "I never really thought of it that way, but I guess you're right."

"Well heck yeah I'm right. In fact, when I think back as to what all this boat actually started, it really makes me wonder," he added with another look around.

"About what?"

"Oh you know, me an Willie an Foster, an all the things that'd happened."

"Why, is that when they finally got back together?"

"Well, not really," Otis chuckled. "But that's pretty much when all the pieces that'd brought em back together started fallin in to place."

"Really? How's that?"

"Well, if I remember correctly, I think it was right around the middle of August, Willie was in her last week of that finishin school."

"Again?"

"Oh yeah, see that Mrs. Portman, well, I guess she'd gottin it in her head that she wanted Willie to do that whole debutante thing."

"Whoa whoa whoooa... debutante thing?"

"Yeah, you know... debutante," Otis repeated.

"You mean where all them high society types go an get all dressed up an then have their little so-called comin out party?"

"Yep, that's exactly what I mean. See Willie, I think she was about twenty at the time, was without a doubt one of the prettiest girls in Mobile an ol Mrs. Portman really wanted to present her at that upcoming Christmas Ball."

"Whoa whoa whoooa," Jim drew Otis into another stop and then narrowed his eyes. "Let's just hold on a minute here. Willie was a sharecropper, an even I know that a sharecropper ain't gonna get invited to a debutante ball. Stuff like that don't happen, an I don't care how pretty she was."

"You're right, that is true," Otis agreed. "That is, unless you can get someone who's powerful enough to step in an make it happen. See, back then it wasn't what you knew, but who you knew."

"Oooh," Jim raised his brow. "An just who in the hell would that of been, Foster?" He laughed.

"No, but you're pretty close."

"Then who?"

"Well, you really ain't gonna believe this," Otis began to laugh and shake his head. "An to tell ya the truth, when I first heard about it, I didn't either, but it was ol Judge McAlister an his wife."

"Whaaat?" Jim blurted. "You, you mean his in-laws!" he exclaimed with a slap to the table.

"Yep, that'd be the ones."

"Are you shittin me?"

"Nope," Otis shook his head.

"An ol Foster... he didn't know nothin about it?"

"Nope, or at least not that I ever knew."

"Okay, so tell me," Jim shook his head as if he still couldn't believe what Otis had said. "Just how in the hell did all that come about?"

"Well, I guess it all began earlier that year when Mrs. Portman started puttin the pressure on her husband to get a hold of ol Judge McAlister. See, by then I guess ol Willie had become jus like a daughter to her an she wanted him to say somethin to the Judge so he'd say somethin to his wife cause she sat on that committee or whatever the hell it is that sends out all a them invites."

"But wait a minute, that was Foster's in-laws," Jim's voice rose along with his sense of hypocrisy. "An she knew it, didn't she?"

"Oooh yeaah, she knew it all right," Otis grinned. "But the McAlisters was real blue bloods if ya know what I mean, an if ol Mrs. McAlister recommended to the committee that someone be invited to the debutante ball, well, it was pretty much a certainty that that's exactly what'd happen an ol Mrs. Portman knew that. Anyway, an I ain't exactly sure as to jus how or when they did it, but her an Willie even went over to their house one Saturday afternoon, you know, for tea, so Mrs. McAlister could meet her an size her up so to speak."

"Are you serious?" Jim rolled his eyes. "She actually had the brass to take Willie over there knowin that that woman was Foster's mother-in-law?"

"Yep."

"An this, Mrs. McAlister," he probed further. *"I'm taken it that she didn't know who Willie was?"*

"Nope, or at least I don't think she did."

"An Willie, she didn't know who this woman was either, huh?"

"No, I really don't think so, an I don't believe that that Mrs. Portman said anything either."

"Jesus, that's unbelievable, I mean..." his voice trailed off in disbelief.

"Oh hell, tell me about it," Otis grinned.

"So then what happened?"

"Well, I guess this Mrs. McAlister must of really been impressed with Willie, specially after she'd learned how her momma had died in the fields an then of how she'd come all the way to Mobile on her own to get an education. Yes sir, she must of really taken a likin to her cause it wasn't to awfully long after her visit that she got her invitation to that up comin Christmas Ball."

"Really, just like that?"

"Yep, jus like that."

"An how'd you find out about it?"

"Willie told me."

"She did?"

"Yep, her an that Daphney an that Angela gal had all become pretty good friends after our little trip up river an they was all out runnin around one day when they stopped by the boat. Willie wanted to tell me the good news, an that Daphney girl wanted to bring me another cobbler an thank me again for what I'd done for her. I remember it real well too cause me an Foster had jus gotten back from checkin on all the ships in his shipyards. He liked do'n that jus so he could see how things was go'n.

"Anyway, an I don't know how in the heck they missed each other cause no sooner had he left than the three of them came walkin down. I'd jus finished wipin down the boat an was gettin ready to close it all up when I heard em comin an looked up. They was all excited an was gigglin an carryin on cause Willie had jus gotten her invitation an they were all gonna go to that party together."

"So you knew the whole story?"

"Oh yeaah, I knew it all right," Otis grinned again.

"But you never said anything to Foster... or Willie?"

"Oh hell no, shit I wasn't gonna get mixed up in the middle of that mess," he laughed.

"So what happened?"

"Well, not much other than the summer kind of came to an end. Willie, she ended up go'n back to school to her first year of college I think it was, an ol Foster, well, he finally took off for Washinton again, but boy did he really have a lot on his plate."

"What-a-ya mean?"

"You know, that other shippin company that was tryin to ruin him. See, I got to hear a whole lot of what was go'n on cause I was always driven him around an if I wasn't do'n that, I was workin on somethin at the offices. So I knew that that other company had been tryin to run him out of business. But ol Foster was really smart, an even though he never did say much about it, you could sure tell that he was up to somethin. I didn't know what it was, but by then, I knew him well enough to know that he wasn't gonna jus lay down. No siree. You could see it in his eyes an the way he acted, like he was some sort of great white hunter who'd been stalkin his prey an was about to make that prefect kill. Specially after he'd gotten back from that trip to New Orleans. Yes sir, he was up to somethin all right, but then, an right around the end of September, well, that's when he got the news. Actually, that's when we all got the news."

The door to his office flew open without a knock and as soon as he looked up from his desk, Foster could tell that something was terribly wrong. "Suzanne?" he instantly asked as she rushed into the room. "What's wrong?"

"It's Melinda," she replied as she choked back her tears. "She's on the phone. It, it's your father-in-law," she stuttered as she began to cry. "He's..."

Instantly grabbing the phone, Foster called his wife's name then listened to the horrible news of how her father, Judge Robert Randal McAlister, had just died of a sudden heart attack. It was a sad and torturous conversation that hurt more than anything, for the Judge had been like a father to him. He felt an anger and rage boil up inside, but then with a hushed and compassionate voice, he assured Melinda he would be home immediately.

The next morning, Foster, Adell and Suzanne, along with a number of other politicians who knew the Judge well, boarded a military DC-2 and headed to Mobile. Four days later, the church was over flowing with people who'd come to honor and pay their respects in what'd become one of the largest funerals that the city had ever seen.

Everyone had come; there were family and friends, the Governor and Senators and Congressmen. There were other Judges, and state and local officials. The Reverend R. L. Stone officiated and blessed his passing, and after that Foster stood before the crowd and gave one of the best eulogies anyone had ever heard. They wept and cried as he gave praise and remembrance to the man that they all had known, then laughed when he told stories, imitating and mocking the Judge as only he could do. They were his final words to a man he revered above all others, and so it was that in the early fall of 1935, everyone said goodbye to Judge Robert Randal McAlister.

He was laid to rest under a bright blue sky, and after the funeral, the entire family and many of their friends gathered back at the house. Monique as always did her best to see to the needs of everyone, but she too had been greatly affected. She'd been struggling and Foster knew it. He could see it in her eyes from across the room when she looked up after pouring a glass of tea for an elderly woman. She was holding the pitcher at her waist and looked both sad and scared, as if she were now lost and didn't know what to do now that her master was gone.

Staring for just a moment, he slowly crossed the room toward her. He'd had just about all of the small talk he could take. The, *'Oh I'm so sorry for your loss,'* and *'He was such a great man,'* and with a discrete whisper to her ear, Foster quietly left and made his way to the Judge's library to honor the man in his own special way.

Slipping inside, he closed the doors behind him and then leaned back in a moment of solitude and surveyed the room. Yes, this room he thought, here within the confines of its four walls where he'd spent so many hours with the Judge. Here, where the decisions of so many cases had been rendered, and then handed down in true Robert McAlister fashion. Here, where he himself had been chosen and then made a Senator. It was an emotional moment that hit without warning, but with a heavy breath to settle his feelings he made his way to the liquor hutch, grabbed a heavy tumbler from the shelf and poured a scotch.

Lifting it to his nose, he inhaled its aroma then touched the burning liquor to his lips and took a sip. Closing his eyes, he savored in the taste for just a moment then swallowed, and even though the drone of muted voices could still be heard outside, the Judge's voice suddenly overrode them all. *'Well son, what-a-ya think?'* His gravelly growl echoed inside his head. *'Damn good, isn't it?'* Looking up into the mirror, Foster nodded and smiled as if he were actually there. "Mother's milk sir," he answered. "Mother's milk," he repeated as he turned toward the windows and crossed the room then took a seat in one of the chairs.

It was the first time that he'd sat alone, and suddenly the room felt strangely empty. Opening the box of cigars setting on the table, he thought of the last time that he and the Judge had sat and talked just before he'd left for Washington. And of the advice he'd given him on how to finish off Crandell and the Lucass Brothers. But the man was gone now and they would never talk again, nor would they share a drink or a smoke. He missed him already, and with the strike of a match he lit his cigar.

Puffing to ensure a good light, he snuffed his match then drew in a smoke filled breath deep into his lungs. The first was always the best, and as the nicotine-laden smoke saturated his lungs, he tilted his head and closed his eyes, savoring and drawing upon it as if it contained the very essence of the man's spirit and all of the memories they'd shared. Fond memories of a man who'd given and taught him so much, and who'd guided and counseled him first as a friend, and then later on like a father. But just like the smoke in his lungs as he exhaled into the air, the memories disappeared and were replaced by the soft sound of the doors as they opened and then lightly closed. It was Monique returning with a bowl of ice.

A moment later, she stopped beside his chair with her bowl and tongs in her hand. Catching her gaze as she looked down, he pushed his tumbler to the edge of the table then lifted his hand and stared at it in the strangest of ways. He remembered the day he had watched the Judge and with the subtlest of glances back up, he caught her gaze again and smiled. The thought was implied and they both knew it. He could see it in her eyes that'd become locked with his. The time had come when neither one owed anymore to the man they'd both cared so much for. He was gone, and without a word Foster dropped his hand off the side of his chair then ever so slowly reached up under the hem of her uniform.

He knew she would submit, yet even so he felt her flinch and clutch her bowl then drop her ice into his glass as his hand found the insides of her thighs. They were smooth and silky, and as he slowly raised it between her legs, he felt her knees weaken and then bend ever so slightly, allowing his access as he asserted his dominance and took the Judge's position. A second later he felt the tangled mat of thick dark curls beneath her cotton garment and then the moistened heat of her sex as it permeated onto his hand. She'd wanted this for as long and as bad as he had, and in her own unspoken way of saying so, she pushed herself against him.

There were no words spoken, but submissively and willingly, the mysterious dark-skinned beauty changed masters. She had been the Judge's possession for almost twenty years, but now the dusky jewel was Foster's. Foster's to obey and to serve in any way he wanted as she dutifully left the house later that evening and drove across town. There was no way Melinda would leave her mother, and as she quietly stepped from her car and looked up, Monique smiled at the sight of the dim flickering light radiating from the second story window.

CHAPTER 52

———◆———

THE FACT THAT THE JUDGE had died, gave absolutely no reprieve from the attacks that Crandell and the Lucass Brothers had been waging. They were unrelenting in their quest to destroy him, but by the beginning of the Thanksgiving holidays, to Foster it no longer mattered for the trap that he had set earlier that spring was about to close around them. He'd wagered everything he had in a game with out limits and his gamble had finally paid off, he owned fifty six percent of their stock and they didn't even know it.

It was the controlling interest that he had needed to take over their company, and now it was just a matter of time before he attended their very first shareholders meeting and fired them all. Scheduled for the first week in December, it was the moment he'd been waiting for and one he would relish as he brought them all to their knees and then beheaded them one by one. But Crandell and the Lucass Brothers wouldn't go easy, and the executions would be messy. And even though they were bound by the governing laws of the Securities and Exchange Commission, they would fight and argue in an attempt to manipulate and challenge their very own by-laws.

It would be a valiant but futile effort for Foster had prepared as if he were going to trial, and he knew that at their very first meeting, they were required to elect a new board. It was one of the first orders of business on the agenda, and one that would trigger their instant demise. A death sentence that'd been created by the rules of their own making as he replaced each and every member of the board, then, and in the most methodical of ways, dismantled their company piece by piece until there was nothing left.

It would be retribution at the highest level and in the most ruthless of ways as he destroyed them from within. First, by sliding the entire debt of his stock purchase onto their balance sheets, then by directing the board to pay it all back in the wholesale liquidation of all twenty-eight ships to the various corporations and holding companies that held their stock.

It was a brilliant plan and one that the Judge himself had helped devise. They would sell the ships at greatly reduced rates then alter the bill of sales with over inflated prices and secure their government subsidies. After that, the corporation or holding company that'd bought them would transfer the ownership of their ship back to Siler Shipping, the bank would then be paid and the rest would go in to Fosters' pocket. It was a deal that would net him almost fifty thousand per ship, and now nothing stood in his way. But even so he thought of it constantly, replaying the events that would take place at the meeting and then afterwards. He could leave nothing to chance, and it consumed him even as he watched his brother-in-law do the honors and carve the Thanksgiving turkey.

Two weeks later, he left for New Orleans and the bloodletting began. It was just after lunch on a Thursday when Foster, accompanied by Ralston DuPree', Henry Fletcher, Jasper Cummings and Morgan Sinclair, strolled into the fourth floor meeting room of the Lucass Brothers' corporate head-quarters. They were the men who would sit on his new board, and since he'd expected trouble from the very start, right behind them was a police officer, a locksmith and a New Orleans district judge.

The meeting had just been called to order and Foster could tell in an instant that the men behind the table were surprised. It was the expression on Crandell's face when he looked up and saw Foster and his entourage enter. It was the first time that they'd seen each other since the debates, and even though it had been years, there was still an obvious disdain to his welcome.

"Well well well, if it isn't the man himself," Harlen declared as they took their seats. "Gentlemen," he went on after a quick glance to Lenoir and Lefont. "I'd like you to meet the one and only Senator Siler." Gaining an instant round of light but audible chuckles from the rest of the board, Harlen paused for a second then continue on. "And so what pray tell brings you all the way to New Orleans, Senator?"

"Well," Foster replied as he stood and looked around the room at the twenty or so people. "This is a shareholders meeting, isn't it?" he retorted as he settled with his eyes back on Crandel.

His answer was a simple one, but even so, it was how he'd said it that caused the board to instantly change their mood. "Yes it is," Harlen answered with a curious curtness. "But why would that concern you?"

"Well," Foster replied with an unflinching gaze. "I came here to vote."

"Vote?" Crandell scoffed.

"Yesss, you know, exercise my rights under the terms of your by-laws. You are getting ready to elect a new board, aren't you?"

"Yes, we are. But are you telling me that you're a shareholder?"

"Yes, as a matter of fact... I am." He grinned.

"Oh really," Harlen smirked and took a breath. "Now isn't that interesting?" he added as he studied the man before him. "Well, if you think that your vote here is actually going to count, I'm sorry to say but you've wasted your time. See, between Lenoir and Lefont and the rest of us here on the board, well, we pretty much hold all of the stock we need to do whatever it is we want. So your vote, or your voice, however important you thought it might be, means absolutely nothing."

"Well Harlen," Foster drawled in a calm and undeterred way. "That's what I thought you'd say, but I happen to disagree, so that's why I brought this along with me," he turned and grabbed the folder from Ralston.

"And what's that?" Harlen's interest suddenly peaked.

"Well," Foster began. "It's a list of all the companies that I own along with the number of shares that you've issued to each of them over the last ten months. Would you like to see it?" He held it up with another grin. "See, when you guys decided to come after me you'd just taken your company public and over the course of this year, through a number of various holding companies and corporations that I've created, I've been buying up your stock.

"In fact, as of last week, I believe that I own right at fifty-six percent of all your outstanding shares, which, if I'm not mistaken, gives me controlling interest of your company. It seems Harlen, that you and your bosses have been trying to destroy me with the very money that I just took over your company with. Now isn't that just about the most ironic thing you ever heard?" He smiled and then looked straight at the two brothers. "So now let me tell you as to why I'm really here. See Harlen, I came here to fire you. Actually, I came here to fire you all."

Lenoir Lucass was a large and simple man in his late sixties, a bully of sorts, who along with his brother had built their company from the ground up into what it was today. He was the older brother and chairman of the board, and just as soon as he realized what Crandell had done and what had happened to his company, a crimson wave of color swept across his face and he flew into a tirade.

"You son-of-a-bitch," he stood and roared at the man beside him. "You told us that this was the way to ruin him and run him out of business! Take it public, you said! And now look at what you've done!" His voice bellowed throughout the room as he berated the man with an ever-increasing rage. "Lefont an I spent thirty-five years building this company and you just destroyed it in one. You Goddamn idiot," he roared. "I ought-a kill you right where you sit!"

A second later, his rage boiling over, Lenoir slipped his hand inside of his suit coat, pulled out a nickel-plated derringer and without a moment's hesitation, shot Harlen dead in the chest. It was an ear-shattering crack that resonated throughout the room and for a few fleeting seconds everyone sat in disbelief. It was as if time had suddenly slowed and everything had turned surreal. The bang and the smoke from the gun, then Crandell clutching his chest as he slumped into his chair, and then Lenoir as he turned back toward Foster and raised his arm.

"Now nobody's takin over my company, you hear," he threatened as he cocked the hammer and then pointed his gun at Foster. "And I'll kill any son-of-a-bitch that tries... and that includes you."

He tried to move, but before he could, another shot rang. A deafening shot, that somehow seemed louder than the first. Staggering backwards, Foster instantly grabbed for his chest, he never had a chance. He was going to die and he knew it, but just as suddenly, he regained his footing. Lenoir Lacass had missed... or had he?

A man with a gun less than twenty feet away had just tried to kill
him. He'd heard the shot, yet there was no pain or blood. Was he
dead and didn't know it? He checked himself, patting and touching
his body just to be sure, then cast his eyes back to the man at the
table and stared in a state of confusion. Someone had shot someone,
and for a fleeting moment Foster looked on until he suddenly realized what'd happened. He could see it in the contorted expression
of pain and disbelief growing on the man's face as he looked down
at his chest.

He'd already shot one man, but before he could pull the trigger a second time, the police officer sitting in the back, had drawn
down on him and sent a 38-caliber slug straight into his heart. It was
a shot that caused him to instantly drop the gun and grab for his
chest. A second later he coughed and staggered then turned toward
his brother and calmly called his name. He was hurt and he knew it.
The pain was excruciating, and as he gasped for air and the blood
oozed from beneath his hand, he heard his brother frantically call
out for a doctor.

But it was to late, and all too quickly Lenoir Lucass's world began
to darken and fade. He tried to speak but his words were garbled
and incoherent. A moment later, he faltered and fell to the floor
then closed his eyes and exhaled for the very last time.

*"Damn Otis," Jim exclaimed. "That sounds like something straight out of an
old western. I mean, a real honest to God gunfight," he finished with a slug
from his beer.*

*"Yeah, I guess when you really think about it, it kind of does doesn't it,"
he chuckled. "An let me tell ya, from everything that I heard after they got
back, ol Foster was damn lucky to be alive. In fact, they said that if that ol
police officer hadn't of drawn down on that Lucass feller right when he did,
that he'd be dead too. Yes sir, he was one lucky son-of-a-bitch all right."*

*"No kiddin," Jim agreed. "But what happened to that Crandell guy who
got shot. Did he die too?"*

*"No, I don't believe that he did actually, they said he was too goddamn
mad at Foster to die," he laughed. "But from everything that I was told, I
don't think that he was in to good a shape. I mean face it, he jus got shot
in the center of his chest an even though the bullet had missed his heart,
it pretty much tore the hell out of em. Anyway, ol Foster had really gone an*

given himself one hell of a Christmas present this time, an jus as soon as him an Ralston had gotten back they went out on the town an proceeded to get drunk... an I mean real drunk."

"Really?"

"Ooh yeaaah. See, there was a whole lot-a people that'd heard about what'd happened an wanted to hear all about it, so they grabbed me to drive em around while they drank an told their story. It was actually a lot of fun, but after they'd seen jus about everybody that wanted to see em they were so drunk they couldn't tell their story no more," he laughed. "Yes sir, them two had a real run-away, but by then it was late an I was tired, so I took Ralston on back to the office where I think he spent the night an then I took Foster's drunk ass home.

"Anyway, the next day an needless to say, neither one of em was worth a shit. In fact, it took em both almost two whole days to recuperate to where they could function again, but boy when they finally did, did they ever go back to work."

"What-a-ya mean?"

"Well, you gotta remember, ol Foster had jus taken over a company that was damn near three times the size of what he already had an jus as soon as he had, he fired every single person there was except for the office manager an a secretary. Then, after they'd gone through the books an learned who, what, an where everything was, they drained all the bank accounts, packed up almost everything that they had an then moved their whole entire operation back to Mobile.

"I'll tell ya, he gutted that company like a fish an when he was finally done there wasn't nothin left except for two employees, all them ships an a whole lot of empty offices. Which, he also sold."

"Jesus," Jim shook his head as the true extent of what Foster had done sank in. "He really did destroy em, didn't he? I mean literally?"

"Ooh yeaah," Otis agreed as if it were an understatement. "He destroyed em all right... an he did it in a way that I never could of imagined. I mean, who would of ever thought that you could buy a company an take it over the way he did? It was unheard of."

"No shit," Jim agreed even as he continued to shake his head. "But what'd he end up do'n with all the ships? I mean... how many of em were there?"

"Twenty-eight."

"Yeah, what'd he do with all of them?"

"Well, before he came back home he left orders with that office manager that jus as soon as each one of em got back to New Orleans an had unloaded their cargo, they was to bring their ship over to Mobile an report in."

"All of em?"

"Yep all of em, ya see Ralston wanted to inspect each one of em personally before he sent em back out to sea again, an I don't mean jus the ships either, but the captain an the crews too. See, he was a real captain's captain, an he knew exactly what life was like out on the open ocean, an he knew what it meant to breakdown out in the middle of nowhere in forty foot seas too. Yes sir, I don't think that there wasn't nothin that he didn't know about them ships an he wanted to make damn sure that each an everyone of em an their crews, was ready to go back out to sea."

"Ya know, I never really thought of it, but that was actually a pretty smart thing to do, I mean, I sure as hell wouldn't wanna breakdown out in the middle of the ocean."

"Oh, hell nooo," Otis agreed. "Nobody would. An that's exactly why ol Ralston did it. Besides, they had their own damn shipyard to fix whatever needed fixin. I'll tell ya, he was real smart an it was real easy to see why Foster had picked him to help run the company. Anyway, shortly after they got back them ships started comin in jus like they'd been ordered an after about the fifth or sixth one, well, that's when they ran into a little bit of trouble one evenin."

"Trouble?" Jim rolled his eyes. "Now what?"

"Well, if I remember correctly, I think it was right about a week before Christmas. I'd jus picked up Foster an Melinda an her mother, an was taken them in to town to that Christmas Ball or whatever the hell it is you wanna call it."

"You mean that debutante thing that you told me about?" Jim queried.

"Yep, that was it," Otis nodded. "Anyway, Foster was real aggravated cause right before I'd picked him up he'd gotten a call from Ralston that he was havin trouble with one of the captains an crew that'd jus come in."

"On one of their new boats?"

"Yep, ya see there was some of them guys from that other company who really didn't like what'd happened in New Orleans, or the fact that they now worked for someone else. Specially after they found out that they had to report in to Ralston an that he was changin things all around."

"Changin things, what-a-ya mean?"

"Well, like I jus said, he was smart an he really knew that shippin stuff, an it didn't take him long before he started changin some of the routes an the way some of the things was done onboard the ships, an that's when all the trouble started.

"See, some of those captains had worked for the Lucass Brothers for a pretty long time an there was a few of em who'd become jus a little too comfortable an set in their ways. In fact, it was the captain of that ship who'd told him that he an his crew wasn't gonna sail back out until after the Christmas holidays was over that started it all. Ralston wanted to put it right back to work on a new route an this captain didn't wanna go."

"You gotta be kiddin?"

"Oh nooo."

"So what'd Foster do?"

"Well, we went an headed into town to that debutante Christmas thing an dropped Melinda an her mother off, an then jus as soon as we did me an him drove straight over to the pier. Now, if there was one thing that I knew about Foster, it was that he didn't like anyone tellin him what he could or couldn't do, an that was specially true when it came to his own company. It was his an he was gonna run it jus the way he wanted, an no son-of-a-bitch that worked for him was gonna tell him otherwise. I remember him tellin me that on the way over to meet Ralston. Anyway, this whole ordeal had jus about ruined his evening an by the time we pulled up to that ship out on the pier he was in a real, real bad mood."

"So what happen?"

"Well," Otis continued. *"I hadn't even gotten the car all the way stopped before he was out the door an standin next to Ralston. I couldn't hear what they were sayin, but they was both shakin their heads an lookin up towards the back of the ship. Now by then, ol Foster was jus about beside himself an that's when I heard him yell an point to a bunch of those great big burly dock workers that was out there, an then before I knew it, they was all stompin up the walkway to that ship.*

"Now I'm not exactly sure as to what all was said or how it actually happened cause I was standin by the car waitin. But I guess that jus as soon as Foster an all them fellers had gotten up to the back of that ship where everybody was, he gave the order for all them dock workers to grab a hold of that captain an throw his ass off the back of that boat."

"What!" Jim exclaimed. *"You gotta be kiddin? He threw the guy overboard?"*

"Yes sirr," Otis chuckled. *"Right off the back. I remember it real well too cause I was listenin to all the hollerin an yellin that was go'n on an was already lookin up, when all of a sudden I saw him fly right over the railin. An boy was he ever screamin. I tell ya, he sounded jus like a mashed cat, an he didn't stop until he hit the water."*

"Oh my God. So then what happened?"

"Well for me, nothin, other than the fact that I did step over real quick an look down to see if he was okay. I really don't know why cause I wasn't gonna do nothin. I mean, it was kind of cool out that night an the water was cold, so..." he grinned an shrugged his shoulders.

"So was he okay?" Jim asked with a genuine concern. "I mean, he didn't drown or nothin right?"

"Oh no, he was fine. Although at first I wasn't quite sure until he finally came back up to the surface a coughin an carryin on like you couldn't believe. I'll tell ya, was that man ever mad, an jus as as soon as he'd got himself a breath of air, he started yellin an callin Foster jus about every name in the book there was."

"Jesus Otis, do you know how crazy that is to actually throw someone off of the back of a ship. I mean, it's gotta be at least what, thirty forty feet to the water?"

"Oooh at least, an let me tell ya, he made one hell of a splash too."

"I'll bet, but didn't anyone try to help the poor guy?"

"Oh sure, Foster did."

"Foster?" Jim laughed. "Really? After he just threw him off?"

"Yep."

"How?"

"Well," Otis chuckled and shook his head. "He threw em one of those life savin rings an told him to catch it. An then, right after it had hit the water, I remember him tellin em real loud an clear that, oh an by the way... you're fired."

It was an amazing story and for a fleeting moment Jim just sat and shook his head. "So what'd he do with the crew? Did he fire all them too?"

"No, I don't believe he had to cause after they'd jus seen what he'd done to their captain, I think they all kind of decided that workin durin Christmas wasn't such a bad idea after all. I mean, I don't think any of em wanted ta go swimin," he laughed.

"Anyway, right after that Foster disappeared from the rail an for about the next five minutes or so I could here him talkin. An although I couldn't hear exactly what all he was sayin, I'm pretty sure that he was havin one of those real come to Jesus meetins with that crew if you know what I mean. Then, after he was all done, they came walkin back down. Him an Ralston went inside to talk an have a drink, all them dock workers went back to work, an the crew of that ship came down an fished their old captain back out of the bay."

"*An what'd you do?*"

"*Well, after I watched the men from that ship pull their captain back out of the water, who by the way was freezin cold an still madder than a hornet, I went back to the car an waited until Foster was done with Ralston an came back out. It wasn't but about fifteen minutes or so, but by then his evenin had pretty much been ruined an he was jus about as disgusted as I'd ever seen him. In fact, he couldn't of cared less if he went back to that Christmas party, but Melinda an his mother-in-law were already there, so we got in the car an drove on back. I remember when we pulled up an--.*"

"*Whoa whoa whoooa,*" Jim interrupted as if he'd just realized the obvious. "*Isn't that the one that Willie got invited to by Foster's mother-in-law?*"

"*Yep, that's the one.*"

"*An she was there?*"

"*Ooh yeah, she was there all right,*" Otis chuckled.

"*An so did they see each other?*" He raised his eyebrows and dipped his head.

"*Ooh yeaaah, they saw each other all right,*" Otis chuckled again. "*In fact, from what all Willie'd told me later on, it was Foster's wife Melinda who'd come an found her an then insisted that she come an say hello to her mother an meet her husband.*"

"*Ooh my God, you've got to be kiddin,*" Jim rolled his eyes. "*His wife introduced them?*"

"*Yes sir, an to be right truthful with ya, I don't think that it was to awfully long after I'd dropped him off an he'd walked inside.*"

"*Oh my God,*" Jim began to laugh. "*Can you just imagine?*"

"*Oh, I know,*" Otis joined in. "*I'll tell ya, what I wouldn't of given to have been there to see the look on ol Foster's face when Melinda walked up with Willie.*"

———————————◆———————————

CHAPTER 53

IT HAD BEEN WELL OVER an hour before Foster had returned and by the time he had, the girls had all been announced, the father-daughter waltz was over and the party had begun. He could've cared less about the first two events, in fact, he was actually glad that they were over for he'd always found them to be stuffy and boring. But now the party had started, and as he stepped through the doors into the lavishly decorated ballroom, he looked around for his wife and smiled.

It was the event of the year for all in Mobile society, and the room was festive and abuzz with activity. There was a band and people were dancing, some were talking and laughing, and some were sitting and eating. Surveying the room amidst an exchange of friendly greetings with people he knew, he finally spied his wife and mother-in-law sitting at one of the many large round tables scattered throughout the room. They were looking and pointing across the room as if they'd seen someone they knew. Curiously turning his head, he stared and scanned the crowd more out of curiosity then anything else. There were people he knew but no one of interest and after only a few moments, he turned to the bar.

"Oh Mother... look," Melinda said as she craned her neck to see across the room. "Isn't that Elizabeth Portman?"

"Wherrrre?"

"Over there, with Frank Posey's wife," she pointed. "See."

"Why yes, yes I do believe it is."

"And the girl that's with her," she went on. "Isn't she the one that you recommended?"

"Yes, remember I told you that when she was presented."

"Oh that's right, I guess I forgot. Oh my," she gushed as she continued to stare. "I still can't believe how pretty she is. Mother... she's beautiful."

"Yes she is, isn't she, and just as sweet and gracious as you could ever imagine, too. In fact, I don't believe that I have ever met a nicer young lady."

"Really?"

"Oh my yes, and to think that she turned out that way even after everything she's been through."

"After everything she's been through? What-a-you mean?"

"Oh Melinda honey, that poor little gal over there has had such a harsh and tragic life it just breaks my heart to even think about what all she's had to endure. See, she has come from a world and a way of life that neither you nor I could ever imagine... or for that matter understand. But she's a spirited one, and true to the promise that she'd made to her mother when she died, she picked herself up and left home and then came all the way here to Mobile, all by herself."

"But why here?"

"To get an education, in fact, I believe she's in her first year of college right now. She said that it was her mother's last wish just before she died. That she go to a big city and get an education so she could make a better life for herself. Anyway, that's how she ended up here."

"Ooh mother, that's so sad. So how did her mother die... did she tell you?"

"Yes, she did," Martha replied in a somber tone as she stared across the room. "She said it was the fields. That it was the fields that'd killed her."

"The what?" Melinda turned back as if she'd not heard correctly. "The fields?" She looked on with a confused expression. "I don't understand, what fields?"

"Why the cotton fields," her mother replied. "Didn't I tell you that her mother was a sharecropper."

"A what?" Melinda gasped. "A sharecropper?" she repeated, then stared as if her mother had just committed the gravest of sins in southern social etiquette. "Mother, are you serious!" her voice rose. "I mean, I know you mean well and all, but are you actually telling me that you recommended to the committee that the daughter of a sharecropper, whom you didn't even know, be invited to the Christmas Ball?"

"Well," she replied with a casual indifference. "Yes... actually I did."

"Mother, how could you? I mean, do you have any idea what people will say if they find out?"

"Oh hush, and stop your frettin," she waved her hand. "And the hell with what people say, cause if you really wanna know the truth, it was your daddy bless his heart, who told me to go ahead an do it. Now he was one of the most respected Judges around, and even though he isn't here your husband is, and he's already one of the most powerful Senators that we've ever had, so I doubt that anyone is going to say anything really. Oh, and let's not forget about Tom Portman, who the President has just appointed to take your daddy's place. Besides, look at her with all those other girls over there," she nodded toward the other side of the room. "Now I don't have my glasses on, but if I'm not mistaken I believe that that's Angela Posey and Daphney DeWeese isn't it... and they don't seem to mind."

"Okay, okay, but how did she come to be with the Portmans?"

"Well, I think it was about four or five years ago that Tom found her at an orphanage and took her home with him one day. I kind of like to think that maybe it was the good Lords way of helping them both. You know poor Elizabeth, she never was the same really after she lost her Becky, and this poor girl, well, after she lost her mother, she didn't have anybody. Anyway, whether it was the good Lords work or not, someone put those two together for a reason."

"Someone put who together for a reason," the familiar voice suddenly came from behind.

"Oh honey," Melinda turned. "There you are. Mother and I were just talking about the young girl she sponsored. You should see her, she is absolutely beautiful and she's right over there with all those other girls, see!" She turned back and pointed.

Staring, Melinda scanned the crowd but Willie was nowhere to be seen. A little perturbed that she'd vanished, she stared for a moment longer then finally gave up and turned back to her husband. "Well, she was right there just a second ago. Anyway, where have you been? You were suppose to be right back and now look, you've missed the entire presentation... and the father-daughter waltz."

"I know, I know, and I'm really sorry, but Ralston was having a lot more trouble than what I'd really expected."

"Well, just imagine that! I told you what I thought of all those silly ships when you started buyin em didn't I... and see!" she huffed then turned and looked back out into the crowd. "Now, if you'll excuse me," she smiled and rose from her chair. "I'm going to go find her and introduce myself."

As the months had passed, Melinda's mood swings had been increasing, and as she wandered away into the crowd, Foster could only sigh and shake his head.

"Oh, don't mind her," Martha waved her hand in an effort to dismiss her daughter's ridicule and console her son-in-law. "She's just crabby and tired of being pregnant. Besides, she doesn't have the slightest idea as to what it takes to run a business anyway. Heck, even her daddy said so," she sighed. "So don't you fret none about it ya hear, your shipping company is a good thing and everyone here in town knows it."

"Yes ma'am, and thank you. That means a lot, and I really appreciate it. I'll tell ya, she has been kind of hard to live with lately," he chuckled.

"Ooh really," Martha rolled her eyes. "Well if you think she's bad now, you should've been around for the first twenty-five years," she laughed.

"I can only imagine," he agreed as he joined in her laughter. A few seconds later, and after their amusement had subsided, he turned to her with a curious gaze. "So tell me," he probed. "Just who is this young lady anyway?"

"Oh, just a girl that I met earlier this spring really," she replied and waved her hand as if it were no big deal. "At first I wasn't going to get involved, but after I met her and then learned of what a harsh an tragic life she'd had, I changed my mind."

"Oh really, and why was that?" He leaned toward her.

"Well, I'll tell ya," she sighed and then slowly looked around the room. "She really touched my heart. I mean, when you look around here and you see all of these little princess's that've been born with silver spoons in their mouths... including Melinda I might add," she chuckled. "And then you take this young girl who came from absolutely nothing and has managed to overcome just about every single obstacle that life had placed in her way, well, I just had to do something."

"Wow, I'm impressed. So who is she, and how did you meet her?"

"Well, to tell you the truth, I'm a little surprised that you don't already know."

"Know, why should I know?" he asked and then took a sip from his drink.

"Well, I just figured that since you and Tom Portman were such good friends that you'd know."

The second he heard his friend's name, Foster choked and coughed his drink back into his glass.

"Oh dear," Martha leaned forward with a genuine concern. "Are you okay?"

Glancing back to his mother-in-law, Foster hit his chest and cleared his throat then tried his best to smile. "Yes ma'am," he replied in a raspy voice as he reached for a napkin. "I, I think," he coughed again. "That it just went down the wrong pipe, that's all."

Gazing at her son-in-law, Martha stared for a fleeting moment then continued on with her story. "Anyway, it was his wife Elizabeth. She came to me earlier this year... and that's how I met her."

"Elizabeth?" Foster repeated as the blood in his head began to drain.

"Yes, it was her and Tom who took this poor girl in about four or five years ago and then raised her just like their own bless their hearts." She continued on but then stopped and looked at him again in the most curious of ways. "But I just can't believe that you don't know about all of this already. It seems to me that as close as you and Tom are that--."

"Well," Foster interrupted in an attempt to defuse and contain her curiosity. "You have to understand, I have been kind of busy the last four years, and to tell you the truth, I really haven't seen that much of Tom or Liz," he chuckled as if it were no big deal. "But, if they have a foster child and she's the one you helped, well, I'd be delighted to meet her."

He'd said it with all of the conviction in the world, but in reality Foster was unraveling, for he knew that the girl she was talking of could only be Willie. It had to be, and of all the unbelievable things that could have happened, his wife had gone to get her. He felt a horrible feeling envelope him and for a few fleeting moments his entire world seemed to drop into slow motion and fall silent as he envisioned the scenario that was sure to unfold. The confrontation that was certain to come just as soon as she saw him, and then the embarrassing aftermath that would immediately follow as he tried in vain to explain and apologize.

He cringed at the very thought and wanted to leave before she got back, but for some reason he couldn't move. He'd been sucked into the vortex of a silent world where the only sounds that he could hear were those of his own voice. And although it was no more than a few fleeting seconds, he stayed where he was until the sound of Martha's voice brought him back into reality.

"Well good, I'm glad to hear that because I'd really like you to meet her. She is such a dear, and I just know that you're going to like her. In fact," she suddenly glanced up to the sound of her daughter's voice. "Speaking of our girl, there she is with Melinda right there."

"So you really weren't kiddin when you said Foster's wife actually went an found Willie an then took her back to the table?"

"Oh hell nooo," Otis grinned great big. "An what was so funny about the whole thing was, was that when she first introduced herself, she jus told Willie that she was Martha McAlister's daughter an didn't say a word about be'n Foster's wife. Willie said that they talked for a bit an then before she knew it, Melinda had hooked her arm in hers an had drug her all the way back across the room to their table."

"Oh my God, can you just imagine Foster when he looked up an saw his wife an Willie comin toward him?" He laughed. "I mean, your wife an your old girlfriend that you dumped, hooked arm in arm. Damn Otis, it just doesn't get any better'n that. I mean, you couldn't make that up if you tried." He laughed again. "So what happened? Did she make a scene an yell at him?"

"Well, to tell you the truth," Otis drawled. "No she didn't actually."

"Whaaat?" Jim raised his eyebrows. "You mean she didn't freak out or nothin?"

"Nope," Otis shook his head as he thought back. "I don't believe she did, but boy let me tell ya, was she ever surprised when she walked up to that table. An from everything she told me, I guess Foster was too. See, if I recall

correctly, I don't think neither one of em knew the other was there, an right after she heard ol Mrs. McAlister call out her name, well, I guess that's when she finally saw him."

"Willie," Martha called out as she rose from her chair. "How nice to see you again. And just look at you. Why, you're absolutely ravishing... and I just love your gown."

"Oooh Mrs. McAlister," Willie smiled and blushed as she took the woman into her arms. "You're way too kind, but thank you, and how nice to see you again too. I was just telling Miss Liz that I needed to find you and thank you again for everything you've done when all of a sudden your daughter here found me." She glanced to Melinda. "Anyway, I'd like you to know just how much I," she began but then suddenly stopped and froze at the sight of the man sitting in the chair behind her. A man who she instantly recognized and one who she'd vowed to hate for the rest of her life.

She'd never expected to see him again, but yet there he was, and in an instant a crimson wave of color swept across her face as her mind took off and ran wild. Was this a trick or some sort of joke, she thought as the memories of a love that once was came flooding back? She wanted to turn and run but her body wouldn't move. She wanted to spit in his face and scream, but she didn't, she just stared in a daze until the sound of Melinda's voice suddenly snapped her back into reality.

"Oh Willie," she said as Foster rose from his chair. "I'd like for you to meet my husband Foster. Or," she rolled her eyes. "As we like to call him around the house, just Senator. And honey," she turned back to her husband. "This here is Miss Willie Mae Dawson. She's the young girl that we were just talking about. The one that mother helped, and in my opinion, the prettiest young lady here at the ball."

He'd dumped her without even a goodbye and hadn't seen her in four years, yet slowly and somewhat sheepishly Foster stepped toward her. Gazing upon her as he did, he could see that she'd changed and that she was no longer a little girl in boots and overalls, but a mature and vibrant young woman of unbelievable beauty. A woman who was gracious and elegant with her hair and makeup perfectly done, and who now stood before him dressed in a beautiful white gown with elbow length gloves and a single strand of pearls draped around her neck. She'd blossomed far beyond that of anything he ever could've imagined, and was without question, a stunning depiction of everything a debutante was to be. But even so, Willie had always been spirited and strong willed, and he could clearly see by the expression on her face and the glare in her eyes that it was a trait she still possessed. He was in serious trouble and he knew it. And he could only hope and pray that when he took her hand, that she could see and read the hidden message in his and wouldn't make a scene.

"Well Miss Dawson," Foster greeted and extended his hand as if they'd never met. "I must say, it is truly is a pleasure. Martha here was just telling me all about you, but I must say I didn't expect to meet someone quite so lovely. In fact, I do believe that this is one instance in which I may have to agree with my wife."

Taking a breath, Willie hesitated for just a moment as her mind whirled and she quickly assessed the situation. It was clear what he was doing and why he was doing it, but even so, she was boiling with contempt and wanted nothing more than to slap him in the face and then leave. It was a scenario that she'd played out over and over in her mind, and even though it would've brought her great joy and satisfaction, she knew that this was neither the time nor the place. It was a debutante ball, with dozens of influential people, and she would never disrespect or embarrass Mrs. McAlister or the Portmans by doing so. They'd both been far to kind to her, and so without another thought, she cleared her throat, then smiled ever so graciously and took his hand.

"Well Senator," she replied as she joined in his game of charades. "Thank you so much, you are way too kind. But if I could be so bold as to correct you, I do believe that the pleasure is all mine. I mean... I have never actually met a Senator before." She smiled demurely then continued on. "This is truly an honor, but for some strange reason," she paused as if she were deep in thought then quickly went on as if what she was about to say was silly. "And I really don't know how or why I feel this way... but for the life of me, it seems as if we have already met before." She finished with the flash of an angry smile as she released his hand.

Willie had always been incredibly gifted and quick and it was clear that under Elizabeth's watchful eye and vigilant tutelage, the uneducated sharecropper in her was completely gone. She was refined and articulate, and had caught him completely off guard by the hidden innuendo she'd so eloquently slipped into her greeting.

"Yes, well I'm sure that it's just the newspapers and all," Foster chuckled and stammered as he tried to divert the subject. "I get that quite often. You know... with me being in them all of the time."

"Yes, I'm sure you're right now that you mention it," Willie retorted with yet another wry smile. "In fact, now that I think about it, I do see your picture in there quite often."

"Oh, I'm sure that's it," Melinda laughed. "Heck, he's always in one of them for some reason or another," she added as the band picked up and began to play. "Oh honey," she turned. "Listen, isn't that that song you like?"

"Yes, I believe it is," he replied and turned his head, elated that she had changed the subject. "And if I'm not mistaken, I think they played that at our wedding too, didn't they?"

"Yes they did, and if I wasn't so darn big and clumsy I'd drag you out there so you could twirl me around again, but I'm afraid my dancing days are over for the next few months. But," she widened her eyes and turned to Willie.

Melinda never said a word, but Willie could clearly see just by the expression on her face as to what she was thinking. "Oh noo Mrs. Siler, I, I just couldn't," she stammered and protested. "I mean, it really wouldn't be proper. You're married and--."

"And pregnant," Melinda interrupted as she rubbed her belly.

"Yes."

"Well, don't let that worry you none," she waved her hand. "It's fine really, besides you'd be doing me a favor. Foster just loves to dance and right now I really don't believe that I'd make a very good partner. I mean look at me, I'm fat and my feet hurt, so please, I insist... really, it's okay."

"Oh honey, don't be so bossy," Foster quickly interceded in an effort to sidetrack his wife. "Maybe Miss Dawson doesn't want to dance, or, would rather dance with one of those handsome young men over there." He nodded to the other side of the room in hopes that it would appease and change her mind.

"Oh Foster, don't be ridiculous," Melinda pressed. "Besides how many girls ever get the chance to dance with a real life Senator? Now go on before the song is over."

To have argued any further would've been pointless and Foster knew it, and so with a fabricated smile in hopes of hiding his fears, he anxiously took Willie's hand and led her out onto the dance floor. She was the most unlikely of girls to be there, yet even so here she was walking out into the midst of swirling bodies with one of the most handsome and important men there.

In many ways, she felt as if she were a beautiful princess in a fairytale, smiling at the many people who were now staring and whispering, and then before she knew it, Foster had taken her into his arms. But Willie had four years of pent up anger to let off, and as soon as they'd spun into the crowd and out of view, her radiant smile and sparkling eyes changed into a scathing glare. She'd waited a long long time for this moment, and now that it was here, she was determined to have her say.

"Sooo, it's Senator Siler now, is it?" she seethed beneath her breath as they swirled amongst the other dancers. "Oooh, or should I say Senator Liar."

"Liar?" he repeated as if he'd just been offended.

"Yes liar, you know, someone who doesn't, or shall I say, can't tell the truth," she continued with a hushed but growing disdain. "See, I've learned a great many things over the last four years and one of them is, is that that is exactly what you are. A liar! But I guess it should really come as no surprise, after all, you are a politician, aren't you?"

"Willie please, at least let me explain," he pleaded.

"Explain, explain what?" Her nostrils flared as she dropped into her diatribe. "That you told me that you loved me and I believed you. Or, that you took my virtue from me when I was just fifteen then lied and tricked me into thinking that I was married. For over a year!" Her hushed voice jumped an octave higher. "By adopting me! With some, some little piece of paper that you typed up to make me believe that it was official!" She rolled her eyes and then changed her tone into one that mocked him. "It's just like being married Willie, except that you can't ever tell anyone. God, I can't believe I was such a fool."

"But you don't understand, I was--."

"What," she scoffed and cut him short. "I don't understand! Are you serious?" She narrowed her eyes and glared. "Just tell me what part I don't understand. The part where you lied to me and used me, or was it the part where when you were done with me and wanted to become a Senator you dumped me and gave me to the Portmans. You discarded me as if I were nothing more than a dog that you'd found on the streets, and of all things, you didn't even have the decency to do that... you had Otis do it. How could you? What was it that I did that was so bad?" She finished and then stared with a lingering gaze.

She was right in everything she'd said, and she had every reason in the world to say it. He had betrayed both her trust and her love, and he felt terrible for what he'd done and for the pain he'd caused, but even so he hadn't expected the truth to hurt so much. He could see the look of hurt in her eyes even after four long years, and in the most heartfelt and apologetic of ways he tried to explain.

"You didn't do anything bad, it's just that I... well, I really didn't mean for it to happen quite that way and I'm sorry. See, I was--."

"Sorry," she cut him off again and rolled her eyes. "Is that all you have to say to me after four years? Is, is that you're sorry! God Foster, do you have any idea as to how I felt or how much it hurt when I finally realized what you'd done and that you were never coming back for me?" She paused and stared then continued on a second later in a much softer voice. "To know that the person who you loved more than anything else in the world had abandoned and left you without even so much as a goodbye." She paused again and waited. "Well do you?" She demanded.

It was a question that Foster couldn't answer, and without a moment's hesitation Willie proceeded on. "I ask you again, what was it that I did that was so terrible to make you want to do that to me? I loved you with all my heart and you broke it, but did you ever even give a damn about me? Or care for me at all?" She took a breath to settle her emotions then went on in a heartfelt voice. "Or ever think or worry about me? Or wonder how many nights I'd cried myself to sleep, waiting and wondering why it was you never came back for me?"

But Foster still couldn't answer and Willie knew it, he could only swallow his pride and look away in a moment of shame. A guilt-ridden moment of silence that seemed to grow with each passing second until Willie finally spoke as if somehow and in someway she were now satisfied.

"Yes, I thought sooo," she surmised with a smirk as she stared into his eyes. "Well, I want you to know that I am over you and have been for quite some time, and now that I know who and what you are, I guess I should really be grateful that you did. You see, the Portmans are truly wonderful people, and Miss Liz has opened my eyes in ways that I never could've imagined, so I guess in a way, I really do need to thank you. But still I do wonder," she lightened her tone and then glanced toward their table. "Does your lovely wife and mother-in-law know of your philandering ways? Or about us?" She raised her eyebrows, then laughed and pressed her point. "My guess is that they don't, but maybe we should tell them, huh? What-a-you think? Or hey, I know, I have an even better idea," she continued on with a mischievous smile. "How about if I just tell your wife how lucky she is to have such a wonderful lover as a husband, you know, kind of girl to girl so to speak now that we know each other. Yes, that's it," her eyes lit up. "Oooh my... what a delightful little Christmas present that would make, don't you think?"

"Willie," Foster glared. "That isn't funny and you know it, now stop! That's enough."

"Yes, just as I thought," she added with yet another glance to the table. "She doesn't... does she? Well, just imagine that," she giggled. "But I can't say as if I am really that surprised," she looked back and regained his eyes. "I mean, after all, you lied to me, didn't you?"

"Willie please," he pleaded. "Come on... I said I was sorry. What more do you want?"

"Nothing!" she snapped and scowled then slowed her moving as the song came to an end. "You've said quite enough and I don't want anything from you, ever again. And now that your song is over," she finally stopped and looked around as the final notes were played. "Well, so is our dance. Now, if you could be so kind as to applaud and then smile as if you've just enjoyed yourself," she released her hold and began clapping. "There are people who are looking at us."

Applauding just as he'd been instructed, Foster stared at Willie for just a moment, then turned with a painted on smile and nodded to some of the people he knew. He'd just received one of the worst tongue-lashings of his life, yet somehow he'd managed to endure her wrath. She was a viper and had sunk her fangs deep, injecting some of the most potent venom he'd ever seen, yet even so he couldn't help but admire the alluring young beauty before him. Elizabeth had done an amazing job, and for one of the first times in his life, he felt the pains of regret fill his emotions. It was a feeling he hadn't expected, and as the band struck up another song, he took her arm in his and returned to their table.

"Oooh you two," Melinda gushed as they approached. "You should've seen yourselves, you were just wonderful."

"Yes I agree," Martha quickly added. "The loveliest couple out there, and I might add, the best dancers too."

"Ooh Mrs. Siler... Mrs. McAlister," Willie blushed as she presented Foster back to his wife. "You both are way too kind, but if we were, it was all because of your husband here. I must say he is truly a wonderful dancer."

"See, I told you," Melinda beamed.

"Yes you did, and now all of my girlfriend's are going to be so jealous. They were watching you know," she said with a quick glance to her friends across the room.

"Yes, there were a lot of people watching," Martha interjected.

"Well, I am sure that if they were it was because of the Senator here and not me," she took a breath. "But if you would be so kind as to excuse me, I really do need to be going now. And Senator," she turned and then extended her hand in the most formal of ways. "I can't tell you what a pleasure it was to finally meet and talk with you. It was truly a dream come true." She stared and then smiled wryly.

"Yes, well, I couldn't agree more," he stammered as she dropped his hand and turned.

"Oh, and Mrs. McAlister, I want to thank you again... for helping me."

"Well, you're quite welcome young lady," Martha replied. "It was nothing really, and if I might add, it was my pleasure, because if there's anyone that deserves to be here tonight, it's you. But I want you to know that after tonight and after the holidays are over, I do expect for you to stop by and visit from time to time, hear?"

"Yes ma'am," Willie replied. "Thank you, I would like that very much." Then with a final glance to each of them, she turned and left.

It was the moment he'd been waiting for and with each and every step she took, he felt as if the weight of the world was being lifted from his shoulders. It was relief to a degree in which he'd never imagined. It was finally over, and although he was bruised and battered, he was still alive. She could have killed him, but she didn't. She had allowed him to live, and as he watched her fade into the crowd, he could only wonder why. A moment later, she disappeared completely and with that he turned back to Melinda and his mother-in-law. He needed a drink in the worst of ways and after he'd excused himself, he hastily made his way to the bar.

It took the bartender less than a minute to serve him, but before he could even pick up his glass to take a sip, someone from behind reached up and tugged on his arm.

"Foster," the man hissed into his ear as he tightened his grip and pulled. "What in the hell are you doing? Are you out of your goddamn mind?"

Turning to the all too familiar voice, Foster smiled and started to speak but was instantly silenced by the onslaught of Tom's whispered rant. "Dancing with Willie? Are you serious? I thought we talked about this? Jesus," he shook his head. "Liz is over on the other side of the room going nuts. Goddamn, what in the sam hell is wrong with you?"

"Oh God Tom," Foster gushed. "I'm really sorry, I really am. But you gotta believe me, I didn't have a choice," he declared in defense of his innocence. "Melinda made me!"

"Melinda?" Tom repeated as he drew his eyes into a skeptical frown. "Your wife?"

"Yes my wife," Foster emphasized as quietly as he could. "You know, the woman I'm married to. She insisted when the damn band started playing."

"You're kidding?"

"Noo!" he cringed as if he still couldn't believe what he'd been through. "Shit, I didn't even know you guys were here until she went and found Willie and then brought her back to our table. It's the truth, so please tell Liz. I know she probably hates me, but this time I'm really innocent, I swear."

"So you're not...?" Tom looked on with an insinuating stare.

"Oh God, no," Foster shuddered and shook his head. "Not a chance. Not after the damn ass eatin that I just took. Christ, I'm just glad she didn't have a knife," he laughed.

It was the last few words he had said that seemed to relax his friend and put him at ease; in fact, they'd even made him smile. "Yeah, I know what you mean... she is a little head strong isn't she?"

"A little?" Foster cringed as if it were an understatement. "Shiiit, she's more than just a little I can tell ya that," he laughed and then took a sip.

"But wait a minute," Tom suddenly asked. "There's something here that I don't quite understand. Why did Melinda go and find Willie, and then of all things take her back to your table? I mean, they don't know each other do they?" he pried as his curiosity deepened.

"Nope," Foster grinned with another sip. "But they sure do now."

"So are you telling me that she just got up and went and introduced herself?"

"Yes sir," he replied as he rolled his wrist and glanced at his watch. "Right about ten minutes ago."

"Well what in the world possessed her to go and do something like that?" Tom persisted as if he were trying to solve some great riddle.

"You mean, you really don't know?"

"Know... know what?"

"How Willie got her invitation to come here. I mean, come on, you know how all of this debutante stuff works, don't you?"

"Well sure I do," he scoffed as if it were a silly question. "You send them to one of those finishing schools like Miss Winfield's, and after a few summer sessions and after they've graduated, you get an invitation? But still, what in the hell does all that have to do with your wife and Willie?"

"Oh come on Tom," Foster replied as if he really couldn't believe his friend. "You absolutely amaze me sometimes, as smart as you are and you don't even know how this debutante stuff works. Shit, even I know that those finishing schools don't send out the invitations." He laughed.

"Oooh, and just who does... your wife? Is that why she went and got Willie?"

"No, but you're pretty close. It's some sort of committee that does it."

"A committee?"

"Yeah, a bunch of women from here in town actually, you know, mostly old money and blue blood types. Anyway, I guess they have these meetings or something where they all get together in the spring and then start picking and choosing from all of the girls that are coming of age to see who's going to get an invitation and who's not. It's all suppose to be kind of real hush hush and secret like but I'm pretty sure that that's how it's done."

"Really," Tom looked upon his friend with a genuine surprise. "And who all sits on that?"

Lifting his arm ever so casually, Foster just rolled his eyes and then pointed toward his table. "Well, one of them ladies would be that woman sitting right over there."

"Who, your mother-in-law?" Tom asked as he stared across the room.

"Yes sir, and if I'm not mistaken, I believe she chairs that committee. And, I'd be willing to bet that she was the one who got Willie her invitation. Well, her and the Judge that is," he added. "In fact, I think that he's probably the one who gave the final nod if you want my opinion."

"Wait a minute, what-a-you mean gave the final nod?" Tom quickly questioned as if he were offended. "Why would he have to do that? Wasn't Willie good enough?"

"Well," Foster drawled with a bit of reluctance. "Actually, no she wasn't."

"What? What-a-you mean, she's the prettiest girl here tonight. Hell, anyone can see that."

"Oh I know, I really do," Foster quickly agreed in an attempt to quell Tom's growing resentment. "In fact, I couldn't agree with you more, but just think about it for a second and look around will you," he lowered his voice as he began to scan the room. "You see all of these young ladies?"

"Yeah... sooo," Tom replied as he too looked around.

"Well, even though Willie is probably the smartest and is by far prettiest girl out there, we both know that she is still a sharecropper. And Tom my friend," he paused and gained his friends eyes. "Sharecroppers don't get invited to debutante balls. It doesn't happen, or that is, it doesn't unless someone steps in and makes it happen," he rolled his eyes toward his table. "Someone who's powerful enough to tell the committee that they want this girl to receive an invitation."

"Wait a minute, are you telling me that Martha and the Judge made that happen?"

"Yes sir, that's exactly what I'm telling you."

"But why would they do that?" he asked as he turned and looked back across the room. "And just how and when in the hell did they meet Willie?"

"Well," Foster drawled with a chuckle and a pat to his friend's shoulder. "Since you obviously don't know, I think that that would be something you'd want to ask your wife."

"Elizabeth?" Tom turned back with a blank expression.

"Yes sir," Foster assured with another pat. "That'd be the one all right."

"Damn Foster," Tom sighed and shook his head. "I really don't know what to say. I mean, I truly had no idea. She never said a word about any of this."

"Well," Foster grinned as he took another sip from his drink. "You sure know now don't you. And we're all here now, too."

"So what-a we do now?" Tom asked as he looked out and searched for Willie amongst the sea of swirling dancers.

"Well," Foster finally replied after a moment of thought. "Why don't you try and keep Willie on that side of the room and I'll see if I can keep Melinda on this side. And since she's pregnant and Martha is already tired, and since I really couldn't give a damn as to whether I was here or not, I'd say that in about an hour or so we're going to be leaving. Then, you and Liz, and Willie," he emphasized. "Can enjoy the rest of the evening like you should. This is her night and Martha was right, if anyone deserves to be here... it's her."

Somewhat surprised by his comment, Tom turned to his friend and smiled. "Well damn Foster, thanks, I really appreciate that, that sounds great, and I'm sure that it'll put Liz at ease too."

"Well good, because I sure as hell don't need her chewin on my ass too," he laughed.

"Yeah, I know what you mean," Tom chuckled. "I'll tell ya, she really wasn't too happy when she looked up and saw you and Willie out on the dance floor."

"Oooh I can just imagine," Foster grinned. "And with that being said, I think that maybe it's time I slipped back to my table before she comes over here. She's been watching us you know, but hey, how about after Christmas we have lunch," he added as he stepped away.

"Sounds great," Tom replied. "I'll give you a call next week."

"Good, oh and by the way," he stopped and turned back. "I almost forgot; congratulations. I know that it's probably a little early, but the word on the hill is, is that just as soon as the holidays are over and we're back in session, the judiciary committee is going to hold your confirmation hearings. I've been invited to sit in and help move them along, so get ready my friend cause before you know it, you're going to be hearing your cases on a Federal level. You did me one hell of a favor four years ago and I told you I'd never forget it."

"Yes you did," Tom drawled as he stuffed his hands into his pockets. "But you know Foster," he sighed and stared with a thought filled gaze. "When I look back on that day in the diner and I think about it. And then I look at my wife and Willie, and I see how happy they truly are, I wonder sometimes as to who really did who the favor."

It was something he hadn't expected to hear and for a moment Foster just stared at his friend. He was at a loss for words, and after a moment he just nodded and turned back to his table. But what Tom had said seemed to haunt him, even after he'd taken his seat, and for the next half hour as the music and the dancing continued, Foster for the first time in his life began to experience the feelings of rejection and jealousy. Feelings that seemed to have come from nowhere, and that had a life of their own. Feelings that he'd never had before with any other woman, not even his own wife. That tore at his insides as he watched the endless parade of young men vie for a dance with Willie.

He'd really thought that he was over her, and that the four years that they'd spent apart had been his cure. That he could see her and be fine, and that he could let it be, but as he watched her dance it soon became clear that he couldn't. The four years had only served to enhance her in ways that he never could've dreamed, and to compel him to think of the unthinkable. She was a woman now, and she was hauntingly beautiful, and even though he had made a promise to stay away, he desired her now and in a way in which he never had before.

The band continued to play, but after another couple of songs, and even though the gala was in full swing, they took a much-needed break. It was the moment that he'd been waiting for, the perfect opportunity to make his exit. He'd seen and talked to just about everyone that he needed to, and now true to his word, he gathered Melinda and her mother, said their holiday well wishes and good-byes, and then quietly left the ball.

Later that evening, unable to rid his mind of Willie or the dance that they'd shared, Foster lay in bed unable to sleep. She was haunting him like a ghost from the past, and as the minutes slowly turned into hours, he tossed and turned in an effort to rid his mind of his thoughts. He could see her smile and hear her voice; he could even feel the tender touch of her hand and smell her perfume.

She had always been amazingly beautiful, but now she was so much more. She was mature and smart and witty, and now... he wanted her back. He wanted to hold her and to taste the sweetness of her mouth once again. She'd been his once, completely and without question, and now he wondered if he could win her back. He punched his pillow and rolled to his side, then stared out through the window at the twinkling stars. There had to be a way, but how? She hated him. He thought of it for a few minutes more then closed his eyes with a long heavy sigh and smiled.

⚊▪⚊

IT WAS WELL AFTER MIDNIGHT before Willie and the Portmans had returned home, and even though Elizabeth was tired, after she had readied for bed, she headed straight to Willie's room. She'd waited almost all year for this event and now that it was over, she was dying with curiosity and wanted to talk, girl talk, like one could only have between a mother and daughter without the presence of a nosey husband.

Scurrying down the hall, she turned the corner and with a gentle knock to Willie's door, quietly slipped inside. She was sitting at her dresser and had just pulled the pins from her hair when she looked up into the mirror.

"Well young lady," Elizabeth whispered as she stepped up behind her and placed her hands on her shoulders. "Did you have fun tonight?"

Gazing back at their reflections, Willie smiled and nodded then turned her head and cast her eyes upwards. "Yes I did," she sighed with a dreamy drawl. "It was just wonderful and so much more than I expected, but my feet..." she made a face and began to laugh. "They hurt something awful."

"Your feet hurt?" Elizabeth mocked as she reached for the brush on the dresser and then sat behind her. "Well it's no wonder. Heck, every time I saw you, you were out on that dance floor twirlin and swirlin, I swear you must have danced just about every dance there was," she said as she tenderly pulled the brush through her hair. "I mean, it seemed as if those boys just wouldn't leave you alone would they? Especially that Danny Mitchell."

"No they wouldn't," Willie smiled again. "But I didn't mind really, they were all real nice and polite, even Danny, but still they all only want one thing."

"Ooh, and just what would that be?" Elizabeth teased.

"Miss Liz," Willie blushed. "You know!"

"Yes, I dooo," she laughed. "Well, that's just how young boys are... and men too if you really wanna know the truth," she laughed again. "But still you never refused any of them and that was very gracious of you. In fact," she added as she stopped her brushing and then stared into the mirror. "I saw that you even danced with Foster Siler. Is there anything that you wanna tell me?"

Gazing back at Elizabeth's reflection, Willie took a heavy breath and then stared in a moment of silence. She knew that Liz still resented Foster for what he'd done and was only asking out of concern. A concern that had been forged by her love, and one that now deserved an answer.

"Yes ma'am," she answered along with a nod. "But he didn't ask me, his wife did."

"His wife?" Elizabeth repeated. "Melinda?"

"Yes ma'am," Willie nodded again. "In fact, she insisted."

"She insisted?" Elizabeth raised her eyebrows. "That you dance with him?"

"Ah huh," Willie answered with yet another nod. "I really didn't want to but as soon as the music had started, she wouldn't take no for an answer. She said that Foster loved to dance and that I'd be doing her a favor cause she was fat and pregnant and her feet hurt. He even argued with her but it didn't do any good."

"I seeee," Elizabeth replied as she envisioned the scene. "So he really didn't ask you?"

"Ooh, no ma'am," Willie shook her head. "And I'm sorry if I upset you, but I didn't know what to do. So instead of making a scene an embarrassing Mrs. McAlister, I just pretended like I didn't know him and then went ahead and danced with him."

"Well," Elizabeth sighed and resumed her brushing. "I guess there really wasn't any harm done was there?"

In many ways what Willie had said seemed to ease Elizabeth's concerns, and for the next couple of minutes as she brushed her hair, they talked and laughed. But the early morning hours were upon them, and after several uncontrolled yawns from both of them, Liz finally laid the brush back on the table.

"Well young lady," she said as she stood and looked into the mirror. "I think it's time that we went to bed. It's late and we still have chores to do in the morning, remember."

"Yes ma'am," Willie replied with yet another yawn. Then with a tender kiss to the top of Willie's forehead, Elizabeth turned and left. A few minutes later the tired young debutante crawled into bed and laid her head on her pillow. Her night had been like that of a fairy tale come true, and for the longest time as she laid and quietly gazed out through her window, she couldn't help but smile and think of everything she'd done.

She'd had more fun than she had ever dreamed possible, but the one thing that kept repeating itself was her unexpected dance with Foster and the feelings that had risen the moment he'd taken her into his arms. Feelings that until tonight she never realized she still held. Feelings that had lain deep and dormant inside of her, that now and no matter how hard she tried, she could not dispel. Why, she really wasn't sure and before she realized what she was doing, she'd reached to her neck and had taken her locket between her thumb and forefinger. It was an old habit she had developed right after he'd given it to her. A subconscious eccentricity, that seemed if only in mind and spirit, as if it brought them together when they were apart.

It was the only thing that Foster had given her that she still had, and even though she hadn't thought of him in years, it seemed as if now he was all she could think of. She hated him for what he'd done yet deep in her heart where she'd buried her feelings, she found that in a way she still cared for him. She was confused and torn, and could not understand how or why she could feel this way, yet as she searched her heart and stared out through the window, she found herself wondering. Wondering, as the minutes slowly passed, if he'd missed her too?

"So after that... after that debutante ball I mean, is that when they finally got back together?"

"Well, not exactly," Otis chuckled. "But that's pretty much when it all started. See, at first Willie didn't wanna have nothin to do with him."

"She didn't?" Jim seemed surprised.

"Nope, an let me tell ya, it drove ol Foster jus absolutely crazy."

"Really?" Jim chuckled.

"Oh hell yes, see there wasn't nobody that told Foster Siler no, an if ya wanna know the truth, I think that that jus made him want her even more. He'd always been pretty crazy over her an I guess the four years that they'd been apart hadn't changed a damn thing. In fact, after that Christmas ball I think he was even worse than before cause ol Willie, well, she'd gone an grown up an had become a young woman. An let me tell ya, she was jus as beautiful as you could of ever imagined. Anyway, that's right about the time I ended up gettin involved in the whole thing."

"Whoa whoa whoooa," Jim waved his hand as if to stop. "What-a-you mean, you got involved? Why'd you get involved?"

"Well, I was their go-between," he replied. "You know, how they first started talkin back an forth to each other. Ya see, ol Foster knew that she still came an seen me every once an a while, an he knew that he jus couldn't pick up the phone an call her. So he came up with this plan to try an see her again. You know, to try an get her back."

"But wait a minute, wasn't he still married an about to have another kid?"

"Well sure he was, but shit, that didn't matter none to a dog like Foster. Besides, I really don't think that him an Melinda was gettin along to well if you really wanna know the truth. I mean, face it, he was never really home, an whenever he was he was always workin.

"Anyway, if I recall correctly, I think it was jus a week or two after the first of the year an right before he went back to Washinton that him an I had gone out to check on a couple of boats that'd jus come in from New Orleans. I remember we'd jus pulled up an were watchin while the tugs pushed the last ship into its slip when he came up beside me an started askin me all about Willie."

"Otis," Foster said as he placed his hand on Otis's shoulder. "I wanna ask you something."

"Yes sur boss," Otis replied. "You jus name it."

"Well, I was just wondering if you still saw Willie? You know, if she still comes by the boat?"

"Oh yes sur, in fact, I jus saw her right before Christmas. She brought me a present, another book. It's called, *The Call of the Wild*; it's about a dog up in Alaska. She's still helpin me with my readin an writin. In fact, I can read an write pretty good now."

"Yes I know, and that's good, I'm glad. But tell me, how often do you see her?"

"Well, pretty regular now, mostly on Saturday mornins when she gives me my lessons. In fact, after the first of the year she's gonna start teachin me how to add an subtract," he beamed.

"Well good Otis, that's good. In fact, that's perfect because I have something I want you to do for me. Something very, very important but that you have to keep secret. You can't tell anyone, hear. Now, I can trust you to do that, can't I?"

"Oh, yes sur," Otis assured. "You can always count on me boss, I won't never lets you down."

"Good, now listen closely because here's what I want you to do."

"So wait a minute, are you tellin me that he used you to help get her back?"

"Well, I never really thought of it that way, but yeah, I guess in a way he did actually."

"God Otis, how could you? I mean, first he used you to dump her an then he used you to help get her back. Jesus, didn't you have any kind of conscience?" he scolded and then took a gulp from his beer. "I mean...?"

"Well sure I did," Otis defended. "But you gotta remember, I really didn't have much of a choice. It was 1936, an even though I had a great job workin for one of the wealthiest an most powerful men in Mobile, it was still the depression an I needed it. So let me tell ya, whatever Foster Siler told me or asked me to do, well, that's exactly what I did."

"Yeah, I guess you're right," Jim's demeanor seemed to ease. "I guess I just didn't think about it that way. So tell me, what was the big plan?"

"Well," Otis chuckled. "As Foster had put it, he wanted to try an mend things with Willie."

"An just how in the hell did he propose to do that?"

"Well, Willie always did like openin them gifts he used to get her an he remembered that. So, an as corny as it may of sounded, he decided to try that first. An so while we was out that day, we went over his plan again an again until he was absolutely certain that I understood jus how he wanted everything done. In fact, we even had our own secret way of talkin to each other."

"No way."

"Oh yeaaah."

"Okay Otis," Foster looked on. "Now you understand everything I just told you, don't you?"

"Oh yes sur," Otis assured and then repeated his instructions. "You want me to go by the office every Friday while you're gone an check to see if Miss Vicki has a package for me."

"A package for the boat," he corrected.

"Right, parts for the boat."

"Yes."

"An then you want me to give it to Miss Willie when she comes by an sees me right?"

"Right. And?" he insinuated with the pull of his thumb and forefinger across his lips.

"Ooh, yes sur," Otis added. "An I ain'ts sapposed to say nothin to nobody cept Miss Willie."

"Riiiight. Annnd?" he dipped his head as if to lead him on.

"Oh yeah, an I'm sapposed to let Miss Vicki know how the new parts fit an if they worked okay, or if we need to change em an get different ones right?" He finished then looked on with a grin.

"So that's how he started workin on her, huh?"

"Yep, pretty much. He thought that that was a good way to kind of break the ice an smooth things up a little, an let me tell ya, he didn't waste no time either cause it wasn't but about a week or so after he'd been gone that I got the first little box at the office. I remember when I first gave it to Willie an how surprised she was, an then of how she jus kind of sat there an stared at it real quiet like for the longest time."

"Well, didn't she open it?"

"Oh yeah, she opened it, but boy it sure took her long enough," he chuckled and shook his head.

"An so what was in it?"

"Well, if I recall correctly, I think it was a box of chocolates. You know, those real fancy kind that are all decorated with the nuts an the fillins in em. Oh, an it had a card in it too. Now, I don't know what all it said or nothin like that, but I do remember the look on her face after she read it."

"So she liked it?"

"Oh yeah, she liked it all right," Otis grinned as he thought back. "You could tell jus by the way she started smilin."

"Anyway, after that, he started sendin a box about every week or so. Usually chocolates or perfume or somethin like that. I'd pick it up durin the week, an then give it to Willie that Saturday when she came an gave me my math lesson on the boat. Then, that next Monday or Tuesday, I'd stop back by the office an let Miss Vicki know how the new parts fit an if they worked okay. See, that was our secret way of talkin to each other so he'd know if she liked what he'd sent or not."

"You're kiddin," Jim scoffed. "That was your secret way?"

"Yep."

"An it actually worked?" He raised his eyebrows with a dubious gaze.

"Yee... ep." Otis grinned again. "Sounds pretty silly, doesn't it?"

"Silly!" Jim laughed. "I'd say! An so then what happened?"

"Well, Foster kept sendin them packages. In fact, after about the second or third one ol Willie got to where she even started lookin for em."

"Really?"

"Oh hell yes. See, she jus loved to open presents, an every time she showed up to give me another lesson, well, that was one of the first things that she'd ask me. An then after a while she even started askin about Foster. Now of course it was all real casual like, like she couldn't of cared less about him, but still, she was askin, an I think that that is exactly what ol Foster'd wanted."

"So are you tellin me that she actually fell for this present thing?"

"Yep, I'm afraid so," Otis drawled. "See, deep down I think that she still cared for him, an Foster, well, he really knew how to push her buttons. An as those weeks slowly passed an she opened those gifts, you could see her heart open up jus a little more each an every time."

"But wait a minute, what about Foster, what in the hell was he do'n besides sendin you boxes to give to Willie? I mean, I know politicians don't do a whole hell of a lot, but wasn't he supposed to be workin? You know, do'n that Senator crap?"

"Oh sure, an I think he was actually cause jus as soon as he got back to Washinton he got real busy makin that Tom Portman a Federal Judge. Then, an jus as soon as he was done with that, I think it was around the end of February by then, he came back home an him an Melinda had their second baby. William K. Siler. He was real happy, but he didn't get to stay very long cause jus a few days later he got called back to Washinton. By the President himself."

"Really... for what?"

"Well, if I remember right, it was cause he wanted Foster to head up some committee or somethin that was gonna change the way the shippin an ship buildin industry worked. Anyway, it was..."

CHAPTER 55

———•———

His FIRST ORDER OF BUSINESS upon his return to Washington was to meet with the President. From the very beginning Roosevelt had wanted a strong Merchant Marine for the country, but after three frustrating years, he still didn't have one. The programs that'd been put in place when he took office were not working, they were antiquated, and he wanted a new and stronger bill that would change them and achieve a multitude of goals.

He wanted to formulate a bold new shipbuilding program that would bring them into the modern era and ease the current rules and regulations that'd prevailed within the industry. Restrictions that were time consuming and convoluted, and that although well intended, in hindsight had stifled its growth. There had to be a way to ease the process and entice the private sector into coming forth, and in doing so the President called on Foster.

It was just a day after he'd returned when he and the President had lunch. Roosevelt knew that Foster, not only understood the private world of shipping, but also the government's role as well. His successes in both the Senate and the business world were without question, and he was highly respected in both arenas. They talked at length, and after two and a half hours, the newly appointed chairperson of the Merchant Marine and Fisheries Committee, left with his directives.

Their goal was simple; to create a new and innovative long-range construction program to build five hundred new ships over a ten-year period, and to ease the way in which the private sector could do it. Ships that could replace the slower and older vessels of World War

I that thus far had made up the bulk of the fleet. Armed with a large degree of latitude with in which to work, along with the President's complete support, Foster went work as the leading architect for the bill.

It was a challenging task that took several months, but he understood the intricacies of greed better than most and when he was finally finished, he and his group had radically changed the way in which the government's operational and construction subsidies were administered. They'd cut the process in half and had opened up the nations coffers in a way and in which no one had ever thought of before. It was new and unique and creative, and for those who found their way into the system, a treasure trove of untold funds laid in wait to buy and build as many ships as they wanted.

Then on June 29th of that year and much to the delight of the President, the 74th Congress passed in to law the new Merchant Marine Act. A bill that in its design would create thousands and thousands of new jobs throughout the country and that in its passing would also create the United States Maritime Commission. An independent executive agency comprised of five men who'd been selected to oversee and administer the new programs that'd just been approved.

Nominated by the President to temporarily chair the committee, Foster quickly established its protocol, then went back to work and began to implement its policies. It was without question a monumental task to think that they could completely reshape the entire industry and its thinking, but Roosevelt had always wanted a strong Merchant Marine fleet for the nation and now, Foster was going to give it to him. He had the power and the tools to do it, and not only for the country, but for himself as well. He'd drafted almost the entire piece of legislation on his own and he knew the process better than anyone else there was. But more than that, he knew the ways in which it could be used and manipulated through its many provisions.

The Judge had been right, greed and power drove everything and everyone in Washington, and as the depression continued on, the ways in which he began to do business became even easier. Times were still hard and he knew just who to bribe and how to do it. Both the Sec. of Transportation and Navy had become good friends, and

it wasn't long before his twenty-eight new ships quickly found themselves at the front of the line. But now with the summer recess upon
them it was time to go home; he was tired and needed a break. He
wanted to see his wife and his kids, and if things worked out as he
hoped... to even see Willie.

He'd thought of her constantly over the months that'd passed,
and as he sat in his office and waited for his ten o'clock, he stared
out through the rain soaked windows. It was a dreary day, and with a
heavy yawn he rocked back in his chair, plopped his feet on his desk,
and in the quietness of his office, closed his eyes and drifted back in
time. Back to the days when he would visit her on the river and she'd
shared her love.

But his dream world of yesteryear didn't last long, and all too
soon he opened his eyes to the sound of voices coming from the
other side of his door. It was his receptionist who seemed to be greeting someone who'd just come in. Was this his ten o'clock, he wondered as he pulled his feet from his desk and glanced at his watch?
Yes, it had to be, he was certain of it, and even though the man was
early, he was glad he was here. He remembered how he had agreed
to the visit in haste and without much information, but still he wondered; what in the hell did a geologist from Texas want with him?

His appointment with Senator Siler was for ten o'clock yet Everett
Hayes, a tall easy-going Texan and head geologist for the Gulf Shore
Oil and Drilling Company, was early. "Good morning, may I help
you," the girl behind the desk greeted.

"Why yes ma'am, and good mornin to you," Everett drawled and
tipped his hat. "I'm Everett Hayes, and I know that I'm a little early,
but I have an appointment with Senator Siler for ten."

"Oh yes sir," she replied. "The Senator is expecting you. He told
me to send you right in, so please, if you'd like to follow me."

A knock on the door as they entered instantly refocused Foster's
attention. "Senator," Carolyn called as she stepped inside "Mr.
Hayes, your ten o'clock is here. And Mr. Hayes," she continued as
they crossed the room and Foster rose from his chair. "Senator Siler."

Extending his hand as he walked from behind his desk, Foster
smiled and repeated the man's name. "Mr. Hayes... Foster Siler. It's a
pleasure to meet you."

"Yes sir, and you too Senator," he said as they shook. "And I want you to know just how much I appreciate you taking the time to meet with me this mornin. I know that you're busy and that you're suppose to be on break already, but I think after you hear what I have to say you'll understand why our company was so insistent."

"Well, it's not a problem really," he laughed. "Heck that's what we're here for, but please have a seat would you." He gestured to the two large leather chairs in front of his desk. "Could I offer you a cup of coffee?"

"Yes sir, thank you, a cup of coffee would be great. Strong and black, if you don't mind."

"And you sir?" Carolyn asked as the men took their seats and she prepared to leave.

"Yes Carolyn, please," Foster said as he turned back to the man in the chair and cleared his throat. "Now Mr. Hayes, how is it that I might help you today?"

"Well sir," Everett began as he pulled a map from his folder and opened it up. "I have actually come for a couple of reasons. First, I was wondering if you've ever heard of a little town that lies just north of Mobile called Citronelle," he asked and pointed to the map.

"Can't say that I have really," Foster leaned toward him and peered with a curious gaze. "Why, is there something special about it that I should know and don't?"

"Well actually," Everett drawled matter of factly. "Yes there is. See, this little town sits pretty close to a giant salt-cored anticline in the eastern portion of the Mississippi Interior Salt Basin. That's a large underground area between that town and the city of Mobile where layers and layers of sedimentary rocks from the Mesozoic and the Cenozoic periods have sagged thousands of feet below the ground to form a great big giant bowl that we're guessing is somewhere in the neighborhood of about 200 million years old. We're calling this the Citronelle Dome, you know cause of the little town that's up there an all."

"Yes, well I'm sure that this geological formation or whatever it is that you're talking about is an amazing feat of nature, but what in the hell does all of this have to do with me? I mean...?" He smiled and shrugged his shoulders then spread his arms in an open handed gesture.

"Yes, you're absolutely right, please forgive me. Sometimes I get a little carried away because it's so exciting to find something like this. But if I could have just a few more minutes of your time, I would really like to try an explain its significance."

"Ooh, by all means, please do," Foster smiled again and then gestured with another set of open hands. "You're killing me."

It was a subtle yet serious hint and Everett instantly picked up on it. He could see the man's growing impatience, and with that he quickly proceeded on. "Yes, well thank you. Now, as I was just sayin, located at the crest of that dome which is directly above that bowl, is what we call the Citronelle oil fields. Now we believe that these fields, or that bowl as you might imagine it to be, is filled with oil."

"Oil?" Foster raised his eyebrows with a renewed interest.

"Yes sir," Everett nodded. "Oil... you know, that black gooey stuff that comes out of the ground."

"Yes, I'm familiar with it," he replied and then narrowed his eyes. "How much oil?"

"Well, we're not exactly sure at this point because it's still a little too early to tell, but from most of our preliminary estimates, we think that there's somewhere between a 100 and a 150 million barrels. It's down there, I know it is," he asserted in a voice that'd suddenly turned serious. "In fact, we believe that we just may have discovered what could possibly be the largest oil fields ever found east of the Mississippi. Now oil is sellin for about a dollar twenty-five a barrel and what we'd like from you is permission to test drill."

"Permission to drill... from me?" He threw the man a confused look. "Why me? I don't have any dealings with those committees."

"No sir, we're well aware of that, but you do own approximately two thousand acres in between those two towns," he paused and took a breath. "And we believe Senator... that almost all of that oil sits directly beneath your ground."

It took only a second for the meaning and magnitude of what the man had just said to sink in, but still he couldn't believe it. Oil... on his ground? It was like finding a hoard of buried treasure without even searching for it. And did he really say, between a 100 and 150 million barrels? The largest oil fields ever, east of the Mississippi? It was an almost inconceivable thought, and for a few fleeting moments he sat in sort of a dumbfounded daze, his mind whirling with an ever increasing giddiness until the sound of Carolyn's voice jolted his senses and brought him back into reality.

"Okay gentlemen," she called as she walked into the room with a tray. "Mr. Hayes, Sir," she said as stopped and then lowered the tray in front of them. "Now if everything is okay and you don't need me," she added as they took their cups. "I'll just slip back outside."

Looking up at his assistant, Foster stared for just a second then slowly turned his gaze back to his newfound business partner. "No Carolyn," he drawled as he held up his cup and smiled. "We're just fine. In fact... everything is just finnne."

———————

Reaching into the cooler, Jim grabbed two more beers and set them on the table. Then with a curious expression growing on his face he slowly slid one toward Otis. "Okay," he began as he popped his top and took a sip. "Now let me see if I've got this all straight again. First he made that Tom feller a Federal Judge an then he had another kid, right?"

"Right."

"An then after that, he became buddy buddies so to speak with the President an they passed all them new shippin laws?"

"Yep, that's pretty much it," Otis replied then downed what was left in his can. "I remember he was real busy the whole first part of that year an was gone a real long time."

"I'll bet. An so when'd you finally see em again?"

"Well, if I recall correctly, I think it was jus a few days before that 4th of July. In fact, I'm certain of it. I remember cause Vicki had called me into the office earlier that week to give me a message from him. She said that he was gonna be home in a couple of days an he wanted me to get the boat all cleaned an ready to go because jus as soon as he got back he wanted to go up river."

"Wait a minute," Jim cocked his head. "The guy's gone for months an the first thing he wants to do when he got back was go up river? Are you serious? What in the hell did he wanna do that for, I thought he wanted to see Willie?"

"Ooh he did," Otis assured. "An real bad too, but he had somethin up river that he wanted to see first. Even more than Willie."

"What the house?" Jim scoffed and rolled his eyes.

"Well, not exactly," Otis drawled with a light-hearted chuckle. "Although we did go by there an work a bit. See, the real reason was to see his new oil well that they were gettin ready to drill."

"His what?" Jim exclaimed. "His new oil well?"

"Yes sir," Otis grinned.

"You've gotta be shittin me? An oil well, as in like the black stuff that comes out of the ground?"

"Yes sir," Otis chuckled again. "That's the stuff all right."

"So are you tellin me that he just up an decided to drill an oil well one day?"

"Yep, pretty much," he answered with another grin as he popped his top and then took a slug.

"An when in the hell did he do that?"

"Well, if I remember right, I think it was jus before he took his summer recess an came back home," he replied and looked to the ceiling. "In fact, I'm certain of it," he dropped his gaze back to Jim. "I remember cause he told me all about it when we went up river. He said that this ol boy from Texas jus up an strolled into his office one mornin an told em that they thought that there might be oil on his ground. That worthless piece of swamp land as he use to call it," he chuckled.

"An was there?" Jim pried.

"Ooh yeaah, it was there all right. In fact, I think they found it on their second hole not more than three or four thousand feet down. An I don't mean jus a little either... but a lot."

"Oh my God, that's riiiight," Jim said as if he suddenly remembered. "The oil fields just north of here, up towards that little town of aah, oooh, what in the hell's it called?" he paused and scrunched his face then blurted it's name. "Citronella."

"Yep, them are the ones," Otis nodded. "An true to his word the very next mornin after he'd gotten back, me an him took off an went up river. I remember we left bright an early cause he wanted to get a good start which turned out to be a pretty good idea cause by the time we finally found them boys an then got out to where they was gettin ready to drill it was damn near noon.

"Now I'd never seen a drillin operation before, an I really don't believe that Foster had either. In fact, neither one of us had any idea as to how you got oil out-a the ground. But that ol foreman was a pretty nice feller an he sat us down an explained it all real simple like. I remember Foster an how excited he got after he was all done cause he really wanted to see that oil. In fact, I

really believe if he could of picked up one of them pipes an drove it into the ground, he'd a put his mouth over the end an sucked that oil out himself," he chuckled and shook his head.

"Anyway, we screwed around there for a little while longer lookin an talkin until Foster finally decided that we were probably more in the way than anything, an after that we headed back down river to the old house. He wanted to check on it an do some work. You know, clean it up a bit an cut the grass, stuff like that. Then, an jus as soon as we was done there, we headed back home. I remember that it was really gettin on into the afternoon an that it was hot... damn hot."

"Okay Otis," Foster called out as he came up from below and set an ice-cold bottle of beer down in front of the wheel. "Look what I found. This ought-a make our ride back a little more enjoyable don't ya think?"

"Oh, yes sur boss," Otis instantly replied. "Thank you."

"Ah, don't mention it," he replied as he turned and stared out the front. "It's Friday and it's too goddamn hot not to be drinking one. Besides, it's the forth of July weekend, our nation's birthday and we're suppose to celebrate, right?"

"Ooh, yes sur," Otis nodded as he grabbed his beer. "Specially if you say so."

It was to go without saying that even the notion of a rich and powerful white man serving a black man a beer was still unheard of, yet neither Foster nor Otis thought anything of it. They were just two men returning home after a long hot day on the river and they were thirsty, and without a moment's hesitation, the thirty-one year old black man tilted the bottle upwards, took a long sizable swill and then set it back down with a satisfied sigh.

"Pretty good, huh?" Foster asked as he raised his bottle and then took a slug.

"Yes sur," Otis agreed. "In fact, I think that's jus about as good as it gets boss."

"Yes it is," Foster smiled as he took another slug and then turned his gaze out front. "But tell me," he asked and instantly turned back. "Tell me about Willie? Does she still come an see you?"

"Oh yes sur," he grinned great big. "Pretty much every Saturday mornin when she can. She's been teachin me math since the beginnin of the year, you know, how ta add an subtract."

"Yes I know, and so how's that going?"

"Well, at first it was real hard cause I didn't understand how all those number things worked. But Miss Willie is a real good teacher an it's go'n good now," he beamed at the conquest of his new found numerical skills. "In fact, I can add an subtract all the way to a hundred now, an she says that I'm almost ready to start dividin em. You know, that's when you take the number an--."

"Yes I know," Foster interrupted. "So is she coming to see you tomorrow?"

"Yes sur, usually about ten o'clock or so after she gets all her chores done for that Miss Liz lady."

"I see," he nodded. "And that's good, but listen, I have something that I want you to do for me."

"So wait a minute," Jim interrupted. "He had you set her up?"

"Oh nooo," Otis shook his head. "It wasn't a set up."

"Oh really," Jim retorted. "Then what was it, cause to me it sure sounds like it was."

"Well, it was his plan... you know, on how he was gonna try an see her."

"An just how in the hell did he propose to do that?"

"Well," Otis chuckled. "It was pretty simple actually, he jus had me stay home an when she got to the boat that next mornin to give me my math lesson, he was there waitin for her."

"No way?" Jim rolled his eyes.

"Oh yeaaah," Otis assured along with a nod. "It was the 4th of July an ol Foster was gettin ready to light that fuse all over again."

———◆———

CHAPTER 56

HE HEARD THE SOUND OF her voice as she called out for Otis, that sweet irresistible drawl that he'd missed so much and could never get enough of. And then the clamoring noise as she stepped on board and called again. "Otis, I'm here," she said as she stuck her head in the doorway and stepped inside. "Where are you? Come on, I don't have all day. I have to be back early cause we're havin a cookout this afternoon an Miss Liz needs my help," she added but then suddenly stopped at the sight of a small neatly wrapped box sitting on the table.

"Oh wow, did Foster send me another present?" she asked as she set her books on the table and picked up the box. "I wonder what's in this one?" She brought it to her ear and shook it.

But the box didn't rattle or make any noise; there was only the sound of what she thought were Otis's footsteps descending from the pilothouse. "Well," the all too familiar voice finally came from behind. "I guess you'll just have to open it, won't you."

Snapping her head toward the voice, Willie sucked in a breath then froze with a disbelieving stare. "That is, if you still want to see what's in it?" he finished with a hopeful smile and a step towards her.

It was clear that he'd caught her completely off guard, and in a startled reaction to his presence Willie instantly set the box back on the table and turned to leave. He'd frightened her and he knew it, but he had waited far too long to just let her walk away and before she could take a step, he reached up and took hold of her arm.

"Willie wait," he pleaded in a voice that exuded an urgency she'd never heard before. "Please," he quickly added along with a gentle tug. "We need to talk. I need to talk," he paused and took a breath. "To you. Please. I'm begging you... don't go."

It was the sincere and almost desperate tone of his voice that caused her to stop and stare out through the doorway. She knew that his being there was wrong and that she should leave and run just as fast as she could, but she didn't, she stayed and battled her feelings. She'd dreamt and thought of this moment for months and now it was here. It was what she had wanted, but even so she was afraid. Afraid that he would see through to her heart and the feelings she still harbored. Feelings that were as strong now as they ever were, and that try as she may, she could not dispel.

The boat was quiet, and for a few fleeting moments the only thing she could hear was the pounding of her heart, until, and after what seemed like an eternity, she took a long deep breath and turned back to Foster. He was staring with a forlorn expression, and even though her eyes were defiant and heavily glazed, he quickly reached up and grasped her other arm.

"Willie," he began with a sigh. "I know that you probably still hate me, but I want you to know how truly sorry I am. I know that what I did to you was wrong and I'm sorry, I really am. I didn't mean to hurt you... please, you've got a believe me. I just thought that I was doing what was right and best for you because I was going to Washington and I couldn't take care of you anymore. I want you to know that, but most of all," he took a breath and stared deep into her eyes. "I want you to know how much I've missed you. And how much I still love you."

"Nooo Foster," Willie cried and shook her head.

"Yes," he hissed and drew her closer. "And more than you'll ever know. I've been thinking about it, about us, and I know that this is going to sound crazy, but we can be together now. Again, like we use to be. I can make it happen and make it all up to you and we can--."

"Nooo," she shook her head again and cut him short. "We can't! Don't you see, it's wrong! You're married and a Senator, and we can't, we just can't," she argued and looked away. "Besides, I'm seeing someone now."

Her reasoning made sense but Foster wouldn't have it, he couldn't, it would kill him, and just as quickly as she'd turned her head he turned it back and regained her gaze. He could see that she was confused and that her conscience was telling her to run. The expression on her face said it all, but before she could turn back Foster pulled her tight and kissed her.

It was a short and brazen kiss that quickly broke when she pushed herself away and turned her head. Yet even so he could sense that what she'd done and what she wanted were two different things, for no matter how much she feigned and protested she still loved him and he knew it. "Yes we can," he insisted as he turned her back once more.

"Nooo," she cried and shook her head. "We..."

But before the beautiful twenty year old could utter another word in remonstrance, Foster pulled her tight and kissed her again. Softly at first, then more pressing as her resistance slowly began to fade. That increased in its passion until she'd surrendered completely and had ceased to speak. Until he felt her arms ever so slowly encircle his shoulders and then pull.

"An so that's how they finally ended up back together, huh?" Jim seemed a little surprised but delighted that he now knew.

"Yes sir," Otis replied. "That's pretty much how it happened, or at least how it all started. Why, you surprised?" he grinned and took a sip.

"Well yeah, actually I am. I mean, I just can't believe that she fell for him again."

"Oh yeah, I know what you mean," Otis agreed. "In fact, I'd thought about that myself cause at the time she supposedly had this boyfriend that lived jus a couple of farms away from her that she'd been seein an really liked. His name was Danny... Danny Mitchell, an if the truth be known, I think that she actually liked him a whole lot more than she cared to admit. In fact, I know she did cause she would always talk about him whenever she gave me my lessons, you know, how much fun they had when they were together an what all they were gonna do later on that day.

"Most of the times if the weather was nice, she said that they'd go out to the airport an jus lay in the grass at the end of the runway so they could watch the airplanes take off an land over the top of em. She said that that was all he wanted to do was to learn how to fly. Anyway, like I jus said, I really think that she liked that boy, but I guess deep down in her heart she still loved Foster in a way that she jus couldn't get over, an after that weekend the two of them started meetin down at the boat real secret like whenever they could. I remember

thinkin at the time that there wasn't nothin but no good that was gonna come out of it all, an that between Foster an Willie, an his wife an the Portmans, somebody was gonna get hurt an there wasn't no gettin around it."

"Really, an why was that?"

"Well shit, jus think about it," Otis replied as if Jim should've known. "Foster was a rich an powerful Senator with a wife an two kids who had absolutely no intentions of changin any part of it. Shiiit he had it all, an all he wanted to do was get back in her pants. An poor Willie, well, I don't know what all he started fillin her head with, but it wasn't to awfully long before she started dreamin about havin a life with him all over again."

"So he just out an out lied to her again didn't he?" Jim looked on in disgust.

"Well hell yeah he lied. I mean shit, he was a politician, wasn't he?" he laughed.

"Yeah, I guess he was," Jim chuckled. "So then what happen?"

"Well, as it turned out ol Foster found himself jus a little busier with his shipyards than what he really wanted to be. They were gettin ready to build a couple of brand new ships, so he really didn't have a whole lot of spare time that summer. But him an Willie still managed to meet a couple of times after the 4th an then a couple more in August.

"Now from everything that I could piece together at the time, you know, from what all Willie'd let slip whenever she was givin me my lessons, I think that Foster was really workin on her. See, all he wanted to do was to get her back in the sack again jus as fast as he could. I think he thought that she was jus gonna let him pick back up where he'd left off four years ago. But ol Willie wouldn't have it cause there was jus somethin about sleepin with him on the boat down at the marina an then go'n back home like nothin had happened that she jus didn't like.

"Now I don't know whether it was all that church go'n an all those new moral values that that ol Mrs. Portman had instilled in her or jus what it was, but let me tell ya she didn't wanna have nothin to do with it. She told me that too, an even though Foster had really tried an had put the pressure on, she didn't budge. Anyway, I guess when he finally figured out that he wasn't gonna get what he wanted, well, that's when he came up with the idea of taken her back up river. Back up to the little house where it had all started."

"An she went?"

"Oh heck yeah, in fact, just as soon as she agreed to go ol Foster sent me up one day about a week before to clean it an make sure everything was okay.

Then right before she went back to school to go to her second year of college I think it was, we all went up river an spent the weekend at the house."

"But wait a minute," Jim stopped him and stared. "How in the heck did she get away for a whole weekend without that ol Mrs. Portman knowin what was go'n on? I mean, I thought she kept a pretty close eye on her, didn't she?"

"Oh she did. Or at least she tried. But you know how them young girls can get when they think they're in love. Shiiiit, they'll do an say jus about anything to get their way, an ol Willie wasn't no different."

"Yeah, I'll bet she wasn't," Jim laughed. "So what'd she do?"

"Well, you remember that Daphney an that Angela girl don't ya?"

"Yeah."

"Well, I guess she told her that they were havin an end of summer camp out on one of their farms before they all had to go back to school an she wanted to spend the weekend with em."

"An she believed her?"

"Well," Otis thought for a second. "Yeah, I'm pretty sure she did. I mean, she let her go."

"An them other two girls, did they know what she was really do'n?"

"Oh heck no, shit, Willie knew better than to tell them the truth. Hell, if they'd of known what was really go'n on, why that whole damn town would've known before we'd reached Chickasaw Creek." He laughed.

"So what'd she tell em?"

"That she was go'n up to see the witch, an not to tell anyone."

"An so you guys went up?"

"Yep," Otis nodded. "It was a Friday, a real pretty day with hardly a cloud in the sky. Willie showed up real quiet like right at two o'clock jus like Foster had told her, then about an hour after that, he came walkin down an jumped on board. Then, an jus as soon as he checked everything to make sure that I'd stocked the boat like he wanted, we took off an headed up river with that little fishin boat followin right behind us.

"I remember Willie had insisted on takin it so she could go an see that damn witch. It'd been right at three years since she'd last seen her an she was all wound up about gettin to visit with her again. In fact, she'd even packed up a whole box of stuff for her. You know, some clothes an shoes an even some canned goods that she'd talked Foster into buyin to take along. Yes sir, she was all excited, but by the time we got up there it was gettin on into the afternoon so she decided to jus go an see her the next mornin when she had more time. Actually, I think it was Foster's decision if ya wanna know the truth cause

he had plans an I don't think that they had anything to do with that witch."
He laughed.

"Oh yeah, I can just imagine," Jim rolled his eyes.

"Anyway, after we got all unloaded, me an Willie gathered up some wood an made a fire, an after it had burned down, Foster cooked us all a real nice dinner. I tell ya it felt jus like old times all over again sittin there grillin an drinkin beer, heck, even Willie had a few. Then after we were all done, she got up an took our plates an went inside. She said she wanted to take a bath so me an Foster jus laid out there an drank another beer until it started gettin dark when he finally got up, told me that he'd see me in the mornin an went inside."

———◆———

They made love that night for the first time in four years and then again the next morning when they woke. Willie felt like a young bride on her honeymoon and could have lain for hours basking in the afterglow of their union. She was in heaven all over again, and it was clear that she'd missed the act of sex. But she'd also come to see her old friend, and even though Foster pleaded for her to stay, she finally rose and dressed. A short while later, and after a simple breakfast of steak and eggs, she made a generous plate for Otis and Foster then kissed him goodbye and walked down to the pier.

"Morning Otis," she hollered as she stepped onto the pier. "I made you some breakfast, are you hungry?"

"Ooh, mornin Miss Willie," he turned on his bucket to the sound of her voice. "You bet I am. What'd ya make?"

"Last night's dinner, some cut up steak and potato with a couple of eggs on top. It's good, here," she stopped and held out her arm.

"Oh thank you," he gushed as he took the plate and brought it to his nose. "It smells great."

"It is," she replied as he dug in and took his first bite. "So are ya havin any luck?"

"Ah huh," he mumbled and nodded. "Caught two nice ones already."

"Really," Willie seemed surprised. "Well don't catch em all, I wanna help you when I get back and then maybe we can catch enough for supper."

"When you get back?" Otis cocked his head. "Ya means you're go'n to see that witch right now?"

"Well sure I am, heck, that's one of the reasons I came up here. I haven't seen her in three years. Why, ya wanna go with me?"

"No!" he scowled. "An you know I don't!"

"Aaah, come on Otis," Willie teased and rolled her eyes. "You know she'd like to see you. A big ol strong black man like yourself... um ummm," she licked her lips and giggled.

"Noo!" he repeated and clutched his plate then looked away. "Now stop it, I'm serious!"

Otis's words left little doubt as to his lingering fears of the witch, but even so Willie couldn't resist the temptation of giving her friend one last jab. "Well," she said as she plopped her hands on her hips. "I guess since you won't go see her, I'll just have to let her know that you're up here again and then she can come an visit you tonight while you're sleeping on the boat," she giggled again.

"Miss Willie," Otis glared. "Now you knows that that ain't funny, now stop it."

"Oh sure it is," she replied with a dismissive wave. "Heck, you know Hadie wouldn't hurt you. She wouldn't hurt anybody. Anyway, I'm gonna go an see her. Is my shotgun still in the boat?"

"Yes ma'am, in the closet by the sink," he said and shook his head then dug back into his plate. "An it's loaded too," he added as she jumped on board.

"So Willie finally got to go an see the ol witch?"

"Yep, it was that next mornin, she came walkin down with a big ol plate of food an after she finally got done teasin me an givin me a hard time, she jumped on the boat here an got her shotgun an all her stuff that she'd brought along. Then, after she got it all loaded into her little boat, she checked her gas, gave her motor a couple of pulls, an after it'd started an she was sure it was gonna run okay, I untied her an she took off up that little tributary with a great big smile on her face."

"I'll see you in a couple of hours okay," she hollered over the noise of the motor.

"You got it," Otis replied and tossed her line. "Oh, an you be careful out there, ya hear?"

"I will," she assured as she turned to the front and gave her motor the gas.

It took a little longer to reach Hadie's hideaway than what she'd remembered, but even so Willie finally rounded the last bend to her campsite and called out her name. She was excited that in another minute she would be sitting with her friend, but as she drew closer to her camp and it came into view, she could see that something was wrong. That there was something unusually quiet, and that the swamp had begun to reclaim her once clear campsite. It was as if she'd moved and had abandoned the area, yet all of her things were still there. "Hadieee," she called again as she pulled her boat on shore and looked around. "It's me, Willie."

Listening for an answer that never came, she finally turned and settled with her eyes on the hut. Partially hidden by a growth of sawgrass, it was clear that Hadie was gone but even so she took a few steps closer for a better look. "Hadieee," she called again in a voice that was now growing with apprehension. A second later, Willie's heart suddenly sank at the sight of Hadie's skeletal remains lying on her mat. A skeleton still covered in what looked to be the tattered remnants of one of the last dresses she'd given her. A growing lump instantly welled in her throat and she wanted to leave but she didn't, she stayed and then slowly stepped closer. What'd happened, she wondered? Did she get sick or bit by a snake? It looked as if she'd died in her sleep and knew she would never wake. The bible and rosary still clutched in her hands told her so.

"Oh Hadieee," Willie quietly whispered as she slowly went to her knees. "What'd you do...?"

It was sad to think that she'd died out in the middle of nowhere so all alone, and even though she was heartbroken, Willie knew that Hadie had finally found the peace that she'd so desperately sought. That the demons and the nightmares of the war, that had afflicted her, would haunt her no more. But even so, no one had missed her, or had even known that she was gone. No one had said a prayer or even cried. No one cared. No one that was, except Willie, and it bothered her immensely.

She thought back to the day that they'd first met and smiled, then reached up and touched her scar. She remembered how frightened she'd been at the time and how she'd thought that she was going to be eaten. She smiled again then thought of how Hadie had eased her worries, and then of how quickly they'd become friends. She thought of her humor and the goodness in her heart and of all the times that they'd spent together. She remembered them all, and then she began to cry.

It wasn't right for her to have died and then to have just lain out in the middle of the swamp like an animal. It was sacrilegious and she knew it, for without a proper burial, Hadie's soul could never go to heaven. She had to be put to rest. She deserved it, and without another thought, Willie wiped the tears from her cheeks then got up and went to her boat. Retrieving one of the dresses she'd brought, she then picked some water lilies at the water's edge and returned to the hut. It was cramped inside, but even so she tenderly unfolded the dress over Hadie's remains then laid the flowers on her chest and said a prayer.

It was one of the hardest things she'd done since her mother had died, but after she was finished asking God to forgive Hadie's sins and accept her soul, she got up and began to gather wood. She gathered everything she could until she had filled the inside of the hut and had piled it high on top. Finishing with a mass of grasses and leaves on the bottom, she knelt and said a final prayer. Then, in the quiet backwaters and reaches of the swamp, she set fire to the little hut. A few moments later, a thick white smoke billowed into the air and in the raging inferno that quickly ensued; Willie said a sad and final goodbye to her friend, Hadie Gertrud Grossman.

"Oh man. So the witch was dead?"

"Yep," Otis replied. "An ol Willie was real sad about it too."

"Yeah, I can just imagine," Jim shook his head. "I mean, to go out an to find her like that."

"Oh I know," Otis sighed. "I'll tell ya, I felt real sorry for her too, cause that was when I finally realized jus how close they'd become while she'd been up river. I guess be'n out there in the middle of that swamp like she was, Willie was the only friend that she had."

"So what happened?"

"Well, if I remember right it was about a half hour or so after Willie'd left when Foster came down drinkin a cup of coffee. We were sittin there talkin

when we both looked up an saw all this smoke risin up into the sky not more than a couple of miles or so away--."

"No no no," Jim interrupted. "I mean, what happened to the witch? How'd she die, do ya know?"

"Oh, nooo... not really. All Willie said was that she'd found her lyin in her little shack all real peaceful like. Like she'd jus gone to sleep one night an knew that she was never gonna wake up. Anyway, like I said, she was real sad about it an for the rest of the afternoon while we fished, she was pretty quiet. Foster sat up at the house an did paper work out on the porch an after dinner we jus kind of laid around the fire for a while pokin it an drinkin beer until it got dark an we all went to bed. Then bright an early the next mornin, we loaded up an headed on back."

"An nobody ever found out that you guys went up river?"

"Nope, or at least not that I knew of."

"But what about Foster an Willie, what'd they do after that weekend? I mean, that wasn't just a one time thing was it?"

"Oh hell nooo," Otis laughed as if it were a silly question.

"So they kept seein each other?"

"Oh yeah, although I don't think that it was as often as they wanted cause Willie had gone back to college an ol Foster, well, he was so damn busy he didn't have time for nothin."

"Why, what-in-the hell was he do'n now?"

"Well, like I said earlier, he was gettin ready to build himself a couple of brand new ships."

"Oh yeah," Jim scrunched his face as if he'd forgotten. "Oh, an let me guess," he added in what was clearly a contemptuous tone. "Compliments of the Federal Government, I presume?"

"Yep, you guessed it," Otis nodded. "Who else? It was in that new shippin law or whatever the hell it was that he'd helped the President with. He called it a construction subsidy or somethin if I remember right, an he was one of the first people in the country to start usin it."

"You mean the government actually paid him to build ships for himself?" Jim probed.

"Yes sir, or at least a pretty big part of it they did. I heard him an Ralston talkin about it one day while we were out in the boat. He wanted to watch the men in the shipyard lay the keel to that first ship before he went back to Washinton. In fact," he added with a hearty chuckle. "An you really ain't

gonna believe this, but that's when he told Ralston to start hirin more men an to start lookin for as many old used ships as he could find."

"Old ships... for what? I thought you just said he was buildin new ones?"

"Oh he was, but the government had started buyin em. See, accordin to Foster, in that new law that they'd passed they really wanted everyone in the shippin business to have new ships, you know, for the good of the country an all. So if you had an old ship back then that they considered slow an obsolete, they'd buy it from you an then build you a brand new one. It was a hell of a deal, an jus as soon as he could, ol Foster had Ralston lookin for all of the cheapest old boats he could find."

"Wait a minute, are you tellin me that he actually went out an started buyin old junk ships just so he could sell em back to the government? Are you serious?" He finished with a wide-eyed gaze.

"Yep," Otis drawled. "That's exactly what he started do'n. He'd find him an old ship that'd barely make it into port an then fix it up jus enough so that it'd make one trip across the ocean an when it got back he'd trade it in for a new one. You know, kind of like you'd do if you was tradin in your old car for a new one."

"Jesus, didn't anybody say or do anything? I mean wasn't anybody watchin this guy?" Jim's sense of outrage seemed to rise along with his voice.

"Nope, or at least not that I ever knew about."

"Jesus Chrissst, what a bunch of goddamn crooks. Oh, an let me guess again," he continued on with a cynical overtone. "The taxpayer's paid for all of em too didn't they?"

"Yes sir, our good ol federal government was spendin their money in ways that you jus wouldn't believe, an let me tell ya, ol Foster was right there taken it jus as fast as he could too. In fact, it was right about that time that a lot of us that worked for him like Ralston an Vicki, an heck even me, started gettin raises. An big ones, too."

"Anyway, after he'd gotten everything all set with Ralston, he took off an went back to Washinton. He stayed in touch with Willie through me, an whenever he came into town he did everything he could to see her as many times as he could. He had a suite on the top floor of the Battle House Hotel that he kept cause he was always wine'n an dine'n the hell out of someone an that's where they'd meet. She'd drive over to the marina an then get in with me, an then I'd drive her over to the hotel an drop her off in the back where she'd sneak in so nobody saw her.

"I remember he saw her once over Thanksgivin an then a few times durin the Christmas holidays. Then after the first of the year, after the holidays was all over, she went back to school an he took off an went back to Washinton. I think he started workin on his campaign for re-election about that time, an me, well, right about the end of January or so, after I'd finally finished addin on all the new office space that he wanted, I started makin signs all over again."

CHAPTER 57

THE NUMBER OF BUSINESS PEOPLE that'd come forth in support of his re-election was immediate and almost overwhelming. He'd brought thousands and thousands of jobs into the state and the people remembered it, and by the spring of 37 he'd garnered all of the support he needed. His opposition was an unknown and poorly funded, and from the very start he led in the polls by an almost two to one margin. The papers were quick to pick up on it and tout his almost certain victory, but even so Foster crisscrossed the state campaigning for each and every vote as if he were behind.

It was an exciting time yet even as busy as he was, he kept his eyes focused on business. He had a consortium of companies and was building an empire, and even though he was wealthier now than he'd ever imagined himself to be, the always ambitious an often times ruthless Senator wanted more. He wanted it all, and by the summer of that year he had fifty-eight ships sailing throughout the world and over four thousand men working twenty-four hours a day at Siler Shipbuilding.

His stevedore company, the loading and unloading of cargo, had acquired complete control of all the docks and the fruits of his oil fields had begun to pour in. And as always, Ralston ruled beneath him with an iron fist and unflinching loyalty, proving again and again to be an intelligent and competent leader to his ever-growing empire. It seemed as if there wasn't anything that the thirty-five year old sea captain couldn't handle, and for his efforts and allegiance, Foster rewarded him generously.

Ralston was his man, but it was always Foster who truly led. He was smart and calculating, and in the five years that he'd been in office, he'd become a powerful and well-respected Senator. He'd maneuvered himself like a master chess player and in doing so he'd created ties on both sides of the aisle. Strong ties that had served him well on many occasions. But it was his even stronger ties to the White House that had gained him the favorable nods and preferential treatment that he needed from both the Secretary of Navy and Transportation to do business in the manner in which he was doing. Roosevelt liked him and people knew it, and that very fact seemed to go a long long way in everything he did.

He'd begun to operate in ways and on a level that was completely different from anyone else, above the fray of normal business where the funneling of money into secret off-shore accounts for the two Secretaries had gained him more ships in a shorter period of time than anyone else in the nation. Yet for all of the success and wealth that he had accumulated, his world was far from perfect and he soon found that there was a price to pay for the life he'd chosen.

His relationship with Melinda had become strained over the last few years, and even though they appeared in public as the perfect couple, behind closed doors their marriage had been falling apart for some time. She was discontented and resented the fact that he was never home, and that when he was, he spent little if any time with her and the children. They quarreled, with accusations of his blatant and growing infidelities. The list was long, and in her loneliness and depression that seemed to follow, she'd begun to drink to numb the pain.

She knew of his whores in Washington as she'd come to call them, and had suspected for some time that he had a mistress in Mobile as well. Rumors and gossip that had come back to her, that her husband had been seen in town on several occasions with an unbelievably beautiful young girl. She hated it, and was embarrassed that other people knew of his philandering ways, and that they were talking and laughing at her behind her back.

She was suspicious and Foster knew it, yet even so, and even though he knew of the dangers that an affair could bring to his re-election, as the months turned into summer and the heat and humidity intensified, so did his relationship with Willie. Her job that summer as a clerk in the circuit court system allowed for their discrete yet ever increasing liaisons. It was her second year, and on days when the docket was short or the lawyers or judges were unprepared, they would steal away for an afternoon of passion at the Battle House Hotel.

He tried to stay away but couldn't, for he was attracted to her in ways that he'd never dreamed of before. Willie had grown into a beautiful and intelligent young woman, a stunning example of every single thing that he looked for and before the summer's end, he was professing his love to her again and again. Promising that after the election and after he was sworn in for another term, that he would finally tell Melinda and file for divorce. It was music to her ears and that fall the twenty-two year old intoxicating beauty from Hale County returned to her third year of college with the hopes and dreams that soon after the first of the year, the man she loved would file for divorce and then ask for her hand in marriage. But even so Willie was a realist, she knew that it would be difficult and take time. Foster had an election to win first, and the days were closing fast.

The months passed quickly and even though his opponent had fought a hard campaign, the results of the November ballots gave credence as to the immense popularity of the forty-three year old Foster. The people had given him another six years, and after the holidays were over, he flew back to Washington. Then in mid January of 1938, he took his oath and was sworn in for a second term.

Melinda flew in for the event but left after the ceremony and the photo ops were over a few days later. She really didn't care much for Washington or the people in it, and since Foster had persuaded her to return for another visit in February with the children, she returned to Mobile.

"So ol Foster won re-election?" Jim shook his head and then took a sip from his beer.

"Yep," Otis nodded as he thought back. "An if I remember correctly, by a pretty big margin too. I'll tell ya, he was jus about as popular as you could ever get. I mean, people really loved him an they told him that everywhere we went which actually made it kind of hard for him to sneak around an see Willie."

"But wait a minute," Jim interrupted. "What about his old lady? I mean his wife. Didn't she suspect anything that whole time? I mean?" He looked on with a curious gaze.

"Melinda? Oh heck yeah... she was real suspicious. In fact, she always use to ask me real sneaky like if I knew where Foster was or what he was do'n cause she knew that I drove him around everywhere."

"Really?"

"Oh yeah, shiiit, she wasn't stupid. She knew he was seein someone... she jus didn't know who."

"Really?"

"Oh yeah."

"An you never told her?" Jim raised his eyebrows.

"What, an get my ass fired? Are you crazy?" Otis chuckled. "Anyway, right after his election the holidays came an before I knew it, we'd dropped into the new year an he headed back to Washinton for his second term. I remember Melinda flew there about a week later for the ceremony but then came right back jus a few days later. She really didn't like it there an I guess couldn't hardly wait to get back. Then right around the end of February or so I think it was, I drove her an the kids back to the airport so she could go see him again."

"Again?" Jim scrunched his face. "But I thought you just said that she didn't like Washington?"

"I did, but Foster had insisted that she go back with the kids."

"For what?"

"Well, accordin to Melinda, so he could show em off."

"Show em off?"

"Yeah, you know, parade em around town so to speak so everyone there could see what a prefect little family he had."

"You've got to be kiddin?"

"Oh hell no, shiiit, I think he even had a lunch date set up with the President."

"The President?" Jim looked on with a curious gaze. "What the hell was he up to now?"

"Well, I'm not exactly sure to be right truthful with you. All I know is that anytime Foster Siler did somethin he always had a real good reason for it, an if Melinda an the kids were flyin all the way back to Washinton an were go'n to meet the President of the United States an have lunch with him, you could damn well bet that he was up to somethin.

"Now president or no president, Melinda jus flat out didn't wanna go, an I mean not at all cause she knew that it was nothin more than a dog an pony show. She'd told me that too on the way to the airport. Actually, she griped an bitched about it the whole way there but I guess ol Foster had really

laid down the law an before she knew it her an the kids had climbed into that
big ol twin engine airplane an were on their way."

———◆———

The weeks seemed to fly by and before she knew it Melinda found herself back in Washington with the children to do her duty. It was supposed to be a vacation of sorts, but her week there had been just about what she had expected. She was tired of being paraded around, and now that it was over, she was more than ready to leave. She'd been arguing on and off with Foster almost the entire time, and their drive to the airport proved to be no different. In fact, it had escalated until out of pure exasperation she grew quiet until they had pulled up to the plane and stopped. Then with a scathing glare to Foster, she wrapped her soon to be two-year-old in her arms and got out of the car in a huff.

She was angry and upset with him for staying in town after he'd promised to fly back with them and wouldn't drop the subject. She knew that he could do and did whatever he wanted whenever he wanted, and as she waited by the trunk for the chauffeur, her anger only increased.

"Dammit Foster, I just don't get it. You promised that you'd fly back with us, and now out of the clear blue you've changed your mind," she argued as Foster began pulling their bags from the trunk for the chauffeur. "William will be two on Saturday and I have a party planned... remember? I need help, and it would really be nice if his father was there for his son's birthday."

"Good God Melinda," Foster sighed with an exasperated breath. "We've already been through this a dozen times. I told you I'll be there, I just can't leave today."

"You can't or you won't," she snapped and narrowed her eyes into a scathing glare. "You promised me, remember. If you come Melinda," she mocked in a contemptuous tone. "And let me parade you and the kids around like little puppies, I'll fly back home with you. Oooh, but wait," she stopped and smacked her forehead then rolled her eyes. "How stupid of me. I forgot that you're a politician and you don't have to do what you say. Isn't that how Washington works? Say and promise one thing, then do another?"

"Dammit Melinda, I told you I can't. Suzanne has me scheduled to--."

"Oh yes, and let's not forget about your Suzanne," she cut him short then glanced to the sky and laughed. "How could I have forgotten about your precious little Washington whore?"

"What are you talking about? Suzanne is my assistant and a damn good one, and nothing more. And you know that!"

"Oooh, so that explains it all," she laughed again. "I guess that's why you bought her a flat downtown and a car. Oh, and let's not forgot her collection of hats and shoes too, shall we. Every woman needs those," she sneered in disgust. "Tell me; is she really that good in bed?" She paused for an answer she knew she wouldn't get. "You sleep with her more than you do me and don't you deny it, I know you do."

"Listen, this is not a conversation I am going to have standing out in the middle of a damn airport. Now I've told you that I have business here in town and that we'd talk about this when I get home."

"Yesss, this town," Melinda replied as she looked away and surveyed the skyline. "It's always this town, isn't it?" She lowered her voice to a calm and unemotional level then slowly returned her gaze to her husband. "You know, my father was right," she went on with a cynical disdain. "He always use to tell me that Washington was nothing more than a cesspool of thieves, liars and whores," she smirked. "A gathering spot for the biggest bunch of crooks an self-serving hypocrites he'd ever met, all pretending to do what was right for the people of this great country." She paused and pulled a wisp of hair from her face. "And now after all of these years, I finally realize what he meant. You an everyone else here think that just because you've been elected to help run this country that you have the right to do whatever you want. Well, I have news for you Senator; your job does not include the right to screw around with other women. I am your wife, and I'm sick and tired of your whores."

"Oh really," Foster replied with an opened armed gesture. "Well, if you're so damn worried about who I'm gonna be sleeping with for the next two days, then why don't you just leave Robert here? He can keep and eye on me for you, besides he's big enough that he can hang with Dad now. Right buddy?" he smiled and looked to his son who'd been curiously watching. "What-a-ya say?

You wanna spend a couple of days with ol dad and then fly back home by ourselves."

"Oh yeaaah," Robert's little eyes lit up at the thought of spending a few more days with his dad. "That'd be great. Can I Mom, huh?" he instantly asked with a glance to his mother.

"No," she snapped. "Now go and get in the plane. It's time to go."

"Ah, come on Mom, pleeease," he pleaded.

"Yeah Mom pleeease," Foster quickly added with a hint of sarcasm.

"I said no," she reiterated with a growing impatience. "Now go and get in the plane like I said, you hear me."

"Come on Melinda," Foster argued without the sarcasm. "Let him stay, he'll be fine."

"I said no," she snapped again and pointed. "Now go."

But the young boy didn't move, he just stared at his father until Foster finally nodded with a defeated look and backed up his wife. "Go on buddy," he drawled. "Do what your mother tells you okay, and I'll see you when I get home in a couple of days," he promised as he bent and opened his arms. "You can help me and Ralston go look at a couple of new ships that I'm buying okay."

"Yes sirrr," the disappointed lad sighed as his dad scoop him up and lifted him from the ground. "But can I help the men fly the plane back home?"

"Well," Foster smiled at the audacious request of his son. "I don't see why not, but I think that you better ask the pilots first to see if it's okay."

"Oh good, thanks Dad," he grinned excitedly as he wrapped his arms around his father's neck and squeezed. "I love you."

"And I love you too," Foster repeated with a kiss to his cheek and a squeeze.

There was no doubt that he adored his young son, and as soon as he'd lowered him back down and his feet had touched the ground, he watched his pride and joy scurry to the steps of the plane and then climb onboard. Little Robert was a precocious young boy far beyond his years and the powerful Senator had plans for him, big plans. He was building an empire, and his hopes were that one day in the not too distant future, his son would rule in his place. A few seconds later and after his son had disappeared inside, he turned his attention back to Melinda.

"Now like I said," he began as if he were issuing a directive to a subordinate. "I'll be back in a couple of days and we'll talk about this then, do you understand?" He finished with an icy finality then suddenly turned his attention to his son now yelling from the plane.

"Dad," the little voice came from the stairwell. "The pilot said I could sit on his lap and help him fly the plane, do you wanna watch me."

"Sure buddy," Foster hollered back. "But you better let your mom and William get in first, don't you think?" He chuckled.

"Okay," he answered then instantly yelled to his mother with the impatience of a five and a half year old. "Come on Mom, let's go...!"

Turning her head toward her son, Melinda sighed with a disgruntled breath. "Robert, I'm talking to your father... now just hold on, you hear?"

"But the pilot said he was ready and that we needed to go."

"Robert," she huffed with a motherly glare.

"Yes ma'am," he replied then turned and disappeared again.

"Well, I guess it's time to go," she said as she turned back to Foster. "Now, if you could give your son a kiss, we'll be on our way."

"Melinda I promise," he said as he bent and kissed William's cheek. "I'll be home on Friday."

"You'd better be," she glared but then quickly turned before he could kiss her and began walking to the plane. "Oh, and one more thing," she suddenly stopped and turned. "When you get back, you get rid of your little whore that you've got in Mobile, too. I've put up with your women here in Washington, but I'll be damned if I am going to be humiliated right in my own hometown, you hear me. I won't stand for it!"

The copilot was standing by the steps waiting and after a polite and pleasant good morning to the two as they approached, he assisted Melinda and her son into the plane. Foster used only the best from the Army Air Corps, and the two today were both well seasoned and well trained. He'd used them many times before and the captain had no problem in letting the son of Senator Foster K. Siler sit on his lap. The copilot was more than capable of flying the plane and after a couple of slaps to the door as it closed and latched from inside, Foster stepped back into the view of the pilot.

He could clearly see his son sitting on the man's lap, smiling and waving, and with a big thumbs up and final wave back, the pilot engaged the starters. Turning with the all too familiar whine, the giant propellers began to spin until the big radial engines of the sleek new Beech 18 crackled and popped then roared to life in a cloud of smoke and exhaust gases.

A few moment later they were ready to roll and with all due haste, Foster walked back to the car and watched as they slowly pulled away. He could see Melinda sitting in the back with William and was going to wave but she never turned her head. A few moments later the plane turned away and with the shrug of his shoulders, he stuffed his hands into his pockets then watched as they taxied to the end of the runway and did their run-up.

It was standard procedure, and after what he knew was a final call to the tower for takeoff, the pilot pushed the throttles forward and the twin Beech began to roll. The nine cylinder Pratt and Whitney's were powerful motors, and after only a few moments its twin tail left the ground. Accelerating faster and faster as it rolled down the runway, the big plane finally defied gravity half way down and lifted into the air. A few seconds later, it retracted its gear and began on its slow but steady ascent into the cold winter sky.

Foster had always found the power of flight to be fascinating, and as soon as they were in the air he imagined his son sitting on the captain's lap jabbering with an endless barrage of questions on how to fly. He smiled and chuckled at the thought, then watched as the plane turned and banked to the southwest on its long flight home, climbing ever skyward until it began to disappear in and out of the puffy white clusters of low-lying clouds.

Until it had vanished above them into the vast open sky and all that remained was the heavy drone of the big radial engines, resonating their distinctive sound as they faded into the distance. A sound that grew harder and harder to hear until there was nothing left at all. They were gone, but he would see them in a couple of days. Then, and with casual glance to his watch, Foster turned and opened the door to the car. Suzanne was waiting.

———•———

CHAPTER 58

IT WAS LATE AND THEY were in bed when the phone rang for the second time within minutes of the first. The first had awakened them and with a heavy sigh of disgust, Suzanne finally rolled to her side and answered it. She was irritated and answered as such, but within seconds both her voice and demeanor changed. The person on the other end sounded urgent and grave, and with the look of trepidation pulling at her face, she turned to Foster and handed him the receiver.

It was highly unusual for anyone to call for him here, and even more so for Suzanne to answer it and actually admit that he was, yet even so he brought the receiver to his ear, said hello, then listened to the voice on the other end. For a moment he said nothing, until he coughed and gasped for air then emitted an anguished cry and curled into a ball. The gut wrenching pain that shot through him was overwhelming, and for the first time in his life Foster reeled in an inescapable sorrow greater than anything he ever imagined. The plane with his wife and children had gotten caught in a thunderstorm and had gone down in the swamps just east of Mobile.

"Oh my God," Jim stared in disbelief. "They crashed?"

"Yep," Otis nodded with a somber expression and a voice to match. "I'm afraid so. At first I thought that somebody had made a mistake, but it was true. In fact, it wasn't but a hundred miles east of here where they went down.

"I remember when I first heard about it an how I thought that it jus couldn't be cause Foster always had the very best pilots that there was. An I mean the best," he emphasized. "He wouldn't settle for anything less. Anyway,

632

I was waitin at the airport for em, you know, to take em home when all of a sudden all these people in the tower buildin started runnin around real crazy like.

"Now I knew right off that somethin was up to get everyone all stired up like that, but for the longest time I didn't know what until one of the men who worked there an knew me, an knew that I was waitin for Melinda an the kids, finally came up an told me. I remember he said that they'd been talkin to the pilots on the radio an knew that they'd run into trouble when all of a sudden they jus quit talkin. He said that they was still tryin to reach em but that nobody was answerin. Anyway, they kept callin an callin while everybody sat there an watched the skies an listened... but that plane with Foster's family in it never came.

"Now at first everybody thought that they might of turned an went to another airport so they started callin around to all of the places where they could of landed. But nobody had seen or heard of em, an as those minutes slowly ticked by, well, that's when everybody, includin me, started to think the worst."

"So what happened?" Jim asked. "Do you know?"

"Oh yeah," Otis nodded again. "It was the weather, an if you'd of seen what they flew in to, you'd understand. An that's what was so damn sad about the whole thing cause all day long it was jus as pretty as you could ever imagine, you know, sunny skies with a light breeze, springtime. But that afternoon it all changed jus about an hour or so before they got there when this storm came rollin in from out in the gulf like nothin I'd ever seen before.

"I mean, it turned real dark an real ugly real quick, an they flew right into it. Yes sir, it was really boilin up there, an even though those two army air corps pilots were as good as you could get, that storm closed around them as they were comin into Mobile an they got trapped up there in the middle of all those thunderheads.

"Anyway, an I ain't exactly sure as to what happened or jus how they crashed, but they did... an it killed em all. Now of course we didn't know that until the next day when they finally found the plane, but that afternoon while we all waited at the airport an that storm set in, there wasn't no doubt that every person there was thinkin the same thing."

"Oh my God. His whole family?"

"Yep, an the two pilots... it killed em all."

"Jesus, that's horrible. I mean, I can't even imagine losin your wife an kids like that."

"Oh I know, me neither," Otis agreed. "An let me tell ya, it really tore ol Foster up too. I remember the next day when I picked him up at the airport an then drove him over to the McAlister's house, an how he tried to put on one of those real brave faces like he was okay an all. But by then I knew him well enough to know that deep down, that deep inside of him... he was a real mess."

"Damn Otis, how in the hell do you go on after something like that?"

"You know Jim," he took a heavy breath. "I really don't know. An to be right truthful with ya, I don't ever wanna know. Not after what I saw Foster go through. I'll tell ya, he was jus about as broken up as you could get. In fact, it was on that drive over to the McAlister's that I realized jus how bad he was.

"I remember we talked a little bit, actually he talked an I jus kind of listened cause I really didn't know what to say an that's when he started ramblin on about how he was actually suppose to be on that plane, an that if he would of been he could of told those two pilots to turn around a whole lot sooner. I think in some strange way he felt guilty an blamed himself, an you could see that it was really eatin on him. Specially after he started thinkin of what'd probably happened.

"An what was that?"

"That Melinda had threatened them two pilots with their jobs."

"She what?" Jim scrunched his face. "She threatened em?"

"Yep, ya see she'd always been pretty spoiled an use to gettin her way, but over the years, an with all of Foster's money an power behind her, she'd gotten to the point where she was jus down right demandin."

"Really?"

"Oooh yeah. See, an this was all accordin to Foster, she really really wanted to get back home, an even though those guys knew better than to fly into weather like that, he was pretty convinced that that was what she'd done."

"You mean threatened em?"

"Yep, now nobody really knew that for certain, but as far as me an Foster were concerned after we'd talked an thought about, we both kind of figured that that was what she'd done. Then right after he told me that, he jus kind of laughed an shook his head an quit talkin. I remember I was lookin in the mirror waitin for em to say somethin else but he never did, he jus turned his head an stared out the window with this real lost look on his face an for the rest of the ride he never said another word till we got to the McAlister's."

"But wait a minute," Jim narrowed his eyes. "It wasn't his fault the plane crashed."

"Oh I know, but that didn't stop Foster from thinkin he could of changed things if he'd been there. He was like that, always thinkin that if he was there or involved in some way, that he could make things different. But that time he wasn't, an like I said before, I think that that really ate on him."

"So he really blamed himself?"

"Oh yeah... or at least I think he did. In fact, I think he carried that guilt with em all the way up until the day he died. He never really was the same after that accident I don't think. Anyway, about four or five days later they had one of the biggest funerals that I'd ever seen, even bigger than the Judge's. I'll tell ya, people came from everywhere, an after the Reverend Stone had blessed em an had said their final prayers of passin, Foster laid Melinda an his two little boy's to rest right next to her daddy."

"Now that whole week was jus about one of the saddest times that I can ever remember, but after the funeral was over an after everybody'd gone an the weeks slowly turned into months I really started to get worried about him."

"Why... what'd he do? He didn't go crazy did he?"

"Oh no, but it was like he, well... it was like he'd jus shut everybody out an bottled all that grief an anger up inside of him so nobody could see it. An then he started drinkin. Now Foster always did like his liquor, but after that crash he started in on the bottle pretty heavy an that's when he really began to change."

"What-a-ya mean?"

"Well," Otis sighed as he thought back. "To me, an I was jus about as close to him as anyone, it seemed as if he hated the whole goddamn world an didn't give a shit about nothin or nobody anymore."

"Really?"

"Oh yeah, see, you gotta remember his whole world had jus been ripped apart an his most treasured possessions had jus been taken from him. An even though he had all the money an power in the world, he couldn't get em back an that was somethin that really pissed him off. In fact, I think it was pretty much at that point that he'd decided he wasn't ever gonna care about anyone again."

"But wait a minute. What about Willie?" Jim asked. "Where in the heck was she? I mean, I thought they were supposed to be really hot an heavy? Didn't she like try an save him or anything?"

"Oh they were, an I think she did actually," Otis replied. "Or at least as best she could, but if I remember right they really didn't get to see much of each other until the beginnin of that summer. See, she was still in school

an it wasn't but about a week or so after the funeral that Foster took off an went back to Washinton, an that's where he pretty much stayed until summer cause to be right truthful with ya, I don't think he liked, or for that matter, could handle be'n in his house all alone. But that summer when he finally took his break an came back home, well, that's when him an Willie really started to see a lot of each other. I'll tell ya, she really helped him through a terrible time. In fact, I think that that's when she finally became a real part of his life."

"Ah haa," Jim smiled and blurted as if he knew what Otis was going to say before he could tell him. "An that's when they got married, isn't it?"

"Actually," Otis chuckled and shook his head. "No it isn't, but I'll tell ya, they sure weren't sneakin around anymore like they use to."

"What?" Jim exclaimed. "What-a-you mean they didn't get married? I thought they were in love an all that stuff? An Foster's wife was gone, so what was the deal?"

"Oh they were," Otis agreed. "Or at least Willie was I know that for sure. An you're right, Foster's wife was gone. But you gotta remember it'd only been about five or six months since the crash an to tell you the truth, I really don't think he was ready to get married again. Or, for that matter... really wanted to."

"So they really didn't get married?"

"Nope," Otis shook his head.

"Not ever?" Jim raised his eyebrows.

"Nope," Otis assured for a final time. "Not ever."

Sitting for a second in thought, Jim took a sip from his beer then narrowed his eyes and stared as if he were trying to figure everything out. His mind was whirling, but after what was clearly a frustrating moment of thought, he emitted a heavy sigh and then shook his head.

"Okay okay, so they didn't get married. But I don't understand, what the heck happened?"

"Well, at the time I really wasn't sure. But the real reason, an of course this was all accordin to Willie, was that Foster had told her that it was jus too early. That an elected official like he was needed to wait at least a year or so before he got married again so that it didn't look so bad."

"An are you tellin me that she actually bought that line of crap?" Jim scoffed.

"Well," Otis drawled. "I really don't think so, but she was in love an you know how young girls can get when they're like that? Anyway, like I was jus sayin, they really saw a lot of each other that summer an even though he didn't *marry her, she was his girl an it didn't take long before everybody in town knew it, includin her foster parents or whatever it was they were."*

"Oh yeah, I almost forgot about them," Jim nodded. "I'll bet ol Mrs. Portman didn't like that very much did she?"

"Well," Otis grinned. "Accordin to Willie, no she didn't. In fact, I think it'd be pretty safe to say that she was jus about as upset with her as she could get. See, she knew Foster for who an what he really was, an even though she felt sorry that he'd lost his family an all, Willie said that she'd tried jus about everything she could to keep her away from him. She said that they'd had a couple of pretty big arguments where Mrs. Portman had tried to convince her of how wrong it was an how he was jus use'n her like a whore but it didn't do no good cause Willie didn't wanna hear it. She always was jus about as stubborn an bull headed as you could get," he laughed.

"Anyway, I think she must of ended up winnin the biggest part of them arguments cause for the rest of that summer she continued to see Foster. An even though I think it broke ol Mrs. Portman's heart that she was go'n against her wishes, she stood by her."

"So they were out in the open?"

"Yep, wherever Foster was, Willie was. An let me tell ya, they was together a whole lot. Willie was livin life like she never could've dreamed. We boated an checked his ships that were waitin to be loaded or repaired an for the first time in her life she began to travel."

"Travel? To where?"

"Hell, to wherever they wanted. Most of the times it was jus one of those quick little weekend get aways to the beach in Destin or to the Keys in Florida. Shit, I was always taken em to the airport to go somewhere. Then that September, she went back to her last year of college an ol Foster, well, he finally climbed back up in the saddle an went back to do'n business like he use to.

"Now like I've said before, he was always thinkin an plannin way ahead. I don't know how he did it but he did, that's jus the way he was. Anyway, it was later that fall when I overheard him an Ralston talkin one day. I was drivin em over to look at a new piece of property that he'd jus bought for his new office buildin when I heard him tell Ralston two things. One, was that he wanted all of his oil wells that were up on the Davenport property pumpin away slowed down to a trickle, an two, was that he wanted his new buildin built jus as fast as it could."

"Wait a minute. Why in the hell did he want his buildin built so fast for, an why'd he wanna shut down his oil wells?" Jim scrunched his face. "That just don't make sense."

"Well," Otis began. "He said that war was comin an he wanted it built before it started cause he was afraid that when it did, that there wouldn't be any materials left to build it with. That everything that this country had would go to the war, includin all of his oil which would then be in real high demand an go up in price."

"War? You mean as in World War II?"

"Yep... that's the one. An let me tell you, he was damn serious too."

"An what year was this again?" Jim narrowed his eyes into a dubious gaze.

"The fall of 38," Otis replied as he took a sip.

"An you're tellin me that he knew war was comin?"

"Yep, that's exactly what I'm tellin you."

"Oh come on," Jim laughed and rolled his eyes. "Give me a break. How in the hell did he know that? I mean, that was over three years before Japan even attacked us."

"Well, that's exactly what I wanted to know too, so I asked him when I took him home later that day an I'll tell ya, what he told me scared the hell right out-a me."

"Really?"

"Oh yeah, see, I guess for years he'd been sendin ships loaded with aluminum oxide or whatever the hell it was over to Japan an Germany an he knew exactly what they were do'n with it."

"An what was that?"

"Buildin airplanes, lots an lots of airplanes to attack people with an he said that they was never gonna stop. Yes sir, what he told me in the car that day really got me to thinkin. Then right about a year later an jus like he'd said it would, it all started over there in Europe in the fall of 39. I remember I'd jus taken him an Willie to the airport. See, she still wanted to be a lawyer in the worst of ways an right after she graduated from college earlier that spring Foster enrolled her in another one up in New York. It was a law school, you know, one of them real fancy ones. Anyway, ol Willie was all excited cause he had her an apartment an a car an--."

"Whoa whoa whoaaa," Jim interrupted then looked on as if once again he'd heard incorrectly. "He did what? He enrolled her in law school? In New York?"

"Yep," Otis replied.

"But what about the Portmans? I thought they were sendin her to school? What'd she do with them, just dump em?"

"Oh heck no, Willie loved those people, an they loved her too, an she wasn't gonna go nowhere or do nothin without their blessins. She told me that too, but she really wanted to go an I guess she must of jus kept on arguin an whine'n until she'd worn ol Mrs. Portman down to almost nothin. An although she still didn't like the idea of Willie an Foster be'n together, or of her jauntin off to New York to go to school, she knew what an opportunity it was an after Foster had offered to pay for everything, an I mean everything, well, I guess that that's when she finally broke down an gave in."

"Damn, that sounds just like something one of my kids would do," Jim laughed.

"Yeah, mine too," Otis agreed.

"Anyway, like I was sayin, we'd jus gotten to the airport an was loadin their bags onto the plane when I overheard one of the pilots ask Foster if he'd heard the news yet. Now for some reason, an I really don't know why, but when that young boy asked him that it really caught my attention. Maybe it was the way he said it or maybe it was the tone of his voice, I ain't really sure, but jus as soon as he had I stopped right there on the spot an turned around."

"Senator, ma'am," the young pilot greeted as Foster and Willie approached, his eyes lingering on Willie a little longer than what they should have. "Good morning. Senator, did you hear the news?" he asked before either could respond, unable to contain his excitement.

"The news?" Foster drawled with a casual indifference as he helped Willie to the first step.

"Yes sir, the news."

"And what's that son?" Foster asked and turned back.

"Well sir," he began with a quick and somewhat awkward glance to the beautiful young woman who'd stopped and turned to listen. "The mad man, the one they call Hitler over in Germany, they say he attacked Poland this morning. Can you believe that?" He finished then waited with an anticipating gaze.

To Foster the young man's words were music to his ears; war was profitable, very profitable and he knew it. He'd predicted it over a year ago and now it was finally happening, and as a sense of self-satisfaction slowly enveloped him, he took a long deep breath and stuffed his hands into his pockets. "Yeah son," he nodded ever so slowly. "Actually I can."

"Well, I'm sure glad we're not over there," he voiced his opinion. "I mean, we sure don't need to be fighting in no crazy war again."

"No we don't," Foster agreed with sort of a solemn gaze as he glanced between the young pilot and Willie. "But we will," he added in a tone that'd turned grave and serious. "An you can bet on it. Yes sir, we'll be over there just like we were before... and a whole lot sooner than anybody thinks."

"So he really did know?"

"Oh yeah," Otis nodded. "He knew all right, an when he told that young boy that it wouldn't be long before we'd be over there too, well, that's when I really got to thinkin cause over the years I'd come to learn one thing, an that was that jus about every single thing that Foster Siler had ever predicted or said was gonna happen... happened."

CHAPTER 59

———◆———

FOR THE LAST FEW YEARS Foster had been sending heavily loaded shipments of alumina to Europe and Japan and was well aware of the
turmoil that was building throughout the world. The clouds of war
had been gathering for some time, and in doing so they'd created
a dark and stormy sea of unrest between countries. Countries that
would soon wage war on an unprecedented scale against each other
in a quest for global domination.

Japan had already invaded China in 37 in what they had perceived as their sovereign right to rule Asia, and in Europe the winds
of war had begun to blow as well. For years Hitler had been rearm-
ing Germany with one of the greatest military and industrial expan-
sions their country had ever seen, and in doing so his aggression had
grown into a fanatical state that would soon plunge the planet into
another world war.

His war machine was ready, and in an act that had been
emboldened by his earlier uncontested conquests of Austria and
Czechoslovakia, he quickly set his sights on Poland. Then on
September first of 1939, and just three days before Willie walked
into the halls of Columbia College to begin her first year of law
school, Hitler mobilized his armies and invaded their country. Two
days later, Britain and France declared war on Germany and the
Second World War began.

The fighting was instant and vicious, and in his determination
to win, Hitler struck hard at the heart of the merchant vessels that
were bound for Britain. His U-boats decimated the slow moving convoy lines and by the end of January of 1940 they'd sunk more than

a hundred vessels. They had an aggressive and unrelenting goal to sever the supply lines, and the need for new ships to aid and assist the British became an instant concern. It was the lifeblood to their very existence. They were an island nation and highly dependent on imported goods, requiring more than a million tons of material a week to fight and survive.

But to the cold and uncaring Foster it was nothing more than a golden opportunity that'd just been presented on a silver platter. War was profitable, and even though he knew that the German U-boats prowling the Atlantic could sink a large percentage of his ships, he ordered his older more heavily subsidized ones into the dark and dangerous waters of Europe. To help and assist the English in their time of desperation and growing need for supplies.

He would make a small fortune for what many would perceive as an act of benevolence for it was through the Treasury Department and the Bureau of War Risk Insurance that he had acquired his government backed policies on all of his ships. Policies that had been grossly over inflated in values and that were paid in full almost as soon as the ships had hit the ocean floor. The proceeds of which instantly spawned new ones at Siler Shipbuilding.

Then in June of 1940 Hitler invaded France. The German war machine with its Luftwaffe fighters and Stuka dive-bombers quickly overwhelmed the French and the country fell after only two weeks of fighting. The Fuhrer was overjoyed, and almost overnight he established new submarine bases on her shores and intensified his attacks. Now with a direct and unimpeded access to the Atlantic, he changed his tactics and began to attack the slow moving convoys farther to the west.

The British responded with the best and most advanced anti-submarine escorts they had but it wasn't enough and by October of that year the U-boats of the Kriegsmarine, who were now operating in wolf-packs and with almost complete impunity, had sunk another two hundred and seventy more ships. There seemed to be no end to the devastation and the need for new ships quickly exceeded anything anyone had ever expected. And even though orders had already been placed by the British with U. S. shipyards to replace their wartime loses, it wasn't enough.

The Battle of the Atlantic had begun and so had the Battle of Britain. Hitler was determined to control both the seas and skies over England, but the British, in a fight for their very survival, rose with great courage and in a stance against tyranny, fought back with a tenacious perseverance. The times were tense and quickly growing worse, and while the people and the politicians of America watched and argued as to whether or not the country should become involved, the British fought on and the ambitious Senator from Alabama quietly prepared his companies for war.

Pulling two more beers from the cooler Jim set them both on the table then pushed one toward Otis and looked on as if he were deep in thought. "Okay, so let's just hold on a minute here," he said as he popped his top and tried to clarify his thoughts. "Are you tellin me that your boss actually sent his ships into those convoy lines cause he knew that they'd get sunk by those U-boats?"

"Yes sir," Otis replied as he grabbed his beer and popped his top. "That's exactly what I'm tellin you, an every time one of em did he had Ralston hire more men cause he got to build himself a brand new one. See, everyone of em was insured through the good ol Federal Government, an before they'd even hit the bottom of the ocean floor he was orderin more steel."

"But wait a minute," he stared with a concerned look. "What about the men? You know the guys on the boats? I mean Jesus, what a son-of-a-bitch, didn't he give a shit about anybody?"

"Well," Otis drawled matter of factly. "To be right truthful with you, after he lost his wife an kids, an other than Willie, I really don't think so."

Exhaling with a heavy sigh Jim took a short sip from his beer, shook his head in disbelief then sat back and continued to listen.

"Anyway, by the summer of 1940, Foster had over five thousand men workin for em an they were buildin the hell out-a ships. Then that fall, an right before Willie went back to New York to go to her second year of law school, he moved into his brand new seventeen-story office buildin. His worldwide corporate headquarters as he called it. Complete with a great big beautiful two-story open lobby that had a fourteen-foot round globe set right smack dab in the middle of it. I remember it was settin down in this square hole in the floor that looked like a little swimmin pool with a little knee wall around it that was made out of granite or marble or somethin."

"Damn, he built that thing quick?"

"Yep, an let me tell you, he was damn proud of it too. I remember right after it was done, it was jus a few days or so before the grand openin. He wanted to do a walk through, you know to check an make sure that there wasn't nothin left that needed to be done before everybody saw it. Now most of the time when I drove Foster around I usually waited for him by the car, but for some reason that day, an I ain't really sure as to why, he invited me to tag along with him an Miss Vicki. He jus did things like that every once in awhile. You know, kind of like time when I followed him around on his first boat, nice things that he didn't have to do but did.

"Anyway, we started on the top floor with him an Ralston's offices lookin out over the bay an for the next hour an a half we went from floor to floor until we'd worked our way back down to the bottom. Miss Vicki took notes on everything an after we was all done, we stopped in the lobby so he could watch the men put the last of all his little black ships on that globe."

"His little black what?" Jim cocked his head.

"His little black ships," Otis repeated and laughed. "You know, little cardboard cutouts that showed which countries his ships went to. One for each an every ship that he had, an let me tell you he had a whole bunch of em. An not only that, he also knew where everyone of em was suppose to be."

"You need another one there," Foster barked at the workman on the ladder.

"Where's that sir?" The young man quickly turned to the sound of Foster's authoritative voice.

"There." He raised his arm and pointed to the country of Great Britain. "Right there."

"Herrre?" The man questioned and touched the globe where Foster was pointing.

"Yes," Foster huffed as he stuffed his hands in his pockets and frowned. "It's called England, and if you knew what was going on in the world today, you'd know that our country is helping them in their war against Germany. And I'm sending ships there. Lots of ships, so stick another one up there you hear."

"Yes sir, but my paper says that it only gets one."

"Dammit son, I don't care what your paper says," he growled. "I want two ships up there you understand. Now, if you could be so kind as to stick it on and then get down and turn this thing on, I would really like to see it work before I leave. Lord knows I've spent enough money on the damn thing."

"Ye ye, yes sir," the young man stammered as he hastily stuck another ship to the globe then scurried down the ladder and flipped the switch to the giant ball.

"Now in all my thirty-five years of livin, I'd never seen anything quite like that globe, an when that ol boy turned that switch on an it began to turn I really couldn't believe it."

"Believe it? Believe what?" Jim questioned and took a sip.

"All of his little black ships," Otis replied. "That he had stuck all over it. I mean, I knew he had a lot of em, but these damn things were everywhere an it wasn't until that globe had started to spin that I finally realized what ol Foster had actually done."

"An what was that?"

"That he'd gone an built himself a real honest ta God empire, an that globe was his monument to let everyone know jus how big it was," he laughed. "Anyway, I can still remember standin there with him an Miss Vicki, watchin an starin as it slowly turned. An I can stll remember how proud I felt too. I was there when he'd started it all with his first ship, an now here he was one of the richest men in the whole state an I was standin right there with him."

"So is all a them little black boats yours boss?" Otis asked as the globe began to spin. "I mean, are all them your ships?"

"They sure are Otis," Foster replied with a smile as he continued to stare and admire the spinning orb. "All one hundred and sixteen of em."

"Wow boss, that shor is a bunch."

"Yes it is," Foster replied as he continued to smile.

"An so is that where all those people are fightin?" he asked and pointed. "Where that man jus put your boat?"

"Yes, it is actually," Foster answered with a casual glance to his long time employee. "A man named Hitler is trying to take over all those countries over there. See, that whole area right there is called Europe," he pointed to the globe. "And England is just about the only one that he hasn't defeated yet."

"An is he gonna win?"

"Well Otis," Foster sighed as if he were deep in thought. "He just might because I'm afraid that the British can only hold on for so long. They're a good people and a strong brave nation, but they need our help. More help than what they're getting. They need the industrial might and manpower that our country has to offer, and if they don't get it and get it pretty soon, I'm afraid that eventually they'll fall just like the rest of those other countries. And then over here," he pointed to the globe again as it continued to spin. "We have the Japanese raising hell in the South Pacific."

"Well ain't we gonna do that, I mean go over there an help em? You know, them England people."

"No," he answered with a smile in light of Otis's comment. "No, we're not."

"We're not?" Otis cocked his head and then stared with a confused look. "But why not?"

"Well, it's kind of complicated, and controversial really. See, there's a whole bunch of people back in Washington who don't wanna get involved because they think that the Germans, and the Japanese for that matter, will just stop after they've conquered all those little countries and that they'll just stay on their sides of the oceans." He took a heavy breath then went on. "But they're fools, all of em. And they're wrong, dead wrong. They'll never stop. Hitler's a madman who is absolutely obsessed with power, and the Japanese, well, to tell you the truth, they're just as bad if not worse. And if you want my opinion, I think that what they both really want, and what they really have plans for, is to try and conquer the whole goddamn world. And let me tell you, that includes us too.

"Anyway," he took another breath and continued to stare as if he were studying the globe. "For our country to actually go to war, the Senate and Congress have to approve it and vote on it. Now that's really a good thing, but right now we have just a few to many indecisive idiots back in Washington who couldn't agree on whether the damn sun was going up or down. In fact, they're just about the biggest bunch of misguided morons I've ever met. There are some of them who think we should and some who think we shouldn't, but my bet is, is that in the end, we'll end up going to war too. And my guess is... is that it'll be a whole lot sooner than what anyone thinks.

"Now to actually get everybody in Washington to agree to that, well, that's really gonna take something, and by that I mean something big. You know, something that'll gain the attention of the entire nation and unite us like we've never been before. Now I don't know exactly what that'll be or when it'll happen, but I do know that it's coming. Trust me Otis, it's coming... I can feel it."

"Now to me it seemed like Foster had hardly gotten those words out of his mouth before another whole year had passed by an Willie was taken off to go back to New York again. It was her third year up there an she was do'n real good. Like I always said, she was real smart. In fact, if I recall correctly, I think she was second or third in her class. We were all real real proud of her too.

"Anyway, it was early fall of 41, an jus like ol Foster had said they would the Germans an the Japanese kept on attackin country after country. Hitler was completely out of control an the Japanese, well, they was jus as bad but still nobody wanted another war an nobody thought that it'd reach all the way over here. But all that changed jus a few months later in December."

"That's right," Jim blurted and banged his can onto the table. "Pearl Harbor!"

"Yep," Otis nodded. "Sunday December 7ᵗʰ, 1941. Ol Foster had always said that it'd take somethin real big to bring this nation together an get Congress off their asses, an I guess Pearl Harbor was jus about as big as it got. I remember I was at home an had jus finished eatin lunch when I got a call from Miss Vicki to go an get Foster right away an to take him to the airport--."

"Whoa whoa whoaaa," Jim interrupted and then scrunched his face. "You gotta what? A callll? You mean, like on the telephone?"

"Well yeah," Otis retorted and grinned. "That's usually how you get em isn't it?"

"Well sure," Jim laughed. "But how'd you get a phone? I mean shit Otis, come on, you're black an that was 1941."

"Oh thaaat," Otis chuckled. "Yeaaah, well, their was a lot of people that wanted to know that," he chuckled again and shook his head. "An I really wish that I could take credit for it but I can't cause it was Foster. See, he had one put in my house years ago so he could always get a hold of me if he wanted. Shit, for years I was the only one in my neighborhood who had one.

"Anyway, jus as soon as I got that call I went an got Foster an then took him straight to the airport so he could fly back to Washinton. I remember we

talked a bit on the way about how he'd always said that it'd take something real big to bring this nation together an without even knowin how bad it really was he told me that this was it. That this had to end the debate an before the week was out, he was certain that we'd be at war. That even the most reluctant ones that'd kept us out of the fightin in Europe would have to bow to the pressure for revenge. But I'll tell ya when he told me all of that, he looked real worried an that scared me, but I guess at that time... everybody was scared.

"Then the next day, I remember listenin to Roosevelt's speech on the radio. A date which will live in infamy," he imitated the man's voice and then shook his head. "I tell ya, I'll never forget it."

"Oh hell no," Jim quickly added. "Me neither."

"An then what was it?" Otis paused and squinted as if he were concentrating. "Jus an hour or so after that speech an pretty much jus like Foster had said they would... we declared war."

"Oh yeaaah, I remember that too," Jim nodded. "Hell, three days later I was in the Navy. Ended up drivin landin crafts of all things. Shit I even got shot," he grinned and then proudly pointed to his left shoulder. "Right here. It was D-Day, Omaha Beach. We were one of the first ones to hit the sands an took some of the heaviest machine gun fire that you could ever imagine. I'll tell ya, there was bullets flyin everywhere an I jus knew that I was gonna die right there in that boat." He shook his head and then lowered his voice into a more somber tone.

"But ya know, I was one of the lucky ones that day cause most of the men I carried in that mornin never even made it across the sand." He sighed as if to give homage to the dead. "Anyway, that pretty much took me out of the war cause by the time I healed up to where I could function again we were on the back side of it an there wasn't much use for landin craft drivers." He finished with another sigh and then changed the subject. "So what about you? What branch were you in?"

"Well," Otis drawled as if he were still disappointed that he never served. "The Army... but it was only for a day or two."

"A day or two?" Jim cocked his head. "What-a-you mean?"

"Well, I'd gone an joined up so I could go kill me some Germans an some Japanese jus like everybody else when I went an told Miss Vicki. You know, to say goodbye an all to her an Dawn, an to tell her to tell Foster cause he was in Washinton. Anyway, before I could even make it back down an out of the buildin I was stopped by one of the security guards in the lobby an told to go straight back up to her office."

"*For what?*"

"*Well, I guess she'd picked up the phone before I was even out the door an had called Foster. She told me when I told her that I'd joined that he wasn't gonna like it an good God was she ever right. I remember as soon as I walked back into her office an her handin me the phone with this look on her face that said boy was I ever in trouble. Now in all the years that I'd work for him, that was the first an only time that he'd ever yelled at me an let me tell ya, did he ever chew my ass. Yes sir, was I ever glad that he was in Washinton an I was in Mobile.*" He laughed.

"*Anyway, after he was all done yellin, he told me that what he really didn't want was for me to go traipsin off to war an get myself killed cause he didn't wanna have to train anyone else to take my place. Sooo, he said that he'd fix it.*"

"*Fix it, how?*"

"*Well, I believe he called up some general or somebody an that was it. See, ol Foster was real real powerful an if he wanted somethin done or somethin to happen, you could bet your sweet ass that it was gonna happen. Anyway, before I even got the chance to report in an get myself killed, I had my discharge papers.*"

"*Really, just like that?*"

"*Yep, jus like that. I think the official classification was 2-A, you know, deferred due to critical civilian work.*" He laughed again. "*An then jus as soon as school had let out at the end of that semester, he had Willie come back home too. He was real worried about her be'n up there in New York cause he already knew that the Germans could reach across the Atlantic. An like he said, if the Japanese could bomb us the Germans could too, an since we'd declared all out war on both countries, anything an everything was fair game. Includin New York City.*"

The attack on Pearl Harbor for the most part came as a surprise and not only stunned a sleeping nation but filled it with a tremendous resolve. America was now at war, and as the young men and women from around the nation rose to the call for revenge and flocked to the recruiting offices, the gears of the country's giant industrial engine came to life and slowly began to turn.

The need for wartime goods was instant and overwhelming, and it didn't take long for Foster to use his political influence and position his company in front of the U. S. Maritime Commission. The Navy needed ships on an unprecedented scale, and as one of the leading ship builders in the nation, the committee quickly designated Siler Shipbuilding as one of their nine emergency shipyards that would focus solely on warship production.

Its first wartime contract called for twenty liberty ships. A four hundred and forty-one foot long cargo vessel that had been specifically designed to handle the mass transportation of men and equipment across the oceans of the world. They were America's lifelines to her armed forces, ensuring that they were well supplied. Foster hired men by the thousands and by March of 42 he had over eighteen thousand people working for him. Their goal was simple, to build and deliver ships faster than the Germans and the Japanese could sink them.

They innovated and developed new building techniques, and by October of that same year his company had built all twenty ships. The Navy couldn't have been happier, but with its heavy losses on the open seas, a shift in production was necessitated. They needed tankers to carry fuel and before the last Liberty Ship had even been splashed, Siler Shipbuilding had secured another new contract to build a hundred and two T-2 Tankers. A five hundred and twenty-foot long fuel transporter.

The war raged on, and as the young men and women were deployed onto the battlefield around the globe, the death toll quickly began to mount. The Japanese and the Germans proved to be both a cunning and ruthless enemy that would stop at nothing to win, and as the fighting progressed it soon became clear that it would be a long and bloody battle.

The cost in lives was great, and the news and propaganda that came back from overseas reflected the worst. It seemed as if America could lose, and even though the Battle of Midway in June was a victory and had boosted morale, the future looked grim and uncertain. The country was fighting on two different fronts that were thousands of miles away from her shores. It was an unimaginable undertaking, but the American people in support of their troops banded together with a tremendous resolve and rose to the challenge. National pride soared and along with it, so did the productive output of its industries.

The entire economy had shifted into a wartime production with plants and factories operating at full capacity twenty-four hours a day seven days a week. Planes and tanks and equipment rolled off of assembly lines from around the country in record numbers and soon found their way into battle. America had finally awakened from its long long slumber and was now applying the full force of her industrial might towards the war. Everything that she had went to the war and the troops, and as the fighting intensified, rations were implemented and enforced. Consumer goods took a backseat to the needs of the military and it soon became a time of perseverance and sacrifice.

"So as soon as the war hit ol Foster started buildin ships for the Navy huh?"

"Yes sir, right after Pearl Harbor. See, he was in pretty tight with all them fellers up there in the war department, an right after we were attacked he got them to designate his company as one of the nine emergency shipyards in the nation that was to focus solely on warship production."

"Oh really?" Jim rolled his eyes with a hint of cynicism "Well, who could've guessed that one."

"Ooh I know," Otis agreed. "But that's how he worked. Anyway, from what all I can remember, jus as soon as he'd built all of those Liberty Ships, he started buildin oil tankers. An not jus a few of em either. In fact, what was it?" he squinted and cocked his head in an effort to recall the past. "By about the end of 42 I think it was, he had close to thirty thousand men workin for em an after they got their production line rollin, they was splashin a brand new ship jus about every ten days or so."

"No way," Jim set back.

"Oh hell yeah. I'll tell ya, I'd never seen anything like it in my life. It was like that whole shipyard was one great big giant assembly line. I mean, there was men an cranes everywhere, an boy did they ever work em hard. Twenty-four hours a day seven days a week. They never stopped. It was the war, an ol Foster was determined to build ships faster than anyone else there was."

"Damn, I didn't know that," Jim replied. "I mean, I didn't know that they could build a ship that fast. Jeeesus Chriiiist, that's unbelievable."

"Unbelievable?" Otis repeated. "Shit it wasn't jus unbelievable, it was unheard of. I mean their wasn't anyone in the world who'd ever built an delivered ships that fast, but boy they sure did. An let me tell ya somethin else too. Somethin that was really amazin."

"An what was that?"

"Was to think that they kept that pace up for another two an a half more years."

"Goddamn, that is amazing," Jim shook his head. *"But wait a minute,"* he suddenly asked as he'd forgotten about her. *"What about Willie? What'd she do after the war hit?"*

"Willie?" Otis grinned.

"Yeah Willie," Jim repeated. *"You know, the gal that we've been talkin about for the last couple of hours. What'd she do? Did she go back to school?"*

"Well," Otis drawled. *"No she didn't."*

"She didn't, why not? I thought she wanted to be a lawyer."

"Oh she did, but ol Foster wouldn't let her go back to New York. See, he was still all worried that the Germans were gonna come over an bomb us so he made her stay here in Mobile."

"Really?"

"Yep."

"An what'd she think of that?"

"Well," Otis chuckled. *"She really didn't like it. In fact, she didn't like it at all, but we were at war an so jus like everyone else had done back then, she put down her books an went to work to help our boys overseas."*

"Really... do'n what?"

"Workin for Foster. In fact, she even moved in with him. Not too awfully long after she'd gotten back. See, he'd finally proposed to her over the holidays an had promised to marry her jus as soon as things settled down an he could get all of his companies in order. I remember the day she told me an how happy she was, an how she kept showin me that big ol diamond ring that he'd given her."

"But wait a minute," Jim looked on curiously. *"I thought you said that they never got married?"*

"Oooh, they didn't."

"They didn't?"

"Nope." Otis shook his head.

"Well what happened?" He shrugged his shoulders. *"I mean?"*

"Well," Otis sighed as he thought back. *"I believe it all started right around the end of 42. Almost a whole year after she'd moved in with him. I guess the war in some way or another took its toll on everyone, an Willie, well, she wasn't no different than anyone else. An even though she was without a doubt one of the most striking twenty-seven year old women that you'd ever seen, an lived a life of unheard luxury with one of the wealthiest an most*

powerful men in the country, I think she felt lonelier than she had ever been before."

"Lonely?" Jim scoffed. "What-a-ya mean lonely? What in the hell she have to be lonely about?"

"Well for one, Foster was never home an when he was I guess they were hardly ever together. She told me one day that for some reason she felt as if they never would get married, an that they were driftin apart, an that he'd grown cold an distant. Now naturally she blamed it on the war an the fact that he worked so much, but that wasn't it at all, it was him. See, I really don't think that he wanted to get married, an in the chaos of a world that'd gone completely mad, he kept puttin Willie off with one excuse after another."

"Well then why in the hell did he propose to her? I mean, that just don't make sense stringin her along like that."

"Oh I know," Otis agreed. "An to be right truthful with you, I really ain't sure as to why he did it. I knew he had other women all over the place, but he'd always had them, even when Melinda was alive. Anyway, I really felt sorry for her cause in a way I think she felt trapped between what she had an what she'd always dreamed of havin."

"An what was that?" Jim narrowed his eyes.

"A husband... an kids," Otis replied. "You know... a family."

"Anyway, they never did get married, an jus about the time that ol Willie had had enough of Foster's crap an of him stringin her along, well, that's when she met the new liaison officer from the Navy in charge of quality control. It was jus a couple of weeks before Christmas when he stepped through the doors of Siler Shipbuilding."

"The whooo?"

"The new investigator for the Navy. See, right by about the end of that year Foster started havin trouble with some of the ships he'd built, an let me tell you, I ain't talkin jus a little trouble either. In fact, one of em had actually broke in half an sunk."

"No way?"

"Oh yeah. An the Navy an the War Department, well, they both wanted answers."

CHAPTER 60

———◆———

THERE HAD BEEN NUMEROUS REPORTS and claims of structural defects on many of the ships that'd come from Siler Shipbuilding. Cracks and fractures in the decks and the hulls that'd occurred on the open seas, broken welds and missing rivets that'd gone unnoticed, and that'd resulted in serious damage. One of the ships had even sunk because of them, and even though they had most often times been grossly overloaded and the problems had occurred during storms at sea, the Navy wanted answers and quickly launched an investigation.

Suspicion fell directly to the shipyards that'd been using inexperienced workers and new welding techniques to produce large numbers of ships in great haste. It was thought by all to be the reasons the problems had occurred, yet even so, and in their quest for the absolute and undeniable truth, a team of special investigators was dispatched to the corporate headquarters of Siler Shipbuilding.

Their job was simple, to do a thorough and sweeping review of the ways in which the ships were built and then report their findings back to the war department. Led by Captain Daniel Ryan Mitchell, the six-member team of metallurgists and engineers entered through the doors of Siler Shipbuilding just two weeks before Christmas.

"Good morning ma'am," Dan's easy going drawl greeted the young receptionist as he approached her desk. "I'm Captain Mitchell from the Navy and we're here to see Mr. DuPree."

"Oh, yes sir," she smiled and blushed at the handsome man in the uniform. "I believe Mr. DuPree' is expecting you. Please if you would like to have a seat, I'll let him know that you're here," she added as she rose from behind her desk then turned and left.

A few moments later she returned with the man who was second in charge of everything Foster owned, including Siler Shipbuilding. "Captain," Ralston called excitedly as he approached and extended his hand. "I must say it is truly an honor to meet you... truly an honor. Your exploits in the Pacific and the way you saved that aircraft carrier was really something. You're an inspiration to us all and exemplify everything that is best in our military. And I for one, am damn proud to meet you."

"Yes sir, and thank you sir," Dan replied in a humbled tone as he took Ralston's hand. "It's a pleasure to meet you too, but really, I was just doing my duty."

"Duty," Ralston scoffed. "I'd say that what you did was a little more than that," he finished then looked on with a profound sense of admiration. "Anyway, the Senator has instructed me to see that you and your staff here receive the full cooperation of Siler Shipbuilding. Anything that you need or want, you just ask. He even has some office space for you to work out of if you'd like. Believe me, he wants to find the answers to these problems just as bad if not worse than everyone else. His name is on those ships.

"Now, if you'd like to follow me, I'll introduce you to some of the men in our drafting and engineering departments who can assist you and your men with your investigation. They have the plans and specifications to every ship that we're building and refitting."

But just as Ralston had turned to lead the group away, Willie came walking through the door, smiled and said good morning, then froze in a state of disbelief. "Danny?" she cried out in surprise. "Oh my God! Danny!" she repeated as she lunged toward him. "It's you... you're alive!"

"So wait a minute, are you tellin me that the head guy that the Navy had sent out to investigate how Foster was buildin his ships was Willie's old boyfriend?"

"Yes sir," Otis drawled fondly. "Captain Daniel Ryan Mitchell."

"Now wasn't he the boy that lived a couple of farms down from her? You know, the one you said wanted to fly. That she liked a whole bunch."

"Yep, that's the one all right. An boy let me tell ya, did he ever learn to fly. In fact, I believe he was one of our countries first real war time heroes."

"Really?" Jim seemed intrigued.

"Oh yeah, shit he not only received the Air Medal, the Distinguished Flyin Cross, the Silver Star, an the Navy Cross, but also the Medal of Honor, our countries highest award."

"Jesus, what in the hell'd he do? Shoot down every plane in the sky?"

"Well," Otis smiled. "He really didn't talk about it a whole lot, but from what all Willie had told me, he started out over in China with the Flyin Tigers, an then after about a year or so there he got sent to the Pacific as a new squadron leader on one of our carriers. Now I really don't know which one he was on or where exactly they was fightin, but I guess he was one bad ass son-of-a-bitch in an airplane. They say he shot down fourteen enemy fighters the first month he was there an then went on to collect twenty-eight confirmed kills before he finally bought it himself."

"Oh no, what happened?"

"Well, from what all I was told, I guess they got into one of the biggest dog fights that you could have ever imagined tryin to take over one of those islands over there. It had a runway on it that the Japanese had jus built an I guess we really wanted it. Now they must of really wanted to keep it an must of known that we were comin cause by the time our boys got to that island they were already up in the air with every airplane they had, an every one of em was headed straight for our carriers.

"Now even though we had better pilots, they had more planes an it wasn't too long before some of those dive bombers an fighters had slipped past our fighter protection an were in sight our ships. Which meant that not only were they in danger, but that our boys now had to fly straight into their own anti-aircraft fire to chase after em."

"Jesus," Jim sighed. "An I thought landin at Normandy was bad."

"Well, I really wouldn't know," Otis admitted with a profound sense of respect. "I never got that chance. An let me tell ya, after hearin all those stories about the war, I'm not to awfully sure that I would of wanted it. Anyway, some of those dive-bombers that'd slipped through were carryin five hundred pound bombs an Dan knew it, an I guess that's when he noticed one of em drop out-of the clouds an dive straight for his own carrier."

"Ah-hah, he shot em right out of the sky didn't he?"

"Well, not exactly," Otis chuckled and shook his head. "An you really ain't gonna believe this. But, they say that he turned his plane jus as hard as he could an came screamin down out-a the sky through all that anti-aircraft fire an then flew right through the tail section of that dive-bomber right before it dropped its bomb."

"He did whaaat?" Jim looked on in disbelief. "He flew his plane through the other guy's? Jesus, what in the hell'd he do that for? I mean, why didn't he just shoot the guy down?"

"Well," Otis chuckled and shook his head again. "As he put it to me real simple like one day. He was out of bullets an he had to do somethin to save that aircraft carrier an all those men on the deck."

"Out of bullets?"

"Yep, ya see by the time all this'd happened I think he'd already shot down two or three planes an after his first burst of machine gun fire he was empty."

"An so are you tellin me that he just up an flew his plane right through the other one cause he was out of bullets?" Jim's tone seemed to reflect his sense of awe.

"Yes sir," Otis chuckled. "That's exactly what I'm tellin you, cause like he also said, he needed a place to land."

"Jesus, that's crazy."

"Oh hell, tell me about it."

"An so did he saved the carrier?"

"Oh yeah, he saved it all right. They said that that dive bomber spun out-a control an went right over the top of that flight deck an crashed jus on the other side of the ship."

"An so then what happen?" he asked excitedly. "I mean to him?"

"Well," Otis chuckled again. "He crashed. He said he knew jus as soon as he'd hit that ol boy that he was go'n down, an since he was way too low to parachute out, he jus went down with his plane in the ocean. Anyway, after that, well, that's when all of his real troubles started."

"His real troubles?" Jim mocked as if it were an understatement. "Jesus Christ, what in the hell else happened?"

"Well, I guess by the time the fightin had finally stopped, you know, to were they could send out their search planes an look for him, he'd gotten swept out to sea by the wind away from all the ships an was unfortunately spotted an picked up by a Japanese submarine that was leavin the area."

"Oh my God, an they took him prisoner didn't they?"

"Yes sir, an before he knew it, he was on some little island some ninety miles north of the one that they'd jus fought over. It was some sort of hidden base that the Jap's had been operatin out of an they needed to resupply before headin back to Japan, but I guess with the American Navy crawlin all over they decided to lay low an hide out for a few days."

"But didn't we try an look for him?"

"Oh heck yeah, in fact they sent out all kinds of planes. See, the admiral in charge of that battle group was on the carrier that Dan had saved an had actually seen what he'd done. He even saw him crash an climb out of his plane, so they knew he was alive. But unfortunately for him, nobody had seen him get picked up by that sub an after about the third day of searchin an scourin the ocean, they finally gave up an listed him as missin in action.

"Now from everything that I could gather, I guess the Jap's must of jus about beat him half to death tryin to get information out of him, you know, where all those carriers were headed next an stuff like that. But he never talked."

"So how'd he get away? I mean, how'd he escape?"

"Well, by about the third day the Navy had taken complete control of the area an he could see that the commander of that sub was gettin real anxious. Anyway, I guess he knew that they was gettin ready leave, an he knew that they were either gonna kill him or take him back to Japan as a prisoner of war. I remember him tellin me that one day, an that there wasn't no way in hell that he was go'n back to Japan, dead or alive, an so that's when he decided to try an escape."

It was late and the entire camp was asleep including the guard that'd been left to watch him, a sick and sadistic brute who seemed to derive a great pleasure out of inflicting pain. Pain that had been delivered by both feet and fist and by his obvious favorite, a four-foot long bamboo cane that'd left welts and lacerations on Dan's back and arms and legs in an effort to make him talk.

They wanted to know where the American Navy was headed next, and for two straight days he endured beating after beating. They were sadistic and inhuman, a cruelty on a level he never could have imagined and he knew that he couldn't take much more. He had to escape before they killed him or took him back to Japan as a prisoner, but how? He was caged and guarded and on an island in the middle of the South Pacific. He watched the sun set and then later on the moon slowly rise; and then an idea hit him. An idea that would either set him free or end in his death.

The moon was full and although it was still low in the sky, he could see the coil of rope that they'd used to build his cage lying in the sand by a coconut tree. Smiling, he turned his gaze to the beach some fifty yards away and the few large pieces of driftwood laying at the water's edge. Yes it would work, and all he had to do was entice the guard into letting him out of the cage, kill him, then lash the wood together into a make-shift raft and swim out to sea. Then hope like hell that the Navy had taken over the island, and that the patrol planes that protected the battle group and searched the seas and skies for the enemy would somehow spot him.

It was a long shot and he knew it, but he also knew that the guard was slow minded. A dim-witted brute who would delight in showing his superiors how he'd extracted the information they had been wanting all by himself. It would be a dangerous game of life and death, but one no different than what he had already been playing in the air. He thought of it some more and finalized his plan then reached through his cage and dug down into the moistened sand. Packing it into a ball, he then threw it with an audible *'pssssst'* at the guard sleeping some thirty feet away.

But the guard didn't move, and after a long and agonizing moment of uncertainty, he gathered his courage and did it again. Awakening with a startled grunt, the big man shook his head and then sat upright. Brushing the sand from his body, he looked first to the sky and then all around. He was clearly confused and after a check of his surroundings, he turned his head toward Dan. Focusing his eyes, he watched as his captive reached through the cage and then motioned with his hand. A little perturbed that he'd been awaken but drawn by curiosity, he finally rose with a disgruntled huff and grabbed his cane.

Submissively bowing as the big man approached, Dan then sheepishly reached through the cage and began to draw a map in the sand. It was what they themselves had been doing for the last two days in an attempt to communicate and find out where the American Navy was headed. It was an act that instantly changed guard's demeanor, but just as it did Dan stopped drawing and looked him in the eyes then pointed to his canteen.

He needed water like never before but the guard wouldn't have it, and with another disgruntled huff as if to say no, he poked Dan with his cane, spoke in a harsh demanding tone and then pointed to the sand. Shaking his head Dan stood his ground and once again pointed to the canteen. The guard looked furious but even so he finally relented and unsnapped his canteen. He knew that Dan had not had any water in almost two days and he wanted him to continue. Holding the canteen inside of the cage he poured a few gulps of water into Dan's mouth then quickly pulled it back, spoke in an even harsher tone and then pointed to the sand.

Obediently complying, Dan began to draw a map of the area as he knew it. First the island they had attacked, then Australia to the south and Japan to the north. But still his arm was only so long and he could only draw so big from inside the cage. His figures were small and hard to see, and with every intent of frustrating the guard in hopes of letting him out, he feigned his disgust, erased what he had done and then started all over.

He could see that the guard was anxious, yet even so he erased his work once more as if it wasn't good or clear enough. A second later and just as he'd hoped, the frustrated guard grunted and poked him with his cane to back away then unlocked the cage. His plan had worked, he was being let out yet he knew he couldn't just run for there was no way he could beat the guard without a weapon. He saw his gun and knife, but in his weakened condition there was no way he could take them without being killed. He thought for a moment longer and then it came to him; he could use the cane.

Cowering like a frightened animal that'd just been freed, Dan crawled from his cage on his hand and knees then quickly began to smooth out a large area of sand. Turning after he'd finished he looked at the guard then gestured for the cane as if to draw with. He needed it as his weapon but the guard was wary of the young pilot and just stared in a moment of uncertainty, glaring until his desire for information finally overrode his sense of caution. Then, and with an arrogant smirk and a grunt to match, he unsnapped his pistol and patted its side then handed over his cane. Nodding and bowing at his implied action, Dan took the cane then turned away as if he were going to draw.

He knew that this was it and there was no turning back, and that in the next few moments he would either kill or be killed. But to the young lieutenant his freedom was worth it, and without another thought he drove the end of the bamboo rod into the sand and fell forward as if he'd lost his balance. Snapping the cane in half as he landed on top of it he groaned and then stirred as if he couldn't move. A moment later and just as he'd hoped the guard barked and kicked him to get up then knelt in the sand and grabbed the back of his collar.

It was exactly what he'd wanted, and as he rose to his knees with one half of the cane clenched in his hand, he turned to face the big man with a glaring gaze. A split second later, and with all of the strength he had left, Dan flashed a smile then drove the splintered end of the stick up into the man's jaw and through the roof of his mouth. "Take that you black eyed son-of-a-bitch," he whispered in a vengeful voice as he locked eyes with his captor.

The sound of bamboo splintering against bone could easily be heard as the powerful man grabbed at Dan's hands and tried to pull down. But try as he may he failed, for his mind no longer controlled his body and it instantly went limp. He was helpless and could no longer brutalize Dan with his strength, he could only look on and gurgle in what was clearly a plea for his life. A plea that was ignored for after the beatings he'd inflicted, Dan was without mercy, and in a gratifying moment of revenge, he shoved the stick through the man's brain to the top of his skull.

Jerking into uncontrolled spasms as death took its hold, the big man's eyes instantly snapped back into his head. A second later and without another sound, his hands dropped to his side and he fell over into the sand with a deathly thud.

Collapsing in the sand next to him, Dan rested for just a moment then quickly rose back to his knees, took the man's canteen and guzzled another much needed drink. Then taking his knife and gun, he scrambled to the coil of rope. Grabbing it with a nervous look around, he turned and then headed to the beach. He knew that this was his one and only chance of escaping, and with all of the remaining strength he had left he lugged the heavy pieces of driftwood into the water then lashed them together as quickly and as quietly as he could. A short while later, along with the canteen of water, the knife and the pistol that he'd taken from the guard, Lt. Daniel Ryan Mitchell pushed his make shift raft from the shallows and swam out into the vast open ocean.

An hour later, completely exhausted from his ordeal, he finally climbed onboard, tied himself to his raft then rolled over and stared at the stars. They were different than the constellations back home, and as he gazed up at the heavens and the gentle breeze blew his raft farther and farther from the island, he began to wonder as to what fates awaited him. Would he be found, or would he die out here and drift forever? He prayed and hoped that the Navy was still in the area, and that they would somehow find him for he knew that he wouldn't last long. He was at the mercy of the sea, and with that thought lingering in his mind, the daring young aviator from Mobile Alabama closed his eyes and drifted off to sleep.

"Jesus, that's amazing," Jim's voice seemed to reflect his continued sense of awe. "So he did escape?"

"Yep, in the middle of the night on a pile of driftwood that he'd lashed together after he'd killed that guard. He swam out into the ocean an then tied himself to his raft."

"So how'd they find him? I mean how'd he get rescued?"

"Well, I believe he was spotted by a small group of fighters that was out on patrol. I'll tell ya, he was real lucky too cause without even knowin it he ended up driftin straight south, damn near ninety some miles right back down toward that island that they'd all been fightin over. An let me tell ya, it's a damn good thing he did too cause by the time they picked him up he was damn near dead."

"Really?"

"Oh yeah, shit I don't know how long he'd been out there but they said that he wouldn't of lasted another day at sea. In fact, they didn't know if he was gonna make it even after they'd picked him up an got him to the hospital ship. I guess he was pretty much touch an go for a while, but that Admiral that was in charge of that battle group refused to let him die. They said that he had jus about every doctor an nurse on that ship watchin an workin on him twenty-four hours a day.

"Anyway, he finally pulled through, an when he did he came back home a real honest to God war hero. I'll tell ya Jim, that boy was bigger than life, he was handsome an brave, an boy did the women ever love him. Yes sir, he was really somethin. Anyway, after he did a promotional tour for the war effort around the country he came back here to Mobile. An then shortly after that, well, that's when he got assigned to head up the investigation team to Foster's ship buildin company."

"But wait a minute," Jim looked on with a confused expression. "I don't understand. How in the hell'd he go from fighter pilot to investigatin Foster's ship buildin company?"

"Oh hell, that was easy. See, he was actually some sort of structural engineer, an since the Navy wouldn't let him fly combat anymore they assigned him to that."

"Oh, well that makes sense. But still, why'd they clip his wings? I mean, if he was that good an the war was still go'n on."

"Well, I guess those Japs had done a pretty good number on him when they was tryin to find out where all those carriers were headed, an in the beatins that they'd given him they had pretty much destroyed the peripheral vision in one of his eyes. Now he could still fly, he jus couldn't fly combat anymore. Anyway, that's how he got assigned to head up the investigation into Foster's company, an that's how an when him an Willie met up again. An then after that, well, it wasn't too awfully long before the two of them had run off an gotten married."

"They what?" Jim laughed. "They got married?"

"Yep."

"But wait a minute, I thought Willie was engaged to Foster?"

"Oh she was, or at least she was until she caught him with another woman."

"Another woman?" Jim blurted and laughed again. "Are you serious?"

"Oh yeah."

"You mean, he was screwin around on her before they were even married?"

"Yep, that's exactly what he was do'n."

"Well, I can't say I'm that surprised, but damn, didn't the guy ever keep his dick in his pants?"

"Well," Otis chuckled. "To be right truthful with ya, no, I don't believe that he did."

"But he was engaged an supposed to get married," Jim insisted.

"Oh I know," Otis agreed. "But hell, that didn't make no difference to a dog like Foster."

Shaking his head with an amused yet puzzled expression growing on his face, Jim sat for a moment as if he were contemplating some great question. Then, and with a long heavy pull from his beer, he sat back in his seat, swallowed the cold foamy mixture and began to smile.

"Okay, so just how'd she catch him? I mean... I really gotta hear this one."

"Well, if I recall correctly it was jus about a week before Christmas. It was a Saturday, an me an Willie had been shoppin. See, Foster was supposed to be in Washinton an couldn't come back home until after the weekend so he asked her to do some shoppin for him.

"*Now Willie really loved Christmas cause it was somethin that she never had as a young girl, so while I drove her around from store to store she bought gifts for jus about everybody you could think of. Anyway, we'd been gone pretty much all day when we finally finished up an decided to head back home, an that's when we jus so happened to drive by the old Battle House Hotel. An right as we did, well, that's when she yelled at me to pull over an stop.*"

"*Stop... for what?*"

"*Well, at first I wasn't sure until I got stopped an had turned around to see what was wrong. I remember she was lookin straight across the street, an that's when I turned an saw him.*"

"*Who?*"

"*Foster, see he'd told her that he had to stay in Washinton which was really no big deal until she saw him comin out of that hotel. Now even that wasn't too awfully bad cause he was always changin plans an wine-in an dine-in the hell out of someone. But when she saw him help some gal out of a car that'd jus pulled up an then kiss her in a way that he really shouldn't of been a do'n, well, that's when I think every dream that she ever had of livin a life with him disappeared.*"

"*Oh nooo... for real?*"

"*Yep,*" Otis nodded. "*Shit, I saw him myself.*"

"*An you guys just happened to be drivin by?*"

"*Yep. We were on our way home.*"

"*Well, wasn't he just a real piece of work?*"

"*Oh yeah, he was a piece of work all right,*" Otis agreed. "*Anyway, Willie knew exactly what be'n at that hotel meant cause if you remember right she'd been there plenty of times herself, an when she saw him kissin on that other girl the way he was, well, I think it jus about broke her heart right in half. I remember her coughin an then cryin out like she'd jus been hit in the stomach, an then her gettin real real quiet.*"

"*Now I'd been lookin at Foster too, but as soon I heard her I looked back up in the mirror to see if she was okay an that's when I saw her bite her bottom lip an then look back up at me all teary eyed. Now even though she never really out an out cried, I knew that she was hurtin an upset so I tried to talk her into leavin. But she wouldn't have nothin to do with it an for the longest time she jus sat there an stared at the door to that hotel.*"

"*Ah man, that had to be tough.*"

"*Oh it was. I'll tell ya, her seein Foster with that other gal like that really hit her hard an I couldn't help but feel sorry for her.*"

"So what'd you guys do? I mean, what'd she do?"

"Well, like I said I wanted to jus get the hell out of there cause Foster an that gal had gone inside, but Willie wouldn't have nothin to do with that so we stayed right where we were an waited."

"Waited? Waited for what?"

"Well, at first I wasn't sure cause she was jus sittin there real quiet like with her head down, like she was lookin an playin with her engagement ring. Then after about three of four minutes of that she opened her door, told me to wait for her an that she'd be right back, an then marched straight across the street. I think that her heartbreak had finally turned into some real anger an before I knew it, she'd disappeared through the doors of that hotel."

"Jesus, what'd she do confront him right in the lobby?"

"Well," Otis chuckled. "There wasn't no doubt that she was upset, an I mean really upset, an I really think that if she'd of had a gun she'd of walked right in there an shot him. But no she didn't, she kept her cool an instead of confrontin him an makin a scene, she jus went in real calm an quiet like an went straight over to the front desk.

"Then, pretendin to be Senator Siler's personal assistant who'd forgotten to do what she'd been told, she got a hold of the front desk manager all embarrassed like an explained her problem an the very special occasion that the Senator had planned. She said that he was real nice an understandin, an after she'd slipped him a fifty dollar tip of Foster's own money for his help, she ordered the most expensive bottle of champagne that they had, charged it to his room an then sent it up to him an his little girlfriend with her big ol diamond engagement ring tied right around the neck of the bottle."

"Oooh my God," Jim laughed. "You've got to be kiddin... she didn't, did she?"

"Yes sir, she sure did."

"Oh man, that's unbelievable. I mean, can you just imagine the look on Foster's face when he got that?" He laughed again as he envisioned the scene. "Oh, an the girl too! What-a-ya think she thought when she saw that ring? I mean wow... what a classy way to tell someone off."

"Wasn't it?" Otis agreed. "I'll tell ya, ol Willie, she really had class."

"So then what'd she do?"

"Well, jus as soon as she got back in the car she told me what all she'd done an after we finally quit laughin, she had me take her back to the house. Then after we got there, she had me help her pack up three or four big suitcases full of her clothes an things, throw em in the car an leave."

"Leave? To where?"

"Well, I took her over to the Portmans."

"To the Portmans?" Jim seemed surprised. "Really?"

"Yep."

"An so what'd ol Mrs. Portman think of all this?"

"Well, at first she was sad cause Willie's heart had been broken, you know, like any mother would've been. But deep down, an if the truth were to really be known, I think that she was jus thrilled. See, I don't think that she ever did like the idea of Willie an Foster together."

"So when'd Foster find out that she had left him?"

"Well," Otis began with a chuckle. "I really ain't for certain, but my guess would be right about the time that room service delivered that bottle of champagne with Willie's engagement ring on it."

"Yeah, I guess you're right. I mean, that is pretty obvious," he laughed and shook his head. "An so what'd he do... I mean after that? Did he try an get her back?"

"Oh sure, in fact he tried the very next day after he got home an saw that she'd actually moved out an left him."

"Wait a minute," Jim cocked his head. "The next day? You mean he actually stayed at the hotel with that other gal? Even after he got that bottle of champagne?"

"Yep, till about noon if I remember right. Which was jus about the time that I got called."

"You... what'd you get called for?"

"Well, even as smart as ol Foster was," Otis chuckled. "He couldn't figure out where in the hell Willie had gone. Or at least that was until I filled him in on how she'd seen him an all."

"Wait a minute, you mean he actually thought that she'd still be there?"

"Oh heck yeah, an he was real surprised that she wasn't too. In fact, I think he thought that he'd jus come home, have an argument, apologize, spend a whole lot of money on her an then everything would be jus fine again. I think he thought that Willie was a whole lot like Melinda an that she'd put up with his crap, but she wasn't, an she wasn't there, she was gone. She'd left him, an that's when I think he finally realized jus how much he cared for her. An that's when he told me, that afternoon, Otis jus as soon as I get her back I'm gonna marry her."

"But they never got married?"

"Oh no."

"*But he did try? I mean, to get her back?*"

"*Oh heck yeah. He tried callin, an sendin flowers an candy, heck, he even had me go over an talk to her an deliver his letters cause she'd quit her job, an since he really didn't wanna see ol Mrs. Portman, I was the only way he had of actually reachin her.*"

"*Really?*"

"*Oh yeah. Anyway, ol Willie, well, she didn't wanna have nothin to do with him. An like she told me, she was tired of his crap an she didn't give a damn about his money. She was a free woman an was out from under his thumb, an besides,*" he added with a growing smile. "*I really think that before the holidays was even over, that she'd gone an fallen head over heels in love with somebody else.*"

"*Ah haaa,*" Jim pointed his finger. "*Let me guess, her old boyfriend right?*"

"*That's right,*" Otis replied as he fondly envisioned the man. "*Captain Daniel Ryan Mitchell of the United States Navy.*"

CHAPTER 61

———◆———

HER THOUGHTS OF HIM HAD materialized almost as soon as she had arrived, and for the next two days as she helped Elizabeth bake and ready for the Christmas holidays, she wondered whether or not to visit. Whether it was proper or befitting in light of her situation. She tried to reason with herself that they were just old friends and nothing more, but something deep inside of her told her that there was more to her desires than just a visit. More to it than just the delivering of Christmas cookies and fudge that she'd made.

She had feelings that were stronger and that touched her in ways she'd never felt before, even with Foster. Feelings in her heart as well as her loins that she couldn't shake and wouldn't go away, and even though she'd already changed her mind twice, she rose this morning determined to see him. She remembered the very first day that they'd met at church all those years ago. The cute young alter boy with the sandy blonde hair and boyish grin who kept staring at her from behind Father Ruggeri. And then of how she would smile and blush then avert her eyes as if she were embarrassed, only to return them a few moments later to see him still looking and smiling.

Then of the sunny days years later, when they were older and would go to the airport and lay in the grass at the end of the runway. Where they would sometimes kiss and make out while the planes took off and landed over the top of them. She remembered his dreams of becoming a pilot, and then of how they'd drifted apart when she'd become involved with Foster and he'd gone away to college. She smiled at the memories and with a final loop of the cinch strap through its ring, she pulled it tight and finished saddling her horse. A second later, she turned to the sound of Elizabeth's voice as she came walking into the barn with a cup of coffee.

"Well, young lady, you're sure getting an early start," she chirped and took a sip.

"Yes ma'am," Willie replied as she flipped the reins over her horse's neck. "It's such a beautiful morning, I thought I'd go for a ride."

"Oh that's nice. And so just where are we headed?"

"Oooh I don't know," Willie smiled and shrugged her shoulders. "No where, really. I just thought that I'd go for a ride since it was so nice out."

"Oh really, just a ride to nowhere, huh?" Liz raised her eyebrows.

"Yeah, you know," Willie drawled and rolled her head. "Just down the road a ways."

"Oooh I see, well surely you're not going to ride that same old trail down to the Mitchell place again are you?" she jested and rolled her eyes. "Heavens to Betsy, I just can't imagine how boring that would be."

It was easy to pick up on the innuendo laced in Liz's voice as well as the knowing but curious gaze that came along with it, and as she checked the cinch strap on her saddle one last time she couldn't help but shake her head and smile. Elizabeth always did have a way of sensing the truth about what she was going to do, and it would have been futile to deny the obvious. It was her built-in motherly instincts and she knew it, and so with a turn and a step toward her, Willie opened her arms and embraced the woman she'd come to care so much for in a warm and loving hug.

"I made him some cookies an fudge," she admitted along with a kiss to her cheek and a reassuring look that she was okay. "Just a little box of goodies for Christmas. Nothing special," she added as if that were all she was going to say. "And now," she smiled as she dropped her stirrup from the horn and then swung up into the saddle. "I'm going to take them to him."

"Well, I'm sure he'll enjoy them, but you be easy on Cricket ya hear," Liz said as she reached up and gently patted her horse's neck. "She hasn't been ridden much since you've been gone and she's gettin pretty old."

"Yes ma'am, I will," Willie replied as she pulled the reins and coaxed her horse to turn.

"Oh, and one more thing," she raised her voice as Willie began to ride away. "You stay out of that hay loft too. I've already heard stories of Mr. Mitchell's conquests, and I don't mean the aerial kind either. I've heard that he has a real smooth way of talkin young ladies into to doing things that they really shouldn't be doing, and war hero or not, that isn't any place for a proper young woman."

"Yes ma'am, I know," Willie turned back with a radiant smile and a devilish gleam to her eyes. "Only he's not the one you have to worry about." Then with the gentle touch of her heals to the flanks of her horse, she kicked Cricket into a trot.

She knew the shortcut all to well and in less than an hour Willie had arrived at the Mitchell's farm. She'd thought of their meeting almost the entire way, worrying with an almost schoolgirl mentality about what she'd say and do when she finally saw him. What his reaction would be when he saw her again. She was nervous and for good reason; she'd rejected his advances for years, and as far as he knew, she was still engaged to one of the wealthiest and most powerful men in the country. A man who's company he was in the midst of investigating.

But everything was different now, for she was no longer bound by the strings of a matrimonial promise she'd given. Yet even so, as she emerged from the trees and into the fields of their farm, she stopped to quell the butterflies growing in her stomach. It had been a long long time since she'd seen the place, and as she looked around and the memories of the times that they'd shared came flooding back, she began to smile. A few moments later, and with a heavy breath of cool morning air for courage, she coaxed her horse with a gentle kick and headed toward the barn.

Yes, the legendary barn she thought, complete with its infamous hayloft which had been rumored to contain the names of almost every girl in town inscribed somewhere inside of it. Every girl, that was, except her. She'd held out against his best and most tenacious efforts and smiled at the thought, and as she slowly crossed the newly plowed fields, she could see that someone was working on the corral that encircled it.

Was it Dan she hoped with the flutter of her heart? She rode on and soon saw that it was. He was nailing a board on top of the fence and had his back to her, yet still he heard her as she came up from behind and turned. "Well," he greeted with a surprised but pleasant drawl as he raised his hand to block the sun. "Good morning."

"Morning," Willie replied with a grin and an inviting gleam to her eyes as she slowly rode up to him. But instead of stopping and talking like he thought, the girl who'd occupied his dreams for so many nights when he was young, rode right on past without another word and headed straight to the barn. Quietly staring as she rode on, he set his hammer on top of the fence and then leaned back against it. What in the hell was she doing he thought? And what in the hell was with that look that she'd just given him? She was engaged to be married, or so he thought. And even though she'd said good morning as if it were just another day, her smile and the look in her eyes as she passed said something completely different. They were wanton and daring and inviting, and left little doubt as to the message that they contained.

It was a look he'd never seen in her before, and with an ever-growing curiosity, he watched as she slowly rode to the barn. Willie had always been a hard one to figure, and this morning was certainly proof that she hadn't changed. Then, and in an action that confused him even further, she stopped her horse some twenty feet short of the barn, looked up to the opened doors of the hayloft and stared. It seemed like forever but it was only for a few short moments until she finally turned her horse back and then stared with a smoldering gaze.

To Dan her message couldn't have been clearer, and it took only a second to decipher its meaning. It was her invitation, and although she'd never said a word, he knew by the look in her eyes exactly what it was. For years he'd tried to entice her into climbing the ladder into the loft and now here she was, beckoning with her eyes for him to join her. A few seconds later, the sultry twenty-seven year old turned back to the barn, coaxed her horse with a gentle kick and then slowly rode into the darkened shadows.

"So ol Willie went an saw him right after she'd moved back in with the Portmans?"

"Yep."

"Well, that sure didn't take her very long did it?"

"Oh hell no," Otis replied. "Like I said earlier, I really think that she liked that boy a whole lot more than she'd ever let on. An after that first visit, they was pretty much together all the time."

"An then they got married?"

"Yep," Otis nodded. "In fact, it wasn't but a couple of months after she'd left Foster."

"Really? Damn, that was quick."

"Yep."

"An so what'd ol Foster think of that?"

"Well, to be right truthful with ya, he really didn't say a whole lot, or at least to me he didn't. But deep down I don't believe that he liked it cause in a way I think he actually thought that Willie still belonged to him. That she was his an nobody else's. Anyway, their marriage," he sighed. "Well, it didn't last but about a year."

"A year?" Jim scoffed. "Why what happen... she catch him with another woman too?"

"Oh nooo. Heck, it wasn't nothin like that. Shiiit, that would've been somethin that they could of worked out an lived with," Otis paused with a solemn expression as he reflected on the events of the past. "No, what ended their marriage was a chain of events that'd been set in motion an was so over-whelmin that neither one of em stood a chance of stopping it. See," he paused with another heavy sigh as he continued to reflect back. "Sometimes people an things, well, they jus ain't quite what they seem."

"Really?" Jim narrowed his eyes into a curious gaze. "How do you mean?"

"Well, if I remember right, it all started about four or five months after they'd gotten married. I think it was somewhere around late July of 43, they was livin in a little house that they'd rented out on the edge of town. Dan had jus finished up his investigation into Foster's ship buildin company an was waitin to be reassigned when, well, that's when they came an got him."

━━━◆━━━

Sauntering to the table with his breakfast, Willie laid the plate to the side then raised her robe to her thighs and straddled his lap. "So tell me there mister fly boy," she cooed with a loving kiss. "Do you think we made a baby last night?"

Reaching a hand beneath the folds of her robe, Dan couldn't help but stare into the depths of his wife's beautiful green eyes. "A baby," he coughed as he rubbed her belly and thought of their night of passion. "The way you were last night?" He raised his eyebrows and chuckled. "I think we made two."

Their marriage was one of a love that was long over due, and with another loving kiss and a hug Willie rose from her husbands lap and then slid his plate in front of him. "Well, just in case we didn't you better eat up, because you, Mr. Mitchell," she smiled wantonly as she stepped back to the sink. "Are going to need all the energy you have when you get back home."

"Well, it may be kind of late because if you recall, today I'm suppose to get my new assignment."

"Oh that's right," she turned and smiled. "You're finished, aren't you?"

"Yes I am, in fact I finished my report just the other day and submitted it."

"Annnd?" Willie raised her eyebrows.

"Well, the bottom line was, was that I cleared your old boyfriend and his company of everything."

"Really?"

"Yep. You see, contrary to what a lot of the higher ups in the Navy had thought about the way he was building all of those ships, he didn't do anything wrong."

"Oh really... well then what was the problem with them all? I mean, why were they breaking?"

"It was the steel that they were using from the foundries."

"The steel?"

"Yes. See, it was changing on a molecular scale and was becoming brittle when it hit the cold waters of the Atlantic. And that's where all of the cracks and fractures were coming from."

"And you figured all that out by yourself?" she asked proudly.

"Well, not exactly," he chuckled. "Although on a hunch I did push the investigation in that direction. It was actually the scientists who figured it out."

"Well, I'm glad you're done," she sighed as she stared out the window. "I really didn't like the fact that you had to be there every day like that. I know Foster, and I know how he is. He has a lot of power, and I know if he thought for one second that you were going to hurt one of his companies, well..." She stopped talking and then turned back with a worried expression.

"Well, you can stop your frettin," he assured. "Because like you just said, I'm done, right? Besides, they couldn't have been nicer to us, especially after we cleared them of any wrong doing. In fact, we even got a letter from Foster himself thanking us."

Gaining a smile and a nod as if his words had eased her mind, Willie slowly turned back to her dishes as her husband picked up his fork and took a bite. The bacon and eggs she'd prepared went down in minutes and after he'd finished Dan sat and enjoyed a last cup of coffee before heading to work. He was listening to a news report on the radio when both he and Willie suddenly jumped at what sounded to be an urgent knock at the door. A second later and before either could move, it came again only louder and more insistent. It was odd that someone would knock so loud and so early and with one last hasty sip, Dan set his coffee down then rose and went to the door.

"Captain Mitchell?" one of the uniformed men sternly asked as soon the door opened.

"Yes," Dan answered with a degree of apprehension as he eyed the men before him.

"Captain, Daniel Ryan Mitchell?" the man repeated as if to ensure he was correct.

"Yes," Dan answered again with an even greater degree of concern.

"I'm Commander Sutton from the Judge Advocate General's office and I am here to inform you that under article three, section three of the Constitution of the United States, that you are hereby under arrest for the crime of treason against your country."

At first he thought it was a joke and had even started to laugh, but something quickly told him it wasn't. The man was deadly serious, and before he could even answer the Commander had turned to the Military Police officer standing next to him. "MP," he barked in a tone that was clearly an order.

Reacting without the slightest degree of hesitation, the MP quickly pulled his weapon and raised his 45. Then with an unflinching gaze, he pointed it straight at Dan's head and cocked the hammer.

"Danny?" Willie's frightened voice called out as she stepped up from behind. "What's going on? What do these men want?"

"Ma'am, step back please," the Commander ordered as one of the MPs stepped up and cuffed her husband's hands behind his back.

"I don't know baby," Dan answered. "It has to be a mistake," he said as he turned to the man giving the orders. "What in the hell is this Commander?" he demanded. "I want some answers, do you hear!"

"Wait a minute. They did what?" Jim looked on as if he'd misheard. "They arrested him?"

"Yes sir."

"For what?"

"For treason."

"For treason?" Jim repeated. "You're kiddin right?"

"Oh hell no, in fact, it wasn't but a couple of days or so after he'd finished his investigation. I guess they had gotten a tip that there was some plans missin an that's when they came an got em an took em to jail."

"But for what? I mean, what'd he do?"

"Well, after the Navy did their little pre trial investigation or what ever the hell it was called, they charged him with sellin ship buildin secrets to the Japanese."

"Ship buildin secrets?"

"Yep."

"An they had proof?"

"Oh yeah," Otis nodded. "They had the proof all right. In fact, they had more damn evidence than you could ever imagine."

"Really, like what?" Jim asked as if he were now ready to judge.

"Well, I wasn't at the trial or anything like that, but from everything that I'd heard an read in the papers, I guess when they really got to diggin into what he'd been do'n an started puttin all of the pieces together, they found hidden bank accounts an post office boxes that he'd opened up here in Mobile an Los Angeles an Honolulu. All of em places that he'd been. They said it was a trail of money an correspondence that led all the way back to Japan, an that'd started right about the same time he'd started investigatin Foster's ship buildin company."

"No way?"

"Oooh yeah. Shit, they even found an offshore bank account that he had over in the Bahamas with a hundred an fifty thousand dollars in it. Now back then, that was some real serious money. An then if all of that wasn't enough, an this is what really made it bad, was that they also had evidence that he was showin em right on the plans where the weakest an most vulnerable points were on all of the ships that Foster was buildin an refittin. You know, so that they knew right where to direct their guns an torpedoes to do the most damage. Ships that he actually had the plans to at his house," he finished and then shook his head as if he still couldn't believe the events of the past.

For a moment Jim sat in a stunned silence as the magnitude of what Otis had just said slowly sank in. "Jesus, they really had him, didn't they?"

"Oh yeah, they had him all right."

"An so what happened?"

"Well, let me tell ya, the Navy wasn't there to screw around, specially with someone who'd gone bad an betrayed em, an they proceeded on with a full blown court marshal. Now that didn't start until about a month later if I remember right, but in the mean time, well, that's when the newspapers picked up on it an went wild with the story. Heck, I can still remember readin the headlines. 'War Hero Arrested for Treason!' 'War Hero Sells America Out!' 'War Hero Betrays his Country!' *I'll tell ya, those papers did jus about everything they could to find him guilty before he even went to trial. In fact, I think they even made some of the stuff up.*

"Anyway, it wasn't long before the whole goddamn town had turned on the both of them like a pack of wild dogs. I mean, you couldn't go nowhere without readin or hearin someone talk bad about Dan Mitchell the traitor. Everybody was jus shocked, an I mean shocked. They couldn't believe that he could do somethin like that cause we still had boys overseas that were dyin by the thousands an to them, he couldn't of done anything worse. An poor Willie, well, she couldn't go nowhere without someone givin her a hard time. In fact, it got so bad an she got so scared, she moved in with her in-laws. Yes sir, there was a real lynch mob out there... an I mean a real one."

"Really?"

"Oh yeah, I'll tell ya those two was livin a real nightmare, an then if things couldn't of gotten any worse they started talkin about arrestin her too."

"Who, Willie?" Jim asked. "Why her, she didn't do anything did she?"

"Oh heck no," Otis shook his head. "But that didn't stop that prosecutor. An that's when, after they'd drug her in an raked her over the coals for about the third of fourth time that she finally broke down an called Foster.

"Now as far as I knew, I don't believe that she had seen or talked to him since she'd sent her ring up to his room, but she swallowed her pride cause she knew that he was the only one who was powerful enough to help her. Anyway, about a week or so before her husband's trial started, I got a call from Foster to go an get her an bring her to his office."

He was standing by the windows with his hands in his pockets waiting and watching as the rain fell out across the bay when he turned to a knock on his door.

"Senator," his receptionist quietly called as she entered. "Mrs. Mitchell is here."

"Yes Jenny, thank you. Bring her in, would you please."

"Yes sir," she replied and then disappeared.

She was gone for only a few moments before the door reopened and Willie appeared. It had been right at seven months since he'd seen her, yet even so as she walked into his office he could easily see that she was still the radiant beauty she'd always been, still one of the most beautiful and remarkable women he had ever met. He'd missed her, and for a fleeting moment as she crossed the room and approached, he held his breath in an awkward silence. Staring as if he were unaffected by her presence, until she'd stopped in the middle of his office.

"You look tired," he said in an effort to express his concern and hide his emotions.

"I am," Willie replied and sighed. "I haven't really slept much lately."

"Yes, I can imagine," he nodded as if he understood. "I've been reading the papers. They haven't been very kind, have they?"

"Nooo," she shook her head. "No, they haven't."

"Well, tired or not, you're still the most beautiful woman in Mobile. I was a fool to do what I did."

"Yes you were," she answered and glared.

Pausing in thought, Foster stood for a moment then nodded as if she were right. It was an apology of sorts, his way of saying he was sorry but that was as far as he went. Then in typical Foster fashion, he changed the subject. "Well, you are all right, aren't you?" he asked as he stepped away from the windows toward her.

"Well," Willie began with a fabricated laugh. "To tell you the truth, I really don't know anymore. One day I think that I just might make it, and then one day I'm a complete wreck. I guess it all depends on which paper you're reading and what they're printing that day. You never know what they're going to say really. I mean, they've twisted the truth so much I don't think anyone knows what it is. In fact, I don't even know what to think or believe anymore. That's why I called you, I need answers and I need your help. I know that we didn't part on the best of terms, but still, if you have ever held an ounce of love for me, you'll help me. I don't know where else to go and I need your help; my husband needs your help, and so here I am. You know people, important people," her passion grew. "And you can get answers with the snap of your finger. I can't get anything from anyone."

"Well, I don't know about the snap of my finger, but you are right, I do know a few people and after you called the other day, I did look into it and make a few inquiries."

"And what'd you find out?" Willie's voice rose with hope.

"Well," Foster stared with a somber expression. "To honest with you, the news isn't very good."

"What-a-you mean, it isn't good?" Willie anxiously challenged. "It can't be, Dan is innocent. Don't you see? This whole thing is some sort of mistake," she insisted. "They have the wrong man. Surely you found that out, didn't you?"

"No I didn't," Foster replied and shook his head. "I thought that maybe they did, but after seeing the evidence that they're going to use, I really don't believe they do."

It was clearly something she had not expected to hear, and for a few fleeting moments Willie just stared until the sound of Foster's voice regained her attention. "Willie, did you hear me?" He took another step closer and narrowed his eyes. "I said they have proof that your husband collaborated with the enemy. Do you know what that means? I mean, do you really understand what I'm telling you here?" He took a breath then continued on even though she didn't answer. "They're saying that he's a traitor, a traitor who sold out his country for money."

"Nooo," Willie protested and shook her head. "No, he didn't. Dan wouldn't do that."

"Yes, he did," Foster argued. "They have the proof, and I've seen it. I know that it hurts because you love him, but I'm telling you he's a traitor. He's not the man you think he is. Whatever the Japanese did to him when they captured and took him to that island, it changed him. It really did, and even though no one will ever know, or for that matter understand what he went through, those are the horrors of war and I can assure you that your husband is not the same man you use to know."

"But he is," Willie defended even as her doubt began to rise. "I know it, I can feel it."

"No, he isn't," Foster argued. "Did you know that he'd been taking the plans to our ships home with him."

"Yes, I did. He was studying them to find out what was wrong with them. It was his job and he cleared your company of any wrong doing."

"Yes he did, and I'm extremely grateful. But did you also know that he was selling them to the Japanese? Did you know that? Jesus, do you have any idea as to how much shit he is truly in? And now the prosecutor wants to charge you too... as a co-conspirator. They're saying that you helped set it all up. Which means if you're convicted you could get the death penalty, or at a minimum spend the rest of your life in prison. Now, if I'm going to help you I have to know," he asked as if he were now questioning a witness on the stand. "Did you have anything to do with this?"

"Nooo," Willie cried. "No, I didn't, I swear," she turned away then walked to the windows and stared out at the bay.

He'd hit her breaking point, and as she stared out though the rain soak panes and fought to hold back her tears, Foster slowly stepped up behind her. "Willie," he finally said in a comforting voice as he gently touched her shoulder. "It's okay, I believe you. I really do, and I'll help you. I'll help you get to the bottom of this if you want."

His words were comforting but more than that, it was the knowledge that he could actually do what he'd said that made her turn back and give a subtle nod.

"Good, now listen to me. I know the Judge Advocate General and the Secretary of the Navy both pretty good, and I think I can get you out of this because I really don't believe that you knew, or had anything to do with what he was doing. But I'm afraid that I can't do much for your husband. I'll try though for you, I really will, but it'll have to be off the record because it is my company that's involved in all of this. See, I can't appear as if I'm interfering, you know, all of that government and war department stuff. You do understand that, don't you?"

Gaining another nod along with a tight-lipped smile, Foster continued on. "Good, now give me a week to see what I can find out. But Willie," he paused and stared deep into her eyes. "Don't raise your hopes too high because they really do have a lot of evidence against him. And, he really is going to stand trial for treason."

His words seemed to resonate with an almost hopeless finality and for a few fleeting moments Willie could only stand and stare as if in a daze. The last four weeks had been an absolute nightmare, a terrible dream that at any moment she knew she would wake from. But she didn't, and as the days slowly turned into weeks, the nightmare for her and her husband continued. He was in jail, but in a sense so was she. The press had already convicted them before the trial had even begun, and all she could do now was hope and wait and pray. Pray that the man whom she had once loved could now save the one she did as their day in court slowly arrived.

"So was ol Foster actually able to help Willie?" Jim asked.

"Oh yeah," Otis nodded. "Like I always said he wasn't jus rich, he was powerful, real powerful, an if he didn't want somethin to happen it didn't happen. An right after he got involved, both that prosecutor for the Navy an the newspapers backed off of her real quick. But her husband... well, that was a whole different story."

CHAPTER 62

———◆———

THE TRIAL, ONCE IT HAD begun, moved swiftly. The evidence that was presented against Willie's husband was indisputable and overwhelming, and before she new what was happening the twelve-man panel had returned with their verdict and the Judge was calling for order. They'd returned far faster than anyone had expected and as they reentered the courtroom and took their seats a deafening silence fell across the room. A second later the Judge called to Dan and his lawyer.

"Captain Mitchell," the man began in a gravest of tones. "Would you please rise." Rising from behind their table, Dan and his lawyer stood and faced the Judge then listened with emotionless expressions as he turned to the jury foreman. "And what says the jury, have we reached a verdict?"

"Yes your honor," he replied as he rose. "We have."

"And how do you say?"

Clearing his throat, the man slowly turned his gaze toward Dan and then read the verdict in a loud clear voice. "Your honor, we the jury, after a careful review and consideration of all of the evidence that has been presented, find the defendant, Captain Daniel Ryan Mitchell, guilty as charged on all counts."

It was at that very moment that every dream Willie ever had of living a life with the man she loved disappeared. A moment later, and even though she'd prepared herself for the worse, she began to shake her head and cry at what she knew was coming next.

"Captain Mitchell," the judge began with a heavy breath. "In one of the most deceptive and heinous of acts that I have ever seen, you've deceived this nation and its people into thinking that you were a highly decorated war hero when in fact by the overwhelming and irrefutable evidence that has been presented here in this court-room, you are actually a traitor who has been collaborating with the enemy.

"For me personally, and in all of my years as a judge, I cannot think of anything that has ever been perpetrated against this great country that could be more reprehensible. You have not only deceived this nation, but you have betrayed her and her people by aiding and abetting the enemy during a time of war, a crime for which the prescribed penalty under the Articles of War is death. To me, I can think of no greater crime that you could've committed. And so, it is here by the order of this court that you are to be hanged by the neck until you are dead. May God have mercy on your soul." A second later, his gavel rang out and the judge dismissed the court.

"Oh my God," Jim looked on in disbelief. "They gave him the death penalty an then they really hung him, didn't they?"

"Yeah they did, an let me tell ya, it was real sad too," Otis nodded as he thought back. "I think it was around May of 44, an not to awfully long after he'd exhausted the last of his appeals.

"See, the military was pretty quick about stuff like that back then, an even though he fought an kept professin his innocence, I heard all the way up until they put the rope around his neck, nobody believed him. He'd had three trials in seven months an had been found guilty at each one of em, an each time the jury came back with their verdict, I think Willie lost a little more hope. In fact, the evidence that they had against him was so overwhelmin by the end of that third trial I think that even she'd begun to doubt him. But I'll tell ya, she never left him. Not for one minute. Or for that matter... ever stopped lovin him either.

"Anyway, about a week before D-Day, well, that's when they finally carried out his sentence up there in Fort Leavenworth. I'll tell ya, I felt so sorry for her, she'd been through so much durin those eight or nine months, losin first her baby an then her husband like she did."

"Her what?" Jim asked as if he'd misheard.

"Her baby," Otis replied in an even sadder tone. "It was right after he'd lost his first appeal if I remember right. She had a miscarriage from all of the emotional stress that she'd been under.

"Now Willie was a pretty strong girl, she really was, but I gotta tell ya, I think that that one really hit her hard. See, in all the years that I'd known her, all she had ever wanted was to have kids an a husband an a big white house, but one by one all of those things had been taken away from her. I remember seein her jus shortly after she'd gotten out of the hospital an how we talked for the longest time. I'll tell ya, it jus didn't seem fair."

"Oh man, how sad. I mean, poor Willie, I can't even imagine what her husband must of thought not be'n able to be with her?"

"I know what you mean," Otis agreed. "But to tell you the truth, I don't think that he ever knew."

"You're kiddin?"

"Oh noo, see Willie, even with everything that had happened, well, she didn't want him worryin about her so I don't believe she ever told him. That she was pregnant, or that she'd lost their baby."

"Anyway, right after his execution, Foster had his very own DC-3 fly up an get Willie an his parents an his body, an bring em all back to Mobile. He took care of everything real quiet like an when they got back, they buried him in a plot with just a few family members an friends who'd come to grieve. It was real sad too cause there wasn't no flag or trumpet, or honor guard, an as they said his final words of passin, well, I think that that was when Willie finally began to find some comfort in the fact that Foster was standin right there with her. For years he'd always been there for her, an when they lowered her husband's body into the ground he was still there."

"But I just don't understand. I mean it just doesn't make sense," Jim shook his head. "You know. He was a hero, he had everything, he had a career an Willie an, so... so why'd he do it?"

"Well, that was a question that a lot-a people wanted ta know, specially Willie. But nobody could ever figure it out, cause like you jus said, it jus didn't make sense. Anyway, shortly after he was executed we landed on the beaches of Normandy an after that I think that the country as a whole pretty much forgot all about Dan Mitchell. But Willie, well, she was still havin a pretty hard time cause there was still a lot of people around town who thought that she was involved an should've at least gone to jail. Now that was really hard on her an she was actually gonna leave town, but Foster, well, he some-how talked her into not only stayin but movin back in with him."

"Really?"

"Yep, ya see in a way I think she felt like he was the only one powerful enough to protect her an take care of her, an since she really didn't wanna

bother the Portmans or her in-laws any more than what she had, she went an moved back in with him. It was the fall of 44 if I remember right."

———◆———

After the death of her husband, the war wore on and at times seemed as if it would never end, and although D-Day had come and gone and was touted as the beginning of the end, people continued to die on an unprecedented scale. The fighting was intense, but even so the allies pushed on across Europe and into the Pacific and as they did, the tide began to change. The German war machine was in full retreat and everyone knew that the end was near. But Hitler wouldn't quit and it wasn't until May of 45, and after his suicide, that the fighting in Europe finally came to an end with Germany's surrender. Then on August 6th of that same year, the Enola Gay, a B-29 super fortress, dropped *Little Boy*, the first atomic bomb the world had ever seen on the town of Hiroshima.

It was an unimaginable force that destroyed the city and killed seventy five thousand people, but even so the military leaders who were ruling the government refused to surrender. Three days later, another one fell on Nagasaki. Six days after that the Emperor Hirohito issued a radio broadcast declaring Japan's surrender and the Second World War as we'd come to know it, came to an end.

It was the deadliest conflict in human history, and by the time it was over, an estimated sixty million people had lost their lives, hundreds of cities and towns lay in ruins, and the political and geographical maps of the world had been redrawn forever. The war was over and as the men and women who'd fought so bravely returned home and reunited with their loved ones; a time of jubilation and celebration enveloped the country. But for Willie who'd turned thirty that September, the war's end was bittersweet. For even though she'd moved back in with Foster and had been acquitted of all charges, she still carried the stigma of having been the wife of a traitor.

It was something that haunted her and seemed as if it wouldn't go away, even after she'd taken her name back. She was sad and lonely, and as the year slowly came to a close her depression only deepened. There had been so much sadness and heartbreak, untold casualties in a world that'd gone completely mad. She felt lost and all alone, and as if she were somehow one of them. All she'd ever wanted in life was to love someone, to be Mrs. Somebody someday, and to have a family. But life in a sense had been cruel to her, holding the realization of her dreams just out of reach, teasing her and giving her hope, then pulling them away.

She thought that they would've married long ago, but it never happened, and now it was almost as if she'd become nothing more than a possession for him to use or look at whenever he wanted. Like a painting on a wall, or a prized horse that you would sometimes ride. She wanted to leave and go where no one knew her, but she didn't. She stayed with a man who was now one of the wealthiest and most powerful men in the country. A man who by many was both feared and revered, and whose draconian rein of power now ran unchecked. A man whose ship building company had built a 125 new ships and refitted 2800 more for combat all by the end of the war. A man whose business empire stretched around the globe with over a 135 ships roaming the oceans of the world and whose only interest now seemed to be that of his next deal. For if Foster K. Siler was anything, he was first and foremost an opportunist, and even though the end of the war had signified the end of the ship building boom, it wasn't the end of his dealings.

The fighting had left most of the world in shambles, and as the war torn countries around the globe picked themselves up and began to rebuild, the powerful Senator from Alabama began to work on one of the biggest deals he'd ever done. He knew that out of the 2751 Liberty Ships that'd been built during the war that over 2400 of them had survived. And as was typical with government, they were now sitting in great idle fleets scattered around the country. Mothballed and rafted together by the Navy into huge flotillas, and now no one knew what to do with them.

It was hard to imagine such a large number of ships just sitting and it wasn't long before the Sec. of the Navy began to grow concerned. Eventually his concerns made it to the President and then to Foster who was once again summoned to the White House. There wasn't anyone in the government or the private sector who knew more about the shipping industry than he did and President Truman wanted his help.

It was an unprecedented opportunity for cargo ships to carry goods was now just as great if not greater than it was during the war. Whole countries had been torn to shreds and now lay in ruins. There was no food or supplies, and people were starving. Thousands had already died and the winter wasn't even over. Something needed to be done to help the shipping industries of the other nations that were struggling to recover and replace their wartime losses. They needed ships in the most urgent of ways and the United States Navy had them.

Answering the call for help, Foster quickly assembled a bipartisan group of Senators, wrote a new bill and then pushed it through congress. A bill that would allow the Navy to sell off a large portion of their cargo fleet to aid and assist the commercial buyers of allied nations. It was a win win for everyone, and so it was that in the spring of 1946 the Merchant Ship Sales Act was passed. A week later and in a closed-door deal with the Secretary of Navy, Foster was quietly awarded an option on two hundred and fifty of their best ships. It was a deal that would net him millions and before the ink was even dry on the contracts he had word of his ships out on the open market.

He knew more people around the world in the shipping business than anyone else there was and it didn't take long for news to spread that Siler Shipbuilding was brokering cargo ships from the U. S. Navy. Times were desperate and it wasn't long before a young opportunistic group of Greek and Italian entrepreneurs made their way across the ocean to Washington.

"Senator," Carolyn called as she entered. "Your one o'clock is here."

"My one o'clock?" Foster looked up with a blank expression.

"Yes sir, you remember, that man from Greece and his two friends from Italy, the ones who want to buy some of your ships."

"Oh yes," Foster nodded. "Thank you Carolyn, send them in would you please. Oh, and Carolyn," he called before she could turn completely around.

"Yes sir," she stopped and twisted her head.

"What'd you say his name was again?"

Looking at her tablet, Carolyn scrunched her nose. "Ar-is-totle," she said, then shrugged her shoulders as if she wasn't quite sure. "O... Onasis, I think is how you say it."

"Yesss, Aristotle," he repeated as he rose from behind his desk. "Send him in, would you."

"What?" Jim scoffed and rolled his eyes. "Onassssis? You mean, as in Aristotle Onasis?"

"Yep, or at least I think it was him."

"The shippin dude, right?" Jim narrowed his eyes. "The one that's married to Jackie Kennedy?"

"Yep," Otis nodded. "I'm pretty sure that's the one. I heard Foster tellin Ralston one day while we were drivin over to his office buildin about these guys that'd come over from Greece an Italy an bought a whole bunch of those ships from him. I remember him sayin his name several times to Ralston cause as part of the deal he said that they had to convert all of em to civilian use before they could take em an he was the man that he'd be dealin with."

"Wow, now that's unbelievable. I mean, who'd of thought? Him buyin ships from Foster."

"Oh I know, but you gotta remember there weren't a whole lot of cargo ships to be had cause the biggest part of em had been sunk durin the war an ol Foster, well, all of a sudden, there he was with two hundred an fifty of em. Anyway, those ships that he bought or brokered or whatever the hell it was he did from Navy, well, that was one of the last deals that he ever did."

"Really? The last one?" Jim seemed surprised. "Why, did he finally retire?" He laughed with a hint of cynicism.

"No, an you really ain't gonna believe this, but," he took a breath. "Well, that's when the real truth about Willie's husband be'n a traitor finally came to light."

"The real truth?" Jim shunted forward and narrowed his eyes. "What-a-ya mean? I thought you said earlier that it was an open an shut case? An besides, what in the hell did all that have to do with Foster's last deal?"

"Well," Otis sighed. "You remember when I told you a jus a bit ago about how sometimes people an things ain't quite what they seem."

"Yeaaah," Jim looked on with curious gaze.

"Well," he began as he reflected back to what'd actually happened. "If I remember right, it was around late August of 46, a Saturday, an Foster'd jus made a pretty big deal with these two fellers from Russia to sell the very last of

those ships that he'd bought when I got a call to come an pick em all up at his office buildin. It seemed that they wanted to celebrate, an as soon as they were in the car we took off for an afternoon on the town.

"Now what really surprised me, an I didn't know it until that day, was that ol Ralston actually spoke what turned out to be pretty good Russian. I think he learned it from his mother, you know, her be'n from Russia an all. Anyway, it really loosened things up an got the party started, an before I knew it the four of them was all laughin an carryin on jus like old friends.

"Now let me tell ya, those two fellers from Russia could really drink an they didn't have no problem at all holdin their own with Foster an Ralston. Yes sirrrr, they was havin a hell of a time an after they was all good an liquored up, Foster fixed em up with a couple of real fine lookin women an we took em back to their hotel. Then after that I dropped Ralston off at the office buildin so he could get his car an then took Foster on home an dropped him off.

"I remember it was right about sundown when we finally pulled into his drive. Now normally at the house ol Foster'd jus get out of the car by himself, but he was pretty lit up an I knew it so I got out real quick to help him. I think he must of really liked that cause right away he started tellin me what a good employee I'd always been an how, come very first thing Monday mornin that he was gonna tell Miss Vicki to give me another raise.

"Now right off I tried to tell him that he didn't need to do that cause he already paid me good enough, but there wasn't no arguin with Foster Siler drunk or otherwise, an deep down I really knew it. I'll tell ya, he always did treat me good. So jus like I always did, I thanked him real politely, told em to tell Willie that I said hello an that I'd pick em up on Monday. Then after that, I got back in the car an drove off.

"But he never saw Monday mornin, cause when he walked through the door to his house that evening he started somethin that you jus wouldn't believe. An in all my wildest dreams as I drove off an glanced up into the mirror, would I of ever guessed that that'd be the last time that I ever saw or spoke to him."

"What?" Jim blurted and sat forward. "He died?"

"Yep, in fact, it was the very next mornin if ya wanna know the truth."

"Jesus, how? I mean, what happened?"

"Well," Otis began as if he were still saddened by the events. "I guess it all started when he found Willie packin upstairs. See, she was finally gonna leave him an..."

CHAPTER 63

SHE'D MADE UP HER MIND weeks ago and had decided to leave, for their love that once was, was no longer. It had disappeared in the wake of Foster's abuse and possessiveness that'd grown to an intolerable state. A state of cruelty that had continued on until she no longer loved or cared for him. She could take no more, but that evening before she could finish her packing and leave, he returned home and found her upstairs standing by the bed with her hands on her suitcase.

He'd been drinking all afternoon and at first was confused, but in what quickly turned into a heated and bitter exchange of words, he suddenly realized her intentions. She was leaving and for good, but to Foster it was completely inconceivable to think that a possession of his would try and leave without permission. He was one of the most powerful men in the country and nobody did anything without his approval, including Willie. He controlled everything and everyone in his life, and in his drunken and angry state a violent confrontation quickly ensued.

"What in the hell do you think you're doing?" he demanded.

"I'm leaving," she snapped and turned with a defiant glare. "And it's for good. I'm tired of your crap... and I'm leaving," she finished then slammed her suitcase close and locked the latches.

"You're leaving? Bullshit," he snarled as he approached and then grabbed her arm. "You're mine goddammit, and you don't leave unless I say so."

"I'm what? I'm yours? Are you serious?" Willie scoffed in mockery of his claim. "And just what am I Foster?" she demanded as she jerked her arm from his grasp and then the suitcase from the bed. "Huh, tell me?" she elevated her voice. "I'm certainly not you're wife... or your maid! No! Hell, I'm not even your damn girlfriend! In fact, I don't know what I am to you anymore? You're never here, and even when you are, we're never together. So tell me... just what am I?"

She was right and he knew it for even though he had taken her back after her husband's death, he'd always resented the fact that she'd left him for another man. It was something he just couldn't get over, and after a momentary pause he began to smile in sort of a twisted and malevolent way. "You're my whore, Willie," he sneered in hopes of provoking her. "That's what you are, and you always have been. Haven't you figured that out yet?"

"Fuck you!" she retorted and slapped his face.

It was something Foster had expected, and without a second's hesitation he struck her back. Catching her cheek with the palm of his hand, he hit her hard and sent her head sideways. It was a blow that resonated throughout the room, and as Willie stumbled backwards, she grabbed her face and cried out in pain. At first she couldn't believe it, but her spinning head and stinging cheek told her otherwise. It was the first time in all the years that they'd been together that he'd ever hit her, and even though he could see the hurt and the pain that he'd caused in her eyes, he seemed to glory in the fact that he was finally overpowering the one thing he could never control. Willie had always been a free and independent spirit, but now he was determined to teach her a lesson and before she knew what was happening, he stepped toward her and began to tear at her clothes.

"And now," he snarled. "It's time you earned your keep!"

She was still in a daze, but even so Willie fought back with every ounce of strength she had. She hit and clawed, but Foster was strong and drunk, and before she could stop him or get away she felt another blow to the side of her face that struck even harder than the first.

"Nooo Foster," she cried out as she fell to the floor and began to plead in terrified gasps. "Don't!

She was begging, but something inside of Foster had snapped, and before she knew what was happening she was being jerked up by her hair and thrown onto the bed. Then in an uncontrolled and drunken rage, and just as her stepfather had done to her mother years ago, the man whom she'd once loved with all of her heart, forced himself upon her and took her against her will.

It was without question a violation of the worst kind, and for hours and hours afterwards Willie raged with a boiling hatred. She thought back to the time when her mother had endured the very same fate, and of how she'd listened through the thin walls of the cabin to the sickening sounds of her beating, and then to the haunting sound of her voice as she pleaded over and over again for him to stop. But he didn't, and neither had Foster, and as both the physical an emotional trauma festered inside of her, Willie closed her eyes and cried herself to sleep.

Although his needs had been satiated, Foster brooded and continued to drink until he'd emptied his bottle and passed out in bed. The next morning when he woke, he quietly rose and dressed as if nothing had happened then left the house and headed to Connie's Diner. He'd started drinking early in the afternoon on an empty stomach, and now all he could think of was food and coffee to cure the pounding in his head.

Watching from her window as he pulled away, Willie hurriedly dressed and then finished her packing. She couldn't wait to get away, and with a final check of her room, she descended the steps with the last of her bags. She was leaving and never coming back, but just as she reached the front door and grabbed the knob, she suddenly stopped and then turned to Foster's office.

It was clearly an afterthought, but one she knew she had to do. One she wanted to do, her final words to dissuade him from ever trying to find her. She'd leave a letter for him to find, but as she took her seat behind his desk and glanced around, she found no paper. It was clean and neat with nothing but a large felted desk pad, a phone, and a cylinder of pens and pencils. Looking down undeterred, Willie grabbed a handle to one of the drawers and pulled. But the drawer was locked and wouldn't open, as was the one just below it. She tried the other side and found the same. Her anger and frustration grew, and as it did she began to jerk and pull on them all until the bottom drawer on the right hand side flew open with a crack. She'd broken the lock, and without a second's hesitation she reached inside for whatever she could find and pulled a folder from the bottom.

Setting it on the desk with a huff, she opened the flap in search of paper but then stopped and stared with a curious gaze at the name inscribed inside. A name she knew all too well, and one that the entire nation had also come to know. A name that'd become synonymous with the word traitor, her husband's... Captain Daniel Ryan Mitchell of the United States Navy.

Curiously pulling some of the papers from within, Willie quietly began to read? Was this Dan's record of heroism that his lawyers had tried to use? Or, was it what Foster had compiled to help exonerate him after she had asked for his help? She wondered, but still she was confused and didn't understand. The records of offshore bank accounts with dates and transactions addressed to Foster. Post office boxes and more bank accounts, in Mobile and Los Angeles and Honolulu, all made out in her husband's name. An offshore account created in the Bahamas, also in his name. But what did all of this have to do with his defense? They didn't make sense, and now with a growing feeling that something was terribly amiss, she pulled the entire stack from the folder.

At first, it was difficult because of the secretive and complex nature in which Foster had compiled everything. It was his way, but Willie continued on and it wasn't long before she'd pieced together a diabolical and methodical trail of deceit that led straight back to the very desk at which she was sitting. There were even papers with her name on them, additional bank accounts that'd been created but had never been opened. Her blood ran cold at the thought and at first she couldn't believe it. It couldn't be, but it was, and the more she read the clearer the circumstances involving her husband's court martial became. It was all there, everything. An entire folder proving that Foster had not only fabricated the charges against him, but had also been the driving force behind his court martial. A court martial that'd led to his execution... the execution of an innocent man. A man she had loved.

She remembered his words and how he'd so vehemently defended his patriotism and professed his innocence to her. Over and over again, along with his undying love, all the way up until the day he was hanged. It was one of the most heart-wrenching moments she had ever endured; yet even as the tears of her heartbreak fell onto the pages, she forced herself to read on.

It was inconceivable to even think that a man whom she'd once loved with all of her heart could do such a thing, but the facts were undeniable. He'd taken her husband, a war hero who'd fought with honor and bravery and destroyed his name, then killed him in the most cowardly of ways. It was more than she could endure, and as her anger and pain welled, she pulled the papers tight against her chest and began to shake her head. Then with a long deep breath, Willie cried out in a moment of heartache and pain. A long and anguished cry that resonated throughout the house and left little doubt as to the torment and sorrow it carried. She felt empty and lost in a way she couldn't explain, and in the quiet of the house, Willie lowered her head and began to cry in heaving sobs. Why she wondered? Why...?

——◆——

He had just finished his first cup of coffee when a bruised and battered Willie quietly walked up the steps to the diner. She was in a daze, but even so as she reached down and grabbed the tarnished knob to the door she couldn't help but think back to the day when she'd first opened it all those years ago. This is where it had all started, where they had met so long ago when she was so young. When he'd filled her with the hopes and dreams of a better life at a time when she'd been so sad. A second later, she slowly turned the knob and then stepped into the diner.

She knew exactly where he'd be sitting and without so much as a glance to any of the other people there, she walked straight towards the back as if in a trance. She could see him sitting in his usual spot, and saw him motion to Connie with a finger-pointed gesture for more coffee then return to his paper. He was completely oblivious to her presence until Connie stepped out from behind the counter with a pot of coffee and saw Willie walking toward them.

"Oh Willie," she greeted cheerfully. "Good mornin, I didn't know you were joining Foster. Heck, he never said a word, but let me pour him a cup real quick an I'll," she went on but then suddenly stopped at the sight of Willie's bruised and battered face. "Oh my God. Oh Willie... you poor dear. What happened, are you okay?"

Glancing to Connie, Willie stared for just a second then quickly turned back to Foster just as he looked up and laid his paper to the side. She'd been crying and was upset, but without a moment's hesitation as to what it was she'd come to do, she reach down into her purse and pulled her husband's nickel-plated memento from within. Glistening in the bright morning light as she raised it up, she pointed the gun straight at Foster then put her thumb on the hammer and slowly pulled it back.

It took only a second for the unmistakable click of the gun to silence the room and for Connie to cry out. "No, Willie!" she pleaded as she stood with her pot of coffee. "Don't! He's not worth it." It was a heartfelt plea, but still Willie didn't move, she just stared with an unflinching glare and waited as the two tables next to Foster instantly rose and scurried past her.

It was a scene that was reminiscent of an old western where the gunfighter draws on his opponent and then instantly empties the saloon. But to Foster, it was as if he'd just been abandon and left for dead, and with the gun still pointed straight toward him, he swallowed hard then ever so slowly rose from his seat with his hands out in front. He knew she was upset for what he'd done, and in a way he couldn't blame her, but even so, he really hadn't expected her to walk into the diner with a gun. And even though her actions infuriated him like nothing before, he tried his best to remain calm. She was more than capable of pulling the trigger and he knew it. And even though he was staring straight down the barrel of a Colt 45, he was hoping and praying that she wouldn't, and that she would listen to Connie.

"Willie please," Connie pleaded again. "Put the gun down, okay. Come on. Whatever he's done he's not worth it, I promise. Please, listen to me... pleeease."

"Yeah Willie," Foster smirked with a glance to Connie. "Listen to Connie. I'm not worth it, see." He spread his arms and exposed his chest as he slowly approached and closed the distance between them. He knew that he had to get the gun before she snapped, but the closer he got and the more certain he became that she wouldn't shoot, the more his anger rose.

"Now, like Connie said, put down the gun," he demanded with another step closer.

"Nooo!" Willie refused.

"What?" Foster snapped. "Listen I've had just about enough of this shit, and I'm telling you to put down the gun. Just who in the hell do you think you are anyway? I mean, do you really think that you can come in here and threaten me just because I slapped you around a little last night?" His voice rose with an air of indignation. "Well, do you?" he went on before she could answer. "You need to remember just who in the hell you are."

"And just who am I Foster?" Willie demanded as she re-gripped the gun and stiffened her arm in what was clearly a gesture to stop. "Huh? Tell me... I forgot!"

"You're my whore," he sneered. "Remember? I thought I made that clear enough to you last night. And you always have been. Ever since I picked you up at that little table right there, all those years ago," he turned and glanced back to his seat. "Remember?" He smirked. "I've given you everything you've ever wanted, and even saved you from going to jail. Shit, I even tried to help your no good husband, but he ended up being a traitor after all didn't he. And now this is how you pay me back?" he snarled. "Now, for the last time, put the Goddamn gun down, you hear!"

She'd come with every intent in the world to kill him, but for some reason Willie still couldn't pull the trigger. She loved him, but hated him even more for everything he'd done to her over the years, and as the heartbreak of what he'd done to her husband returned, she let out an anguished cry. "Nooo!" she refused as her tears began to fall. "And no you didn't help him. You killed him! I know you did. You killed him and I hate you!" She sobbed in a voice filled with pain. "You used your money and power, and you set him up to make him look like a traitor! He kept telling me he was innocent and that someone had set him up, but I never believed him. I didn't know what to believe then. There always seemed to be so much evidence against him. But now I know! It was you; it was you all along! I know it was!

"Danny was innocent, but you couldn't stand the fact that I'd left you and had fallen in love with another man, so you set him up out of spite for me. And the whole time that I begged and pleaded with you for help, you led me on and pretended as if you really cared. As if he'd meant something to you too, while you were actually just waiting until they executed him. You coldhearted coward. How could you? How could you do such a thing?"

"What are you talking about?" Foster feigned with an expression to match. "That's absurd, you're crazy and you know it," he argued with a dismissive glance to some of the other patrons looking on. "Your husband was a traitor and everyone knows it. He betrayed this country and he got exactly what he deserved."

"No, he wasn't," Willie defended as her emotions welled. "And he did not betray this country. He was a hero who fought for us, for all of us, but you set him up to make him look like he had. It's true," she cried as she wiped her eyes with the palm of her hand. "And you know it. I found your folder in your desk and I have the proof. I have it all, and now I'm going to use it to see that you rot in jail for the rest of your life and that when you're finally dead, that you burn in hell."

She was distraught beyond words, and as an unbearable wave of heartache and pain took hold of her emotions, Willie slowly lowered the gun and then her head. She wanted to scream and cry out in rage, but she didn't. She couldn't, for the truth of her husband's innocence and what Foster had done left her numb, and in the fleeting seconds that followed, she finally broke down and began to sob.

It was the moment that Foster had been looking for and in an instant he closed the gap between them and grabbed for the gun. He was in serious trouble and he knew it. The evidence was there, it was undisputable and it was overwhelming, and he knew that he had to get it back and stop her in any way he could. But Willie had chambered a shell and had cocked the hammer, and even though she'd decided not to shoot, when he jerked on the gun, she squeezed it tight and her finger pulled down on the trigger.

"Nooo," she screamed as they struggled. An instant later, her husband's 45 exploded with an ear-shattering bang and sent its lead projectile deep into Foster's stomach. At first he couldn't believe it, but the gut-wrenching pain that quickly followed was something he couldn't deny. He staggered backwards and almost instantly a violent rage seemed to rise from within. His eyes went wild like a man possessed. He could kill her now and he knew it. She'd come into the diner with every intention of shooting him, and if he could take the gun away, he could kill her and claim self-defense. He had all of the witnesses he needed and there wasn't a jury in the state that would convict him.

A split second later, he lunged at her in another attempt to take the gun and turn it against her. And although Foster was strong, the gun was an automatic and had chambered another shell, and Willie held tight in an uncommon display of emotional strength. She knew that he wanted to kill her, she could see it in his eyes, and when he pulled on the gun for a second time, her finger squeezed down on the trigger.

Firing with another ear-shattering bang, the gun exploded once again and sent its red-hot slug dead into the center of his chest. Staggering backwards for a second time, Foster instantly exhaled in excruciating pain then clutched at his chest and collapsed to his knees. He felt as if a ladle of hot molten metal had just been poured into his chest and stomach, and he frantically ripped at his shirt to extinguish the fire burning deep inside. He had all of the money and power in the world, yet there was nothing he could do to stop it. A few seconds later, he looked back up at Willie and stared as the realization of what was about to happen suddenly set in. He was going to die, and it was just that simple. They both knew it, and as the blood slowly oozed from his body, Foster coughed and gasped then closed his eyes and slumped to the floor.

There wasn't a sound from anyone or anything except for the chair scooting on the floor as Willie backed into it and took a seat. It was unimaginable to think of what'd just happened, and for a few fleeting moments she just sat and stared in a state of shock. The man who'd taken her when she was just a child and who'd promised her the world, now lay dying before her in the very diner where they had met. She felt a sickening feeling envelope her and as it did she gently laid the gun on the table and then lowered her head until the sound of Foster's voice gained her attention.

"Connie," he gasped as he raised his head and reached out with a hand. "Help meee."

It was without question a desperate plea, yet even so Connie didn't move, she just stood with her pot of coffee and stared through the eyes of a woman whose heart was filled with disdain. She'd always blamed him for the death of her niece, and even though she was a compassionate and God fearing woman, she just turned and looked to his table. To her, he'd finally gotten what he deserved and with a callous disregard to his plea, she walked to his table and picked up his cup. For years she'd filled it to a finger-pointed gesture that had followed just as soon as he'd turned it over and this morning was no different than any other. But now those days were over, and in an act of spite for him to see, she turned and gained his gaze then turned it over and gently placed it back in its saucer.

To Foster, it was as if she'd just stuck a knife in his heart, and with all of the remaining strength he had left, he struggled to speak. He wanted to curse and to tell her off, but the words never came. A moment later, Senator Foster K. Siler exhaled a long final breath then laid his head back down on the floor and closed his eyes for the very last time.

The entire scene seemed as if it had gone on for hours, but in reality it was only a few short minutes. And no sooner had the shocked and disbelieving patrons began to stir, than the door to the diner flew open.

They had heard the shots from out on the street and had their guns already drawn when they burst inside. Battle hardened from the war, the two city cops then slowly and cautiously made their way to the back of the diner and the direction that everyone was staring. Following their telltale gazes until the sight of Willie sitting at the table with a gun and the lifeless body of Foster lying on the floor told the story.

"Son-of-a-bitch! Are you shittin me? Willie shot him? I mean... actually shot him?"

"Well, technically speaking," Otis drawled as if what Jim was inferring to were some sort of minor infraction. "In a way, I guess she did."

"In the very diner where they met?"

"Yes sir," Otis nodded. "Right in Connie's Diner. Right where they'd first met all those years ago when Willie first came walkin into town."

"Jesus, that's unbelievable. I mean, ho-leee ja-moleee," Jim rolled his eyes. "But ya know, after what he did to her an her husband," he added with a finger pointed gesture. "The son-of-a-bitch got exactly what he deserved. Shit, I'd a shot em too if it'd been me."

"Oh, I know," Otis agreed with another nod. "In fact, jus about every person in Mobile felt the same way after they finally found out the truth, includin me. I'll tell ya, what ol Foster had done was jus about as cruel an dirty as you could get, even for him. I mean, who in the world would of ever thought after all the years that they'd been together that he could of done somethin like that? It was jus crazy."

"So what happen after that? I mean, to Willie?" Jim pried. "What happened to her?"

"Well, from what everybody had said, I guess there was these two cops that jus happened to be right outside the diner when her gun went off."

"Oh really?" Jim looked on with a skeptical gaze. "Two cops?"

"Yep."

"An they just happened to be there?"

"Well actually, they'd jus stopped."

"Stopped, for what?"

"Well apparently, Willie hadn't bothered to park her car when she got there an had jus left it out in the middle of the street with the door wide open," he chuckled and shook his head. *"Anyway, I guess they must of seen it or somethin when they was drivin by an had stopped to check it out when they heard the shots. Now from what all I was told, I think they must of thought that it was a robbery or somethin an came runnin in with their guns drawn ready to shoot. I think they were a couple of ex marines from the war an--."*

"Whoa whoa whoooa," Jim interrupted. "They didn't shoot Willie, did they?" he asked as if he were almost afraid to hear the answer.

"Oh nooo," Otis chuckled. "No, they didn't shoot Willie, but from everything I heard they was sure wantin to shoot someone." He chuckled again. "I think they were still a little antsy from the war an all but after they'd made their way to the back an saw her sittin there at the table cryin an Foster dead on the floor, well, that pretty much told em what all had happened."

"Jesus, I still can't believe it," Jim shook his head. "I mean, she actually shot him?"

"Yes sir, she shot him all right," Otis smiled wryly. "An he died too."

Taking a long deep breath, Jim sat for a moment as if he were contemplating the entire sequence of events. Then, and as if he'd finally accepted the facts as unbelievable as they were, he slowly exhaled and began to smile. "An so when'd you first hear about it?"

"Well, it wasn't too awfully long after it'd happened really. See, I was the one who got the call to go an get the car."

"The car? You mean the one she left in the street?"

"Yep, Miss Vicki called me jus all upset. She was cryin an carry'n on an tellin me how Willie had jus shot Foster an how I had to go over to the diner right away an get that car an... Anyway that's how I found out about it, an that's how an when I found that big ol folder that she'd taken."

"Folder? What folder?"

"The folder. You know, the one that she'd found in Foster's desk. That had all of the evidence in it that proved how he'd fabricated everything an

set her husband up to look like a traitor. It was layin right there on the front seat."

"Oh that," Jim nodded. "So she'd taken it with her?"

"Oh hell yes she took it. Shiiiit, she was gonna burn his ass. An that's how I ended up with it. When I took the car back to Foster's house, I took the folder home with me. I didn't know what it was at the time, but it had her husband's name in it so I jus kept it cause I thought it was hers."

"But I still don't understand. Why'd he do it? I mean, he had it all. He was rich an powerful, an had everything. So why?"

"Jealousy," Otis answered.

"Jealousy?" Jim repeated.

"Yep, see, the one thing that his money couldn't ever buy was Willie's love. So in order to win her back, or punish her, an I'm not sure as to which one it was really, he set her husband up to look like a traitor."

"Jesus, what a son-of-a-bitch. An through all three of those trials he stood by her an pretended to help while they tried an convicted him... an then executed him?"

"Yes sir, that's exactly what he did."

"Good God, no wonder she shot the bastard. He really did deserve it, didn't he?"

"Oh yeah," Otis agreed. "No argument here. After what he did, I think he got exactly what he deserved. Anyway, it didn't take very long for word of Foster's death an who'd shot him to get out an around. In fact, I think it pretty much shot through the city like a shock wave from an atomic bomb. They said that the switchboards down at the phone company lit up like a Christmas tree an inside of fifteen minutes the whole town knew an both the prosecuting attorney an the chief of police had been pulled from church.

"Yes sir, ol Willie'd really gone an done it. She'd jus shot an killed one of the most important men to ever come out of Mobile an by Monday mornin his death had become the front page headline of every major newspaper in the country an the city started fillin up with reporters. I'll tell ya Jim, I never seen anything like it. I mean, there was news people everywhere an from every-where, an it seemed like everyone of em was tryin to dig the same dirt out of the same hole at the same time."

"Really?"

"Oh heck yeah, shit, jus think about it. A Senator as rich an as pow-erful as what Foster was, who had supposedly been shot by his mistress of almost fifteen years right after she'd found out that he'd actually set her *husband up to look like one of the biggest traitors that this country ever had. I mean, come on...shiit, you couldn't make up a story like that if you tried."* He chuckled. *"An man did the press ever love it, cause boy-o-boy did it ever sell newspapers."*

"So what happened? I mean to Willie."

"Well the next day, the prosecutin attorney announced that he was chargin her with first degree murder an that he was also gonna ask for the death penalty. I think that he really liked all the press that'd come into town cause every time he got a chance he was spoutin off about somethin in the papers. They said that what he was really tryin to do was to make a name for himself cause he wanted to run for attorney general or somethin like that an Willie's trial was gonna do that for him. Anyway, for the second time, poor ol Willie got pulled into court to try an defend herself."

"Annnd?" Jim looked on with a set of opened hands. "What happened?"

"Well," Otis drawled with another sip from his beer as he reflected back. "I gotta tell ya, at first it didn't look real good. See, an as far as most of the people in town were concerned, Willie was still the wife of one of the worst traitors that the country had ever seen, an now she'd jus killed one of the most important men in the state. A man that a lot of people had actually come to love for everything he'd done. In fact, I think she jus may have been about the most despised person in all of Mobile right about then.

"Anyway, like I jus said, it sure didn't look very good, specially after her arraignment hearin or what ever in the hell it was called. I'll tell ya, that ol prosecutor was really out to bury her ass an I don't think he cared one bit for the truth. An the papers, well, they was jus as bad if not worse cause every time you picked one up they was crucifyin her... jus like they'd done to her husband."

"But wait a minute," Jim sat forward. "Where in the hell were the Portmans, or her lawyer? I mean, good grief, didn't he object to all of that crap?"

"Her lawyer?" Otis scoffed. "Shit, Willie didn't have no lawyer."

"She didn't?" Jim seemed surprised.

"Oh hell nooo. Or at least not for the first week or so she didn't, cause to tell ya the truth, I don't think there was anyone in town who wanted to defend her. An as far as the Portmans, well, other than Mrs. Portman visitin every couple of days, ol Tom was a Federal Judge so he really couldn't do nothin. His hands were tied so to speak, an in a way I think Willie really understood that. Besides, I think he was all tore up over the whole ordeal.

"Anyway, like I said, it didn't look good for Willie cause as far as most everybody was concerned, she was guilty an that's all there was to it."

"Damn Otis, what in the hell kind of justice was that?"

"It wasn't," he replied. "They were out to convict her."

"So what happened, I mean, what'd she do?" Jim's sense of injustice seemed to reflect in his voice. "Shit, she had to have a lawyer. Didn't court appoint one, or anybody help her?"

"Well," Otis drawled and shook his head as if he still couldn't believe it. "Sometimes when you least expect it the most unlikely of people come walkin back into your life. An out of that whole damn town an of all the people that Willie knew, there was only one person who came forward an actually had enough guts to walk through the doors to the county jail an help her."

"Really," Jim sat forward. "An who was that?"

"Well, you really ain't gonna believe this," he shook his head again. "An to tell you the truth, I didn't either when I first saw her, but it was right about the second week that Willie'd been in there when they came an got her one mornin."

CHAPTER 64

———⬦———

SHE'D JUST FINISHED HER BREAKFAST when the guard returned to her cell and called her name. "Miss Dawson," he said in a monotone voice as he stuck his key into the door. "You have a visitor."

"A visitor?" Willie curiously repeated.

"Yes ma'am, you have someone who wants to see you. Come with me, would you please?"

Stepping through the door, Willie dutifully followed the guard through the bottom of the court-house to the rooms where the lawyers met with their clients. Small rooms, with nothing more than a table and a few chairs where the deals were made. She remembered them from her days as a clerk for Judge Summerford, and the smiles and the disgruntled looks that would often accompany the attorneys as they emerged from within. But why was she being brought here? Had Miss Liz hired a lawyer or had she finally been given a public defender? Was she here to tell her a bit of good news, she hoped as the guard finally stopped by one?

"You have fifteen minutes," he said as he opened the door and stepped back.

Thanking the guard, Willie stepped inside but then suddenly stopped at the sight of a nicely dressed lady looking out of the window. She had expected to see a man, and immediately questioned the wisdom of a woman attorney until the lady turned and a whole new array of thoughts entered her mind. It had been years since she'd seen her, but even so she instantly recognized her. "Daphney?" she asked and then stared.

Nodding with a smile, Daphney paused for a second then took a nervous breath. "Hello Willie," she drawled and stepped toward her. "How are you?"

"Well," Willie finally answered after she'd regained her senses. "I would really like to tell you that I'm doing just fine, but the simple truth of the matter is, is that I'm..." she suddenly stopped and shook her head. "But wait, what are you doing here? And where've you been? It's been ten years."

"Yes, it has. And I've been living in New Orleans. And the reason that I am here is... is that I've come back to help you."

"Are you a lawyer?" Willie asked with a hint of hope.

"Nooo," Daphney replied and shook her head. "I'm not."

"You're not?"

"No," she shook her head again.

"Well then what are you doing here? I don't understand? I mean?"

"Well," Daphney began as she pulled a chair from the table and took a seat then watched as Willie did the same. "You remember all those years ago when I got into trouble an out of nothing more than the kindness of your heart you came and helped me? When you and your friend took me up river?"

"Yes," Willie answered inquisitively.

"Well, in all of these years since, and as far as I know, you've never said anything to anyone, nor have you ever asked for anything. You kept your promise just like you said you would, an to me that is not only rare, but it is also a mark of a person's character and is something that I have never ever forgotten. And I just want you to know," she reached across the table and took Willie's hand. "That I wouldn't have had any kind of life at all if it wasn't for you and your two friends, especially the one that I am living now. And I know," she continued on as if she were confessing her sins and seeking redemption. "That that boy that I'd been with, most certainly wouldn't. They would've killed him without even thinking about it; you know it and I know it, and it's hard tellin what all they would've done to me." She lowered her head as if she were still ashamed of what she'd done. "I don't think that they would've actually killed me, but I know that it wouldn't have been very pretty.

"Willie, I owe you a debt of gratitude I'd always thought I could never repay. That there was nothing I could do to equal what you'd done for me, and that life would pass us by and you would never know how I felt. That is until now. You were an angel who'd been sent to me at a time when I needed somebody the most, and for years I promised myself that if I ever had the chance to help you and repay even a small part of your kindness that I would."

"But how?" Willie asked as if she were a hopeless cause.

"Well, to start with," Daphney began. "I have money, lots of money, so we can afford to get you the best attorney in the country. See, my husband just happens to be the son of Andrew Twiggins. You know, Twiggin's Boats. The ones who built all a those little landing craft things for the military during the war."

"That's you?"

"Yes ma'am," Daphney admitted. "Well, actually it's my father-in-law if you wanna know the truth, but I do get to enjoy some of the benefits."

"And your husband knows that you're here?"

"Knows," Daphney laughed. "Heck, he not only knows, he's agreed to pay for it. Especially after I told him how you and I'd been friends and what I wanted to do. See, he really didn't have a whole lot of love for the late Senator. Something to do with how he tried to prevent us from getting our Navy contracts an all during the war. So yeah, he knows all right.

"Anyway, I don't believe a thing that they're saying about you in the papers, I just don't. It's not the Willie that I know or used to know. In fact, I have a feeling that there's a whole lot more to what has happened here in Mobile than anybody really knows. And I don't mean just including what happened to your husband, but especially what happened to him. That is, everyone except you.

"I've heard rumors and stories that Foster had set him up, but nobody seems to have any proof. Is that true? I remember Danny, and I really liked him, and I'm sorry for your loss, I truly am. I remember reading all of those stories about him in the papers and I want you to know that I never believed any of them, not for a minute. Not then, and not now. It just wasn't him. It wasn't in his heart to do something like that. He never could've betrayed this country like they said."

"He didn't," Willie quickly asserted.

"He didn't?"

"No," she replied and shook her head.

"But how do you know? I mean, after all three of those trials?"

"Because I have the proof," Willie said at the thought of the folder. "Or at least I did," she sighed then turned and stared out through the window.

"You did?"

"Yes," she nodded. "I found a folder that Foster had in his desk," she turned back with a glassy-eyed gaze. "At first I thought it was all of the evidence that he'd put together to help Danny, but it wasn't."

"Well what was it?" Daphney pried.

"It was everything that he'd done to set him up and make him look like a traitor," she wiped her eyes and then took a breath to quell her emotions. "The bank accounts, the post office boxes, and the money. All of that goddamn money that the juries could never get over. It was all there, the proof of what he'd done to my husband."

"And you have it?" Daphney asked then waited.

"No," Willie shook her head. "I left it on the seat of my car when I got to the diner, and now I don't know where it is... or who has it."

"Oh dear God," Daphney gasped. "Willie, if what you are telling me is true... I mean, really, really true, we have got to find that folder."

"I know, I know. But I'm afraid to say anything to anyone because they'll take it and destroy it." She looked on with a helpless gaze. "I know they will. There are people here who want me gone, powerful people. I know there is, I can feel it, and that's why I haven't said anything to anyone about it. I don't trust anybody. I'm just hoping that I can somehow find it and get it before anyone else does. It can help me, it really can. I know it can, and you have to help me find it."

"So wait a minute, are you tellin me that that Daphney girl, the one that you guys took up river to the witch, was the one that came an helped her?"

"Yes sir," Otis nodded. "In fact, I can still remember the day that she drove over to Foster's house lookin for the car that Willie had driven to the diner. I'd been told to take care of the place an keep everything lookin good, so I was over there cuttin the grass when she came pullin into the drive real slow like an then stopped. Now right off I thought that somebody was lost so I walked on over to see if I could help em an that's when I saw her gettin out-a the car."

"Yes ma'am," Otis called as he approached and the lady opened her door. "Can I help you?"

"Oh yes," Daphney drawled as she stepped from her car. "Good afternoon. And yes, yes, I think you can. See, I'm an old friend of Willie's, I mean Miss Dawson, and I was just wondering if..." she suddenly stopped and closed her door then took a step closer to Otis. "Oh my, and please forgive me if I'm mistaken, but aren't you Mr. Brown?"

"Yes ma'am," Otis nodded with a curious gaze.

"Otis, right?"

"Yes ma'am," he nodded again.

"Well, hello Otis. I don't know if you remember me because it has been so long, but I'm Daphney. I'm Willie's old friend," she paused for a reaction. "You remember, the girl that you took up river all those years ago?" She raised her eyebrows and lowered her voice. "The one that was in all of that trouble."

"Ooh, yes ma'am," he finally said as the past came flooding back. "I remember you now. But surely you don't need to go up river again do you? Miss Hadie the witch is... well, she's dead. She passed on some years ago."

"Oh my heavens no," Daphney blushed and waved her hand. "But I do thank you for asking."

"Oh, yes ma'am," he replied as if he were relieved.

"And I do want to thank you again for everything that you did all those years ago. That was not only very kind of you, but also very brave. I know what a risk it was for you to take three young white girls up river like that and I have never forgotten it. And, I never will either. Remember that if you ever need any help, ever. And I mean it."

"Oh yes ma'am, an thank you. I'll remember that. But how can I help you? If you're lookin for Miss Willie... well, she don't live here no more. She's in jail."

"Yes, I know," Daphney replied. "I saw her this morning. We had a nice long talk and before I left she told me that if I happened to see you, to tell you hello and to let you that she was doing fine and not to worry about her."

"She did?" Otis's eyes brightened at the news. "An so Miss Willie is okay?"

"Yes," Daphney nodded. "Miss Willie is just fine."

"Well, I sure am glad to hear that," he sighed. "But still, she don't need to be sittin in jail like that. An I don't care what all they said she did to Mister Siler."

"No she doesn't," Daphney agreed. "And that's why I'm here. I'm here to try and help her."

"To help her," Otis repeated. "But how is you gonna help her here?"

"Well, it's kind of a long story, but the bottom line is, is that I really need to see the car that she drove to the diner the day that Foster died."

"The car?"

"Yes, the car. It is here, isn't it?" She looked on with a hopeful gaze.

"Oh, yes ma'am. It's right over there in the garage," he turned and pointed. "Right where I parked it after I went an picked it up. Come on, an I'll show you. But why do you need to see the car?"

"Well," Daphney said as she began to follow. "Willie said that she'd left a folder in it and I need to get it for her. It's very very important because we think that it can help her."

"A folder," Otis stopped and turned. "You mean like the one with her husband's name on it?"

"Yes!" Daphney exclaimed. "That's it. Do you know where it is?"

"Oh, yes ma'am," he nodded as if it were no big deal. "I took it home with me after I brought the car back here cause I thought it was hers. I thought that she might want it after she got out-a jail."

"Oh my God... and you still have it?"

"Oh, yes ma'am."

"So I'm takin it that this Daphney gal was pretty surprised that you had it?"

"Oh yeah," Otis nodded. "An pretty happy too."

"An so what'd you guys do?"

"Well," Otis began as he thought back. "After she finally finished thankin an huggin on me, we got into her car an drove straight over to my house. Then after we got there, me an her sat right at my kitchen table an read through that entire folder. Page by page until we'd pieced together the whole picture of jus how an what Foster'd done to Willie an her husband."

There was a short moment of silence as the two men sat and contemplated the true meaning and magnitude of what Foster had done. Then with a heavy sigh, Jim began to shake his head. "Man, I still can't believe that he did it. I mean, to have actually set somebody up like that an then to have stood by an watch while they executed him... it, it's just crazy, ya know."

"Oh I know," Otis agreed. "But I'll tell ya, he did it. He really did, an the proof was all in that folder that Willie had taken from his desk."

"So then what'd you guys do, I mean, with the folder an all?"

"Well, the next day that Daphney took it back to Willie at the jail."

"Oh Daphney," Willie gushed as she set the folder down in front of her. "I... I just don't know how to thank you. This has to be the best birthday present ever," she added as she rubbed her hands over the leather binder.

"It's your birthday?"

"Yes, today is the eleventh, isn't it?"

"Yes, September eleventh, I do believe it is."

"Well that's it, although it is kind of hard to believe that I'm thirty-one and I'm spending it in jail."

"Well heck," Daphney drawled with an air of disappointment. "If I'd of known that, I would've brought you a cake too, but happy birthday anyway."

"Thank you, that would've been nice, and if we really would've been thinking," she looked back up with a mischievous grin. "We could have baked a hacksaw inside of it so I could escape."

"Yes," Daphney agreed. "Well at least you have the folder now, but still, I don't understand how it's going to help? I mean, I know that it proves that Foster set your husband up and all, but that's a crime that he committed and he's dead, and you're being charged with murder. His murder. I mean, you went into the diner and shot him, and there is nothing in there that proves that you didn't."

"Yes, I know," Willie replied as she gripped the folder in both of her hands. "But if I learned anything when I was in law school, it was that if you can get a jury to sympathize with you and to judge you with their hearts," she paused and then turned to Daphney with a determined look. "You can change the outcome of almost any verdict in almost any trial."

"Oh really?" Daphney replied with a skeptical gaze.

"Yes," Willie nodded then refocused her eyes back on the folder.

"And just how in the heck are we going to do that?" she asked as she pulled out a chair and took a seat. "I mean, come on, don't try and fool yourself. "Even with this folder, do you really think that you're going to change anyone's mind? I mean, just think about it, you're the wife of a traitor who just shot Foster Siler, and as far as the prosecutor and the people of this town are concerned, you're guilty. And your trial I'm sorry to say, is going to be nothing more than a sham... you know it and I know it. A dog and pony show that they'll put on just so all of the morally righteous and God fearin people of this town can hold up their heads and look to each other after you've been hung and say that yesss... you really did have a fair trial."

"Yes, I know," Willie shifted her eyes back to Daphney. "And I've been thinking about that. A lot actually, and even though what you say is true I still believe that I have a chance."

"Oh really?"

"Yes."

"And how's that?"

"Because now I know who can help me."

"You dooo?" Daphney seemed surprised.

"Yes, I do."

"Annd?" she prodded.

"Well, it's kind of a long shot, but while I was still in school up in New York there was an attorney from Kansas who came and gave this two day seminar. He was a criminal defense lawyer, and his talk was on the tactics and methods he used to defend people who were being tried for capital crimes. I saw him work in a mock trial that the school had put on, and I remember how compelling and brilliant his arguments were, even when he couldn't win. I've seen a lot of lawyers work in a lot of courtrooms, but I've never seen anyone win over a jury like he did. Ever. He was amazing, and in a setting that had been specifically designed against him, you know, for him to lose, he secured a winning verdict." She finished and then looked back to the folder.

"So is this the guy you wanna use?" Daphney asked.

"Yes, I've seen him work."

"Well then," she took a breath and grinned. "Tell me, does this white knight of yours have a name so I can go and find him?"

"Yes, he does," Willie looked back to Daphney and narrowed her eyes. "It's Hawk. Just like the bird... Clayton Hawk."

"So wait a minute," Jim stopped Otis. "Are you tellin me that they actually went all the way to Kansas to get an attorney?"

"Yes sir. Well, I mean Willie didn't, but that Daphney did. In fact, she chartered a plane the very next day an flew up to see him."

"An he took her case?"

"Oh yeah, in fact he even flew back with her. See, he was one of those real high profile types where the biggest trials with the most publicity an the most money were his. He was Willie's hired gun so to speak an when he got to town, things for her finally started to change."

"Really, an how's that?"

"Well, one of the first things he did was to stop that ol prosecutor from beatin up on her to get a confession out of her. They said that he was really tryin to break her before the trial, but Willie be'n Willie, well, that didn't happen," he grinned. "An then the second thing that he did was to start a publicity campaign use'n the very same papers that'd been given her such a hard time."

"A publicity campaign?" Jim scrunched his face.

"Yeah, you know, to try an change everybody's opinion of Willie."

"But wait a minute. How in the hell'd he do that if the papers were all against her?"

"Well, about a week after he was there, an after he'd gone over everything that was in that folder, he had that Daphney take copies of some of it to the papers over in New Orleans."

"To New Orleans? Why there?"

"Well, for one they really didn't trust the papers in Mobile to print the truth, an two, when one paper picks up on a lead or a scoop as they say, I guess all of the others pick up an run with it too. I'll tell ya, he really turned the tables on those boys." He laughed. "Anyway, about once a week they'd spoon-feed somethin to the papers an after they investigated it an all they'd print it. See, he wasn't jus tryin to change peoples minds, he was tryin to get that ol prosecutor to drop the charges."

"An did he?"

"Oh hell nooo. Shit, that man liked the attention too much."

"An so when'd she finally go to trial?"

"Well," Otis cocked his head. "By the time they actually walked into the courtroom an sat down, I think it was right about the second week in December. It was a hell of a scene, the courtroom was packed an for three *whole days that prosecutor an her lawyer battled it out, but when it was all said an done, that Hawk feller actually got her off."*

"You're kiddin? You mean like in not guilty?" Jim seemed surprised.

"Yep."

"Of nothin?"

"Yep, not one single thing. Ya see, he was really really good, an right after that jury heard how Foster had set her husband up an then stood by an watched while he was executed, they had a real change in attitude. An then when they heard of how she'd lost her baby an how he'd raped her the night before he died, I don't think that there was a dry eye in the place. I'll tell ya, he had jus about everyone there wipin their eyes, includin me. Then when they heard from all of the witnesses that was at the diner, you know, tellin how Willie had actually lowered the gun cause she really couldn't shoot him, they stepped out, an after deliberatin less than half a day, they came back with a not guilty verdict."

"Really? Just like that?"

"Yes sir."

"So she was free."

"Yep, but even after she got out, it was almost as if she was still in jail. See, there were still a lot of people in town, powerful people, who didn't like the verdict an wanted her gone. An let me tell ya, they didn't make no bones about it either."

CHAPTER 65

———◆———

ALTHOUGH ACQUITTED OF MURDER, FREEDOM for Willie was bittersweet, for it had certainly not come without a price and it had certainly not come without controversy. Controversy that seemed to have no end, and that followed her wherever she went. There were a lot of people who liked her and felt sorry for what Foster had done to her and her husband. It was an unconscionable crime, but even so, many believed she'd gotten away with the murder of one of the most prominent men in the state. A man who'd done so much for a town that now seemed to resent her in the most hostile of ways.

Shunned by a city she loved and hounded by a press that continued to vilify her, Willie, by the beginning of 1947, had finally had enough. There were people that wanted her gone, wealthy and influential people who'd made it abundantly clear that her welcome in Mobile had come to an end. And even though the Bishop of her Church had so graciously offered her sanctuary within its confines, she could take no more of the constant scrutinization and had decided to leave town.

"Now it wasn't until around the middle of January that I saw Willie again when she showed up at my house one Sunday lookin for help. I remember she looked jus terrible, like she hadn't had a good night's sleep in weeks. In fact, she was--."

"But wait a minute," Jim interrupted before he could finish. "Where in the heck had she been? I mean, that was almost a month, wasn't it?"

"Oooh," Otis replied as if he'd forgotten. "The Catholic Church, here in town. She told me that she'd gone there to go to confession an to pray one day

right after the trial an that while she was there she'd run into some Bishop feller. Actually, I think it was her old priest Father Ruggeri. Anyway, I guess he must of took her confession or whatever it was an then afterwards, after she was all done, they got to talkin.

"Now whatever it was that Willie'd told him, it must of really worried him cause after she was all done an he realized what all she was go'n through, well, that's when he insisted that she jus stay there at the church. That they had a little guest house there where she could stay until things around town had died down a bit an she felt better. He was real kind to her that Bishop man, an he really helped her cope with a lot of the things that she'd been through. You know, first her baby, an then husband, an Foster--."

"But wait a minute," Jim interrupted again. "Why in the heck didn't she just go to her old in-laws or her foster parents? You know, to the Portmans. They were all still pretty close, weren't they?"

"Oh heck yeah, but I guess Willie didn't wanna bother em with all of the crap an controversy that kept followin her. She said that they'd been put through enough. Besides, you gotta remember that Tom an Foster had been best friends for years an when Willie shot Foster, well, an even though Mrs. Portman wanted to help her an I think actually had in a lot of ways, her husband I guess had a pretty hard time with it."

"Yeah, I guess I can see that," Jim surmised.

"Anyway, by the time that trial had run its course an was over, it seemed as if every single person that Willie had ever known had abandoned her in some way or another. Yes sir, there wasn't nobody left that'd help her except for that Daphney girl, but she finally had to leave an go back to New Orleans. I'll tell ya, it was really sad too, cause she didn't have nothin no more. No money an no car, no place to live or call home, an most of all no friends.

"I remember she told me that she'd tried callin some of em, but nobody ever called her back. That was a real shock to her, an I think deep down it really hurt her, an then after awhile she said she jus quit tryin an that's when she finally came to me. I guess I was jus about the only friend she had left, or at least the only one that she could turn to that'd help her.

"Anyway, I think she ended up stayin with us for about a week, an after she'd rested an put some of Momma's food in her belly, I scraped together close to five hundred dollars that me an my wife had saved over the years an gave it to her. It was damn near everything we had, but I knew that someday she'd find a way to pay me back when she got the chance.

"Then after that, I gave her my son's car to use. Me an him had been fixin it up, but he was in the military an overseas so I knew he wouldn't mind. Now granted it wasn't much to look at, but even so it ran pretty good an was dependable. Then early one mornin, we loaded her up with a whole bunch of food an some household things that she was gonna need for her new home, an after a great big hug an a promise to see me real soon, Willie got in my son's car an headed off to Florida.

"An that's pretty much how she ended up leavin Mobile. I remember standin there with my wife as she drove off down the street an then seein her wave out the window one last time jus before she disappeared around the bend. An then I remember be'n real worried an hopin that she would be okay. I knew she would cause that's jus how she was. She was tough, but still, in the back of my mind, I worried about her. In fact, I worried about her a lot."

It really wasn't much compared to what she'd lived in before but it was quiet, it was on the beach and the rent was cheap. Her search was over and she'd moved on, but even as she settled into her new home she couldn't help but think of the past. Memories she cherished and now reflected upon as she began to unpack what few belongings she had. Trinkets and keepsakes that she'd collected over the years, and of course her most prized and coveted possession; her large leather bound scrapbook of pictures and letters.

It was one of the only things left in her life she could still call her own and she was glad she had found it after the trial. Smiling as she pulled it from the box, she held it up with a contented sigh then turned and took a seat on the sofa. Settling in as the afternoon drizzle continued to fall, she curled her legs beneath her, laid the book on her lap and then opened its cover. It had been a long, long time since she'd looked inside, but as she slowly began to thumb through the pages of the past, she smiled at the memories that came flooding back.

Memories of her life that seemed so long ago, yet somehow, seemed to instantly bridge the span of time. Of happier times, that gave her a soothing comfort if only for a moment as she slowly turned from page to page and reflected on the past. Reminiscing of days that were long since gone until she'd turned to a page with a yellowed and tattered typewritten paper taped neatly inside. A paper, that at the time was to have symbolized her marriage when she was just fifteen.

'*This is just like being married,*' the sound of Foster's voice echoed inside her head. Smiling, she stared for a moment then ever so lightly brushed her hand across the page and thought of that day. That day that had meant so much to her when they had stood in the grass by the river and he'd said that he loved her. That special day so long, long ago... that had made her so incredibly happy.

She remembered it all as if it were yesterday, but along with the memories came a sudden and overwhelming flood of emotions. Emotions of heartache and sorrow that she'd buried deep inside, but that now seemed to have a life of their own as they began to well from the depths of her inner core. That try as she may, she could not control. She was sad and lonely, and weak and tired from her struggles, yet even so she battled to suppress her tears and quickly turned her gaze outside.

It was an attempt to clear her mind but it failed, for her memories of the past were too strong. She felt lonelier now than ever before, and as she stared out through the rain spotted glass and into the vast open expanse of a gray empty ocean, she felt her throat tighten and her eyes fill with tears. She thought of her life when she was young, and then of her hopes and dreams, then wondered as to how it had all gone so terribly, terribly wrong. She tried to make sense of it all but couldn't, and now it seemed as if it just didn't matter. A few moments later she returned her gaze back to the page and stared. But it was a watery and unfocused gaze, and as the onset of tears escaped from their salty reservoirs and rolled down her cheeks, Willie gently closed her book and then lowered her head.

CHAPTER 66

———◆———

THEY'D BEGUN BEFORE THE LATE Senator was even in the ground, yet even so it had taken the lawyers and greedy business partners who had been looking to seize control of Foster's companies, almost a year of arguing to finally come to their agreements. Led by Ralston DuPree', who for years had been Foster's ruthless right hand man and who now sat as the new court appointed administrator, the dozen separate entities had bickered for months.

At first each had started off wanting just a certain piece, but as time slowly passed and the true extent of Foster's staggering wealth was revealed, the greed within them all took over. It became ugly really quick, but just as quickly as their talks had disintegrated, the group soon realized that if they didn't change their ways, an estate worth millions could be tied up in court forever.

Colluding together, they established a hierarchy with Ralston clearly in charge and things slowly settled. They worked hard and by the mid-summer of 47 and the onset of the trial, the jackals and hyenas that'd been circling and vying for the most coveted and succulent pieces of Foster's empire, had finally figured out a way to divide it all and make everyone happy.

They would manipulate the very system itself. The legal process in which it had to go through, then take it to the slaughter-house where they would then butcher and carve up his companies into neat little pieces. Pieces from a carcass of an unimaginable size, that they would then divide amongst themselves to feast upon. The ships and shipbuilding, the banking and real estate, and of course the still untapped riches of his oil wells. Each one claimed a piece of

Foster's fortune, including plans to drain and divide his off shore bank accounts that were loaded with cash.

They had thought of it all, including a big meaty bone to the Judge and some scrapes to a few of the distant but gold digging relatives, just to ensure that the proceedings went without a hitch. They had planned it all with a meticulous and unprecedented zeal, all of it behind closed doors and away from the prying eyes of the media and the public. Everything with an almost arrogant certainty, even down to who got what from his personal effects and mementos, and now it was just a matter of time and formality. They drooled like ravenous dogs, and as the trial approached they began making plans for the money. They even began to celebrate. But the one thing that they hadn't thought of nor ever imagined, was for the mistress of Foster K. Siler and her attorney to come walking into the picture. No one did.

It didn't take long for Willie's attorney to investigate her request and then immediately file a claim with the Mobile County Probate Court. It was just two weeks before the trial and in his petition he laid claim to every single thing that Foster Siler owned. It was an unprecedented move and it didn't take long for word to get out and around that there was another player in the game. A player that every one of them knew all too well.

Enraged at what they considered as nothing more than an intrusion into their plans and a ploy for money, the group postured and then threatened. They were powerful men and were determined to complete the scheme that they had worked so hard on. But Willie's lawyer was confident and undeterred and quickly returned their threats with his own.

Shocked at the sheer audacity of his actions, they quickly reconsidered their options. They thought of vilifying her in the press but knew that if she were to play her role correctly that she could garner sympathy in the form of public opinion and drag out the trial indefinitely. They had to be careful and in doing so they backed off, but even so, they'd worked far too long and hard to have someone stop them now. They offered a bribe, five hundred thousand to go away, to leave and never come back.

Incensed, Willie scoffed at their offer and told them all to go to hell. She knew Ralston DuPree' for who and what he was; a greedy and overly jealous tyrant, and she despised him vehemently. He had always been resentful of Foster and she knew it, often claiming that it was he who'd built Siler Shipbuilding and Siler Shipping into what it was. Besides, she knew now that it was he who'd wanted her out of town, and now she knew why. He wanted Foster's fortune.

A few days later, and after their talk's had broken off, one of the local papers got wind of the story and instantly went into print. It seemed as if they just couldn't get enough of the beautiful and controversial Miss Willie Mae Dawson... the woman who'd shot Senator Foster K. Siler. She'd sold more newspapers than anyone else in their history, and as word spread of her impending plans, the rest of the press from around the country picked up and grabbed hold of the story.

Once again returning to Mobile, they descended into town filling room after room until they had transformed the city. It'd quickly and clearly become the second biggest event since her murder trial, and everyone who was anyone was there. There was TV and radio, and newspapers, all vying for the latest scoop. There was gossip and opinions and speculation. They interviewed people, some who'd known her and some who had not. There were those who defended her and those who ridiculed her, but all of them waited. They waited until the day finally came when Willie and her lawyer pulled up in front of the Mobile County Courthouse.

She was a stunning depiction of everything beautiful and elegant in a woman, and without question a photographer's ultimate dream. And as she stepped from the car in the most regal of ways, the flash bulbs from over a hundred cameras seemed to go off at once. But this wasn't some Hollywood premiere, nor was it a press conference, and with all due haste Willie and her lawyer ascended the steps without a word to fight for her rightful inheritance. They were the last to arrive and just as soon as they had entered through the set of double doors, an instant hush fell across the entire courtroom. A second later, the buss of rising whispers swept from person to person as every eye in the room followed them to the front. Shortly after that, the bailiff called out for everyone to rise.

The Judge had been an easy target for the influential businessmen, and the proceedings began as if they had already been rehearsed. The trial was nothing more than a charade and a show for the press, but even so he pretended to listen to each attorney, shaking his head and making notes as one by one they presented their cases. An hour and a half later, and after they had all finished, he turned to Willie and her lawyer with a smug indifference. He knew who she was and even though he really didn't care for her or her east-coast lawyer, he had to let them speak.

"Well now," he began with a heavy breath. "I really didn't expect this one, but what the hell, you might as well throw your hat in the ring too. It seems like everyone else around here has. So tell me counselor," he continued in a condescending tone as he shifted his eyes from Willie to her lawyer. "What little piece of Mr. Siler's estate would you like to take a bite out of today?"

"Well your honor," he stood and smiled with a casual but unwavering confidence to his voice. "If it pleases the court, and with all due respect, we're not here just to take a bite out of Mr. Siler's estate," he said as he looked around the courtroom then settled with an unflinching gaze on the band of lawyers sitting at the other tables. "We're here to declare a claim against his estate in its entirety. Everything."

"Oh you are now, are you?" the Judge replied with a smirk as he racked his gavel to quiet the courtroom.

"Yes sir," he answered as he turned back to the Judge with another smile. "We are."

Shaking his head, the Judge racked his gavel once again and then took a disgruntled breath. "Now counselor, I'm not exactly sure as to just where it is that you're tryin to take this, but I want you to know something. I know how this all works. See, I was a lawyer long before I was a judge, and if you are deliberately trying to disrupt these proceedings in hopes of making some sort of deal or settlement with regards to the late Senator's estate, I'm warning you, do not try my patience here, for it has been a very, very, lonnng couple of weeks."

"Oh, no sir, I wouldn't think of it."

"Well good, then tell me please, just under what grounds are you proposing to make such a preposterous assertion."

"Well, your honor," he began with a taunting smirk to the other lawyers before turning his attention back to the Judge. "We're filing our claim under the inheritance provisions of the State of Alabama. You see, I've just recently discovered that Miss Dawson here is in fact, and without question, Mr. Siler's closest living relative."

"Oh she is, is she?" The Judge chuckled and shook his head as another wave of humor swept the courtroom. "Well, I really don't recall Miss Dawson and Mr. Siler ever being married. Sooo?"

"No sir, they weren't. And they never had any children together either."

"Then what pray-tell, are you basing such an outlandish claim upon? Please, if you would be so kind as to enlighten this court and humor us all. I think we would all find this very, very interesting, not to mention amusing."

"Well sir, I know that you might find this just a little hard to believe," he paused with a glance to the other lawyers now sitting on the edge of their seats. "But the simple truth is, is that Miss Dawson here is Mr. Siler's daughter. His adopted and only daughter."

It was at that very moment and in one simultaneous gasp from every person there that the entire courtroom fell silent. There wasn't a sound from anyone and you could've heard a pin drop as his words slowly sank into each and every person there. But all of that changed just a split second later, when, and in almost perfect unison, it erupted into absolute chaos. Every lawyer along with their client instantly stood and yelled in vehement objection as the flash bulbs from over a dozen cameras flashed again and again. The Judge called for order and struck his gavel, but no one was listening.

He pounded harder then stood in a rage, threatening to empty the entire room until everyone had quieted and order was finally restored. Glaring as if to ensure that they really understood what he meant, the Judge took a moment to gather his composure then turned and took his seat. Fixing his robe as he settled, he took in a long deep breath, then removed his glasses and shook his head.

It was a curve ball that'd come out of nowhere and had caught everyone off guard, especially him. They'd worked out everything or so he'd thought, but now here was Willie and her lawyer, making one of the most absurd and outlandish claims he'd ever heard. Good God, he thought as he cleaned his glasses and then put them back on, what more could these people possible throw at him? Then clearing his throat, he narrowed his eyes and looked to Willie and her lawyer.

"Counselor," he began with a finger pointed warning, the humorous disposition that he'd displayed earlier now completely gone. "I know that you're not from around these parts and I'm sure that you and your friends back east probably do things a little different than we do down here, but let me warn you sir. Don't you even think of making a mockery out of my courtroom here or I'll hold the both of you in contempt. Do you understand me?"

"Oh yes your honor," he answered with a contemptuous tone. "I wouldn't dream of it."

The Judge knew that his tone was a challenge, yet even so he let it slide for curiosity had taken its hold. "Good. Then I really hope you have something that can substantiate your claim cause I'm warning you, you are beginning to tread on some very, very thin ice here."

"Yes sir… that I do. If I may?" He held up a folder as if to present.

Receiving a nod along with a hand gesture to approach, Willie's lawyer crossed the room and handed the folder to the Judge.

"Now as you can see your honor," he began with a glance to the band of lawyers still glued to his every word. "I have brought with me a copy of the records from the Mobile County Probate Court clearly attesting to such adoption. Recorded as of record, showing that in the month of December of 1930, that Foster K. Siler did in fact, without duress or coercion, and upon his own free will, legally adopt Miss Willie Mae Dawson as his very own child. Which under the provisions of the law your honor, as I am sure you are well aware of since you know how all this works," he grinned. "Accord her the very same rights and privileges of inheritance as if she were his naturally born child."

Grabbing his glasses the Judge opened the folder, gazed at the papers for a just a few seconds then peered down upon the man with a scowl. "Counselor," he directed his voice at the man in a brutally stern warning. "This better not in any way be a hoax or where you are tryin to pull some sort of fast one you hear, or I can assure you that it will be a very, very long time before you make it back home. Do I make myself clear?"

"Yes sir," he grinned again. "Perfectly."

"Well good then. Now, let's see just what it is that you have here, shall we?"

"So wait a minute, are you tellin me that Foster actually adopted her?" Jim's sense of shock seemed to resonate in his voice. "I mean for real?"

"Yep, that's exactly what I'm tellin you."

"Oooh my God, what a bombshell that was."

"Oh hell, tell me about it."

"An did you know that? I mean, before the trial?"

"Nope, not a clue. But when Willie's lawyer started talkin about it, you know, how ol Foster had adopted her all those years ago, I jus couldn't help but think back to that day. Back to all those years ago when the two of them had stood in the grass next to the river an he pretended to marry her. Tellin her how he'd found a loophole in the law that would let them get adopted to each other but that she could never tell no one cause she was too young. Now back then when he'd done all this, neither me or Willie had any idea what adopted meant. We jus thought that it was another word for be'n married. But boy let me tell you, we sure knew what it meant by the time that trial had rolled around... oooh yeah. An let me tell ya somethin else too, so did that Judge an all them lawyerin boys sittin at them other tables.

"Yes sir, by the time her lawyer had finished with his little presentation there was a whole lot-a real unhappy people sittin there in that courtroom. An not only includin that Judge, but specially that Judge, cause everything that they'd been plannin had jus been brought to a screechin halt. See, Willie's lawyer was really smart an had actually put that crooked ol Judge an all them lawyers right on the spot cause with a claim like that an with all of them people an reporters watchin, they didn't have a choice... they had to stop.

"Anyway, I remember him sittin up there behind his bench after Willie's lawyer gave him all them papers. There wasn't a sound from anyone, an every single eye in that whole room was locked right on him as he started shufflin through them. Now you could see that he was real disgusted, an with each an every page that he looked at I think he got a little worse. Yes sir, he wasn't very happy an after he'd seen all he wanted, he looked back up at Willie's lawyer an then warned him again about spendin a real long time in jail. An then right after that, I remember him sayin somethin about how in light of such compellin evidence that'd jus been presented, that the court had no choice but to postpone their proceedins until they could substantiate Willie's claim. An with that, that ol Judge slapped his gavel down real hard an dismissed the court."

"So you were there... again? An saw it?"

"Oh yeah," Otis nodded as he recalled the day. "Sittin right next to Willie. See, her lawyer had wanted me there jus in case he needed me to testify or somethin, but I never had to talk or do nothin which suited me jus fine really."

"So then what happened? You know, after the Judge dismissed court."

"Well, all them lawyers that was sittin at those other tables shot right out-a their chairs an rushed out of that room straight down to where the county kept all their adoption records. I'd heard a few days later that they'd tried every which way they could to discredit Willie's claim, includin destroyin all the records. But it was iron-clad cause her lawyer had made damn certain of that before he ever let anyone know about it. Like I said before, he was smart.

"Anyway, it didn't take but a about a week for that trial to reconvene, but boy by the time it did, ol Willie had the whole goddamn city stirred all back up." He chuckled and then took a sip from his beer. "Yes sir, jus as soon as word had gotten out that she was actually claimin to be his daughter an had proof of it, that whole town went plum nuts all over again an by the time that trial had started back up, she'd created a real honest ta God circus."

"Really?"

"Oh, hell yes. I mean shit, jus think about it. You couldn't make somethin like that up even if you tried. Yes sir, it jus didn't get any juicier than that if you was a reporter, an within days I don't believe that there was a hotel room left in the city. I'll tell ya, there was more people comin into town than you could of ever imagined. People from all over the country, who'd come jus to see the woman who had shot Senator Siler. The gold diggin mistress as some had begun to call her, who was now claimin to be his daughter, an who'd actually carried on an incestuous relationship go back into court to battle all of them big shots over his fortune. A fortune that at the time was rumored to be between a hundred an thirty an forty million dollars."

"Whooooa," Jim widened his eyes great big. "You're kiddin?"

"Oh hell no," Otis grinned. "See, ol Foster wasn't jus rich, he was real rich. Yes sir, by the end of the war that man had built himself a real honest to God empire. Shit, he had ships an ship-buildin, an bankin an real estate, an oil an gas an... well hell, you name it an I think he was into it. An now, everybody was fightin an squabblin over it."

The courtroom was packed to standing room only and as the judge slowly lumbered toward his place at the bench, the bailiff called out for everyone to rise. Slowly taking his seat in front of the silent yet suspenseful crowd of onlookers, he opened his folder and looked around then rapped his gavel. A few seconds later he cleared his throat, and in a tempered voice that seemed to match his mood, he began to read his findings and then his decision.

"Let it be known that in light of Miss Dawson's claim, that the probate court of Mobile County has rendered a decision. That under the Alabama Adoption Code of 1923, Article 2, Section 9302, any person desirous to adopt a child so as to make it capable of inheriting his estate, real and personal, may make such declaration in writing, attested by two witnesses, setting forth the name, sex and age of the child he wishes to adopt. Which after being presented by the declarant before the judge of probate of the county of his residence, filed and recorded as prescribed by law, has the effect to make such child capable of inheriting such estate of the declarant.

"Furthermore, it is the findings of this court that after a complete and exhaustive review of the records from the Mobile County Probate Court dated December 9th of 1930, that Foster K. Siler did in fact willfully and lawfully adopt Miss Willie Mae Dawson as his legitimate daughter, whereby rendering her capable of inheriting his entire estate. And so, and in light of the indisputable evidence of record attesting to such, it is the order of this court that Miss Willie Mae Dawson," he paused with a reluctant sigh then continued on. "Be awarded sole and exclusive rights of inheritorship, personal and or otherwise, in the estate of Foster K. Siler. And," he pounded his gavel and raised his voice to the erupting crowd. "That all real estate holdings, companies, bank accounts and monetary funds, including any and all stocks and bonds, and every damn thing else that the man owned, be released immediately and remanded into the exclusive custody and control of Miss Dawson without further delay," he hastened his words as the drum of voices grew louder. "That is the decision of this court; it is final and so concludes these proceedings. Court dismissed."

"Now jus as soon as that judge had read the verdict an had banged his gavel down on his bench, that whole courtroom went jus plum crazy all over again. An I really believe even worse than the first time. I tell ya, I'd never seen anything quite like it. Everyone of them lawyers jumped up an started hollerin an objectin, actually, an now that I think about it, cryin an whinin like a bunch of babies was more like it." He chuckled and took another sip.

"Anyway, it wasn't but a second later that I glanced back to Willie jus as she'd closed her eyes an lowered her head as if she really couldn't believe it. It had really been a fight, but her ordeal was finally over an she'd won. She had gone up against every single one of them crooked bastards tryin to get at Foster's fortune an had beat em all. Now in all the years that I had known her, I'd never ever seen her shed a tear. Not once I tell ya, an not over anything. She was tough, but right after the judge had read that verdict an we sat there, I watched her cry.

"Now I couldn't even begin to imagine as to what was go'n on in her head right about then. But I can still remember to this day thinkin to myself of all the years that'd passed an how it was that we'd come to be sittin there. Foster really had adopted her. Why?" He sighed as if he were deep in thought. "Nobody knew... not even Willie. Did he love her? I'm not really sure, but in a way when I look back, I like to think that deep down that he did. That he really did love her, even after everything that they'd been through. An that maybe, in some strange kind of way, this was his way of showin it. But who knows really, that was so long ago."

"So that's why he never married her after his wife died?" Jim surmised as if he'd just solved some great riddle. "He couldn't, she was his daughter. I mean, in the legal sense."

"Well, I never really thought of it like that, but yeah, I guess so," Otis agreed. "An that's how she ended up gettin everything too."

"Everything?" Jim raised his eyebrows.

"Yep, everything. Although there was some of those guys that had tried to contest the judge's rulin right after the trial, they failed an then if I remember right, I think it was right around the spring of 48 that Willie began to wind up all of her affairs so she could finally leave Mobile for good. She said that she was jus gonna sell everything that Foster had an was gonna move to someplace nice, that she was tired of the spotlight an of all the attention, an that she jus wanted to live a quieter life.

"She mentioned somethin about go'n back to Florida to Destin I think it was. On the beach, she said. An hell, ya really couldn't blame her after everything she'd been through. You know, all three of those big trials an all of that publicity. First her husband's for treason, then Foster's for murder. An then after those, that big ol probate trial." He shook his head. "I'll tell ya, poor ol Willie couldn't go nowhere around town without somebody botherin her.

"Anyway, one of the first things that she did after she started gettin rid of everything was to up an donate the boat to the Catholic Church. Actually,

gave it to that Bishop feller is more like it. See, the two of them were actually pretty good friends an after church, weather permittin, they'd have me take em for cruises. Now he really like boatin an Willie knew it, so that summer before she left, she jus up an gave it to him with a promise that it would stay with the church an he would hire me on as its captain.

"So that's when you started workin for the church?"

"Yep, all the way up until last week." *Otis chuckled and then took a sip from his beer.* "Anyway, right after she did that, she went on a real sellin spree an by mid fall of that year had sold jus about everything that Foster ever owned. You know, his shippin company with all those ships that sailed all over the world. Some said there was over a 135 of em. An then the shipyards an the dry docks with all them Navy contracts he had in place, an that big ol office buildin he was so proud of. Hell, she even sold his house. Yes sir, by the time the dust had all settled an you could see again, she'd sold everything. Everything that was, except for some stocks an the Davenport property up river."

"Really? An why'd she keep that?"

"Cause it had all those oil wells on it that were still up there pumpin away. An like she said, all she had to do was to collect a check once a month from the oil company. But it wasn't as if she really needed it cause all told, rumor had it that she was gettin ready to leave town with right around a hundred an twenty-eight million an some change."

"A hundred an twenty-eight million?" *Jim choked.* "Are you serious?"

"Yes sir, in fact I think it was right about then that ol Willie became one of the wealthiest women in the state if not the nation."

"Jesus," *Jim gushed.* "Can you just imagine? I mean... a hundred an twenty-eight million?"

"Oh hell, tell me about it," *Otis agreed.*

"So is that when she finally took off to Florida?"

"No it wasn't actually. In fact, that's right when she took off an went up north."

"Up north?" *Jim looked on with a bewildered gaze.* "To where?"

"I ain't sure really. All I knew was that she had some business to take care of an that she wanted to visit an old friend that she hadn't seen in a real long time. I remember her tellin me that when I was over at her house helpin her pack up the last of her things but that when she got back later on in the week that she'd come by an see me an we'd go to lunch. You know, to say goodbye before she really did leave. Anyway, as best I can recall, I believe she left the very next mornin."*

———◆———

CHAPTER 67

IT WAS STILL DARK BUT the breaking day was close at hand when Willie and her chauffer pulled up to the hotel. She wanted to get an early start, and just as soon as the two men had descended the steps and had settled in for their journey, they were off. A short while later they reached the outskirts of town, turned left onto highway five and headed north to Hale County. Leaving the city behind as they drove into the country, they could see the crimson glow of the rising sun on the far off horizon. Slowly replacing the dark of night with a colorful array of pinks and pastels, they watched as it grew steadily brighter until its brilliant orange light broke over the horizon and spread itself across the landscape. Bringing with it a glowing warmth and a clear blue sky, it gave every indication of the beginning of a great day.

Later that afternoon, they finally turned off of the highway onto an old gravel road. It had been eighteen years since she'd seen the area, but as she clung to the back of the seat and peered through the windshield, she gave directions as best she could. At first she wasn't sure, but as soon as they crested the high rolling hill and rounded the curve she recognized the spot.

"Here Charles," Willie suddenly called out.

Rolling to a gentle stop, she quickly opened her door and stepped from the car. Was this it, she wondered as she walked to the edge of the road and then gazed at the valley below? It looked familiar, but it had been so long. She turned back toward the car and gazed past it in search of the old dead tree that'd once stood in the field. She could see that it had fallen and was now nothing more than an indiscernible log slowly decaying back into the ground as the years had passed. Yes, this was it. She was certain of it. She remembered the owl and how it had scared her all those years ago. Hooting loudly at her from high above, then dropping from its jagged perch as it took flight and descended silently across the fields into the forested trees below. She remembered it all.

She turned back and cast her eyes out across the valley, and then to the cotton fields she knew all too well. That she'd worked so hard in, and that in a cruel and unforgiving way had taken the life of her mother. They looked smaller than she remembered, and were cornfields now, but seemed as if they had been abandoned with rows of broken and withered stalks. Her curiosity rose. What had happened after she left? Did Mr. Johnson die?

She put a hand to her forehead to block the afternoon sun and surveyed the terrain until she saw the small grass covered mound that use to be her home. Yes, it was still there. Her heart leapt with a twinge of joy but just as it did she caught her breath as she envisioned the glowing pile of embers and how it had shimmered in the far off dark. A radiating red, glowing and pulsating with a life of its own as it slowly cooled and entombed her mother and stepfather. She remembered being afraid and sad and crying, and then of pushing on all alone in the dark.

Now overgrown with weeds and briars, it hardly seemed a fitting place for her mother. So far from everything, so all alone and so forgotten. She felt ashamed and remorseful at how she'd forsaken her memory for so long then dropped her head as a growing lump welled in her throat and her eyes filled with tears. She'd never even said a prayer for her. No one had. She stared for a moment longer then wiped her eyes and cleared her throat. A moment later, she turned and walked back to the car.

Following the road, they made their way to the valley floor then finally stopped at the cross roads where Willie had begun her journey all those years ago. She told the men that she needed a few moments alone and that she wouldn't be long. It was something that she'd been thinking about for a long, long time and as she walked what remained of the long dirt path that led to their house, the three men waited by the car and watched.

At first she was reluctant, but Bishop Ruggeri had finally convinced her to do it. She remembered how he'd said that in the eyes of the Lord it was most certainly the right thing to do, even after she'd confessed her sins of what she had done all those years ago. Granting forgiveness, he then blessed a beautiful wooden cross and wrapped it in clean white linen. *'This is to mark your mother's grave.'* He had told her. *'God would want this. Plant it where she lays and say a prayer, then be at peace my child.'*

Slowing as she approached, Willie finally stopped just at the edge of the mound where her home had once stood. There were still signs of a house, but with the effects of time and how Mother Nature eventually reclaimed everything that man had taken, there was very little. Just remnants of the old corrugated roof, partially exposed under a blanket of dirt and grass as it slowly disintegrated back into the earth. And then the old cook stove sticking out of the rubble, now rusted and pitted as if it had been eaten away by some cancerous disease. She looked for other signs but saw nothing then turned her gaze to where her mother's bedroom had been and where she might still lay.

Yes, that was it, right where a beautiful little oak now some twenty feet high had taken root and was providing shade. It was a sign from God, she was certain of it. A living marker that he himself had put there as a continuation of her life yet in another form.

Making her way closer, Willie instantly spied a spot at the base of the tree. A grassy area, with just a few weeds, that was highlighted by a filtered shaft of sunlight. It was perfect, and with a contented smile she dropped to her knees, laid her cross to the side then weeded and cleared a small area until all that remained was a patch of grass. Then grabbing a short sturdy stick, she drilled a hole into the soil, unwrapped the twelve inch long cross from its linen and stuck it into the ground. Packing dirt around its base until it stood on its own as her own little memorial, Willie then brushed her hands with a satisfied sigh and bowed her head to pray.

It was a short and simple prayer, but one that she'd recited a hundred times in her head. It was the closure she needed to ease her aching heart and as soon as she had finished, she felt a sense of relief. As if the heavy burden of guilt she'd been carrying all of these years had suddenly been lifted and was replaced by a feeling of peace and warmth. A radiating glow, emanating deep from within that seemed to touch her soul and give her solace as she closed her eyes and raised her head to the sky. She'd found her peace, and as she knelt in her moment of silence, she began to listen to the sounds around her. To the sounds of the soft gentle breeze as it blew across the landscape and into the trees, rustling the fall foliage and then touching and caressing her face with its warmth and familiar smells. And then, to the long lonesome cry of a red tailed hawk high above the fields.

Opening her eyes, she put a hand to her forehead in search of the winged raptor. Nothing. She heard it again then a second later, the alarmed calls of a half dozen crows squawking wildly as they flew into the distant trees, no doubt looking for protection. They were the sounds and smells from her youth and she remembered them well. Smiling, she closed her eyes once again and drifted with her thoughts to a time that was long long ago. To happier times with her mother, when she was a little girl and they'd made her very first dress out of their leftover flour sacks. And of how she had lovingly cut and sewed it by hand, and then bleached and softened it. And then of the little wide belt that they'd braided from the twisted twine of hay bales to go with it as a sash.

She remembered how proud she'd been when she put it on and wore it for the very first time. And then of when she was older, and had gone to the creek for her bath and shaved for the very first time. Then of how she'd proudly returned home with her arms held high and twirled for her mother to see, only to be teased in a loving kind of way when she began to count her nicks and cuts. Twenty in all, she recalled with a smile. And then she thought of how her mother had fallen ill shortly after that, and then that night after dinner. That horrible night when her stepfather had violated her on the porch, and then later on when he finally went to bed in a drunken stupor and beat her mother into an incoherent daze and raped her.

Snapping her head in the direction he laid, Willie stared with a glaring hatred at the evil that was so close... too close as far as she was concerned. She'd been told by the Bishop to forgive and forget but she couldn't; it just wasn't in her. She hated him for what he had done, and would never forgive him, ever. She was glad she'd burnt the house, and glad that he was in it. But as she stared at the weeds and briars where he lay, the haunting vision of his memory soon faded and was replaced by the discolored white rocks that had once made up her mother's small flower garden. Staring blankly at first, Willie focused her eyes then began to smile at the cluster of the little white flowers growing miraculously out of the corner.

It was her mother's much beloved daisies, all still in bloom. That against all odds had survived the fire and then sprung forth through a rusted cancerous hole in a piece of corrugated tin. It was another sign from God that he had been, and still was, watching over her mother.

Rising from her knees, she made her way to the small rock outline and picked a handful of the nicest ones. She was glad she'd seen them for in her haste to leave Mobile she had completely forgotten about flowers. She felt a touch of guilt run through her, but then thought of how it was just God's way of guiding her, of helping her to choose the ones her mother loved most.

Returning to the site of her mother, she knelt back down and tenderly laid the clean white linen in front of the cross. Spreading it out like a blanket, she smoothed and patted it free of wrinkles then pulled a light blue ribbon from her hair. Wrapping the stems twice around, she tied the flowers together with a delicate bow and then laid them in front of the cross.

To her it was the final and befitting touch to a moment in which she'd sought for many years. A moment that seemed to bring a soothing contentment as she sat upright and then stared down at the flowers. They were beautiful, and just what her mother would've wanted. And with the afternoon sun beaming its filtered rays of light through the leafy canopy of the young oak, bathing her miniature memorial in a shimmering mix of moving shadows and sunlight, she smiled. Yet even so, her heart still ached with a dull and empty sadness. It had been eighteen years and here she was, still all alone. It weighed heavily on her mind that she'd forsaken her mother for so long, and in an effort to ease her pain she closed her eyes and reached instinctively for the small silver locket that'd slipped from beneath her blouse. A locket she'd worn for years. That now was more precious to her than anything else in the world for it contained the only picture she had of her mother.

Looking down, she thought of the photos she'd put inside all those years ago; of her and her mother that she'd taken from the dresser the night she died. A second later, she snapped it open and quietly gazed at the black and white reminders of a time long, long ago... of her as a little girl, and of her mother as a beautiful young woman. She thought of how pretty she was and of how much they resembled each other and smiled. And then she began to hear the haunting sound of her soft sweet voice resonate in her head. Whispering in the wind as if it had been carried to her from the hereafter on the soft gentle breeze. The last words she'd spoken before she died as they lay together on the bed. *'I love you sweetie. An don't you never forget it, ya hear.'*

"I love you too, Momma," Willie coughed and looked to the sky. "I love you too..." her voice faded as she lowered her head and wept.

CHAPTER 68

THE TOWN WAS ONLY AN hour away but by the time they arrived the sun had set and it was getting dark. It wasn't very large and in short order they found a nice hotel at the edge of town and settled in for the night. Early the next morning they woke to another beautiful day, strolled to the local diner and leisurely had breakfast. It reminded her a lot of Connie's, catering mostly to the local farmers with good food and lots of it.

"Now, the Jacksons are gone right?"

"Yes ma'am," Walter answered. "Talked with Mr. Jackson Sunday morning and he assured me that they would be out by that evening."

"And they don't suspect anything?"

"No ma'am, except that…" he smiled with a glance to Harold then chuckled and shook his head.

"What?" Willie instantly asked. "Tell meee?"

"Well, it's just that they think that you're some kind of kooky crazy rich lady from the city that's got way too much money and doesn't know what in the hell she's doing."

"Well, there just might be a little more truth to that than one thinks," Willie replied with a laugh. "Cause I'll tell you, who in the hell else would come up here an do something like this? Now, what about the survey and the title work?"

"Done, all prepared just like you asked."

"And the truck?" She raised her eyebrows and then took a bite of her toast.

"A forty-six Ford half ton, sitting right in the drive. It's used, but in good condition."

"Good. Oh, and what about all of the farm equipment?"

"Left in the barn."

"And their stuff in the house?"

"As far as I know, just as we discussed. Their pictures, clothes and personal items all went with them. Everything else should still be there. You know, the furniture, beds, pots, pans... everything."

"Good," she replied. "Now, what about my friend?" Her voice turned serious.

"Well, as far as I know, he was told that the new owners wanted him to stay on and that on Tuesday they would be coming by to meet with him."

"And he stayed?"

"Yes ma'am."

"Good," she sighed. "Thank you Walter. That's perfect. Now, what about our appointment at the bank?" she asked, directing her eyes to Harold.

"That's taken care of too ma'am," he replied as he swallowed his food and wiped his mouth. "Ten o'clock with the president just like you requested."

"Good," she smiled at the two clearly pleased. "Good, thank you both so much. Now gentlemen," she said as she downed her coffee and then wiped her mouth. "If you're finished... shall we?"

It had taken weeks and weeks of searching, but they finally found him living with his family in a small dilapidated house just at the edge of the very fields he worked. She was glad for she'd never forgotten what he'd done all those years ago, yet still it weighed heavily on her that his life was no better now than what it had been when they first met. A father with a wife and two daughters, his life as far as she could discern, had been a constant struggle. Dirt poor with no education, he and his family were hopelessly bound to the farm by the invisible chains and shackles of the times that they lived in. A harsh reality that for him, she knew would never change. That was until now.

She was going to change it, and as they ventured out of town onto the main highway, it seemed as if in no time Charles was turning the car onto the long dirt road that led to the Jackson farm. A rolling two thousand acres of some of the most coveted land in the county. Land that he'd worked and slaved on almost his entire life. Just as his daddy and his daddy before him had, for a family that treated their help no better than the slaves of the eighteen hundreds. But as they drew nearer and the small desolate looking house came into view, Willie began to feel the onset of butterflies in the pit of her stomach. A growing sense of doubt and anxiety, that seemed to have started just after they'd left the diner. Would he remember her after all these years? Or for that matter, would he even care? She felt in her heart that he would, but it had been so long and she was so young. She hoped and fidgeted then inhaled a breath to quell her nerves and stared out the window.

She saw the house sitting just off the road, surrounded by acres and acres of cotton fields. A single level home with a small front porch and a rusted corrugated roof that reminded her of what she'd grown up in. She looked at Charles in the front and cleared her throat. "Is that it?"

"Yes ma'am," he replied with a glance into his mirror. "We'll be there in just a moment."

The girls had spotted the car coming long before it had ever hit the property line. They'd been watching and waiting all morning, and as soon as they saw the huge plume of dust rising up from behind the shiny black Cadillac, they knew in an instant that the new boss man was on his way.

Watching for a moment as it barreled toward them on the dry dusty road, they jump and giggled then bolted through the door to get their dad setting at the kitchen table.

"Daddy daddy," they called excitedly. "The new boss man's a comin. Com on. He's comin down the road! Git up," they insisted as they took his coffee cup and then pulled on his hands. "Hurry!"

Rising from his chair with a groan, the big man slowly walked to the door, stepped out onto the porch, then watched as the big black car gradually slowed and then finally stopped in front of his home. Staring as the trailing dust cloud slowly settled onto the car and then lazily drifted across the fields, he tried to think of what would've compelled the Jacksons to sell but he couldn't. He could only think of how the family who'd owned the farm for the last seventy-five years, and had always said that they would never sell... had sold. And now here he was with a new boss man after all these years, parked right in front of his house. He felt anxious, and wondered what his new boss man was like? Would he be good, or cruel and harsh like Mr. Jackson? And most importantly, did he still have a job and a place to live? He worried, but even so he watched with his family gathered closely around as the driver got out and stepped to the back.

Looking through the glass as the dust slowly cleared, Willie finally set her eyes upon the man she had come to find and smiled. It had been right at sixteen years since she'd last seen him, and now there he was just as she'd remembered. Dressed in dirty and worn coveralls, and a tee shirt that looked a size to small. And although he'd aged, he still stood as a pillar of insurmountable strength. A giant of a man with a heart to match, patiently waiting and watching beneath the rusted corrugated roof of the porch with his family. She'd found him, and as the door slowly opened and her chauffer extended his hand, Willie reached out and stepped from the car.

But to the big man and his family standing on the porch, the woman getting out of the car was not the boss man they'd been expecting. Staring as she emerged from the shadows of the vehicle into the bright morning sun, they watched as she took a couple of steps toward them and then stop. Who was she, they wondered? This white lady who was dressed so nice, with the sunglasses and the long auburn hair flowing from beneath a beautiful wide brimmed hat. Was she lost, they wondered as she quietly removed her glasses and then her hat?

Squinting against the morning sun, Duncan stared for a second then took a slow uncertain step off of the porch toward her. He sensed that for some reason he knew her, but from where and when he could not remember. He could see the faint resemblance of a person he'd known a long time ago, the hair and the eyes, but so many years had passed he wasn't sure. He was confused and could only stare, until the woman spoke and called out his name.

"Hello Duncan," Willie drawled and smiled.

It was all he needed and just as soon as he heard it, he knew. He knew it was Willie, the scared little girl from the train whom he'd saved all those years ago. Yet even so, he hardly recognized her for she'd changed so much. She was so beautiful and grown up. "Miss Willie?" his deep baritone drawl resonated with a curious surprise. "Ii... is dhats you?" he stammered as he shuffled another step closer.

"Yes," she nodded as she stepped toward him and opened her arms. "It's meee."

She'd forgotten how big he truly was, and as his giant arms encircled and closed around her, she couldn't help but think of how safe and secure he'd made her feel all those years ago. Like nothing in the world could hurt her as long as he was there, and of how his guardianship of her had delivered her safely to Mobile. But those days were gone, she could see that now, and so were his days as a productive farm hand. They were behind him and coming to a close, and soon he would be discarded like a worn out work mule.

He was tired from years of long hard labor in the fields and it showed in his face and how he moved. And it pulled heavily on her heart as the stark reality of his life truly came into light. It was poverty on a level she knew all too well, but she was here now and she was going to change that, for now it was her turn to protect and to help him. To give something back to the man who'd saved her life all those years ago, and to remove from his life the hardship and squalor that he'd endured for so many years.

"It's Miss Willie Momma," he turned to his wife excitedly. "See!" He turned back and held her at arm's length then suddenly stopped and cocked his head as an endless barrage of questions exploded in his mind. "Bu... but, whut' s are you do'n here Miss Willie? An how did you finds me? Ii... is you the new boss man?"

"No," she smiled and shook her head.

"Well, is one a thems the new boss man?" he asked with a deep concern as he cast his eyes toward the other two men emerging from the car.

Glancing toward the car and then back to Duncan, Willie smiled again then lovingly placed her hand on the center of his chest. "No," she said as she patted and brushed his dirty overalls in a soft and comforting way. "They're not either. But I promise you'll meet him shortly. He's very nice, and he's going to treat you and your family real good from now on."

"So you knows him?"

"Yes, I knows him," she nodded and teased. "But we can deal with the new boss man later, okay. I have something else that we need to do first."

There was no doubt that Duncan was worried about meeting the new boss man, but as important as it was, something else seemed to override his thoughts. He'd always hoped in the back of his mind that someday his family could meet the brave little girl he'd helped on the train, who'd then in turn gotten him out of jail. He was overjoyed and with a great big grin, he snapped his head toward the porch and then back to Willie.

"Well okay," he began. "But firs you gots to come with me cause I wants ya ta meet my family. See, I's told the misses an dha girls all abouts you. Of how, how nice ya wus ta me, an how ya gave me all dhat money when we got ta Mobile so's I could eat. An then of how you had dhat real nice man come an help me get out-a jail so's I could get back home," he stopped and then cocked his head with a curious gaze. "Dhat wus you, wusn't it? Dhat sent dhat real nice man ta help me?"

"Yes, it was me," she nodded.

"But I never gots ta see ya like he said I would afor I left."

"I know," her voice softened. "But I'm here now."

"Well then," he said and tugged on her arm. "Come on... I wants ya ta meet em."

Sitting on the porch with Duncan and his family, the two talked and reminisced of their journey all those years ago. A short while later and after they'd finished, Willie ever so slowly began to explain to Duncan as to why she was there. First, she told him of her life in brief and of how she'd come to find him. Then, of how she'd come into some money and had purchased the farm, and how the new boss man she'd hired would be moving into the big house later on in the day. She assured them all that he was very nice but that she needed Duncan to go with her into town to the bank. She said that it was just for a short while and that his wife and daughters could wait for them up at the main house. That when they got back they would all meet the new boss man there and help him move in. It was a simple request but that was something that was never allowed, and with looks of apprehension and protests, they resisted until Duncan intervened.

A few minutes later, Willie and Duncan returned to the car to find the men still conversing and smoking their cigarettes. Staring in awe as they approached, Willie quickly introduced them and then loaded back up. Her appointment was at ten and she wanted to be on time. She asked Harold to ride in the front, giving room for their new passenger in the back. Closing the doors with a final wave to the three on the porch, they took off and just as quickly as they'd left town, they were back and pulling into the parking lot of the bank.

It was really nothing more than a typical small town bank located right in the center of town. The kind that serviced the entire rural community and that many of the local businesses and farmers had become dependent on. That dictated new terms and conditions to the poor and unfortunate the minute they faltered for it was the only bank in town. In fact, it was the president of the bank and a few others who pretty much ran the county from the commissioners on down. They were greedy and dirty, and tales of their corruption abounded.

But Willie knew this before she had arrived, for she had studied the bank for months. It was something she'd learned from Foster, the master himself. A tactic he used before ever doing any kind of business with anyone. Seek out the weaknesses and desires of your adversary he'd taught her, and you will always have the upper hand. She'd watched him for years and had learned from him well. She knew everything about Frank Krewitt and his little bank that she needed to know, even down to the fact that he'd been sleeping with his secretary for the last five years. And now, she knew exactly how to deal with him.

He'd been waiting for weeks to meet the new owners of the Jackson farm. The new owners that had reportedly paid almost twice what it was worth, and that now, as it had been put, wanted to open up a sizeable bank account with him. He remembered the story that Jim Jackson, a good friend and one of his best customers had told him. Of how some accountant from Mobile had come to him one day out of the blue and made him an offer to buy his farm he couldn't refuse then wrote out a check right on the spot. He loved people like that, and had been salivating for weeks at the prospect of a new depositor. He looked at the clock on the wall. It was just after ten. He fidgeted then looked to the lobby through the glass wall of his office. A second later, he smiled.

Yes it was them, but for some reason Frank failed to even notice the towering giant following the group as they came into the bank. He should have but he didn't, for he'd become fixated on one person and one person only. Leading the group, Willie had caught his eyes just as soon as she'd walked through the door and now he couldn't pull them away. He was mesmerized, for she was as beautiful and as elegant as any woman he'd ever seen. And as she strolled across the lobby floor with the confidence and prowess of a lioness on the hunt, he stared in a silent daze.

Was this Miss Dawson, his ten o'clock? He wondered as he rose from behind his desk and stepped to his door then watched with a schoolboy fascination. He felt giddy, almost to the point of foolishness. She looked like a movie star, and as she stopped at the reception desk and removed her sunglasses and hat, he looked into the glass at his reflection and slicked back his hair. Satisfied after a last lingering look, he cleared his throat and then hurried toward them.

"Good morning," Willie greeted the young girl with a refined and pleasant drawl. "I'm Miss Dawson, and I have an appointment to see Mr--."

"Oh Miss Dawson?" Frank called out before she could finish.

"Yesss," Willie turned as he stepped up from behind and she met his gaze.

"Good mornin, I'm Frank Krewitt," he smiled and extended his hand. "I must say it is so good to finally meet you," he continued as she took his hand.

"And you too," she replied politely.

"Yes, and I do trust that your journey up from Mobile was pleasant?"

"Well actually," Willie rolled her eyes. "To be right truthful with you, it was quite long and boring. The roads are just terrible, but we're here... finally."

"Well good, I'm glad to hear that, and now that you are, why don't we step into my office and see how it is that our bank can be of service to you." He replied with an extended arm toward his door. He was excited, but just as he had Frank suddenly stopped at the sight of the towering giant standing behind Willie. It was as if he had been hit by a truck and for a few fleeting seconds he just stared until he regained his composure and looked back to Willie. "Ah ma'am," he whispered beneath his breath as he leaned towards her. "I kind of feel a little awkward askin you this, but is that big ol negro with you?"

Turning to Duncan, Willie stared at her friend for a just moment then turned back to the banker and smiled. "Why yes, yes he is. Why?"

"Well ma'am," he hesitated slightly. "I know that you're from the big city and all, so I'm sure that this is probably just an oversight on your part. But out here in the country see, we like to leave our workin negroes outside. You know," he added with an insinuating look around the room. "Kind of as a courtesy to all our other valued customers. So, if ya don't mind, could you be so kind as to have your buck wait outside," he finished politely.

Looking at the banker, Willie stared for just a moment then turned her gaze to Duncan. The look in his eyes said it all and without a second's hesitation she turned back to the banker. "You mean my good friend Mr. Haywood here?" She raised her eyebrows.

"Well, yes ma'am," he answered as his eyes shifted from her to the black giant. "If that's what you wanna call him," he continued with a smug yet humorous indifference. "Your good friend, then. See, people around these parts, well, they just feel a little more comfortable leavin the black folks outside away from all this money and temptation. You know what I mean? Besides, their kind ain't got no money anyways."

"Well," Willie replied with an air of indignation. "My friend does. In fact, he was just about ready to deposit $750,000 of his money into your little institution. But since you've put it that way, I guess we'll just have to find another bank in another town that is, shall we say, a little more understanding. You know, one that is a little more accommodating and appreciative as to the wishes of its larger account holders." She smiled with a pleasant finality and turned, knowing that the man would buckle under the crushing surge of his own greed.

It took only a second for the impact of what she'd said to sink in for no one in all of his banking days had ever made such a deposit. Ever. And even though he didn't care much for the black kind as he called them, he was still a banker and a greedy one at that. And true to her intuition, before she could even take a step, he reached out and touched her arm.

"Oh Miss Dawson! Wai wai waaait... please," he stammered. "Di, did you just say se, seven hundred and fifty thousand?" he asked as a salivating grin began to pull at his mouth.

"Yes sir," Willie stopped and turned as if it were nothing. "Seven hundred and fifty thousand... in the form of a certified cashier's check drawn on Alabama Federal and Savings."

"Well," he began as if he had completely misunderstood what she'd said. "My apologies ma'am. See, I think I must of misunderstood you. I'm sorry, but you did say your friend here correct?"

"Yes sir, that is correct."

"Your good friend, right?" He raised his eyebrows.

"Yes sir, my gooood friend," Willie retorted.

"A...aaah," he declared as if he'd just been enlightened. "Well see, that makes all the difference in the world. See, here at First National, we like to think of everybody in our little community as friends. And of course it should go without sayin, that a friend of yours is most certainly a friend of ours," he laughed with a sheepish yet hopeful glance. "And those friends are always treated in the utmost of accommodating and appreciative of manners. You know, sensitive to all of their needs and wants."

"Even my friend?" Willie dipped her head with a scowl.

"Oh, yes ma'am," he nodded anxiously. "Especially your friend."

Pausing in thought as she digested his plea, Willie looked to Duncan, studied his expression for just a second then cast her eyes back to the banker. She was enjoying the fact that he was groveling and sucking up to her, but now it was time to continue on. "Well," she sighed and waved her hand. "I guess since you put it that way we may as well. After all, we are here already, aren't we?"

"Yes ma'am," he smiled in relief. "Please please come in, won't you. And," he emphasized with an implied glance to Duncan. "I do mean all of you."

Taking their seats, Willie took a moment to introduce everyone and then started right in. She knew Duncan's heart was huge but that his mind was slow and simple, and she knew that he would need protection from the vultures and hyenas that would descend upon him and try to get at his money in any way they could.

There would be the con artist and scammers that would prey upon his ignorance, and then the bottom feeders and the poor-pity-me's that would prey on his sympathy. They would come and she knew it. She knew it without question, and she also knew that if word really got out as to what he had and what he was worth, there would be an overwhelming amount of resentment and hatred. They would try and hurt him, and that was something she couldn't allow.

"Now Mr. Krewitt, like I just said. What I would like to do is to open an account in the amount of seven hundred and fifty thousand dollars. You know, one of those interest-bearing kind, at say two percent adjusted annually. Oh, and I'd like that to be a joint account too if you don't mind, with my name and Mr. Haywood's name on it. See, I like to think that I can withdraw my money just as fast as I have deposited it. But before I do, and if it's not too much of an imposition, I do have just a few little requests that I would like to ask of you if it's okay. You know, courtesies that I would like your bank to extend to my friend here."

"Oh, yes ma'am," he grabbed his pen and prepared to write. "It's no imposition at all. You just name it. Like I said before, we're here to accommodate all of our account holders, but our larger and most valued ones... well, we like to take care of them on an even more personal level if ya know what I mean?"

"Oh, how wonderful," Willie smiled as she began with her list. "Now first of all, I would like for my friend here to be treated with the utmost respect and courtesy at all times. Agreed?"

"Agreed." He nodded.

"Good. Then second, once every two weeks after you've closed on Saturday, I would like for you to personally drive out to the farm and dispense to Mr. Haywood in the form of cash, an advance in whatever amount the interest on our money has earned for that particular time period. Understand?"

"Yes ma'am, no problem."

"Then third, I would like for you to set up charging privileges at all of the local businesses that pertain to farming as it may be. You can set them all up under Dawson Farms, that way people will think it's for me. But I want it managed and the bills paid from here. And fourth, I would like for there to be a two-signature requirement before Mr. Haywood can withdraw any of the principle. Oh, and one more thing, you'll also need to provide a monthly statement to my accountant of all his transactions as he will be monitoring this account for me. You know, just to ensure that there are, shall we say, no unauthorized withdrawals or egregious expenses that have occurred. Agreed?"

"Oh yes ma'am."

"Well good. Now Harold," she turned to her accountant. "If I may?"

"Yes ma'am," he replied as he reached into his folder and pulled out the check. "Here you are."

Examining it for just a second, Willie smiled and then handed it to the banker. "Here you go Mr. Krewitt, just as I said earlier, seven hundred and fifty thousand in the form of a cashier's check drawn on Alabama Federal and Savings."

Taking the check, Frank stared with a grin then slowly turned his gaze back to Willie. "Ya know Miss Dawson," he began with a concerned expression growing on his face. "It ain't none of my business and all, but this being a small town, people around here ain't gonna like it much that you're just given seven hundred and fifty thousand dollars to this negro. I... I mean your friend like that. Hard tellin what all might happen when word about this gets out. You do understand what I'm tryin to say here don't you?"

He was being serious, but not in a bad way and Willie knew it. He was concerned, and for good reason. She could tell by the tone of his voice and the look in his eye. "Well yes, actually I do. And I do appreciate you bringing that to my attention and all. But you see I've already thought about that, and that's why you're going to help me."

"Help you?" He cocked his head curiously.

"Yes sir," she replied. "See, you're going to see to it that the community here does not besiege upon my friend."

"I am?" His eyes widened.

"Yes, you are."

"And jus how am I go'n to do that?"

"Well, first you're going to keep the real truth about all of this money stuff very hush-hush, and two, you're going to personally keep an eye on everything for me. You know, kind of like a watchdog of sorts to keep, let's say, the local sheriff or some of his boys from harassing or throwing my good friend here in jail on some kind of trumped up charges. Or to ensure that something like, shall we say, a fire or some sort of mysterious accident doesn't befall him.

See, I would find that to be very disheartening, and quite frankly, I just don't know what I would do. And that's why if anyone in town asks you, you're going to tell them that," she stopped and turned to Walter. "What did you say the Jackson's called me at the diner?"

"That kooky crazy lady," he replied and smiled.

"Oh yes, thank you," she laughed. "That that kooky crazy lady from the city, that bought the farm has deposited all this money into your bank. And that after finally meeting her, you are absolutely convinced that she has more money than sense, and that for some reason, which you have no idea as to why, she took a liking to Mr. Haywood here and hired him to take care of the farm and run it for her. And that as part of their agreement, he will be living in the big house until she can move here in a few years. And then after that, gossip will do the rest and before you know it, why nobody in town will have any idea as to what the real truth is… that I can assure you of."

Contemplating what she'd said, Frank Krewitt sat for a moment staring at the four in front of his desk. He knew everything that Willie had said was true, and he knew that if he wanted to keep her account he would have to do as she said and watch over Duncan. To extend the courtesies of his bank farther than he ever had, and to protect him like she'd asked. It was that or nothing, and with the shift of his eyes to the big black man squeezed into the chair, he cleared his throat.

"Mr. Haywood," he said, gaining the man's attention.

"Yes sur," Duncan answered with a polite nod.

"You do know how to manage a workin farm, don't you?"

Swallowing nervously, Duncan turned to Willie as if seeking permission to speak. Receiving a pat to his arm along with a smiling nod, he slowly turned back to the man. "I know's how ta grow cotton if'n that's whut ya means."

Shaking his head with a heavy sigh, Frank stared at Duncan for just a moment then slowly turned to Willie. She never said a word, but he knew just by the tilt of her head and look in her eyes asking him to do so, that his services would now include help in managing the farm. Shaking his head once again, he called to his secretary. The papers and process were simple, and after everyone had signed and Duncan had made his mark, Frank Krewitt welcomed his two newest customers to his bank. Standing with a round of handshakes and a reiteration of his good will, he escorted them all to the door and bid them farewell.

The drive back to the farm was filled with an endless round of questions from Duncan. He'd been there and had heard it all, but even so it seemed like a dream. He felt lost and numb and confused. Just how much money was seven hundred and fifty thousand dollars? He had no earthly idea for it was a number he could not imagine. And why was that banker man going to be bringing him money every two weeks? He wasn't working for him, was he? And was he really going to be living in the big house like he heard? Surely not... what about the new boss man? Where was he going to live?

His mind whirled in a confused and worried state, but with each and every question Willie answered, he settled a little more. He listened as she slowly explained the truth as to what she'd done and what they were doing. Of how she was now very, very rich, and how she'd bought the house and the farm to give to him, and that he was now the new boss man.

She explained how the money that they'd put into the bank was there to help, and how it would work for him and make him money every day. She explained how and why the banker would then bring it to him twice a month. She told him he could never spend the money in the bank, only the money the banker had brought him. She told him of how important it was to keep quiet about it all, and to just let people believe that he worked for her. And then she told him of the people that would come. The ones who would try to get at his money and the farm in any way they could. She told him everything, and by the time she'd finished and the true extent of what she'd done began to sink in, they had turned into the driveway and were pulling up to the house.

Looking out of his window as they came to a stop, Duncan stared in a surreal daze. He could see his family sitting in the grass next to the house, waiting patiently beneath the shade of a giant oak. And he could see the looks of nervousness and uncertainty pulling on their faces as they rose and came toward him. He knew what they were thinking, and as he opened his door and stepped from the car, he looked around at what Willie had said was now his.

The modest two story white house with its covered wrap around porch. The barn and out buildings setting off to the side, and then the hundreds and hundreds of rolling acres that fell away in every direction as far as the eye could see. Fields that he knew all too well.

It was an emotional moment knowing that the farm he'd worked and slaved on most of his life was now his, and it was almost more than he could bear. He felt humbled and overwhelmed, and as the true reality of what Willie had done began to sink in, his heart welled under a crushing gratitude he knew he could never repay. A kindness that'd come from a little girl he'd almost forgotten. An angel of mercy who'd found and come back to him in a way that he never could've imagined. He thought of how they'd met and of all the people in his life that'd treated him so harshly, and then he looked at Willie standing by his side.

Gazing back, Willie could clearly see the look of uncertainty and a reluctance to go forward. Like an animal that'd been caged for far too long, and that now stood before its opened door, free yet afraid to venture out. "It's okay," she assured as she slipped her arm inside of his. "Come on, and I'll walk with you," she insisted along with a gentle tug to his giant limb. "Let's go see your new home."

Her words were comforting, and as he continued to look down into Willie's eyes, Duncan could clearly see the protective nature in her gaze. As if she were now his guardian and would let nothing in the world hurt him. A second later and with another gentle tug to his arm, he finally took a step and began walking toward the house.

"It's okay Momma," Duncan assured his wife as they approached. "Miss Willie's made everything all good."

"But where's the boss man Daddy?" his eldest daughter piped up from behind. "We's been sittin here ever since you left, an we ain't seen nobody. Not nobody!"

Grinning great big, Duncan and Willie traded glances and then looked back to his daughter. "You're looking at him Emma," Willie answered with the pride of a doting mother and another glance to Duncan. "Your daddy here's the new boss man," she added along with a pat to his giant arm. "And this here is your new home. What-a-you think of that?"

At first they just stared as they tried to comprehend what Willie had just said. It was unbelievable, but with a nod from Duncan in answer to their doubts, all three women erupted into screams of joy. They were ecstatic to the point of tears, but after few minutes and after they had calmed, they all continued on toward the house. Climbing the short set of steps to the porch, they headed straight for the front door and then stopped.

To Duncan it was a somber moment, for in all of the years that he'd worked for the Jacksons, he'd been in the house only once. They had just bought a new china hutch, and once it was set, he was quickly ushered out. But today was different; today he wouldn't be ushered out. Today he would be staying, and with an oversized fist he grabbed the worn black knob and turned it until it clicked. Yet even so the Jackson rule of never entering the house was strong and he hesitated until he felt the gentle touch of Willie's hand on his push and swing the door open. Then with a reassuring nod as if to say it was okay, Duncan took a giant stride and entered the home as its new master.

Following directly behind him, his wife and daughters stepped through the door but then paused and looked around as if they'd just entered the sanctity of a church. They'd never been in the boss man's house before for it was forbidden, until, and with yet another nod from Willie, they ever so slowly began to move from room to room. Looking at each and every item that'd been left behind as if they were in a museum, they would then look to Willie as if to ask permission to touch or sit. Relaxing a little more with each and every nod they continued on, smiling at the turn of every corner and each new discovery. They were amazed, and relished in the newfound delights of modern living; an inside bathroom with a flushing toilet and a stove that worked on gas. They opened doors and cabinets and rummaged; they sat on the beds and chairs. They turned on the lights then ran the water and flushed the toilet. They lit the stove. They laughed with joy.

It was almost a half hour before they finally made their way back out onto the porch but as they did and gathered, Duncan could sense that it was time to say goodbye. That it was time for him and Willie to go their separate ways once again. Separate ways that would part them only in the physical sense, for even though they had met only once and had known each other for just one day, they'd forged an enduring bond. A special kindness that against all odds and in its own mysterious way had transcended the passage of time and eclipsed the barriers of racial bigotry.

Yet even so, and even though the times had changed, they were worlds apart and Duncan knew it. He knew that she had to leave, and as they slowly shuffled toward the steps to say goodbye, he began to feel a sad upwelling of emptiness rise from within. As if his own daughter was leaving and he knew he would never see her again. It was a daunting thought and he wanted to tell her how he felt, but before he could speak Willie's attorney ascended the steps. "Excuse me ma'am," he said as he stepped toward them. "But it's time."

Nodding her head, Willie stepped back and let him continue.

"Mr. Haywood," the man said with another step closer.

"Yes sur?" Duncan drawled with a curious expression.

"I have some papers for you, important papers, that you need to keep."

"Whut kinds of papers?" he asked with a glance to Willie.

"Well first," he began as he lifted the stack in his hand. "I have the address and phone number to Mr. Simons office, you know, Miss Dawson's accountant here." He nodded toward Harold. "She wants you to have them just in case you ever have any questions or problems in the future. So you can call if you ever need us to help you, okay. And second, this here is the title and the keys to your truck. It's a forty-six Ford, sitting right there," he pointed to the black pickup beside the house. "And then these here are the deeds and title work to your property showing that you and your wife are now the new owners of all this. The house the barns and all two thousand acres... everything."

"The whut?" Duncan cocked his head.

"The deeds," Walter repeated. "Ah, I mean the papers that say you own all of this now. That you're the new owners," he slowed his voice. "They're very, very important, and you need to put them in a very safe place okay," he paused and stared then continued on like the lawyer he was. "You do understand... don't you?"

Nodding as he took the papers, Duncan stared blankly for a moment then slowly looked to Willie with a lost expression. He was searching for the words that he felt in his heart but they eluded him and he could only stand before her as the simple and humble man that he was... a man who was now eternally grateful.

"I don't knows whut ta say Miss Willie," his deep voice began to falter as he tried to express his gratitude. "I, Iiii's--."

"Shussh," Willie quickly interrupted as she stepped toward him and opened her arms. "You don't have to say anything," she smiled in an attempt to mask the sound of her own voice that was now beginning to waver. "Just accept these as my gifts to you and your family."

Bending slightly at the waist, Duncan could feel her arms as they encircled his huge neck in a warm and tender embrace. He could feel the softness of her cheek on the side of his face and smell her perfume, and as he straightened and wrapped his arms around her, lifting her feet from the floor, he heard the sound of her voice as she whispered into his ear.

"Besides, you do remember our train ride, don't you?" she added as she stared out over his shoulder. Out past the barn and out buildings, and into the vast open fields through eyes now brimming with tears.

Nodding his head ever so slowly, Willie closed her eyes and then tightened her squeeze even more as the heartache within her instantly rose to an unbearable level. She hadn't expected it to be quite like this and all too quickly the hard-shelled exterior of her outer defenses began to crumble. She could feel the tears that'd welled in her eyes escape and then roll down her cheeks, and then her throat as it tightened and stopped her from speaking. But she was determined to tell him, and with a heavy breath, she summoned her will and forced herself to continue. "Well see," she choked in a broken voice as she turned her mouth to his ear and began to cry. "I told you I'd never forget what you'd done."

She'd told herself that she wouldn't cry, and that she could and would remain strong. Yet as his giant limbs tightened around the small of her back and his body heaved in an emotional reaction to her words, she quickly unraveled and lost her battle. They both did, and as Willie descended into an emotional meltdown, Duncan reeled as if the words themselves had shot through him like a burning spear. A spear, that instantly opened a porthole to a time that he'd all but forgotten.

Closing his eyes tight, he shook his head as his mind began to whirl and flash back to that fateful day all those years ago. To that hot August morning when he'd first met the sad and grief-stricken little girl. A girl not much more than a child, so vulnerable and so all alone... so afraid.

He did remember, and remembered it all. He remembered that morning when she'd tried to board the train and how he'd saved her from falling beneath the wheels. He remembered her kindness and the food she'd shared later on, and then of the three thugs that had tried to hurt her and how he had dealt with them. He remembered the railroad bulls when they'd pulled into the Mobile yard and then the stormy night that they'd spent together in the boxcar, and of how she'd taken a spot between him and the wall to sleep. He remembered how he had watched over her all that night, and then the next morning after they'd made their way to the edge of the train yard and said goodbye. How he'd knelt and she'd wrapped her arms around his neck and squeezed him then told him how she'd never forget what he'd done for her. He remembered how sad he had been, and of how he'd worried about her when they finally parted. And then he remembered the money she'd given him so he could eat.

His throat tightened and his knees weakened under the emotional onslaught of feelings that truly staggered him. He felt as if his heart had just been ripped from his chest and then torn in half by the feelings of both sadness and joy as they each battled for control of his emotions. But they were evenly matched, and with one last warm-hearted squeeze, he inhaled a heavy breath and relaxed his hold. And with one last tender kiss to his cheek, Willie slowly relaxed her grasp and slipped back to the floor. She was crying and so was he for they both knew that this was goodbye. But that was a word she couldn't say without completely unraveling and she knew it. She could feel a hardened lump grow in her throat at just the thought. A moment later she bit her bottom lip and drew it into a smile then wiped the tears form her cheeks. Then with a small but reassuring nod and a gentle pat to the center of his chest, she dropped her gaze and turned then slowly walked away.

Watching as she descended the steps and dropped into the car, Duncan knew deep down that he would never see her again. That the fates that had caused their paths to cross so long ago and that had brought them back together would never come again. That the powers of destiny that had ruled and had guided their lives was now over. He knew it, and as he stood on the porch with his family gathered tightly around, a trail of tears running down his cheeks, he watched with a heavy heart as the shiny black car slowly pulled from the drive.

They were leaving, and with a final wave from Willie through the glass as they turned onto the road, Duncan and his family watched as it quickly sped away. They watched as it passed the shack that just earlier in the day they'd called home. They watched as a huge plume of dust rose high into the air behind it and then followed like a boiling cloud. They watched under the shimmering blue sky as it grew tiny and then quiet, and then finally disappeared over the distant rolling hill. They watched as the cloud of dust that had been left behind drifted lazily in the gentle breeze and then slowly settled out and across the vast open expanse of empty fields. Across fields... that they now called their own.

CHAPTER 69

———◆———

"Wow," Jim SHOOK HIS HEAD. "So that's why Willie went back up to where she was from. To help that guy that'd saved her on the train?"

"Well, that an to say goodbye to her mother too. See, that was real important to her. Anyway, an jus like she said she would, when she got back later that week she came an got me. I remember I was workin at the church rakin leaves when she pulled into the drive in that big ol long black car."

"Oh yeah," Jim interjected. "She was going to take you to lunch, right?"

"Well actually, I thought that she'd jus stopped to tell me when we was gonna go, you know, like she said we would, but that wasn't it at all."

"Really... then what'd she want?"

"Well," Otis grinned. "She said that she had a surprise for me an wanted me to go with her. Now right off I told her that I had to work an I couldn't go but she kept arguin an insistin, tellin me that she'd already talked to the Father until I finally agreed." he laughed. "I'll tell ya, she never did like to lose an argument. Anyway, after I put my stuff away, I followed her back to the car an climbed in behind her. There was two men already sittin there which kind of surprised me but right quick Willie introduced me to them. The one man I remembered him from her probate trial. He was her lawyer, an the other, well, he was her accountant. They was all dressed up real nice in suits an ties an shook my hand, an didn't seem to mind much at all that I was black or that I was ridin in the car with em. An then, jus as soon as we'd closed the door, we was on our way.

"Now by then I had a pretty bad case of curiosity gnawin at me, an jus as soon as we turned onto the highway, I started askin Willie where we were go'n. But Willie be'n Willie, well, all she'd do was jus smile an then pat me on *the arm an say that it was a surprise. I'll tell ya, it was enough to drive me almost plumb crazy. An those two men, well, they didn't exactly help matters either cause every time I ask her they would jus grin an look at each other with these funny little smirks.*

"Anyway, I kept askin, but she never did answer me straight. She jus kept grinnin an glancin at me with her eyes all sparklin an happy like. That was until we finally came to a stop right in front of one a those great big banks downtown."

"Bank?" Jim raised his eyebrows.

"Yep... bank. I remember lookin out of the window an thinkin, whaaat-in-the-hell are we do'n here? An then before I knew it, they were all pile'n out of the car an hollerin at me to come along. Now I still didn't know what was go'n on, but I followed em right up the steps to the front door an that's right where I stopped an then watched as they all went inside."

"Stopped?" Jim asked. "Why'd you stopped?"

"Cause it was a white man's bank," Otis postured as if he should've known. "Shit, it wasn't for black people. No sir, not back then it wasn't, or at least that was unless you was cleanin it an it was after hours. An God forbid if you thought that you was jus gonna go walkin in through the front door in the middle of the afternoon," he scoffed.

"Yeah, I guess I forgot about those times," he shook his head. "So what'd you do? I mean, what happen? What'd Willie do?"

"Well to right truthful with you, I jus kind of stood there an watched through the glass as the three of them strolled on in. Now they really hadn't gone more than fifteen feet or so before Willie realized that I wasn't with em an that's when she stopped an turned around. I remember her lookin back at me with this... this real funny look on her face, like she was confused an a little hurt that I wasn't at her side. I could see it in her eyes an not more than a second or two later, well, that's when she came walkin back toward me real slow like an opened the door."

"Otis?" Willie called as she stepped outside. "What are you doing? Come on," she insisted and extended her hand. "Your surprise is inside."

"I, I can't Miss Willie."

"But why not?" She cocked her head and stared. "What's wrong?"

"Cause it says no colored folks," he replied and then pointed to the white cardboard sign that'd been taped to the door. "See, right there. An I know that you want to give me a surprise an all, but I best jus wait out here by the car till you're finished if ya don't mind."

Gazing into Otis's eyes, Willie could clearly see the effects of the racial bigotry that she detested so vehemently. The ignorance of a people who'd put one race superior to another. She remembered what Foster had told her on her sixteenth birthday after he'd given her the book by Mark Twain. When she had questioned him about how and why the black people were treated in the way that they were. She remembered his explanation, and how he had said that all men are created equal, and that no matter what color they were, everyone's blood was red. She thought of it all in the flash of a second and with the snap of her head back to the door, she jerked it open and ripped the sign from the glass. "Not any more it doesn't!" she huffed defiantly as she tore the sign in half and threw it to the ground. "Now come on," she said as she grabbed his hand and jerked her head. "We have us some business to take care of."

"An that's when Willie took my hand, actually grabbed it is more like it, an then pulled me inside. Now it didn't take us but a second to join up with her lawyer an accountant, but I gotta tell ya we didn't get no further than half way across that lobby floor before this big ol security guard came strollin up an stopped us. I remember he tipped his hat an greeted us real pleasant like, but then right after that he looked straight at me an made the terrible mistake of tellin Willie that she really needed ta leave her nigger outside."

"Oh man," *Jim grimaced as he envisioned the scene.* "You're kiddin?"

"Oh nooo."

"So what happen? I mean?"

"Well," *Otis chuckled and shook his head.* "I really don't know jus where to start, but jus as soon as he'd finished ol Willie took a great big breath an then started in on him like you couldn't believe. I remember she got up in his face an started poken him right in the chest an by the time she was done railin an chewin on that poor man's ass, he was stammerin an apologizin, an answerin yes ma'am an no ma'am to jus about everything she said. I'll tell ya, she had everybody in that whole goddamn lobby lookin an starin at us, an then before I knew what was happenin, he was leadin all of us right upstairs to the president of that bank.*

"Now at first there was a little bit a confusion with the secretary an all cause we didn't have no appointment or nothin. But after Willie got done explainin everything to her, this real nice lady led us right on in to the man's office. You could see that he was real surprised that I was there, but he let us all in, includin me, an after he introduced himself, we sat down an he took a seat behind his desk.

"I remember as soon as he sat down, him claspin his hands together on top of his desk an then leanin toward us. An then him lookin at Willie while she settled in an crossed her legs an fixed her skirt. Actually, stared like a dog was more like it cause he had a real hard time takin his eyes off of her legs. Anyway, when she was finally all done, well, that's when he turned his attention to her accountant an lawyer an took on this real serious no-nonsense look."

"Now gentlemen, how can I help you?"

Looking first to Harold, Willie's lawyer cleared his throat then turned his attention back to the banker. "Well Mr. DeWeese, thank you for asking, but I believe that that is a question you need to ask of Miss Dawson here. You see, we are here just at her behest, you know, for legal and financial advice if she needs it."

"Ooh, well my apologies then," he said as he turned back to Willie. "And so, how is it that I might help you today ma'am."

Her eyes had been focused on the picture behind him, but his question quickly regained her attention. "Well," Willie began and then turned her gaze to Otis. "As you can see I have brought a friend along with me and we would like to open up a small savings account for him. You see, Mr. Brown here has come into a tiny sum of money and I would like for your bank here to handle his account. You know, kind of as a personal favor... to me."

"Well Miss Dawson," he began in a patronizing tone. "We do appreciate you coming in and thinking of us. Really, we do. And I'm sure that Mr. Brown there is no doubt a fine gentleman... of color that is," he smirked. "And we would like nothing more than to have and to safeguard his money for you. But you must understand our bank policy is really quite clear. You see we just don't serve his kind here. Never have, and never will." He rocked back in his chair and then smiled with a smug indifference as to her request.

"And just what kind would that be, Mr. DeWeese?" Willie retorted with another glance at the picture on the shelf behind him. The one of his daughter and her first born baby. If only he knew, she thought with a twinge of spitefulness, that his very first grandson was actually black.

"Well, that would be the negro kind ma'am," he replied with a glance to Otis. "And from everything that I can see, I'd say your friend sitting there is just about as negro as you can get."

Taking a breath in an attempt to compose herself, Willie thought of the irony of what he'd just said then flashed a smile. "Well, I can truly appreciate your policy, really I can. But you see, Mr. Brown here is a very close friend of mine. And like I just said," she reiterated with a firm politeness. "I would take it as a great personal favor if you could reconsider your policy just this once."

"Well, I really don't believe that that is going to be possible ma'am," he replied with a curt and icy finality. "Like I said before, our policy is quite clear."

"Now when Willie told that man that I'd come into a small sum of money, well, that's when I finally realized why we was there. But for the life of me, an as hard as I tried, I sure as hell couldn't figure out how or when I'd gotten it. I didn't remember gettin any money from anybody, but then I thought of ol Foster an how maybe he might a left me some. You know, in his will or somethin, an Willie was jus now gettin around to it. I thought maybe he'd left me ten or fifteen thousand or heck, maybe even twenty-five cause he was real rich an had always treated me real good from day one. An so right about then, I actually started to get pretty excited. But when that ol banker told Willie for the second time he really didn't want me there, well, money or no money, that's when I was ready to jus get up an leave. Ya see, I could tell that he didn't like havin a black man in his office even though he was tryin to be real polite. An he sure as hell didn't want me havin a bank account there. No sir. But for some reason Willie did, so I jus sat there fidgetin an squirmin while I tried to figure out where in the hell I'd gotten all this money.

"Anyway, I think it was right about then that she must of sensed jus how nervous I was cause that's when she turned an looked at me then smiled an winked an reached over an patted the top of my arm. You know, one of them reassurin it's gonna be okay kind," he laughed and then took a sip from his beer. "An then right after she did that, I remember seein the look on her face change an I knew right then an there that we wasn't done, no sireee, not by a long shot. Cause if there was one thing that Willie didn't like, it was to be told

*what she could or couldn't do an that's when she began to really put the pres-
sure on that ol banker. An then when she still didn't get her way, well, that's
when she jus out an out threatened em."*

"Threatened him?" Jim stared.

*"Yep, threatened him. Like I said, she was really determined to get her
way, but most of all, she didn't like be'n told what she could or couldn't do.
Hell, she never did."*

It took only a second for Willie to clear her throat and continue
undaunted. "Well, I am truly sorry to hear that because I was really
hoping that you would see things just a little different. You know,
being that it's 1948 and all. But please, if you don't mind, could I ask
you just a couple of questions before we go? I promise to be brief."

"Go right ahead," he nodded amicably.

"Thank you. Now forgive me if I'm being presumptuous, but I
am assuming you do know who I am, don't you?"

"Yes ma'am, and I believe just about everyone here in town
knows who you are too," he answered in an insolent tone. "It seems
as if you've made quite a name for yourself here in Mobile over the
last few years."

"Well good, then since you seem to know who I am, as you so eloquently put it, I take it then that you've also heard of a little company
I now own called Dawson Holdings?"

"Dawson Holdings," he mumbled and shook his head. "No, I
don't believe that I have. Why, is there some great significance as to
why I should?"

"Yes actually, I believe that there is," Willie continued on. "And if
I might have just another minute of your time, I'll explain. You see,
Dawson Holdings over the summer has acquired and now controls
all of F. K. S. Enterprises. Which not only includes all of their companies, but all of their investments as well. You know stocks and bonds
and well, just a whole lot of stuff that I really don't understand." She
laughed. "Were you aware of that?

"Anyway, I'm not sure if you really know who F. K. S. Enterprises
is, so let me enlighten you if I may. You see, that was the poor late
Senator Siler's sole holding company that owned and operated
just about everything he had. You know, Siler Investments and
Financial Services, and Siler Shipping with all those ships that

he had sailing all over the world. And let's see, there was Siler Shipbuilding and Dry Docks, and all those oil wells he had up in the delta. Oh yes, and I almost forgot, that little ol seventeen story office building he had too. You know, the one right down the street from here. All of which, excluding the oil wells and some stocks and bonds that is, were sold this summer, and I might add, for a great deal of money."

There was no doubt the Gordan DeWeese was all about money and by the time Willie had finished, she'd certainly gained his attention. "And so what does any of that have to do with this bank and its policies?" he asked and narrowed his eyes.

"Oh Mr. DeWeese," Willie gleamed. "I'm so glad that you asked because if I am not mistaken, I believe that F. K. S. Enterprises even owned a little piece of this here fine institution," she cast her eyes upwards and looked around then dropped her gaze back to the man. "In fact, if I recall correctly, it was somewhere around thirty percent. Isn't that right Harold?"

"Aaah, thirty-five ma'am, to be exact," Harold sat forward and quickly interjected.

"Oh yes, I'm sorry, thirty-five. How silly of me," she looked to her accountant and laughed then turned her gaze back to the banker. "Now, since I own thirty-five percent of your bank, I was wondering. What would the board of directors think if they were to find out that you were, say, not cooperating with the wishes of one of their largest shareholders?

"Well ma'am," Gordan began with an emboldened breath. "Just for your information, that policy, with regards to your friend sitting there, is made by the board of directors. Now you're quite welcome to inquire and see if they would be inclined to change it, but I doubt seriously that they would. You see they pretty much go along with the guidelines that I recommend if you know what I mean," he smirked as if he were done.

"Well yes, actually, I do know what you mean Mr. DeWeese. And although I am a bit disappointed with your decision, I can assure you it is not my desire nor intention to bother the board with such trivial matters. You see, I was really thinking of something entirely different. You know, something that would just kind of circumvent all those silly rules," she waved her hand in a dismissive manner.

"Circumvent the rules, are you serious?" He chuckled at the audacity of her suggestion. "Ma'am, with all due respect, like I said before, that's just not going to happen, not in this bank. You see," he went on in a voice that'd clearly grown impatient. "I'm not about to ruffle the feathers of the board or our account holders just to please you and your friend there. Now, if you have nothing further?" He finished as if to conclude their meeting.

"I see," Willie exhaled with an humph. "Well, I am truly sorry to hear that. But I guess if you insist, then I shall just have to revert to the golden rule."

"The golden rule?" he scoffed with another laugh. "You mean, as in do unto others?"

"Yes sir, the golden rule, but no, not quite in the sense that you're thinking. See, if there was one thing that I learned from the late Senator, it was the golden rule in which he lived by. You know," she paused with a quiet confidence and a growing smile. "He who has the gold, rules. And now with all this money I have from all of those businesses that I've just sold, and the fact that you are clearly unwilling to accommodate us, well, I was really thinking that maybe I would just acquire another little piece of your bank here. Say about another fifteen percent or so. I could do that, couldn't I Harold?" She turned and looked to her accountant.

"Yes ma'am," he instantly replied. "Actually, you could. I believe their stock is currently at--."

"See," Willie interrupted before he could finish. "And then we wouldn't have to ruffle anybody's feathers like you just said because I would then have, as you men like to say... controlling interest? And then," she finished sardonically. "Well, that would make me your boss, wouldn't it?"

It was clearly a threat and he knew it. And now that he knew the true extent of her wealth, and the fact that she was willing to use it, Gordan DeWeese took a heavy breath and cleared his throat, then ever so slowly rocked back in his chair.

"Well now," he began, his lofty sense of superiority shattered at the thought of her intentions. "I've never really thought of it that way, but since your reasoning seems to make so much sense, I don't see why we couldn't bend that old rule just a little. You know, just this one time to help out such a valued customer. After all, I am the president. And like you just said, it is 1948," he finished with a manufactured smile.

"Oh good, good," Willie replied. "I must say Mr. DeWeese, you are such a wise man, why it's no wonder that you're the president of this bank," she retorted. "Now Harold," she turned to her accountant and extended her hand. "If you could be so kind as to hand me that check, Mr. DeWeese here can deposit it and then we can put this whole messy affair behind us."

Taking the check, Willie examined it and then looked back up to the banker. "Oh, I'm sorry," she feigned politely. "You will accept a certified cashier's check, won't you? It's drawn on Alabama Federal and Savings"

"Yes ma'am," he nodded. "Alabama Federal is a fine institution."

"Good. Now like I said before, Mr. Brown has come into a tiny sum of money, and what we would like to do is to deposit it into a savings account. You know, one of those interest-bearing kind where he could draw a small monthly stipend to kind of help him out in his older years. We could start at say two percent and adjust it annually if that's agreeable with you," she finished and sat forward, then handed him the check.

"That'll be just fine," he conceded as he reached across his desk and took the check.

"Now Willie had called it jus a tiny sum of money, so I really wasn't expectin much. An shit, to be right honest with ya, I was still tryin ta figure out how I'd gotten it. But when she handed that check to that ol banker an he finally took a look at it, I thought he was gonna have a heart attack right there on the spot. Heck, I can still remember him suckin in his breath an then poundin his chest an coughin. I really think that right about then he was tryin ta say somethin but there didn't seem to be no words comin out of his mouth. He jus sat there real quiet like an stared at that check.

"I remember it seemed like a real long time, but it wasn't but a second or two before he looked back up to Willie, took a great big breath, an then really went off on her. But by then ol Willie had had jus about enough of his crap an she tore right back into his ass jus like a junk yard dog an set him right in his place. Yes sir, he'd finally crossed the line. An right about then, well, that's when I found out jus how big that check was."

It took a moment for the actual figure to sink in and for him to regain his composure, but just as soon as he had Gordan DeWeese looked back to Willie and went into an instant tirade. "What?" he snarled. "Is this some sort of joke? I mean, do you really expect me to believe that you're just going to walk in here an give this to some stupid negro?" He held up the check. "And that this is actually good!"

"Well Mr. DeWeese," Willie snapped back with an incensed glare. "Let me assure you that one, no this is not a joke. And two, yes, the check is quite good."

"But that's two and a half million dollars!" His voice rose with an air of indignation. "Jesus Christ lady. Are you out-a your ever-lovin mind?"

"No, I'm not, but you Mr. DeWeese!" She instantly threatened. "Will most certainly be out of a job if you do not do as I wish. That I can guarantee. Do you understand? See, I've had just about all of the sanctimonious bullshit from you that I can take, and believe me when I say this," she glared with vicious and unwavering gaze. "That I will make it my mission in life to see that the only banking job that you hold after today is that of a teller! Do I make myself clear?" She finished and then waited.

But the man didn't answer; he just stared in a state of disbelief at how he'd just been threatened by a woman. By a woman who was as vicious as she was beautiful, until Willie regained his attention.

"I'm sorry," she feigned as if he'd replied but she didn't hear. "But I don't believe that I heard you. What was it that you said?"

Glaring at her from across his desk, Gordan DeWeese finally cleared his throat and choked on his pride. "Yes ma'am," he answered with a defeated tone.

Smiling with pleasure, Willie paused for a second then sat forward in her chair. "Well good, I'm glad to hear that. You know, it's always so nice when everyone can get along don't you think? Oh, and one more thing if I may," she continued with an icy steadfastness. "Just to ensure shall we say, that the integrity of you and your fine institution here is maintained to the highest of standards under which you profess to operate. And that there are, let's say," she glanced to the ceiling then quickly brought her eyes back to him. "No unauthorized withdrawals or egregious expenses to Mr. Brown's account. I would appreciate it if you would send copies of all of his monthly statements to Mr. Simons here at this address. In fact, I insist. You know," she finished with a dismissive disdain. "Just to ensure that the moral compass in which you proclaim to be guided by stays pointed in the right direction."

"What!" Jim blurted and widened his eyes. "You gotta be kiddin? She gave you two an a half million dollars? Just like that? She just gave it to you?" His voice rose higher. "Two an a half million in 1948? Jesus Chrisssst, I don't believe it," he shook his head and laughed.

"Yes sir, two an a half million dollars," Otis nodded. "I didn't know it at the time, but that's a two an a five followed by a whole bunch of zeros," he paused then smiled wryly. "Five to be exact."

"Goddamn Otis, you're rich! I mean, or at least you were?" He looked on curiously.

"Oh, I still am. In fact, I've got more now than when she first gave it to me. I'll tell ya, her ol accountant really kept me on the straight an narrow."

"But I don't understand," Jim cocked his head. "Why'd you keep on workin for the church?"

"Oooh Willie wanted me to," he sighed. "See, I think deep down she worried that all that money would change me somehow, so she made me promise that I'd stay on with the church so I wouldn't get into no trouble or nothin. She said she didn't want me thinkin that since I was rich that I didn't have to work anymore. An she was right really, a man does need to work.

"Anyway, after we left the bank we went an had lunch, an that's when she told me that she was finally leavin. The next day, first thing in the mornin she said. Now, I knew that she needed to leave, but boy I sure didn't want her to. Then after lunch, she took me back to the church an that's where she finally said goodbye to me for the very last time.

"She seemed really sad by the time we got there but she still wanted to see the boat one last time, so we walked on down to the water an jumped onboard. See, that's where it had all started, all them years ago, with this here boat," he looked around. "It was the first time that I'd met her. She wasn't even fifteen years old yet, an now here we were.

"Anyway, after she'd played with the wheel for a bit an had finally finished reminiscin, an after she'd made me promise to always look after it, we slowly made our way back to the car. I remember her tellin me all kinds of

things while we walked like how glad she was that I'd been there all those years an of how much I'd meant to her an stuff like that. An then of how right as we got back to the car an her chauffer had opened her door, her turnin an squeezin me around the neck real hard. Like she was never gonna let go, an then the tears in her eyes after we finished huggin. But most of all, I remember how she told me in a real broken up voice how she'd never forget me. Not ever she said.

"Now for me, that was one of the happiest days of my life an also one of the saddest. Ya see, I had jus become one of the wealthiest people in Mobile, an yet at the same time I was losin one of the few people in my life that I cared the most for. It was as if your mother an your sister an daughter was all leavin at the same time an somehow, deep down inside of you, you knew that you were never gonna see em again. Then with one last kiss on the cheek an a promise to write jus as soon as she got settled, she turned an got in the car.

"I remember watchin her as she settled in an how right before that chauffer could close the door, her reachin back out an grabbin my hand as if she was gonna tell me somethin. I could see her eyes were all red an watery an she was bitin her bottom lip. It was somthin she did whenever she was sad or upset, I'd learned that much about her over the years. But she never said nothin, she jus squeezed my fingers real tight an then gave me a gentle shake as if to say goodbye one last time. Then, an with one last tight-lipped smile, she slowly let go an nodded to her chauffer.

"That was her final goodbye, an with that I stepped back out of the way, an when he closed the door, well... that was the last time that I ever saw her. I remember be'n real sad an havin this big lump in my throat that I couldn't get rid of, an then watchin an wonderin as they slowly drove away if I'd ever see her again. An then I remember thinkin of how every once in a while in your life, if you're real lucky, someone special comes along an changes it for the better. Someone good, with a good heart, that gives you hope an lights it up in a way that nobody else can, an for me that person was Willie Mae."

"So she finally left?"

"Yep," Otis nodded and then took a sip from his beer.

"An did she ever write like she said?"

"Oh yeah, in fact I got a letter from her shortly after she left tellin me how she'd found this real nice place on the beach. Oh, an she also told me that her husband Danny was now lyin in Arlington Cemetery. That he'd received a full Presidential pardon along with an apology, an that his record had been completely exonerated. Now I was really glad to hear that cause he was a good man, an he really was a hero... an if anybody deserved to be there it was him. Then about a year later I got another one from her tellin me how she'd fallen in love again an was gonna get married. I think she said he was a doctor or somethin. Anyway, she asked me all about the boat an if I was do'n okay, an that she sure missed go'n out on her an hoped that it still had her name on it.

"I really enjoyed those letters an for quite awhile we wrote back an forth, but after a couple of years or so they jus seemed to keep gettin a little farther and farther apart, until one day, they jus stopped altogether." His voice trailed off as if he were still saddened by the fact. "Anyway that was the last I heard from her until about fifteen years later when I heard a rumor that her husband had died. An after that, I don't think nobody really knows what happened to her," he sighed.

"Well," Jim finally replied after a moment of silence. "That sure was some story. I mean, I gotta tell ya, in all my wildest dreams when I bought this last weekend, I sure as hell never thought that this boat had that kind of history, or that I'd be sittin here with you like this, no sir."

"Well, it does. An it's all true too... every bit of it."

"Well, she sure sounded like quite a gal," Jim shook his head. "It's a shame I'll never get to meet her. I would've liked that. At least just once, ya know?"

"Oooh she was," Otis replied. "She really was. An you'd a liked her too. An what would really be neat," he smiled and looked around. "Is if she could see this when we get her all finished."

"Oh yeah," Jim's eyes lit up. "That would be cool. Ya think she'd like it? Or go for a ride?"

"Oooh yeah," Otis nodded with another look around. "Willie loved this boat."

Contemplating the story in another moment of silence, the two men sat quietly until Jim finally downed the last of his beer and then looked to Otis. "Well my friend, there's only two left. Shall we have one more an finish off this cooler?"

"I don't see why not," Otis answered as he too downed his beer and then crushed his can. "No since in lettin a good beer go to waste. But I gotta tell ya somethin, if today is any indication of jus how much work we're gonna be gettin done, we're gonna be here for a pretty long time. Hell, at the rate we jus started, we'll be here for the next three years."

Laughing together Jim turned without another word then reached into the cooler and pulled the last two beers from their icy confines. Then setting

them on the table he popped his top and held up his can. "To the Willie Mae,"
he said.

Quickly doing the same, Otis popped his top and held up his can. "To the
Willie Mae," he repeated and touched his can with Jim's.

It was a befitting toast, and for a short moment the two sat and enjoyed
the quiet as they reflected upon the boat and its incredible history. There was
nothing left to say, and as the late afternoon sun streamed its soft rays of light
through the dirty panes of glass, and the neighbor's lawn mower buzzed with
a monotonous drone in the distance, they each drifted with their thoughts.
Each conjuring images from the past until their moment was broken by a
sudden banging on the hull and then the sound of Jim's wife from outside.

"Jim... Otis," they heard her call from the stern. "You boys still in there?"

"Yeah honey," Jim turned and answered with a cringe.

"Well if the two of you are finally done screwin around an drinkin beer,
I got a whole mess a fried chicken with some mash potatoes an gravy sittin on
the table. So come on now an get your asses in here before it gets cold. An now
means now dammit, I ain't gonna tell ya again, ya hear."

They did hear, and they laughed, and as the two carefully climbed out
of the boat and then shuffled toward the house, they continued on with their
lighthearted banter.

"So how long did you say?" Jim asked but answered before Otis could
speak. "I say two."

"Twooo?" Otis repeated and chuckled. "The way you pulled them beers
out-a that cooler today," he smiled and shook his head then placed his hand
on Jim's shoulder. "Three..."

THREE YEARS LATER

―――――――

OTIS HAD BEEN RIGHT; IT had taken them right at three years and a hundred cases of beer to complete the boat, yet with a tender and painstaking tenacity, the two men labored on and off almost every weekend until there was only one thing left to do. The final and fitting touch that would return the 1926 Cruiser back to its original glory. To repaint its name on the back. A name that had been conceived, in part, out of the lust for a beautiful young girl.

Watching as the painter put the final brush strokes on the back of the boat, the two men finally stood back and admired their finished product. "Looks jus like it did back when ol Foster had it put on all those years ago," Otis drawled.

"And now it's done my friend," Jim added as he put his hand on Otis's shoulder. "Cheers," he raised his beer in a final toast.

Touching their cans together, the two men toasted and took their sips then turned to the young man behind them. "Now gentlemen," he said as he lifted his camera. "If you don't mind, I'd like to get some pictures of the both of you standing on each side okay."

Positioning the men on each side of the stern, the novice newspaper reporter then stepped back and took several quick shots. "That's great gentlemen, thank you, but really," he pleaded with a laugh. "Could we take just a few without the beers? Please."

Laughing, yet relenting, Jim and Otis set their cans on the ground and then posed for several more.

"That's great guys thanks," he said as he set his camera down and then turned to Otis. "Now Mr. Brown, I'd like to ask you a few questions for the article next week, if you don't mind."

"No sir," Otis replied just a little surprised. "I don't mind at all. We can jus sit right here an you can ask away all ya want."

"Good," he began with his pad and pencil in hand. "Now, from what I understand, you use to be the captain of this boat, is that correct?"

"Yes sir," Otis replied. "I was the captain from about 1928 all the way up until, oooh, about 1958 I think it was. Right at about thirty years or so, an for three different owners."

"Wow, that's a long time," the reporter beam. "Could you tell me about it?"

It was well over an hour before the young man finally rose from his chair and then shook his head in disbelief. "Some story, huh son," Jim chuckled and then took a sip from his beer.

"Oh my gosh," he gushed. "Story? It's incredible! I mean, holy cow, you should write a book. I'll tell you, this is going to make such a great article in next weekend's paper. I had no idea when they sent me out here to do this that the boat had so much history an..." He paused as if he'd just ran out of words, then extended his hand. "Well, I really don't know how to thank you. In fact, I'm going to ask the editor if I can do a full page spread," he smiled great big. "This is really, really great."

"Well," Otis drawled as he took the young man's hand. "It was our pleasure, really."

"Same here," Jim added. "An maybe next weekend if you ain't do'n nothing, you can come by the marina an go for a ride. We'll be droppin her in the water next Saturday an you can do a follow up."

"That sounds great," he said as he turned away. "I'll see you then."

ONE WEEK LATER

———

IT WAS RIGHT AROUND NOON by the time they got the boat to the marina. Checking and re-checking, they finally backed the antique beauty down to the water's edge to a small crowd of onlookers. It hadn't seen water in over fifteen years yet before they allowed it to float, they stopped to do the traditional maritime honors and christen the boat. To break a bottle of champagne across its bow and for-mally name her. To Jim, it was something he'd thought about for a long, long time. In fact, as the days had turned into months and then years, and Otis had told of the boats colorful history, he had become certain of his decision. Even his wife agreed, and so after carefully taping a towel to the leading edge of the bow, Jim turned and handed the bottle to Otis.

"Who... me?" Otis asked as the man nodded for him to do the honors.

"Yeaaah you," Jim replied. "Meredith an I have both talked about it an we want you to have the honors. In fact, we couldn't think of anyone else in the world that we would rather have break this than you. Sooo," he gestured with his arm and took a step back.

It was the moment they'd all been waiting for, but just as Otis prepared to swing, he hesitated then slowly relaxed his stance and lowered the bottle.

"What's wrong?" Jim asked. "Go on."

"I can't," Otis shook his head and began to laugh.

"Can't? What-a-ya mean you can't?" Jim retorted. "Sure you can," he assured with an elevated zeal. "It's okay. We want you to have the honor, really."

"No no nooo... not that," Otis rolled his head.

"Then whaaat?"

"The champagne," he raised his arm and gestured with the bottle. "We'd be wastin it, wouldn't we? Shit, we ought-a at least drink some of it first, don't ya think."

"Well," Jim surmised after a moment of thought. "I never really thought of it that way, but yeah, I think we should," he conceded. "I mean it is alcohol. An after all the work we've done, it does kind of make sense. Here, give me that. An Meredith, go grab us some cups would ya?"

Handing the bottle to Jim, Otis watched as he removed the wire and foil from around its neck then held it out and put his thumb against the cork. A second later and with an audible pop, it shot into the air and was instantly followed by a white foamy mixture that spewed forth like an erupting volcano. They were having fun, and after the bottle had finally settled they poured a small amount into their cups and then held them high.

"To the Willie Mae," Jim said as he touched his cup with Otis's and then his wife's.

"Amen," Otis grinned then looked to the boat with an admiring gaze. "To the Willie Mae."

Downing their drinks with a single gulp the two men quickly realized that cheap champagne was not their drink of choice. And really cheap champagne was even worse. Yet even so, just as soon as they'd finished cringing and making faces, they poured two more. But the fruity bubbly just wasn't for them, they were beer drinkers, and as soon as they'd finished their second cup Jim retrieved the cork, pushed it back into the bottle and then turned to Otis.

"Maybe we ought-a jus stick ta beer," he laughed as he handed it back. "What-a-ya think?"

"I think you're right," Otis agreed as he took the bottle and shook his head. "That stuff's horrible. Where in the hell'd ya buy it anyway, the paint store? Shiiit, no wonder they use it for this," he laughed as he stepped back in front of the bow and raised his arm. Then with a nod from Jim, he smiled great big and swung his arm. "The *Willie Mae*," he shouted as the bottle shattered into pieces.

The boat with its new diesel engine ran better than Otis could ever remember. She was faster and quieter, but after several hours out on the water, they finally returned to the marina and called it a day. Carefully secured into her new slip, the two men lovingly wiped her down and then made plans to meet the next morning for her maiden voyage. A voyage that Otis had promised to take them on, to a place up river that he knew all too well. "I'll see you around nine," he said as they walked off the pier.

———◆———

It was mid-afternoon by the time she had returned from her shopping trip. Grabbing the weekend paper as she struggled through the door with her bags, she threw it onto the kitchen counter then dropped her bags on the sofa and headed to the bedroom. A little worn out from her arduous journey through the shops and boutiques, she changed her clothes then quickly returned to the kitchen.

Opening her blinds, she gazed outside and smiled. It was Saturday, and it was sunny and warm, and the beach was calling to her. A relaxing cocktail beneath one of its umbrella's and the Florida sun, along with the weekend edition of her beloved Mobile paper, and she was certain she had the perfect cure for her tired and aching feet.

Grabbing a lime from the refrigerator, she made a vodka tonic then took a long awaited sip. Aah yes, she sighed... just right. Now what does my paper hold? Curiously flipping it over, she glance at the headlines then grabbed her lime and tonic. Turning to the refrigerator, she took a step but then suddenly stopped and turned back. Directing her eyes to the picture in the upper left hand column, she silently stared at the photo of a boat. A boat with a name on it that she knew all too well and a caption below it that read, *'History returns to Mobile Bay.'*

THE NEXT MORNING

———————

MOORED STERN FIRST IN A slip halfway down the pier, the forty-foot cruiser glistened like brand new under the hazy rays of the early morning sun. Now completely restored, the Willie Mae as she had remained, floated calmly within the serene and protected waters of the marina. Neighbored on all sides by modern fiberglass trophies of the newly rich, she stood as a pristine and idyllic reminder of an era that'd long since passed. And as Jim took his first sip of coffee and began wiping the night's dew from the newly varnished woodwork, he smiled with an almost parental pride at what he had come to see as the finest restoration job he'd ever done.

Finishing some fifteen minutes later, he grabbed one of the Adirondack chairs setting in the stern and then spun it toward the transom. Pouring a second cup, he took a quick sip then set his cup back down on the table next to the chair and took his seat. Reclining back into the comfort of the chair, he propped his feet on top of the gunnel, exhaled with a contented sigh and closed his eyes.

Leisurely basking in the warmth of the rising sun while he waited for Otis, Jim could easily hear the gulls and pelicans noisily fishing for their early morning meal. They were always noisy, yet before he knew it the sounds of the birds battling for food were replaced by the overpowering and unmistakable sound of footsteps steadily approaching. 'Damn Otis,' he thought with his eyes still closed. 'It's about time you got your sorry ass here.'

But it was unusual to hear a hard-soled shoe such as this clonking down the boardwalk, for most boaters, if not all of them sported some sort of boat shoe and it quickly caught his attention. Maybe it wasn't Otis after all, he surmised. Yet even so, he sensed that the steps had meaning and purpose and he listened intently as they noisily approached, growing louder and louder until they suddenly stopped just behind the boat. Smiling as the looming shadow swept across his face and blocked the morning sun, Jim sat for a moment and then cleared his throat.

"Well it's about time ya got your sorry ass here you ol son-of-a-bitch," he drawled with his eyes still closed. "Hell, the damn day's half gone already. I thought for a bit there I was gonna have to take her out all by myself."

He'd said with all of the orneriness in the world, and was ready to continue on until he heard the soft sweet drawl of a woman's voice reply back. A voice that was laced deep in its own southern heritage, that was both charmingly polite and articulately refined.

"Excuse me," the lady replied with a surprised but curious smile.

Instantly opening his eyes, Jim pulled his feet from the gunnel and sat forward then raised his hand to block the morning sun. Squinting intently at the darkened silhouette before him, he focused his eyes until they had cleared and he gazed upon a very attractive woman. A little younger than himself he guessed, she was elegant and smartly dressed with a thick mane of auburn hair that flowed from beneath a beautiful wide brimmed hat. Adorned with a delicate sprinkle of fine jewelry that glittered in the morning light, she exuded an aura and mystique unlike anyone else he'd ever met. She was, in his eyes, reminiscent of the timeless beauty he occupied. Standing motionless on the edge of the pier, she stared down at him from behind a pair of darkened glasses as if she were admiring the boat.

"Oh heck, I'm sorry ma'am," he apologized. "It's just that I thought, well, I thought that you were someone else. A friend of mine actually. Didn't mean to offend you."

"Oh, that's quite all right," she waved her hand. "No offense taken, but good morning to you," she greeted warmly.

"Mornin," he drawled politely as he pulled his two hundred and seventy-five pound frame from his chair. Standing with a slight but definite groan, he shuffled back into her shadow then raised his hand once again against the morning sun. "Can I help you?" he asked.

"Oh nooo," she replied as she slowly removed her sunglasses. "I was just looking actually," she added, only to change her mind a second later in what was clearly an after thought. "But tell me," she asked inquisitively. "Is this your boat?"

Beaming proudly, Jim turned his head ever so slightly and surveyed his work. "Yes ma'am," he answered. "Bought it three years ago at an auction in New Orleans. Been restorin it ever since."

"Three years," she repeated. "Oh my, well it certainly appears as if you've done a marvelous job. Why, it's just beautiful."

"Thank you... sure was a lot of work though."

"I'm sure it was," she replied as she looked down at the black and red lettering painted across the transom. Silently reading the words, she stared for a moment as if she'd just found a long lost friend then cleared her throat and looked back to Jim. "It looks old," she finally said in a scratchy voice. "I'm sure that it must hold a great deal of history."

"Oh yes ma'am," Jim chuckled then turned and stared at the boat. "Thaaat it does," he added as he looked back to the lady. "I'll tell ya, if this ol boat could only talk."

Now if there was one thing that was an absolute certainty, it was that Jim was always eager to talk to anyone who expressed an interest in his boat. He loved to show it off and retell the stories that Otis had told again and again. It was a passion to a fault, and without realizing just what she'd done, and that she'd opened the proverbial door, the old riverboat pilot instantly dropped in to a colorful narration of the boat's long history.

Listening intently as he told his story, the lady stood quietly and fondly reflected on the many years that'd long since passed. A few minutes later and after he'd finished, she began to wonder as to just how it was that he knew so much. How was it that the details of something so long ago and known only to a few had come to pass? She thought of the picture in the paper, and of the black man standing by the stern. But was it him? She tried to imagine his face and how he might have aged, but it had been so long since she'd seen him she wasn't sure.

"Well, that was indeed a delightful story," she sighed. "And I must say it most certainly seems as if you are very well informed, but I was wondering if I might ask another question if you don't mind."

"Oh, no ma'am, not at all," Jim answered with an accommodating smile. "Go right ahead."

"Well," she began. "I really don't mean to pry into your affairs or anything, but it's just that you spoke of so many things and in such great detail, that I was wondering just how it was that you have come to know so much of its history."

"Oooh that," Jim laughed and nodded. "Heck, that's easy. I learned it from a friend of mine who helped me restore it... an ol black man. He's the one who told me all about it. See, he use to be the captain of it way back in the thirties and forties. Back when some real rich Senator use to own it who by the way, then got shot by the very gal he named the boat after. Can you believe that?" He laughed and shook his head.

It was at that very moment that the lady on the pier, now overwhelmed with memories of the past, suddenly knew who the man in the paper was. It was Otis, for he was the only one who knew, and who could've shared such stories. He was alive and well, and with both a profound sense of sadness and joy enveloping her, she slowly reached into her purse and pulled out a handkerchief. "Well," she finally mumbled as she wiped her eyes. "I really don't believe that it has ever looked this good."

"Excuse me ma'am," Jim curiously cocked his head and scrunched his brow. But the lady didn't answer; she just stared at the back of the boat with a blank expression, looking at the name until he called again. "Ma'am?" he asked in a concerned voice. "Are you okay?"

"Oh yes," she feigned with a nod and a smile. "Yes, I'm just fine... thank you. And thank you for sharing such a wonderful story, but I can see that I have already taken enough of your time. I'm sorry to have been such a bother to you."

"No bother at all ma'am," Jim replied, only to stare as if there were still some question he wanted to ask. "No bother at all. An you're welcome too."

"Well then," she said with a final glance back down to the transom. "I really must be going. Please, enjoy the rest of your morning won't you."

"Yes ma'am," he replied as she slipped on her sunglasses and turned to leave. "You too," his voice trailed off as she turned and began walking back down the pier. She was leaving, yet as the mysterious lady slowly walked away, Jim began to anguish over a feeling that seemed to have suddenly risen from within. An overwhelming sense, that something or some unanswered question was leaving with her. Unable to shake or collect his thoughts, he shook and scratched his head with a disgruntled huff then stepped to the back of the boat and placed his hands on top of the rail.

Gazing into the water, he tried to discern his feelings. There was something about her and he knew it, yet for some reason he couldn't make the connection. He concentrated and stared at his reflection while the sound of her hard soled shoes clonking on the pier slowly faded toward the gate. He raised his head and glanced toward her then quickly lowered it back to the transom. Shaking it in a defeated gesture he agonized for another second then suddenly inhaled in wide-eyed disbelief.

"I'll be damned," he uttered at the revelation that was just below. Could it really be, he thought as he read the name on the back? Was it her? Was it really her? Raising his head just as she approached the gate and reached for the handle, Jim stared in a moment of uncertainty. It couldn't be, could it? Surely she would've said something, he reasoned? And if it wasn't her, then who was she?

Watching as she grabbed the handle, his mind whirled and his anxiety grew. He had to know. She just couldn't leave without his knowing; it would haunt him forever. He wanted to run after her but he didn't, he just watched as she pulled on the heavy metal gate. Swinging the door ever wider until he inhaled a heavy breath and anxiously called out.

"WILLIE MAE!" his deep voice boomed down the walkway in a curious but commanding way.

Frozen by his words as they resonated down the pier, the lady instantly stopped with the door half open and her head slightly lowered. She hadn't heard her name called out like that in a long, long time and for a few fleeting seconds she silently contemplated her response as it echoed in her mind. She'd thought she would just come and see the boat and then leave. And that nobody would know who she was. But she was wrong, and with that she slowly removed her sunglasses then turned and raised her head high in the most regal of ways. Proud of who she was and what she stood for, and with a radiant sparkle emanating from the depths of her beautiful green eyes, she gave the big man in the boat a warm and friendly smile.

It was at that very instant that time for Jim seemed to stop and he suddenly knew. He knew it was her, the woman who Otis had so often and so fondly spoken of, the woman who'd occupied so many of his thoughts and dreams for the last three years. She was real, and without question everything he had envisioned. And she'd come just to see the boat. He realized that now, and suddenly he felt an immense sense of pride as he recalled her words. 'I really don't believe that it has ever looked this good,' her honey smooth voice echoed in his mind as it then instantly raced with a flood of questions. 'Did she like it? Did she wanna go for a ride? Did she...? Oh, and what about Otis? Yes, where in the hell was Otis? He was late, dammit.'

He wanted to stop her but he didn't, for in some strange way he could sense that it was not what she wanted. She'd come for her own reasons, whatever they may have been, that was clear. And so with all of the courtesy and respect of a true southern gentleman, he just smiled and let it be, content that he now knew as they both stared in a fleeting moment of silence. Communicating with their eyes as if somehow they were now friends. Friends who'd been mystically and magically brought together by a common bond, but yet at the same time still very much strangers. Two different people from two different worlds, destined to never meet again, yet certain within their thoughts never to forget that they'd met. Then, and with a subtle nod as a final goodbye, the lady dropped her gaze and turned back to the gate.

Pulling on the heavy iron bars, she opened it the rest of the way and then slowly stepped through the doorway. She was leaving and he knew it, and he knew that he would never see her again. But now it no longer mattered for each of them had in their own unique way, found what they'd wanted. Their moment was over, and as the heavy iron door gently closed behind her, Jim watched as the woman he now knew as Miss Willie Mae Dawson... disappeared to the other side.

———◆———

Made in the USA
Lexington, KY
03 July 2016